It was at that precise moment that she saw him.

He was walking towards her, wading through the thick forest of talkers and drinkers. He had dark eyes bright with energy. That was the first thing she noticed. His face was vivid and compelling. His eyes stormed hers, held them fixed. The roomful of people receded and she saw only this stranger, dark and quick and alive.

When he was close enough, he took her hand.

'I've come for you. It's our dance.'

'Yes. I think it is.'

Just like that. So simple. He took her gloved hand and pulled it through his arm. She felt the warmth of his shoulder as it brushed against her own.

'My name is Armand, *ma petite*. Armand St. Amour.'

'I'm sure you know my name,' she said.

'Since you are the only woman at the ball worth looking at, I found out immediately. I was told it was Honey. In French that is *miel*.'

As they moved onto the floor, people made way for them, staring. Honey was conscious of the looks, the whispers, but she smiled directly into Armand's face, into his dark, sparkling eyes, into his heart. Yes, it seemed to her that she touched his heart.

PROUD BLOOD

Joy Carroll

MAGNUM BOOKS
Methuen Paperbacks Ltd

A Magnum Book

PROUD BLOOD

ISBN 0 417 03770 8

First published 1978
by Dell Publishing Co. Inc., New York
Magnum edition published 1979

Copyright © 1978 by Joy Carroll

Magnum Books are published
by Methuen Paperbacks Ltd
11 New Fetter Lane, London EC4P 4EE

Made and printed in Great Britain by
Hazell Watson & Viney Ltd
Aylesbury, Bucks

For my children—
Anne, Barbara, Scott and Angus

ACKNOWLEDGMENT

To reconstruct any period in history, so many authors are consulted that it is impossible to list them all. However, I would like to acknowledge some of the sources I found so valuable: Peter Quennell, Philippe Julian, Peter B. Waite, Mason Wade, Marcel Rioux and Yves Martin, Edgar A. Collard, Thomas E. Appleton, Leslie Roberts, Joseph Schull, W. G. Hardy, Gustavus Myers, J. M. and EDM. Trout, and Ralph Allen. Throughout the writing my researchers, Jean O'Heany, M.D., Barbara Carroll and Ruth Bernard, were always helpful. I am especially grateful to Peter C. Newman for his imaginative and wise advice. Finally, I wish to thank Henriette Neatrour, who encouraged me from the moment the book was undertaken, as well as Linda Grey and Beverly Lewis, who were as enthusiastic and creative a pair of editors as any writer could wish.

JOY CARROLL

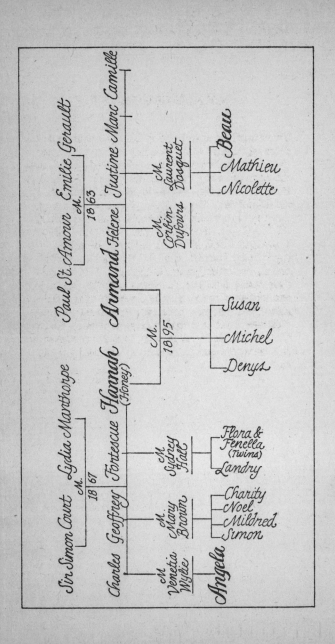

PART ONE

1895–1899

CHAPTER ONE

The Mountain dominated the island city of Montreal. As the English had taken possession of the west side, so the French clustered to the east, spreading out from the base across the plateau and into the countryside.

It was not only language that separated the two cultures. The French were solidly and devoutly Roman Catholic, their lives supervised by the Church in meticulous detail. The English were Protestant and independent. There was also the bitterness of a conquered people; the French had felt humiliated by England and betrayed by Mother France ever since 1759, when English troops had defeated French troops on the Plains of Abraham. And so the two peoples spun slowly in their separate orbits.

Pride's Court was a half-Gothic, half-Italian Renaissance castle entirely surrounded by houses of similar style and of nearly equal size. On the shaded streets easing up the southwest slope of Mount Royal, the houses of *les anglais* overlooked the busy harbor and the broad sweep of the St. Lawrence River below. The nearer the summit the house stood, the more influential the family within. Pride's Court was near the top.

High tea was just over. The tea wagon still stood in front of the bay window, where the thick crimson-and-gold curtains had been pulled tightly against the brutal cold outside. The remains of the meal—plates of small meat sandwiches, buttered scones, cream buns, and thin slices of dark fruitcake steeped in brandy—were still spread out. The fat teapot, resting snugly in its quilted pink satin cozy, was warm.

The Red Sitting Room was almost always used at teatime. It was small enough to hold the heat from the huge radiators with their cast-iron lace covers, yet large enough to seat a dozen people in comfort. A crackling cedar-log fire scented the air pleasantly. The Raeburn over the mantel (picked up at Harrods in London), the pieces of Japanese pottery carefully collected over the years, the exquisite Louis XV clock fashioned of tortoiseshell inlaid with brass floral motifs (tolling the hour—seven o'clock; the day—December third; and the year—1895), all these things combined to give the room a rich texture. It was easily the prettiest of the fifty-odd rooms in Pride's Court. Sir Simon had such a fondness for it that most evenings he would spend an hour there, filled with tea and satisfaction, and it would seem to him that the world was good.

Even when the Montreal weather was at its worst, as it was today, with the thermometer outdoors registering a chilling forty-eight degrees below zero, he could sit in his maroon leather armchair, feet up on the matching footstool, and gaze into the fire, mulling over his successes. A brandy helped against the cold, too. Not that Sir Simon minded the winter. If a man dressed warmly enough the cold could be positively bracing. It was one of the advantages he always stressed on his visits to London when he talked to immigration authorities about British settlers coming to Canada. "Tell them the cold weather kills diseases," he would say emphatically. "Tell them it's invigorating." Quite a different thing from those arid outbacks of Australia, for instance, and not a bit like service in India where strange diseases festered in the incredible heat and filth, killing off people in droves. Yes, he liked the Canadian winter and he usually could spend a very agreeable hour after tea. But not tonight.

Tonight Sir Simon did not see any of his treasures. He saw only his daughter, a slim, fair-haired girl with riveting blue eyes and the temper of a shrew if she didn't get her own way. A girl who dreamily read bad poetry, scoffed at the stuffiness of business, and yet who, judging by the fine cashmere of her tea gown, accepted the luxuries a dull, plodding businessman could provide.

"Hannah," he said loudly (he always spoke loudly), "what's the matter with you these days? Why are you mooning about the house like a sick colt? Why didn't you finish your tea?"

"There's nothing the matter, Father."

But his question alerted her. The mere fact that he had called her Hannah instead of Honey indicated just how upset he was. Members of the Court family (Honey was the youngest of four, and the only daughter) always reverted to her baptismal name when they were angry with her. She noticed, too, that her mother had retired quickly to her boudoir, leaving a cream bun half finished on her plate. And her brother, Charles, had already left for his club. Perhaps Papa had warned them of the coming storm.

Honey's glance drifted past her father's bulky figure toward the fire. She did not need to record his physical image to know how Sir Simon looked: burly and overwhelming, a man with an air of importance even when he was at ease, with thick gray hair, a matching mustache and pointed beard, and the booming voice of an enraged drill sergeant.

"Are you pining after that damned Frenchie?" he demanded, rising heavily to his feet and standing before the fire with his hands behind his back, coattails lifted to the heat. He rocked back and forth on the balls of his feet, glaring at her.

"How *can* you talk like that?" Honey asked sharply. "Really, Papa, it's terribly out of date. No wonder the French hate us!"

"How can I talk like that? Because that's how I feel. I know how to treat 'em, keep 'em in their place. If Fort hadn't brought that Frenchman to the ball last June, you wouldn't have met him in the first place! I meant to lunch with old Mr. St. Amour at the Windsor to talk business, but young Fort took matters into his own hands. What do we get in return for our hospitality? It's damnable! The cheeky devil makes my daughter the object of gossip all over the city."

Honey was furious. Any other night she would have matched his temper with her own, but there was no time now for a long argument. He might stay another hour, and that would destroy her carefully laid plans. She tried a more moderate tone.

"That's ridiculous, Papa. All we did was dance."

Sir Simon had worked himself into a mild rage. His words tumbled out faster than his tongue could form them. In his mind's eye he could see his daughter at another ball, the St. Andrew's Ball, only three nights before, whirling about with Armand St. Amour while everybody whispered. In his anger, he half stammered, "Dance? You call that dancing? I call it a disgusting exhibition. And in front of *everybody!* The way he looked at you . . . my God, it's useless to try to tell you how revolting it was! I ought to kill the bloody bastard, I ought to challenge him to a duel—they had some common sense in the old days, you know, a man could get satisfaction when he was insulted. And Charles tells me you stood up God knows how many perfectly eligible young men just to dance with that . . . that *Frenchman* . . . you don't seem to understand who we are, how important the right marriage is for someone in our position . . . and then this . . . this *St. Amour* . . . ridiculous name . . . this *Frenchman* . . ." His words finally tumbled to a halt. When Sir Simon said "Frenchman" the word became synonymous with murderer.

"But, Papa . . ."

"Don't 'But Papa' *me!* Who would want to marry you after an exhibition like that? Nobody who counts for anything in the city of Montreal, or anywhere else that's civilized. How did that damned Frenchie get into the St. Andrew's Ball? . . . It used to be only the best people. That was the whole point of the ball. Now they're obviously letting in riffraff—anybody with a decent suit of clothes—it only shows how right they were in the beginning to keep everybody else out."

"If they kept everybody else out," she said reasonably, "the Courts wouldn't be there either. Because in the beginning it was only the Scots. We happen to be English."

"That isn't the point, goddamnit! I mean keeping out scum. Like young St. Amour. I must admit his father was civilized enough when I spoke to him, and had quite a bit of spunk, too. But the son . . ." Sir Simon broke off helplessly, incapable of adequately describing Armand St. Amour's complete degradation. He poured himself a brandy.

Honey looked anxiously at the clock. She ought not to have started any kind of argument with him, especially on the subject of old French families vis-à-vis old English families. It would be enough to start him off on a two-hour diatribe.

"The St. Amours are bankrupt," Sir Simon said, as if that finished the matter, "and we're in the middle of a depression. A fact which you couldn't be expected to know."

Honey did not listen. Every second was precious to her

now. She must escape from her father, and quickly. Papa usually went straight to the Mount Royal Club after one brandy; there he could be sure of meeting the right men and presumably of talking business as he had done all day in his office and over the ritual long lunch at the Windsor Hotel. Why was he lingering tonight? She and Armand had worked it out so carefully. She was to wait in the shadow of the gate by the coach house, out of the wind, until he arrived with his cariole. At eight o'clock. What if Papa didn't go to the club tonight? What if he suspected her secret? What if he caught her, carrying her valise, as she tried to escape the house by the servants' door? She couldn't bear to think of Armand out there waiting in the cariole while she was locked in the house.

"Aren't you going to your club, Papa?"

"When I'm good and ready, Miss. I'm not finished with you yet. Have some more tea. It's still hot. You scarcely ate a bite tonight."

"I don't want any more tea." God's eyebrows, but he was pouring himself another brandy!

"Meeting the right sort of men may seem a dull occupation to you, but we aren't discussing one passing ball, you know, we're talking about the way you'll spend the rest of your life. Marriage isn't supposed to be fun; it's business pure and simple. You marry somebody of your own kind. Otherwise, you get nothing but disaster from beginning to end. Oh, I know how you girls moon around, stuffing your heads with cheap novels about undying love with some handsome stranger and that kind of rubbish. I'm not blind, you know. But marriage is a day-to-day proposition. A successful marriage takes a hell of a lot of effort. Look at your mother and me. It isn't a dream."

"It certainly wouldn't be a dream to be married to Tom McPherson or Mark Wyndham; it would be a nightmare," Honey said sharply. "They're both sissies. Tom is chinless and Mark's eyes water all the time. Even indoors," she added somewhat irrelevantly.

"The Wyndhams have the largest bloody flour mill in Quebec," her father shouted, "and young McPherson's father is a director of the Canadian Pacific, to mention only one of his connections. There's not a thing wrong with either of those lads. They go regularly to Christ Church Cathedral."

Honey groaned. "Tom has the mind of a flea. I know because I tried to discuss Byron with him. And Mark's voice sounds like a girl's. He ought to be in the boys' choir still. That's where he belongs."

Sir Simon's cheeks turned red above the line of his neatly trimmed beard. His eyes changed, took on a harsh gleam of cruelty, a buried look of fierce determination that he usually kept well concealed.

Sir Simon was approaching a towering rage. He did not like to have his judgment questioned for a moment or to be frustrated in his designs in even the smallest detail. His daughter, nineteen years old and without any knowledge of life, was setting herself up against him. She did not seem to grasp her value to the family. Nor did she appear to realize that the only daughter of the Courts was, in many ways, like a royal princess. It was not her place to act rashly or to consort with unsuitable people. The St. Amours, while they could not be fairly described as nobodies (the French aristocracy did have some historical background, however slight), were Roman Catholics, non-British, and practically at the end of their financial resources. Sir Simon had good reason to know. On the other hand, an alliance with the Wyndhams or the McPhersons or any one of half a dozen other good, solid British families in Montreal would be advantageous in every way. Flour and lumber must be transported. Railways must be built. Virgin land must be opened up. Settlers must be encouraged. The Court Shipping Line might just as well get the big contracts as any other firm, and family connections helped.

He had to admit that the girl was attractive. Not pretty in that pink-and-white way so popular in the drawing rooms, of course, and certainly not pliable. But she had a good face and a reasonable figure. Lady Court had received some discreet requests for introductions not only from Montreal families but from Toronto people and even from as far away as New York. Charles had confessed to him only last night that several of his friends had asked to be formally introduced since they had not been able to attend the Court ball the previous June at which Honey had been presented to society. Charles had pointed out irritably that rich girls were seldom beautiful and that at twenty-eight he had yet to find a suitable wife. There were too many plain women in the right families.

"You behaved badly at the ball," Sir Simon now shouted, referring once again to the ball held only three nights before in the Windsor Hotel. "I happen to know you danced seven times with St. Amour. And each time was more lurid than the last."

"We were always in plain sight of everyone," Honey protested.

"I devoutly wish that you could not be seen by anybody at all," Sir Simon said, setting his empty brandy glass down with a thump.

"It's seven-thirty, Papa."

"Time means nothing to me," her father said, but he moved toward the door just the same. "I'll tell you one thing, Miss Hannah Court. I'm going to personally see that that damned Frenchman isn't invited to any more dinners or balls where you will be a guest. And now, Miss, ring for Yvette to take away the tea things."

Sir Simon took one last, parting shot, his hand gripping the brass doorknob.

"You do look most odd, Hannah. You have an unbecoming flush. Do you need a tonic of some kind? Perhaps you ought to see Dr. Baker. You haven't caught some foreign kind of influenza from the damned Frenchman, have you?"

It was Sir Simon's firm belief that all influenzas were foreign and could only be contracted by contact with people of non-British extraction. He had been known to speak for several minutes on the subject, allowing only that members of foreign aristocracies might not present such a threat.

"I have a headache, that's all," Honey said.

"Too much reading. Stop reading that tripe."

"Yes, Papa. Goodnight."

He nodded to her then and closed the door with a bang meant to indicate that he was still angry. When he had gone she pulled the bell cord for Yvette and waited until the maid had taken away the tea wagon. Then she hurried out into the chill of the great hall. There was no sign of her father, so she assumed that he had gone to the cloakroom first to put on his beaver coat and hat. She could imagine him, even now befurred and booted, gold-headed cane in hand, ambling along in the frosty night like a great domesticated bear.

Honey walked quickly across the vaulted hall. The flickering jets of gaslight in their clear glass bowls cast uncertain shadows on the high white walls and the dark ancestral paintings. At the top of the curved marble staircase, she paused for a moment before the portrait of her grandfather, Cathmor Court. In the heavy night silence she thought she felt his disapproval. His eyes had always fascinated her, and, like her brothers, she had used to think that they followed her down the stairs or along the corridor. The idea had made her shiver as a child. She remembered how Fort, always the most rebellious of her brothers, had used to shout crazy dares at the picture and wiggle his fingers in his ears, then run away. Tempting the portrait to come alive. In those days, the gesture had seemed oddly brave. The old man's eyes (rather like Sir Simon's, now that she thought about it) *did* seem to move.

Her own bedroom was warmed by a small coal fire; her bed had been turned down, her cambric nightgown with its wide revers of tucking and embroidery laid upon the bed.

She hurried across the dark-patterned carpet to the dressing room. Her clothes hung in deep closets, her shoes and boots and hats were placed neatly upon shelves, her gloves, underthings, and nightgowns sat in tiers of drawers. She hesitated before a tightly packed row of gowns and suits. Earlier, she had thought of wearing the bottle-green velvet suit. Was it right? She pulled it out nervously and threw it on a stool. Anyway, the white fox coat was perfect. Her father had given it to her last Christmas, along with the matching deep, round hat. And of course she would wear her muskrat-lined boots. And yes, the fine-woven white wool scarf, which she would wrap about her head like a misty veil, warm and mysterious. It was flattering, too. Most definitely she would wear a cloud.

She was interrupted by a light rap on the door.

Good God, what now? Surely her father wasn't coming back to continue his boring lecture?

"Come in."

She clutched the suit and stared at the door, but it was only Yvette.

"Excusez-moi. Lady Court wishes to see you."

Honey had developed the habit of speaking to Yvette in a mixture of English and French. Since the ball in June when she had met Armand St. Amour, Honey had been taking French lessons. And since none of the Courts spoke a word of French, nor did they see any need to learn, Honey had been forced to practice on the maids.

Lady Court had objected to the French lessons from the beginning. So unnecessary, she said pointedly. Why did Honey want to do such an odd thing? (Sir Simon was not informed, it being quickly agreed between mother and daughter that the knowledge might raise his blood pressure.) Honey had foreseen objections, and so had argued that many members of the English aristocracy spoke French fluently. Some of them even spoke German and Italian. Lady Court had been somewhat mollified, although the idea of actually learning to speak Italian was too farfetched for her to contemplate. She considered a second language an affectation, like working on a large tapestry, perhaps, or learning to blow glass.

Yvette was obviously waiting for Honey to respond to her message.

"Maintenant," the maid said firmly. She was staring at the heavy velvet suit that Honey had aimlessly picked up and was clutching somewhat desperately.

"Oui. Je viens," Honey said.

Yvette's small, hooded eyes were black and expressionless. She had a pointed, thin face and straight lips set tightly, and there was about her the reserve of an aborigine. Remote. Secretive.

"I have a headache," Honey said in English, as if this somehow explained the outdoor suit she was holding.

Yvette stirred the fire before she left, then slid out quietly, closing the door against the cold air of the corridor. Honey felt trapped. What on earth could her mother want at this hour? It was so unlike Lady Court to have a visitor after tea. She always retired to her room to read a novel. And teatime was considered quite sufficient for family discussions unless there was a crisis.

When she entered her mother's bedroom, she found that

Lady Court had retired. She was propped up in the enormous Regency bed with its circular canopy, leaning back against a mountain of pale blue satin pillows. Her nightgown and bed jacket were of a slightly deeper shade of blue, the jacket elaborately trimmed with wings of Valenciennes lace from neck to shoulder and with the same lace on deep cuffs that drooped gracefully over her slender hands. Her gray-blonde hair was bound in two thick braids, one on either side of her face. She had been reading a novel by Marie Corelli and it lay open on the bedcovers.

Honey bent over to kiss her mother on the cheek.

"You wanted to see me, Mama?"

Her mother smelled of lavender; sweet and sharp and eminently suitable to the blue of the room. Lady Court's cheek was still smooth, the skin fine and surprisingly unwrinkled for her age. It struck Honey that her mother must have been quite beautiful when she was young.

Lady Court looked at her daughter with eyes that were still bright blue and mischievous.

"Darling, I only wanted to say . . . don't worry too much about your father's little talk tonight. He's terribly upset about young St. Amour. But I told him it was nothing but a tempest in a teapot. I suppose he went on and on about it?" She sighed.

"Yes, he did. It was awful. I thought he'd never stop, Mama. You'd think I'd danced naked at the ball."

"Well, he's only thinking of your own good, Honey," Lady Court said mildly. "You mustn't mind too much. I told him it was nothing, but you *did* make yourself conspicuous, you know. Charles was quite cross, too. You stood up several of his friends. However, as soon as you accept some invitations from the right people, your father will calm down again. There's a skating carnival at Victoria rink soon, isn't there? A costume party? Charles could arrange a partner for you. Wouldn't that be nice? You skate very well, darling."

"Yes, I know about the carnival," Honey said noncommittally.

"You could have Grace make you a costume especially for the party. Something splendid. Perhaps Queen Victoria as a young girl. Wouldn't that be nice? And that would please your father, we'd calm him down again. Especially if you're with the *right* partner."

Lady Court's eyes were conspiratorial. Honey often joined her mother in some harmless plot against Sir Simon. They had been doing it since she was old enough to speak clearly. But it was far too late for that now. There was nothing she could do but try to escape her mother's presence without actually lying.

"You will do that, won't you?" Lady Court's voice took on a hard edge, and she frowned. She sensed that the link had been broken, that she had lost her daughter's confidence.

"But they're all such bores!"

"I know that, darling, but so often one must *marry* a bore, you see. There's not much else one can do, really." Lady Court sighed, a long, drawn-out sigh.

Honey felt a wave of sympathy for her mother. It was an entirely new emotion for her. Imagine being married to Sir Simon! Imagine spending one's whole life listening to him huff and puff, with only occasional thunderstorms of anger to break the monotony. He was no fun, and he danced badly. He didn't even like *classical* music. He paid no attention to the flowers that Lady Court and the gardener planned for hours on end. And she could not recall ever hearing her father give her mother a compliment before a ball or a dinner. Poor Mama! No wonder she spent every evening reading a novel. And this was exactly the same fate they planned for her. Tied to some great lump who owned a sugar refinery or a few miles of railway. It was horrible!

"Oh, Mama, why can't some of the *right* people be charming and fun?" Honey cried in exasperation.

"I suppose some of them can be, but it's very hard to find one of them."

Honey glanced at the clock on her mother's dressing table, an ornate gold ball supported by two cupids. She had always detested the clock. It was twenty minutes to eight.

"I'm tired, Mama. I do have a headache, and I think I'd like to go to bed."

"Run along, then, darling." Lady Court picked up her book, watching her daughter go before turning her eyes to the page. Honey blew her mother a kiss. Lady Court said impulsively, "I do understand what you see in young St. Amour. But darling, he's completely unsuitable."

For a brief moment they were once again in communication. But as Honey ran back to her own room she wondered just how sympathetic her mother would be when she found out the truth. Armand as a son-in-law would probably be quite another story.

Once more secure behind the closed door of her room, Honey took off the tea gown and threw it on the bed. No time now to be tidy. As she eased herself into the tight velvet suit, a flash of vision fired her nerves and she saw herself in the traditional white gown—billows of tulle and tiers of heavy lace and satin embroidered with a thousand seed pearls, topped with a veil and train that followed her down the aisle of Christ Church Cathedral from the altar to the door. How Papa and Mama and Charles would have loved the pomp of a huge church wedding, with *all* the right people watching, and perhaps even the artillery band from Charles's reserve regiment. Not that having the band would be as glorious as it would have been in the old days her father liked to recall. One of the few times he became enthusiastic over a subject unrelated to business was when he described Montreal as a garrison town before 1870. His excitement was almost touching. In those days the regiment had paraded to Christ Church on snowshoes. The band had followed the men down the main aisle of the church right up to the pulpit, where they'd made an enormous pyramid of their drums and trumpets. And when you had looked up any aisle in the entire church, you had seen a great heap of bearskins at the end of each pew: those big black beehive hats that the troops wore on ceremonial occasions. How Sir Simon would have loved to have the regimental band strike up the wedding march!

But it wasn't to be like that for her. It was to be the dark cold of a December night and a lone priest speaking French and Latin in some bare, candlelit room. Armand had warned her. All very secret and a little foreign. Perhaps frightening. Except that Armand would be there.

It would be enough for Armand to be there. How different he was (even her mother had noticed) from the men Charles brought around for her to meet, from the brothers of her girlfriends, and from her own cousins.

Armand, with his thick black hair, shining eyes, full lips, and tawny skin. Armand, so tall and graceful and quick-moving (not like those solid, thick-legged boys Charles was trying to palm off on her), and yet as strong as any woodsman who worked at the St. Amour lumber camps. Armand, who danced and sang and laughed, whose eyes held a promise of something she could only guess at now but that tonight would surely be revealed to her.

She got out the valise she had packed that morning, not sure if she had the necessary items but too hurried now to double-check. She knew she had put in the ruby-and-pearl collar her father had given her at the coming-out ball, her Teaberry tooth powder, and her own soap. She had only to meet Armand, really, because he had made all the arrangements for the wedding, and the honeymoon, and for where they were to live afterwards. He had applied for the dispensation that would allow them to be married by the clergy even though she remained a Protestant, and he had made the appointment with the priest to perform the service. Armand knew how to get things done. He seemed dashing and worldly. He had been to Paris. Perhaps that was the explanation for his confidence.

She pulled on her boots, and then the soft white fur coat and the beautiful hat, and she wound the white cloud around her head. She picked up the small valise. There was no turning back now. If she were caught, she could give no explanation but the truth.

Out in the wide spaces of the upper hall, everything was dead silent. No sounds came up from the blue-pierced darkness below, or from the room where her mother lay reading. She crossed to the guest wing and found the back stairs. It was years since she had ventured into the servants' area, and the cold linoleum that covered the stairs, the sparse lighting, surprised her. The stairs creaked. They were alive with sounds: loose boards and rising nails and shifts in supporting walls. It seemed to her as she descended breathlessly that every servant in this part of the house must surely hear her. But she reached the foot of the stairs undisturbed. Straight ahead was the door to the stableyard. The heavy bolt screamed out for oil. She pulled the door open in silent agony, expecting a horde of alerted maids to flock from the kitchens and the scullery. Nobody came. It did not say much for the security of Pride's Court, she thought as she went out into the night, closing the heavy door behind her.

Sharp cold air struck her between the eyes like an icy

needle. She leaned back against the closed door for a moment to get her bearings, to let her eyes adjust to the night. Deep snow piled around the outbuildings up to the level of the window ledges threw off a lighter color than the sky. A few windows in the coach house and a row of kitchen windows gave off a weak yellowish glow. She saw, gratefully, that one of the stable hands had dug narrow paths from building to building and out to the gate. Her own moist breath rimmed the edge of her cloud with white, damp frost, and her eyes watered from the intense cold.

She was in the shadow of the great stone gatepost when she heard the friendly jingle of harness and the unmistakable slip of metal runners on packed snow. When she ventured out to peer down the street into the wind, she could make out the shape of the cariole coming up the hill, the single horse trotting smartly. Then she saw Armand, his scarf blowing behind him in the wind, his beaver hat set at a jaunty angle.

When he stopped and waved, she could not at first reach him. Walls of shoveled snow from the sidewalks cut off the roadway, and she ran along the barrier until she found an opening. The horse was breathing frost-smoke, snorting at being made to stand in the cold. Armand reached out for her and pulled her up beside him, laughing silently into her numb face. He pulled a buffalo robe over her knees and clucked up the horse.

"*Merveilleux!* Perfect timing, my love."

"Oh, Armand, I thought I'd be late!" She was out of breath, her heart tightening with nervous fear.

"*Ma chérie,* I would have waited all night. I would have turned into a human icicle before I gave up."

"Papa insisted on a long, serious talk. About our disgraceful behavior at the ball." Honey's blue eyes were merry for a moment.

"I wish I could see his face when he finds out about tonight," Armand said.

"I don't! I'd be terrified. My, how he'll shout and rage!"

They were driving down Beaver Hall Hill toward the ice-covered river, and occasionally the fur-hatted head of some single brave pedestrian would pass by on the other side of the snow wall as if it were not attached to a human body at all, but had a life of its own. Honey peered at each fur hat nervously. What if Charles were underneath it? Or one of Armand's many relatives?

"We might be seen. Oh, Armand, I'm afraid we'll be caught."

"Not long now, darling. Are you cold? Everything is arranged. We only have to get to the church, that's all."

"But what if the priest isn't there? What if he hasn't received the dispensation? Doesn't it have to come all the way from Quebec City?"

"But he *has* the dispensation, my darling. It came this morning. I called on Father Leguen myself to find out."

"You're sure that all I have to do is sign it, Armand? That's all? And then he can perform the ceremony?"

"That's all. You do remember what it means?"

She remembered. She knew the guarantees by heart. She must promise not to have any other wedding ceremony following this one, and she must educate her children in the Catholic faith and offer no interference to Armand's practice of his religion. It all sounded quite simple. A simple promise in exchange for Armand's love.

"But what if something goes wrong?" Suddenly the night seemed mysterious and threatening, the streets filled with nameless obstructions. Would they never reach Notre Dame Church?

"Nothing will go wrong. Father Leguen will be waiting in his study. My God, my fee will buy his wine for the next three years. And Father Leguen does like his wine, *chérie*."

"You shouldn't talk like that. I thought you were supposed to be respectful of your priests."

"I am, I am. But I also understand them. They are men, after all. If you notice a faint odor of port hanging over the wedding ceremony, pay no attention. It is only the *best* port. Depend on the Father for that."

Armand leaned down and kissed her cold cheek. She felt the familiar shock of excitement at his touch, but she could not be carefree as Armand was. It was different for a man. He would still have his family, even if they were furious, but she was running away from hers.

"Do you think your father will try to have the marriage annulled, Armand?"

"Not if it's consummated," Armand said, giving her a comically lustful look, and then laughing at her.

Really, she thought, his eyes were wicked and funny and loving all at the same time. He was behaving like a small boy stealing a sweet. *Consummated.* It sounded so official. Not at all the way she had imagined her wedding night. But if consummation meant that Armand's father could not have the marriage dissolved by the church, then she was in favor of it.

They had reached Place d'Armes, the square dominated by the great Church of Notre Dame. Armand climbed down from the sleigh and hitched the horse to a post barely visible in the snow. Then he led her through the gate in the stone wall beside the church to the Sulpician Seminary where Father Leguen lived and worked.

A thin little man with close-shaven hair answered the bell. He wore a plain black robe. He was obviously expecting them and led them straight to Father Leguen's study. The room was tiny, scarcely large enough to hold a desk, a few chairs, and a handful of people. It was stuffy with fire smoke, and, just as Armand had predicted, Honey could smell a hint of wine in the air. Two fat yellow candles in brass sconces provided the only light. The desk was covered with papers and the walls were lined with shelves of dark-bound books that looked as if they were never taken down and read.

Father Leguen stood before his desk with his hands folded over a protruding stomach. In fact, his soutane bulged alarmingly so that the cross hanging on his chest was tilted at an odd angle. He was red-faced and wore spectacles. The hands were folded, but they moved in a gentle, wringing motion. His smile was feeble, but he managed to greet Armand with an attempt at warmth. He spoke quickly in French, and Honey could not follow what he was saying.

Armand translated.

"He can't offer Mass under the circumstances. It's against the rules."

The thin priest who had ushered them in remained as a witness. A second priest, darkly handsome and faintly rebellious, was summoned as well. The ceremony was brief and without dignity or emotion. A skulking kind of thing, in which words ran together meaninglessly, the monotonous flow broken only by Father Leguen's raspy breathing. Honey was glad when it was over.

Father Leguen offered them port from a cut-glass decanter that appeared to be the only thing in the room that wasn't dusty. Honey was aware that Armand put money into the priest's hand, and that this brought a momentary flash of pleasure to the fat face. And then, somehow, they were outside in the cold again and Armand was kissing her. The horse protested noisily. He was shuddering with cold. Armand handed her up and unhitched the horse from the post. This time, they went up narrow St. Urbain Street for two short blocks and then Armand stopped to point to the house. "There we are," he said. "My friend's city house. One of the old ones. Do you like it?"

It was a French-style frame cottage with a steep roof and small rectangular windows with six panes in each. Icicles hung from the edge of the roof and shimmered in the light from a gas lamp on the snowy sidewalk. It looked small, and snug, and secretive.

"Oh, Armand, I've never been in a house like this one. I've only seen them from the outside."

"You'll find it's comfortable. At least it is possible to keep these cottages warm," Armand said. "They were designed for the climate."

"I know I'll love it."

Armand had driven the sleigh down a narrow alley to the stable behind the house. There was no sign of life. Armand pulled on a leather strap and a bell jangled noisily somewhere in the far corners of the building. There was a scurrying of feet, muttered curses, and then a sleepy boy appeared, his narrow face crumpled with irritation.

"Take the horse in," Armand said. "Why are you asleep? It isn't late. You were supposed to be expecting me."

"I'm sorry, sir." The boy took the reins and pulled the horse toward him. They had spoken in French.

"Look to your manners," Armand said, "or I'll report you. And see that the horse is given a blanket. He's cold. Mind, I'll check on you in the morning."

"Yes, sir." The boy sulkily began to take off the harness.

"Mioche paresseux!" Armand said as they crossed the snowy stableyard to the back door of the house. "Lazy brat! That type doesn't want to work, but he's good for nothing else. The horse is more intelligent."

"Where is your friend? The one who owns the house?"

"Oh, Grande? He's in Quebec City on business. We can stay here for a week if we want. And the housekeeper goes with the house. So you won't have to worry about cooking, my love. Not that I think you know how. I don't suppose you can boil water, eh? This house is only a convenience for him if he comes to Montreal on business, anyway. He lives in the country."

Armand had a key to the back door. She followed him down the narrow hallway that cut the house in two, and Armand stopped before a closed door.

"Here we are, if I remember."

"You've been here, then?"

"Oh, yes, sometimes Grande has parties here." Armand laughed, remembering. "Very elegant parties indeed."

"I suspect you have been very wicked."

"As wicked as possible."

He set down her valise and picked her up, carrying her easily over the threshold and into the bedroom.

"You're quite a bundle in that coat," Armand said, thumping her down unceremoniously. "Let me take it off."

He opened a pine armoire that stood near the door and put both their coats into it. The room was pleasantly warm. The low ceiling, painted white and sectioned with smoke-stained beams, trapped the heat from a birch fire. A single oil lamp in a milk-glass globe lighted the room. Cozy, Honey thought. Cozy, and very different from her own bedroom at home. She felt exhausted suddenly, and flung herself into an upholstered chair by the fire. Armand came to her quickly and knelt on the carpet beside her, taking her hands and kissing them, and putting his still-cold cheek against hers.

"Wait until I lock the door, my love. Then we'll have wine to warm us up." He put down the thick wooden bar across the door and poured them each a glass of wine from a decanter left on a tray by the fire. "Madame Gillon might just be curious. You know how old women are about newlyweds. Lascivious."

The wine was hot. Thoughtfully, Madame Gillon had mulled it.

Armand sat on the floor, his head in her lap. The hot, spiced wine was making her giddy. She wondered how it would be when they finally were together. How, in fact, they would manage to go from their present romantic but only slightly improper pose, both of them fully dressed, to getting into the great four-poster in the corner, already turned down by a foresighted Madame Gillon.

She leaned down to him, her pale hair falling toward his face. He pretended concern, examining her pink, cool cheek but finding no telltale white marks to denote freezing. He was conscious of her thick brown lashes and the sharp blue of her eyes, and for just a moment he thought he could not wait to take her. But he fought down that thrust of desire, breathing hard, and forced himself to drink his wine slowly.

Honey leaned back in the chair and closed her eyes. She wanted a little time to think. There was no retreating now. She had run away from her family, from the security of her position, from the absolute right to rank and money that her birth had given her. She was now a married woman: no longer the Honorable Hannah Court, but a *madame*. It sounded very foreign. She shivered despite the warmth of the fire.

When she opened her eyes again, Armand was standing in front of her, looking down into her face with his familiar, intense gaze. It was as if his eyes were trying to swallow every detail of her face. He was as handsome here in the firelight as he had been at the ball three nights ago. She had been almost afraid that somehow when they were alone, safely married, he might change. Become plain. Less romantic. His face looked tense, perhaps a little thinner, but the black eyes shone as eagerly as ever. She saw the cleft of his chin, the olive skin that looked permanently sun-kissed, the long black hair that fell over his forehead, the full-lipped mouth so suggestive and yet so firm.

"Madame St. Amour," he said.

She stiffened with surprise. He had voiced her own disturbed thoughts.

"It sounds odd. I don't feel . . . very different."

"I hope you like the name," Armand said.

"I love the name." But she wondered if she really did. She had always been a Court.

"Did you know that you are easily that most beautiful woman in Montreal?"

"Nobody mentioned it."

"Liar. Every man who danced with you at the ball mentioned it." And he grinned at her. "Finish your wine, *ma petite*. There's a bath waiting for you in the dressing room. We don't want the water to get cold."

"Armand, you thought of everything!"

"I hope so."

He brought a pale green satin robe from the armoire and handed it to her. Then he carried her valise to the dressing room. There was a small coal fire in the grate and, on the thick white carpet, a hip bath filled with warm water. A towel was laid over a rack to warm before the fire.

"Hurry up, darling," Armand said. "I'll be waiting."

Honey accepted the robe and clutched it defensively. She tried to relax. A bath would be lovely, and how lucky she was to have a husband who thought of such details. The small dressing room was cool, but she closed the door to the bedroom and began to undress slowly, close to the coal fire. She found Pears soap and a washcloth on the stand. She sat soaking in the hip bath, reluctant to get out, but she could hear Armand moving about restlessly in the other room.

When she finally came out, smelling of patchouli, Armand was in a dark blue silk robe, standing by the bed, a wineglass in his hand. He set the glass down.

"You are beautiful, my darling." And he stared at her, not moving for a few seconds, until he shrugged as if to awaken himself and said briskly, "Sit by the fire again. I want to look at you. And take off your robe."

Take off the robe. She found it difficult to do as he said. Nobody had seen her naked, not even her mother, since she was a child. The idea echoed and re-echoed in her head. She recalled, suddenly, whispered speculations with her girlfriends about what men actually did. Terrible tales of suffering and agony to be endured, handed down from old women. And grossness beyond belief. And yet she had married Armand, had given up everything for him. She did have a beautiful body. It must be all right to show it, surely?

She slowly took off the robe, feeling wicked.

Armand just looked at her. He didn't speak. Or appear to breathe.

She sat in the chair, motionless, exposed, vulnerable, and yet strangely excited by doing something that she had never imagined for one moment was possible. The first faint stirring of desire crept into her thighs. A hint of sensuality, a slow, invisible dance of nerves in her blood. Armand was smiling a little. He took off his silk dressing gown and let it drop to the floor.

Honey looked at him, fascinated and at the same time terrified. Nothing was the way she had imagined it. There was Armand, covered with black hair (it seemed to her) from chest to ankles, and at the same time insistent, huge and very male. She pressed back into the chair as if seeking escape, but as he moved closer, her excitement rose, making her feel ill. And yet she would not have turned him away. She realized that, returning Armand's plunging look right back into his eyes. There was no retreat.

There was a looseness in her limbs, in her throat, in her mouth, and she relaxed, sighing, falling into Armand's look as into soothing water, sinking like a swimmer who dares to drown. Her legs fell apart slightly in invitation.

Armand knelt impulsively on the carpet and pressed his dark head into her lap, into the warm skin of her thighs. They sat like that for a moment while he groaned and muttered something she could not hear, and then turned to press his lips against the soft flesh. At last he rose and picked her up easily and carried her to the bed, her breasts pressed like silken buds against his chest. His mouth traced her face in exquisite detail as if recording it forever in his mind. And then his mouth slid down over her neck and shoulders, over the pale breasts and the flat, inviting stomach. A wash of delight turned her pink as he blew out the lamp and she moved to take him in.

"If it hurts, my darling, you must be patient. *Ma cherie*, that part will be over soon. Be patient."

She did want him. A miracle of the senses overcame her reluctance, her shyness, her astonishment at what men were really like. The darkness covered the pain. And yet she took the pain well, only biting her lip and moaning into Armand's own heavy sighs. She wanted to get closer to him, she wanted to blend into him, she wanted to kiss him and touch him endlessly. When her eyes became accustomed to the darkness, softened a little by the dying fire, she saw that his eyes were closed tight and that he looked rather like the pictures she had seen of tortured saints.

A dark current ran beneath the surface delight, a

knowledge passed along in the blood. She felt that there would never be enough of Armand, not enough of his love no matter how long they both lived. It was a discovery that shocked her into an even wilder return of his caresses. Was this sinful, was it normal? To feel like this about a man was surely wanton. Nice women did not act like this. But the waves of sweet need poured over her, and she was climbing to some unreachable but very desirable peak. There would be release. Somewhere, there would be release.

"You do like it, my darling," Armand whispered to her.

She did not answer. Armand himself was like a mountain climber who has gone too far into a rarefied atmosphere and is gasping in pain. She felt his struggles, and, in a milder way, duplicated them, but when he cried out at last in triumph, she still ached with longing.

He held her close, knowing.

"You will have to learn that, *ma cherie,* as we go along," Armand said, when he could speak. "It will take time to learn but you *will* learn, from me."

Honey waited somewhat impatiently for him to recover. She saw him in the semidarkness, boyish and spent, smiling vaguely, eyes closed, forehead damp. But it was not long before he was wide awake again and as forceful as before.

When they fell asleep at last it was almost dawn. She was exhausted, and happy and afraid. She sank into an uneasy, restless sleep, aware of sounds, eyelids closed but fluttering. And then it happened, while Armand lay blissfully unaware beside her, and the room shook to the rumble of wheels. She sat up wild-eyed. Across the carpet, between the bed and the fire, flew an enormous black coach pulled by four black horses wearing tall black plumes. The horses plunged across her vision. There were black plumes on the corners of the coach. It was a hearse. She struggled to see who lay in the coffin inside, but it was impossible. Yet it was someone she knew. She almost, but not quite, identified the body. At any second she would know. She would know. Desperately she tried to see again and again, wanting to know, but at the same time terrified that she would find out. She screamed shrilly.

The scream cut the dawn, a sharp obscenity. Armand, deep in the folds of sleep, fought his way up to air in sudden panic, not understanding what had happened. He saw Honey standing on the carpet by the empty grate, her hands clasped to her head. She screamed again. He grasped her, shaking her violently until she looked into his eyes. Then he took her in his arms, soothing her like a small child, stroking the long light hair, kissing the trembling mouth.

"What is it, my darling? What happened?"

"Somebody is going to die, Armand."

And that was all she could say. She sobbed against his chest for long minutes, wracked, until at last she fell into a shadowed sleep. He did not really understand what had happened, but he knew that he loved her more than ever.

Madame Gillon was eager to have morning coffee. Her next-door neighbor, Madame Didier, was more than willing to oblige. The houses were close together, sharing the same stableyard. Madame Didier, keeping house for a deaf old gentleman now retired, had heard the scream. She was anxious to discuss with Madame Gillon the newlyweds who were temporarily living in Monsieur Grande's house. Because it had obviously been the scream of a young girl.

Madame Gillon called upon Madame Didier at ten o'clock instead of the usual eleven. And Madame Didier, anticipating, had brewed coffee that might have felled a *coureur-de-bois* in earlier days. They sat down together at the kitchen table.

"Cream as usual?" Madame Didier's eyes suggested that the strain of the night might have altered the habits of her friend. Something stronger might be in order. She was rustling with impatience.

"Thank you, yes." Madame Gillon sighed heavily. "I am tired. As you can imagine."

"I'm not surprised. I heard it."

Madame Didier's eyes did not leave her friend's face. She waited, silently deploring Madame Gillon's need for dramatics. But Madame Gillon took her time, stirring the brew with a small pewter spoon.

"One could hear it well enough through the walls," Madame Didier went on. "Frankly, I was afraid. A maniac is loose in the neighborhood, I thought. Then I remembered your honeymoon couple. Holy Mother! Is there no limit to the brutality of men?"

"Think," Madame Gillon said slowly, "how it sounded to me, sleeping directly above!"

"What could he have done?"

"The good Lord only knows." Madame Gillon rolled her eyes and shrugged in despair. Nameless bestialities thickened the air over the coffee cups.

"On the other hand," Madame Didier suggested somewhat delicately, "if she is a *virgin* . . . it may not be as bad as we think. It is often the case."

"She *could* be a virgin. She is from a wealthy family, one of *les anglais*. Monsieur Grande told me that much. The groom is a friend of his, and has, in fact, been at . . . various *parties* in the house in the past. If you follow my meaning. He is rich and handsome. He is paying well."

Madame Gillon dwelt upon that for a moment, thinking with satisfaction of the money that had changed hands for her services. Well, and she had done everything asked. More, if you counted heating the wine, and turning down the bed. A small pleasure she had allowed herself in anticipation of the night to come.

Madame Didier, while fascinated by the hints of parties of dubious respectability (did not the neighbors all realize that Monsieur Grande was a man of odd tastes?), was not about to abandon the horror of the past night. She savored her coffee, sucking it in, and stared hard at Madame Gillon to impress upon her certain possibilities as yet unmentioned.

"He might be one of those who are . . . unusual. While some men could not hurt a midget, others . . ." She trailed off suggestively, making a little motion in the air with her plump, brown-spotted hands.

"I thought of it myself. We've heard of these men. Built like stallions."

There, it was out. The point they had both been striving to make without seeming to be overly coarse. Silence, while they speculated upon the groom's possible dimensions.

"If that is the case, she is ruined. Judging by the scream. A woman can be turned to stone on her wedding night," Madame Didier said knowingly.

"Men are pigs. I've said it before. If that is the case it will be a tragic marriage, poor little thing. She is quite small, you know. I've seen her. And beautiful, too, for one of *les anglais*. They are pale, of course."

"How did you come to see her?" Madame Didier was quick to seize on the tone of Madame Gillon's statement. It implied more than had been said.

Madame Gillon allowed herself a slow and meaningful smile and poured another cup of coffee. Then she leaned forward, whispering her message across the table, not daring to voice it aloud although there could scarcely be a soul within hearing distance.

"I saw her in the bath."

"In the bath?" This was indeed more than she had expected, and Madame Didier wanted every detail. "I don't understand how you saw her in the bath."

"I was to have the room warm and the bath ready. I put out hot wine for them. I had the fire in the dressing room just right. I did everything he asked," Madame Gillon said.

"Yes, yes. But the bath?"

"I was not *in* the room, of course. Still, when you've lived in a house a long time and you've cleaned it thoroughly, you get to know every little corner. I expect you know *this* house very well, Madame."

"I clean as thoroughly as anyone."

"I know you do. The place shows that, and I've always said you were one of the best housekeepers I know. Now, I know my house well. And that room—that dressing room—is very special."

Madame Didier's eyes sparkled and she expelled her breath slowly and deliciously. So it was one of *those* rooms. She had suspected that the house had certain features. There had been rumors about the parties there. About the men who came. About the women who came.

"And so you actually saw her? In the bath? And was she pretty?" Madame Didier wanted to know.

"Very pretty indeed. White skin, ah, light-colored hair. Yes, you might say she is truly a blonde. Not a mark on her anywhere. Beautiful skin."

Madame Didier could imagine the scene. The naked girl stepping into the bath, not knowing she was being watched. It added a great deal to the whole evening; it provided fuel for many future tellings of the wedding night.

"Monsieur Grande *would* have a room like that, I suppose. It's very common in Europe, they say. And he's been to Paris. More than once," Madame Didier said.

"I think I will have a little more coffee, Madame."

"Of course, of course."

Madame Didier poured out another lethal serving and Madame Gillon took it gratefully. A complete description of the bathing scene was not beyond her abilities, but she needed to strengthen herself for the ordeal. Madame Didier was, after all, in no hurry.

CHAPTER TWO

Armand had been outdoors. He brought a gust of cold air with him into the bedroom. He also brought three yellow tea roses wrapped in a copy of the *Dominion Illustrated News* to protect them from freezing. Honey was still in bed.

Armand took a small china vase from the mantel and went into the dressing room for water from the ewer. When he came back he stuck the roses in it and put them by the bed. Honey leaned over to sniff them. She was still half asleep but the vision, or dream, of death still hung like a cloud in her mind. She tried to shake off the uneasiness.

"Where on earth did you find roses at this hour?"

"Can't you guess?"

"Guess?" Honey frowned. Then she laughed, amused at his audacity. "Oh, Armand, you *didn't!*"

"Why not? I told you last night that I would deliver a letter to your father before his breakfast. Otherwise, *ma petite,* he would have the police out looking for you. *Quelle horreur!* There would be a hell of a fuss, no? Can't you imagine it? And while I was in the house, the smell of flowers from the conservatory tempted me. So I snipped these for you."

"Jamie will be furious! He guards his flowers like jewels. Even Mama isn't allowed to cut tea roses!"

"Don't worry. We will not be there to be punished."

"No, but still . . . how did you get into the house? You didn't ring the bell, did you?"

"Pride's Court isn't difficult to enter. I've had quite a bit of experience entering certain large houses on the Mountain. Now you take the Belmonts', for example, that's a difficult house. Although I admit that Madame Belmont was well worth the extra effort. On the other hand, the kitchens at Pride's Court are an open invitation. Nobody bothers to bolt the doors. A woman who gave her name as Catherine was preparing Sir Simon's tea tray when I walked in. And we came to an understanding. For a small gratuity she promised faithfully to deliver my letter on his tray."

Armand was building a fresh fire. The room was cold. He cleaned the ashes out with a brass shovel, adjusted the draft, which had been closed down a little for the night fire, and built a pyramid of kindling. The logs would be put on later when the kindling blazed.

"But the flowers?" she prodded him. "You must have gone through to the conservatory. What if you'd run into Papa? Or even Mama?"

"I knew I'd be safe, since his tray hadn't gone up."

"That's true." She nodded.

She could imagine the sun coming through the broad bay window of Sir Simon's bedroom, and her father having his tea in the mahogany four-poster. (Later, he would take breakfast with Lady Court down in the morning room—a lavish meal that required at least a dozen serving dishes. They would hold fish, chops, ham, rissoles, pickles, rolls, cheeses, fried potatoes, crumpets, toast, and biscuits. There would also be a jug of milk and a big vessel of strong coffee. Sir Simon ate heartily in the morning.)

"After I arranged about the letter," Armand explained, stirring the kindling to get the fire going, "I walked through to the front of the house. I thought I would leave by the front door. Why not? The smell of flowers lured me into the conservatory. That's when I decided to cut the roses and bring them to you. I hope Sir Simon had read the paper. I stole it from the front vestibule."

"Armand, the risk!" She was still a little frightened when she thought of him prowling about Pride's Court like that.

"No risk is too great if it makes you happy." Armand made a mock bow.

"I love the flowers. Tea roses. I would never be allowed to have them in my room at home."

"And now, my darling—" Armand threw two logs on the burning kindling and waited for them to catch— "I will look for that old woman. She wasn't around when I came in. I'll order some breakfast for you in bed. Would you like that?"

"Yes, please."

"Stay in bed until the room warms up."

When he was gone she closed her eyes, trying to accustom herself to this new life. She was not at Pride's Court. She was no longer a young girl to be wooed, but a married woman in a strange place, among strange people. People whose language she could barely understand. Was it only six months since she'd first met Armand at the ball? Only last June? It was impossible. And yet it was true.

The ball, given by the Courts at Pride's Court, had been in her honor. It had been one of the major social events of the summer season in Montreal. Ten thousand roses, their delicate scent wafting through all the rooms that would be open, had emphasized the splendor of the occasion. The roses had been imported from florists in Quebec and Ontario, and even from south of the border. In the conservatory at the far end of the double drawing room, a fanciful cascade of red and white blooms had been cruelly secured to the spikes of a giant organ-pipe cactus (a particular pet of Jamie's). Red and white were the Court family colors.

It had not been only the flowers that had demonstrated the care the Courts had taken over the arrangements. There had also been the steady flow of French champagne and the cheerful wheeze of Strauss waltzes from thirty violinists stationed on one side of the grand staircase. And there had been carriage-loads of guests, representing all the English families in the city of Montreal that truly mattered.

Sir Simon and Lady Court had given the ball for several reasons. It had been Honey's coming-out party—that was the first thing. The Lieutenant Governor of Quebec had been one of the guests, adding a vice-regal splendor to the occasion. Also, all three Court sons had been home, and that didn't happen very often . . .

Charles, the eldest, lived at home still, unmarried at twenty-nine. It was not unusual that he be present. But Geoffrey, at twenty-six, was in charge of the Liverpool office of the Court Shipping Line—the other end of the transatlantic run from Montreal. Geoffrey happened to be in the city for a two-week conference with his father and with Charles, now a vice-president of the line. Most unusual of all was the fact that Fort happened to be in the city, since he was a sea captain learning the business from the inside.

It was a glorious June night—rain-washed air stirred ever so slightly by an uncertain breeze, stars hanging so low over the Mountain that they might have been ornaments for the ball, and cicadas singing wildly in the flower gardens around Pride's Court. It seemed that Sir Simon Court controlled not only his seventeen prospering business enterprises, but the weather as well. Several guests made such a remark, laughingly giving Sir Simon credit for the perfection of the evening.

The great house might have been designed for just such a night. A huge limestone portico with thick pillars stretched across the gravel driveway like a magnificent canopy. Black oak double doors opened first on a square anteroom, and beyond that, framed by a high, polished mahogany arch, was the octagonal reception hall. It was an elegant room, with its eight white walls, four featuring niches holding marble statues—highly idealized and very innocent-looking human figures. And beyond that, again, the great hall itself—sixty feet of shining oak floor overlaid with colorful Turkey carpets. But that was on ordinary days. For the ball the oak floor had been stripped bare for the dancers. The great hall had been transformed into a ballroom, lined conveniently with handsome benches and small chairs with carved backs bearing the Court coat of arms—two lions combatant, three lances on a shield. The light that radiated from the gilt bronze and marble gaslamps set at suitable intervals along the walls was designed to be flattering, mellow with a bluish cast. A regal setting for handsome women dressed in pastel gowns and wielding busy fans, and men perspiring a little as they struggled with the waltz in their tight tails and white gloves.

The long dining room was on the left, its ceiling decorated delicately with pale blue molded medallions and flowered pendants, and its windows swelling out into gentle oval bays. To the right of the great hall was the double drawing room and, at the end of that, the enormous conservatory with its hundreds of tropical plants. There were also smaller sitting rooms, a smoking room, and a card room.

In the green-chintzed smoking room, Sir Simon was

drinking Scotch and soda and talking to Paul St. Amour. St. Amour and his son, Armand, had been invited to the ball by his son Fort. Sir Simon had not been pleased to learn of the invitations. For some time he had wanted to speak to St. Amour briefly, to sound him out about a business deal, but he saw no need to bring Frenchmen into his own home.

Sir Simon studied Paul St. Amour with intense curiosity. The French were a bit of a mystery to him, with their closed society (they did not entertain lavishly, but he understood that some of the houses were extraordinarily well-endowed with family relics of great value) and their reputation for dash and gallantry. He couldn't see any evidence of it in St. Amour. The man needed a new tailor. He was unprepossessing—a thin, worried-looking man with receding gray hair and dark, pocketed eyes.

Sir Simon offered St. Amour a cigar from the porcelain box on the table beside him. "Have a cigar, sir?"

"Thank you, yes."

St. Amour clipped his cigar carefully and studied it before lighting it. Sir Simon noticed, with an inner snort, that St. Amour was drinking champagne; that fact registered as an automatic debit on the invisible balance sheet he was keeping in his head.

"Splendid party," St. Amour said. "All the English who count. And then some."

His voice had the cadence of the French Canadian speaking English: a rhythmic rise and fall of pitch, always recognizable.

"Aha. Yes. Glad you could come. I hope you're feeling better? I heard you were sick."

Sir Simon's voice, although lowered from its usual boom, as befitted a tête-à-tête, was still penetrating. St. Amour shuddered inwardly.

"Nothing serious. I only had the influenza. There's been quite an epidemic, you know. The immigrants bring it over on the boats. As well as cholera and typhoid. A man my age has to be careful."

"Not on *my* boats," Sir Simon said at once.

"I don't think the influenza recognizes the name of the shipping line," St. Amour said, allowing himself a smile.

Sir Simon obviously did not agree. His boats were clean, the immigrants well-treated (or so he thought), and he did not expect that disease would be found there. And if it did happen to be found there, it was some foreigner's fault, that much was clear.

"Anyway, I'm glad it was nothing serious. Ross told me he was worried about you."

"Oh, yes, Ross. He's on the board of directors of one of the railroads I'm connected with. The Quebec and St. John Railway Company. My son, Armand, went to the director's meeting last month in my place. I suppose he mentioned to Ross that I was ill."

"Right. That's what Ross said."

Sir Simon knew he was making St. Amour uncomfortable. The man was lying about his health, but he could understand that well enough. It didn't pay to let people know you were seriously ill. Destroyed confidence. Ross had said the old boy was supposed to have had a slight stroke or a heart attack, he wasn't sure which. St. Amour's hands were trembling and he had a look of fear in his eyes.

"Are you opening up the area around Lake St. John? Ross tells me that that railway might be a small gold mine."

"We're adding forty-nine miles of track this year. And, of course, settlement is going ahead. It's great country up there."

A waiter came by with a tray of drinks. St. Amour set his empty glass on the tray and took a fresh glass of champagne. Sir Simon replenished his supply of Scotch.

St. Amour was pleased to see that his hand was steadier. The heart attack had not impaired his speech and there had been no paralysis—as from a stroke, for example. The shaking was a weakness he was trying to overcome. He hoped that Sir Simon had not noticed it.

"So you are encouraging settlers to go up to Lake St. John, then?" Sir Simon pursued. "That's pretty rough country, isn't it? Can they grow anything on the land?"

"When you see trees like that, you know the soil is good. No problem there. They're growing wheat, oats, barley, vegetables. You know, about six years ago we asked the clergy in some parishes in the province to send in delegates to look at the possibilities in the Lake St. John area. The reports were good. They went back home, many of them, to encourage some of their people to move up there. Some of the parishioners in the older communities are sending their sons north to settle. Land is cheap. Then there are the saw mills. Good lumbering."

"What trees do you have up there?"

"Everything. Elm. Ash. Black birch. Maple. Pine. Everything."

"Are you building any sawmills yourself, or just leasing your land to people who want to cut lumber and build mills?"

"No, we won't build any mills. But we're encouraging businessmen to come in. We lease the land cheap. And give them good rates on the railroad when they take the lumber out."

"Ross tells me there's good fishing in Lake St. John," Sir Simon said.

"Excellent fishing. *Mon Dieu,* that lake is is so full of fish it'll be years before it can be fished out! Maybe twenty years. It's a big lake, you know. There are landlocked salmon, dore, pike."

St. Amour was waiting for Sir Simon to get to the point. Men like Court always wanted something. They did not spend time in idle chatter, especially at a party like this. Could Sir Simon have heard about the St. Amour financial difficulties? If the man knew Ross well, it was possible. As things stood, Paul St. Amour might have to sell his block of shares in the railroad. But if he did, St. Amour thought angrily, it would not be to any goddamned English. He would at least find a *French* buyer.

Sir Simon was anxious to move along. He wanted to talk to James Kirkpatrick about mining in Ontario. (Somebody had come up with the idea that there might be gold in the north.)

"How important do you really think the railroad is, then, in terms of lumber?" he asked, staring into his now-empty glass.

"Important? Well, right now we're taking out twenty-five million feet of sawn lumber in a single year. And when we finally get the line completed we'll take out six hundred million feet. Think of it! It goes by rail to the Ottawa River, and then by water to Europe and South America. No limit to the market."

"At any rate, if you ever decide you want to get out of the Lake St. John project, let me know. Or let Charles know. He's my lieutenant here in Montreal, you know. Good man. We'd be interested to hear from you."

"I don't plan to sell," St. Amour said coldly.

"Not now, perhaps. But who knows about the future?" Sir Simon badly wanted to free himself now that he had made his point. He twirled his glass impatiently. St. Amour was butting his cigar, a promising sign. It was as good a moment as any to disengage himself. His thoughts had moved along to his daughter, and he wondered if Honey was dancing with any of the fellows Charles had earmarked as suitable. Mark Davidson, now, was a particularly eligible chap. A merger between the Courts and the Davidsons would be most welcome. The Davidsons had, among other holdings, a large ironworks.

St. Amour, however, was still talking.

"Should I decide to sell," he was saying somewhat heavily, "I hope you will understand me when I say it will be to a *French* Canadian."

Sir Simon allowed himself a cross between a guffaw and a harrumph, abridged slightly with a cough.

"Well said, sir."

"I don't mean to be rude . . ."

"Not at all. I see your point perfectly. Only three French Canadians on the board of directors now, eh? I believe Ross told me that. Quite."

Sir Simon knew how things stood. He would have to use a front if he were going to buy out St. Amour's shares. But he would have to be careful. He could use Pierre Tellier. Tellier was a sell-out—a *vendu*—but nobody knew that yet, so he was still useful. Sir Simon despised Tellier, of course, but there was no getting around the man's value. At the moment, Sir Simon held eighteen percent of the shares in the Quebec and St. John Railway, through Ross. He knew that St. Amour held forty-three percent. If he bought up St. Amour's shares through Tellier, he would control the company. Tellier would be a director, of course, but he would do as he was told. At the same time, Sir Simon admired St. Amour's spirit. Yes, it was commendable even if it was a nuisance.

"Excuse me, sir, but I must go along and see how my daughter is. Tonight's her big night, you know. Being presented to the Lieutenant Governor . . . I wonder if he's arrived."

Sir Simon drifted off, his mind quickly seizing on other problems in other rooms with other people. Honey was no doubt up to some ridiculous trick or other. She was a rebellious and unreliable girl and required a good deal of control. When he reached the edge of the ballroom, he saw that Mark Davidson was standing alone. Damn the girl, she had disappeared! Absolutely nowhere to be seen. The Davidson fortune—ironworks, sugar, textiles—was all acceptable. Mark was a good enough chap. Had gone to Oxford with Charles. And the Davidsons would be pleased. They belonged to Christ Church Cathedral, too; not part of that dour Presbyterian bunch. He wouldn't wish that on Honey if it could be avoided.

Honey was too precocious for a girl, too independent by far. She must be put in her place before it was too late. She didn't realize how important her marriage was, and that was partly his own fault; he had spoiled her when she was small. A girl after three boys. Well, it wasn't so surprising. And now he had only Charles to help him here in Montreal. Geoffrey off in Liverpool, doing well enough, but a dry stick. Not much to him, actually. And Fort, at the other extreme, buzzing about the world like a demented sailor without a penny to his name. Some of his escapades were a bit much, but at least the boy was adventurous. He'd been a bit like that himself as a lad. As for his wife, Lydia, she was inclined to be vague. Always involved in a book, or organizing some damned hospital fund, or rooting about in the gardens with that great oaf of a gardener, Jamie. Not that Jamie was a bad gardener. No, he was good. But still. Well, as usual, he would have to straighten things out himself. You couldn't trust anybody else, that was the difficulty. Now where in hell was Honey?

While Sir Simon thrust his way through his guests, making slow progress in his search, Honey was in the conservatory carefully setting her full glass of champagne in the pot of a huge white jasmine bush. She was bored with dancing and the champagne was going to her head. Papa had allowed her wine at table since she was sixteen, but only in small amounts. Tonight everybody wanted to bring her a fresh glass of champagne before she had finished the one in her hand.

From her retreat behind the jasmine plant, Honey looked

out at the guests clustered in the drawing room. A forecast of life to come. Bunches of overripe matrons sipping wine and ogling the young people and puffy men with glassy eyes pretending to be wise. It must be awful to be old and fat like Mrs. Lewis-Graham, or poor Lady Bolt, all got up in purple satin with an ugly ostrich boa.

As for the music, it wasn't very good. Poor Papa didn't know about things like that and assumed that if the orchestra were large and expensive, it must be good. Honey sighed, hoping that Mark Davidson would not find her. He had the oddest, droopiest mustache that gave him a permanently sad look. Rather like a bloodhound she'd had as a child. The hound's name had been Charlie and he'd worn exactly the same expression. How on earth could she make love to a man who looked like a dog she had owned ten years ago?

Several young men with names she could not remember had told her she was beautiful. One had kissed her hand. He hadn't been so bad; it was the one who had spent the whole dance looking down the front of her gown who had annoyed her. And the other who had managed, somehow, to accidentally touch her bosom, and then turned red as a pomegranate. Why couldn't Papa and Charles see how hopeless these men were? Perhaps Fort might know some interesting men. Of course, they would all be foreigners, since Fort was always sailing to some strange country. But at least they would have a spirit of adventure, even if they weren't rich and suitable.

Such a waste of a pretty gown! She wore white silk with ruffles of off-white Chantilly lace around the shoulders and hem. Papa had imported it from New York for the occasion. And the pearl-and-ruby necklace (the family colors)—a gift of Papa's for her coming-out. Fort had made fun of the necklace when Papa wasn't within hearing, saying Papa was placing it on her so that all the young men would see how much she was worth—like a ribbon at one of the cattle exhibitions. Fort was sometimes quite amusing. He often told her stories of life at sea and in the ports he'd visited. Once he actually had seen a sea monster, off the coast of Ireland. It had been lying on a deserted beach, he said, until the word had spread and then a great crowd had gathered to see it. It had had arms and legs, and one ear, and a horn and a beard and a single glowing eye. But you couldn't always believe Fort, of course.

Reluctantly she left the conservatory. She couldn't stay hidden all night. She ventured into the drawing room, pushing through the crowd, nodding and smiling at some of the women her mother knew. She saw her mother across the room for just an instant, but then, as if a curtain had come down, her mother disappeared behind a woman in jet black.

It was at that precise moment that she saw him.

He was walking toward her, wading through the thick forest of talkers and drinkers. He had dark eyes bright with energy. That was the first thing she noticed. His face was vivid and compelling. His eyes stormed hers, held them fixed. The roomful of people receded and she saw only this stranger, dark and quick and alive.

When he was close enough, he took her hand.

"I've come for you. It's our dance."

"Yes, I think it is."

Just like that. So simple. He took her gloved hand and pulled it through his arm. She felt the warmth of his shoulder as it brushed against her own.

"My name is Armand, *ma petite*. Armand St. Amour."

"I'm sure you know my name," she said.

"Since you are the only woman at the ball worth looking at, I found out immediately. I was told it was Honey. In French that is *miel*."

As they moved onto the floor, people made way for them, staring. Honey was conscious of the looks, the whispers, but she smiled directly into Armand's face, into his dark, sparkling eyes, into his heart. Yes, it seemed to her that she touched his heart. When the dance was over, he said, "Where can we go to talk? I must talk to you alone. Everything here is boring. I hope you don't think I'm rude to say that about your father's party, but . . ." He shrugged.

"I know exactly what you mean. I was bored too, until you came. I don't know what most of these people get out of it, do you?"

"Well, they drink and eat. They talk business. The women watch and gossip. They wear fancy clothes. Some dance. And some, like us, fall in love. So you see, it isn't all bad. Now, where can we go?"

"The gardens are filled with people," Honey said.

"Then we don't want the gardens. Come, Miel, you can think of a place. This is a huge house. There must be many places for a tryst."

"I know! The tower."

"Ah, yes. Is it open?"

"Yes, Papa keeps it open. He goes up there in the day-time to watch the ships come up the river. And there's a telescope. We can look at the stars."

They stood in a well of music, the sounds of "The Blue Danube" enveloping the tower, reaching up sweetly through the soft, dark air. The stars hung close outside the win-dows, and below, the orange lights of ships glowed like stationary comets.

Armand took her hand and they stood together, close, leaning slightly toward each other in the warm night. For a long time they did not speak. At last Armand said, "We'll have to elope."

"Anything else would be impossible," she agreed, smil-ing.

"They'll find a way to stop us if they can."

"They mustn't find out. Oh, Armand, they mustn't find out."

"You're sure?"

"There's nothing else to be done, is there?"

"Nothing else, *ma chérie*."

That was how it had begun. Up there in the tower they had both known that it was only a matter of time. And they had been patient for almost six months, meeting secretly, making plans. It had ended, finally, with the visit to Father Leguen, and now here she was, waiting for her breakfast on a tray, to be brought by her husband, Armand.

Remembering, she smiled. The smile covered a tremble of fear when she thought of Papa, reading that letter this morning. And for an instant, she knew doubt. Then Ar-mand opened the door, carrying a tray with a pot of steam-ing tea on it. And she knew that she made no mis-take.

"First, tea," Armand said, setting the tray down by the bed. "And then, how shall we spend the day?"

"Perhaps I ought to shop for some clothes."

"Excellent. Well, let me see. First tea. Later shopping. In between . . ."

Armand began to take off his clothes. Honey decided that the tea would keep.

CHAPTER THREE

"I have nothing to say!" Sir Simon said loudly.

Actually, he had dozens of things to say, each more bitter, more graphic than the last.

"Surely, sir, it can't be as bad as all that!" Armand protested. He tried a half smile, but it met with such a wall of cold blue ice from Sir Simon's eyes that he let it die a mercifully quick death.

Sir Simon, glowering before the fire in the Red Sitting Room, turned an even deeper shade of red until his face was a perfect match for the crimson curtains. He looked about his favorite room, a room that had given him so much comfort in the past, and saw that Christmas was already in evidence. It was two weeks away, but already swatches of tinsel hung across the deep valances of the bay window, dripping with handmade angels and silver balls dangling from silver threads. Two enormous poinsettias, one red and one white, stood in green china pots on either side of the bay. A red velvet Santa with a sheep's-wool beard sat jauntily on the Sheraton side table.

Lady Court loved Christmas and every year whipped the servants into a frenzy of preparations for entertainments of every conceivable sort—formal dinners, high teas, gala brunches, a New Year's Eve ball, and even a children's party for an orphanage of which she was chief patron. She adored making decorations and was constantly searching for new ideas and materials. The Court Christmas tree, standing strategically in the great hall, was a miracle of color, size, and style, a legend in the city.

Sir Simon, too, had grudgingly admitted that he liked the Christmas season, especially after the children came along and were able to take part in the fun. He liked to buy them model trains, tin soldiers imported from Germany and France, a pony cart, and English dolls. In the last few years he had begun to project further, to the grandchildren. A nice touch, he thought, when he could reign over three generations and would be able to create new family customs, endorse additional rites of celebration.

And now *this*. The word "grandchildren" now pierced his soul. Grandchildren, half French—and all Catholic, by God. His bile stirred again. He swung his fiercest look at Hannah, his only daughter, standing there so innocently, as if she had done nothing wrong. Nothing wrong?

"It's worse than anything I could have imagined!" Sir Simon said, moving from the fire to the cigar box and selecting a cigar without even looking at it. "What about my grandchildren?"

"I hope there will be children," Armand said.

"I would have hoped so, too, before this happened. But now . . . now . . . do you realize, Hannah, what you've done? They'll all be little Papists!"

"Well, Papa, the children will be brought up as Catholics, of course. I agreed to that. But I'm not converting. I'm still a Protestant. Armand won't interfere with that."

"A hell of a lot of good that will do you," Sir Simon exploded. "Married to a Frenchie! You might as well have gone all the way!"

"I didn't want to go all the way. I chose to remain a Protestant."

"You *chose* to rebel against everything I've taught you. Against everything that you were born to. Against everything this family stands for. You don't understand what you've done."

"She married me because she loves me," Armand said quietly, although he was keeping his temper with some difficulty.

"You, sir, have stolen my grandchildren!" Sir Simon said. He puffed on his cigar, almost annihilating it in the process.

"Oh, Papa, really . . ." Honey began.

But Sir Simon interrupted her and drove on with his tirade.

"Do you think for one moment that *his* family will accept you? Eh? Have you called on *them* yet? They're the worst of all, the Catholics. They'll treat you like dirt because you're a heathen. Do you think they'll take you in, be loving, be kind?"

"They couldn't behave any worse than you are, Papa."

Armand put his hand on Honey's arm as if to restrain her. Sir Simon, seeing the gesture, rose to it like a tormented bull, his voice booming louder in the confines of the room. He waved his cigar.

"You'll find out what it's like to live with foreigners! What it's like to be alone, cut off from your family and friends, cut off from everything you're used to. Goddamnit, Hanah, you haven't any idea . . ."

"I'd like to see Mother," Honey said. Her voice was still calm, but she was beginning to tremble a little. Her fingers dug into Armand's arm for support.

"Your mother is indisposed," Sir Simon said curtly.

"Please, could I go up?"

"She's ill."

"She's not seriously ill, is she? Does she know we're here? Did you tell her?"

"She doesn't wish to see you. She's not seeing anybody. She took to her bed when I told her the news, and she's not seen anybody since."

"I'd like to speak to her myself," Honey persisted.

She had never known her father to lie. Yet she could not believe that her mother would not see her. Did not *want* to see her.

"Absolutely not. I forbid it."

For a moment, Honey thought of running out of the room, across the great hall, and up the stairs to her mother's bedroom. But Sir Simon, standing there like a medieval tyrant, prevented her from moving. Her will seemed to drain away. It occurred to her that she might arrange a visit with her mother on another day, when her father wasn't home. That ought to be possible. But for the first time, some of the bravado left her. A thin edge of doubt and fear broke through the rosy cloud of her happiness.

"Anyway, Papa, I'd like to get my clothes. I'll just go upstairs and pack some of them, if I may. Armand has the sleigh, and we could get one of the stable hands to help with the trunks."

"Your clothes will be sent to you when you provide me with your permanent address."

Honey was incredulous. She had not foreseen this implacability. She had expected him to be furious, to rant and rave, yes. But she had assumed that she would be able to get around him, as she had always done in the past, and that he would at least let her take some of her clothes and books.

"You mean I can't go up to my room to get my things, Papa?"

"I mean you cannot go upstairs. You don't live here anymore. Why should you? I'll have your things sent along. No doubt you'll need them, my dear. Your new husband won't have told you, I'm sure, but his family are in certain financial . . . ah . . . difficulties."

She whirled on Armand, suddenly feeling afraid and cheated. He hadn't mentioned anything about money troubles. The idea that there might be hardship, as well as family anger had never occurred to her.

"Is that true, Armand?"

"In a way. I didn't want to tell you on our honeymoon, but yes, there are many troubles in the family. However, nothing as serious as Sir Simon is suggesting. Please, darling, don't worry about it."

"But, Armand . . ."

"*Je t'aime, ma petite.* Do not worry."

"Perhaps," Sir Simon said heavily, "you can live on French phrases."

"There will be no need for that, sir," Armand said stiffly. "I am perfectly capable of looking after my wife."

"I hope so. Because if you think you'll get any help from me, you're badly mistaken. The Courts will not pour good money after bad. And as for Hannah's inheritance, she will not be able to count on that. I'm not leaving any of *my* hard-earned money to a bunch of bloody Catholics."

━━━━━━

Camille St. Amour opened the door to them. Honey saw at once how like her brother she was. Her hair was black and thick, with a few unruly curls that fell over her forehead in the same childish way as Armand's. Most of her hair, however, was caught in a black net at the back of her neck as if she were attempting to look prim. The style was at complete odds with her brilliant black eyes and sensual mouth. All together, the pale heart-shaped face, the intense gaze, and the restless hands gave her a distinctly feverish look.

"We've looked for you for hours, Armand," she said in French. "I sent Jacques out to the house on St. Urbain Street, but you were gone."

"But my dear, I told you this morning that we'd be here for Christmas Eve supper and that I'd go to Mass with the family. Why were you looking for me?"

He kissed his sister on the cheek, not waiting for her answer. Snowflakes from his hat melted against her face and she drew back from him, wiping away the cold water. Outside it was a postcard Christmas with large, soft snowflakes blurring the shapes of trees and buildings and deadening the city sounds. Armand and Honey stamped snow off their boots, and then Camille quickly shut the door behind them.

"You don't know," Camille said.

"Know what, for God's sake?" Armand said impatiently. He helped Honey take off the snow-covered fur coat and hat, and then her boots.

"About Father."

She seemed incapable of forming a complete sentence. She was intent on giving off bits of information in spurts. Armand straightened up from taking off his own fur-lined boots and stared at his sister.

"What about him? He knew we were coming. I planned to introduce Honey to the family tonight. I gathered there was no objection. Isn't Helene here? I suppose Marc has come in from Oka? Isn't he here for the holiday?"

"Yes, Father knew you were coming. Helene is here. Marc is here. We have sent to the country for Justine. She wasn't coming until the day after Christmas, bringing Laurent and the children with her. You know how Laurent hates to leave the farm for more than a few hours."

Armand grasped Camille by the shoulders and shook her.

"What's the matter? What is this about?"

"Father. It's Father. He's had a heart attack. When he heard you were coming, bringing . . . bringing your wife, he became quite odd. And then . . . I think it was an hour later . . . he had great pain. We sent for Dr. Lanctot, and . . . he says Father may not live."

"Father had a heart attack in the spring. Attacks often

follow one another, I've been told. Surely you aren't suggesting that I'm responsible for this?"

Armand was angry. Camille closed her eyes as if to close him out. Her face was even whiter than before and a deep crease of tension appeared between her eyes.

"Where's Helene?" Armand demanded. "Is Corbin here yet, or is she here alone?"

"Corbin is still at the office. Helene is alone in the drawing room having coffee."

"Let's go there, then. I'd like a brandy. We're cold. I suppose Helene is waiting to have a scene?"

"She's had one scene with Marc already," Camille said wearily. She led the way through the central hallway to the drawing room.

"Knowing Helene, I'd say she's quite capable of having another scene as soon as she sees me. I'm sorry, Honey, I'd hoped you could meet the family under pleasant conditions."

He took his wife's arm, pressing it to his side for comfort.

Camille said, "We sent a message to Corbin as soon as we could. He'll be here soon, but he had a court case that went right through the day."

The St. Amour house was not like Pride's Court. It was more than a hundred years old, built of unyielding limestone, with a perpendicular front and small, graceless windows. The rooms were boxlike and opened off twisted hallways. Along the dark walls there were paintings of various saints, and statues of the Virgin. Honey thought the house looked dingy and infinitely old.

The drawing room was decorated in navy blue and brown, giving it an austere, unwelcoming look. Even the mantel was inordinately dark, having been stained at some period in the distant past so that now it was almost black. It reached the ceiling and dominated the room. The fire was blazing but there was no sign of any Christmas decoration except a rather crudely made crèche on one of the tables.

Helene was standing in front of the fire with a cup in her hand that had been taken from the tray of coffee on a nearby refectory table. She was heavy, with a high-piled mass of black hair generously streaked with silver. Her well-trussed figure bore witness to years of good eating. She glared at all of them when they entered but directed her remarks to Armand in French.

"Well, Armand, you've arrived at last. It's always difficult to find you when you're needed. You know that Father's had a heart attack? I expect Camille has told you?"

"Yes, she told me. I sent word this morning that my wife and I would be here for supper. I didn't know there was any urgency. Anyway, I'm here."

"You can see what your wretched behavior has brought on the family!"

Honey had trouble following Helene's rapid and emphatic French. She could grasp the general meaning but not all the individual words. It would have been polite of Helene to speak in English, under the circumstances, but she was making a point.

"I'm not going to take all the blame, Helene," Armand began to protest. But his sister interrupted him.

"This is the last straw, really! You've always been unreliable, a worry to Father, particularly considering that you're the eldest son and will be head of the family. A thought I can't bear, at the moment. I don't know what Corbin will say. He knows how difficult it is for me to keep the family together, when you're such a . . . a *roué*. Ever since Mother died . . . I've done my best. But I have my own family. My own house. I can't be here all the time. And Camille, well, she runs this place, I'll admit, but *really* . . ." Helene paused to emit a painful groan and rolled her eyes. *"You've* acted against the will of God and *we're* all being punished for it. I hope you intend to come to Mass with us tonight."

"For God's sake, Helene, shut up!"

Helene had always been the same; passionless, harsh in her judgments, but heavily armed with religion. Armand had always preferred Camille, even with her touch of madness, to the coldly self-righteous Helene.

"How dare you speak to me like that? I wish Corbin were here. He wouldn't stand for it."

"You're very rude, my dear sister. Let me introduce my bride. Honey . . . my sister Helene. Helene . . . my wife, Honey."

Helene stopped talking long enough to acknowledge the introduction and to excuse her lack of welcome on the grounds that the family was upset. Despite this belated attempt at civility, there was no outward yielding in her manner, and Honey felt that Helene was determined to make her feel an outsider.

"Who is with Father now?" Armand asked.

"Dr. Lanctot and Marc," Helene said.

"Has Marc given him the last rites?" Armand felt the first real stab of hard reality, and death became more than a word.

"He's given him absolution, yes," Camille said, speaking for the first time since they'd come into the drawing room. "Father was quite lucid, so it's perfectly all right. Please sit down, won't you . . . Honey? Can I get you some coffee?"

Camille spoke in English. Honey accepted, although she would have preferred a cup of black, strong tea. At Pride's Court they would be having a special tea at this moment, with all the usual scones, crumpets, jellies, and Christmas mincemeat pies made by Mama for the occasion. Mama would have put out the Christmas figures on the mantel and there would be cedar boughs in the halls. After tea, Papa would herd everyone to the smoking room to listen to Christmas carols on the phonograph. (During the rest of the year he sometimes played a noisy version of the "Anvil Chorus" and some American Civil War songs. He also dearly loved a humorous selection elaborately entitled "A Meeting of the Ananias Club at Pumpkin Center.")

"I'll go up to see Father now," Armand said to Camille, "I'll come down for some coffee later. But first, I'd like a brandy, please."

Camille waved a hand toward a commode.

"Over there."

Armand found a bottle of French brandy and poured himself a drink.

"I've given you and . . . your wife . . . the room you had when you were home, Armand," Camille said. "I thought that would be best. Blanche put a fire on."

"Thanks, yes, that's a good idea. We can all go up together and you can show Honey to the room. We only brought a small bag each. I hadn't planned to stay more than a couple of nights."

Helene sniffed in the background, but since she had a

mouthful of hot black coffee, she refrained from comment.

"Will you excuse us, then, Helene?" Armand asked politely.

His sister gave him a cold look and poked at the fire. As she put more wood on she said stiffly, "Do as you like. Corbin will be here soon; I won't be alone for long. Justine may arrive tonight, since we sent for her, but the roads will be snowed in. Will it ever stop snowing?"

Armand had stayed with his father. Alone in the bedroom, which like the rest of the house was boxlike and dark, Honey stood by a window with small leaded panes of glass and stared down into the street below. The lamplight was diluted by steady drifts of snow. Every tree, every post, every fence was edged in white. It was quiet in the street until suddenly a group of youngsters well wrapped in long woolen scarves and wearing woolen toques in the French manner came by laughing, pushing each other in the snow, and singing snatches of an old French Christmas Carol. Christmas. How different tonight was from what she was used to, what she might have expected as a young bride! At Pride's Court, she thought wistfully, the huge Christmas tree would be ablaze with candles, and Papa would have placed three buckets of water beside it, just in case of fire.

Camille climbed to the fourth floor. The nursery was her retreat—always waiting, a shrine to past and happier times. Nobody in the house seemed to recall that the room was there; it was so far removed from the downstairs rooms that were in daily use. When she and her brothers and sisters had all been very young, the entire fourth floor of the house had belonged to them. A governess imported from Quebec City had lived in a large, cold bedroom separating the children's bedroom from the nursery. She had had a trunk that had smelled of mothballs.

The nursery itself was on a slightly different level, five steps up from the corridor where the bedrooms were lined-up, cell-like. Camille still kept it free of dust so that the rocking horse, with his tight black leather skin and bedraggled but real horsehair mane and tail, looked as if he had just been ridden. His glass eye hinted at it. A game of chess was set up on a wooden table. The slate stood on its easel. A train waited on a track in one corner.

The nursery was a vault of stored dreams, of flights back into that diffuse but brightly colored world of childhood. Sometimes in the early evening when the light reached a certain moment of purity, when it turned the red saddle of the rocking horse, Tonnerre, to a sensuous crimson, when the stale green carpet became translucent as grass under dew, when the wax doll's painted face pulsed with the need to be touched, then Camille was back in that other time. That time of mysterious, cryptic secrets, that place knit together by subterranean desires embroidered with the fluted laughter of children, laughter born of untouchable, unknowable subjects.

Camille stood in a circle of light from the single lamp she carried. The corners of the room receded into distant shadows. Earlier in the evening she had taken time to build a fire in the grate, and now she set the lamp down on one of the wooden work tables and threw some coal on the flames.

Then she sat in the wooden rocker to stare at the fire and wait. She could see snow filling up the windows, building on the ledges and on the leaded strips that separated the small panes of glass. On the white-painted mantel, a red velvet Santa Claus was the only sign of Christmas. She had taken him out of the toy box that afternoon. Her gift to Marc lay on the mantel beside him. A very precious gift; one she had planned for months.

Downstairs, Marc would probably be searching in the kitchen for something to eat. He had been in Father's room for hours without food. He would eat some bread and cheese and drink some red table wine. Marc didn't eat much. He never had. He was excruciatingly thin. His handsome face, especially his cheeks, looked sunken as if he were ill. Well, perhaps he *was* ill. She sighed, thinking about him.

Perhaps Marc wouldn't come up here. Perhaps he would go to Mass with the others. She wasn't going to Mass, herself, but intended to say her prayers in her room. She was sure the Virgin would excuse her tonight (and as if for confirmation, she looked toward the wall where a painting of the Virgin in a light blue gown hung, just as it had hung when she was too young to understand). If the Virgin did not understand, what good was it to pray to Her?

Her thoughts returned to the days when she and Marc had played in this room as children. They had formed an alliance against the others. Against Armand and Helene and Justine, who pushed and bullied and had their own way. She and Marc had always been different—imaginative, sensitive to the moment. She wrote poetry; Marc was obsessed with religion, with being a priest, a martyr, even. Well, you could be a martyr in this life without trying very hard. But whatever the cause, they had seen things in the same way. They had *known* certain things, been born knowing. She loved Armand. After all, he was dashing and handsome, and no doubt he would be successful. But he was not like Marc. Not like her, either.

She heard the door open and swung around. Marc stood in his own pool of lamplight, dark, brooding, and wearing a look close to tears.

"Father's asleep," he said, moving toward her.

"What does Dr. Lanctot say?"

"If he doesn't have another heart attack in the next twenty-four hours, he may recover. Rest is what he needs."

"Who is with him?"

"Armand."

She nodded. Marc pulled up a stool and sat beside her.

"Did you eat anything, Marc?" Camille asked after a short silence.

"Yes, I had something in the kitchen."

"I'm not going to Mass. I've prayed to the Virgin to explain it. I'm sure She understands."

"I'm sure She does."

"Marc, if Father dies . . . what will happen? Will Armand come to live in this house, with his bride?"

"I suppose so. He'll be head of the family then."

"But what will become of *me?*" Camille whispered. It was a whisper with a broken wing. Her voice trailed off until it was nearly inaudible.

"Perhaps you will get married. Why not? You're very beautiful, Camille. You're not like Helene and Justine. Perhaps you'll find somebody who is right for you."

"No," Camille said.

Marc nodded, but he felt it necessary to protest.

"I have my Church, my vocation; it isn't the same for me. For you, for a woman, it's quite different. Unless you join an order. Have you thought of that?"

"Yes, of course. I've thought of it many times."

"It might . . . might be the solution. Although, Camille, you should not give up the idea of marriage altogether. Not yet."

"Marriage! What good is there in talking of *that*?"

"You realize that I'll be in Montreal now, instead of in the country at the monastery. I won't be far away. You must tell me when you need help. I'll have my own parish, you know."

"Will you miss the life at the monastery? Will you miss the solitude, and the prayers, and the time for thought, and the silences?"

"Yes. I expect I will."

"It must be very peaceful there."

"Wonderfully peaceful. I think going to Oka saved my sanity. But still, I felt called to the world again. I decided I wanted to take part in a mission to the people themselves."

Marc got up and wandered across the half-dark room to one of the front windows and looked down into the street.

"Christmas Eve," he said. "Do you remember that Christmas when we were very young, about ten and eleven? Everyone had gone to Mass. One of the maids was supposed to be in charge, but I think we were completely alone in the house. And you were frightened? You came to my room."

"We had rooms next to each other. Mine was closest to the nursery because I was youngest. You let me come into your bed, I was so frightened. The others would have laughed at me if they'd been home. But you didn't laugh."

She closed out the memory of it. The memory of an act born of innocence that somehow revealed a thick stirring in the depths of her being more frightening than the silence and darkness of the empty house.

"That Christmas you gave me a top," Marc said.

"It's on the shelf—it isn't lost, you know." She went to the shelf where some of the toys were laid out: a large French doll with a bisque head and kid body, dressed in pink satin; a suite of furniture for a doll's house; a Noah's ark complete with giraffe; and a heavy, coin-shooting mechanical bank. The top was there. Faded pink, a voluptuous, perfect shape with a dark red tip. Her hands slid over it fondly, remembering.

"Here's the top."

Marc took it from her.

"You bought it yourself."

His dark, prophet's eyes fixed on hers, eating her glance and swallowing her whole face. She felt herself slipping into him as she'd used to do, slipping into that delicious oneness that offered such security and comfort.

"Here, I've got a present for you this year too. I worked on it a long time."

She broke the spell of the moment harshly, walking jerkily to the mantel for the gift she had placed there earlier. It was a book.

"I had it printed. There are only two copies in the whole world, Marc. One for you and one for me."

He took the book from her with trembling hands and opened it, leaning toward the lamp he had set down on the square table so that he could read it. Poems. So, she was still writing poetry.

He opened the book at random (it was bound in dark red leather and the title—*Numbered Poems*—was embossed in gold letters) and found:

"Poem Four"

Someone said to me,

"If there is a death,
Then love is meaningless.
Reject it, for there is only emptiness
When the end comes."

Another said to me,

"Yet if there *is* a death,
then love is everything
Cling to it, for there is only sorrow
when the end comes."

My heart cries;

"Take it!

Rest upon its warm blood,
Weep upon its flesh,
Give it your most deeply hidden secrets.
Death, or no death,
You need the hurt of love."

He shut the book and looked away from Camille's intense white face toward the fire. He cleared his throat of some unexpected constriction.

"I've always liked your poems."

"Thank you. I don't want anybody else to like them, really. I write them for you."

"I brought you something, too. Father Lazare gave it to me at the monastery just before I left. I helped nurse him when he was very ill and he wanted me to have something as a token of his affection. It's a family ring. Very old."

He brought it out, a star sapphire set in gold, and showed it to her.

"Oh, Marc! It's beautiful."

"Father Lazare said it has the Pope's blessing. It's a protective ring."

He took her hand, looking at the thin fingers, the pale, carefully tended nails. The ring slipped easily onto the fourth finger of her left hand. Her fingers were cold, almost icy, as were his own. Touching, they warmed slightly. Her dark eyes met his, hollow with forbidden fancies, with a flight too close to the sun of her life.

They walked to the window, hand in hand, and looked into the white, silent night. They were both shaking. There was nothing to say.

CHAPTER FOUR

Death came in the frost-gray light of Christmas morning, cutting sharply through the suffocating medicinal air of the sickroom.

Armand was sleeping lightly, folded into an armchair by his father's bedside. It had been a restless vigil. Only after a disconnected discussion of the will had his father finally fallen into a drug-induced sleep, allowing Armand himself to doze off. Still, his father had seemed much improved.

The lamp was fluttering dimly on the night table, almost as exhausted as the air supply in the room, when Paul St. Amour suddenly jerked upward, pulled by invisible strings of pain. Armand came awake with a jolt and leaped up to try to help his father to a sitting position. His arm was around the thin shoulders and he could sense the terrible struggle for breath, could almost feel the squeeze of pain on his father's chest cavity. His father's face was as gray as the ashes in the grate.

Within moments, the old man fell back on his pillows as if his spine had cracked.

A clock in a far corridor struck six.

Armand reached for the decanter of brandy on the night table and poured a small amount into a glass, as Dr. Lanctot had instructed him to do. He tried to force the liquor into his father's mouth, but the lips were blue and tightly pressed together. The brandy dribbled uselessly down his chin.

Armand drew back sharply, aware that death had taken over from him. He felt stripped, frighteningly helpless in the face of the only truly insoluble problem. He wanted to fight back, as if there were indeed a real contest. But death was now a chimera, a monstrous fancy too frightful to face. He, Armand St. Amour, was alone. When his

mother had died it had been different. His father had still
been alive in that earlier time, a solid bastion between the
youth and the blackness of the unknowable void. But now
the old man was gone, too. And he alone was responsible.

He picked up his father's flaccid wrist, searching vainly
for a pulse. Making one more attempt to turn back the
truth. He found no sign of a beating heart.

He thought of Honey's nightmare on their wedding
night. Was this the death she had foreseen, then? The
weight of guilt crouched against his neck and his head
seemed too heavy to hold upright. Helene and Justine
would both try to make him feel responsible for his father's
death. He could expect that. They were a mediocre, frustrated pair, suited up in the cold armor of righteousness;
forever proper matrons, good mothers, and devout Chris-
tians. With hearts of ice. Hearts that might well have been
cut from the same dazzling green blocks of ice that formed
the Ice Palace every winter in Dominion Square.

He stared wildly around the darkened bedroom as if he
were seeing it for the first time. It was now part of his inheritance. It was his house. He was going to control the St.
Amour properties and the business enterprises that his
father had put together over the years when he had tried
not only to hold the family fortune but to expand it in the
face of English greed. And the debt, the family debt was
his, too. He mustn't forget the debt.

Before he had fallen asleep, his father had told him
briefly about the will. The debts might exceed fifty thousand dollars. That meant that some shares, some of the
properties would have to be sold to salvage the rest, and
although Paul St. Amour had known that, he had held on
to everything until the last moment. The house must be
kept in the family, he had said over and over. It had belonged to the St. Amours since 1780, and if the family
was to remain an important entity in the French community, they must not lose the house.

And it wasn't only the debt, Armand thought angrily,
but the difficult terms his father had insisted upon, if he
were forced to sell the shares. He had promised his father
that he would sell only to other French Canadians. As
things stood, French families controlled very few of the
important assets in the province of Quebec; a small piece
of the railroads, which were growing rapidly; a little of

the shipping, the banks, and the communications. Anything that Armand could do, that the St. Amour family could do to prevent *les anglais* from getting more power, must be done. There was to be no sale to an *anglifié*, either, one of those despicable Frenchmen who collaborated with the English, who were tools of the English, who even imitated the English. That was yet another obstacle.

He took one more long look at the dead face, already shrinking in upon the skull, already looking so old that the body might recently have been taken from a long-closed tomb. And then he knew that he wanted to see Marc. Not as a brother, but as a priest. He had never felt more in need of the Church's comfort than he did at this moment.

"Mary, Mother of God, where is my brother?" It was a desperate whisper into the grayness of the morning.

Marc wasn't in his bedroom. The bed had obviously not been slept in. Where in hell could he be at this hour? Armand became suddenly confused. He tried to clear his mind; he made an effort not to run out into the halls shouting for Marc.

Was he off praying somewhere? But if so, where would he be if not in his room? Where did Marc go for solitude in this house? What had been his retreat as a child, when he had lived here, in the years long before he'd gone to the monastery, in the years when priesthood had been only a word and a not-too-well-understood word at that? Then it came to him—a pinprick of recognition. The nursery, of course. Marc had somehow retained his special attachment to the nursery, abandoned by the adults and the servants as they went about their adult business.

Armand ran to the flight of stairs leading to the upper floors and went up two steps at a time. On the fourth floor he could see light around the crack of the door to the nursery, and he was aware that in that room there was warmth and human life. He knew that he had been right.

Marc and Camille were sitting side by side, like puppets with no puppeteer to pull the strings—sagging, silent, staring at the fire. The fire had been freshly fed and was blazing up. But they sat unmoving, only Marc's dark eyes seemed to be alive, and Camille's own burning look was mute testimony to her consciousness. Armand halted near the door, picking up the aura of some binding mystery that clung to them like moss. Eager as he was to unburden himself of his dreadful message, he hesitated, looking at them as if they were strangers. But he could not decipher what it was that struck him as mysterious. Finally, he heard his own voice, harsh in the quiet of that private room.

"Marc, Camille—Father's dead."

A stranger's voice, so coarse and broken in that cocoon of silence. Marc stood slowly, as the words fell into the fire, and, taking Camille's hand in his, pulled her to her feet beside him. They stared at Armand, not breathing, as if he were some messenger from another land, another time. And then, without speaking, they both put their arms around him, and the three of them stood in a peculiar, closed circle, a brief but comforting embrace. The communion lasted such a short time that it might never have happened at all, and yet it was long enough to give Armand the lifeline he needed to reach a familiar shore once again.

━━━━━━

In the spring of 1896, the ice went out of the St. Lawrence River early. The sweep of water traffic, which began at the mouth of the broad river, thrust westward from Quebec City to Montreal in early May: great iron steamships; sailing vessels with peeling paint that were sadly out of date but still capable of hauling heavy cargo from ports all over the world; a few of the first adventurous, steel-hulled liners with red and green and blue smokestacks; and the vast, faceless cloud of small gadflies of every make and shape the mind could imagine.

Montreal, the port farthest inland on the river that could accommodate ocean-going ships, was bustling with activity. Dock workers sweated ceaselessly as they unloaded vast cargoes of raw sugar and oil for the new refineries. There were tons of iron, coal and leather, tea, wine, furniture, and textiles for the growing populations of Quebec and Ontario. Fresh hordes of immigrants, many of them sickly, inadequately clothed, and with insufficient cash left to pay their way to the land they had come to claim, camped despondently on the riverbanks. There was no organized body to help them on their way; they received only the spasmodic handouts from charitable institutions and church groups, and the ineffectual promises of the government. The hope in their eyes had died somewhere out on the Atlantic as they had been squashed helplessly together against the rolling and heaving of the ships, sometimes feverish and almost always hungry.

Mount Royal, like some ancient, mystical fortress, was as serene as ever. It stood above the sordid struggles of the crowd. Its trees were lace-green, its grass sprinkled with purple and white crocuses and patches of unused sunlight. The roads winding up the mountainside had dried from sloppy mud to hard, black cement, and the wooden sidewalks of the lower town were now dry in the gentle May breeze.

Honey and Armand had moved into the St. Amour house on Christmas day. Honey did not really like the big house, but she understood that it was necessary for Armand to live in it. She had taken over the second-floor apartment that had once belonged to Armand's mother, rooms that had been closed off when Emilie St. Amour had died ten years before. They would have to be redecorated. Honey had chosen the apartment because, while most of the rooms in the house were unrelievedly boxlike, this monotonous symmetry was broken in the sitting room of Emilie St. Amour's suite. There a deep, corner tower with tall glass windows held a semblance of charm.

Once she had stripped away the ancient maroon curtains and had the glass cleaned, the room came alive. It offered only a faint echo of the delights of Pride's Court, but it pleased her. Faced with the St. Amour house, which seemed to have been decorated to produce a determinedly dreary effect, she was trying desperately to imprint her own embryonic taste on the small apartment. Anyway, it was a beginning.

She had the plain mantel in the sitting room painted a pale cream, and in one of the shops along St. Paul she found a pretty piece of apple green China silk for the windows. She sent the sofa out to be re-covered in green velvet, bought a huge aspidistra and put it in a porcelain stand in a corner near the tower. She had all the dark-stained small tables and chairs removed to the attics and replaced them with fragile Florentine pieces in cream and antique gold.

It was while she was supervising the storage of banished furniture in the attic rooms that she made her greatest discovery. It was a large oil by Ricci, called, appropriately, "Courtyard of an Italian Villa," and the colors were so lighthearted and delicate (pale greens, pinks, and the bright blue of an Italian sky) that she had it cleaned and hung over her own fireplace. It pulled the entire color scheme of the room together. While digging curiously in one of the old dusty trunks, she found a fine Meissen piece marked on the bottom as "Pair of Lovers," and it seemed so suitable that she took the ornament downstairs as an addition to the sitting room. Sir Simon's eclectic taste in china and pottery had rubbed off on his daughter.

Now that she was five months pregnant, she stayed in bed most mornings until eight o'clock. Armand, of course, couldn't wait that long for breakfast and took his in the morning room quite early, but he always came up to share coffee and a roll with her and to discuss plans for the day.

On a May morning, as they drank their coffee together, Honey told Armand her great news. It had come in a letter with her breakfast tray.

"Armand, I've had a note from Fort! He's here in the city. Isn't that marvellous? He's going to call on me. He wants to know if tomorrow will be convenient."

She was terribly pleased. Although she wouldn't for the world admit it to Armand, she often missed her family. She missed Charles with his pompous manners and desperate caring about the right people, and her mother's Sunday morning collaboration about which bonnet to wear to church, and even Sir Simon's harangues. Visiting with Fort would be like opening a door on her familiar world again. Fort was good with gossip, and with details; he noticed things about people, and he remembered conversations.

Armand smiled at her affectionately. He worried often that Honey might regret their elopement. This house, he well knew, was not a beautiful house to manage, not in Honey's terms. And she no doubt missed her friends. She was only nineteen, after all, and would have her twentieth birthday a month before the baby was to be born in September. She was really not much more than a child.

"But that's good news, *chérie!* My poor darling, you do miss your family, don't you? Even the growls of the old bear himself."

"I'm beginning to miss them. But until now, I've been so busy fixing up the apartment, I haven't had time to think about life at Pride's Court."

"I hope you do not regret . . ." Armand began hastily.

But she cut him off instantly. "No, no, Armand! You mustn't think I regret it. Don't even think it for a moment. I can imagine what my life would have been like if I'd married one of *them*. But I do miss Mama sometimes. And, yes, even Papa, though it's nice not to have to worry all the time about what his opinion will be."

She must not let Armand realize, even for a moment, how much she disliked this house. It was large and should have been gracious, but instead it was cramped and dark. There was not even a garden, just a walled stableyard and a few shrubs. It could have been gardened, but apparently the St. Amours were not interested in landscaping. Inside, there were no open spaces, no great French doors leading onto balconies or green lawns. The paneling was all dark, and the carpets must have come over with Jacques Cartier. Besides all that, she was tired of French cooking. She longed for rare beef with horseradish and Yorkshire pudding and a bit of English trifle soaked in sherry, or a big boiled pudding with fruit in its heart.

Armand came around the table and bent to kiss her forehead.

"How are you feeling, darling? Well enough?"

"All right, I guess," she said a little petulantly. "But I don't much like being pregnant. I don't know how women can say they like it. Being fat is boring, and I get very tired."

"I'm sure it'll all seem worth it when you have a son," Armand said. "And there's no other way I know that we can have a son."

"It's all very well for you to be so cheerful," Honey said crossly. "I've often noticed how philosophical men are about these things, but *you* haven't lost your figure."

Armand helped himself to rolls from the silver-covered dish and began to spread them lavishly with black currant jam.

"Armand! You're eating too much jam again! You *will* lose your figure if you aren't careful, pregnant or not."

"It's you who needs to worry, not me," Armand said, looking down at his trim waist. "You're just jealous."

"Yes, I *am* jealous. It seems to me men have all the advantages in this world."

"I wouldn't say that," Armand said gloomily. "At least women don't have to worry about money. I worry about it every day. I can't believe how badly things have gone with my family in the past few years. And there is a very real depression in the economy, you know."

"You didn't know how badly things had gone because you were too busy having a good time," Honey said, repeating what she had heard every member of the St. Amour family say since she'd married Armand. "And now you're paying for it. Or *not* paying for it, if it comes to that."

"When's Fort coming to call?" Armand was quick to change the subject.

"I told you, darling. Weren't you listening? He's coming for tea tomorrow, and I wish I could manage a real English tea for him. But Suzanne is hopeless."

"Why don't you prepare it yourself, then?"

"I can't cook. Armand, you know perfectly well I can't cook a thing. I scarcely know how to make tea in a pot."

"If things go on as they are, you may have to learn. We may not be able to keep all the servants."

"Don't joke, Armand, please."

"Well, the bit about the servants is a joke, *chérie*. But I feel we are heading for the *hospice*. The poorhouse. Are you studying your French these days? I hope so."

"A little, darling. I pick up quite a lot from you, you know, so I'm getting lazy with my books."

"We *will* have to spend less money, Miel. That part is serious. I'm going to sell the railroad shares so we can keep this house. And I think I have a suitable buyer lined up, I promised Father I would only sell to one of our own, you know, and that isn't always an easy thing to do in this business. The English have the money. Even a few Irish have money these days, but the French . . ." He made a face.

"Is it somebody who's been here? Somebody I may have met?"

"No, I don't think you've met him. I hate like the devil to sell the shares in the St. John Railway. That part of the country is just opening up. It's a shame to let those shares go."

"You can't lose the house, darling," Honey said with a tinge of regret. "The whole family would be upset. Although it would be lovely if we could buy a house on the Mountain. But what's his name, this man who might buy your stock?"

"Tellier. Pierre Tellier. He owns shares in the telegraph company, and in at least one of the sugar refineries here."

Honey stopped eating. She frowned.

"Tellier? I feel I should know that name. What does he look like? I mean, is he old, or young?"

"He's in his thirties, I suppose. Tall and thin and clean-shaven. He has pale eyes and he wears a pair of gold-rimmed spectacles on a black cord."

"Of course! I remember. Armand, does he fiddle with his glasses all the time he's talking? And does he take them off and put them on like a nervous, fussy person? And does he speak excellent English?"

"Yes, he does speak excellent English. And I think you're right about the glasses. Why? Where did you meet him?"

"Darling, he's a business friend of Papa's! He came to the house once and another time I heard Charles talking about him to Papa just as I came into the room. He's . . . one of *them*. Don't you see, darling, he's a *vendu*. You can't sell your shares to Tellier—they'll probably end up with Papa!"

"Are you absolutely sure? You couldn't be wrong, could you? It's terribly important, *ma petite*."

"I'm sure. I remember how he flirted with me that night, and how laughable it was. Because he reminded me of an old aunt we have in the family. I also remember the way Charles and Papa spoke of him, as if he were almost despicable. They use such people but, of course, they don't respect them. I told Charles once I thought it was disgusting to use people, but he said that was business and women simply don't understand these things."

"Goddamnit, it makes sense!" Armand said, pounding the breakfast table with his fist. "I knew Sir Simon wanted to buy out the St. John shares, because Father told me months ago. Now Tellier comes along and makes a good offer. It all fits together."

"Probably all the shares Tellier holds really belong to Papa," Honey said.

"I shouldn't be surprised." Armand groaned and rolled

his eyes toward the ceiling, as if asking some invisible presence there to witness his problem. Then he put down his napkin and walked around the table to his wife to kiss her on the cheek.

"Miel, you have probably saved me from a regrettable mistake. It's a good thing you remembered."

He slid his hands slowly along the sides of her neck to a spot just below the earlobes. Her skin was warm, velutinous, like some expensive silk imported from Elysium. She smelled faintly of violets. Her hair was still hanging loose from the night before, pale and thickly curled against the curve of her neck. He buried his face in it, suddenly drowning in the touch and smell and feel of her.

Honey leaned against the chair back, her eyes closed.

"You deserve a reward for saving me from a very serious mistake, Miel," Armand murmured, "and I think you should have that reward now."

She made indefinite sounds of pleasure. She was easily aroused in the morning. The idea of Armand making love to her when other people were at work added a touch of wickedness that seemed to intensify all her most sensual feelings.

Armand left her in order to lock the door. Some over-zealous servant might arrive at any time to take away the breakfast tray. Honey went into the bedroom and pulled the curtains against the harsh yellow of the morning sun. The bed was still unmade and she took off her robe and gown quickly and then lay between the sheets, waiting. Armand came through the door already undressed, his clothes strewn in a crazy path across the carpets of two rooms. The sight of him like that, overeager, almost exploding with need, always excited her. She felt the voluptuousness of fine skin on fine skin, of body crevices fitted to body crevices, of hungry flesh against hungry flesh. And she knew her choice had been right. There was nothing in the world so valuable as a lover whom one loved.

CHAPTER FIVE

Honey was determined to produce a decent English tea when Fort came to call. She had always preferred Fort to the others. He had a touch of ferment about him, as if something highly secretive were brewing constantly in his mind, some risqué adventure that he dared not reveal.

Fort had always enjoyed his tea. When they had been small children, it had been Fort who had usually managed to get an extra share of the cream buns. He had known how to get round Papa for one more chocolate drop, how to delay for an extra fifteen minutes before all of them were banished to the nursery for the night.

Fort had now been at sea for months, eating God knew what feisty concoctions on board his ship and poisonous messes in foreign ports. He would be doubly ready for a good, solid English meal. The trouble with Suzanne, the St. Amour cook, was that she refused to try to understand what an English tea was about. Ordinary meals, yes. *French* meals, that is. She had a long repertoire of thick hot soups, and endless recipes for fiery stews. Her stock of perplexing meat sauces was formidable, but she couldn't or wouldn't, grasp the simple ingredients of an English high tea. How could one expect to offer Fort some special treat when he came tonight, with only Suzanne as a recruit?

The answer was obvious. She would prepare tea herself, and not only that, she would shop for it so that at least some of the items on the menu would be correct. She did at least know the names of the right brands to buy, because Lady Court had always been most particular about that, and as long as Honey could recall, there had been earnest family discussions about the comparative merits of Keiler's orange marmalade as opposed to Robertson's, and whether Ceylon black tea was preferable to China black tea. The Courts, on the whole, favored Keiler's over Robertson's, and Lady Court swore by Assam Pekoe when it came to a good bracing cup.

Although the weather was pleasant and the sun promised to shine all morning, Honey decided to take the gig and drive down to the shops instead of walking. She had no idea how heavy her purchases would be, and there would be a boy at the store to tie up the horse and fetch parcels for her. As she drove across Notre Dame, she noticed how many of the new-style bicycles were about, and wondered vaguely if Armand would let her have one after the baby came.

It was somewhere on the hill that Honey conceived of the desperate need for real Scotch scones for tea: the flat, tasty ones, cooked on a hot, smooth iron griddle. Fresh from the fire, Scotch scones had always been considered a great treat at Pride's Court and before hiring a new cook, Lady Court always made a point of asking each applicant if she could guarantee light scones for the tea table. But how could she, Honey, possibly produce real Scotch scones by six o'clock tonight?

At Pride's Court, Honey had not been encouraged to visit the kitchens. Court cooks never seemed to care for children. So the closest she had ever come to cooking was during her regular weekend visits to Emily Ross, her closest friend. The Ross family had somehow managed to keep the same cook for twenty years—a fierce, intractable Scotswoman trained in a series of important London hotels. Mrs. Mackie ran the kitchens of Ross House as if she were working for the Savoy, and she never appeared to age or even to get tired. She had a redoubtable manner and a limber tongue. It was an amusing experience for Emily and Honey to hear her expound upon the absurdity of Mrs. Ross's hiring a chef to make the main dishes on the menu when the Rosses held a ball or an especially important dinner.

Underneath her seemingly impregnable armor, however, Mrs. Mackie had a soft spot for children. Once in a while she would let Emily and Honey watch her prepare a particularly exquisite dish, or allow them to whip the cream for tea, or even turn the handle of the metal ice-cream freezer. And even when a chef was brought in for one of the great events, Mrs. Mackie was still in charge of supplies, lesser items on the menu, the kitchen help, and the great Aga stove that had to be constantly stoked. She operated always without fear or favor, and there did not appear to be a grain of sentiment in her being. Honey well remembered the day Mrs. Mackie had been preparing dozens of tiny songbirds for roasting and how she and Emily had wept over the naked little bodies. But Mrs. Mackie had said flatly that a bird was a bird. Neither more nor less. And it didn't matter a jot to *her* whether it quacked or trilled. If somebody wanted to eat it, she would cook it.

Thinking of Mrs. Mackie and her skills, Honey had an idea. Why not call on Emily Ross, the one friend she had seen a few times since her marriage? Then she could ask Mrs. Mackie to show her how to make scones. Surely if she practiced all afternoon, she could produce an edible batch?

Greatly cheered by this thought, Honey proceeded to purchase potted shrimp, lemon snaps, fig bars, Callard and Bowser's butterscotch and some buttercups with nut centers that Fort had always adored. Fondly eying her parcels, she drove the gig to Pine Avenue, where the Rosses resided in a whimsical stucco castle complete with colonnades, parapets, verandahs, and a balustraded dry moat.

Emily was delighted to see her, and eager to impart her own great news; she had just become engaged to James Cuthbertson (sugar and textiles) and was anxious to talk to Honey about marriage. Well, actually about the going to bed part of marriage. Her mother only fenced when questioned. Her older sister, Hester, was an impossible stuffed turkey who had already developed a sense of remoteness after only one year of marriage, a trait that Emily and Honey had noticed was common among all the married women of their acquaintance. So Emily wanted the truth. They therefore had a delicious morning cup of tea with thin toast and apple jelly. And Honey delicately implied that making love to a man was not the painful, dull chore hinted at by one's elderly aunts. In fact, marital duties could be quite exciting, depending on who the man was, and *if* the man had experience. They both giggled a lot at that and Emily managed to ask the worrisome question of how one managed the weight. Since men almost always weighed much more than women, wasn't it all very uncomfortable? How could one breathe? Honey assured her that if it were properly done, there seemed to be no problem at all, and she could always breathe quite nicely.

"Do you mind Armand being a Catholic?" Emily asked gently. "We've always thought of them as so different. Almost like heathens. With their statues, and incense, and bells ringing under priests' skirts. And all that rubbish about the Virgin and everything."

"I don't mind, most of the time. But there is the problem about having lots and lots of children. The Pope says one must, you see. Other than that, well, Armand goes to church with the others, and I suppose he confesses, although I can't think what he confesses *these* days. His brother is a priest, and I find that a bit odd. In fact, some of his family are *quite* odd. But then, so are some of mine, if you don't know them. But most of all, Emily, I hate being pregnant."

"I've often thought it must be awkward. All that fat. But you don't look very pregnant, Honey. You look quite lovely."

"Thank you; I wish I felt lovely . . . I must say I was pleased when Armand's sister Camille went to the country. She's the unmarried one and she ran the house before we got married. So I imagine she dislikes me. Anyway, she's even more peculiar than the rest of the family. Very dark and mysterious and intense. I wish she'd fall in love and get married. It would solve the problem of what to do with her. At the moment she's visiting Justine—that's the married sister who lives on an estate in the country. They're always telling me how the land was granted to their great-great-great-grandfather by Intendant Talon and was an original Seigneury. It's so boring."

"Have you seen the farm, then?"

"Not yet. Justine isn't very friendly and I've only met her husband, Laurent, a couple of times. They make it clear that they don't approve of Armand's marriage. And they refuse to speak English. Of course, I understand a little of what they say, but when they jabber on so quickly, I can't follow."

"Do you miss your Mama and Papa?" Emily asked, her round blue eyes widening into doll's eyes.

"Sometimes. But I don't regret what I did."

"Do you think they'll come to see the baby?"

"I hope so. He'll be their first grandchild. By the way, did I tell you that Fort is back in Montreal to live and work at the head office? He's coming to tea today, and I'm sure he'll have news about all the family."

"Will he like it here, after being at sea?"

"That's what I wonder. Look, do you think Mrs. Mackie would show me how to make real Scotch scones?"

"You don't think you can learn to make edible scones in one afternoon, do you?" Emily said, laughing. "Poor Fort, if that's what you're serving for tea."

"Why not?" Honey asked confidently. "It can't be very hard. Papa always says that servants are not very intelligent. That's why they're servants. So if Mrs. Mackie can make scones, why can't I?"

Emily was still amused. "But the first time, Honey! I mean, surely one must practice."

"I plan to practice all afternoon."

"But why can't your own cook make them?"

"She only makes French things. Great thick sandwiches for tea, and no crumpets or hot biscuits. I'll admit she makes good little cakes. Really rich ones. But that's all. I long for Mama's teas, with all the right cookies, and cream buns, and luscious fruitcake. Oh, Emily, sometimes I *do* miss it all! Pride's Court is such a pretty house. So much light, and such big rooms. You and James will have a pretty house, too, right here on the Mountain. I envy you that. You can't think how boring these old French houses are. All little square rooms and dark wood. And the family goes on and on about how old the house is and how their ancestors were aristocrats in France, and how the English have mistreated them. Then they glare at *me* as if it were my fault that the English won the war. I mean, it was a hundred years ago. But they still go on about it. And the house . . . there are religious statues and pictures every place. Every time you turn a corner you bump into a tortured saint!"

"The house sounds ghastly, but I'd love to see the tortured saints. Why don't you invite me for tea?"

"Will you come? Really? Oh, Emily, come tomorrow. I get lonely sometimes."

"I can't come tomorrow, but the next day, for certain," Emily said. "Mother's taking me for fittings tomorrow and they go on for hours. Madame Fréchette is making my wedding dress, and dozens of gowns and wrappers and nightgowns. You're lucky you eloped—you didn't have all this worry. Mother supervises every detail to make sure it's all proper. What difference does it make if a nightgown's proper if you're going to . . ."

"No difference that I can see," Honey said, thinking of her own wedding night.

"Did I tell you we have a telephone now? It's such fun, but you can't call many people because so few people have one. Oh, Honey, why don't you get one? Then we could talk on the telephone."

"I'll ask Armand. It sounds like a lovely idea. Do you think we could see Mrs. Mackie about those scones?"

They found Mrs. Mackie in a dark, Gaelic mood. A huge dinner was being planned for the next night and she was in the midst of her menus.

"She doesn't want much, does she?" Mrs. Mackie inquired, referring to Emily's mother with heavy sarcasm. "Only veal cutlets with mushrooms, roast beef cooked so there's both rare and well-done, and how's that to fit in with roast lamb, I ask you? We could use two more ovens. Ducks, too. There's always such a fuss with ducks, draining off the grease. And turkey with oyster sauce. I don't know if I can get oysters at the market fit to eat . . ."

The menu appeared to go on forever, Honey thought, peering over Mrs. Mackie's shoulder at Nora Ross's spidery handwriting. The list included boiled tongue, roast ham, venison (taken out of the ice house and now slowly thawing in the pantry), chicken, guinea hen, and lobster salad. And for dessert, plum pudding, Charlotte Russe, Italian cream, and a variety of fruits.

The girls explained their mission. Mrs. Mackie professed to be astonished, but she was not totally displeased.

"Even if I do show you today, you don't think you're going right home to make scones anybody could eat, do you?"

"But why not?" Honey asked.

Mrs. Mackie made a strange noise meant to illustrate complete disbelief, but sounding more like an old man with a serious sinus problem. However, she agreed to give the lesson to both girls, since she felt that Emily should learn something about housekeeping before her wedding.

Mrs. Mackie insisted on giving Honey half a dozen

scones to take home with her as a sample; this was fortu-
nate for Honey, since three full hours spent trying to
achieve the same result in her own kitchen produced
scones like paving stones. Only Mrs. Mackie's scones could
possibly be served to Fort.

Fort arrived with his brown hair longer and his beard
more abundant than ever. Honey thought he looked stylish
and quite European, somehow. His Scotch tweed suit was
fashionably single-breasted with a high-cut vest. While he
looked a bit of a dandy, there was no mistaking the old
familiar gleam of mischief in his eye, or the ever-so-slightly
sardonic smile on his well-shaped mouth.

"Honey! Nobody told me you were pregnant!" he said,
after he had given her a hug in greeting.

Honey was a little miffed. She had hoped that her condition didn't show that much and she had planned to tell
Fort as a surprise.

"Yes, I am," she admitted.

"Papa doesn't know. Or he would have told me."

"There really isn't any way he would know unless Emily
Ross has told her mother. I don't see him. Or Mama
either. I thought she might relent, but she hasn't."

"I'm sure she'd like to see you, but she won't go against
him. Give Papa a grandson and he'll be dying to see the
boy. That might fix everything."

"I thought of that."

She took Fort upstairs to her own apartment, apologiz-
ing for the rest of the house. Fort said he'd been in several
of the old French houses and they were all pretty much
alike. Built for the cold climate and to keep out the Indians, as far as he could see. When they were sitting.
in front of her fire, she rang for tea.

"I shopped for some of the food myself," Honey told
him. "And I went over to Ross House to get their cook to
teach me how to make Scotch scones for you. But . . ."

"My God, I hope you're not planning to serve them,"
Fort said, pretending horror. "I've eaten enough hardtack
to last me for the rest of my life."

"How did you know what my scones would be like?"

"I'll wager they were like bricks. Fit only for a garden
path."

Honey smiled. "Well, maybe, but don't worry about it. Mrs. Mackie, that's the Ross's cook, gave me some perfectly delicious ones to bring home. But Fort, I had no idea cooking was so hard!"

"Never mind. I brought you a present, anyway."

He handed her a small blue box. Honey opened it to find an oval cameo, pink with a white carved head, set in gold.

"It's beautiful, Fort! Where did you find it?"

"In Venice. Do you really like it? I saw a lot of women wearing them over there."

"I have a perfect gown to wear it on. Black velvet. Now, tell me all about the family. And what you're doing back in Montreal."

Over tea, Fort explained that he was back in Montreal at Sir Simon's request. He was going to handle the Court Shipping Line's bid to the government in Ottawa for an important Royal Mail contract.

"They're calling it the new Fast Line," Fort explained. "A weekly service between Montreal and Liverpool. The tender calls for a guarantee that a shipping line can produce four ships that do twenty knots, each to weigh at least eighty-five hundred tons. Ships must be built to British Admiralty standards, too. It's a combination deal between the British government in London and the Canadian government in Ottawa. England sees it as a link between parts of the Empire, so she's putting up a share of the money."

"Is it worth a great deal?"

"A million dollars. So Papa is eager to get it, as you can imagine. He's an old school friend of Joseph Chamberlain, you may recall, and Chamberlain's now Colonial Secretary in London."

"And what about your influence here, in Canada?"

"We've got influence as long as the Conservatives are in power. And now that Bowell's been thrown out of office, and Tupper's the new P.M., things should go well for us. Papa and Tupper are great pals. The only problem is, the government might fall and there would have to be an election. And if the Conservatives lose, we might not get the contract. However, nobody thinks the Liberals have a chance in an election this year."

"I'm glad I'm not a man. I'd hate to have to get into

that kind of business struggle," Honey said with a sigh. "But Fort, what exactly do you have to do, if Papa is already set up with both governments?"

"Well, we have to make a formal submission, just like every other shipping line. Frankly, I don't think any of the others have either the capital or the experience to get a contract like that. But we must present our case just the same. I'll make the submission in Ottawa soon. We have to declare how much capital we have, how long it will take to build the ships and man them, how soon we can start the actual service. Imagine! Mail once a week across the Atlantic! That's an exciting idea, you know."

"Yes, I suppose it is. Have another scone, Fort. Doesn't Mrs. Mackie make heavenly scones?"

"It was damned clever of you to get them for me." Fort said appreciatively. "I like all kinds of food, but there's nothing like English home cooking, is there?"

"And what's Charles doing? And Geoffrey?"

"Geoffrey is just about the same as always. Handling the Liverpool end of things. Papa is getting anxious for him to marry. God's britches, he's getting anxious for all of us to marry, for that matter. Especially since you married your Frenchie and crossed him up. Poor Charles has gone to England to handle the Whitehall end of things. You know, butter up Chamberlain and quaff a few with some of the influential people there, tell them what a great line Court Shipping is, so there'll be no hitch. At the same time, he's actually looking for a bride."

"Oh, no! Not going shopping for a bride!" Honey giggled. "How like Charles!"

"Papa says that's ridiculous. There are plenty of suitable girls in Montreal."

"And what does Charles say to that?"

"He says they all look like brood mares."

"That's very rude of him, but I expect he's right. You know, Fort, that's exactly how I felt about the suitable men. None of them was attractive. Papa said marriage was a business proposition and not supposed to be fun, and Mama told me that most women marry bores, and they accept it. So I can understand how Charles feels."

"Poor old Charles is going hunting in London. Hunting

for a beautiful woman from an acceptable family. I hope he has better luck than I did, frankly. The only really beautiful women I met were in Paris. And one in Venice, I mustn't forget her. But you know Charles. He's methodical. I'm sure he'll come up with a bride who'll make Papa's heart burst with pride. I can see it all now. Charles with promises from Chamberlain in one hand, and a gorgeous, eminently suitable wife in the other."

"If he does, then Papa won't be so worried about me," Honey said, frowning. "But do you think that's good or bad? I mean, will he relax because it isn't so important anymore? Or will he just not care?"

"Hard to say, with Papa. But I'd be willing to put money on his coming round soon, Honey. When you've got that son and heir, he won't be able to resist. So cheer up!"

"Oh, Fort, it's good to see you! I'm glad you're back to stay, I really am. Will you come to dinner some night with Armand and me?"

"Of course I will. I have nothing against Armand. We may be rivals in the business world, but I hope I'm a little beyond that narrow position about foreigners that Papa and Mama take. As a matter of fact, I have a letter of introduction to a French countess now living in Montreal. I hear she runs a fascinating salon, if you happen to be one of the right people."

━━━━━━

The Countess of Redon, who in more conventional circles would have been addressed as Lady Redon, was familiarly known as Countess Leda. Nobody knew exactly what her baptismal name was, but her friends generally supposed among themselves that it was Alice. No matter. She was now Leda, and the name was particularly apt, since she had a strange predilection for swans.

Having been driven out of Paris (and before that, London) for reasons that were never fully explained, Countess Leda was at present intent upon bringing to Montreal that touch of the exotic so obviously lacking in an infant city. She claimed to have known Wilde and Beardsley in London and had been rather more than a passing acquaintance of Moreau, Huysmans, Rossetti, and Verlaine in the studio salons of Paris, Florence, and Venice.

Certainly she had all the credentials—a mysterious source of income; an obscure title; a bizarre taste in clothes, music, and the arts; and a memorable face.

The countess was more than striking, she was electrifying. Under an umbrella of orange hair, her face was chalk white, its bone structure exceedingly prominent. Her eyes were large and their naturally dark color was emphasized by a ring of kohl around the rims so that in the greenish-blue lights so often affected by herself and her companions, she looked like a reincarnation of Nefertiti.

She had a liking for long, loose, diaphanous gowns the folds of which did not entirely conceal the sensual outline of her figure, or for solid black dominos with the hoods cut off so that her white face and brilliant red hair seemed to grow out of the top like a macabre plant out of a tall black pot.

While her appearance might strike the newcomer dumb with shock upon first meeting, it was likely to become utterly distracting very soon. Strangers were frequently torn between looking at the face and the body, or the hands and the feet, or closing their eyes and just listening to the voice. She spoke English fluently but with a highly provocative accent, and the timbre of her voice was an odd mixture of whiskey and mysticism, so that the slightest thing she said was likely to sound portentous, wise, or charming. She was exceedingly tall (although her height varied somewhat because she vacillated wildly between bare feet and specially constructed slippers with thick wooden soles and heels), and when her figure was revealed, as it sometimes was in the thin gowns, it was seen to be voluptuous—huge protruding breasts that appeared to need no support and hips like slices of watermelon. Visitors to her salon often remarked that even if nothing amusing took place during the evening, the mere sight of the countess was enough to make the encounter live forever in their memories.

She had a talent for collecting around her the wealthiest most adventurous, most garish, and handsomest men and women in any given city. A discreet pursuit of vice (whether real or imagined) was her vocation, and she talked about it at length. How much she practiced, no one person knew. Her salon provided an elegantly fertile setting for the care and feeding, and eventual flourishing, of bizarre tastes.

At present she occupied a huge stone fortress in the older part of the city, a structure that had formerly been a bishop's palace and, before that, the site of a particularly bloody Indian massacre. Bloodstains on some of the stones in the west loggia testified to its history. Such marks of violence were cherished by the countess, who felt that such intimations of death varied the otherwise shoreless plateau of life.

Fortescue Court found the residence without much difficulty. Even if it had not been well-known, he was an old hand at ferreting out obscure addresses with veiled doorways and buildings that seemed to melt into a river of stone fronts in the densest alleys of foreign ports. The absence of any name or number on the gate cut into the high limestone wall of the countess's fortress provided no puzzle to him.

He was admitted by a black boy dressed as a Blackamoor, who took his card from him with delicate ceremony and placed it upon a gold platter. Fort gave him, as well, his letter of introduction to the countess. The boy went off bearing the platter on one hand, gliding like a dancer who has taken his turn at center stage and is disappearing temporarily into the wings.

While Fort waited in the anteroom, he took stock of the place. Money had obviously been spent here. The walls of the squarish room were covered with forest-green silk caught at regular intervals with brightly colored cabochons that sparkled like gems taken from the rings of giants. There were two elaborately carved dark benches, two potted palms, and a green marble-topped side table with heavy pillared legs. Nothing about the furniture or the atmosphere hinted at unusual happenings in the rooms beyond. Yet Fort knew from his London friend, Ivan Blake, that there was more to Countess Leda's salons than a few spidery palms and ersatz gems.

As he sat, a flutelike voice reached him—high-pitched, sharply sweet as only a young boy's voice can be. He was singing a madrigal. And with this sound, Fort began to sense in the air a hint of some gilded blight that would not, perhaps *could* not, quite be brought into the open. As a world traveler, Fort was tutored to some extent in the effects of Byzantine decor and certain social convolutions of the East. So he waited impatiently for the Blackamoor to return, marveling at the nerve of the countess in reviving the old custom of dressing up a black boy as a lackey and plaything.

The boy was quick. He came back grinning and beckoned Fort to follow him through a leather-padded door into the interior of the palace. The plan of the building had been violently altered (the countess considered a mere bishop's needs to be mystifyingly Spartan) and rooms had been extended, staircases moved, corridors redirected, gardens created, ceilings raised. Over every room hung the scent of wet tropical flowers bred in rich black earth.

The sound of sensuous violins replaced the boy's madrigals. Each room through which they passed was thickly carpeted and ornamented with arches, mosaics, elaborately painted screens, enormous Chinese vases that properly belonged in museums and murals that fell just short of outright pornography: ample but pale women lay in grassy glades wearing golden collars and nothing else while they fondled apparently hypnotized unicorns, and whole fleets of long-haired maidens with well-defined breasts but indistinguishable nether parts floated mournfully on murky seas.

None of the rooms seemed to have any windows. Occasionally a tapestry depicting a garden of poisonous-looking plants would hang where a window ought to be, but there was no way of telling. Greenish-blue light came from opaline globes set in gold wall brackets, or from large, painted-glass trumpets held aloft by statues of sinuous black women of monumental proportions.

In the fourth room they entered, Fort saw the countess for the first time. She lay stretched out on a curved divan upholstered with brocade and supported by serpentine legs, her head propped up against green satin pillows. Although he had fully expected to see an unusual woman, he was startled by the vivid red of her hair and by the black-lined eyes with their intent gaze. At the same time, he was intrigued by the vision of her rounded, sloping flesh beneath the transparent green gown: a gown designed, it seemed, to offer fleeting morsels of intimacy while maintaining a façade of decency.

This was by far the most extravagant room he had yet seen. Its circular shape was broken by a number of arches that led to other greenish-blue rooms and flowered groves. The vaulted ceiling was supported by gilt groins (perhaps it had been the bishop's private chapel, thought Fort) all of which directed the eye to a central painting of smug cupids teasing languid and very fleshy women. At floor level there were plump hassocks covered with velvet and satin, potted orange trees laden with fruit, and palms with open-mouthed blue trumpet vines growing about their trunks. The air was warm and humid.

Behind the countess a young man stood casually eating black grapes from a gold platter. His sun-browned skin contrasted sharply with Countess Leda's white face and arms. Fort thought the boy looked like a Greek fisherman who had been captured and brought to the house in a net; he looked greedy and confused at the same time.

"I'm delighted that Ivan gave you a letter to me," Countess Leda said, her voice husky with welcome. "He's such a sweet man. I'm sure you'll enjoy the salon, though I don't know who is here tonight, or what might transpire."

She gave him a mysterious smile that froze him mid-carpet. But her hand was gracefully extended as if she expected him to kiss it. He moved forward and caught her fingers to his lips.

"My pleasure, dear Countess, I assure you."

The scent of flowers was almost overwhelming. It swayed the senses, lulling the mind into a state of lethargy. Fort noticed the lilies—jars and jars of white, waxy lilies—adding their sweet odor to the dark red roses on small, heavily laden bushes set in stone tubs among the fruit trees against the walls. There was a madness in the combination.

"And how *is* Ivan?" the countess asked.

"About the same as always. World-weary. Critical of events and governments. Quite disabused of the idea that the Russian aristocracy could be called civilized, and desolate in view of the prospective downfall of Paris. 'A reluctant Babylon,' he calls it. As for the Germans and Berlin, he has washed his hands of them."

Countess Leda laughed and nodded, recognizing the symptoms.

"He enjoys despair," she said. "That's why I like him."

"Well, the diplomatic service is the right place for encouraging despair, I should think."

"Did you know he writes verse?"

Fort was genuinely surprised. He could not imagine the sophisticated Ivan Blake playing with words.

"No, he's never mentioned it to me. I thought he found it hard enough to write his name at the bottom of a document."

"He once read me some of his verse," Countess Leda said thoughtfully. She broke off in her musing to turn to the silent young man. "Marius, bring us some wine . . . now let me think for a moment." She closed her huge eyes, folding the purple lids down like butterfly wings, and appeared to be searching about in the cubbyholes of her mind, drawing her fine brows together in a frown.

"Yes, I remember how one of his verses began: 'I have been closed for many years like the smug rose taken early from a gardener's locked heart, ready to open some day and be measured but always fearful. Petals folded upon petals . . .' "

"It doesn't sound like a threat to the poet laureate," Fort observed drily.

With some difficulty, the countess brought herself to the point of curiosity.

"What is it that you actually *do?* So many young men feel compelled to *do* something these days. It's a communicable disease, I often think. For my own taste, I much prefer young men who do absolutely nothing, but do it well."

"I work for my father. Perhaps you've heard of him. Sir Simon Court."

"Ah, yes, of course, But I thought Ivan's letter mentioned *the sea.*" The Countess pronounced "the sea" as if it were a distant star in whose existence she did not quite believe.

"I was at sea, but I've come home to work in the head office. You know how it is for sons."

Countess Leda appeared to acknowledge the need for shipping lines in general. "But we need shipping, and ships," she cried enthusiastically, "to carry the mail, and such things. Somebody must take one's letters about. I see all that. So you have money! That's always a suitable beginning for a young man, although it's seldom a suitable ending."

At this point, Marius arrived with a tray on which sat

three wineglasses and a cut-glass decanter filled with pale yellow liquid. Behind him, a peacock strutted self-importantly. Countess Leda clucked encouragingly at the bird while Marius poured the wine.

"Isn't he a pretty boy?" the countess asked, referring to the bird who had just spread his tail obligingly. "His name is Parsifal."

The bird turned a cold eye upon her and walked off behind a clump of roses. Fort tasted the wine and found it dry and cold. The countess explained that it was a special wine for new guests at her salon, and then went on to talk of the rigors of the Canadian climate and the difficulty of finding workmen who could do the kind of alterations and decorating she desired.

"Perhaps there are some amusing people in one of the other apartments," the countess offered finally. "Marius will take you to meet them. Anyway, Sydney will be there. You'll find her fascinating. She was a model to Rossetti, you know. And Sara Bernhardt met her once at Rossetti's studio and instantly detested her. They were too much alike."

Fort realized that the countess was dismissing him. The interview was at an end.

"Will I see you again, Countess?"

"My dear, of course. You must come to our masked ball. Sydney will tell you all about it."

Fort bowed to her and followed Marius out of the room. They ventured deeper into the house, up a short flight of stairs, and through several doors. Eventually they reached what seemed to be a forest grove, and Marius abandoned him abruptly. He was left alone to absorb the sight of real trees planted in great stone tubs, of wall paintings of trees that seemed to extend the room for miles into black forest, of thin tendrils of damp Spanish moss and the strange effect of a black, forbidding pond ornamented by a decaying rowboat.

When his eyes became adjusted to the gloom, Fort saw that he was not alone after all. There were at least three other people standing in the grove. One was a young man wearing a white robe with a gold belt. He wore his yellow hair as long as a child's. His extravagantly curled eyelashes were oddly black against the paleness of his hair and skin. He was talking with enthusiasm to a dark, portly, middle-aged man in a tight-fitting black suit with velvet piping around the collar. Each held a silver goblet. The third person was a woman.

She stood beside the pond, one hand on the prow of the rotting rowboat, which was tied to a post on the small wooden dock. If she was smiling, and Fort could not be sure that she *was* smiling, it was a smile of rejection rather than of welcome. In cataloging her appearance, he couldn't find a single remarkable feature. She was of medium height and wore a plain, high-necked gown of some indefinite shade of blue. Her hair was light brown, straight, hanging almost to her waist, and she wore no ornaments either in her hair or on her person. She had a pale, oval face, wide-spaced eyes, a classically straight nose, and a full bottom lip that gave her a slightly pouty expression. Yet her features and her clothing combined to create an effect of mystical innocence, of a soul untouched by the vagaries and vulgarities of human life. Fort could easily imagine her standing in the ruins of Rome, or of Sodom, or of Babylon, in the midst of chaos and horror, unburned, unraped, unscathed.

"Are you Sydney?" Fort asked, approaching her through the trees.

She looked at him with no expression—neither with interest, nor surprise, nor even indifference.

"Yes, I'm Sydney."

"I'm Fortescue Court, a friend of a friend of Countess Leda's. She said I might find you here."

"As you see, I am here."

Fort cleared his throat. He suddenly had a sailor's thirst. The atmosphere of the place was stifling, the air warm and damp and motionless. He could hear the sound of violins coming from some distant place. A swan had appeared on the pond and was floating effortlessly in a vague circle.

"I wonder if I could get a drink," Fort said, eying the goblets the two men held.

"I'll get *you* one," Sydney said, walking toward a side table he hadn't seen before. It blended into a rose bush, but now that he'd spotted it, he could see glasses and bottles. Fort could hear the young man drawling, "And do you know what he said? He said, 'I don't need drugs, I *am* a drug.' "

"He's a mesomorph," the dark man said with decision,

"and they're all the same. Completely turned inward upon themselves. I've seen it time and again. You can see it in his paintings. They revolve incestuously about his own doings, his own feelings—never anything that contains a grain of universal truth. The series on masks, for example. So personal. Hellish."

"Hell is a personal carnival," the young man said.

Sydney interrupted them.

"I'd like you to meet our new guest, Fortescue Court. This is his first visit here."

The two men turned to look at him. The dark man held out his hand.

"I'm Edgar Kent. You're not one of *the* Courts, surely?"

Fort shook the offered hand.

"I'm Sir Simon's son, if that's what you mean."

"I've run into your father. We belong to the same club, you know. But you won't find Sir Simon at a place like this."

"I'm Felix Martin," the blond young man said, extending his hand rather too languidly and barely squeezing Fort's hand in his fingers. "One of *the* Martins."

"We should have met somewhere before, then," Fort said, frowning. He knew some of the Martins. Coal in Nova Scotia, if he remembered correctly. A bank in Halifax. Holdings in England and Germany.

"No, I think not. I've been abroad since I was ten. I'm the son they kept out of sight. They don't approve of me. Even when I was ten they didn't approve of me. Which only shows how right my father always is."

"It's wonderful to find a salon like this in Montreal," Edgar Kent said. "One can't always find time for London or Paris. Rather too far for an evening's conversation, you know."

"I long for Paris," murmured Felix. "I don't think there's much hope of turning this crude colonial backwater into a great city, do you, Court?"

Fort shrugged, thinking quickly of Rome, of Venice, of Cairo, and he was forced to agree with young Martin.

"Unlikely. But I hope the countess won't give up too easily."

Sydney handed Fort a goblet of wine.

"Don't you drink wine?" Fort asked her, noticing that she didn't have a goblet herself.

"I don't drink wine or smoke. I very seldom eat, if it comes to that."

He noticed that her voice was smooth, even, without much expression and yet not unpleasant.

"The countess said you were a model. What do you do here in Montreal?" Fort asked.

"I exist."

She led him away from the two men, back to the dock, where they sat and watched the swan sailing about in the semidarkness. There was a musty smell from the Spanish moss. The violins had been replaced by the siren sound of a seductive female voice humming.

"Then you have an income, I assume," Fort said, tasting the heavy wine.

"I'm a companion to Countess Leda. She brought me with her. She couldn't possibly travel alone. She needs certain people about her."

"I can see why painters like to paint you."

"Can you? I can't."

"Montreal must be rather dull for you, after Paris."

"Most places are the same."

"But this atmosphere . . . you should be in a place with a healthier atmosphere. It doesn't seem the right setting for you."

"Oh, dear, you aren't one of those do-gooders, are you? You aren't going to try to take me away from all this, I hope?"

Fort realized with surprise that he had been thinking just that. She wasn't the kind of woman he usually found attractive. She seemed so negative. Still, there was a wistfulness about her . . . he wanted to know what created that virginal air. What it was that implied a strange and secret life, a life that she would not expose easily.

"Have there been other knights, then?"

"Dozens. Every one of them wants to carry me off, marry me, and keep me in a more suitable castle where I'd be safe. I don't understand it at all. I ask for nothing."

"Still, it isn't safe for you here."

"Safe? I'm perfectly safe."

He wanted to ask her about her life as a model, and whether she had been painted in the nude. He wanted to ask if she'd had affairs with the painters and whether they had smoked opium. A terrifyingly puritan mood was seizing him. It was so unlike him to engage in this kind of confidential conversation when he first met a woman.

"I don't think you can be safe here. I'm new, of course, but the salon seems extremely sophisticated. Certain tastes seem to be catered to. The mood of the place is anything but correct for a young woman."

"I'm not concerned with correctness, but with freedom." She turned her green eyes upon him and gave him a clear, steady look that unnerved him; that wide gaze suggested such innocence that it seemed unlikely to him that she understood what went on around her, much less took any part in it.

"You must come to the masked ball," Sydney said suddenly. "It's next Saturday."

"Perhaps I will."

"Oh, you must promise to come. We put a great deal of effort into planning a ball like this. It begins after ten o'clock. And everybody must come completely masked. All the guests will be in costume, and there's no limit to the imagination when it comes to what sort of costume you might choose."

It was the first time she had showed any enthusiasm. Fort was at a loss to understand. He would have liked to coldly refuse the invitation, but he knew that curiosity would probably drive him to attend. It wasn't that he was seriously interested in the girl, it was simply that he wanted to know just how far the countess would go in her search for excitement. As for Sydney, he ought to try to help her if he could. It was only a matter of time before she would fall. A fallen angel. The idea struck him as comic. When he left the palace, however, he realized with some dismay that he had neglected to ask her her last name. She was merely Sydney.

CHAPTER SIX

Armand took a hansom cab from the hotel to the corner of Fifth Avenue and Fifty-Seventh Street. The driver found the house quite easily; Armand had passed along to him the explicit directions he'd received from Max DeLeon in the reply to his request for an interview. "An immigrant French chateau," DeLeon had written in barely legible handwriting, "brought stone by stone from the Loire Valley."

It was a graceful house, with three high peaks across the central façade, acres of green creeper covering the turrets and bays, and three symmetrical clusters of chimney pots worked into the overall design of the roof. A broad gravel driveway swept across the front, crowding both rhododendrons and rose bushes, and on the east side of the building a large wing of matching stones and creeper housed kitchens and servants. It was evident that Max DeLeon lived in high style. At the back of the property Armand could see a coach house for three carriages and a stable large enough to accommodate six horses. The whole effect was pleasing to the eye and to the heart.

Armand felt relieved. Everything he'd heard about De-Leon appeared to be true—that he had limitless financial resources, spent lavishly, and was important in banking and mining. As he rang the doorbell, Armand sent up a little prayer that he would be able to convince DeLeon to go along with him on a couple of business ventures.

He'd come alone to DeLeon's house. But Honey was in New York, back at the hotel on Central Park, resting. The rail journey from Montreal to Portland and from Portland to New York had been tiring. Honey had been excited about her first train ride; there had been so many new experiences. If she'd waited a year or so before marrying, Sir Simon would no doubt have sent her to Europe on a Grand Tour. But her elopement had ended that possibility, and now travel was a completely fresh experience. She had been amazed at the speed (sometimes the train had reached thirty miles an hour) at the elegant green plush seats, at the long stops made at small country stations while boxes and mail were unloaded, at the urgent train whistle cutting through the June air to remind passengers of departure. Armand had opened the window to let in a bit of a breeze, but of course that had also brought in great clouds of grit and coal dust. So in the end they had both felt dirty and exhausted . . .

Armand's thoughts drifted to Sherbrooke, Quebec. He had a special interest in the country around there. Sherbrooke was the terminal point he had in mind for the railway up to Thetford, seventy miles to the northeast. That was one of the projects he was going to mention to Max DeLeon.

As he waited for an answer to his ring, he found his heart beating a little too fast from an injection of hope. But he knew he must remain calm. DeLeon must not know just how important this meeting was to him.

He was let in by an elaborately liveried fellow in maroon with gold trim and gold buttons and shown to a formal library. The book-lined walls, thick carpet, and antique furniture were to be expected; the paintings took him aback. Each contained an element of ferocity: a portrait of a pointer in a do-or-die pose; an old man with an expression suggesting cannibalism telling tales to three small children; a matched pair of portraits of a stiffly posed European couple with eyes like those of starving demons. Armand suppressed a heavy surge of doubt as he viewed them. Max DeLeon's fondness for threatening pictures might be a clue to his personality. He would probably be a difficult man to sway.

Before he could dwell too long on this discomfiting thought, however, a short, bald man in a brown suit with the bottoms of the trousers turned up like golf pants detached himself from a gloomy corner of the room and thrust out his hand.

Armand was momentarily surprised. Surely this affable, unimpressive little man was not the great DeLeon he had heard so much about? Surely this was not the intrepid adventurer who had first made his fortune peddling trifles to the natives along the Ivory Coast? Could this be the man who had coaxed dilapidated steamers up the Sassandra and Bandama Rivers to jungle villages with names like Douékoue and Zouénoula to bring out rare hides, ivory, and exotic wood? He had visualized a darker man, a fiercer man, a man with more presence.

"I'm Angus McKie," the man said, sticking out his hand and smiling to reveal two alarming gaps in his front teeth. He was rough, out of place in the formal library.

"Armand St. Amour." Armand shook his hand.

Armand must have shown his puzzlement, because McKie said quickly, "I'm advisor to Max on some of his mining ventures. I was a prospector up around Sudbury way. Had a bit of luck. So Max thinks I know a hell of a lot about Canada."

"Didn't they find some copper and nickel deposits up there ten years ago?"

"That's right. Nothing much has come of it yet, but Max had some claims up there. He has an instinct about mining, and he's hanging on to what he's got in that area. That's part of Max's way—his instinct."

"He seems to have been remarkably successful."

"Yes, you can say that all right. What are you interested in yourself, sir? I take it has something to do with mining, or Max wouldn't have asked me to come today."

"Asbestos," Armand said.

McKie looked interested. "You know about Max's roofing plant, then. Right now we mine asbestos on Staten Island, but it's low-grade stuff."

"Exactly what I was told. I've got a line on something that I think will really interest M'sieur DeLeon. Top-quality asbestos. And the mine can be bought, I think. But there are certain difficulties."

McKie gave a short bray of laughter. "Where is it, at the North Pole, laddie?"

"Not quite. But there's no way of bringing ore out or taking supplies and men and machinery in."

Max DeLeon interrupted them. He was no more than five feet four inches tall; his dark, curly hair was graying and was parted carefully in the center. His black eyes were sharp, inquisitive, his nose noticeably hooked, and his chin and mouth almost concealed by a thick handlebar mustache and pointed beard. He was dressed nattily in a dark suit

with matching vest, heavy gold watch chain, white shirt
with deep cuffs showing, and broad silk tie pinned with a
spectacular diamond.

"St. Amour?"

"Yes, M'sieur. I am Armand St. Amour."

Armand bowed slightly. Despite DeLeon's shortness and
his rather vulgar appearance, he commanded respect.

"Vell? You haf a deal? Tell me aboud id."

It was immediately apparent that his accent was unman-
ageable, almost shocking for a man who had reached such
a pinnacle of success. Armand took a moment to recover
from his surprise.

DeLeon offered cigars and selected one for himself.
McKie refused, taking out a pipe instead. When they had
lit up, Armand began to talk. He could be extraordinarily
charming when he chose. This was such a time.

DeLeon, who had been born in Europe of Dutch parents, responded to Armand's Old World manners. He listened attentively while Armand explained about the asbestos mine at Thetford. It was presently being mined
on a small scale by Joseph Barber, a man with little capital,
who presumably could be bought out if enough money was
available. The other aspect of the deal was to obtain a
charter to build a railroad into Thetford from Sherbrooke,
and this Armand felt he could do, since the St. John Railway, of which he was a forty-percent owner, was so successful.

"Und how far is id from Sherbrooke to Thetford?"

"About seventy miles."

"What is de cost, now, per mile?"

"About fifteen thousand."

"You can get dis charter?"

"That depends," Armand said. He outlined the situation. He must hang on to the stock he now had in the St.
John Railway in order to prove that a railroad he was involved with was already a success. They must buy the mine
outright. The promise of encouraging settlement in the
area, of providing jobs and bringing out ore, would be an
incentive for the government to grant the charter. But with
a charter, there was always an enormous and valuable land
grant; forty years earlier, the Grand Trunk Railway had
been granted three million acres of free land along its extended right-of-ways, and the great Canadian Pacific had

been granted twenty miles on either side of the transcontinental line.

"Dis man Barber, vill he sell?"

"I think so, for a price. He's only dabbling at the moment."

"How sure are vee of the quality?"

Armand had expected this question. He brought out a sample of the ore wrapped in a heavy silk handkerchief. McKie handled the piece of asbestos; it was gray with long crystalline flakes like a mass of fine needles. He whistled.

"That's top quality," McKie said.

"Vee need more zamples, but id looks good."

"How do you stand with the government?" McKie wanted to know. "Have you friends there?"

"Some, yes. There's a federal election coming up in a month. If the Liberals win, it will be easier for me. The Liberals are leaning more to the problems of the French Canadians. Also, my brother-in-law, Corbin Dufours, is running for a seat in East Montreal. If he gets in, it will be helpful. But even if the Conservatives are returned, I think they will listen. They want development, they want railroads, they want settlement. But I *must* hold the shares I already have in the St. John. That is imperative. It's my base."

"Eggsagtly how many shares do you hold now?"

"Forty-three percent. My proposition is this. You buy half my shares and I'll negotiate another ten percent from other shareholders. Together we'll have fifty-three percent. Believe me, you won't lose. The railroad is making money. I've brought statements with me to show that. With this success to my credit, I can approach the government for the other charter."

"Vere is dis St. John Railway? Led me see a map, Angus."

McKie, familiar with this routine, brought out maps of American and Canadian territories. He spread them on the polished surface of a Hepplewhite satinwood desk, and DeLeon bent over to examine them carefully. There were marks drawn on areas of northern Ontario, showing where he held claims.

"You ship lumber now to Ottawa?"

"That's right. Then it goes down the river to the St. Lawrence and is taken on by boats," Armand said.

"I vould like to see a railroad northwest of Ottawa."

"There's nothing there, at the moment," Armand protested.

"Someday, you vill see. Dere vill be reason for a railroad. Copper and nickel is dere, and maybe gold. Don't you dink so, Angus?"

Angus agreed.

Max DeLeon said, "How aboud a drink, Angus? Perhaps you could give our guest a drink? I don'd drink myself. I haf stomach trouble."

He held one hand to his stomach, as if he had a pain. His face was crowded now with frowns and fleeting expressions of discomfort.

"Sometimes I dond eat, either," DeLeon said, making a rueful face. "Life is hard."

Angus McKie offered a glass of very old brandy. Armand accepted it. DeLeon still looked unhappy.

"Did you come to New York alone?" he asked.

"No, I brought my wife with me. She's at the hotel. We've only been married a few months."

"Ah. Dad is nize. I used do dake my vife along on my journeys. My vife is a beautiful voman, Mr. St. Amour. I took her to India. My advice to you is, dond dake your vife to India."

Angus McKie looked a little embarrassed. He began wrapping up the maps, ready to put them away.

"I hadn't given the matter any consideration, M'sieur."

DeLeon sighed heavily, one hand on his stomach, rubbing the front of his vest as if to soften some invisible blow. He looked unhappy.

"In India, Mr. St. Amour, they have maharajahs. Maharajahs are unusual men—they are vat the vomen call romandic. You see vat I mean? Vomen are romandic, too."

Angus McKie drained his brandy glass.

"I think you ought to consider this asbestos mine seriously, Max. Do you want me to go up there and look at the place?"

"Oh, yes, I do. Ve'll haf anoder meeting tomorrow, Angus. Now, Mr. St. Amour, vould like you to come to dinner. You could bring your vife?"

"With pleasure."

"My vife likes visitors," Max offered, as they walked

out into the large central hallway. The huge square staircase dominated the room. Armand looked up, noticing the intricate carving of the balustrade and spindles, the large paintings in heavy gilt frames that hung against the richly flocked wallpaper. Then he saw a woman he could only assume to be Mrs. DeLeon. And at first, he was puzzled. He had supposed that DeLeon's veiled references to his wife and to maharajahs meant an affair. And when he first saw Velma DeLeon, he could not imagine why any man would be so indiscreet. She was a large woman, as pink as a cabbage rose, overly plump, fussily rather than tastefully dressed. She came down the stairs heavily, so pink and white of skin and of gown that he mentally placed her in a music hall. It was incredible to him that a maharajah had so lost his head over this woman that he would offend an important and wealthy guest.

She was halfway down the stairs when she smiled at him. It was a smile so piercing and so beautiful that he knew instantly what had possessed the maharajah, and what had possessed Max DeLeon in the first place. Suddenly he was glad that he would have his wife along tonight, and that he would be prevented from any folly in this direction. He looked away from her smile just the same, and even when her husband introduced them, he contrived to look slightly aside, rather then address his look to her directly. He had seen many women—many beautiful women, talented women, clever women, rich women—but he had never seen a woman with a smile like Velma DeLeon's.

The sound of distant hammering interrupted the stillness of the June afternoon. Lady Court, arriving in the Green Room before high tea, was impatient. The noise was distinctly irritating, and especially so since the idea of having Pride's Court abandon gaslight in favor of the new electric light had been Sir Simon's idea and not her own. She did not trust electricity. Not enough was known about it, she felt. And the gas was perfectly adequate.

The coolness of the Green Room, however, did much to calm her nerves. It was screened from the gardens by a deep, shadowed loggia covered with creeper and filled with green plants. There was a fountain in the garden framed by the doorway, and the illusion of tumbling water helped to make the room feel cooler still.

She sat down to wait for Sir Simon and Fort, and, despite the hammering, fell into a thoughtful mood. With Charles gone to England, she was lonely. He was not as gay and amusing as Fort, but he had been more often home, and now, more than ever, she missed Honey. She ought to have been in the throes of planning a grand wedding, she thought fretfully, like Nora Ross. Why couldn't Honey have behaved reasonably, as Emily Ross had done? There Emily was, making a perfectly good match with James Cuthbertson, having a perfectly lovely wedding in Christ Church in July. It was heartbreaking, really.

It made her nervous, too, that Charles had announced that he would be actively looking for a wife while he was in London. Suppose he showed up with some stage girl, or some artful climber from the shops? But no, Charles was much too sensible to be taken in that way. She must have faith. Please, God, not another disaster like Hannah's, she prayed. I couldn't bear it, really I couldn't. Poor Honey, she would find out soon enough what a ghastly mistake she'd made, but it was far too late for second thoughts.

Lady Court sighed heavily.

She considered having a sherry by herself, but that was "giving in," and she didn't approve of giving in. Once you started it there was no telling where it might lead.

Her melancholy mood was shattered by the sound of Sir Simon and Fort approaching from the front of the house. She automatically rang the bell for tea.

"What the devil is all that racket?" Sir Simon asked testily, settling himself into the one comfortable chair he used in the room. "It's damned cool in here, eh, Fort? The streets are like a furnace. We ought to move down to the summer place soon, Lydia. But I suppose you can't very well do that with all this work going on."

"You know perfectly well what the racket is. It's *your* carpenters. Fixing up after the men who installed the electric lights. And no, we can't go just yet. Drake House will have to wait."

Drake House was their summer house on the south shore of the St. Lawrence. A number of the English had places there.

"They can't go on forever," Sir Simon said, closing that subject. "We've had rather bad news today, Lydia. Fort, pour me a Scotch, will you? I'll have it before my tea."

Lady Court stiffened. If Simon needed a Scotch before tea, then it was bad news indeed. She thought of Charles, who had sailed on the *Corsican*.

"It isn't Charles, is it?"

"No, no. Nothing quite so serious as that. But bad enough. The *Highland Princess* hit an iceberg off Newfoundland. Terrible business, from what I can make out. We haven't the details yet, but the ship is lost. No loss of life, I'm glad to say."

"Thank God. I thought it might be Charles's ship."

"Everybody rescued. Splendid effort, really. Some fishing boats helped, and the lifeboats were all manned, I gather, according to the rulebook. So there's no doubt Captain Peters did a good job. But it costs money just the same."

"Aren't you insured, Simon?"

"Yes, yes. But what people don't understand is, we're insured for what it cost to build the damned ship. That was eighty thousand pounds. But to replace her, it'll take a bit more, don't you see? At least a hundred thousand, wouldn't you say, Fort?"

"Yes, perhaps more. Here's your Scotch."

Fort poured himself one as well.

"Sherry, Mama?"

Lady Court hesitated. Then: "Yes, darling, I think I *will* have a sherry."

Somehow, she managed to make it sound quite decadent. Fort was amused, but refrained from teasing her.

"How we're going to crowd the passengers onto another eastbound liner, I damn well don't know," Sir Simon went on. "But we have to, just the same. We can't leave them there. Peters had just navigated the Straits of Belle Isle, and was out in open sea, running between pans of ice, but no sign of a real berg. Anyway, the passengers and crew are back at some little fishing village called Raleigh. Nothing there, I gather, but a few huts. We're getting the *Sardinian* to stop by and pick them up, but where they'll all be berthed is beyond me."

Sir Simon was heartily displeased at the loss of a ship and at the loss of money. But he savored any kind of trouble that was well-handled (he would have preferred a naval battle of some kind, but there was none going *this* year), and he would be talking about the loss of the *Highland Princess* for weeks to come.

"I sympathize with Peters," Fort said. Having been a captain himself and having felt the responsibility for ships and crew and passengers, his emotional response was to the men in charge. He could almost hear the sounds of panic, the ripple of fear, the grinding and the banging, the shouts, the pounding of feet. He could smell the terror.

"From what we know, Peters did the right thing all the way through. We'll take note of that, Fort. When we get the details, of course."

"The Atlantic at this time of year is bloody cold," Fort observed, taking a mouthful of Scotch, "and uncommonly black. I never fancied dropping into it."

Sir Simon fished a letter from an inner pocket of his coat.

"By the way, Lydia, there's a letter from Geoffrey. Just arrived today. He says he's engaged."

Lady Court, having finished her sherry, said she thought she might well need another.

"Before you tell me any of the details," she added.

Fort laughed. "Oh, don't worry, Mama. She isn't *completely* unacceptable."

"What do you mean?" Lady Court's hand trembled as she took the refilled sherry glass. Please, not another one. Not some perfectly hopeless woman, a shop girl, perhaps, or . . . but no, Geoffrey wouldn't look at somebody of another race. There was no need to worry about that.

"There doesn't seem to be anything objectionable about her, from what Geoffrey says," Sir Simon said hastily, glaring at Fort. "You have an odd sense of humor, Fortescue. You know how your Mother worries."

"She's English, Mama. In fact, her name is Mary Brown," Fort said.

Lady Court's first thought was, "How like Geoffrey."

"Yes, she comes from Lancashire. Not too far from Liverpool. Her father has some land, I believe. They come from a place called Bootle," Sir Simon added.

"Bootle," Fort said musingly, "sounds like a limerick. There was a young lady from Bootle . . . but what rhymes with Bootle? Tootle?"

"Be quiet, Fort. Let your mother read the damned letter," Sir Simon said loudly. "As I say, Lydia, she appears to be from a sound English family, although I doubt if they're particularly well-connected, or Geoffrey would have mentioned it."

"He wouldn't mention it if she were half-caste, either," Fort observed. "What about half-caste? Just because her name is Brown, that doesn't prove she's true-blue white, you know. Old Geoff might be slipping one over on us."

"I wish you would keep that kind of humor for your friends. Whoever they are," Sir Simon said.

Lady Court was allowing her eyes to glide quickly over the letter. She did not find it particularly riveting. Geoffrey was a boring boy, and he wrote boring letters. She had never been able to convince herself that she missed him very much after Simon had sent him off to Liverpool.

"Yes, Fort," Lady Court said, with a touch of self-pity, "you know what I've been through with Hannah. God knows, a Frenchman is bad enough, but at least he's white."

"But *is* he?" Fort asked no one in particular. "I mean, there are anthropologists who insist that the Latin races are partially black, you know. And the French . . ."

"Be quiet, damn you!" Sir Simon roared. "The girl is British, and that's enough of that! Just see that you pick a suitable wife *yourself* when the time comes. And make the time soon. *I'm* not getting any younger."

"Ah, but *you* don't have to father the children, or keep the bride happy," Fort pointed out.

Sir Simon had had enough. He turned from red to purple.

"How dare you say such things in your mother's presence?" He could scarcely articulate the words. "Years at sea have turned you into a bloody . . ." He could not think of a word ugly enough to fit the case.

"Sailor," Fort supplied. "Sorry, Mama, I didn't mean

to offend you. Papa's right. I've been with men too long. Good thing you brought me home again to get civilized, don't you think?"

"I'll ring for tea again," Lady Court said. Secretly she found Fort's humor quite pleasing. If she hadn't been so concerned about Hannah, and about Charles, and about Geoffrey's prospective bride, she might have laughed.

Lady Court pulled the bell once more.

"I'll read the letter more carefully after tea," Lady Court said, sinking into her chair. "Perhaps we've overlooked something."

"I wouldn't count on it," Sir Simon said gloomily. "Geoff is almost illiterate. However, I'm sure everything will be fine. If Miss Brown's father has land in Lancashire, he's bound to be solid enough."

He was anxious to put the best possible face on it, although a girl with the name of Mary Brown from a place in Lancashire called Bootle did not provide much material with which to work.

"Bootle. Let me see," he went on. "What have I heard about Bootle?"

"At least Geoffrey is getting married," Lady Court said consolingly. "It's time you thought about marriage too, Fort."

Fort's mind went to Sydney, and he smiled. He tried to imagine bringing the wispy, remote Sydney home to Pride's Court and presenting her as his fiancée. He could not envision just how Sir Simon would react, but he decided without much effort that the reaction would not be enthusiastic. However, he was not serious about Sydney. He was intrigued, nothing more.

"I'm thinking about it," Fort said noncommittally.

"I couldn't bear another marriage like Hannah's," Lady Court said, closing her eyes as if that would shut out the memory.

"Speaking of Honey," Fort said, grasping at the chance to pass along information that he thought would be news to both his parents, "I saw her."

Sir Simon paused in his sipping of Scotch, his hand arrested in midair. Nobody had mentioned his daughter to him since that awful day when he had caught her sneaking into Pride's Court. Lady Court was anxious for news.

"You saw Honey? How is she?" Lady Court asked quickly.

"She seeems fine."

"You actually visited her in her home? I thought this family had agreed . . ." Sir Simon began angrily. But nobody had actually agreed not to see Honey, they had simply been told not to do so.

"Naturally. I had tea with her. It isn't an interesting house, I'll admit, but it's large enough and quite comfortable. I thought Mama would like to know about her state of health," Fort said quickly.

"Yes, I do want to know," Lady Court said, ignoring her husband's glares.

"Well, she's having a baby. Pretty far along, in fact. That's the big news. She would like to make up the quarrel, I think, on that account. After all, a grandchild should be welcome here. You ought to make some move to patch things up, Papa."

"I'll have another sherry, darling," Lady Court said.

Sir Simon drank off his Scotch and gave his son a freezing stare. No member of the family was allowed even to *suggest* what his mode of behavior ought to be.

"I hope you aren't going to be tipsy before tea, Mama," Fort said, getting his mother the wine. "Anyway, I told her I thought you might both be interested in the grandchild when it arrives. Especially if it's a boy."

"I have no interest in a half-French grandchild," Sir Simon said scornfully.

"Come now, Papa," Fort protested.

"She *is* well, though? You're sure of that?" Lady Court said quickly, hoping to prevent another outbreak of temper from Sir Simon. She was flushed with the wine, and with this latest piece of news.

"So sure that I happen to know she's gone traveling with Armand," Fort said. "I heard it at the club."

"Traveling? In her condition?"

"They went to New York. Armand has some business there, apparently."

Lady Court was appalled. Pregnant women did not appear in public once their condition became noticeable. It was in bad taste. Also, the train could be dangerous. The whole thing was lacking in sense and propriety.

"What can you expect from barbarians?" Sir Simon

bellowed, voicing, for once, his wife's exact thoughts. "I don't want to hear any more about it. I don't want to see the child. Why should that change my mind? What does it alter, can you tell me that?"

Mercifully, the tea arrived, and Sir Simon was distracted by the sight of some Melton Mowbray pork pie, sliced, with pickles and hot mustard to accompany it. Evidently, then, it was high tea, and there would be no dinner. But he was not unhappy. He saw that there were scones, and plenty of cakes and hot muffins.

"Scones," Sir Simon said. "My favorite. Did you notice how the food has gone off at the club, Fort? My beef at noon was a bit offish. Have they changed the chef, do you think?"

"Scones," Fort said. "I had delicious scones when I had tea with Honey."

"*Impossible!*" Lady Court said with conviction. "She has a French cook."

Fort didn't explain. He began to think, instead, of Sydney sitting in this room, pale, unreachable, and somehow exquisite in her remoteness. Such pale skin, he thought, must be very beautiful when seen without clothing of any kind. While he ate his scones, he tried to remember whether or not Sydney had large breasts. He did not like his women to be too thin. If she had been an artists' model, surely she must have some flesh on her. Artists didn't usually like skeletons. Yes, he was sure, now, thinking back on the bluish dress she had worn, that her breasts were quite pleasantly rounded.

He was dragged out of his reverie by his father's next remark, which concerned the election.

"If the damnable *rouges* get in, we'll have more problems than you can shake a stick at. Not only with the Royal Mail contract, but with my bank expansion plans as well. Not that I think they have a chance, mind you," Sir Simon said, glaring over his teacup at his son.

"The Tories ought to win with Sir Charles back at the helm. He's an old hand in the field," Fort said in an attempt to comfort his father, who so obviously needed soothing. "And the bishops are with us all the way. Since they tell the people how to vote, Quebec ought to go Conservative."

"Right. Right. But I wanted to see the legislation passed

before the election, just to be sure. I know it's sitting on the Governor General's desk, waiting for his signature. Damn it, His Excellency is just stalling. He's a Liberal at heart—everybody knows that."

"And if the Liberals do by chance get in, you think the Governor General won't sign it?" Fort asked.

"Not likely. It'll get lost in the shuffle if I know anything about political plums," Sir Simon said moodily. "We'd do the same thing ourselves, if the situation were reversed."

"But the Liberals can't possibly win, can they?" Lady Court asked. "With that young upstart Laurier leading them? Anyway, Simon, I don't understand it. You say the Roman Catholic bishops are supporting the Conservatives —and yet Laurier, the Liberal leader, must surely be a Catholic, since he's a French Canadian. Why aren't the Bishops supporting *him*?"

"Ah, my dear, I can explain it, although I doubt whether, as a woman, you can understand it. Put briefly, the bishops, who represent the authority of the Catholic Church, don't like rebels. And Laurier is a rebel. He's on record against the Catholic Separate Schools in Manitoba, for example. The bishops have always supported British authority. And the Conservative Party represents British authority. And so the bishops, who know when they're well off . . . haven't they, as a conquered people, been allowed to keep their religion and their own language? Absolutely unheard of when you lose a war. It just shows how damned just the British are and always have been. Anyway, the bishops know they're more than just tolerated by the British. The Church is positively *entrenched*. You have to admit that the Catholic Church has always understood that power and authority go together. Keep people in their places, instruct them in their duties, tell them they should be grateful for what they've got. I admire that in the bishops, much as I'm against Papists and always will be. But, damn it, they understand law and order. They understand sound politics."

"Oh, I see," Lady Court said. But she did not really see. "Well, darlings, I think I'll go up to bed. I'll read Geoffrey's letter again." She picked up the letter pretending interest. In actuality, she wanted to get back to her novel, in which things happened that she could understand, and which had the advantage of being romantically presented.

When Lady Court had said her good nights and finally retired from the room, Sir Simon settled in for a serious talk with his son. Over brandy, he became more explicit.

"We've got the bishops on our side, yes. And they'll direct the priests to tell the people how to vote. And the word is Conservative. But we've still got plenty of greasing to do. Our man, Tellier, for example, is running against a French Canadian Liberal in East Montreal. The question is, how much are we prepared to put up for Tellier's campaign? Things cost more than they used to, you know. What do you think of fifty thousand dollars? Is it enough?"

Fort was surprised. "Things are as desperate as that, are they?"

"*More* desperate. I want you to get out and see if you can arrange something with the papers. I wouldn't trust just anybody on my staff . . . it could be a sticky thing if it gets out. Bribery has a long-lasting smell."

"You'll go that far? Paying newspaper writers to print what you want?"

Sir Simon allowed himself a half laugh, half growl. "There's always *somebody* for sale. I leave it to you to find out who, and how much. The truth is, we can't afford to lose this election. We've got too many irons in the fire. If the *rouges* come out on top, we're going to suffer, make no mistake about it. And the Royal Mail contract isn't the whole story. I told you I'm expanding the bank, didn't I? I've got Smith working on that now, but we need government support to do it. I want to get into railways. The Canadian Pacific may be a reality, but it isn't the end as far as railways in this country are concerned. Believe me, Fort, we *need* the Tories. Not only for ourselves, of course—" Sir Simon added hastily, in a last-minute attempt to show concern for the country—"but for the whole country, you see, for the *people*."

"Everybody at the club seems to think Tupper will bring the Conservative government back in."

"Rubbish! My dear boy, nobody feels confident. If they did they wouldn't talk so much. Do you realize that there are four vacancies in the Senate right at this moment? Tupper's got his list of nominations ready, but the Governor General is stalling. Until after the election, of course. He dislikes Tupper intensely, and *His Excellency*—" Sir Simon spoke the title with heavy scorn—"*His Excellency* was a Gladstonian, so he's really a dyed-in-the-wool Liberal. And in addition to the Senate vacancies, there're judgeships and key diplomatic posts and God knows how many other contracts. All waiting—waiting until after this damnable election."

"Tell me what you want me to do," Fort said, lighting a cigar and preparing for a long session (there would be no escaping the house tonight, he could see that), "and I'll do my best."

"First, we've got to get Tellier elected. He'll get a cabinet post if he takes that riding, because it's one of the most important in the country. Then we're going to have to contribute to the overall campaign, perhaps even to Tupper's personal campaign, although I can't stand him myself."

"How much are you prepared to spend?"

"Half a million," Sir Simon said calmly.

Fort stared at his father. All other thoughts fled from his mind and he prepared to concentrate on a strategy that would assure success. Dispensing half a million dollars lent a man a certain aura of self-worth. Fort was not immune to the satisfactions of wielding power.

"Now, here's exactly what I want you to do," Sir Simon began.

CHAPTER SEVEN

"Monsignor Marois has pronounced it a mortal sin to vote Liberal in the election," Marc said.

"I didn't realize it was as strong an edict as *that*." Corbin Dufours was a little shocked.

"Oh, it is, I assure you. The bishops are taking the strongest possible stand. I know, because I've already been given my orders."

The St. Amours were gathered in the drawing room to discuss Corbin's election campaign. He was running on the Liberal ticket in the riding of East Montreal, and every member of the family who could contribute something was being asked to do so. Armand and Honey were present, and even Laurent Dosquet (Justine's husband) had come in from the country. Helene had seen to that. She was acting as unofficial campaign manager.

"That's going to be tough to beat," Corbin said doubtfully. "People are accustomed to listening to their parish priests during elections. So when the bishops tell the priests, and the priests tell the people, they listen."

"Very true, I'm afraid," Marc agreed. "Or, at least, it's always been true in the past. But this time there's a French Canadian leading the Liberal party, and even the bishops may have trouble making people vote for an Englishman with a choice like that. Bishop LaFleche, by the way, has completely condemned Wilfrid Laurier, our great hope, and the whole Liberal party along with him."

Helene, sitting stiffly in an armchair by the empty grate, allowed her plump face to set in lines of anger. She had respect for the bishops, for the Church, of course—who hadn't? But when the Church's will crossed her own (and it was *her* will that her husband be elected as the Liberal member for East Montreal, whereupon she was sure he would become a cabinet minister) when it came to *that*,

Helene Dufours began seriously to doubt the Church's motives. She was aware, even in her anger, that the drawing room was too warm for comfort. The muggy June air of the city had begun to penetrate the thick walls of the house, to push its way into the dim interior rooms kept so carefully curtained against the sun. Her gown was too tight. She was putting on weight again, and she would have to take care with her diet if she was going to make an elegant appearance in Ottawa when Parliament met. The opening of Parliament was always a grand affair; diamonds and evening dress in the middle of the afternoon. Lord and Lady Aberdeen would be there—the Governor General and the Governor General's wife. And other titled people as well. Laurier, of course, suave as always, would be dominant. She could see it all. And she did not take kindly to the idea that this opulent scene could be erased from her life by a pack of bishops who ought not to meddle in politics at all.

"And what exactly do you propose to say to your parishioners from *your* pulpit?" Laurent asked Marc.

Laurent Dosquet was not usually aggressive. But today he was anxious to draw attention to what other members of the family might contribute and keep in the background himself. He was ready to give his time, but if they asked for money it was going to be embarrassing. So he focused attention on Marc.

Marc looked at his brother-in-law with a touch of derision. He had never cared much for Laurent. The Dosquets were snobs, referring endlessly to their French forebears, all of whom (if you believed the family stories) had been direct descendants of the king. It was all terribly boring. While the St. Amours took pride in their ancestors and their French connections, they did not dismiss every other French Canadian family as insignificant the way the Dosquets did. Laurent was no better and no worse than the scion of any other French family, when it came to that.

"What I am preaching from my pulpit, Laurent," Marc said icily, "—and, by the way, if you took the trouble to attend my church occasionally, you would know for yourself—is in direct opposition to the bishops. But since you are not the most devout Catholic I've ever met, I'm forced to tell you that my flock is being told to vote Liberal."

"You are really going against the bishops?" Laurent asked in amazement. He had been prepared to deliver a severe lecture to a deaf priest. Now the priest had out-maneuvered him.

"Yes, I am going against the bishops," Marc said.

"Splendid, Marc. Splendid," Corbin said. "Since you're in the very middle of my own riding, your support is very important. But what will Uncle Eustache have to say about it when he finds out what you're saying from the pulpit?"

"He could have me removed, I suppose," Marc said gloomily, "or excommunicated."

Uncle Eustache was both Marc's maternal uncle and his bishop. It was through this relationship that Marc had been able to move from the monastery at Oka directly to a parish in the city instead of being sent out into the hinterlands of the province. But uncle or not, Bishop Lavergne would not tolerate disobedience. And Marc knew that.

"That would be terrible!" Helene said, aware for once of somebody's predicament and convictions besides her own.

"I admit I wouldn't like it," Marc said. "But I believe in Laurier. I believe in the Liberal cause. They care about the people. They care about the French Canadians."

During this discussion, both Armand and Honey had remained quiet—Armand because he was waiting to see what everyone else had to say and what they were prepared to do for Corbin's campaign before he himself spoke; and Honey because on an occasion like this she was walled in by her inadequate command of French. Spoken quickly and excitedly, with words overlapping, the language smoth-ered her. Her French was improving, but it was still in-sufficient for a family gathering.

However, she could not resist breaking into the discus-sion at this point.

"But I don't understand. Why are the bishops against Laurier when he's a French Canadian? And Tupper is En-glish, and head of the Conservatives. Surely the bishops favor their own people?"

Marc undertook to explain in careful English. "Perhaps it does sound strange," he allowed, "but not if you know the way power works here. Wilfrid Laurier represents a *thinking* French Canadian group, and there is a certain amount of rebelliousness in them. They do not believe the Church should interfere in politics. But the bishops like to tell people how to vote—it's part of their power. And their strength comes from supporting the British government. Each supports the other, you see, in favor of the upper classes."

"Oh, I see," Honey said. She was not satisfied with the explanation, but she decided to remain silent. It was safer in this family atmosphere to take cover as a woman, and not try to be active or even to understand. As it was, she and Armand were still not very popular with the family. Yet as her father's daughter, she found it hard to be complacent. She wanted desperately to know the whys and the wherefores of things and what could be done to change them.

"Corbin will make a wonderful cabinet minister," Helene said, looking fondly at her husband. He was distinguished in appearance, there was no doubt of it. Equally as suave as his schoolmate, Wilfrid Laurier—thin and aristocratic, with a well-trimmed beard and a high, polished forehead. He spoke English and French equally well and had been first in his graduating class at McGill.

He was too fond of reading the fine print in his law books to be really impressive in court, yet he was capable of a resounding address when his interest was captivated. He was able to charm, too, when he wished and was at home with both men and women. Helene, an utterly sexless woman, regarded him more as a possession than as a husband. He was a fine possession; good to look at, ambitious, and potentially important. She intended, if necessary, to whip the entire family into action to help get him elected. God knew the St. Amours did not have a limitless fund of money, and therefore they must substitute energy, imagination, and, it must be hoped, some style.

"I was hoping, Laurent," Corbin said, cutting off his wife's impending speech about his rare qualities for office, "that you'd run my campaign. We'll need to hire halls, get some posters printed, have people knocking on doors. There won't be too much money. I don't know what we can raise, and I'm not sure how much help we'll get from the party funds. Armand, I depend on you to raise money. How much can you manage to get in the next few days?"

"I'll know better tomorrow," Armand said.

"Oh? What's happening tomorrow?"

"I'm having a meeting with the Canadian representative of my new partner. A man who is based in Montreal. I don't think you know him, Corbin. But whatever money I raise in a hurry will have to come from him."

"I leave that to you, then. But did you think to mention this election when you were in New York? Did you impress on DeLeon—you haven't told me much about him, by the way—did you make clear to him that the election outcome may affect any charters you apply for?"

"Yes, I thought of that."

Armand noticed that Corbin could not quite keep the slight tinge of condescension out of his voice. He'd always regarded Armand as a spendthrift and a dilettante. The image wasn't going to be easy to erase. The fact that Armand had apparently saved the family finances, at least for the time being, did not wipe out the memory of years of spending and pleasure-seeking.

"That's good, then," Corbin said.

"Once I knew DeLeon was seriously interested in my propositions, I explained to him the importance of this election. What do you think you'll need as a minimum?"

"We can't do much for less than thirty thousand dollars, the way prices are these days. I'd like more, but I couldn't manage with much less."

"In that case, I'll ask for fifty thousand and see what the response is. If he has to cut back, we won't be too far out on your estimate. I'll know tomorrow, one way or the other."

"Then we'll meet again tomorrow night. You're sure, Armand, that you can get a reasonable amount? Laurent should be out first thing tomorrow, and if he makes commitments, we'll have to find the money to honor them."

"There'll be something," Armand assured him, although actually he had no idea how Diderot, the banker handling DeLeon's Canadian affairs, would react to his request.

"I hope," Helene said grandly to Laurent, "that Justine won't mind your moving into the city for a few weeks. It will be her contribution to the election, after all."

"No, no. I'm sure she won't." Laurent thought that Justine might welcome the change. She had become increasingly irritated with him lately. She had never been a gay, happy person, nor full of wit or enthusiasm or vitality.

But lately, he had noticed that she was becoming decidedly sullen. Yes, it would no doubt be a pleasant change to get away from each other for a while.

"You can stay here," Armand volunteered. "There's always plenty of extra room in the house. Honey can probably arrange for you to have two rooms, so you can have an office. Is that possible, Honey?"

"Tomorrow, yes. Tonight, I've put Laurent on the third floor, in the blue-and-white bedroom."

"You're right, I'll need somewhere to work," Laurent said with more enthusiasm than he had shown for many years over any subject other than his cows. With a great effort, he had pulled himself out of his rut and made ready to plunge into the election plans. He was aware that the family regarded his cooperation with amazement, that they had fully expected him to hang back. The truth, however, was that he had been terrified that they would demand a large sum of money. He was so relieved that he was being asked to offer time (which he could afford to give) rather than money (which he could ill afford, since he'd lost large sums in the past year on the cattle and had been forced to take out a mortgage on the estate to cover living expenses) that he would have jumped through hoops for them.

"No, Justine won't mind," he assured them again lest they broach the idea that he might prefer to donate money and hurry back to the farm. "She has Camille with her. She won't be lonely."

"Camille isn't exactly the best company," Helene commented. "But Justine must realize that it's her duty to spare you, Laurent. It's only for a short time. The change will do you good."

"You have a man in charge of the animals, I suppose?" Armand asked, noticing his brother-in-law's worried expression and misinterpreting it. "Surely you've got lots of hired help out there in the country?"

"Oh, no problem there," Laurent said briskly. "I've got an excellent man in charge of the herd. An Irishman named Fitzgerald. He used to live in Griffintown here in Montreal, where all the Irish immigrants stay when they first get off the boat. He learned to speak French quite well. A clever fellow, for a working man. It's amazing what they can do if they try, you know. He was a herdsman in the south of Ireland—worked for an Irish lord, I think."

"I'd like to know more about my opponent," Corbin said abruptly, "but he seems to be a bit of a mystery. They say he has shares in the telegraph company, and a textile company, and a lumbering camp in the north. So he'll have substantial resources."

"What's his name?" Armand asked.

"Pierre Tellier."

It was Honey who spoke. "*Tellier?*"

Everyone in the room except Armand turned to stare at her.

"You know him?" Corbin said with some excitement. It was the first time he had regarded his new sister-in-law with any interest.

"He's a business acquaintance of my father's."

"You mean we're fighting against Court money?" Laurent said, with a touch of awe.

"*And* the bishops," Marc said.

"The Court money may be the deciding factor, after all," Corbin said. "Sir Simon has his foot in so many camps nobody knows just how much he's worth, or how many companies he controls. He's a close friend of Prime Minister Tupper—and every other important government figure, for that matter."

"You're sure about this, then? Sure that Tellier is associated with your father?" Laurent demanded.

"I'm positive. Tellier tried to buy the St. Amour shares in the railroad. It was only because I told Armand who he really was that the mistake was prevented. Isn't that so, Armand?"

"It's why I went to New York looking for a partner," Armand agreed. "You know I promised Father I wouldn't sell to an English Canadian. And when Honey told me Tellier was probably representing Sir Simon, I began to look elsewhere."

"Do you think Sir Simon is really interested in the outcome of the election? That he'll spend a great deal of money?" Corbin asked Honey.

"If he's backing Tellier, he'll spend a great deal of money. Papa never loses *anything* if he can help it. He can't even bear to lose at billiards."

Papa. It was the first time the St. Amours had grasped the full significance of just who Armand had married. Honey was, or had been before she'd married, the Honorable Hannah Court, daughter of Sir Simon Court, one of the wealthiest and best-connected men in Montreal. In all of Canada. There was a palpable silence in the drawing room as they digested this fact.

It was Helene who finally broke the spell.

"Sir Simon isn't God," she pointed out. "And Tellier isn't unbeatable, no matter who is behind him. It means we've got to work harder, use our wits. And you, Armand, will have to raise as much money as possible. Any way you can."

This stirred the four men. They began to talk again. But from time to time they shot surreptitious glances at Armand's wife. It was like having a spy in the camp. And yet, perhaps her knowledge could be valuable. Only Armand was smiling.

———

Justine had gone riding early each morning since Laurent had left to live in Montreal and manage Corbin's campaign. The first wave of summer heat had rolled over the riverfront like an invisible, smothering blanket. Only the early morning was bearable. When the air was fresh and the sun still gathering up its strength, the willows bent over the water in emerald fronds and the grass was wet jade in the clear light. Birds—a pair of cheeky cardinals searching for ripening strawberries in the garden, a blue flash of cocky jays, a jabber of industrious sparrows—went their morning rounds. What was left of the purple iris made a hem against the lilacs, and the apple trees promised to turn white at any moment.

Justine loved the morning. Since Laurent was not present to correct her, she had taken to riding with her hair in two thick black braids, and she left off her corset and rode in her habit with only a net waist beneath her shirt. She felt freer than at any time since she had married. But it was a time to think restless thoughts, to let her dissatisfactions gel into rebellion. A time to confront all her frustrations with Laurent and with marriage and with living out here buried in the country.

She did not have to think about her horse. Fripon knew

the route, and stopped at choice spots to nibble at a luscious patch of grass, ambled gently around a pothole in the road, gazed off across the fields to look for animals to greet. Justine paid little attention to Fripon and Fripon paid little attention to Justine. They were a compatible pair in the morning.

It was easy to concentrate on herself with Laurent gone. Camille spent much of her time reading or writing poetry or just gazing off into space. (God knew what she thought about with that intense, almost pained look.) And the two children, Nicolette and Mathieu, were in the care of a nurse . . .

What did she want of life? What had she expected from this marriage, considered at the time to be a suitable one? She did not know what she wanted, but it was certainly more than this dull routine with Laurent. They scarcely spoke anymore except to complain to each other. And Laurent had never been much of a lover. Dimly she had thought that marriage would fulfill all her needs; there would be a house to look after, children, the mysterious ritual of the bedroom. Men must be interesting, and necessary, because everybody said so. The first two years, with redecorating the old farmhouse and the birth of the children, had passed quickly. She had barely noticed the vacuum left by Laurent's dullness, his lack of interest in love-making. She had begun to read a great deal and do needlepoint. She had gardened a little, and learned to ride well. But these activities did not meet all her needs.

When she had first begun to question life, she had not seemed able to isolate the source of her discontent. Then, after reading a particularly glowing passage in *Madame Bovary,* it had struck her that the lack was in her relationship with her husband. It was clearly flat, unstimulating and unrewarding. There was simply nothing to it. Although she had not been taught to expect anything from the bedroom except a performance of duty, some unexplored corner of her mind suggested that there must be more to it than this. Or what were all the romantic poems about? What about the lovely stories, the ancient legends? What about Heloise and Abelard? What about Helen of Troy? If no excitement was to be found in the secret, unspoken relationship of the bedroom, then why had men cared whether or not Helen had had a beautiful face? What possible difference could it make? And what of the stories about knights jousting in the lists, what of Lancelot and Guinevere? Surely it wasn't about a tedious ten-minute ritual in the dark that all the fuss was made? She couldn't imagine lovers risking their lives for the dreary performance Laurent seemed to consider adequate. There was a mistake. Surely there was more to it than the rigid posture she always assumed, the clumsy lifting of the nightgown as she lay unprotesting but cold with boredom and implied inconvenience? More than those half-dozen ugly thrusts and breathy wheezes that Laurent contributed to the ceremony, while she stopped breathing altogether? What, then, had she missed? And *why* had she missed it?

She had heard that men kept mistresses. Did they spend all that money, take the risks, and endlessly intrigue and plot for only a few dull moments of flesh pressed upon flesh? Was it really only a ten-second-long release of male tension that produced symphonies and historic scandals? Had Queen Marie risked her throne and her head for a few vague caresses from the Duke of Buckingham?

Every morning as she rode, she worried away at these momentous questions. And every morning, jogging neatly upon Fripon's back, she felt an alarming stir between her legs (a place with which she was not really too familiar yet, although she had begun to rationalize that it was a part of her just like any other part). Were such thoughts wicked, she wondered, and ought she to confess to Father Huet? But no—she could never tell Father Huet about those stirrings, about that secret place that was beginning to interest her so much. Father Huet would be scandalized. She would, perhaps, be excommunicated. He could not be expected to understand a problem like this, much less give her absolution . . .

The path she had worked out for her rides always took her past the dairy barns—it was a route she had first formulated because she had thought that Laurent would appreciate her checking to see that the cattle were being properly cared for. Also, Fripon liked to fraternize briefly with the cows that happened to be rubbing up against the fence near the road.

Timothée Fitzgerald (the Dosquets always used the French pronunciation of his name), the herdsman, was almost always around the barns at this time of the day, she had noticed. And for the past five days she had briefly discussed with him the weather, and the state of the herd's health, and even the possible outcome of the election on which Laurent was working so assiduously in the heat of the city.

After the first encounter she had begun to look forward to their daily chat with an agitation that was foreign to her. But she told herself that it was merely refreshing to exchange ideas with a man like Timothée, who was so enthusiastic about life despite his ill luck in belonging to the working class. He spoke French remarkably well for an Irishman. He had told her how he'd gotten off the boat at Montreal and found his way straight to Griffintown, that Irish sector of the city where the immigrants banded together before they surfaced and found their separate niches in Canadian life. The Irish, he'd pointed out to her, were a tough breed; otherwise, how had they managed to survive the English, not to mention the famines? They also, he had said with a twinkle, had the touch of magic about them.

In his barely concealed hatred of the English, he was an ally. That sympathy was an almost unspoken thing: sometimes a suggestion only, a set of signals that intimated a deep understanding.

Yes, Timothée Fitzgerald had a zest for life. And he was masculine and handsome as well—dark, with light green eyes and big white teeth and large sunburned hands. He was a large man, his frame muscular and suggesting great strength. He gave an overall impression of capability, as if there were nothing he could not handle and nothing that would daunt him.

This morning she saw him instantly when Fripon rounded the bend and the first barn was revealed. He was standing in the sunlight where it thrust over the roof of a low shed in a bright yellow shaft. His blue work shirt was open at the neck. He looked larger than usual, and his smile was brighter, more urgent, somehow. Her breath was short, her mouth slightly open as if she had been in a race. Fripon must have been jogging awkwardly, she decided.

"Good morning, Madame Dosquet," Fitzgerald said, giving her one of his warming smiles. "A beautiful morning for a canter."

"Oh, yes, it is."

She pulled Fripon up and dismounted. After the first day she had always stopped and dismounted, tying Fripon to the fence where he could communicate with some of the cows. Fripon had become quite enamored of this brief stop, and always hurried up the slope to the barns.

"Only time of day it's fit to ride," he said.

"It's far too hot in the afternoons," Justine agreed.

"Your sister doesn't ride, I see."

"No, no, Camille doesn't ride. She can't bear horses. They make her sneeze."

"A pity. *You* ride well."

"Do you think so?" She blushed. It was not proper to discuss her riding ability with the herdsman. Not proper at all. And yet he was being friendly. What harm was there in that? She fell under the influence of his smile, which was at once boyish and suggestive.

"I know a good horsewoman," Fitzgerald said with authority. "I've watched a good many women ride. Especially in Ireland. I worked for Lord Borthwick. He had a seat near Ballineen in County Cork. A good Catholic, he was, and a good horseman. I've seen them go to the hunt, the women, too. Some of them excellent."

"Do you ever want to go back to Ireland?"

Fitzgerald shuddered. "No, no, ma'am. Never. Mind you, it's beautiful, but only if you look at the scenery. Ireland's a land that doesn't belong in the rest of the world. It was never meant to be. I don't want to remember the poverty, the dirt, the disease. No, I won't go back. Never."

She abruptly changed the subject.

"How are the sick cattle?"

He brightened. He liked to talk about the animals. "Every single one is improving. I thought one would explode, really I did, but she's gone down again, and looks as if she might live. We had to slaughter one, though. Hopeless, it was, and she was suffering, so . . ."

"My husband will be glad to hear that they're improving," Justine said hastily. She had not been brought up to accept the cruelties and the crudities of farm life.

Fitzgerald seemed to hesitate before speaking again. She felt the joyous concentration of attention from his eyes. He was smiling warmly, the cattle forgotten, Ireland forgotten, apparently, in the intensity of the moment.

"Perhaps you'd like to see the new bull?"

Actually, she was afraid of bulls. They always seemed to have red eyes and to be pawing the ground. But she had nothing to do but go on riding by herself or return to the house to look at the strawberry beds and decide how many were ready for picking. It would be like every other morning of her life; dull, even, gratingly tedious. Camille would be there staring at a book or sewing something for the poor. In a flash of outrage, Justine decided that Camille was poor company indeed. Always completely wrapped up in herself. She ought to do something. Get married or become a nun. Anything. It was ridiculous to suppose she could go on living with relatives all her life. First with Justine, then with Helene, then with Armand. Justine sighed, bringing her temper under control.

Fitzgerald waited.

"Very well. I'll look at the new bull. I'm sure M'sieur Dosquet would approve of that."

Nervously she inspected the bull, which was glaring balefully at them from its pen. Fitzgerald suggested next that since she was interested in the dairy herd, perhaps she'd like to see the new cattle in the hill pasture. The hill pasture was a small, well-fenced meadow high up on the slope where a clear, broad stream wound downward to the St. Lawrence and clumps of lush willows provided shade. The grass was always greener and fresher there, and it was reserved for special animals.

Justine hesitated. The pasture lay a quarter of a mile up the grade and out of sight of the house. She really did not think it quite proper to go there alone with Fitzgerald. And yet, the alternative was only strawberry-picking and jam-making. The morning breeze brushed her face and injected her with new energy. She breathed deeply and said in what she hoped was a casual tone, "I wouldn't mind the walk."

"You'll make it all right, in those boots." He was looking at her riding boots. "You're dressed comfortably enough for walking."

As they began the climb Fitzgerald talked about the cattle: Jerseys, just imported at great expense in the hope that they would sire a whole new herd. Holsteins, which the estate had been breeding, but had not worked out. They got the fever too often. They did not give rich enough milk.

She nodded, trying to seem interested. They reached the hill pasture and Fitzgerald opened the gate to let her enter. The cattle were bunched together near a cluster of willows.

"Notice how they stand touching each other?" Fitzgerald demanded. "They like to touch."

"Fripon likes to be near the cows," Justine said.

"Animals have a lot of sense. Humans are afraid to touch like that. We always stand off, keeping ourselves to ourselves. But these animals have a different idea. Just as if they feel safer when they stay together."

She was touched by his attempt at philosophy. It seemed odd to hear a man talk like this. He had such a lilting way with French, making it sound like music.

"They don't feel so lonely, I guess. The world must seem very dangerous to animals," Justine said.

"And to humans, but we don't know enough to stick together. There's just blackness out there. We ought to be close and help each other. Nothing but blackness."

"No, no," Justine said quickly, "I don't believe that, M'sieur Fitzgerald."

Now, why had she called him that? He was not an equal. But she could no longer bring herself to call him Timothée; it suddenly seemed far too intimate.

"This is a lovely bit of property here," Fitzgerald observed. "And out of the way. Nobody around. Close to nature."

They sat down on a log under the willows. The stream flowed beside them over protrusions of gray and white rock, over fallen branches; it sparkled and sang in the morning sun. The shiver of a fish attracted Justine's eyes. A jay swooped over the water and up again, shrieking at its mate. The tall grass, lapping up over the edges of the log where they sat, covered her boots.

The sounds were gentle on the air—a cow yawning, a rustle of wind in the lace of the willows, a bee humming its way to a wildflower. Nobody knew they were there, Justine thought. And the idea caused both a tremor of apprehension and an echoing tremor of pleasure. The children were breakfasting now with Anne-Marie. Camille would be praying, probably. The servants, sensing that she was gone, would be drinking strong coffee and wasting their time. But she did not care. Let them be idle.

She was not really surprised when she felt the warmth of Fitzgerald's hand upon her jacket sleeve. She felt the weight and the warmth of it through the cloth. She had expected it, in a way, because her heart was racing and her breath had caught somewhere in her throat. It would have been possible to scream, she supposed, but a scream in the midst of this beauty would be obscene. Another demand was making itself felt, a demand she could not accurately describe except as a delicious tingling like the one she'd felt in the saddle.

In a last attempt at propriety, she sought something to say. Something about the cattle across the stream dipping into the grass for snacks, dozing in the blue-green shade of the willows, nuzzling one another's necks in a sympathetic gesture of confidence. Fitzgerald's hand (she *could* not call him Timothée, that was admitting more than she cared to admit) moved up the sleeve of her jacket to her bare neck. His fingers sought out the bones at the base of her neck and then moved up toward the black braids.

"Please don't." It was a whisper.

Fitzgerald's fingers did not hear what she said. They traced, warmly in the sunshine, the line of her neck to the lobe of her ear. The tingle moved along her neck, crawling, prickling, eager, and then, by some magic leap, lightning finding the highest point of ground for miles around, settled in that unnameable place between her legs. She gasped, not from shock at Fitzgerald's brazen behavior, but from the unexpected effect it had upon her own body.

"A lovely neck," Fitzgerald murmured in his melodious French, "which ought to be fondled."

She willed herself to stand up, to move away from him, but her will failed miserably. Instead, she sat like a statue while his lips touched the skin at the curve of her neck, just inside the jacket, and then nestled behind her ear where the thick braid started. She was conscious that his shirt was open and that black hair bristled there; and of the faint odor of cattle and sweat, but she did not mind. He took off her jacket.

"It's warm," he said.

"But, Timothée . . ."

She had done it. She had called him by his first name, speaking to him not as an equal (M'sieur Fitzgerald) and not as a servant (Timothée, but said without any intimacy whatever), but as a lover. Without the jacket, she felt naked. The lawn shirt, and the net waist beneath it, revealed the plump breasts with the faint dark circles at the tips. Breasts that jutted out like supplicants toward Fitzgerald's hands.

Timothée drew in his breath, a whistle against his teeth, almost a protest against the bait that caught his eye. His mouth, however, remained soft against her cheek, working its way across the corner of her mouth to rest against the inner edges of her lips. And his hands slid to her breasts, the mounds sinking beneath his fingers—pliable, unresisting at first, and then becoming insistent as the nipples hardened underneath his fingers.

She had been stiff and self-conscious from years of habit, but now she went limp against him. The silent cry from her thighs was maddening her, and instead of pushing him away, she pulled his hands across the bare flesh beneath her shirt, across the pink tips so delicately erect.

He did not hurry. His movements were the movements of a dancer. He took off her shirt, and the net waist, and exposed the full breasts to the sunlight. His mouth, hungrier, perhaps, than his hands, was not so gentle, but she fell gratefully back in the long grass, eager for his flesh to be pressed against her own. She was starving. Her senses overrode any dim protest from her mind. This was what she had been looking for, this sensual feast, the stimulated ache and then the ecstatic release. He was on her, but she rolled back from him, her breasts pleading for his hands. He took a great deal of time, there in the sunlight, to satisfy those breasts.

This, then, was to be no quick and dutiful plunge into cold, resistant flesh. This was to be slow and creeping softness, and a satisfying hardness, like the courses of a banquet. This was to be swallowing, nibbling, consuming, making her mouth go suddenly dry and her genitals wet.

She began to know a little of what men must feel when they finally spewed forth in their climactic delirium. The waves rising and rising up the painful, precious slope broke in sharp releases, little surfs of pain and pleasure. And at last she knew what it was men risked their lives for, paid for, intrigued for, killed for. At last she knew why.

Riding back down to the house, cheeks still burning from the rough caress of Fitzgerald's beard, she was thinking

not of remorse, not of sin or confession, but of how soon
she could again lie in the grass beneath Fitzgerald. How
soon? Would she have to wait, ladylike, until tomorrow
morning's ride? Why, now, should she pretend to be ladylike? Fitzgerald knew what she was, so why could she not
arrange a meeting for tonight? They must make use of
every day while Laurent was in the city. It was less than
three weeks till he came home, after all. She would have
to think of some safe way to meet Fitzgerald after dark.

CHAPTER EIGHT

By midnight, the grottoes were filled with guests, some in purple velvet masks freckled with diamonds, some in black velvet dominos (cloak and hood and half-mask), some dressed like apes and some like fauns, some got up like ancient Egyptian gods and some like lovelorn troubadours from medieval England, some wearing Medusa wigs of scarlet wool threaded with gold, some wearing enormous headdresses of rare feathers, some fully clothed and some half naked, men flaunting long yellow tresses and women in tiny green mustaches as naughty as bee stings.

They milled about the groves chatting or admiring one another's bizarre costumes, or trying to guess the identity of guests who remained elusive. At times there was voluptuous string music produced by a quartet of boys, and at other times a caressing hum from three sirens with bare breasts and fishy nether parts who were perched on a rock. In all the rooms, sideboards were well stocked with decanters of wine, baskets of tropical fruit, and tiny confections made in obscene shapes. In the circular room Fort had seen the first night he had visited the salon, couples were gyrating like wind-up toys to a waltz played excruciatingly slowly. And over everything hung the heavy scent of roses that covered another, more mysterious smell that might have been the odor of hashish.

Fort poured wine for himself and accepted a sweet from the Blackamoor's tray. The boy wore a gold suit and turban and was grinning with obvious delight. The countess appeared almost immediately, dressed as Nefertiti in draped green silk edged with gold, arms covered with gold bracelets from wrist to shoulder, fingers weighted with flashing rings, and wearing a headdress with two sets of horizontal horns and a golden fountain at the top that added three feet to her height and completely covered her mass of red hair. She wore no mask. She was towing Henry the Eighth, a plump gentleman in a scarlet silk capote lined with white fox and a velvet hat with a gigantic ostrich plume. He wore a small scarlet mask and a red false beard.

Fort had managed to borrow a domino for the evening and felt himself well concealed. But the countess, who was maskless, fixed him with her kohl-rimmed eyes.

"With that chin, I'd recognize you in a moment, my dear. I cannot introduce you to my friend because he wishes to be anonymous. But I can suggest that he is magnificent and influential. In fact, sublime."

Henry the Eighth smiled. He wore an enormous emerald on the third finger of his right hand.

Fort wondered if he were a cabinet minister or perhaps a member of the Church, escaping the confines of his somewhat narrow existence.

When he spoke, it was with a French Canadian accent.

"And what do you think of the coming election? Surely there is no hope for this upstart Laurier?"

"I wish I could be sure of that," Fort said fervently.

"Then we are of the same persuasion."

"Do you really think the Church can bring enough influence to bear on the voters?"

Fort had the distinct feeling that he was dealing with a Churchman, and he was anxious for any hint of a forecast that would be favorable to his cause.

"In the country, perhaps." Henry the Eighth sighed and his emerald flashed as he refilled his goblet with cool white wine. "In the city, I am not so sure. There is nothing worse than a heretic, in my opinion. And Laurier is a heretic. But because he is French, they may vote for him despite our . . . that is, the Church's instruction."

He corrected himself hastily, wondering if the man in the domino had noticed his slip. If he had, the other did not remark upon it.

From Fort's point of view, the conversation only reinforced his own growing conviction that the Tories were in trouble. He had been working until late in the evening— it was now midnight—on various schemes that his father was trying to set in motion. He had been in the study of a radical priest not more than an hour earlier (a priest who ought to have been preaching the Church's party affiliations and who was not) trying to bribe him with money to follow the very dictates that his bishop had handed down. It was madness. The priest had refused; money had no meaning for him, and only what he considered the welfare of his flock seemed to count.

It was at this point, as Henry the Eighth turned away from him, and as he sought to amuse himself elsewhere and forget the problems of politics, that he saw a woman whose air of remoteness, of graceful immobility, told him she must surely be Sydney.

From across the room he could not be absolutely sure. But he felt he would know when she spoke. He pushed his way through the crowd toward her, trying not to spill his wine.

"I feel we may have met," he said. It gave him a most peculiar feeling, talking to a woman who was impersonating a peacock. Her head and face were covered with fine green feathers and she wore a green gown, and an enormous peacock's tail fanned out behind her in full color.

"Perhaps," she said.

Only her eyes, nostrils, and lips showed. But he thought the voice was hers.

"Is there somewhere we can sit and talk?" Fort said, looking about him at the shifting zoo. "It's difficult to get one's thoughts in order here."

"That is part of the idea, I believe. People don't want to think all the time. Do you like the music?"

"For me, it's a bit of a puzzle. I'm not educated musically, I'm afraid. Except when it comes to sea chanteys."

She tugged at the edge of his cloak.

"Follow me, and we'll find a place to sit. Don't worry about refilling your glass; I'll find some wine if you want it."

He was glad to thread his way through the connecting rooms until they reached a door that cut them off from the general party. Behind the door was a small boudoir, richly furnished and quite comfortable. It was lighted with thick candles on wooden stands five feet tall.

Fort sat down.

"The countess is amazing. I've been to some soirees in London and Paris, but nothing any more fantastic than this."

"She *is* amazing. She has a wonderful gift for imagining details and then finding a way to execute them."

"It is Sydney, isn't it?" Fort asked as she carefully unhooked the tail from the back of her costume so she could sit down.

"Yes, it is."

"I've thought about you since I met you here."

"Have you? That was foolish."

"I don't think it was foolish at all. There are some things I'd like to discuss with you. But I admit it's difficult talking to a woman who has the head of a bird. Could you take that thing off?"

"Oh, I can take it off, but what can you possibly have to say to me? I made it quite clear when we first met that I'm not interested in being rescued."

"It's one of my characteristics that I don't give up easily. As I say, I've given this matter a lot of thought and I have a proposition for you."

She unfastened the headgear and lifted it off carefully. The long, straight hair was plaited and pinned up on top of her head. She had a long, graceful neck. The wide-spaced eyes he remembered now turned upon him questioningly.

"What is it that you want to propose to me?"

For a moment, he almost backed away from the offer he had come to make. Her look was so cool, so other-worldly that it seemed utterly ridiculous to suggest it. And yet, taking another, harder look, he knew he had been right. He wanted her. He had had many women, women of many classes and many races. This one, who seemed so unapproachable, stirred in him a need he could not describe. He only knew that it was unfamiliar and blinding.

"Will you tell me your last name? I can't think of you only as Sydney."

She shrugged slightly. She took his goblet and filled it from a decanter on a small table near the sofa where he sat and handed it to him.

"My last name is Hall. Very simple. Very English."

He felt a strange relief. He liked to think of himself as a man without prejudice, but if she had given him a European name of some strange extraction, he would have felt it an added difficulty.

"You are English, then? I thought so."

"Yes, but if you are going to ask about my parents, I won't tell you. Just accept the fact that I escaped my background, and I will never go back, I will never discuss it, I will never even think of it. So don't ask."

Actually, he could imagine it. It was probably shoddy beyond belief. Perhaps she had worked consciously to rid herself of some telltale accent that would have given her away. Or perhaps she was from one of those parts of London where the difference in speech was not quite so acute. He would never know. She spoke with such certainty that he realized it would be useless to ask for any more information.

"I also speak French. I went to Paris when I was twelve. The French may have altered the way I speak English. I know what you're thinking, and you're quite right. Now, please, I don't want to talk about that any more."

"I want you to marry me," Fort said.

She laughed. Not heartily. She would never laugh heartily, Fort thought, with a quick flash of insight. It was a light laugh, a passing streak of humor that revealed nothing of her real emotions.

"Marriage? I was expecting you to invite me to be your mistress."

She sat across from him quite calmly. They might have been discussing a play they had both seen or a book they had read.

"No, that's not what I want. Not at this time, anyway. I need a wife."

"Ah, you *need* a wife."

"Yes, and I happen to want you."

"I'm sorry, Mr. Court, but I don't happen to want *you*."

"I know that."

"Then what is the sense of your question?"

"There's a hell of a lot of sense in it, if you'll listen. Look, I don't care about your past . . . well, that's not true, I do care, but I realize it has nothing to do with me. I accept you as you are. I'm not asking what you've done, or who you've been with, or who gave you money or a place to sleep, for whom you modeled . . . none of it. I'm not asking you to tell me anything."

"I am a virgin," she said with no inflection.

It was his turn to be surprised. He had expected anything but that, had been willing to accept anything she was if she agreed to his terms. But he had not for one moment entertained the idea that she was innocent.

"I've no objection to that," Fort said, and laughed at his own joke. "None at all. In fact, I consider it a bonus."

"Only if I accept. Otherwise, it makes no difference to you or to anyone else."

"Sydney, let me explain my position. I want to marry you. I know you don't want to marry me. But then, you don't want to marry anybody at all—you said so yourself the last time we met. And so, it might as well be me. In time, you may come to like me."

"Frankly, I very much doubt that I would ever like you —I don't care much for men, and I don't care much for women. I simply have no interest in the matter at all. And meanwhile, you would expect me to sleep with you and have your children."

"Not until you would do so willingly."

For the first time, she showed genuine surprise. Her eyes widened; her mouth opened slightly.

"You're seriously proposing to marry me without . . . any commitment . . . on my part?"

"Right. Of course, I'll try to change your mind. I'm not such a fool as that. And I'm sure I *can*. But until I do, I won't force myself upon you."

"Why? Why are you making such an offer?"

"I don't know," Fort said quietly. "God forgive me, but I don't really know."

After he left the Englishman, Bishop Lavergne wandered through the astonishing rooms of the Countess Leda's palace, looking for something, for someone who would interest him. He did not often indulge himself in enterprises such as this, but he had been assured by Pepe—and Pepe was a faithful reporter and a faithful investigator—that this salon was perfectly respectable. There was a certain air of licentiousness about it, perhaps, but this was based on nothing that anybody could actually identify. This kind of salon might be a breeding ground for certain eccentric tastes, but it was not the stage.

He had carefully removed his bishop's ring before coming. The emerald, of course, was his private possession. A ring he wore only on rare occasions—times when he wanted to indulge himself.

It occurred to him that he might enjoy watching for a while, rather than actually being part of the parade, and so, with this in mind, he found a corner of one of the grottoes, by some transplanted willows. Near a most peculiar little pond on which a swan floated serenely. People did pass from time to time, but there wasn't too much traffic. From here he could see some of the costumes, watch some of the antics, even hear snatches of conversation, without being observed too closely himself. Earlier, he'd had a fleeting look at a young girl who was serving, and if he was lucky, she might come by. In that event . . .

Despite his attempt to enjoy *himself*, the bishop's mind turned to his affairs, and most particularly to his rebellious nephew, Marc St. Amour. It was beyond his understanding how Marc, whom he had helped get his parish, could be so ungrateful, how he could have become such an apostate. The Church's position was clear: the people must vote Conservative. Yes, he would be forced to see Marc in his study, have a talk with the boy. And if he didn't come to heel after that, there were parishes in the backwoods crying out for priests.

Just as he was falling into a temper, his train of thought was diverted by a pleasant sight. The little girl he had spied earlier in the evening, the one with the tray, was coming toward him. Now the tray held fat red strawberries dusted with sugar.

She could not be more than thirteen, he thought fondly. Her fair hair shone like a true halo. She was naked to the waist, her small breasts hard and almost entirely consumed by the dark red nipples (so reminiscent of the strawberries she was serving) on the pale satin of her skin. His mouth watered at the sight. She wore only a thin band around her waist from which a panel of pink velvet hung between her legs. Her feet were bare.

"Strawberries, sir?" She thrust the tray at him.

The bishop's lips opened involuntarily. His plump fingers selected a berry and lifted it to his mouth, sucking off the sugar slowly. Sugar, now, on *those* . . .

"Did you prepare these yourself?" he asked in English. Not that he cared who had prepared them. But he wanted to keep her talking. He found that his mouth was forming an anticipatory opening, moist and voracious. It was with the utmost effort that he kept his hands on the sugared fruit.

"What's your name?"

"Annabel."

"Pretty name."

He would like to have contrived to have her put down the tray for a moment so he could better study that panel of silk velvet so slimly draped between her legs. Seen from the front he could not be sure, entirely, whether she wore anything underneath. Now, from the side . . .

"Sit down for a moment," the bishop said. "Surely the countess won't mind if you rest a moment. Put your tray down here."

He patted a place beside himself on the rustic bench he occupied beside the pond. The swan swam toward them, eyes bright with what looked like scorn.

"I'm supposed to pass them around," Annabel said dubiously.

"I'll speak to the countess, if she says anything. Don't you worry."

Then he had an inspiration.

"Why don't you offer a strawberry to the swan? Here, put your tray down, child. Now, go gently toward the bird and hold out your hand."

She seemed to like the idea of feeding the bird. She put the tray down beside him (oh, how close the warm and living fruit was as she bent over, almost touching his cheek as she did so!) and picked up a berry. As she moved sideways toward the edge of the pond, the velvet panel fell forward ever so slightly.

The bishop, tearing his eyes away from the confections of her breasts, riveted his gaze upon the thin band of pink as it swung away from her narrow hip. For a delicious moment, it was revealed to him, almost like a miracle for which he had prayed—a patch of golden down, fine as gossamer. Then the vision was gone as she turned from him. The bishop clasped his trembling hands.

"Feed it another, my dear," he managed to say, as she came back toward him, ready to take up the tray. "I'm sure it's perfectly all right. See, he's hungry, poor bird. Nobody thinks of *him* at the party."

"Are you sure I can give him another?"

"Quite sure. Look, he's asking so nicely."

She was smiling. And each time she picked up a berry, asking his permission, doubting the advisability of it, she bent close to him. And each time she fed the bird, the panel shifted ever so slightly and the bishop studied his favorite fruit with mounting interest. He was storing images for future fantasies.

―――――――

Marc had arrived by buggy from the station at St. Cloud. It was after supper, and the children, Nicolette and Mathieu, were playing on the front lawn with a hound pup, watched by their nurse, Anne-Marie. There was no sign of either Camille or Justine.

"Where is Madame Dosquet?" Marc asked.

"She is walking, Father."

He was wearing his soutane, of course, and his hat, despite the heat. The train from Montreal to St. Cloud had been slow and dirty and entirely frustrating. He had had no supper, not even a cool drink.

"Is the cook around, Mademoiselle?"

"Oh, yes, Father. I'll go and speak to her."

He stopped to speak to the children although he was anxious to wash and to have something to drink. In a way, he was glad that Camille and Justine were busy, and that he would have time to calm himself before meeting them.

The pup was playful, and the children were eager to show the tricks they had taught him. Marc struggled to be patient. It was not that he did not like the children, it was simply that his problems were overwhelming.

In a few moments Anne-Marie came back to announce that Cook had been found and that supper would be set, if he did not mind, on the verandah beside the kitchen. Marc thanked her. He knew where he could find a place to wash; the house was familiar to him.

After he had eaten, there was still no sign of his sisters. The children had been taken up to their nursery, and in the distance, he could hear their alternating shrieks and laughter. He decided to go out into the garden and look for Camille. Now that he was fed and clean again and his mind was more organized, he was anxious to tell her his news. It was neither entirely good news, nor entirely bad news. It was a little of both.

He found Camille in the orchard sitting on a rough wooden bench. She had a book open on her lap. The apple trees were white and perfumed and incredibly fragile in the dying light. She was wearing a pale blue cotton gown with a rounded neck and a white sash. Her dark hair was loose, as if she had not bothered to do more than brush it. Her face was pale except for two peculiar spots on her cheeks that glowed as if she had a fever. When she saw him, she leaped up, gulping in air, her dark eyes almost frenzied.

"Marc, what's the matter? What has happened?"

"Nothing, Camille. Don't be so alarmed."

"But we didn't expect you."

"I know, my dear; I came to see *you*. I want to talk to you about something."

He put his hands on her upper arms and pressed his lips against her temple in a brotherly greeting. He could feel the strenuous pounding of her heart through the thin cloth of her gown, through his own robe.

"Who is sick? Has someone died?"

He managed a nervous laugh.

"Don't be so foolish. Isn't it possible that I might come to see you for some reason other than a crisis?"

"No. Not all this way. Not when the election is only three days off. Something has happened!"

Although she was thinner, her cheeks hollow and her eyes overly bright, Camille was still beautiful. Marc thought that she had an intensity that few women he'd met could match. As if everything mattered a great deal. Her capacity to love, to feel, was limitless, it seemed to him.

"Sit down, please. Believe me, Camille, it isn't something terrible. In fact, you may be pleased when you hear the whole story."

"Pleased? But you don't look very happy, Marc."

He shook his head and sat down beside her on the bench. The pink-blue light of evening filtered down through the apple blossoms and gave Camille a magical coloring. She was like a character from a fairytale. Not real. And yet, she was too vulnerable, *too* real, to live in the world, he decided.

"Happiness isn't one of the things I expect in life. Anyway, let me tell you what has happened. First, as you know, I've disobeyed my bishop. I've told my people to vote Liberal, to support Laurier."

"It's about Uncle Eustache!" she cried. "He's terribly angry! I knew it! But Marc, he won't . . . you won't be sent away?"

"Well, he certainly threatened that. He was going to send me to Rimouski. That's what he told me. But I've worked out another arrangement, with Armand's help. You see, in my spare time I've been working down at the docks helping the immigrants. A few people from the St. Vincent de Paul Society, and a handful of other church people, have been giving the immigrants temporary shelter, some soup from time to time, assistance in finding their way out of Montreal to the farmland they're supposed to work. Some are sick, you know. Others have no money. It's all quite difficult. So I asked the Bishop . . . Uncle Eustache . . to allow me to continue my work there. Which is so necessary. I won't be given a place to live, but I'll have a small allowance. That way, I can go on with my work."

"But, Marc . . ."

"I'll still be a priest. He isn't going to excommunicate me, defrock me, but he's taken away my parish. He says he had to do something to punish me for disobeying, and I suppose he's right. Anyway, Armand is going to buy a small house for me on Saint Jean-Baptiste, near the riverfront. What I want to know is, will you come and be my housekeeper? And help with my work down at the docks among the immigrants? We need help so desperately, and Camille, you are so good with people when you want to be. And you do speak English well. It's so difficult to get volunteers who are fluent in both languages."

She could not believe what he was saying. Instead of visiting from one relative to another, she would have a house of her own to manage. And she would be taking care of Marc. It was a dream. The volunteer work was nothing. She would be glad to do that, to do *anything* if it meant being near Marc.

"That would be wonderful. What did Armand say?"

"Armand thinks it's the perfect solution. You know, he seems to have solved the financial problems Father left. He says he will be able to buy me the house I have in mind, although it will come out of my share of the inheritance, of course. But then, before Armand took over I didn't expect to inherit anything at all. There was nothing but debts."

For the first few minutes, her face was ecstatically happy, but then it clouded over. Marc, too, slumped on the bench, exhausted from the journey and from the implications of his plan.

"But I don't know if . . . you know I want to . . . I want to more than anything in the world," she said.

"Yes, so do I."

"But the difficulty . . . it was easier when you were away. It was easier when I was here by myself. Marc, I don't know how we can manage . . ."

She was close to tears.

"We *must* manage," Marc said firmly, taking her hand. "Because there is no other way. If I leave the city, I'll be sent out to some distant parish, and perhaps I'll only get to Montreal twice a year. Perhaps not even that often. While you—you'll be moving from one relative to another."

"Yes, yes, I know. And I want to help. I want to look after a house for you. But Armand doesn't know . . ."

"He doesn't know. Nobody knows. Listen to me, Camille, we will be strong. We will be strong enough to do this. To have what we *can* have and to take nothing else. We must pray for strength."

"I'll pray to the Virgin every night. I'll light a votive candle tonight. I have a prie-dieu in my room. I often light a candle there."

"We must both pray daily for the strength to do the thing that must be done," Marc said.

His face looked drained. He had dropped her hand as if it burned him. She stared at the grass.

"I can do it," she murmured then, standing up and taking his hand in hers to pull him to his feet.

"Of course you can."

He looked greatly relieved.

"How are the meetings?" she asked as they walked along the road leading to the upper pastures. "Is Corbin speaking well? Are there large crowds?"

"Corbin is attracting lots of people. You know, Camille, the Church is wrong about this. I feel it. The bishops ought to be supporting the Liberals. But, of course, they won't. Historically, they never have. And I suppose they never will."

"Helene must be very excited."

"Oh, she is. Helene sees herself as an important hostess in Ottawa. She sees Corbin as a political power. She's far more excited about the election than any of the rest of us, but for an entirely different reason." And he managed a short laugh. "But *you* know Helene."

"And Armand? His business is going well, I take it? If he can buy a house for you, he must have found a way out of debt."

"He has an American partner. A man who already has interests in Canadian mines and communications and who wants to expand up here. Armand feels its the answer to all our problems, and I guess he's right. I wouldn't have expected him to take hold like this, but he has certainly shown that he has ability. He raised more than thirty thousand dollars for Corbin's campaign."

They were passing the barns. The light was fading fast now, and the purple sky was turning navy blue. Soon it would be black. But the air was warm. There were, unfortunately, mosquitoes. Any breeze that might have driven them away had died two hours earlier, and they were noisy in their search for blood.

"Do people ever get used to these insects?" Marc wanted to know, slapping at his face, and at his bare wrists. "I would have been eaten alive if I'd gone to Rimouski. It's better to fight the flies down at the docks. At least you have a chance of killing one before it bites."

"I've never gotten used to the insects. Except for that, it's beautiful here on the farm. But I'd much rather live in Montreal. Tell me what the house is like, Marc, the one Armand is going to buy for us to live in."

He described the house to her. It was a modest affair with two bedrooms, fairly close to Bonsecours Market. She was pleased.

Thy had almost reached the upper meadows and were just about to turn back when they saw two figures coming toward them, materializing out of the gloom.

It was Camille who recognized Justine and Timothée. With a quick motion she pulled at Marc's sleeve.

"Turn around, Marc, quickly," she whispered, pulling

at him as she spoke. "Pretend we were going the other way. That we didn't see."

As he turned on his heel, he realized who it was. But he suspected that Justine could not be sure which way he and Camille had been walking. They hurried down the slope again without speaking.

"Did you know about them?" Marc asked, when they were safely out of range.

"I've known for a week," Camille said. "But Marc, how can I condemn my sister, when I know how wicked *my* secret feelings are? Oh, I know I haven't actually committed a sin . . . well, only in my mind . . . but . . ."

"We will say no more about it," Marc said grimly. "We must pretend, for everybody's sake, that we don't know about Justine."

"Is that lying?"

"Perhaps it is necessary to lie, if the cause is good."

"I don't think Uncle Eustache would approve."

"Uncle Eustache is a great deal more virtuous than I am," Marc said with conviction, "or he wouldn't have risen to be a bishop. I'll never be anything but a priest, and on the lowest rung of the ladder. But you know, Camille, I feel that when I'm working with these poor immigrants, helping them solve their problems, I'm doing more good than I was in my own parish. More than I was in preaching from the pulpit, telling everybody how to behave, more than I was listening to confessions and doling out Hail Marys. I'm really doing some good down there. And perhaps the Virgin will count that in my score."

CHAPTER NINE

She was a beautiful ship. Sir Simon, paying his respects
to her as she berthed after her maiden voyage from Liverpool, felt a quick surge of pride and pleasure. The *Empress
Victoria*. Steel hull, twin screw, rigged for sail and capable
of making seventeen knots on a fair day. Truly she was
a ship to cheer an old man's heart.

Unfortunately, Sir Simon could not sustain happiness
for long. As much as he tried to concentrate on his successes, his frustrations and violent ambitions lurked just
beneath the surface, ready to rise at the slightest provo-
cation. The outcome of the federal election was much on
his mind. He could not forget, even for an hour, the implications of the election with regard to his own plans for
expansion.

But the election results had been confirmed now, he told
himself harshly, and there was no earthly use in mooning
about the dock waiting for a miracle. Laurier, the damned
Liberal, was Prime Minister of Canada, with a safe majority of twenty-three seats in the House of Commons.
Quebec had given him forty-nine of those seats, flying in
the face of the bishops, while she had given only sixteen
to the Conservatives. It was dangerous. It was ridiculous.
It was impossible. But it had happened just the same.

The Liberals could now safely pick the many plums—
four vacant senatorships, numerous judgeships and contracts. The contract for the Royal Mail weekly fast service
between Liverpool and Montreal, which the Court Line had
confidently expected to get, was still sitting on the Governor
General's desk, still unsigned. Sir Simon knew it had been
sitting there for weeks, shoved aside while the Governor
General awaited the results of the election. Lord Aberdeen was supposed to be apolitical, but in England he had
been a raging Liberal; one could hardly expect him to

change his spots overnight because of a royal appointment. He had stalled; and who could push him? Now it was too late. The Liberals were in control, and Sir Simon's friends were now the opposition. No matter how inadequate their ships, some other shipping line would doubtless get the prize. What could you expect from Liberals, after all?

And that wasn't the bloody worst of it. Much as he might gloat over the *Empress Victoria*'s splendor in the morning sunshine, he couldn't forget the earlier loss of the *Highland Princess*. Insurance. Certainly the ship had been insured, but that wouldn't cover the cost of replacing it. And what about the revenue they were losing while another ship was being built? People didn't realize the risks, damn it, when they criticized the very men who put their money on the line, created the jobs, did the worrying, provided the brains. Sir Simon could almost see his dollars sinking to the bottom of the sea while potential passengers, mail, and cargo were transported by his arch rivals.

He brought out his gold watch and consulted it.

"Damned fellow is ten minutes late," he muttered, casting a sharp eye up the dock for some sign of his son. "Young men today don't know the value of punctuality."

Though it was only ten o'clock, the July sun was already beating down hard on the docks. Sweating, swearing workers were unloading the *Empress Victoria,* hauling out great crates of machinery and bales of stinking, untreated wool. Well, he couldn't blame them for cursing the heat. He himself was sweating in his morning coat, even though he was standing idle.

He saw Fort at last, hurrying toward him along the stone surface of the pier, hatless and informally dressed (the young were setting poor precedents) and waving cheerily at some fellow he recognized on board the ship.

"Sorry I'm late, Papa."

"I'll damned well say you are late."

"The gig got into a little argument with one of the electric trams. Nothing serious, but it held me up."

"Ought to allow for unforeseen obstacles in your schedule. My time's valuable. I've been standing here ten minutes."

"You're right, I ought to allow extra time."

Fort turned to look at the new ship, gleaming white in the sunshine, the red pennant worn by all steamers blowing above her house flag in the Court colors. "She's a real beauty. The prettiest ship we've ever commissioned, don't you think? I wish I could take her back to Liverpool myself."

"No chance of that; there's no time," Sir Simon said hastily. "I need you right here. Come along into Thomas's office and we'll have a talk. I have something urgent for you to do."

It was cooler inside the shed, where Thomas, the terminal manager, had his office. Cargo waiting to be transported was piled everywhere so that they had to pick their way through it, acknowledging a ripple of respectful "Good mornings" from workmen as they passed by.

The small office was only a dusty excuse for privacy, with an ill-fitting door and soiled glass windows. There was nobody in it.

"Where's Thomas?" Fort asked.

"I sent him off to have a look at the ship. He was eager to go over her. Anyway, I wanted to have a few moments with you privately."

"I'm afraid to sit anywhere," Fort said, looking with distaste at the worn leather chair, the desk covered with gritty papers, and the odd assortment of items that must belong to Thomas.

"We won't be long," Sir Simon said brusquely.

He did not care what kind of housekeeper Thomas was. This was a place for hard work. If he wanted cleanliness and elegance he would go to his office in the Empire Bank Building on St. James Street. Let Thomas wallow in this dust and clutter just so long as he ran the dock efficiently. Sir Simon seldom ventured in here, but this morning, to save time, he was combining two pieces of business.

"All right, then, Papa, let's get on with it. What's on your mind?"

"Believe me, Fort, it's important. You know that *rouge* rag that calls itself *Le Monde*? Did you see yesterday's edition?"

"No, I didn't. I spent the day talking to people about the Mail contract. Why?"

"Most damnable story in it, about bribery and corruption in the election. Well, you know what a radical excuse for a newspaper it is. Infested with revolutionists—I'm surprised the government hasn't arrested them all long ago.

Well, the point is, Fort, they're hinting at *our* activities. A well-known shipping line, family with important connections, all that kind of bunkum. I ought to horsewhip the sniveling little brute who runs it, but I'm far too lenient. That's always been one of my problems. Anyway, the *editor*—that's how he styles himself, if you can imagine it—wrote this filthy piece of garbage about bribing priests and buying voters. Says he has a letter that proves that an important businessman from the English community actually spent thousands of dollars trying to get his puppet elected in an East Montreal riding. That's the kind of stuff. Says he's going to publish names soon, with quotes from the letter."

"Good God, nobody would put that kind of thing in a letter!" Fort said, laughing. "The man's bluffing."

"Perhaps he's *not* bluffing."

Fort's smile changed to a look of stunned surprise.

"Papa, you don't mean you wrote . . . that Tellier has anything in writing . . ."

"He has. And Tellier has obviously sold the damned letter. He hasn't a seat, he hasn't anything but the business I gave him, he was *my* man, and since he's now useless and happens to have some gambling debts, I suppose . . ."

Fort whistled.

"How bad is it? Is it a wide swipe in the dark, or does *Le Monde* have details?"

Sir Simon spoke heavily, the volume of his normally booming voice forced down with great difficulty.

"Enough details to make me feel the . . . the *editor* . . . has a certain letter I wrote. He mentions paying off members of the press to write favorably about the Tories, he talks of multiple voting, of bribing returning officers at the polls—the whole wretched parade of iniquities. Even hints at the upcoming contract for the mails. It isn't enough that they've got Laurier for Prime Minister. They want our necks as well. Part of it is an attack on the influence of the bishops, of course. Now that the voters seem to have found the courage to go against the Church, there'll be an outcry to end the Church's interference in State matters once and for all. But just the same . . ."

"So you want to get that letter."

"I've *got* to get the letter! Not only because it looks bad for the shipping line, but because I'm expanding the bank, and a scandal will undermine its credibility. I've *got* to get the letter. And after I do, I'll take the little brute out and give him a taste of my whip. It's all people like that understand!"

"What do you propose to do? I don't imagine he carries the letter about with him, do you?"

Sir Simon snorted.

"I cannot imagine how a man of his caliber would act, but I should think that even a chimpanzee would lock up a letter he planned to use as ammunition. I propose, Fort, to buy the newspaper."

Fort exploded with laughter. By God, you couldn't beat the old man! It was a superb idea. There was only one thing wrong with it. The owner, a dyed-in-the-wool Liberal, wouldn't sell the paper to Sir Simon no matter what price he offered.

"You're a genius, Papa. Except that Philippe Grande, whom I happen to know owns the paper, won't sell."

"Not to *me*."

"You'd have to come up with a good Liberal," Fort said, still chuckling. "And if your buyer was a good Liberal, why would he stop the story, once he owned the paper? He'd be just as keen to use it as Grande."

"That, my son, is true. But I have in mind a very good Liberal. And your little chore for the day is to convince my Liberal friend that the paper must be bought for a price Grande can't refuse. The letter will then be in the possession of the new owner."

"And who is this lily-white Liberal whom Grande will accept?"

"My daughter, Madame St. Amour."

"Good God, Papa! I don't quite see . . ."

"Why not? She's a good Liberal now, isn't she? Married to that Liberal Frenchie whose brother-in-law, Dufours, beat our man, Tellier. I propose to offer Hannah the newspaper as a wedding gift. A bit late, but there it is."

"You think Honey will accept such a gift?"

"You said she wanted to be taken back into the fold."

"Yes, she does want to see you and Mama."

"Then this is the first step in making up the quarrel."

"But what about Grande? And that editor who works for him?"

"The price I offer will be so appealing that Grande will

be unable to refuse. Especially since the paper is going to a good Liberal who will undoubtedly propagate more of their lies as soon as she, or her husband, gets a hand on the rag."

"All right, but what about the letter?"

"I think it might go this way. When the editor is informed of the change and the time comes for the exposé, he'll think twice. Probably go and see the owner about it. Do you think he'll risk his job? And Honey won't want a scandal involving her own flesh and blood, particularly now that the family is prepared to take her back."

"I have to take my hat off to you. The editor is a fellow called Beaulne, I believe."

"Yes, one of those names nobody can spell. But you do see the point? Honey will like the idea of owning a newspaper. Mind you, women have no head for that kind of thing, but she can always collect her profits and buy a new hat. That Frenchie she's married to will be delighted. Having a newspaper in the family could be very useful to his brother-in-law. So it works out for everybody."

"And just exactly *when* do you propose to tell Honey that Editor Beaulne must be prevented from running the story about the Court family?"

"After she has accepted my offer. When the paper is legally hers."

"So it *is* a bit of a trick."

"Well, good God, Fort, I'm giving her a valuable present! A present her precious new Frenchie family will think is a miracle. And she does want to come back into the family fold. So it isn't much of a trick."

"But it's still . . ."

"Go over to see her this morning. And tell her about the gift."

Sir Simon was ready to close the meeting. He was now restless, looking at his watch and making motions of departure.

"Graves is handling the legal part of it. See Graves as soon as you've got Honey's acceptance. Then get Grande to a meeting and make him the right offer. I've got Graves finding out how much it's worth. Whatever the figure, we'll double it."

"I can't do it, Papa."

At first, Sir Simon didn't appear to hear. He went on

talking, mentioning a luncheon he was having at the Mount Royal Club, and its connection with the Bank.

"I said, I can't do that, Papa. I'd have to tell Honey why you want the paper, and I don't think you'd want me to do that."

"It's important to protect the Court name!"

"I understand that. But I won't be part of a trick. And that's what Honey will think when she finds out the truth."

"Not just important, but *vital*," Sir Simon said, his voice rising dangerously so that the glass in the wall partition shook. He was fast becoming violently angry. It was one thing to have his will crossed (didn't people do it day and night?), but it was quite another thing to have his will crossed by his own son when he, Sir Simon, was so obviously right.

"Believe me, I see your point of view, Papa, but you'll have to talk to Honey yourself."

"*Myself*?" A furious, disbelieving bellow.

"I won't interfere with your plan, but I can't bring myself to be an accessory. Keeping quiet is about the best I can promise, I'm afraid."

"You're . . . you're an *imbecile*!"

Sir Simon waved his gold-headed cane in a dangerous arc and Fort thought for a moment that either his father's head or the glass was going to suffer. But with an enraged splutter and a crimson face that threatened to precede coronary thrombosis, Sir Simon brought himself under control.

"Good day," he managed formally, his back teeth grinding beneath the shadow of his side whiskers. "I have no more to say to you at present."

━━━━━━━

Honey missed the gardens at Pride's Court. Like many old French houses, the St. Amour mansion was flush with the street, and a carriageway opened through a stone wall into a courtyard behind. Gardens, especially spacious ones, were not part of the old French design. Honey had managed to appropriate a small corner of the inner square for a greenery, and in the evening or early morning she could sit in it and read or sew. However, it was enclosed and allowed scarcely a breeze to enter, so that when the weather became hot and humid the place was unusable. She often longed for the fountains and formal gardens on the Mountain. She remembered in detail the gentle winds of day and the clear stars of night. The smell of migonette, night-scented stock, and roses sometimes haunted her. She yearned for that fabulous tower view—the ever-changing panorama of the river, the damp winds heavy with a coming storm. The few secret visits with her mother were only too brief, merely sharpening her appetite for the graciousness and grandeur of Pride's Court, no matter what the season.

Occasionally she visited Emily at Ross House, but Emily was now so caught up in her own wedding plans that meetings were hurried and difficult to arrange. Honey felt increasingly petulant about her pregnancy, too, and although Armand had suggested that she go to the country to visit Justine, so far no definite plans had evolved. Honey was reluctant. She found Justine enigmatic and harsh at the best of times. There were rumblings in the family that Justine was suffering from a mysterious depression brought on, they thought, by Laurent's long absence while he had worked in the city for Corbin's election. It was thought that Justine had been too much alone, had given herself up to brooding. And although the farm would undoubtedly be cooler than the city, Honey had so little in common with Justine that she preferred the heat and discomfort.

Sometimes she visited with Fort. She had occasionally seen Charles, although this was always more of a strain. But the rift between her and Sir Simon seemed as wide as ever. It was, therefore, with a feeling of astonishment and even hope that she accepted the news of his unheralded visit to her home.

It was Suzanne who brought his card up on a tray. (Blanche, the maid who usually did this, was out shopping.) Honey was resting in her upstairs sitting room. Her first thought was that Fort and Charles had given Papa news of the coming baby. That must be it. He was looking forward to the birth of a grandson, and was even willing to make the first advances. She was a little flushed when Suzanne showed him in.

"Well," Sir Simon said loudly, looking around the room

critically, obviously expecting some heathen statues or paintings to assault his eye, "I see you've made *this* part of the house civilized, at least."

Oh dear, Honey thought, tempted to laugh, he's noticed the pictures of the tortured saints!

"Papa! Please come in. I've told Suzanne to bring up some tea."

Sir Simon sat down gingerly in one of the green armchairs. He wore a distinct air of suspicion and doubt, as if he were a Crusader leading a peacemaking mission into an armed camp of Saracens. His eyes fell inevitably upon the single religious painting in the room, a painting of the Virgin that hung over the Louis XV desk. It was allowed there for Armand's sake.

"I suppose you can arrange a decent tea in this atmosphere?" he inquired.

"Satisfactory, anyway," Honey allowed. "Although I can't promise anything so grand as Mama's teas."

"I shouldn't think so," Sir Simon said positively. "Not with a French cook."

"They do have a slightly different view."

"Ha! A slightly different view on everything!"

He studied his daughter for a moment. Then he said a little more calmly, "Fort told me you were going to have a baby."

"Are you pleased, then, Papa?"

"Pleased?"

He made the idea sound unimaginable. His face reddened a little.

"A first grandchild would be a marvelous thing. Marvelous," Sir Simon went on, recovering a little from the shock of the word "pleased." "But half French? And Catholic? Damnit, Hannah, I don't know which is worse!"

"Then why did you come?"

Her excitement was fading a little, and a trace of anger crept into her tone. Her father was too rigid to change. Why had she ever thought he would be any different? He was unforgiving. Completely and utterly unforgiving. Yet he *had* come. The question was, why had he paid her this visit?

Sir Simon was prevented from replying directly to her question by the arrival of Suzanne with the tea wagon. After the cook had left them, and while Honey poured and

Sir Simon eyed the cakes and sandwiches with a suspicion that might have been shown in former days by the king's taster, Honey repeated her question.

"Papa, I'm so glad you called. But if you didn't come to talk about the baby, to . . . to say I could visit you and Mama . . . that you want to see the baby when it comes— then why did you come here?"

"A matter of some importance." He cleared his throat elaborately, sipped his tea dubiously, and continued, "We do want to . . . to make up this quarrel. I've been talking to Fort about it. Yes, and Fort is a sensible fellow. For a sailor. It's surprising how he's settling down. But that's another matter. Now, it seems to me that your mother and I would like to give you a wedding gift."

A tiny shiver of expectation, even happiness, ran through Honey. She realized how difficult it must be for her father to make this overture, to admit that he had been in any way wrong. She was quite willing to gloss over his familiar and exasperating opinions if it meant visiting Mama and Pride's Court. If it meant taking the baby there, and assuring that all her children would reap the benefit of that atmosphere. Surely, a wedding gift meant a reconciliation?

"A wedding gift? But that would be wonderful, Papa!"

"A bit late," Sir Simon offered, taking a sandwich and eyeing it carefully before biting into it. "Hmph! Not bad. Not good, mind you, but not at all bad. You want to tell your cook that hot mustard is what it needs. English mustard. That's what it lacks."

Honey smiled. The imperfections of her sandwiches paled beside this new possibility. Sir Simon, though he would be the last to admit it, must have mellowed slightly. For allowing her back into Pride's Court would also mean accepting Armand. She felt a surge of hope, a lightness of heart that she hadn't known for a long time.

She longed to know what the gift would be, but dared not ask. She would do nothing to spoil this afternoon, nothing to discourage Papa from making his peace with her.

Sir Simon was not beyond pausing for effect, to dramatize the announcement. He felt that he was being extraordinarily generous, not only in the gift itself, but in coming to the St. Amour house. It was not a question of courage, of course; as to that, he would gladly have slaughtered hordes of foreigners if given half a chance. But it was, after all, the principle of the thing. He had almost forgotten by now (a habit that he had developed over the years and that was most convenient) the real reason for the gift. As he sat condescendingly in Armand St. Amour's house, sipping questionable tea, about to bestow an enormously valuable property upon his rebellious daughter, he felt entitled to make the most of the moment.

"The gift I have in mind will surprise you," Sir Simon began. "But I think it might also interest you. By the way, I'm sure Armand will approve of it."

"Please, Papa, tell me what it is!" She felt almost girlish again. The lightness that had buoyed her spirits earlier had only increased. Knowing her father's resources and his impeccable taste, the gift would be unique. She felt sure of it.

"Ha, ha. You are excited, aren't you?" He was not in the least displeased. Momentarily, she was his child again. But his eye, unfortunately, fell upon the painting of the Virgin, and he was reminded that there was no ignoring the present. The past was the past. He cleared his throat again and said, "It's a newspaper. What do you think of that?"

"A *newspaper*?"

Honey was so astonished that she did not know what to think, except that the notion was amazing. A newspaper. A newspaper of her very own. The idea of being in business, of running some kind of enterprise, had never actually entered her head, although at times she had felt she was cleverer than some of the men she had heard discussing various business schemes. If it had been a question of going out and searching for such a thing, Honey would probably never have done anything about it. She had sometimes offered advice (not always pleasantly received) to Armand. She had listened to her father and her brothers discuss the many Court interests ever since she could remember. But to own something of her very own! That was incredible.

"Yes, it's in operation now. Not being run very efficiently, though. By a friend of your husband's, in fact. A man named Philippe Grande, I think."

"Then that's *Le Monde*. I've read it, of course. It's a Liberal paper. Why would you buy that, Papa?"

"Your husband wouldn't let you own a Tory one, would he? And even if it began as a Tory paper, your family connections would soon turn the scales. This one happened to be for sale. I thought it would give you a sense of being independent," Sir Simon went on, "a little income of your own. After all, in *these* circumstances . . ." He waved his arms around, the gesture encompassing the entire St. Amour clan and all their perfidies. The possibilities for deception in such surroundings, he seemed to imply, were boundless.

It sounded so exciting that she crossed the room and bent to kiss her father's cheek. He sat rigidly in the chair.

"It's wonderful, Papa!"

"You don't have to actually run it, you know. Just keep an eye on it. So they make money. I'm sure your Court instincts for that will come to the fore."

"Oh, but I would want to run it! I'd like to go down there immediately. It's just filled with possibilities for me, Papa! Who is the editor?"

"Fellow called Beaulne. Pronounced 'bone,' as in a dog's bone. But you know how odd these Frenchies are about spelling. I suppose you've noticed it, living among them?"

She was tempted to point out that the English were not without their own eccentricities when it came to spelling, but decided that the gift was far more important than arguing about some silly point that would only make her father cross.

The oddity of the gift made her suddenly uneasy. Why had he hit upon the idea of giving her a newspaper? Why not stock in the Court Shipping Line? Or stock in something else, for that matter? He would know what was safe.

"The whole idea is exciting. I can't help wondering, though, why you thought of buying me a newspaper. You must realize I'll support the Liberals."

"We Tories have our own papers," Sir Simon said, giving a gruff half laugh. "Not afraid of a bit of competition. Why should we be? I don't suppose you can make too much out of it, anyway. But it will be something of your own." (To hold among the heathen, he almost added.)

"Something of my own. Yes, that will be very nice." She realized with a sudden pang how much she had missed being a Court, belonging without question to that special, secure group, knowing there was no fear of losing place, sure of always being looked up to. Yet her long years with Sir Simon had taught her to be wary of his motives. One could never be sure what was really in his mind.

"Of course, if you don't want the newspaper . . ." Sir Simon began heavily, glaring at her.

"I do want it, Papa! Of course I do! I'm sorry I sounded ungrateful. It's just so surprising. How soon do you think I can go and talk to Mr. Beaulne?"

"Mr. Beaulne is not the kind of man you would ordinarily associate with, Hannah, but I'm sure if you make it quite plain that you're speaking to him as employer to employee, then it will be correct for you to see him . . . and your husband . . . he will be glad enough to have a newspaper in the family, eh? Since your brother-in-law, Dufours, was elected, a voice like that could be very useful."

Her first twinge of uneasiness had not entirely disappeared. Still, she could not detect the flaw, she could not sense what motive her father could possibly have except one of reconciliation. And she so desperately wanted to make up and become part of Pride's Court again.

"The whole family was excited when Corbin was elected," Honey said, remembering. "Every member helped in the campaign. I did, too. Then on top of everything, I think they rather liked the idea that Corbin won over your man, Tellier."

"Tellier was *not* my man."

"Now, Papa, you certainly knew him."

Sir Simon snorted. "I know a lot of people. Anyway, people are fools. When they gave the vote to every man on the street, they might as well have given it to the horses. Some people don't know what's good for them!"

Honey was not about to become embroiled in a political and social argument with her father. Something more important had to be settled.

"Papa, does this mean that Armand and I are welcome at Pride's Court? That I can see Mama whenever I wish, and that she can come here? That I'm welcome to bring your grandson, when he's born, to Pride's Court?"

Sir Simon hesitated. He had not reached this crucial point in his own thinking. Forgiveness was not an ingredient of his makeup. He struggled with the vision of Armand as a guest (once when the man had been in the house he'd stolen roses from the conservatory, and Lydia had had a terrible time with Jamie, the gardener). And yet, a guest was always at something of a disadvantage, never fully in control. At least, that was how *he* felt in this heathenish place where the St. Amours lived. It might not be so bad to invite Honey and Armand to Pride's Court. He could not see himself stumping about this cramped, dark house drinking Armand's whiskey and trying to talk railroads or stocks in a place swarming with religious pictures and crucified statues. (He had counted three on the way up to Honey's sitting room). But that was all in the future, since he had not decided how to handle the social end of the scheme. The danger of a scandal must be avoided, and he was taking care of that. Later, other considerations would come along, and he would deal with them appropriately.

"We can arrange something suitable, Hannah, I'm sure. I'll speak to your mother about it. She can send a message round to you. You don't have the telephone, I suppose?"

"Not yet, Papa. Have you had one installed?"

"Just had one put in my study. Good for business, they tell me, though I don't like the damned thing much. If you can't see a man's face when you're talking business, you don't know where you are. How do you even know who's on the other end of the telephone? You only have *his* word for it, after all."

As she poured more tea for her father, Honey smiled inwardly, sensing that despite his protests, Sir Simon probably liked the novelty of the telephone.

"Do you think *Le Monde* makes money, Papa?"

"Not much, but if you were to take hold of it, or put somebody in charge whom you could trust, it ought to make money. Grande is a fool. He's never attended to business properly. All sorts of waste there, mistakes, sloppiness. I had it looked into."

As usual, her father had an instinct for people. While Philippe was charming and generous, Honey had to agree he was a dilettante. It was also typical of her father's thoroughness that he had investigated the state of a business before he'd invested in it.

"If I'm running it, there won't be mistakes," Honey said

firmly. "Armand is away at the moment, but I know when I tell him about the gift he'll be pleased."

She was a little surprised at how quickly she had taken to the idea of attempting to run a business. Already she was thinking that she could make it efficient, that she could improve on the way the newspaper was managed. She intended to supervise it herself, not ask Armand to take over for her.

Sir Simon finished his second cup of tea. He had managed to convey to her that while it was drinkable, it was not up to his standard. Honey noticed, however, that he consumed two of Suzanne's pastries. At the door, he inquired about Corbin Dufours and his plans.

"Helene and Corbin have already moved to Ottawa. She can't wait to entertain in the capital. She's absolutely dying to meet the Governor General, and you know what an old bore *he* is, Papa. Do you remember the night they came to dinner at Pride's Court? But I didn't tell poor Helene that because it would spoil her fun."

Sir Simon frowned, remembering. "Lord Aberdeen is not so much a bore as he is a *Liberal.* Though how anybody in his position could break with the Tory view is utterly beyond me. How can you be a peer and be a Liberal? It only shows he's an ass. Like that Shaftesbury, years ago. Meddling old fool. But you can't acount for everything in this life, I suppose."

"I think Lord Aberdeen means well," Honey said placatingly.

"I'm sure he *doesn't,*" Sir Simon said darkly, his voice rising. He paused at the door so that Honey was forced to shut it again and listen. "By the way, Fort's engaged to be married. Did you know?"

"No, I haven't seen him lately. That's exciting, Papa. Is she a Montreal girl?"

"Good God, no! Fort sent all the way to London for her. I suppose it's in the blood. We Courts always seem to go back to our roots. Your grandparents were the same. You, Hannah, are the exception. Anyway, I told Fort it was like ordering a bride from a catalogue."

"But who is she?" Honey saw herself once more in the family circle, part of Fort's coming wedding, linked to this new family member through marriage. "When is she coming?"

"She's arriving by ship next month. Fort says she's an orphan." Sir Simon sighed. "You'll have to ask your mother about it when you see her. I'm sure she knows the details. The wedding's to be in Christ Church, so Lydia will have her chance at a big wedding after all."

Once again, remembering Honey's defection, he flushed with anger. But she kissed him on the cheek and he calmed down a little before he finally stamped off. Honey smiled as she closed the door. It had been the most exciting day she had known in a long time, in fact for months. She wanted so much to see her mother again—in a proper way, instead of having to sneak around, always hurrying, as she'd done a few times. She wanted to be a part of the marriages of her brothers, to have her own children know their cousins, to have them become members of the family in a real sense. And a big wedding would be fun, especially since it was Fort who was getting married. He had always been her favorite.

She was struck by the thought, however, that she would probably still be pregnant by the wedding date and wouldn't be able to wear a lovely gown. Papa and Mama might even insist that she stay home, since it wasn't considered seemly to appear at public functions when one was pregnant.

This thought dampened her excitement a little. But she thrust the sadness aside, thinking about her wonderful gift and the miracle of her father's visit. Sir Simon had come himself, *in person*, to make up. She knew what that must have cost him in pride. And she would be able to share the experience of having her baby with Mama. What a comfort that would be. And all the power, all the force of the Court name would be restored to her. It was a great weight lifted from her heart. Her thoughts turned to Armand, and she could scarcely wait for his return from Thetford Mines so she could tell him this happy news.

Honey was choosing wallpaper for the nursery bathroom when Blanche announced the caller. (She had found the nursery rooms in extraordinarily good order, toys and furniture all clean and well preserved, but it had seemed diplomatic to redecorate the rooms the new nurse would use.)

"But who is it, Blanche?" she asked irritably, staring at the samples of English tile wallpaper that were varnished and guaranteed to be washable, but the colors of which left much to be desired. "I'm not expecting any visitors this afternoon."

"A gentlemen who says his name is Beaulne."

"Beaulne? Oh, yes, that's the editor of my newspaper." Her voice held a touch of pride. It was a novel feeling, this ownership of something that was completely hers, rather than owned by Armand and merely shared by her.

"Do you want to see him, Madame?"

She sighed and put down the samples. Business, she supposed, must come first. And, feeling a trifle martyred, but enjoying the sensation just the same, she agreed to see Mr. Beaulne.

"Show him to the small sitting room, Blanche. I'll be down shortly."

"Yes, Madame."

The wallpapers for the bedroom were much prettier, she reflected. Tiny pink rosebuds on pale blue stripes. Or geometric, intricate designs in green or crimson with embossed gilt. Well, she would have to decide that later. What could have possessed Mr. Beaulne to come and see her so soon? She had fully intended to visit him in his office and discuss the newspaper with him. Ask to see his work schedule, examine the press, and check the bookkeeping. Meet his staff, and decide whether there were ways in which economies could be practiced. Perhaps even consider buying a new press. It was all very exciting. Now the man had suddenly appeared at the house. It was peculiar and, even though she knew nothing of business, she scented a whiff of trouble.

As she went down the stairs, she considered her costume. It was a pale beige broadcloth wrapper with a cape of green petals. A trifle intimate for an interview with a stranger. Not only that, but it made her look like a giant asparagus stalk. Should she change? But a man wouldn't change for a business conference just because he looked like a vegetable. So she would not change. Let Mr. Beaulne, calling without notice, take her as she was.

She found him sitting nervously on the edge of his chair. He had wispy, carrot-colored hair and a freckled face. His fingers clutched his hat as if it were a lifesaver and he were expecting to drown. She felt a little sorry for him, but her father was quite right. Mr. Beaulne was not someone she would meet socially.

"M'sieur Beaulne? I am Madame St. Amour. You wished to see me about the newspaper?"

He stood up, allowing himself only the rumor of a smile. But she saw that he had a tooth missing in front.

"It's important, Madame, or I wouldn't have bothered you. I'm sorry."

He spoke English, and spoke it well. She did not, therefore, attempt to communicate in her somewhat limited French. This would only have put her at a severe disadvantage.

"That's quite all right. I was coming to see you in your office. But I've only owned *Le Monde* for two days. I haven't had time to do that yet."

"Oh, Madame, I realize my visit seems impetuous. But believe me, I must speak to you. Did you, by any chance, see Monday's edition?"

She shook her head. Until now she had seldom looked at a newspaper. During the election campaign, when everybody was talking about the issues, she had sometimes read a few reports of speeches, of the charges and countercharges. But that had been a short-lived interest.

"Please, read this." He thrust at her a crumpled issue of *Le Monde* that he had drawn from his jacket pocket. Some lines were marked with red ink.

Honey read the two paragraphs that were underlined and then stared at Mr. Beaulne.

"I've read it. Now, just what has this to do with me?"

A suspicion was already creeping along the edges of her mind. The reference to "a prominent English businessman" was not totally obscure. The article had something to do with her father. But now that the piece had been published, what could Beaulne want from her?

"I wrote that story."

"Yes, I gathered that."

"I planned to write another story soon, naming names. I have a letter in my possession, Madame. When the names are named, it will be unpleasant. One of the names—not the only one, of course, but one that is particularly prominent—is your father's."

"I see. And this appeared Monday?"

"That's right, Madame."

"I acquired the paper the next day. It was a gift to me."

"So I was told. Now that you are the owner, and not M'sieur Grande, I must ask you about policy. Naturally, Madame, as a newspaper that supports the Liberal party, *Le Monde* would ordinarily proceed with a story showing the Conservatives in a bad light. But the fact that your father is . . . well, one of those who might be seriously affected . . . I thought it wise to consult you."

"You were quite right to come to me, Mr. Beaulne."

She felt a little ill. After the exhilaration produced by her father's capitulation and unexpected gift, the recognition of his real motive was rather like falling into a well. Quite clearly she had been used as a tool in one of Papa's grand designs. It was not that he loved her enough to forgive her but that he had wanted to use her to prevent a looming scandal.

Beaulne waited. He could see that she was very much affected. Her light-colored skin had turned even paler, and there was a new expression of strain masking her earlier bloom. She sat down abruptly. (Until now she had remained standing.) He was aware that she was pregnant, of course, and it occurred to him how terrible it would be if he had shocked her into a nervous state that might harm the baby.

"Perhaps I should have waited to see your husband . . ."

"No, no, Mr. Beaulne. You did the correct thing. I'll be quite all right."

"Shall I call your maid?"

She stiffened. Making up her mind to behave as a business person should, she breathed deeply, and some of her color came back.

"I'm perfectly well now, thank you, Mr. Beaulne, I would like you to give the letter to me. And you will not publish the story. As far as policy goes, we are Liberals, certainly, and we will support that political party. But I cannot have a story published that will damage my father or my family. I'm sure you understand that. Did you bring the letter, by any chance?"

"Yes, I did. I thought you might want it."

She could see that he was not going to rebel or even argue against her edict. Obviously, the man needed his job.

Or wanted the job enough to agree with whatever decision she made. She knew that the country was in the midst of a rather serious recession and that unemployment was a problem. Perhaps Mr. Beaulne felt that he would have difficulty in finding another job. Whatever his reasons, he was docile. He handed the letter to her.

She took it from him and put the letter in her pocket. She did not intend to open it, ever.

"I'd like to tour the newspaper offices," she said briskly. "Could you arrange that for tomorrow? I'd like to see how you put out the paper, and meet the staff. I want to have things explained to me so that I can decide whether we need to make any improvements or effect any economies."

"Certainly, Madame. What time would you like to come to the office?"

."Shall we say three o'clock?"

"Very well, I'll be ready to take you around. And to show you the press as well."

Beaulne picked up his hat, which in the confusion of the moment he had put down on the chair and then nervously knocked to the floor.

"It *was* a good idea to come to see me," Honey reassured him when he reached the door. He seemed grateful for her smile.

When he was gone she picked up the copy of *Le Monde* he had left on a table and the red ink of the underlining jumped out at her. She would keep it as a reminder of this day.

"I'm not a Court any longer," she thought, half tearful, half defiant, "I'm a St. Amour. Whatever Papa was *trying* to do, he's made me a St. Amour more surely than anything Armand could have done, or the whole St. Amour family put together."

As she went upstairs to finish selecting the wallpaper, the house, for the first time, seemed to be truly hers. And she thought that she would seriously put her mind to redecorating some of the important rooms, transforming them to her own taste.

CHAPTER TEN

Charles Court was bringing his bride back to Canada on the Courts' newest liner, the *Empress Victoria*. She was docking at Portland, Maine, and not at Montreal, and while Charles would have preferred the direct route, taking the *Empress* would bring him home a few days earlier than any comparable booking. He was eager to show off his new wife.

The *Empress Victoria*'s vice-regal suite was rich in blood-red leather. The upper halves of the paneled walls were covered with it, the pillars and even the inside surfaces of the doors matched. The combination of the red leather and the crimson-and-blue-patterned velour on the upholstered furniture, and the thick dark-blue carpet, created a handsome if ponderous effect. The bedroom, with its twin beds, was furnished in dark mahogany and the bedcoverings and slipper chair were done in powder blue satin. Even the bathroom fixtures were exceptional; the white porcelain bowl, basin, and tub were patterned with blue flowers. The taps were gold-plated.

Venetia's mother, Julia, had sent baskets of pink and white gladioli that had survived their days at sea, and her aunt, Mrs. Tate (who had introduced Charles to Venetia) had presented them with a *bon voyage* gift of a huge, rather vicious-looking cactus with a lush red bloom.

By habit, Charles was an early riser. This morning he had risen earlier than usual because he was anxious to sight land. Being there for the ship's landfall meant feeling that much closer to Montreal and the moment when he could proudly present Venetia to his family. He was certain of Papa's approval, and felt deeply that for once he would make a serious impression upon his father. As he looked out the porthole he saw that a thick fog was rolling off the coast and that it was still quite dark outside. He sat down in a chair with a cup of tea he had already ordered from the steward. He wore a blue velvet dressing gown over his pajamas.

Venetia was brushing her hair in front of her dressing-table mirror. Charles marveled each time he watched Venetia dress. The marriage had been so quickly arranged that he still could hardly believe his luck.

He had not been blind to the fact that Venetia Wylie, although incredibly beautiful, had had a serious drawback as a marriage prospect—the drawback was her mother, a woman of somewhat novel ideas and notorious lifestyle. But since Julia Wylie planned to live in England, with excursions to the Continent, and on no account visit the shores of Canada, Charles had been prepared to dismiss her as unimportant. (She had not been dismissed in England, of course, where several sons of well-known peers and the heirs of powerful bankers had toyed with and rejected the idea of proposing to Venetia.)

Canada, a colony without the exotic beauty of India, the challenging wastes of Australia, or the brutal possibilities of Africa, did not interest Venetia's mother in the least. She saw no charm in a visit to Montreal and was now completely absorbed in plans for her own marriage—her third —to the Earl of Twickenham, a man with his own accumulated liabilities. Among them were two divorces and a reputation for wild forays at the gambling tables.

A perfect marriage for Venetia, therefore, was out of the question. A pity, everyone said, but what could one do? There it was. And so Charles Court, with his considerable Canadian fortune and eventual minor title, had been in luck. He had won the prize by default.

Discussion of whether or not Venetia was beautiful was completely superfluous. It was not a matter of opinion, and did not lie in the eye of the beholder. The thick, black curly hair, the glowing, flawless skin, the large gray eyes under gracefully arched brows, the straight nose with slightly flared nostrils, the full lips divided with such precision by a peculiarly sensual curve, the faultless teeth, the slightly cleft chin, the perfectly formed longish neck— everything combined in just the right proportion.

A London wit had remarked that she was a national resource and ought to be confined to England to attract sight-seers. Like the Matterhorn, the Nile, or the bridges of Paris, she ought to be seen. Every painter who had ever seen her had wanted to paint her portrait. Augustus John, always alert to a new beauty, and one of the few who had actually painted her, had observed, "She's too perfect for a serious portraitist, of course, but it's like painting a perfect peach—one ought to do it for the exercise."

Since her coming-out, several possible matches had reached the planning stage. But in the final lap, the duke, the British manufacturer, and the deacon of the church who was definitely slated to be raised to a bishop gave up the idea. Venetia's mother was too much. Julia herself had finally despaired of making a suitable match for her daughter—until Charles Court had appeared. He had seemed a godsend.

There was nothing wrong with Venetia's lineage. Her mother was the third daughter of an earl. Venetia's father, Peregrine Wylie, was the second son of a baronet and an officer in the Horse Guards. But Julia had been divorced when she'd married Captain Wylie, a fact that, in the eyes of the Church of England, cast some doubt about Venetia's legitimacy. Finally, Captain Wylie had stubbornly re-fused to die in an Egyptian campaign and thus had caused Julia to divorce *him* as well. It was all most distressing.

Charles poured himself a second cup of tea and con-tinued to take pleasure in watching his wife brush her hair. He stood up eventually so that he could look into the mirror over her shoulder, his face close to hers. He liked to visualize them as a couple.

"What is it, Charles?" Venetia asked in her low, soft voice. "You look worried."

"I'm not worried, just excited about reaching Montreal. We might be there tomorrow night, darling, and then you'll meet Papa and Mama. And my brother, Fort, too. Not poor Honey, of course."

"I think your father was a beast to disown her."

"That's because your mother is so unlike him."

"I suppose so. But he does sound narrow. Will we stay in Portland overnight, the way things are now, do you think?"

"I'm not sure yet. Depends how soon we make our land-fall. Our agent will have a hotel room for us, at any rate.

But I wish we could get on a train for Montreal immediately."

"It's really too bad we couldn't take a ship that would go directly to Montreal," Venetia said, putting the hairbrush down and trying to decide how to pin up her hair.

"I couldn't wait. This way we saved two or three days," Charles said.

"You're really like a little boy." She spoke fondly. While Charles might be madly in love with Venetia, Venetia was merely affectionate and tolerant of him. But Charles did not ask for anything more. He was quite content.

"If there isn't a suitable house for sale, we'll build. We can live at Pride's Court until it's finished."

"You are sweet, Charles. Building a house would be fun, don't you think? Then we could have all our own ideas. But even if we buy one already built, we can decorate it any way we like. Is your father really a brute? I'm a little afraid of living with him."

"He's not too bad if you ignore some of the bluster and noise. And Mama's kind and gentle. You're bound to get along with Mama."

"Julia says I'll miss London. Will I be able to ride in Montreal?"

"Of course you can ride, darling. I'll buy you the best horse in the city. I belong to the hunt, so we can ride to hounds when you feel like it. And in the winter, you'll learn to skate, and to toboggan down the Mountain. You'll see. There's plenty to do."

"It sounds quite lovely. I'm sure Julia's wrong."

"And we'll have dinners and balls. There are several very elegant balls during the winter. We'll get clothes from New York if you can't find what you want in Montreal. Don't worry, darling, you'll love it."

She was wearing the white peignoir that Julia had brought from Paris, a pyramid of pleated frills from neck to hem. She looked like a queen.

"I'm forever grateful to Mrs. Tate," Charles said, sitting down again to his tea. "When I met her on the crossing to London I thought she was a dowdy old thing, and when she told me about her beautiful niece, I thought she was lying. I nearly didn't call on her in London, you know. It was only because I had nothing to do that day."

"I'm grateful to Aunt Gussy, too," Venetia said. "I wonder what I ought to wear. Do you think it's hot in Portland?"

"Not as hot as it'll be in Montreal, darling, but it will be warm."

"Perhaps the green suit."

"Yes, that's pretty."

"Tell me more about Pride's Court while I dress," Venetia said, bringing out the green suit and laying it on the bed.

She wanted to be reassured about Canada, about Montreal, about Pride's Court. Living in such a godforsaken land was the one obvious drawback to an otherwise good match, Julia had emphasized. Charles, as eldest son, would inherit his father's title, so that was all right, though Venetia clearly deserved a more impressive title. Still, the Courts appeared to have loads of money. Julia had asked a friend in The City to check into it.

"But it's sad to think of *you* buried in the colonies, darling," Julia had rambled on while she'd helped her daughter pack. "Such a waste. You ought to have had at least a duke and a townhouse in London. You should have been entertaining some of the Royals. It's such a shame!"

"Charles says that Pride's Court is a very large house, Julia," Venetia had protested mildly, "so it can't be too bad. And they have a summer place on something called the South Shore. I suppose that means the South Shore of the St. Lawrence. I forgot to ask. And I think they *do* ride. And they must have some sort of entertainment, if they have all that money. I mean, people wouldn't stand for it otherwise."

"Perhaps Charles can buy you a yacht," Julia said vaguely. "Darling, do you want to take this ruby bracelet? It's a bit ugly. I never cared for it on you. What do you think?"

"Oh, put it in, it'll be new to everybody where I'm going. And we don't know about jewelers there, so I'd better take everything I have."

"Did Charles mention the hunt? I mean, other than bears, and things like that."

"I'm almost sure he said there was a hunt in Montreal."

"*Really?*" With a single word Julia managed to throw a cloud of doubt upon the entire Mount Royal Hunt. She was still picking through the jewel boxes with a falcon's eye. "Look at this, darling, a perfectly impossible diamond pin! You can't cart that off—it won't do in winter. And as far as I'm concerned *nobody* ought to wear diamonds in summer. Best leave it here and I'll sell it."

"Buy me a cape in Paris when you next go over, then. That would be lovely. You can always send it along with one of the captains on a Court ship."

"Even if they *do* hunt, they probably don't wear pinks. Or tie their stocks properly."

"One thing they do have in Canada is beautiful fur. Everybody has fur, Charles tells me. Even quite ordinary people like shopkeepers and . . . well, people like that. Fox. Beaver. Mink. Don't you think I ought to get white fox?"

"And black mink. You'll look absolutely divine in black mink. We've never had decent furs, Venetia. They're terribly expensive over here. Perhaps you can send something back for me?"

"I will, Julia. As soon as I can arrange it. Charles will help me—he's awfully good about things like that. He'll understand. And he *does* have money. You mustn't gloom around about the bad things."

"No use pretending money isn't important," Julia said with a touch of regret. "Look at poor Beatrice. Married to that poverty-stricken diplomat, almost on the dole. He had no money at all and no connections that I could see. So he always got sent to some obscure mission nobody else wanted. Sometimes Beatrice had to do her own cooking. And Edward once *rented* a dinner suit. When the baby came it was all they could do scrape up enough for a nanny. And then, of course, Edward was sent to northern India, and . . . well, it was quite sad. But that's what happens when you're poor."

(Poor Beatrice and her husband had both contracted cholera and died. She had been Julia's older sister.)

Venetia, remembering, had to admit that Julia had taken her own advice, for the Earl of Twickenham, while weak on cards and ladies, was strong at the bank. He had a limitless income, it appeared, distributed nicely between Argentinian beef and Australian wool . . .

Charles, about to launch into a description of his runaway sister's marriage, happened to look out the nearest

porthole. He had noticed the fog earlier but it seemed
denser now. The dawn light had turned to darkness again.
He wondered, for the first time, if Captain Barker was well
out in the channel between the Nova Scotia coast and
Sable Island. He hoped Venetia wouldn't notice the fog
and begin to worry.

"We should definitely reach Portland today," he said
in an effort to be cheerful.

Venetia was studying the green suit on the bed.

"Charles, what do you think? This suit? And the straw
turban?" The hat was natural in color with folds of green
taffeta and pale green flowers on the brim.

"Fine. Yes."

She crossed the stateroom and came to stand beside him,
looking out. He could smell her perfume—attar of roses.

"Is the fog worse?" she asked.

"A little."

"That's not good, is it? All that fog when we're so close
to shore?"

"We're probably well out in the channel. Barker knows
this route, knows his business. He's been at sea forty years."

"I'm sure he's very capable. Charles . . ." Venetia hesitated, placing her hand on his arm so that he felt compelled to look into her face. "I *am* happy with you,
Charles."

He was about to reply, to say that while *she* might be
merely happy, *he* was ecstatic, when suddenly there was a
terrible grinding noise, and the wrenching sound of tortured metal; a jangling of heavy objects knocking together
as if some giant were shaking a monstrous rattle; a shuddering, nerve-splitting halt and then a list that put the
stateroom walls ever so slightly out of plumb.

"My God, we've run aground!" Charles cried.

A pause. And then shouts outside on deck and the
ship's alarm cutting through the air with a piercing insistence.

Venetia said coolly, "We'll have to go on deck. Do you
think there's time to take any luggage?"

"Put something over you," Charles said. "It's cold."

She found a black woolen cloak in one of the bags and
put it over her voluminous white gown. The velvet jewel
case that she and Julia had so carefully packed drew her

attention, and impulsively she snatched it up. Charles had turned to the closet and was selecting a suit.

"Charles, I doubt if there's time . . ." she began—but then she stopped, sensing with a whiff of irritation that Charles would not, *could* not go out on deck in his pajamas. She smiled to herself. Fear had not yet had time to replace her natural confidence.

On deck, the fog was so thick that Venetia could see only a few feet ahead of her. Some of the lights on the outer walls of the first-class cabins were still on, but they were completely inadequate in the gloom. Figures moved in and out of her line of vision. Voices rose and fell. Charles, pulling her along by the hand, was saying something probably meant to be reassuring, but she couldn't hear him for the tremendous roar that could only mean that the ship was exploding. She stopped walking along the slanting deck, closing her eyes and waiting for the end.

"That's only the boilers letting off steam," Charles said in her ear, putting his arm around her shoulders. "If they don't do that when the ship stops suddenly, the boilers blow up. It's nothing to worry about."

"I'm so cold," Venetia said, shivering.

"I'm afraid there's no time now to change. You must stay up here on deck so you can get into a lifeboat."

There were a few people on deck, and some of the crew were handing out lifejackets. It was difficult to keep one's balance as the ship heaved over, inch by inch, to the right. She could make out the rail, however, and see that an officer was ordering some of the passengers into the first lifeboat.

"Shouldn't we go to the other side? Where the ship is higher out of the water?" Venetia asked.

"No, no, darling. If the list gets worse, none of the lifeboats on the port side can be launched. They'll all lie on the ship's side and they won't be able to load or lower them."

"Oh, I didn't realize . . ."

There were more people milling about on deck now. Two crewmen were running along, knocking on cabin windows, warning passengers to come out. It was difficult to move quickly on the slanted deck, difficult to keep one's balance. An old woman fell, and a young crewman picked her up and helped her into a lifejacket, then led her toward the rail. Charles said, "Good God, what was I thinking of? Lifejackets! They'll need all they've got here on deck, so I'll go get ours from the cabin. You stay right here, Venetia, till I get back."

With Charles gone, Venetia felt the first genuine twinge of fear, the first uncompromising suggestion of imminent death. The scene about her became startlingly real, evolving out of the mist into a sharp nightmare that could not be pushed away. She saw many figures, shapeless in the moving fog, climbing over the rail and into the first lifeboat. In her strolls about the sunny deck she had given the boats no more than a casual glance. Now she decided that they looked appallingly frail for such a cold and desolate ocean. The ship listed more sharply and she grabbed at a stanchion supporting the rail to keep her balance. A man loomed out of the fog—not Charles—and tried to force her into the boat that was being loaded, but, seeing that she wore no lifejacket, he turned away and spoke to a woman in a kimono, swallowed by the padding of a too-large lifejacket.

Some people still showed reluctance to leave the *Empress Victoria* as if they were juggling the chances of drowning on a large ship with a seasoned skipper and those of drowning in a small boat with an inexperienced crew to guide it. Others were more than eager to get into the lifeboats and began shoving, in a mild panic, near the rail. Venetia recognized Second Officer Arnott, having met him a few days earlier while promenading with Charles on the deck. Arnott was now loading the second lifeboat.

Then Charles was back, holding the lifejackets. He tied her into one, and it bunched curiously over the cloak and gown, pulling them up so that her ankles were exposed. She helped him tie on his own.

"Look, darling, you mustn't miss this boat. I've got to find Captain Barker and make sure that everything's being done that can be done. I'll get away in a boat later. Don't you worry."

"But, Charles, I don't want to go without you."

"Venetia, you must. I'm one of the people responsible here. As one of the owners, I've got to take a hand."

"Yes, I see. It's Arnott who's loading the boat. I recognized him."

Charles shouted through the fog, "Arnott, is that you?"

"Yes, sir, who's that?"

"Court. Charles Court. Get my wife in that boat, will you? Have you room?"

Arnott's face appeared out of the mist.

"Oh, Mrs. Court. Yes. Here, let me give you a hand into the boat. Have you got a lifejacket? Good. Now, don't worry, I've put two crewmen in here to row. And we'll get a couple more men. Here, you, sir, with the child! Hand her up, and get in."

Venetia had not noticed the fellow until now, but he stood in rather skimpy clothes (probably had found his way up from steerage) and was holding a child wrapped in a soiled blanket. He stepped forward quickly.

Arnott helped Venetia over the rail and down the short distance into the lifeboat. She was awkward, with the lifejacket and the long cloak, and almost fell into a seat. Then the fellow gave up his child and, somehow, the little figure landed beside Venetia. The child was whimpering. Venetia pulled the blanket away from the small face and saw that it was a girl. Even in that poor light, she could see that the eyes were wide with fear, and Venetia put her hand on the forehead. The child was feverish. She felt the weight of the small body leaning against her and put an arm around the shoulders involuntarily. She supposed the father had gotten into the boat, although her attention was taken by the sudden appearance of a row of black faces with stark white eyes at the ship's rail. Shouting, they forced themselves over the side and into the lifeboat. Dimly she realized that they must be from the "black gang," the stokers below decks. The ship listed more now, so that the distance between the rail and the water was less. Still, the lifeboat jerked dangerously as the men on the *Empress Victoria* lowered it into the sea.

For a few dreadful seconds the bow pointed straight down to the sea and the passengers were thrust violently forward. The men above, seeing, made a tremendous effort to straighten out the lifeboat. The ropes creaked on the tackle, there was considerable sweat and some cursing, and then, at last, the small boat hit the water with a jolt but in a horizontal position. A fresh panic surged over the shivering group when they found no way to cut the ropes from the tackle overhead. Somebody produced a knife and somebody else hacked wildly until the ropes frayed and spilt. They were free. Several men, among them the black-faced stokers, picked up the oars and began to row. Fortunately it would soon be morning—meanwhile, there were no lights of any kind in the lifeboat.

Venetia, surrounded entirely by fog and fear, could no longer see the outline of the *Empress Victoria*. The lifeboat was moving through trackless, misty space, perhaps in the direction of the shore, perhaps not. There was no way of knowing.

CHAPTER ELEVEN

"This child has a fever."

Marc St. Amour, bending over the flushed little face of the child on the cot, took his hand away from the hot forehead and slowly straightened up. The man who had brought the child wrapped up in a dirty gray blanket stood respectfully to one side. They'd come off the *Brazilian,* which had docked at the Court Shipping Line pier within the last hour. The *Brazilian,* en route from New Orleans to Montreal via Halifax, had taken on some of the passengers from the sunken *Empress Victoria.* They'd first been picked up along the coast by fishing boats and delivered to Halifax. Now, three days later, they were at the Montreal docks.

The long frame shed, a derelict warehouse with cracked walls and a leaky roof, was used as a reception center by Father St. Amour and his volunteers from the St. Vincent de Paul Society. It was roughly furnished with benches, a couple of wobbly tables, a folding wooden screen that could be used during medical examinations, and an iron bedstead on which the sick child now lay.

"How long has she been sick?"

"Three days, Father. She was vomiting just before we got in the lifeboat, but I figured it was seasickness. Out there it was cold and wet. She got worse. Feverish, see."

"What's your name, my son?" Marc said kindly. He could see the man was worried about the child.

"James Smith, Father. And that's my daughter, Janie."

"How old is she?"

"Five."

"And she has no mother with her?"

"Her mother's dead. Janie's all I've got. We came to start over again, see. It sounded good on the posters."

"Where do you come from?"

"Liverpool."

Marc looked at the child again, tossing restlessly on the small cot. Her face was dry and hot, her hair matted, her clothes pitifully thin and soiled. She could be suffering from a number of diseases, of course: anything from typhoid, bronchial pneumonia, or relapsing fever to smallpox. He couldn't see a rash on her face, but that didn't mean much in the early stage. She could even have typhus, the worst sickness of all. He could remember the stories they told about the typhus epidemic during the Forties, when the Irish immigrants had brought the disease to Quebec City, and Montreal, and as far west as Toronto. The Irish had called it "black fever" because the patients had turned a blue-black color. They had smelled so bad that nobody had wanted to nurse them. And sometimes they had gotten gangrene in the fingers and toes, which then had fallen off as they did in leprosy. In the end, they had often died.

"Do you have a headache, Janie?" Marc asked the child.

"It hurts here." The child touched her forehead and then turned away to face the wall. She looked exhausted. But that was understandable after the ordeal of the shipwreck and might not mean anything. Still, she had the air of somebody seriously ill.

"Have you both been vaccinated, M'sieur Smith?"

"Vaccinated? Oh, I have, but Janie hasn't. It didn't seem right to let them give a little gaffer like her the cowpox. For me, it's different, see. I didn't mind. Anyways, nobody asked about Janie when we got on the ship."

"Was there anybody sick when you left Liverpool? Any of your family or friends?"

James Smith allowed himself a short, dry laugh.

"Well, Father, there's always somebody sick, one way or another. I never seen it no other way."

Marc could imagine what it must have been like for Smith, what it was like for all the very poor and unemployed in the large cities of England and Ireland: the tenement with its gross overcrowding, the lice-ridden, unheated rooms in buildings that were sometimes hundreds of years old, the garbage-filled hallways, the rats that infested the cellars and often crept upward looking for scraps of food. Naturally there were always sick people around. It was a foolish question.

"I'm going to send for a doctor to look at Janie," Marc said. "We have a Dr. Grady who helps out here when there's sickness at the docks."

"I'm dead broke," Smith said defensively, just so there'd be no misunderstanding about payment. "I lost everything in the shipwreck."

"Dr. Grady won't charge you. He does charity work for our society, the St. Vincent de Paul Society."

"I'm no Catholic, Father. But I thank you for your help."

"We make no distinctions here. You wait with Janie until I come back. If she wants a drink of water, take some out of the bucket over there. Use the tin cup, but don't put it back with the bucket or use it yourself. Do you understand?"

Marc moved away from Smith, already searching the crowd for some sign of Camille. She would know how to reach Dr. Grady. He knew Camille was in the shed somewhere, probably giving advice about cheap lodgings to newly arrived women, or telling them where to find a train or a boat that would take them out into the country where their free land was located.

He saw her in the midst of a group of women (probably survivors from the shipwreck, judging from the odd clothing they wore, like the bits and pieces from a huge ragbag), and they were listening to her attentively. He could almost sense the waves of gratitude and dependency coming from Camille's audience. It was always like that with the immigrants when they arrived. They came with so little money, so few possessions, such poor health. Many of them were not skilled. The only thing they seemed to bring in quantity was hope, and today even that was in short supply. The loss of the *Empress Victoria* had hit many of them hard. The familiar bleak feeling of inadequacy swept over Marc as he looked at the crowd about him. There was so little he could do for them, really. The odds were against them, but they didn't seem to realize their plight.

He signaled to Camille over the heads of the people, and finally she saw him. She wore that burning look that was her constant expression these days. As if she were being consumed inside by a scarcely contained fire. She pushed toward him.

"What is it, Marc? Do you want me?"

"I'd like you to find Dr. Grady for me. We've got a sick child on our hands. I put her over there on the cot."

"What's the matter with her?"

"I don't know. She has a fever. A headache. She's been vomiting. The father says they were on the *Empress Victoria* and she caught cold on the lifeboat."

"Perhaps it's pneumonia."

"Or influenza."

They exchanged concerned glances. Any disease could be dangerous here, if it were contagious. The immigrants were often in poor health, and this group had been crowded together on the two ships. Still, he found comfort in knowing that Camille would help him in his mission. He wanted to tell her how much he depended on her, how much it meant to him to be able to talk to her, to ask her advice to trust her with special errands.

"Do you know where Dr. Grady can be found?" he asked.

"He usually spends the first part of the morning at the hospital and then makes his house calls. I'll try to catch him before he leaves the hospital. It isn't far. I'll go this minute."

She had taken to wearing gray cotton gowns with small capes, and simple gray bonnets, so that she had the austere look of a nun. Her long black hair was no longer worn loose, but tucked tightly into a bun at the nape of her neck. Despite the severity of her costume, however, the restless passion lurked just below the surface. No gown or hat, whatever the style, could conceal the hunger in her eyes and her full lips. Patches of color ebbed and flowed in her cheeks. Her hands moved a great deal, and the blue sapphire Marc had given her flashed with each gesture. She was never really still. But the same desperate energy that infused her eyes with the tortured look of a tempted saint seemed to endear her to the people she tried to help from day to day. To the poor and the sick and the uneducated who lived, for the most part, in the waterfront area, she was more than human. Not one of them, certainly, but a creature from another world who knew how to communicate with them. Some of them endowed her with supernatural powers, and their childlike belief was reflected back upon themselves so that sometimes they triumphed where they might have failed.

Marc watched her thrust her way through the immigrant crowd to the street, and into the sunshine. She was gone from view almost immediately, and he was left with his thoughts, with his constant moral battle. Should he try to live his life without her? Let her go back to her round of visits with relatives? Or should he allow her to suffer this torment as his housekeeper and aide, every day exposed to terrible temptation? With a short, explosive sigh he made his way back to the cot where Janie Smith lay. The dam of his conscience, he told himself, would force back the tide of his passion. All he had to do was pray.

Dr. Grady was a fierce little man with thick gray hair, a square-cut gray beard, and pince-nez that forever threatened to fall off his nose. He gave honest advice and painful treatments with equal gusto. Issues must be faced, he often said, problems must be tackled head on, words must not be minced. Life was a grueling business. If there was any justice or any happiness to be found, he had failed to notice.

Most of his patients came from the Irish of Griffintown, an area in the southwest portion of Montreal known locally as the "Swamp" and lying between Mountain and Lusignan Streets. He lived in a rundown house on the edge of Griffintown, using the parlor as his office. What the house lacked in cleanliness it made up in the smell of Jayne's liniment, a potion to which Dr. Grady was noticeably attached. He gave a good deal of his advice and treatment free and came out squarely for the Roman Catholic Church in general and the Virgin Mary in particular. He was against advertised cancer curses, Lydia Pinkham's vegetable compound ("there's not much wrong with most of these women that a good long prayer to the Virgin wouldn't cure"), and the Conservative government's loose immigration policy. What the Liberals would do, now that they were elected, remained to be seen. But immigration had long been a sore point with him. He'd lived through the great smallpox epidemic of 1885 and recalled vividly the riots against vaccination, considered a dangerous new medical practice by many immigrants and natives alike. It had been the government's lack of planning that had brought on so many of these terrible problems—encouraging the arrival of immigrants by the thousands without checking into their health or resources, and making no provision for them when they arrived in Canada. It was, to some degree, still the same story.

Standing in the reception shed, staring down at Janie Smith, he was in a position to view the case with a practiced eye. He did not like what he saw. But it was not his way to jump to conclusions. God knew it was easy to confuse smallpox in the prodromal or first stage with influenza, pneumonia, or any one of the fevers.

He took the child's temperature. It was one hundred and five. She appeared to be slightly delirious and so he couldn't ask her about localized pain. As he watched, she shivered violently.

"So far, it could be flu or pneumonia. Let's hope for pneumonia. But unfortunately, her father says she was vomiting before she got into the lifeboat. I don't like that."

Marc stood to one side watching the doctor. He often picked up bits of medical information that were useful to him later in his work among the sick.

Dr. Grady pulled down the blanket so he could examine the child for the rash that, if it appeared in the specified location, would give him another symptom. Yes, the rash was there. A petechial rash that remained fairly constant, as opposed to an erythematous type of rash that came and went fleetingly. It appeared in the groin and spread upward to the navel and downward over the upper legs. If she had been sick for three days, and if it was smallpox, the papular or second stage of the disease ought to show soon.

He pulled the blanket over the child once again and took a closer look at her forehead. It was at that moment that he felt the flicker of apprehension that always struck him hard in the gut when he saw signs of a contagious, potentially fatal disease. The macules were there on the forehead near the hairline. Tiny pimplelike formations on the bulge of the skull, they would grow quickly into full-fledged papules. They would appear next on the lower face and scalp and then on the wrists and on the backs of the hands, spreading slowly downward over the chest, back, abdomen, legs, and feet. The papules might invade the mouth, cover the soft palate and perhaps even the larynx. Complications took many forms: bronchitis, bronchopneumonia, pains in the back due to spinal meningitis, melancholia that might produce a suicide attempt, embolism, and, of course, conjunctivitis that often caused blindness. The kidneys might fail, resulting in uremia, and boils of a particularly ugly and untreatable type might well appear. All this before the final tragic disfigurement that came after the pustules dried up and the deep pits formed in the skin.

"Father St. Amour, come over here for a moment, will you?"

Dr. Grady, who always faced life squarely, did not approve of panic. Even mild panic. He spoke quietly, but left no room for doubt. When the priest came close to him he said, "It's smallpox. The 'classical' type, which is to say the severe type. I think you know what that means. She'll have to be isolated."

"The isolation hospital at Point St. Charles, then."

"Yes. I assume the child wasn't vaccinated?"

"That's right. But the father has been."

"Good. Then he can accompany her to the hospital. He might have to help nurse her, depending on the situation there. Can you arrange to take her?"

"I'll get my own gig. I've been vaccinated. I'm in no danger."

"The best thing to do is to bring a cotton sheet and wrap her completely in it; then you can destroy it later. When we get her admitted to the hospital, we'll see what happens next. Meanwhile, I'm going to get a list of people who were in the lifeboat with her, if I can. Smith will have to try to recall as best he can. They have to be warned so they can be vaccinated. It isn't too late if we get them immediately, but after the papular stage, vaccination doesn't do much good. If some of them are still in Halifax, there's nothing we can do. By the time they get the message to them it will be too late."

"We can try the telegraph," Marc pointed out.

"It's possible, but we can't count on getting the message out there fast enough. I'll talk to Smith. You see about the child, Father."

Marc left Janie Smith's father talking to the doctor while he went to fetch his own gig. Dr. Grady began to scratch out a list on the back of an envelope with the stub of a pencil. Smith remembered the stokers most clearly. And he knew there had been two other crewmen aboard. Perhaps the Court Shipping Line could find out who they were. There had been a woman, but he had no idea who she was except that she had worn a long cloak. He tried to remember something about the other passengers, giving sketchy descriptions that he thought might provide a clue to some official in the Court Line. Dr. Grady left him to care for the child while he hurried off to find an officer of the ship's company.

"Don't let anybody touch the child," Dr. Grady admonished. "And try to keep her covered up."

"Yes, sir. Thank you."

"Be careful now, Smith, and do as I say, or we'll have an epidemic on our hands."

Smith stood by the bed in a stupor. He couldn't believe it. He'd come to this country to begin a new life, and yet his bad luck was following him. Janie was all he had, and now she might be taken from him, or left horribly disfigured. He was slow to react when Janie began to toss about and moan. Before he could gather his wits together, Janie was throwing herself off the bed, and he tried to put her back on it and at the same time keep the blanket over her. Somebody was helping him, and he accepted the help before he remembered what Dr. Grady had told him.

"Poor little girl," the woman was saying, as she assisted Smith in forcing the child down upon the cot. "She has a fever, isn't that right?"

"Yes, yes," Smith said. And then remembered his instructions. "Oh, ma'am, you'd better get back. You're not supposed to touch her! She's got the pox, ma'am. Dr. Grady told me not to let anybody near."

The woman wore a neat gray dress and bonnet. He thought she might be a nun or a nurse. She didn't flinch when he told her about Janie, but said quietly, "I've been vaccinated."

"Still, ma'am, that's doctor's orders, see. I'm only doing what he said."

Janie began to thrash about again. Between them, they forced her back upon the cot. She was unusually strong in her delirium, and Smith was glad enough of the extra hands.

"We must try to keep her wrapped up. It's easy for them to get pneumonia."

Smith realized that the woman was French. She spoke English with a pronounced accent. She was also strangely forceful. He couldn't bring himself to argue with her.

"How are you taking her to the hospital?" the woman asked.

"The priest has gone to get his own gig, he said," Smith said doubtfully. "But the doctor is trying to find the people in the lifeboat. They got to be told about the pox, see."

"The priest is my brother," the woman said calmly, "so I'll stay with you until he comes. He'll understand."

"The doctor will be mad," Smith said stubbornly. "I promised to keep everybody away."

The woman ignored him. She was trying to make the child drink some water.

"They must have water, you know," she explained to James Smith, "or they become even more ill. They must drink."

Smith surrendered. There was no use trying to argue with the woman, as she obviously intended to have her own way. He was secretly comforted; it wasn't so lonely a vigil when somebody was there to help.

━━━━━━

She would have to tell Timothée today, Justine decided as she rode Fripon up the road toward the barns. There was no doubt now that she was pregnant. She'd missed two periods and she would soon have to consult a doctor about the problem. But in her heart she didn't need confirmation from an outside source. She was pregnant, and there was no use trying to pretend otherwise. She was thankful that Laurent had made love to her shortly after he had returned from Montreal so that at least there would be no question about the timing. Telling Laurent would not be difficult (and there was no need to worry about what the baby looked like, at least not for a long time, since Timothée was dark . . . thank God she had not been involved with a red-haired man or a really fair one!), but telling Timothée was something she dreaded. He would have to leave the farm. He couldn't possibly stay here as a constant reminder, a temptation. Not now. Even before she'd known about the pregnancy she had faced the possibility of Timothée's having to leave. Now there was no choice.

Laurent had driven the new spring wagon into the village for supplies. He would be gone for at least four hours and Justine knew that this would be the best time to tell Timothée her news. But she shrank from the scene. He would be angry if she told him to go, and frustrated if he stayed. She didn't want to hear what he had to say, that was the truth.

The morning dragged by and she still could not bring herself to walk up to the barns to face him. She had lunch with the children on the long verandah that had been added to the front of the house fifty years earlier. The central section of the house had been built in 1798 by a fur trader who had dealt with the Indians coming down from the Ottawa River, and there was still a stone vault on the main floor with iron hooks in it on which he'd hung the furs. In summer the verandah was usually cool, catching any passing breezes from the river and at the same time cutting off the sun.

After they'd eaten Anne-Marie took the two children to visit a neighbor along the shore who had three children close to the ages of Nicolette and Mathieu. Justine was perfectly free for the afternoon. She could rest, or sew, or do some preserving. She ought to see Timothée, though, and then put the matter out of her mind. She was tired simply from thinking about it; it was always best to deal with a problem and then go on to something else, she reminded herself.

Still, there were vegetables to pick, and that was of first importance. The crop of tomatoes and cucumbers was extraordinarily large this year, although the past week hadn't produced a drop of rain. If she didn't act now, they would ripen and rot. Or the raccoons and rabbits would get in and clean the place out.

With this plan in mind, she put on a gingham housedress with short sleeves and a bonnet to protect her head from the sun, and, picking up a large wicker basket, walked determinedly to the garden.

The rows of vegetables hung limp in the August heat. At three o'clock in the afternoon, the sun fell directly on the small forest of tomato leaves, shriveling them from the round, red fruit. Plump squash and unripe pumpkins that were not yet a brilliant orange spilled over the dry ground on thick, furry stems. Everything was burgeoning, exploding; erect cucumbers, rosy radishes thrusting above ground in their eagerness to be picked, stiff carrots with probing points, and corn. Corn in tightly wrapped green jackets designed to hide the golden spears from rapacious hands and mouths. She had been right. She must pick vegetables today and then spend the next few hours brewing them on the stove and boiling glass jars.

As she plucked the tomatoes carefully (it seemed they were all threatening to fall off their short, inadequate stems), her mind turned again to Timothée. It would be nice to swim naked in the creek under the willows, safely up there in the hill pasture, with Timothée lunging and splashing, and eventually pressing her to the grass with his irresistible demands. These thoughts only made her hotter, and she wiped the moisture from her forehead and tried to concentrate on the crop she was picking.

But, it was as if she had called him. Called him with her voice instead of her mind. For she heard him singing as he walked swiftly toward her, and then she saw him, rounding the corner of the caragana hedge, grinning at her. His shirt was stained with sweat.

"We need a swim," he said. "How about it? Have you picked enough of those things?"

"No, I've got to take more off, or they'll be wasted."

"They'll keep an hour."

His teeth looked whiter in the brilliant sunshine. He tried to take the basket from her, but she held on to it rigidly.

"It isn't safe. We don't know when Laurent will be back."

"Not for a little while," Timothée said easily. "He went into town. You must know that. We've got plenty of time. And I saw Anne-Marie taking the children off somewhere. Come along and get your clothes off and you'll feel better."

The idea of the swim was tempting. It *was* terribly hot, and Laurent couldn't possibly be back for at least an hour.

"I'll put these in the house first," she said, still not ready to face him. She'd have to tell him after the swim; there was no use postponing it any longer than that.

"Do that. And hurry."

Already she could feel the coolness of the water, and then, refreshed, the coaxing hands, the moist kisses, the searching tongue, and the blandishment of the stiffening flesh. She began to run toward the house with the heavy basket of vegetables. One tomato fell out and she stopped reluctantly to pick it up. It had been split by the fall. The juice ran out over her fingers. She put the basket in the shade by the kitchen door.

When they reached the protection of the willows, Justine hid behind some drooping branches while she took off her clothes; she thought it unromantic to let Timothée see her taking off the white sateen waist that now barely covered her swelling breasts, or the white nainsook drawers with their deep umbrella frill of Swiss embroidery, or the hose supporter of white satin and silk elastic. Nakedness she could understand, though she knew that she had already begun to put on weight; her white breasts were blue-lined with strain, and her stomach was no longer completely flat. It would be only a short time before either Laurent or Timothée noticed.

She slid into the water and came up in the middle of the small creek, so that only the shimmer of her white skin showed in the water. Timothée had no such reservations. He stood on the bank, naked and covered with black hair, proud and exciting in his obvious need. He came close to her in the water, laughing and sputtering. She was by far the better swimmer, but today they both could swim only in the middle, since the creek was shallower than usual due to the lack of rain. Timothée ran his hands over her breasts, pinching her nipples playfully so that they stood up. She struggled away from him, climbed up the bank, and threw herself in the grass underneath the branches. Timothée followed.

"They're bigger," he said, kissing her breasts. "You're eating too much ice cream. Drinking too much Gurd's gingerale."

"No." And she lay back, not wanting to interrupt their lovemaking, but unable to keep back the news now that he had provided an opening. "I'm pregnant, Timothée. It's yours."

That stopped him. For a short few moments he was not ready to make love (and she felt a tremor of fear that perhaps he would never want to make love to her again), but then he stopped frowning and smiled at her. His green eyes were mischievous. He looked very pleased.

"And what are you going to do about *that,* love?"

"Nothing, except to tell Laurent it's his," she said with a directness which surprised him.

"And what about me?"

"You'll have to leave here, Timothée. You can't stay now; it wouldn't be right."

"Go, and not see my own flesh and blood? What do you take me for?" Anger now. Resentment.

"Well, you can't stay. Not only because of the child, but because Laurent might notice something between us. Oh, Timothée, even if we stopped making love today, and I could resist looking at you, he'd still know. I'm sure he would. There's something about people who have been lovers . . . I don't know, I can't explain, but it's there."

"I'm not going."

She felt panic. It was her turn to become angry. Somehow she hadn't taken into account the notion that Timothée might refuse to go.

"You must."

"Your husband needs me here. I'm good at my job. Why should I be unemployed just because you and I have been having sex? It's just as much your fault as mine. You're not going to say I seduced you . . ."

No, she wasn't going to say that. She had no intention of laying all the blame on Timothée. In fact, she had no intention of Laurent's ever finding out the truth. But the idea of Timothée staying, and of the constant danger of discovery, was frightening.

She shook her head. She closed her eyes to the green shade of the leaves. She stretched out her hand toward Timothée's naked body and felt his desire returning. He rolled over on her quickly, and she accepted him with a new hunger. Later she would have to figure out what to do about Timothée . . . right now, she wanted nothing but his urgent body.

When it was over, they dressed and went back down to the house. She was picking up the basket of tomatoes (flushed, but that could have been due to the heat, and damp around the hairline, but that might well have been sweat and not creek water) when she heard the wagon coming up the lane. Timothée stood still. Had he immediately turned away, his hasty departure would have suggested uneasiness, so he stood by the door, looking toward the wagon and its driver.

As soon as she saw Laurent's face, she knew something was wrong. Guilt made her assume that he was angry because she and Timothée had been standing alone, talking. But as soon as he jumped down, and Timothée held the horse while Laurent approached his wife Justine realized that he was worried about something else entirely. He took a letter from his pocket.

"Justine, there's bad news. You're going to have to go to the city, I think. This letter . . ."

Somebody was sick. That must be it. But who?

"What is it? What's in the letter?" she cried with obvious irritation. It was like Laurent to stumble about and hesitate. Why couldn't he simply say what was wrong?

"Camille. She's got smallpox."

She tried to shut out the word. Once the disease was caught, smallpox took its course and there was little anybody could do about it.

"But Camille's been vaccinated!" Justine said, refusing to believe Laurent's ridiculous assertation. "We've *all* been vaccinated."

"Yes, but sometimes in a very few cases—sometimes the vaccination doesn't work," Laurent said.

"That's true, Mrs. Dosquet," Timothée confirmed. "I've heard of that."

"Is she very ill? Who's looking after her? Give me the letter, please. Let me read it."

"It's from Marc. He sounds so upset, it's hard to make much sense of the letter. Frankly, I would have expected Marc to be a little more controlled."

Laurent handed the letter to her. She read it and saw that for once Laurent had reported accurately. The letter was disjointed, almost frantic. Camille had smallpox and was very ill. They thought she had a severe case of bronchial pneumonia. They had no nurse—Marc was nursing her—and he was desperate with worry and with lack of sleep. He needed help. Would Justine come?

"I'll have to go, Laurent. We can't leave Marc to face this alone," Justine said.

"What about Helene? She has no children."

"Helene is still in Ottawa. It will take her much longer to get there. I'll have to go; there's no other way."

"Very well. There's a train in the morning," Laurent said reluctantly but calmly. "I think Timothée will have to take you into town this afternoon, and you can stay overnight at the hotel. You'll be with Marc tomorrow afternoon."

"I'll go and pack, then."

As she went into the house, she heard Laurent telling Timothée to unhitch the horse and bring a fresh one for the wagon. The afternoon was still hot, and it would be a long, slow drive to the village. As she climbed the stairs to her room, Justine wondered dimly if this were some kind of punishment for her behavior with Timothée. But that was foolish. Camille wouldn't be punished for Justine's sin. Camille was innocent. Nothing ought to happen to Camille. And what about poor Marc? He did nothing but good works, even going so far as to oppose the ridiculous bishops over the election. He was almost a martyr, really, and so why would *he* be punished because his sister, Justine, had sinned? No, she decided with relief, it wasn't her sins that had brought this on, it was merely bad luck. And if she prayed, she would be protected from getting sick herself, or from passing the disease along to anybody else.

"Dear Mary, Mother of God," she began silently, as she pulled clothes from her closet and laid them on the bed, "I'll try very hard to do better, but please make Camille well. And protect me for my children's sake . . . and don't let Laurent find out . . . and . . ."

CHAPTER TWELVE

Two of Venetia's trunks and one of her suitcases had been recovered before the *Empress Victoria* had sunk, but the loss of her other pieces of baggage had left her with only a handful of day dresses and walking suits (two bought in Bond Street), while most of her French lingerie and night-clothes, and an impressive collection of formal costumes picked up on both sides of the Channel had been saved. By great good luck, one of the rescued trunks contained the delicate gray lace evening dress that Julia had bought in Paris and several other fashionable reception gowns.

Coming down the grand staircase of Pride's Court for her first dinner with Sir Simon and Lady Court, Venetia was grateful to whatever gods had spared the pale blue foulard silk with the even paler blue chiffon yoke and underskirt of fine accordion pleats. Since she had saved her jewel case by her own wit, she took particular delight in wearing the sapphire pin, an ocean-blue sparkle on a misty blue ground of sheer silk at her throat.

Venetia was accustomed to making an entrance. She was, through constant repetition, almost numb to the ripple of excitement that invariably spread over any group when she appeared. But tonight was so important to both Charles and herself that she was keenly aware of Sir Simon's sharp appraisal. When she recognized approval in his searching look (he beamed at her from his sentry post near the foot of the stairs), she sighed inwardly. She noticed, too, the tiny shock and slow, reluctant pleasure reflected in Lady Court's extraordinary blue eyes. Women, she had noticed, usually succumbed to her beauty no matter what their age, but they did so more slowly than men and with more obvious pain.

She saw Fort standing a little distance behind his father.

He was staring up at her too. She had met Fort, as well as her father-in-law and mother-in-law, earlier in the afternoon when she and Charles had first arrived at the dock, and she had sensed Fort's glittering interest in women. (What an attractive man he was, with his light-brown curly hair, mischievous eyes, and thick beard!) The smile he gave her now was simply friendly, the smile of the appreciative connoisseur rather than the desirous male, and she was pleased. She did not want any complications with her charming brother-in-law.

"Right on time," Sir Simon said heartily, taking a quick look at his gold pocket watch and then giving Venetia the gruff smile of a bear who has been expecting starvation and suddenly sees prey. "That's what I like in a new daughter-in-law!"

"Venetia's a miracle. Always punctual," Charles said with ill-concealed pride. He bent politely to kiss his mother's cool cheek.

"Mama, you look lovely tonight."

"Thank you, Charles, that's kind."

After her first natural stab of jealousy, Lady Court had recovered her sense of proportion. She was grateful to Charles, really, for bringing home such a prize. Beauty and background and taste. The fear of some uncanny repetition of Honey's folly was always with her. Charles had done splendidly.

"May I say you both look lovely?" Fort said. He thought that Venetia was like a perfect rose, lush and vivid and heavily scented, while Sydney reminded him of a lilac; the details were delicate and pale yet the impression was faintly sensual. His mind often took this kind of imaginative turn, and he was quite pleased with his comparison.

Sir Simon had no time for gallantries; indeed he considered them highly suspect. He took a certain pride in never in his life having said anything complimentary about a woman's appearance.

"Let's get on with it, then. Grant announced dinner ten minutes ago. The soup'll be cold."

"Yes, Papa. Mustn't let the soup get cold," Fort said, taking his mother's arm and leading her to the dining room.

Sir Simon led Venetia into the dining room, leaving Charles to bring up the rear. Charles, however, was not displeased. It was a sign of his father's pleasure, and he, after all, had the prize in the end. He could afford to be generous.

The dining room at Pride's Court was the size of an indoor tennis court and was saved from utter bleakness by the thick green carpet and the field-sized landscapes of lush English countryside that were not hung, but rather were worked into the panels of the walls. On the long inside wall of the room, the fireplace consumed a third of the wall space. Because it was August, the grate was empty, but it could take a fifteen-foot log in winter and made the room almost cozy when it blazed away. The Court coat of arms was carved in stone above the mantel: two lions in the act of springing and a shield in the Court colors of red and white, featuring three crossed lances topped by a crested helmet. The lions were gold, as befitted their importance.

Tonight the long table was set with the Royal Crown Derby service (the second-best service in the Court repertoire) with its rich blue-and-red pattern highlighted with gilt; a bowl of late summer flowers from the garden, their ruddy colors appropriately heraldic; and two golden sconces holding five candles each. Unextended, the table seated twelve with ease. The Chippendale chairs with their square-cornered commodious seats and tilted backs with ever so slightly flared uprights were designed for comfort during long meals.

"I hope you aren't completely exhausted, my dear," Lady Court said to Venetia when they were arranged about the table and Grant had served the consommé. "What a frightening experience you've had! It must have been terrifying."

"She was very cool," Charles said proudly. "She didn't panic for a moment. Even remembered to pick up her jewel case. And got into the lifeboat calmly, with no complaints."

"It was Charles who was wonderful," Venetia said. "He made me get into the lifeboat and leave the ship while he went off to help the crew. I didn't see him again until we met in the hotel in Halifax."

"Well, I had to do that," Charles said, shrugging. "But the main thing was to keep people calm enough to load the boats, and to lower them without their tipping. I think the crew did awfully well, not only getting everybody off, but getting a bit of the baggage and mail as well."

"The fishing boats were what saved us, I think," Venetia said, remembering. "I don't know how long the men could have rowed in those small lifeboats. Some stokers got into our boat, and a man with a sick child. I don't know what happened to the child later—I expect they took her to a hospital in Halifax. She seemed to have a fever. But you know, when the fog lifted, the fishing boats simply appeared. They picked us up and took us to shore."

She shivered, remembering her fear in the lifeboat, with the thick fog enveloping the boat so that she couldn't see more than a few feet, and the black-faced rowers from the boiler room looking like figures from some Arabian Nights fairytale. The deathly quiet around the tiny boat had been broken only by the splashing of oars or an occasional shout from one of the men who hoped to hear a responding shout from a boat hidden in the fog. What if they had run into another boat, or a rock? Nobody had seemed to know how far from shore they were. She remembered the child's hot forehead and how restless she had been, how thin. And then when the fog had lifted a little they had been able to see how alone they were on the vast, dark ocean. Where were the other lifeboats? They had drifted out of sight, apparently. And then, on the edge of the world, a fisherman's boat had appeared as suddenly as if a magician had produced it. The fishermen had taken them in, along with other passengers from other boats they had eventually sighted, and somehow they had all reached Halifax.

By that time, Venetia's long black cape and white nightgown had been wet and dirty and had stuck to her like the wrappings of a mummy. She would never be warm again, never safe again, she'd thought at the time. Charles had said she had remained cool, but she had been appallingly frightened . . .

But of course nobody at the dinner table wanted to hear those details. One didn't talk about such things during meals; it simply wasn't done.

"I hate like hell to lose that ship," Sir Simon was saying. "She was a beauty. And the cost to replace her! A terrible loss."

"But no loss of life," Charles reminded his father," and that's good for the shipping line."

"No shipwreck is good for the shipping line," Sir Simon said with asperity. "People only remember the wreck; they forget how many *safe* crossings we make."

"Well, every company on the oceans of the world has its share of shipwrecks," Fort said.

"I don't see how it could have been avoided," Charles said thoughtfully. "The fog was so thick there was no way Barker could have known he was that close to the coast. We can't blame him, in my opinion."

"I suppose not," Sir Simon said. "At any rate, I've given the order that nobody connected with the Court Shipping Line is to discuss the shipwreck. The less publicity we get at this point, the better. Too much at stake. We've got to assess the situation and get Barker's official report. The Commission of Inquiry will do a thorough job, I'm sure."

"Quite, Papa. I've instructed every company official to say nothing to the press, to refuse to discuss details of the shipwreck with anybody who makes inquiries, no matter who they are. Just as you told me. They aren't to release any information. We've got to see where we stand with the insurance, just as you say."

"Good, good! Do you think this hock is satisfactory, Fort? I wonder if it's quite . . . mmm . . . yes, when you get people talking, no telling where it'll all end. Some of the passengers will be making claims against us, if Barker's to blame. Negligence, eh? You did save some of your baggage, didn't you, Venetia?"

"Oh, yes, but some of those poor people must have lost everything they had. That will be awfully difficult for them, you know. You can see why they'd like compensation."

"Compensation?"

Sir Simon bellowed at the exact moment Grant was pouring more hock into his glass. A few drops dribbled down the side of the glass and Sir Simon glared at the offending Grant.

"Well, they've come here with very little with which to start over again in life," Venetia said, remembering how thin the child had been when she'd leaned against her in the lifeboat, and how soiled and tattered the blanket wrapped around her had been.

"That's their own choice," Sir Simon said. "I can't be held responsible for the decisions of every citizen of En-

gland, Ireland, and Wales, can I? We want them to come—
we need workers, we need people to settle the land—but
after all, I can't do more than provide the ships to get
them over the ocean. I can't be responsible for fog, and
rocks, and Barker's judgment, if that's at fault. A man who
is burdened by that kind of thinking wouldn't get out of
bed in the morning."

Venetia could see that compassion for the people beneath him was not one of Sir Simon's strong points. She
decided to refrain from pushing her opinion, at least for
the time being . . . she wondered what she ought to call
Sir Simon. She couldn't imagine calling him Papa; it was
much too intimate. He didn't really encourage that kind of
feeling. Best to ask Lady Court when they were alone.

"Well, thank heaven Venetia and Charles are safe," Lady
Court said brightly, sensing that her husband was on the
verge of an explosive harangue about risk capital and the
laziness of the poor. "We should all be thankful for that.
Now, what I'd like to talk about instead of a depressing
shipwreck is Fort's wedding. And Venetia's introductions to
society. I think the ball before Fort's wedding will be the
ideal time to formally introduce Venetia; what do you
think, Fort?"

"Sounds all right," Fort said. "I've discussed the date
by letter with Sydney, and we've settled on September
twenty-ninth. In Christ Church. Sydney has no relatives
here, of course, but I still think it ought to be a church
wedding, don't you?"

"My, yes, I do!" Lady Court said excitedly. "It's the
only chance I'm ever going to have to put on a large wedding. What with Honey running off the way she did, and
of course Geoffrey getting married in England. And you,
too, Charles. So I'm very excited, darling, about putting
on the wedding. Normally, it would be Sydney's parents
who arranged it, but since she has nobody here . . ."

"If you're sure it's what you want, Mama," Fort said,
"then you can count on Sydney's agreeing to a large
church wedding."

"Marvelous. It's *just* what I want. Leave everything to
me, darling. But we must discuss a guest list. I thought
perhaps two hundred. Since Sydney won't be adding any
names except, perhaps, for a few friends. What about the
people she's staying with in Quebec City? Will they come?"

"The Britton-Fosters? I don't know."

"Who are they, Fort? Should I know them?" Charles asked.

"Britton-Foster is a civil servant. I met Sydney in their house in London last year. They had a place in Eaton Square," Fort said smoothly. (How easily the lies came! How quickly one could construct a whole world for one's love if necessary! The Britton-Fosters were perfectly respectable, but Fort had never met them. Sydney knew them as a connection of Countess Leda's, and she was visiting them in Quebec City so she could arrive in Montreal by boat with a logical story about her activities and whereabouts. Fort hoped that with a new wardrobe and hairstyle, the casual habitués of the salon would not recognize Sydney should they accidentally meet in future.) "Britton-Foster represents the Crown in Quebec City now. I'm not certain what his exact position is. They like to preserve a bit of mystery there, you know."

Charles was satisfied. He was well into his roast lamb and not in a mood for any nice distinctions concerning London officials and their particular roles in the scheme of things.

"I hope Venetia understands about your sister?" Lady Court said, addressing Charles as if Venetia were not present. It was a habit of hers. "Simon is trying so hard to make up the quarrel. After all, she *is* an only daughter. He gave Honey a magnificent wedding present. But she hasn't responded. I don't understand her. It makes me very sad."

Fort choked on his wine.

Charles said quickly, "Venetia understands perfectly, Mama."

And why not, with her own mother running off regularly to marry some totally unsuitable man? But Charles had not given any of the unsavory details of Julia's marriages to Sir Simon or Lady Court. Julia was marrying an earl, they knew that. And it was enough.

"Good. That's the truly nice thing about a house like this," Lady Court went on. "It's designed for large parties. It isn't the same thing to have to engage the ballroom at the Windsor. The Rosses had to do that for Emily, and I thought it such a pity. Ross House is large, of course, but the ballroom doesn't accommodate more than fifty couples. Of course I don't mind a hotel for the St. Andrews

Ball, or some function like that. It's quite another matter. Don't you think, Charles?"

"Yes, Mama. You're quite right."

When they had finished the blueberry tart, Lady Court rose.

"We'll go along to the conservatory where it's cool, my dear," she said to Venetia, "while the men have their cigars and brandy. Now, I want you to tell me all the ghastly details about the shipwreck. Every single one. I'm longing to hear about it."

Venetia felt an instant flood of warmth toward her new mother-in-law.

As they left the dining room, she said, "I do have a problem, you know, I'd like your advice. What should I call you? And Sir Simon? I feel it's so important to begin properly."

Lady Court smiled and took Venetia's arm.

"It is a touchy thing," she said chattily, "I quite agree. You wouldn't want to call me Mama, as the children do, when you have a perfectly good Mama of your own, and no doubt you call her that?"

"Not exactly." In fact, Venetia had always called her mother Julia except in moments of stress, when she had reverted to an exasperated "Mother!"

"What about Mama Court?" Lady Court suggested.

"Yes, I like that," Venetia agreed.

"And Papa Court for Sir Simon. Of course, I don't know what Simon will say, but I'm sure he'll find it quite pleasant."

And on this note, they entered the conservatory to take their coffee. Behind them, the three men adjourned to the library for cigars and conversation.

"I've bought out the Andrews Ironworks," Sir Simon announced over his glass of port, "lock, stock and barrel. We've got full control."

"Good God, Papa, isn't that place operating at a loss? I've heard nothing but bad reports about Andrews since the old man died. Douglas Andrews is letting it go down to nothing. He's no businessman," Charles said.

"How do you think I got it so cheaply?" Sir Simon asked. He did not expect an answer, of course, but went on to say, "I knew Douglas Andrews couldn't run it. He couldn't run a costermonger's barrow. He was glad to sell. I must admit, the men at the works seemed pleased when I announced that they'd all be kept on. I think they expected to be let out any day."

"I presume you have some plan?" Fort put in, mellowed somewhat by the quality of his father's port. "You usually do."

"Oh, yes, I have what I call a master plan," Sir Simon said airily. "It goes this way. We get the majority of shares in the iron mine up near Herouxville—I don't know if you're familiar with it?"

Charles frowned in alarm. "But Papa, that mine's been almost out of production for ten years . . ."

"Yes, yes, but that's why we can get so many shares in it without breaking the bank," Sir Simon said impatiently. "If it were a raging success, it wouldn't be so practical. But on the information I have at present, it produces a fairly high grade of ore and is a cheap mine to operate. The difficulties are not so much in the mine—although it will never be one of the largest mines in the world, I grant you—but in getting the ore out. The railroad from Three Rivers to Herouxville, through Champlain, is in poor shape. Needs a lot of upkeep. A lot of investment. Now, my plan is three-pronged. We control the iron mine that supplies the ironworks, where we manufacture rails and machinery. We get control of the Three Rivers-Champlain Railroad, we supply it with rails from our own works, and we use it to take out more ore. We control all three stages of the process. Do you follow me?"

"Yes, I follow you. But what if we don't get the mining shares? Or the railroad?" Fort asked.

"But we will," Sir Simon said flatly. "And that's what you and Charles are going to accomplish before long."

"I see. But are you sure the ironworks itself is a good investment?"

"Look ahead," Sir Simon said, using his cigar as a sweeping pointer. "What do you see? You see the need for more machinery in Canada. The need for more rails as the railroads expand. Farm machinery for the land being opened up. Where is that machinery coming from now?"

"From England and Germany. In our ships, quite often. That's part of our cargo," Charles said.

"Right. But we'll find other cargo. That isn't a major

problem. We'll manufacture farm machinery right here in Montreal. We'll make rails right here. Now we have to import rails from the United States. But why can't we make our own?"

"Partly because we don't have all the technical knowledge, the men who can manage the works," Fort said.

"Well, you're going to England after Christmas to find a man who can manage the ironworks. And also to find a designer for the farm machinery, Fort. That's one of the jobs I have in mind for you."

Fort poured himself another glass of port. His father's wine cellar was admirable.

"Yes, Papa. And what is Charles going to do?"

"Temporarily, he's going to acquire the necessary amount of stock in the railroad. Before anybody realizes what I'm up to. Once we have the mine we can control the supply, and the price of transporting the ore on the railroad will be manageable once we have control of *that*."

"You're absolutely sure the mine can be developed for a long time?" Fort asked. "I assume you've had some kind of report."

"Yes, I've had a report from a geologist who was up there when it cut back on production. He said there was no need for a cutback. But between poor management and the shaky service provided by the railroad, nobody would listen to him. He wanted them to put more money in then."

"And they wouldn't? Perhaps they didn't believe his report," Fort suggested.

"Well, you're going up there to get another report. You can take a geologist with you. Inspect the place and come back with recommendations. I know it isn't absolutely top-grade ore, but I think the mine can be made to operate profitably. It's all a question of management. You can also take an engineer and get a report on the railroad. I want to know how much we'll need to invest immediately. The ore has to be brought down to Three Rivers. That's where the furnaces are."

"The furnaces must be antiques," Fort said.

"They are. That's another problem. You can give me a report on that, too," Sir Simon said, completely undaunted.

"Who is president of the railroad?" Charles asked. "Do you have a list of directors?"

"Barrett's president. You know him, Charles—he eats at the St. James Club regularly. He was a cavalry officer in the Crimea. Big fellow, big mustache."

"Barrett . . . yes, I think I know who you mean."

"I'll want from you, Fort, a complete report on the rolling stock, the number of locomotives, passenger cars, freight cars, records of the revenue of passenger and freight, that kind of thing."

"And right away, I assume? I'm getting married in less than a month."

"Let the women worry about that. They like it. We've other things to do. You can be up to Herouxville and back before the wedding. The weather may turn nasty in October; you can't depend on it. You know what these northern railroads are like when it freezes up. Hotboxes, brake seizures, all kinds of trouble."

"I'll begin to make arrangements tomorrow," Fort said. "I expect I can find a geologist through McIntyre at McGill University: he'll know somebody we can trust."

"And you, Charles, you get right onto the problem of acquiring stock in the Three Rivers-Champlain Railroad. Before they wake up."

"I follow your plan, Papa, but if we do produce rails and machinery, I can't help feeling we'll be stealing potential cargo from our own ships," Charles said thoughtfully.

But Sir Simon, filled with vision, was not about to be halted by any such picayune considerations.

"Plenty of other cargo. We're such a long way from being self-sufficient in Canada, that's a joke. Did I tell you I've got Geoffrey up in Glasgow right this minute? He's ordering two new ships for the line. I'm finding out about a run from Liverpool to New Orleans. This business of the St. Lawrence freezing up every winter cuts our shipping season here in half. That's not good. Now, New Orleans is open all year round, naturally. No reason why we can't compete down there for cargo, is there? There's a British shipping line for sale at the moment, the Glencairn Steamship Line. Geoffrey's looking into it. A merger, or something of the kind, might be just what we need at the Court Shipping Line to really lift us up to the top. I like the idea. Geoffrey likes it, too."

Fort shook his head. He was smiling. "Papa, you're a

genius of some kind. I have to give you credit for being an idea factory."

"I'll never be able to match your business ability," Charles said. "I haven't the courage. I'm much too cautious."

"You'll learn," Sir Simon said with a chuckle. "That's why you listen to old people like me. Now, I think we'd best join the ladies and say our good nights. I've still got some papers to read. I want to study Captain Barker's report in relation to possible claims from passengers on the *Empress Victoria*. Do you notice how much easier it is to work late at night with the electric light? It's a marvelous thing, electricity. You know, Charles, if it ever comes to the point when the people—that is, the *working* people—have electric lights, there'll be money in it. What do you think? Should we invest in an electric light company?"

Charles, eager to get upstairs with Venetia, refused to consider any more business propositions. The electric light might be a great invention, perhaps the greatest in the world, but it did not compare with being married to Venetia. He felt the first stirrings of desire as he followed Fort's broad back toward the conservatory. Already he could visualize her undressing; the graceful neck, the perfectly formed white breasts with the large nipples of palest pink that she allowed him to see by candlelight, although she would not *completely* undress before him . . . perhaps that would come. Up to now he had had to depend upon his hands to convey to his mind the sweet image, the delicious secrets of her thighs. He trembled slightly with anticipation.

From the conservatory came laughter. It had been a long time since Lady Court had been so cheerful of an evening; in fact, she had not laughed over her coffee since Honey had eloped to join the French.

―――――

The early September days dropped away. Fort left on a small riverboat for Three Rivers to begin his inspection of the railroad and the mine. Charles was already negotiating for the railroad shares, prodded by his father, who, as always, was perfectly confident that his plan was first-rate even without the corroborating reports he expected to receive from Fort.

Lady Court, with Venetia as a willing ally, was shoulder-deep in plans for the wedding. There were guest lists to be made, invitations to order from the printer, the church to engage, the Anglican bishop to cajole and organize to her every whim, the flowers to find (the gardens at Pride's Court would offer autumn blooms, but roses and lilies and orchids must be ordered from New York), musicians to hire and extra servants to engage for the dinner and ball. Venetia was to be matron of honor, but four young women, daughters of Lydia Court's closest friends, were dragooned as bridesmaids on the understanding that Lady Court would pay for the gowns and find the dressmaker, since it was such short notice. Lady Court herself had to find a gown. Only Venetia was free from *that* problem, the Paris lace being declared suitable by her mother-in-law.

Through all this, the family waited with excitement and some reservations for their first sight of Sydney Hall. Nobody had seen her, nobody knew much about her. They were entirely dependent upon Fort's assurances and descriptions before he left for Three Rivers. Lady Court found herself swinging wildly from cheerful confidence (hadn't Venetia been an unqualified success?) to utter despair (how could she expect to have such luck again?).

Nine days after her arrival at Pride's Court, Venetia fell ill after dinner. A severe headache came on as the dessert course was being served. At first Lady Court was not unduly worried.

"It's delayed shock," she said kindly. "You've been so brave about the shipwreck, and that cold, wet experience in the lifeboat. It's bound to affect your nerves."

"But I don't usually get headaches," Venetia said. She had always been in excellent health, suffering none of the ailments that seemed to plague all the women around her. Even Julia sometimes complained of pains in the bones.

"Still, you don't usually spend hours in a lifeboat without even the proper clothing," Lady Court said with some logic. "You don't usually work like a galley slave. I don't know what I'd have done without you in planning this wedding, my dear."

Venetia felt her face draining of blood. She was now almost blind with the pain, and it had come so suddenly that it was frightening.

"I'll have to go up to bed," Venetia said.

Charles came around the table and helped her up. When he began to fuss, Lady Court interceded.

"You take her up to bed, Charles, while I get some pain pills. Radway's Pills will help her, I think. I depend on them myself. Go along, and don't fidget, Charles. Everybody gets a headache sometime in her life. It isn't the end of the world."

But she didn't like the look of Venetia. It suddenly occurred to her that the girl might be pregnant, although headaches were not, in her experience, one of the symptoms.

"Go along, Charles," she said again.

"Yes, Mama."

Dutifully, he assisted Venetia out of the dining room and up the stairs. He had been plunged abruptly into a terrifying fear. It had never occurred to him that Venetia might get sick. That she might even—he hesitated to think the word in case it brought bad luck—die.

As they went up the stairs slowly, Venetia knew she was suffering no ordinary headache. The pain had come so quickly, and already it was almost unbearable. Her stomach was in revolt, and she wondered if she would reach the bedroom before vomiting.

"I'll help you undress," Charles said.

"I'll manage."

But she knew that she could not. By the time Charles had helped her into her nightgown, Venetia was in the bathroom throwing up violently. She staggered back into the bedroom and fell upon the bed. Charles pulled the covers over her. The retching had aggravated the headache. Pains now began in her back and in her legs. She began to shiver violently.

When Lady Court appeared with a glass of water and two pills, Venetia was already moaning and tossing her head from side to side.

"She may not hold the pills down," Lady Court said, "if she's vomiting. But we must try."

Venetia swallowed the pills and fell back upon the pillows. Lady Court motioned Charles to the door and spoke quietly.

"You must get Dr. Miles. Go at once."

When Dr. Miles arrived, Venetia looked extraordinarily tired. Instead of a young, twenty-three-year-old face, the doctor found the face of a middle-aged woman. The skin was white; the muscles had relaxed so that the flesh sagged.

"Influenza," Dr. Miles said, after examining her face and hands and arms. "She has a temperature, but it isn't alarmingly high. The headaches are very symptomatic of influenza and there's a good deal of it about."

"Can you give her something for the pain?" Charles asked.

"Yes, some laudanum. She can take it in sherry. I'll show you. I hope she can keep it down—that's always the problem, you know. If they vomit, it's difficult to control the pain."

"But how serious is it, Doctor?" Charles asked when they were out in the corridor with the bedroom door closed.

"I don't know. It can turn to pneumonia. That's the most serious possibility. So you must keep her in bed, and warm. Give her warm fluids. I'll write out some instructions for you."

"We'll need a nurse, then."

"Yes, I'd engage a nurse for night duty. To see that Mrs. Court keeps well covered, and warm. Your wife may begin to cough. She may run a very high fever. I'll come back first thing in the morning."

Within two days Venetia's temperature reached one hundred and four. She was delirious several times, thrashing about the bed, making strange noises, evidently seeing apparitions judging from her frightened expressions and her jumbled words. She did not, however, begin to cough.

"There's no sign of pneumonia," Dr. Miles said to Charles on the second day. "And no sign of a rash of any kind. I can only diagnose influenza—and that, Mr. Court, takes its own time, goes its own route, so to speak. We must simply wait."

"But she's delirious," Charles protested. "It seems very serious."

"Delirium is often a symptom of influenza. The degree of danger from the disease varies, as you must have heard. It depends on the complications. And so far, there's no indication of pneumonia. I take that as a good sign."

"There must be something else we can do," Charles muttered.

"Keep her warm. She must be made to drink something.

With a fever, the body loses water. That's a danger as well."

To Charles it seemed that nothing was being done to help Venetia. Another doctor was summoned. Charles raged to Sir Simon.

"What good is money? It doesn't help. Look at them—they aren't doing a goddamn thing for her! Where's your power now, Papa?"

"They're doing all they can," Sir Simon said bleakly.

Sir Simon was strangely touched by Venetia's plight. He felt powerless, just as Charles said, but he refused to admit that even to himself. He would not admit it today, nor tomorrow, nor ever. Something would be done to help his daughter-in-law. Logic and science would prevail.

Lady Court had given up preparations for the wedding. It was too soon to decide to cancel the enormous ball, the special flowers, the extra help, the services of the bishop and the church. Yet she was disturbed enough to bring all her activities to a halt. Instead, she supervised the administering of the medicine that Dr. Miles had prescribed (the nurse could not be trusted, that much was obvious), and she went each morning to the cathedral to pray. Sir Simon snorted derisively and refused to accompany her. Church was appropriate on Sundays, but that was the end of it.

On the third day of Venetia's illness, the Courts had an unexpected visitor.

He came unannounced and was rather shabbily dressed. His hair was thick and gray under his stiff black felt hat, and he carried a black bag. His manner was abrupt.

"I must see a member of the family."

Grant was a little taken aback. The man had not even presented a calling card.

"Who shall I say is calling, sir?"

"You can *say* anybody you like. But if you want to know who I am, the name is Dr. Grady. It's very important or I wouldn't be here. I've other things to do. People are sick and they need me."

"Dr. Grady. Yes. I'll speak to Lady Court."

"Be quick, then. I haven't all afternoon."

Grant showed Dr. Grady into the great hall and disappeared in the direction of the second floor. He usually moved slowly and with dignity, but something in the doctor's manner made him hurry. He was soon back, and after taking the visitor's hat, showed him into the library.

"Lady Court will be down in a moment, sir."

"Very well. My business is brief."

The doctor set his bag on a chair. When Grant was gone, he looked around the room with a certain curiosity, noting the paintings, the books, and the furniture. Lady Court came in while he was examining a bronze piece depicting a hunter and two dogs killing a deer.

"You wished to see me? I'm Lady Court."

He saw a slim woman with a worried expression in her bright blue eyes. She remained calm, but he sensed that there was trouble in the house and that the calm façade was maintained at considerable expense. He hoped that he had come in time.

"Dr. Grady, ma'am. I'm sorry to disturb you like this, but it's important. There's a young Mrs. Court, I think, who was a passenger on the *Empress Victoria.* She was rescued in a lifeboat?"

Lydia Court caught the sharpness of his manner. A warning stab below her heart made her catch her breath.

"Why, yes, that's my daughter-in-law, Mrs. Charles Court. How did you know?"

"Is she ill?"

"Yes, she's very ill."

"I was afraid that she would be. Lady Court, I have what may be grave news, although I hope that I am wrong. Have you had a doctor here?"

"Oh, yes, Dr. Miles. And a second opinion, Dr. Edgeworthy. Venetia has influenza."

"I thought she might. It's the usual diagnosis. How long has she been ill?"

"Three days."

"I see. Lady Court, I realize that I am not in a position to ask to see your daughter-in-law, but I hope that you will invite me to examine her. The situation is this, and I wish that I could say something more encouraging, but facts must be faced: your daughter-in-law has been exposed to smallpox."

"Smallpox?"

The word was only a whisper from Lady Court's throat.

"A child in the lifeboat has come down with it. The child was in the early stages of the disease on that morning of the shipwreck, and nobody realized what the trouble was. Her father thought she was seasick. Your daughter-in-law was in that lifeboat with her. I think she may have been sitting next to the child."

"She was. I remember Venetia talking about a sick child. But smallpox!"

"The child wasn't vaccinated."

"Do they let immigrants come in without being vaccinated?"

"Sometimes. The authorities are not too careful. The shipping companies want full ships. The government wants more settlers. Has your daughter-in-law been vaccinated?"

"I have no idea. Really, Dr. Grady, I didn't think of it. Dr. Miles didn't ask."

"He wouldn't be expecting to see smallpox. Since they brought in vaccination the actual epidemics have almost stopped. In the first stage, a diagnosis of influenza is quite common. Now, working down in the waterfront area, I see a great deal more of the fevers, the contagious diseases than your Dr. Miles sees. Fortunately, or unfortunately, I've had plenty of experience with smallpox. I was working in the epidemic of 'Eighty-five."

"I remember." Lady Court was still speaking in a hushed tone.

"The first thing to determine is whether we are dealing with smallpox. The next thing, whether Mrs. Court has been vaccinated. Will you let me see her?"

Lady Court gathered herself up with a tremendous effort.

"Please, Dr. Grady, I would consider it a favor if you'd look at Venetia. Will you come up now?"

Venetia still had a high temperature, but with some sedation (the laudanum had had a calming effect) she had ceased to thrash about the bed so violently. Her eyes looked weary, her facial muscles flaccid.

Dr. Grady introduced himself. "I've been looking for you for days, young lady. All I had was a description of a 'beautiful lady in the lifeboat.' You'd be surprised how difficult it was to find you."

"But didn't the Court Shipping office have a passenger list? Didn't they try to trace the people picked up in the boats?" Lady Court wanted to know.

Dr. Grady opened his bag and took out a thermometer.

"The Court Shipping Line, I'm sorry to say, has been a hindrance, not a help. They refused to give out any information about passengers in the shipwreck until yesterday. I had to get assistance from the mayor himself before they'd release names. Even after I told them about the case of smallpox."

"I see." Lady Court remembered that dinner on the night Venetia had arrived at Pride's Court. The conversation then had been so businesslike. There had been no thought of anything so unspeakable as . . . this illness. Simply a matter of insurance claims, Simon had said.

During the examination, Venetia had lain quiet. The effects of the fever and the drug had combined to produce a half-stuporous state. What difference did it make that one more doctor wanted to look at her? His words had no connection with her own tortured state.

Almost reluctantly, Dr. Grady bent close to the patient's face, peering through his glasses at the fine white skin. He lifted the black curls gently from her forehead. If he had entertained any doubts, those doubts were gone. The first small macules had already appeared along the hairline and were reaching downward toward the eyebrows. Set deep in the skin, they would grow, bloom into papules filled with clear liquid, close together like obscene hills: red, fiery, ugly. The face would bloat and become a mass of these hillocks. Later the sores would turn into full-fledged pus-filled lesions. The whole face would disappear into a horrible mask. The original symptoms might return, and she would be violently ill once again.

"Can you hear me, young lady? Can you understand me?"

"Yes, Doctor." Venetia struggled to pay attention to what the new doctor was saying.

"Have you been vaccinated?"

"Vaccinated?" She appeared to struggle with this question and then, finally, she said, "Oh, no. It didn't seem necessary."

"A vaccination," Dr. Grady explained to Lady Court, "isn't always one-hundred-percent effective. But it usually reduces the severity of the disease, even if it doesn't prevent it."

"But surely it isn't too late? You can vaccinate her now?

It *will* help, won't it?" Lady Court said, grasping at the only hope that occurred to her.

"I can and I will," Dr. Grady said. "But once the papules erupt, the vaccination doesn't do as much good. I ought to have reached Mrs. Court as soon as I diagnosed the child's case of smallpox. Then we could have been reasonably sure the vaccination would help. But now, it may be too late."

He was bringing out the supplies that he had deliberately packed into his bag for this emergency.

"This won't hurt much, Mrs. Court. Just a little scratch."

He was wiping her arm with a piece of cotton soaked in alcohol when she sat up, rigid as a board.

"*Smallpox*?"

And then she screamed and screamed and screamed.

It was some minutes before Dr. Grady could actually achieve the vaccination. And even then it had been possible only after he had managed to force her to swallow some sedation.

Outside in the corridor, Doctor Grady said to Lady Court, "You'd better call Dr. Miles and tell him what's happened. I think Mrs. Court will be hysterical when that laudanum wears off. You're going to have a woman with a sick mind as well as a sick body on your hands."

CHAPTER THIRTEEN

The tiny back room was barely furnished; there were only a prie-dieu placed before a stark black cross hanging on the wall, a square wooden writing table on which lay a leather-bound Bible with silver clasps, and a straight-backed chair. Purple light from the just-sunken sun strained through the one window, turning the air thick with mystical shadow. Only a few muted sounds penetrated the heavy door—a cough from Camille in one of the upstairs bedrooms, the parlor door closing as Marc went in to stir up the fire.

Justine was caught by the mood of Marc's room. It was as if she could feel something, as if she could almost reach into another dimension. She slowly lit the votive candle and knelt on the prayer stool.

"Mary, Mother of God . . ." she began, summoning up her courage for the promise at hand, sure that the Holy Mother was within hearing distance in this darkening, closed envelope of a room. "Please help Camille. Don't let her die. Please, don't let her die. If you let Camille live, Blessed Mother, I will promise never to . . . to be with Timothée again. I know I can resist the temptation—I *will* —if only you'll help poor Camille. And Blessed Mother, protect this unborn child. Don't make *him* pay for my sins, please. I offer him to you, Blessed Mother, and I promise to be faithful to Laurent if only you will help Camille . . ."

Justine prayed in this vein for some minutes, repeating her promise over and over, feeling more sure each time that she would truly be able to keep it. Eventually (the moments slipped together like the single drops in a silken stream) she heard a knocking on the front door, so loud that it penetrated the hallway and even the door of her retreat. It must be Dr. Grady, she thought. They were expecting him.

She shook herself from her half-dream and rose from her knees. The candle had almost burned down. When she reached the hall, Dr. Grady was already talking to Marc.

"Well, how is my patient tonight? Cough any better?"

Marc, standing with a small kerosene lamp in his hand, was thrown into curious relief. Justine saw for the first time how thin he had become, how his eyes had sunk back into their sockets, how his lips moved without voicing words. Marc would be ill next, she thought angrily. He wasn't eating properly and probably not sleeping, either.

"I don't really know how she is," Marc said nervously. His voice had gone up in pitch. There was a tremble in it.

"I'll see her in a moment." Dr. Grady's face was set in a serious expression, his mouth turned down in a warning, it seemed, of bad news. "Marc, that child died this afternoon. Janie Smith."

"Oh, I'm sorry." Marc might have been reciting lines in a play.

"A sad thing. The poor father is in a bad way. Later on, you might find him and give him some comfort. He's living in a boarding house on Mountain Street. I doubt that he'll have the price of burial."

"I'll find him," Marc said tersely. "I'll help. He's not of our faith, however. You realize that. I'll have to direct him to some other minister for a funeral service."

The death of the child was a bad sign. He had told himself that if the child lived it would be a portent for Camille's future.

"The children die most often," Dr. Grady said, sighing. "That is the fact of the case."

Dr. Grady hesitated before climbing the narrow stairs to the bedroom where Camille lay. Because of the connection by marriage, he felt compelled to tell them about Venetia Court.

"Father, I sometimes marvel at the Lord's ways," the doctor said heavily. "Such a time I had, finding all the names of the passengers who might have been in that lifeboat with Janie Smith. The ones who ought to be vaccinated quickly, if they hadn't been vaccinated already. Finally I ran them down. And what do we find? Young

Mrs. Court, just a bride, was beside the child in that boat."

Marc's face took on an even flintier appearance.

"You mean a sister-in-law to Honey?"

"That's right. The son, Charles, apparently married in England. He brought his bride home on the *Empress Victoria*. I can assure you the case is real. I saw her myself."

"It's some kind of justice, I suppose," Marc said tightly. " 'Vengeance is mine; I will repay, saith the Lord.' "

Neither Justine nor Dr. Grady was quite sure what the priest meant by this.

"I don't quite see . . ." Justine began uncertainly.

"Why not? Why not one of *them*?" Marc interrupted, his voice reaching wildly into an upper register that was not familiar to his sister. "Sir Simon is not immune. Why should he be immune to punishment?"

Dr. Grady turned away and began to climb the stairs.

"More like irony, or coincidence," he said roughly.

"Do you want me to come with you?" Justine asked.

The doctor did not turn around.

"No, you can come to your sister after I've had a look. I might need you."

Marc said, "Come along into the parlor. I've started a fire in the grate. It's already chilly at night."

Justine followed him to the parlor. Her mood of certainty, of confidence had disappeared. She was touched by Marc's distraction.

Justine sat in one of the faded armchairs. Marc began to pace up and down the small room.

"Perhaps you ought to pray," Justine said. "That's what I've been doing. I lit a candle and prayed to the Virgin for Camille's recovery."

Marc whirled about to face her.

"Do you think I haven't been praying?"

She realized that she had misjudged him. That he had probably been staying up most of the night (as he had done when their father lay dying) to pray. That was why he looked so ill.

"I didn't mean that," Justine said sulkily. She had been caught out, and suddenly her self-righteous attitude seemed foolish.

"I'm glad you've been praying," Marc said through his teeth. "Believe me, sister, I'm glad of it. But between us we've not reached the Virgin's ear. There wasn't any noticeable improvement this afternoon. Camille looked very ill. The . . . the eruption has closed her eyes. She isn't able to see out. Did you know that?"

"It was the pneumonia I worried about."

"No doubt you were right. But that poor girl cannot see. Can you imagine what that means? God knows how long the wretched disease will keep her eyes swollen and painful . . . it's the filthiest thing I've ever encountered."

Justine got up restlessly.

"I'm going to make some coffee. Perhaps the doctor would like some."

"As you wish."

"You ought to have some, Marc. You may be going out to see the father of that child. You really ought to eat."

"I don't want anything."

Two colored patches had shown up on his cheekbones. The soutane hung loosely on him, as if it had been borrowed from a larger man. His hands, clasping and unclasping behind his back, were all knuckles and tendons.

When Dr. Grady came into the parlor, Justine had just entered with a tray on which were set three cups and a heavy china pot of coffee. He accepted coffee. He looked even grimmer than he had earlier.

"How is she?" Marc demanded.

"The pneumonia is gradually improving. More of her left lung is clear, I judge. The cough isn't quite so tight. That's a good sign."

"Oh, then she *is* improving," Justine said hurriedly. She felt as if her prayers had already been answered. A great wave of relief swept through her chest and stomach. It was as if years of her life were dropping from her in that moment.

"With regard to the pneumonia, yes."

"There's something else?" Marc asked sharply. He made as if to grasp the doctor's sleeve, but Dr. Grady moved away from him and set down his cup.

"Father, there are unpleasant things a doctor has to do, has to say. As a priest, you must surely understand that."

"What is it?" Marc's voice was thin, cold.

"We must look at the thing squarely," Dr. Grady said. "There's no other way to deal with these things. We must face what we have to face."

"What is it we have to face?" Justine began impatiently. "If she's recovering from the pneumonia . . . you said she might die from that, but now . . ."

"The lesions have gone to her eyes. Some degree of conjunctivitis occurs in the severest cases of the disease. Keratitis, followed by ulceration and rapid destruction of the globe . . . sympathetic panophthalmitis of the other eye . . . may result in complete blindness."

For a moment nobody spoke. It was Marc who finally said it.

"*Blind?*"

The word hung in the air like an invisible but living thing. Dr. Grady nodded.

"For the rest of her life?" Justine asked.

"Yes, I'm afraid so. It's a little early to say for certain, but in these cases—and I saw many during the epidemic—damage is usually permanent. There's always the chance that in a year or two she might regain some of her sight, but it's a very small chance."

"Why?" Marc demanded, shaking his fist at the ceiling and staring upward as if he'd forgotten there were other people in the room. "Why? What has she done?"

"It isn't a question of that," Dr. Grady said tentatively.

"Perhaps it's a test of faith," Justine said. Her voice was surprisingly steady. She thought of her earlier prayers. She had asked for Camille's life and it had been spared. The notion of blindness had not occurred to her. But it could be interpreted that the Virgin had answered her specific prayer. "Yes, a test of faith."

"*You* can say that?"

Marc turned on her with the swiftness of a cat. His eyes, piercing and tortured, met hers and bored into her mind. Justine shrank back. He knew. Somehow he knew about her and Timothée. It did not much matter how he knew, but the fact was that he knew.

Marc left them so abruptly that neither of them had time to restrain him or to protest against his going.

In the drawer of the writing table, in the room he had fashioned as a retreat, Marc had long been keeping a revolver. Originally it had belonged to a renegade Irishman he'd once befriended down at Joe Beef's Canteen on Common Street, when Marc had been doing some early missionary work. (Joe Beef sometimes let clergymen in to talk to his customers if they were brave and if they had a brief enough message.) The Irishman had asked Marc to keep the gun for him until he came back to claim it, and since the man had been running from the police on a charge of petty theft, Marc had obliged. It was worth fifteen dollars (a small fortune to the fellow), and on that account alone was valuable enough to store in a safe place.

Marc had never fired the gun but he knew there was ammunition in it. As a boy he had gone hunting a few times with his father and Armand. Firing a shotgun a dozen times had provided the extent of his knowledge of firearms.

Now, he seized the weapon and stuffed it into the deep side pocket of his habit. A kind of mindless fury had taken hold of him as he rushed out into the night. He walked rapidly up to St. Jacques Street, and when he was outside the St. Lawrence Hall Hotel he engaged a hansom cab. The journey to Dorchester Street took hours, it seemed to him, and they were hours in which his mind swooped and dived through an endless parade of fantasies featuring a beautiful Camille destined to a truncated life and a slavering Sir Simon fingering gold coins while he crammed pitifully shabby immigrants into the holds of his ships.

When he reached Pride's Court, which he knew more from reputation than actual location (although the cab driver knew it well and assured him that there would be no difficulty in finding the house), he paid off the driver and mounted the steps without a second thought. The huge front doors were not yet locked for the night. He had no intention of ringing, but merely thrust his way in.

The great hall was now electrically lighted. The grandeur of it did nothing to stop his course. There was no sign of a servant in the front of the house, and he steered unerringly toward the back, where he assumed there would be some kind of sitting room.

What he would have done if Sir Simon had been out, he had never considered. And like a stage play, the plan unfolded without a single hitch. The smell of cigars lured him to the library. Brandishing the gun, he burst in upon Sir Simon. Sir Simon was caught so by surprise that he stood like a statue, lighted cigar halfway to his lips, staring at a handgun flourished by a wild-eyed priest.

"You devil!" Marc cried, knowing this man was Sir Simon even though he had never seen him before. "You've blinded my sister!"

Sir Simon was somewhat more familiar with guns than his assailant, and he was afraid not of the man but of the way he was so carelessly waving the weapon about, always assuming it was loaded. He had no idea who the priest was.

Marc's voice now resounded not only through the library but out into the hall as well. He was shouting a torrent of abuse, of accusations, even of curses. His priestly demeanor had fallen from him in the agony of his concern.

Sir Simon made a step toward him, to seize the gun, but Marc veered to one side.

"Stop waving that gun about!" Sir Simon cried. "You're a lunatic."

"A lunatic who's going to kill you, Mammon!"

This time, Marc leveled the gun directly at his target. Sir Simon raised his arm to protest. The shot blasted in the confined space like a giant explosion.

But Sir Simon did not fall. An arm had appeared from behind and had caught Marc about the neck, pulling him backward so that he almost fell to the floor, and the shot went high, shattering the plaster medallion in the center of the ceiling.

"Give me that," Fort said, grabbing the gun while Marc was still off balance, "and tell me what this is all about. For God's sake, man, you can't go around shooting at people like this. Are you crazy?"

"Thank God you heard the row," Sir Simon said. "I don't know what this is about."

"I'll tell you what it's about," Marc began, his voice still at shouting volume, although he was now disarmed. "It's about your immigrants! Crowding them into boats, trying to make every dollar you can out of human misery. Do you know how they arrive here? *Sick,* some of them. Without money, without a place to go or a means of getting there. I *know*. I work down at the docks trying to help them. And now you've brought in smallpox, because you don't stop to find out if your passengers are vaccinated . . ."

"I know about the smallpox," Sir Simon said in a dead tone. "I know all about it."

"No, you don't," Marc said, his voice only slightly lowered. "I've come to tell you that my sister, who worked like an angel there with the poor, is blind. *Blind*, do you hear?"

"Who are you?" Fort asked.

"Marc St. Amour."

"Honey's brother-in-law?"

"Yes, that's right."

"My own daughter-in-law has smallpox," Sir Simon said again in the heavy, dull voice.

"I know that. I handled the child who gave it to her. The child died this afternoon," Marc said. And then, remembering again his own agony, he shouted, "Camille is blind! Do you know what that means? A young girl? Blind?"

"Blind?" a voice shrieked from the open doorway. "I just wish *I* were blind! I wouldn't have to see this face!"

She stood in the doorway, a bizarre figure in a long white nightgown, her black hair matted to her temples in sweaty patches, her swollen red hands stretched out in a kind of pitiful entreaty. But it was her face that caught the eye and held it. A face without features; the nose and mouth indistinguishable from each other, the eyes mere slits, the skin a blur of yellowish, fevered lumps so tense with pus that they seemed about to explode in an obscene shower.

"Kill him!" Venetia cried into their stunned silence. "Kill him! He ruined my life! What good is being alive if I'm scarred and ugly? He wouldn't let them give out names so we could be vaccinated. He could have saved me, but he thinks money's more important. I wish I were dead. Shoot him! Oh, shoot him . . . shoot him . . . shoot him . . ."

She broke off in a hysterical sobbing. The day nurse appeared in the doorway behind her, breathing hard, as if she had run down the stairs.

"Come along, Mrs. Court. What *are* you doing out of bed?"

Venetia ignored her, but the nurse took one arm firmly and turned her around as if she were simply a naughty child who had said something rude to the adults when she ought to have been in bed asleep.

"Now, now, Mrs. Court," they heard the nurse saying as she took Venetia away, "we must stay in our bed. We mustn't come downstairs like that or we'll get pneumonia. You know what the doctor said."

Sir Simon slumped down on the nearest chair. He appeared to see no one. Fort walked to the commode where the brandy was kept. He poured a glass for his father, and, without a word, Sir Simon took it. But he set it down without tasting it, without even looking at it.

Marc noticed nothing of the other man's torment. He was scarcely aware of his surroundings. He covered his face with his hands and wondered if he would ever pray again as long as he lived.

CHAPTER FOURTEEN

The soft greens and pinks of Honey's sitting room seemed particularly soothing on this late September morning. The air outside the deep bay window was clear and two pigeons scuttled, in busy concentration, in and out of the eaves beneath the shelter of the turret roof. Honey, having finished her third cup of tea, glanced at the painting of the Italian villa over the mantel and dreamed fleetingly of a visit to the Mediterranean with Armand.

In that tranquil atmosphere, the first dull stir of pain in her lower back was so surprising it brought immediate alarm. When the next warning came a few minutes later she recognized the inevitable and felt relief. For some weeks she had been restless; she was anxious to solve the mystery of the baby's sex (Armand was certain it was a boy) and also to return to her own comfortable size and shape. From the first moment she begun to put on weight, Honey had felt trapped in her pregnancy.

After the third pain stabbed her, she felt confident enough to ring for Mrs. Wise, the midwife.

Mrs. Wise was just along the hall making a final check on preparations for the birth. One of the guest bedrooms, long unused, had been completely emptied and scoured and the heavy draperies taken down. A plain wooden bedstead had been substituted for the old four-poster with its dusty flowered curtains, extra kerosene lamps had been installed to augment the gaslight in the event that the birth occured at night, and medical supplies had been laid by. Honey was to have her baby and spend her lying-in period in the guest bedroom while the baby would be installed in the fourth-floor nursery and cared for by a new employee, Nurse Benoit. When Honey was judged fit by Dr. Lanctot, she would return to the apartment she shared with Armand.

Mrs. Wise was a capable person who had, by her own admission, delivered hundreds of fine babies. Honey had engaged her partly on this account and partly because she spoke English. The idea of being completely surrounded by French-speaking people during the birth made her distinctly nervous. True, her French had improved in the past months, but English made her more comfortable. (Secretly she longed to have her mother present, but knowing that was impossible, she had settled for Mrs. Wise.)

Mrs. Wise bustled in looking enormously important.

"Yes, Madame? You sent for me?"

"I think it's begun."

Since the entire household had been waiting breathlessly for this news for days, Honey felt they would all be immensely pleased that the drama was about to begin. Mrs. Wise looked smug. Birth was women's work, in her opinion, and she had long considered Dr. Lanctot superfluous, although she wouldn't have dared to voice such an opinion.

"You've had a pain? More than one?"

"Three during the past hour," Honey said.

"That's good. Though I've known the pains to start and then stop of their own accord. False labor, we call it. But if it keeps up, ma'am, then you'll have the baby by this evening, I'm sure. Now, you just watch the clock over there and tell me how long it is between pains. Later on, we'll notify Dr. Lanctot. There's no hurry."

"Is everything ready? Everything the doctor wants?"

"Oh, yes, everything is in order. It's a fine room for a birth, that much I know. And I've seen a great many."

"You must have had some interesting experiences," Honey said, for she knew that Mrs. Wise liked to recount stories about her past deliveries, especially in the houses of the rich and the important.

"Splendid babies, most of them. And it's funny, the way some people act. I remember a certain Mrs. Walbrook, a little blonde doll she was, skin like fine china, eyes as innocent as a baby's, and so tiny, you couldn't believe she'd ever be able to have a child. All through the birth, she didn't say a word. Never a murmur. Never a complaint. Most peculiar. Just lay there. It was uncanny. And the baby looked like an angel. Came as pale as can be, very sweet and quiet too."

"But that's fantastic!" Honey said, thinking she would never be the stuff of legend if she had to keep absolutely mum throughout the birth. She rather thought she might be quite noisy. "And what happened to the mother and the baby? Was it all wonderful?"

Mrs. Wise shook her head sadly.

"Not really. She died. Just lay there and died."

"Oh," Honey said inadequately. It was not the sort of ending she cared for, not at a time like this.

"Please tell Madame Dufours that I'm in labor, will you, Mrs. Wise?" Honey added.

Mrs. Wise gave her a knowing glance, a glance that conveyed to Honey that they *both* knew this was bearding the lion. Ever since Helene had appeared, to supervise the household during the confinement, she had stormed through the place like a sergeant major—bossing, criticizing, upbraiding, straightening out, attempting to organize. Justine would have been the natural choice, of course, but she was nursing Camille.

Camille's illness and subsequent blindness had cast a cloud over the St. Amour family. Even the excitement over the birth of a prospective heir to the family name was dampened somewhat. The tragedy, it seemed, was always in the wings of family conversations. Armand had been forced to tell Honey about Marc's attack on Sir Simon. For several days afterward, Marc had been depressed and had locked himself in his small retreat. Then he'd gone back to work at docks, but he was almost totally silent. Since he wasn't allowed to visit in Camille's room, he stood in the doorway each evening and talked with her quietly. But it appeared to take every ounce of will he had to go on living.

Mrs. Wise now said from the doorway, "Madame Dufours was downstairs early. She breakfasted with your husband and then she met with Cook. She complained that Cook is using too much butter."

"But Suzanne's so careful!" Honey exclaimed.

"Not only that," Mrs. Wise went on, her mouth firming up with disapproval, "Madame Dufours told Cook that number-two coffee is plenty good enough. Cook had been ordering Maricabo number one, as you well know, and everybody seemed quite satisfied." (Honey found Mrs. Wise to be a divine gossip, knowing everything worthwhile that went on in the servant's quarters.) "Cook was furious. She prides herself on her coffee, and even if I'm not a coffee drinker myself, much preferring tea, I do understand her point of view. Madame Dufours further stated that *your* insistence on buying imported marmalade was a criminal waste, and that any jams or jellies not made in one's own kitchen are not fit to eat, let alone pay those outrageous prices for, but that that was the English for you!"

Honey giggled.

"Oh, I do love Robertson's marmalade!" she protested. "It can't be a criminal waste if it cheers me, can it? Armand doesn't mind my little extravagances in the least."

Mrs. Wise was philosophical.

"You can't account for foreign tastes, ma'am, not that I wish to slight your in-laws. But some people are not brought up to the finer things, more's the pity."

Mrs. Wise was not unaware that Honey was Sir Simon Court's daughter and, in her eyes, Honey was far too good for the St. Amours. A tragic marriage, she secretly thought, though she didn't express this idea even to her friends, preferring to stress her patient's gentility and breeding. "Breeding," Mrs. Wise was fond of saying after she had described some particularly choice scene between the young patient and her French in-laws, "always tells."

"Still, we're lucky to have Madame Dufours to run the house," Honey said, thinking it best to smooth down Mrs. Wise's feathers before she braved Helene. "She's terribly busy in Ottawa, you know. Since her husband became a cabinet minister, she's been practically indispensable in the capital."

"I know that well enough, ma'am. She's told me over and over. Claims she's missing an important dinner with the Governor General tonight on your account. I heard all about it."

Mrs. Wise humphed herself out of the room. Honey weighed the very serious question of more tea. Ought she to have another cup before either Mrs. Wise or the doctor forbade it? Once she was in serious labor, as they called it, they'd probably refuse her anything at all. It would be a long and weary day.

Feeling a little wicked, she poured the tea.

* * *

By five o'clock in the afternoon, Honey was walking with grim determination up and down the corridor outside her apartment. Mrs. Wise wanted her to keep moving, and, in truth, she could not sit still, or lie still either. So it was much better to pace.

Armand arrived in time for tea. He brought with him an enormous load of toys—a boy's velocipede with one large wheel and two small back ones, a vermilion wheelbarrow, a shoofly rocking horse with gray body and black mane and tail, a brilliantly colored top, and a well-made model of a steamship with twin red funnels.

"Do you realize that all the toys are for a boy?" Honey demanded when he had deposited the gifts in the middle of the sitting-room carpet.

"*Ma cherie*, it will be a boy. Denys Paul, as we have agreed."

"But suppose she is a girl? The toys will be useless."

"Trust me, Miel, I have a positive feeling."

At this point, the now familiar giant vise that gripped her pelvis and pulled downward at regular intervals prevented Honey from making any reply. Armand managed to look temporarily distressed at her discomfort but quickly transferred his interest to the top and began to spin it.

"It isn't a very elegant collection, I'm afraid," Armand said apologetically, "but it was the best I could do today."

"*Plus qu'il n'en faut*," Honey said, dragging a common French phrase from some pigeonhole in her mind. Indeed, it *was* more than enough.

Armand was delighted with her reply.

"Even at this time, you try to speak French," he said. "Bravo!"

By nine o'clock Dr. Lanctot had closed the delivery-room door. He was now very much a presence in the house and even Mrs. Wise took orders from him quickly and with respect.

Armand had taken supper in his own apartment. Helene sat with him, telling numerous stories she had heard about childbirth, none of them particularly supportive. But since Helene had no personal experience, Armand paid little attention to her. Instead, he took comfort from a decanter of good French brandy.

Honey, lying on the hard white bed, felt as if her body was one large pain. Try as she would, she could not manage to suppress some groans. Dr. Lanctot said finally, "The baby is coming, Mrs. Wise. Very soon now. You can give her a few drops of ether."

The white pad on her face was not welcome and she did not like the sweetish smell of the gas. But after one or two whiffs she felt herself floating away from the pain-wracked body on the bed, disassociating from the two people who seemed to be doing things to her. There was pain, but it did not seem to matter quite so much. In this euphoric state, she almost liked the doctor, and Mrs. Wise seemed to be a plump angel.

"You can help, Madame, if you push down," Dr. Lanctot said over and over. Honey would have liked to cooperate but she did not feel that she could actually do anything except float. She did this very efficiently, but she didn't think that it would help either the doctor or the baby very much.

Then there was another whiff of ether. A smothering, putrescent perfume that carried with it memories of ancient deaths. It coincided with a tearing pain that reached through the fog about her. She swam through time as if it were molasses, in a seemingly endless marathon, until a shrill animal cry brought the event to a close. That, Honey thought logically, is that.

"A boy!" Mrs. Wise exclaimed. From her new vantage point of sweet reason, Honey wondered why Mrs. Wise was amazed, since there were, after all, only two choices.

"Take him, Mrs. Wise, and fix him up," Dr. Lanctot said.

"It's over," Honey whispered, sinking gratefully into the fog.

"Not quite, Madame," the doctor said hastily. "We have more work ahead. There is the afterbirth to come."

Honey became extremely petulant at this. Nobody had told her there was more, after that dramatic cry. Surely that was all that could be expected of her? Dr. Lanctot ignored her protests. The placenta must come and she must stay awake. Well, she had a son. Denys Paul. Armand would be pleased. But it was quite wicked of people to keep her ignorant of all the ghastly details of childbirth; what a shock to find it all so grossly undignified and totally boring. As she felt the winding sheet tighten around her stomach, Mrs. Wise pulling so tightly on it that she could scarcely breathe, she was glad the toys Armand had bought would be suitable.

Despite its limitations the first month of her confinement offered Honey considerable pleasure. It was nice to lie in bed, to be waited upon, fussed over, to have one's every whim considered. Mrs. Wise looked after her as if she were a Persian princess. She could assist with baby Denys if she wished—Nurse Benoit was quite amenable—or she could read or sew or stare out the window or walk around the hallways and consider future alterations in the gloomy unused guest rooms. She could, as a matter of fact, do anything she wished except take an active part in life.

Armand was attentive, but out a great deal. She understood this; he was deep in negotiations with his American partner, Max DeLeon, with the provincial government in Quebec City, and with the federal government in Ottawa. He brought her gifts of flowers, chocolate, and silk scarves. He gave her a gold locket with niches for four photographs. A place for himself and at least three children. If there were more, he pointed out, he would buy her another locket.

Helene now ruled the household completely. Sometimes the servants were on the verge of revolt (Mrs. Wise reported), but Helene always managed to quell the uprising before it disrupted the routine too much.

At the end of four weeks Honey was restless. Her energy was restored and so was her figure, and she wanted to walk out, to buy a bicycle, to ride in the surrey Armand had bought, to visit Emily, and, most of all, to meet with editor Beaulne about *Le Monde.* The baby was lovely, and she was delighted that Armand had a son, but it wasn't enough. She longed for the outside world.

On November the first, Dr. Lanctot gave Honey permission to return to her own apartment and to take her first walk outside the house. On the same day, Corbin came to collect Helene and take her back to Ottawa for the winter sessions of Parliament.

For her first meal in the dining room, Armand brought out champagne.

"Father put this down," Armand said, examining the

champagne bottle and then setting it back in its bucket. "Honey loves champagne. It's the first drink she ever took seriously."

"We must toast Helene for her help . . ." Honey began pleasantly, a feeling of relief making her smile. But Helene interrupted her little speech.

"Father had some good wine in the cellar," Helene said accusingly. "I was looking at it. And I must say, Armand, I think you ought to let Corbin have some of it."

"Now, really, Helene," Corbin said hastily, "there's no reason to get into a discussion about Armand's wine cellar."

"*Father*'s wine cellar," Helene corrected.

"The house and its contents were left to me," Armand reminded her.

"Nothing was said about the wine," Helene continued. "I'm sure Father overlooked that. There's no reason why all the wine should be yours, Armand. We are all children of the same family, with equal rights. It seems to me you've had more than your share of things, as it is."

"I've had exactly what the will stated," Armand said, getting up and opening the bottle of champagne with a pop that accented his rising anger, "and so have you. I notice you weren't so anxious to take on the debts Father left."

"A few pieces of furniture, a painting, and some jewelry belonging to Mother," Helene said with a sneer. "Very generous. While you get the house."

"You received your shares of the railroad. And they've increased in value. There were also shares in the telegraph company, a venture that will do very well, I think. There was that property in Griffintown. You received your share of that."

"But this house . . ." Helene began again. "Your wife doesn't even *like* the house."

"That has nothing to do with anything," Armand said, not denying her statement. "The will was quite clear. You've done very well, in my opinion."

"Helene, my dear, let's not spoil the evening," Corbin said placatingly, "over a few bottles of wine."

"Oh, it isn't just the wine," Helene said darkly.

"I assure you there are no treasures sewn up in the

furniture, no secret Rembrandts hanging on the walls," Armand said sarcastically.

He glared at his sister with distaste. She had always been domineering. He could remember her as a child, constantly giving orders, tyrannizing the nursery in a hundred little ways, slyly manipulating each and every governess who had ever set foot in the place. Often she had confiscated her sisters' belongings (she had always been acquisitive—one might even say greedy), and had kicked and pinched the boys whenever it suited her.

"Personally, I'm enjoying the wine," Honey said brightly in an effort to divert the quarrel so obviously brewing at the table. "Please pour some more, Armand, and let's stop talking about possessions."

"The nicest thing about champagne," Corbin said smoothly, "is that you can drink it all through the meal."

Helene looked cross, but subsided.

"You did say good-bye to Camille this afternoon?" Honey asked. "You visited their little house? How did you find her?"

"Much improved," Corbin said. "Trying to get around the house by herself. She's facing the whole problem with great strength."

"Marc is such a help to her," Helene said. "You know, the interesting thing is that her face isn't really badly scarred. Did you notice, Corbin? Mostly, the pockmarks are around her eyes, where the disease was worst. But the rest of her face . . ."

"The doctor says there is a chance that she might regain the sight of one eye," Corbin added. "And I think that's giving her courage."

"Marc is praying for her every day. He asked us to do the same, as of course we will. I shall light a candle for her when I get back to Ottawa, the very first time I'm in church. You, of course, can't very well do that," she added pointedly to Honey.

"Even Anglicans pray," Honey said sweetly.

"Very probably. But it isn't quite the same thing," Helene said sweepingly. "It doesn't have the same effect when you don't *believe* in miracles. In healing."

"Do you really think God makes such distinctions?" Honey asked her sister-in-law.

"The Church is the Church," Helene said, as if that closed the matter for all time.

"Anyway, it's wonderful that Camille has Marc to look after her," Corbin said, getting on with his food.

"And that Marc has *her*," Honey said.

They all looked at her strangely. But she had managed to surmount her early nervousness about the St. Amours *en famille*. They no longer frightened her as they once had. She felt quite capable of facing up to them.

"It's nice that some members of the family feel affection for each other," Armand remarked spitefully.

"A nice thing to say when I gave up weeks of my life to come here and manage your house. I ought to have stayed in Ottawa with my husband, where I belonged. But no, the duty of family called me. I gave up everything and came. And what do I get?" Helene demanded.

"Armand is being thoughtless. We do appreciate what you've done," Honey said, speaking in English, as she always did when she was under an emotional strain. The French words and phrases only came to her with great concentration. "I thank you for coming. I don't know what we'd have done without your help."

Armand's expression suggested that they might have done better if Helene had remained at home, but Helene wasn't looking at him, and so seemed mollified.

"Armand, I wish that sometime you could speak to Marc," Helene said portentously. "I wanted Corbin to do it, but since he isn't really part of the family—that is, not by *blood*—he feels it might be impertinent."

"Speak to Marc about what?"

"Well, about his career in the Church. He can't go on like this being a mendicant priest all his life. Living off some little pittance, not having his own parish. After all, the bishop is our uncle. And Marc ought to be moving upward in the Church, not just standing still. It's a disgrace, really. And with Corbin a cabinet minister, it makes it all that much more difficult."

"Where is the difficulty?" Armand demanded.

"I feel I can't really talk about Marc to anyone. How can I tell people my brother is a priest without a parish? I can't explain that he's out of favor with the bishop."

"Perhaps you ought to be out of favor with the bishop yourself, Helene," Armand said.

Helene paid no attention to this remark.

"There's simply no way I can explain that he works among those dreadful people. After all, if Marc hadn't forced Camille to help him down at the docks she wouldn't have caught smallpox in the first place. I'm not surprised he feels guilty . . ."

"Let Marc worry about his own guilt," her husband suggested. "It isn't your problem, my dear."

Armand added angrily, "He's already blaming Sir Simon. Surely you don't have to add to the torment by blaming Marc himself? He could have committed a murder if somebody hadn't stopped him. At least we owe Fort that much."

"But it's true! Camille oughtn't to have been working among those filthy, stupid people. Why do they let them in? You all know that what I say is true, but you're afraid to admit it."

"Perhaps your husband should be in charge of immigration instead of transport," Armand said.

"Marc is coming to terms with his problem," Corbin said quickly. "And I suggest that we let him try to solve it himself. That's what he's trained for, isn't it? A priest is trained to look at problems, to face them and to pray for help."

"Corbin's right." Armand's voice held a note of finality, and when he spoke again it was to change the subject. "Corbin, you know we need the railway charter into the asbestos mine at Thetford. Keep in mind that it's beneficial to that part of Quebec. We'd carry mail, and supplies, and encourage settlers. The mine will provide jobs. As Minister of Transportation you have plenty of influence with the other ministers."

"I have some influence, yes."

"You ought to give Corbin shares in the mine," Helene said, "if you want a favor from him."

"Helene, that would be bribery!" Armand said, half mocking.

"Don't tell me it isn't done," she said.

"Not quite so crudely," Armand allowed, "but there are ways around it. Anyway, that is something for us to discuss."

"Corbin has to think of himself. *You've* made a good thing out of it since Father died, Armand. It's due to your inheritance that you've managed to get your hands on so much money . . ."

"I beg your pardon? You have a short memory! I paid off the family debts and saved all your shares. I've bought a house for Marc and Camille. I've managed to retain the St. Amour name as some kind of force in this city."

"There's nothing wrong with my memory. If you hadn't made such a controversial marriage, Father might be alive."

"So you will forever bring that up?" Armand turned dark with anger. There was the guilt again. Would she never shut up about it? The champagne was suddenly tasteless.

"I think we'll discuss our business after dinner," Corbin said.

"Quite right. It's useless to try to discuss business in front of women," Armand agreed bitterly.

"I object to that," Honey protested. "You know perfectly well, Armand, that I intend to take over *Le Monde*'s management. Your friend Grande mismanaged it almost into the ground. Next year we may even be making money. I see nothing to justify what . . ."

"Arguments are a family habit," Corbin groaned. "Much worse than Parliament. It's always the same. Brothers and sisters—"

"Blame everything on the family," Helene cried, "when obviously the trouble lies in the selfishness of *one man*. Armand wants everything and gives nothing. I could have stayed in Ottawa all this time. My place was there, after all, and—"

"It occurs to me, Honey," Corbin said, cutting through his wife's sermon, "that we could make more use of your power in the newspaper. Now, with editorials, there are things you might say. We have bills coming up that need support, bills that will help the French Canadians."

"With all these loans from England, it's difficult to hear the French Canadian voice," Armand said.

"Yes, that's true. Now, Honey, you could throw some weight in the right direction. Get your man Beaulne to write an editorial or two along the lines I suggest. I'll supply some figures, some facts."

"I'm seriously thinking of trying my hand at editorials

myself," Honey said. "I'm just as clever as Beaulne, after all."

"One of the things we want to promote," Armand said, silently taking note of his wife's extraordinary statement, "is more French ownership, more French control over Quebec affairs and Quebec resources. You can take that line, Honey."

"Yes, I believe that," Honey agreed.

Armand looked pleased. Honey had definitely grown in the last few months. Changed from the childish attitude that "everything British is good" to a more open mind. He decided that as well as being beautiful she was really quite intelligent.

"I'll send you information," Corbin promised.

"Send it to me here," Honey said with conviction, "and I promise it will be my very first project at the paper."

"A woman with a new baby shouldn't need other interests," Helene said flatly. "You can do enough for your husband by entertaining and creating a peaceful atmosphere at home."

"I happen to have a brain," Honey said. "If you are suggesting that *I* stay away from business—"

"After all, Helene," Armand said, grinning, "the newspaper is hers. And she *is* a Court aren't you, *ma petite*?"

Honey glared at him. "Yes and no."

Armand and Corbin laughed.

"How like a woman," Corbin said.

"Anyway, what's wrong with a woman running a business? What can she possibly lose?" Honey demanded of the table at large.

"Her femininity," Helene said.

"*Mon Dieu* . . . I think there are many unfeminine women who stay at home," Armand said pointedly.

"I would be careful, Honey," Helene said, ignoring her brother's remark, "about how much time you devote to your paper."

"*Très bien, ça va*," Honey said placatingly.

Honey rose from the table to indicate that the meal was over. Already Armand had begun to tell Corbin about his latest meeting with his American partner, DeLeon.

"I want to explain some details," Armand was saying, "so you'll know the importance of the railroad and the mine. It can help us in other ways, you know."

"I want to hear. I also want to ask your advice about my own investments. This American partner of yours has so many connections, he must tell you what is good, eh?"

Honey listened to them as they walked to the library. It was going to be boring, sitting with Helene over coffee and listening to her stories about Ottawa, her meetings with important people, her household economies. The women went into the sitting room that Honey used for small, informal occasions. (She vowed once again to redecorate. The wallpaper was a musty brown and at least two generations old. She wondered if there was any possibility of enlarging the window and letting in more light.) Helene was launched, even as they sat down, into a recital of a particularly grand affair at which Prime Minister Laurier had been the guest of honor. Such a brilliant man, and so dashing, so well-tailored! Honey steeled herself for the long ordeal.

Honey sat at her dressing table, pulling a brush through her long, pale hair and staring hard at her reflection. Now that the house was wired for electricity, the lamps on the dressing table gave a less romantic image than the old gaslamps. She searched for flaws in her appearance. Had her looks suffered because of the baby? Would she suddenly turn into an old woman? After all, she was a mother.

Despite the revealing light, her hair hung as thickly as ever and she could detect no aging on her face, no fading of the sharp blue of her eyes, no thinning of the dark lashes, no unwelcome sag around the chin. As for her body, it was slim again. It had returned to its original shape with amazing rapidity, and there wasn't a trace of a bulge anywhere. She had deliberately put the white, half-sheer dressing gown over her nakedness, feeling that it might be an enticement to Armand.

Honey was apprehensive. For one thing, it was the first night she would spend with Armand since the birth of little Denys. The idea of sleeping with him again was disturbing. She would have liked to ask some older, more experienced woman about this problem. That, however, was impossible. There was nobody to ask. (She could not imagine discussing the problem with Justine, for example. They were far from friendly. Helene knew nothing about the situation, never having had children. She was not seeing her mother

sheer gown was provocative. For a moment, she expected him to sweep her up and carry her to the bed, but there was a hesitation, a dangerous gleam in his eye. Instead, he went into the dressing room and began to take off his clothes. His voice came to her from the shadows.

"My darling, I don't want to interfere, but I hope you won't put too much importance on your newspaper. You have an editor to do the work, you know. You can guide him of course, but anything more involving will keep you away from the house and the baby. And from me."

So, the confrontation was to be tonight, Honey thought desolately. There was to be no sidestepping the issue.

"I'll have plenty of time for all those things, Armand," she began calmly, determined to make her position clear without antagonizing him.

"There is so much to do here," Armand was saying. "You must keep control of the servants. There is the baby. I had hoped you would redecorate some of the rooms—"

"I intend to do that, darling. But the newspaper is so exciting."

From the doorway, where he stood in a dark blue dressing gown held loosely together at the waist so that much of his body was revealed, he said, "And the baby? Don't you love the baby?"

"Of course I love the baby! I wanted a son, darling, for *you*. It's quite natural. But we do have the nurse to look atfer Denys most of the time. I love to play with him and pick him up, but he isn't a whole life, after all."

"And the house?"

"I'm running the house, Armand. I ran it before Helene came, and with less difficulty, I might add. Whoever suggested I wouldn't run the house?"

"There's so much you could do with this house if you planned. It would take time, and money, you know."

"The newspaper will make money. Then I can help pay for the decoration."

She knew instantly that she had said the wrong thing. She felt him stiffen across the room. He walked toward her, and the coolness reached her before he did.

"Any alterations to the house will be paid for by me! Do you think I can't afford to keep my wife in the proper style? Do you think I need money from your damned newspaper?"

"I'm sorry, Armand. I didn't mean . . ." She had touched a nerve and she backed down quickly, eagerly. "Very well, darling, the newspaper money can be put back into the business. Into presses. Or something. I won't know until I find out more about it."

"Do as you wish about that," Armand said coldly.

"The newspaper is only an extra in my life, and the family, *your* family, is quite pleased. If Papa hadn't given it to me—"

"As a trick!"

"I know, and I'm furious. You know how angry I am about that, Armand."

"Why not give it back to him, then?"

For a brief moment, it seemed to Armand that he had struck on the solution to the whole problem. Getting rid of the damned newspaper was the easiest way out. His wife would then be back where she belonged, solidly entrenched in running the house, in being his hostess, in having his babies. That was the way it was meant to be.

"Give it *back*?"

Her voice was filled with disbelief. She stepped back, out of his reach. Such an idea was preposterous. She would do *anything* except give the newspaper back to her father. What a *coup* that would be for him. She had been used to prevent a family scandal from breaking into the open, and to protect the Court name, for the sake of Mama and even her brothers, she was willing to accept the sacrifice. But if she turned the paper back to her father he would then use it as a political tool for the Conservatives. No, never. How perfectly that would suit him! Then he would really have the better of her! She would never hand her father that sure, that simple triumph. Perhaps he had counted on it—she wouldn't put it past him. Well, let him count on something a little different: the Court spirit. She would turn *Le Monde* into a moneymaking, Liberal paper, just to spite him. Let him see that not everybody was his dupe.

"Why not give it back to him?" Armand repeated. But he knew the answer. It would show weakness in the St. Amours to do so. The paper could be used by the Liberals as a strong voice, a much-needed voice. Corbin was impressed with the family connection in Montreal's press. The entire St. Amour clan would think him a fool to force his wife to give back such a valuable property. He tried to think of the situation in terms of business.

"I'll never give Papa that satisfaction," Honey was saying, her temper rising at the memory of her father's trickery.

"And what about me?" Armand demanded, switching ground. "As your husband, I must come first. Honey, my darling, we married for love, have you forgotten? Because we couldn't live apart. We alienated your family, and as for mine . . . you gave up so very much, my dear. Is it all for nothing?"

His plea touched her heart as nothing else could possibly have done. She felt her own anger drain away and threw herself into his arms. They held each other tightly, her tears wet against his cheek.

"You're such a child," Armand murmured. "I love you, Honey, you must always believe that. You are a Court, and you will always be one to some extent, but I do love you. Do you believe me, *ma petite*?"

"Armand, let's not quarrel about the newspaper." She brushed her tears from her cheeks, and Armand kissed her eyelids, smiling down at her. "I know we can work this out. Let me try it my way, darling, please."

He helped her off with the dressing gown. In the candlelight she stood naked before him, looking almost like the child bride he had taken only a year before. She seemed untouched by motherhood. She was all pinks, and whites, and shadows. He tore off his own dressing gown as the old passion rose again. Honey's fears were forgotten as he devoured her, as they melted together, flesh into flesh. The world became Armand for her, and Armand became the world.

Yet later, as Armand lay sleeping beside her and she listened to the night creakings and sighings of the old house, Honey realized that they had brought about only a partial truce. Their love was alive, as tender and strong as ever, but she had had a vision of a boundless future. Out in the great world there were exciting challenges; for her, there would be more than decorating, having babies, or even making love. Her mind had been taken out for exercise, and now it was crying for an even stronger, even more vigorous program.

CHAPTER FIFTEEN

By the time they arrived on the south bank of the St. Lawrence, after rattling through the iron tunnel of Victoria Bridge, it was late afternoon. The train puffed to a stop at the wooden platform and small shelter; a cluster of men, horses, and sleighs surrounded it now, but soon it would be silent again. These were the welcomers, picking up passengers from Montreal and taking them to farms and villages along the back roads.

Sydney got out, struck by the sudden cold. The air hung white with frost. There was no sun. Blue shadows washed coldly over the snow banks along the rail line, and dark evergreens pressed close against fences. It might have been a waystop on the lonely Russian steppes instead of a mere train ride away from the city.

"There's Reeves with the cutter," Fort said, piling their bags together on the platform. He hailed a man in a red woolen toque, and Reeves hurried toward him across the snow. "Give me a hand with these, will you?" Fort said to Reeves. He introduced Sydney to the man, and then asked how Reeves and his wife were going to manage while Fort and Sydney stayed at the farm.

"I've made arrangements with Pierre Leduc. My wife is already at Pierre's place, and I'll drive out with him. He's over there getting some supplies off the train, sir." And he nodded toward another muffled figure, sharp against the white, horizonless landscape.

"That's good. Can't have you walking in this cold," Fort said. Reeves carried the bags to the cutter and Sydney followed Fort through the deep snow.

"Mrs. Reeves has everything ready, sir," Reeves said. "She's been preparing all day."

"Thank you, that's splendid."

The train whistle cut through the white air. Most of

the vehicles were beginning to pull away from the platform, and now the train gathered up its strength and chugged forward in clouds of steam.

Sydney had not known what to expect, but a honeymoon on an isolated farm was certainly not something she had imagined. It was unlike Fort, who was gregarious, she had always thought, to plan such a thing.

"Well, Pierre's ready. I see he's loaded up his sleigh." Reeves said. "I'll have to be going, Mr. Court."

"We'll be all right, Reeves. Renegade's getting restless anyway. He's feeling the cold." The horse's breath was smoky on the air. He shifted his feet, tramping down the snow around him.

Fort helped Sydney into the vehicle and Reeves tucked one of the buffalo robes over her knees. Huddling down inside her furs, Sydney felt surprisingly warm and protected; the long drive would delay the question of how Fort would behave toward her.

With a final wave to Reeves, Fort gave the reins a flick and they were off along the snowy, rutted road. Dark green and black trees closed in on either side.

Fort stared straight ahead across the horse's back, and silence, broken only by the animal's heavy breathing and the jingle of the brass harness, folded in around them.

There was a half smile on Fort's face, hidden by his frost-rimmed beard, as he wondered exactly what Sydney was thinking. He had deliberately *not* told her his plans for the honeymoon. How would she react to the isolation and the cold? All through the longish ceremony in Christ Church Cathedral, and later at the wedding breakfast at Pride's Court (a more modest affair than Lady Court had planned before Venetia's terrible illness), Sydney had remained aloof. So aloof, in fact, that Lady Court had taken Fort aside at one point and whispered that she simply did not understand his bride. An almost palpable aura of strangeness clung to her. What was it about the girl that made her so mysterious? Lady Court had puzzled over the question since her first meeting with her prospective daughter-in-law, but so far she hadn't managed to answer it.

Her son could not enlighten her. He was caught up in an unreasoning passion for Sydney, but he did not know himself what lay behind her rather fey expression. Was the mystery an impenetrable one? Perhaps. In any event it was a challenge.

Neither Fort nor Sydney said a word throughout the eight-mile drive to Caughnawaga. That, however, was usual with Sydney. Her remoteness was part of her charm. He could find a pretty woman any time who would lie down for him and with whom he could satisfy his sexual needs. This other thing, this puzzle within a puzzle, was worthy of study. And if, in the end, Sydney revealed nothing, the attempt would still have been worthwhile; it was unusual for a man to find in his marriage an absorbing hobby.

Actually, Sydney wasn't worried by Fort's strange choice for their honeymoon. She was curious, but not unduly concerned. It didn't matter particularly where they spent the honeymoon. Their agreement forbade him to approach her directly with his physical needs. There was to be no pressure, no force, and certainly no attempt at seduction. Still, she mused, as they jingled forward at a pleasant pace, this exile was something of a surprise.

When they rounded a large stand of sugar maples and the farmhouse appeared, she saw it to be a classic example of eighteenth-century Quebec architecture, built to withstand Indians and freezing temperatures with equal success. The square building was topped by a steep roof (originally designed to resist the weight of snow) slashed at intervals by high gables, and across the main façade rows of tall windows formed a soothing, balanced pattern. The house fronted on the great ice-covered river, and so it was the back of the house that Sydney saw first. There was a porch. Smoke rose straight up into the windless air from the two main chimneys. When the horse halted at the steps, the silence was complete. It was almost evening, and the snow was already turning dark blue.

Fort jumped eagerly to the ground. When he spoke, his voice was cheerful but touched with sarcasm.

"Here we are, my love. Now, isn't this a cozy little place for a honeymoon? We're all alone. Except for Renegade, here, and he hardly counts."

The horse swung his head around, recognizing his name. Fort assisted Sydney to the ground and then reached for their bags.

"Romantic, isn't it?" he insisted.

"Oh, *very*," Sydney said, and her voice betrayed neither fear nor excitement.

Fort opened the door. The rectangle of light revealed the kitchen and a large fireplace in which a fire was burning. The smell of cooking food met the cold outside air. Fort picked Sydney up and carried her inside, making a joke about her weight and the slipperiness of her fur coat. He didn't attempt to kiss her, however. Once the bags were inside, he went to stable the horse.

Sydney approached the fire before taking off her coat. Black iron pots were hanging from the fireplace hooks. Something smelled delicious; a stew, she thought. A kettle had been boiled and set aside to keep warm. She rubbed her hands in front of the flames for a while before taking off the bulky fur coat and hood. Although it was warm right around the fire, she knew the corners of the room would be chilly, so she pulled a chair close to the flames.

"Here, I'll put the kettle back on. I see Mrs. Reeves prepared everything for us, and even set the table," Fort said briskly, when he came back.

"Tea would be nice."

"Are you hungry?"

"Not really. But it smells good."

"I'll see that you're fed, don't worry. A sailor gets used to waiting on himself. I don't need servants."

She didn't reply.

They dined on stew and heavy brown bread and drank Beaujolais that Fort had brought along in his baggage. The blackness of the country night wrapped itself tightly around the house. In the intense quiet, each tremor of the old house, each shift of a distant frozen window frame, each fierce spit of burning pine logs was magnified into a miniature catastrophe.

"Mama doesn't know what to make of you," Fort offered over his third glass of wine.

Sydney was staring past him at the flames.

"I suppose she doesn't."

"I'm afraid she finds your charm a bit icy."

"That's because your family is so excitable," Sydney explained. "She reminds me—all of them remind me—of the countess."

"Good God, don't say that to Mama! She doesn't even know that people like Countess Leda exist."

Fort refilled Sydney's glass. They both crouched close to the fender like small children, absorbing as much of the heat as they could.

Fort tried again.

"I've put a bottle of hot water in your bed. And the fires in the bedrooms are set for the night. Coal holds for a long time."

She acknowledged this information with a slight nod. She was dreaming in the flames, seeing visions, Fort imagined. Dreaming what dreams? Seeing what strange parades, what elaborate fantasies?

"Don't you think Venetia's making a serious mistake? Not seeing anybody except for Charles and that odd little maid she's hired?"

"The maid is partially blind," Sydney said calmly.

"Good God, really?" Fort was astonished.

"That's why Venetia can bear to have her around. Josie can't see Venetia's face clearly."

"But that's crazy! She can't live like that forever. What if they have children?"

"I expect they'll have a child. She's pregnant."

"How do you know? Does Charles know?"

"Venetia asked to see me the night before we were married. She told me then. I suppose Charles does know by now."

"And what did she say? How did she behave?" He was curious. He hadn't seen Venetia since the night she had burst into the library and screamed accusations at his father.

"She was sitting in the dark. There was one candle, but it didn't directly light her face. Seen in the half-dark, she is still beautiful. That's the point of it, you see. I could well believe, having seen her like that, what people say about her fantastic beauty."

This was one of the longest speeches Fort had ever heard Sydney make. Shortly afterward, she drifted off to her own bedroom, leaving Fort to mull over what she'd said. Her footsteps echoed loudly in the silent passageway.

Lying night after night between unwarmable sheets, her toes curling hopefully around the warm stone bottle placed at the bottom of the bed in a vain attempt to make it habitable, Sydney fell into despair. It was, she suddenly realized one bleak midnight, a despair that she had kept at bay all her life by surrounding herself with people and movement. In those days, only her own voice had been still. Around her had been the sound of laughter, the rattle of carriage wheels on hard cobblestone, birdsong heard in rustic houses overflowing with old things long unused, the sweetness of madrigals sung by boys in distant towers, and the gravelly voices of lost men droning drunken ditties. Life had moved with the gritty talk of obscene painters and the boring gossip of desiccated aristocrats and sly cutthroats. Life had overflowed with easy women in vivid plumage, with a thousand stained corks popping, with arthritic fat men wheezing, scented youths cajoling, gold coins jingling, and unspeakable smoke sugaring the air with wild fantasies.

Now she was alone.

After the two-week honeymoon, on which Fort had behaved strictly according to their agreement, he had returned to Montreal and to his work. Sydney had been left on the farm. Such a possibility had never occurred to her. She had fully expected to return to Pride's Court until Fort could buy a house on the Mountain. He came to the farm on weekends, and while he remained with Sydney he was always polite. Certainly, she had no reason to criticize his behavior.

During the long, lonely days of the week she read novels or took walks through the deep snow where tracks had been laid. Sometimes she visited the barns. She had also taken up embroidery, and Fort brought her supplies from Montreal. Each weekend she expected him to invite her to return with him to Pride's Court, but each weekend he left her and took the train back alone. At night, in the forbidding cold of her bed, she listened to the wind and the constant shifting of the old house, or the ominous crack of brittle branches breaking under a coating of ice. And while she listened she thought about her life and what to do next.

The most obvious solution was to admit defeat and insist upon returning to the countess. Something held her back. Just what, she couldn't say . . . perhaps a fleeting sense of pride. And so she hesitated about making a decision.

Christmas was now only two weeks away and she wondered if Fort intended to take her to Pride's Court for the holiday season or if she would have to spend it with Reeves and his wife. She realized that she hadn't been a sparkling social success with the Courts before her marriage—actually, they had little in common—but she had not expected to be abandoned. Lady Court was inclined to be fussy and talkative, but she was harmless. As for Sir Simon, he was bossy and rude, but she had endured worse men in her time. No doubt the house would be busy with festivities of one kind or another, and if she were there, she could always escape for walks in the city streets, she could shop for clothes and gifts. There would be people to watch, people to whom she could listen even if she didn't talk much.

On the weekend immediately before Christmas, Fort was late arriving at the farm. For two hours, Sydney knew a chilling despair. What if he didn't come at all? What if she were left here indefinitely, with nobody to take an interest, nobody she could communicate with, no matter how briefly? Not that she and Fort were very close during his visits, but at least he was a fresh face, and he always brought her new books to read, and supplies for her sewing.

She had almost given up hope when she heard the sleigh outside the kitchen door. She ran to the window to peer out, afraid that only Reeves would be there, but Fort had come! She felt a rush of relief. A feeling she wouldn't have thought possible. And when Fort came in the door, stamping with cold, she smiled at him.

"Hello, my dear. How are you?" He threw off his raccoon coat and came close to the fire. "Have you got some mulled wine? I think that's what I need. We had some delays."

Since Mrs. Reeves was busy with dinner (cooking a goose, which always seemed to require extra fussing), Sydney got up to heat the wine herself. Fort looked pleased.

Sydney poured wine into a stone jug and set it inside the fender to warm. Then she procured two eggs, sugar, and cinnamon from Mrs. Reeves so that she could add them when the wine was hot.

"Well, what have you been doing all week?" Fort asked cheerfully, moving closer to the kitchen fire. "Working any more samplers?"

"No. I'm tired of embroidering."

"I see. I brought you a new book. You like Annie Swan's

writing, don't you? This one's called *A Foolish Marriage*."

She wondered if he were trying to be humorous.

"Thank you. I like her work well enough."

"Have to keep you amused," Fort said.

"How is Venetia?"

He was surprised at the question. Sydney seldom inquired after anybody at Pride's Court. He turned to look at her and decided she was paler than usual. Perhaps a little under the weather? Yet she didn't seem to be ill.

"Nothing changes with Venetia. I haven't seen her, but I understand from Charles that she spends her days in her apartment. Dr. Miles has been to see her and says that as far as her pregnancy goes, she is quite well."

Sydney began to mix the eggs and spices into the heated wine. Then she poured a cup for each of them.

"I suppose Pride's Court is ready for Christmas," Sydney ventured. "It must look very gay."

"Yes, Mama's doing the usual. Holly and pine branches. Ribbons. You know how women like to decorate at this season. She's disappointed that Venetia refuses to help. She thought she was gaining a daughter, and all she's gained is a ghost on the second floor."

"Poor Venetia."

"Papa keeps asking me if you're pregnant."

"How ridiculous."

Sydney gave him a cold look and sipped her wine. The tide of restlessness was rising inside so that she wanted to scream at Fort, to vent her hatred of this marriage and his behavior, to tell him how much she regretted having agreed to his proposition. Somehow, she held back her anger. For one thing, the two of them were only alone for a few minutes at a time. They used part of the kitchen as a parlor because it was the only area in the house that could be kept truly warm. And so Mrs. Reeves was always popping in and out from the pantry, or the scullery, setting the table, putting a pot above the fire, boiling a kettle of water. Even if they had been entirely alone, Sydney wasn't sure she wanted to discuss her frustration with Fort. Once she expressed the anger, the growing hatred, there would be no turning back. It seemed to her that, for her own sake, she must be sure what she wanted before she created a stormy scene.

After dinner, when Mrs. Reeves had finally disappeared

into the wing she shared with her husband, they sat for a while before the fire. Sydney had drunk rather more wine than usual. By now the ache of loneliness, the desire to confront Fort with her misery, was submerged by a feeling of simply not caring. She looked at her husband, sitting there happily in front of the fire, and thought that he really was very handsome. Such thick brown hair, such devil-may-care eyes, such a well-trimmed, luxurious beard.

The reflection made her angry.

"Im going to bed."

"Very well, my dear. Although I thought it was quite pleasant here by the fire. Perhaps another glass of wine?"

"No, thank you. I've had enough."

"As a matter of fact, I think I'll go to bed, too."

They walked together down the passageway toward the bedrooms that were their own private bailiwicks. At the door, Fort turned to look at her and bowed slightly.

"Good night, Sydney."

"Good night."

They entered their separate rooms. While she began to undress, Sydney heard Fort go back to the kitchen. He must have forgotten something, she thought. She was tempted to follow him, to have another drink of wine, perhaps. But she couldn't bring herself to do that. She poked up her own fire instead, thinking how much she despised getting into the empty bed. The sheets were always so incredibly cold. A stone water bottle was next to useless against such a formidable chill.

As she undressed, shivering, memories floated through her mind. Scenes from various houses in which she had stayed with Countess Leda, scenes from Paris studios where she had sat to numerous painters (God knows *they* had been cold enough in winter), scenes from English country houses where she had been the weekend guest of how many strange and wealthy landowners? Still, in those places there had always been the warmth of people. There wasn't this terrible starkness of the Quebec countryside. She might as well be living on a solitary star without other forms of life.

Suddenly she wanted to be close to somebody. To feel the touch of reassuring flesh, the unfamiliar simoom of a lover's breath, the insistent heartbeat of another desperate human being.

She stared about the bedroom angrily. Something impelled her to blow out the lamp so that only a patch of silver moonlight fell upon the carpet. Without thinking, she tore off the heavy nightgown and stood in the light, naked.

Looking down at herself she saw once again the slim pale figure so admired by the artists for whom she had modeled. But what good was it? What was the meaning of all that attention, those drawings, those compliments? She still wore the silver chain about her waist, thin and finely worked, that Beardsley had given her one night in London. It was the only line that disturbed the fluidity of her body. She unpinned her hair and let the long strands fall down over her breasts. The hair turned to silver in the moonlight.

Shivering, she made up her mind so abruptly that there was no time to sort out her feelings. She ran across the carpeted floor, flung open her door, and dashed across the passageway and into her husband's room. He had blown out his lamp before she came; she could not see his face. For a few long moments she paused in the patch of light that was identical to the one in her own bedroom. She knew he was looking at her.

She waited, trembling with cold and nervousness.

When he spoke, finally, his voice was thick and strange.

"So you've come, Sydney."

"Yes. I've come." Her voice was shaking and soft but it filled the silence as startlingly as a shriek.

"I'm here waiting," Fort said.

She walked slowly to the bed. He lifted the covers and drew her into the warmth. It was then that they both discovered the voluptuous secrets of her nature, the hidden excesses she had so long denied, the absolute surrender that was, in its own way, a sensuous triumph.

CHAPTER SIXTEEN

In the beginning, Lady Court was ecstatic at the news. Geoffrey and Mary were making their first pilgrimage to Pride's Court for Christmas in this most important year, 1899. She had not seen Geoffrey for two years, not since Queen Victoria's Diamond Jubilee, when she and Sir Simon had travelled to London to witness the elaborate celebrations. Geoffrey and Mary had come down from Liverpool, and they had all stayed at Claridge's.

Not that the Jubilee had been an unqualified success as far as Sir Simon was concerned. He had had reservations. After all, Donald Smith, the architect of the colossal Canadian Pacific Railroad had been raised to the peerage as Lord Strathcona and Mount Royal, and that swaggering upstart, Laurier, had been made *Sir* Wilfrid (a diminishment of all British titles, according to Sir Simon)—and meanwhile, Sir Simon had received no recognition whatsoever. The expansion of the Court Shipping Line to include New Orleans and Rio, the efficient handling of the Royal Mail contracts between Montreal and Liverpool (once the government had finally gotten round to awarding them), the growing influence of the Empire Bank under Sir Simon's direction, not to mention the flowering network of desperately needed local railroads in the Maritime Provinces, had all been sufficient reason for him to expect an accolade of some kind. There had been nothing.

Despite this gloomy vacuum in Court affairs, both Sir Simon and Lady Court had managed to enjoy the pomp and circumstance surrounding the old queen's anniversary. They had been completely united in their insatiable appetite for stiff formal dinners heavily attended by earls, elegant but endless palace receptions, and glittering, trumpet-flourishing reviews of properly polished troops. The Jubilee Procession through London's streets, wildly cheered by the enthusiastic masses, had included scarlet-coated Mounties and the Governor General's Body Guard Cavalry, along with Canadian Grenadiers and Highlanders, and colorful contingents from the outreaches of Australia, India, the British West Indies, Tonga, and, in fact, every spot on the globe that flew the British flag . . .

Lady Court's fervor toward her daughter-in-law cooled a little when she appeared in Montreal in a very advanced state of pregnancy. A baby born at Pride's Court would be welcome, since the event in itself could only enhance family ties; but such a risk! First the long, rough sea voyage from Liverpool to Halifax, and then the bone-rattling train trip, the doubtful hotels en route, the bitterly cold weather!

Mary Court didn't appear to notice either the inconvenience or the danger. She was so stolid and plain in both dress and manner, so lacking in sensibility and passion with regard to people and events, that she seemed frozen in a state of near paralysis. Lady Court wondered, in the deepest places of her mind, if Mary were, perhaps, slightly retarded.

"Mary, dear, you might have brought on a miscarriage!" Lady Court exclaimed when Mary removed her cape to reveal that she was, indeed, very far advanced in her pregnancy. "All that pitching about on the sea and then joggling about in those ghastly trains!"

Geoffrey and Mary had just arrived at Pride's Court from the dock. In the great hall, where the flurry of greetings took place, Mary handed her dark blue woolen cape to Grant in a listless manner.

"I never thought about it," she said, sitting on a bench in order to remove her winter boots.

Sir Simon was already grilling Geoffrey about the Court Line's affairs in Liverpool. Nanny Graham, who had been brought along from England, began to unbutton the coats of the two small children. Simon, aged two, and Mildred, barely a year old, stood transfixed by the awesome combination of the house's grandeur and the explosive conversations of their grandparents. Lady Court dutifully kissed Simon and Mildred and made a mental note to buy some good fur coats and caps for both of them. Mary's lack of taste obviously extended to the wardrobes of her children. Such a shame.

"You must be absolutely perishing for a decent tea," Lady Court went on determinedly. "I know how they make tea in some of those hotels. In tin pots."

Sir Simon, in the background, was bellowing to Geoffrey about a Scotch and soda, and quickly following that offer with a stern interrogation about the train service between Halifax and Digby.

"Tea would be nice," Mary said slowly, as if every word were a priceless gem and must be articulated perfectly. "Do you manage to import good tea here in Canada?"

"Marvelous, yes. We have quite a choice. I've been ordering golden tip orange broken Pekoe, but Cook feels it's rather expensive. However, I insist."

Mary handed her hat and gloves and boots to Grant with a deliberation worthy of pantomime.

"Cooks are all very difficult, I find. I'm always losing mine." Judging by her tone, Mary accepted this state of affairs with complete indifference. She had a marked style of pronunciation, a mixture of her Lancashire heritage modulated by a girls' school somewhere in the south of England.

"You must be starved! The food in most of those small hotels along the river is really tragic. I know, because Simon and I went to Halifax last year—he wanted to see for himself how the immigrants travel. It was quite terrifying. But Simon didn't mind. Anyway, I've got all the treats Geoffrey loves."

"You have some fruitcake, I hope?" Mary turned to watch rather absently over the two children while Nanny Graham at last found time to remove her own outer clothing and give it up to Grant. "I mix my own fruitcake at home. I think Geoff would eat it for breakfast."

Lady Court wondered just how long it took Mary to produce a batch of cakes and if they might not be in danger of going moldy in the lengthy process. Then she felt a little ashamed at her own impatience with Mary and checked herself immediately. It would be kind to say something complimentary. One always needed cheering after an exhausting journey, and even with a good nanny it could be positively beastly traveling with young children. But Mary's dark green gown (the color of muddied grass) and her dull brown hair pulled tightly into a twisted knot left even the imaginative Lady Court floundering for inspiration. Finally she said, "What a pretty pin! Wherever did you get it?"

Mary looked down at the topaz set in gold as if she had never seen it before and it must have appeared on her gown through some mysterious means.

"This? I think Geoff gave me that on my birthday. He often gives me jewelry, though I seldom wear it."

"Come along into the library, then," Lady Court said with strained brightness. "I've had them build a good fire. This weather is simply appalling. You must be cold. Did you bring plenty of warm things? If not, we must shop." Then she turned to Nanny Graham. "You can take the children straight up to the nursery to wash and have tea. Grant will see that the baggage gets up later on. You'll find Angela in the nursery—that's Mr. Charles Court's little girl. She's the same age as Simon. We enlarged the nursery just for this visit, you know, so I'm sure you'll find it comfortable. Ah, there's Angela's nanny now. Mrs. Bigelow, will you show Nanny Graham up to the nursery along with the children?"

Having efficiently disposed of the children, (although little Simon was dragging his heels up the grand staircase and staring at the chandeliers and portraits, while Mildred had to be carried), Lady Court led the way to the library. She rang for tea as soon as they were seated, but it seemed to her that something stronger was called for.

"Geoffrey, dear, I'll have a sherry when you're getting your father's Scotch. And perhaps Mary would like one, too."

"Yes, please. I'll have a sherry."

Lady Court looked across the room at Geoffrey with his reddish hair, pale blue eyes, and rangy figure, and marveled at how different he was from her other children. Listening to his rather thin, high-pitched voice as he described certain business transactions in the Liverpool office, she remembered only too well why she had not been sorry to see him go off to England in the first place. His absence had made her soften toward him, and even the time with him and Mary in London two years before had faded nicely into a pleasant episode. But now it all came back. After only a brief time with both of them, Lady Court realized that this visit would have its drawbacks.

Mary, she decided, after two dips into the Sandeman's,

had carried mere inertness to a distressing degree of eccentricity, and somehow had managed to turn a lack of style into utter drabness. Surely Geoffrey wasn't that stingy with money? What was the excuse? Well, she would find out. The girl had no life in her. She endured. That was about all. Even the rocketing Canadian trains hadn't caused her to complain. Of course, stoicism was good in its way, and truly British. But Mary definitely lacked any hint of yeast. Sir Simon had been absolutely right when (upon Geoffrey's engagement) he had suggested that Bootle, as a birthplace, was totally unsuitable. It was too late now, however; history could not be reshaped.

Regarding her daughter-in-law sitting heavily in the armchair by the fire, Lady Court decided that she must lean heavily on her role as grandmother. The children, after all, were tiny and still open to love, affection, and some enthusiasm for life. She must put her mind to it.

On her second sherry (and third sip of *that* one), Lady Court felt embattled. Mary was patiently describing the house Geoffrey had found for them in Liverpool, and so it was quite easy to let her thoughts wander to other matters. Somehow, through no fault of her own, Lady Court had collected an improbable set of in-laws. Her only daughter (and Honey was so beautiful, such fun compared with a girl like Mary) was solidly entrenched with a family of Hottentots, and she saw neither Honey nor her two children. Imagine, two grandchildren whom she never saw! So unfair, but what could one do with Catholics? It wasn't the Pope so much, or the strange practices, it was what they did to the children. That was the problem. She had always said so, and Simon had always said so. Then there was Charles's wife, who had seemed like a godsend, and suddenly had been tragically struck down so that she appeared to have gone a little mad. Attacking Sir Simon, and then turning into a figure of mystery. Really, it was too much to bear! Venetia did nothing but wander around a darkened apartment (it was lucky Pride's Court was so large and that Venetia and Charles could take over almost the whole of the west wing) dressed like some Arab peasant in a long cloak and scarves all over her head, attended by a maid whose eyesight was in grave doubt, and allowing poor Charles to visit her only by candlelight. Poor little Angela—who looked like an angel, which made her name so appropriate—was wide-eyed with confusion. It was all distressing. How could Angela be normal with a mother like that? It was up to her, Lydia Court, to see that the child was properly reared. That was her task. And then there was Fort's wife. She was pretty enough in an odd sort of way, but there was something about her that escaped one's analysis. She was hard to pin down. Where did she fit? Both Sydney and Fort were so vague about the girl's parents and her home life. At least Fort had had the sense to buy a house. Mellerstain. Fort was so sentimental. He had wanted to call it Mellerstain after a famous Scottish castle the owners of which had been extremely romantic and patriotic. Lady Grisell Baillie had done all sorts of marvelous brave things for her husband's family, and her marriage was a beautiful love affair, according to Fort . . . well, at least she only had to contend with Sydney on family occasions.

Lady Court now came out of her reverie with a sudden start.

"Mary, when is the baby due?" Lady Court sat bolt upright in alarm. How could she have been so nonchalant?

"Any time now," Mary said. "I really don't know."

"Good heavens, we must have Dr. Miles come over to-morrow. We must engage a midwife. We must choose a room for the birth and fix it up. There are a million things to do. Have you brought a layette?"

"No, I thought there would be time to shop here."

"I must make a list," Lady Court said, ringing once again for tea. "Where *is* tea? I must think about all the things there are to do. Why are they so late with tea?"

"It hasn't been very long," Mary said consolingly. "They must have a long way to come with the wagon in a house like this."

"Do you realize, Simon, that we are going to have another baby born right here in Pride's Court? Angela was born here, of course. Isn't that marvelous? We didn't have this house when I had my children, you know. We had a much smaller place. But it will be wonderful, Mary, to have a second grandchild born right here. Don't you think so, Simon?"

Sir Simon thought so. Mary smiled wanly. She was quite content to let Lady Court make all the arrangements for the birth. Thinking about it on the journey over, and remembering Lady Court in London, she had rather thought this would happen. She turned her head slowly toward the door as the tea wagon was rolled in. Persaps it *would* be pleasant to have a really good tea, for a change.

Fort and Sydney had joined the family for dinner on the second day of Geoffrey's visit. Lady Court, in full sail with her plans for the birth in Pride's Court, and having spent part of the day with her three grandchildren ("I took Simon and Angela on a tour of the house. Mildred's too young, of course, but I think Simon might just remember Pride's Court. He was so interested. He and Angela are getting along fine. Naturally, we didn't go near the west wing"), was anxious now to sit down with Sydney and try to draw her out. Mary, she felt, should go to bed directly after dinner.

Charles was in Ottawa, where he was engaged in still another Court maneuver to gain a charter for an East Coast railroad. He would arrive back in time for Christmas Day, although exactly at what time was uncertain. The trains were always balky in the intensely cold weather. Venetia was not present at dinner. She took all her meals in her apartment. When Charles was at home he sometimes drank his after-dinner brandy with her, but since she allowed only the most obscure lighting, he found it a trial.

Following dinner (a saddle of lamb, a favorite with all the Courts), Sir Simon retired with his two sons to the library for brandy and cigars. As usual, there was much to discuss.

Geoffrey went to the commode and brought out the brandy. It had become his task, since his arrival, to pour after dinner. Sir Simon was fond of allocating duties to specific people; ritual was his forte.

"Well, Geoffrey, business has picked up in England as well as here, then?"

"Noticeably," Geoffrey said from the other side of the room. There was the pleasant splash of liquid into glasses. "The depression seems to have lifted."

"Last year was a bad year," Sir Simon opined. "But, actually, the shipping wasn't hit too hard. Immigration to Canada has increased so much that our steerage was not only full, but overflowing. I don't think we could have packed in another body on any of our crossings."

"We need more ships," Fort said, "but I don't know how we can get any built within a year, do you? Even if we ordered two tomorrow——"

"That's it. That's what I want Geoff here to look into when he gets back. He's made some preliminary inquiries, of course, but we need solid figures."

"Oh, what's this? You didn't tell me," Fort said.

"I was discussing it with Geoff, and when Charles gets back we'll go into the scheme in more detail. Briefly put, it's the possibility of a merger with Stanton and Flood Lines."

"S and F? They're heavy on the African runs, aren't they?" Fort asked quickly. "Hurt by the trouble with the Boers, I expect. You want to watch that, Papa."

"The 'trouble,' as you call it, with the Boers won't last. We'll teach them a lesson and get out."

"Now, wait a minute. I know a little about the boats S and F run," Fort said, snipping at the end of his cigar and studying it with care, "and most of their ships are tubs. I wasn't sailing for all those years for nothing, you know. You find out things. You hear things even when you aren't directly involved. They've only about two sea-worthy ships on the whole line. S and F isn't my idea of a great bargain."

"What do you say, Geoffrey?" Sir Simon bellowed across the room.

Geoffrey came back carrying two snifters of brandy and presented one to his father and one to his brother.

"That's a slight exaggeration, Fort," he said. "They have at least four excellent ships."

"Check into it again," Fort said, "and you might find out differently. You don't want to believe everything people tell you. The only way a ship can be judged is by having a look at her. When can you get all the figures in?"

"Not till spring," Geoffrey said. "It's only a rumor now, you know. They haven't announced publicly that they want to sell, or be absorbed, or anything else."

"Find out when those ships will be in British ports and send somebody to look at them. That's my advice," Fort said.

"I fully intend to do that."

"When are you going back?" Fort asked.

"Sometime in February. Mary will have to stay here until she's well enough to travel. I wouldn't want to rush things and take any chances."

"You took a chance coming here when she was so close to having the baby," Fort observed. "Why all the caution suddenly?"

Geoffrey looked annoyed.

"I came because Papa wanted me to come."

Sir Simon, seeing a possible argument between his sons that would lead nowhere and would only waste time, interrupted.

"You knew we gave the *Royal Briton* to the Canadian government for a troop ship, Geoffrey?"

"Yes, you cabled me about that. I certainly approved of that, Papa. You know, recruiting in England was absolutely fierce as soon as word got out that Kruger had sent his ultimatum."

"It was the same here," Sir Simon said with great gusto. He was always pleased when there was a scrap, but on the clear understanding that the British would triumph, of course. "Just three weeks after the bloody Boers declared war on England, we had the Second Royal Regiment sailing out of Quebec City. And the second contingent wasn't far behind. They used *our* ship. I went to see them off. There were the Mounted Rifles and three batteries of artillery. A good effort, I thought, and there'll be more. Plenty more."

"What's the feeling among the French?" Geoffrey asked.

Sir Simon snorted. "Those Frenchies won't fight! Not for England. They're raising the usual stink about fighting wars for the glory of England and the British Empire. Tripe. All of it. But you know how it is with them."

"Some of them will go, surely," Geoffrey said.

"Ha. You won't see any of those St. Amours volunteering! The best they can do is attack an old man in his own house," Sir Simon said darkly. It was one of Sir Simon's talents that he could adopt any age; he could be young, middle-aged, or ancient according to the needs of the current situation. On this occasion, he saw himself as an old man. And yet, in truth, he had never fully recovered from the shock of finding a violent intruder in his own library, ready to shoot him almost without notice.

"I was thinking of volunteering myself," Fort said restlessly.

"What?" Sir Simon shouted in disbelief. "You're needed right here. Don't be an ass!"

"You can't blame a man for wanting to get into a war like this," Fort said defensively. He missed travel and foreign places sometimes, despite the comfort and the power his new life provided.

"Yes, I *can* blame a man like you! There are plenty of fellows to fight who can't do anything else. We need men like you to organize, to plan. Not that I don't admire your spirit. You wouldn't be a Court if you shied away from a fight."

"I was thinking of volunteering as well," Geoffrey put in hesitantly, "but it seemed to me, when I thought it over, Papa, that I could be of more use in an executive capacity."

"Good sound thinking! Get me another brandy, will you? And let me explain some of my ideas."

"Office work isn't exactly what I like best," Fort interjected hurriedly. But his father cut him off.

"Office work? It's a hell of a lot more than office work. I want you to get off company business for a little while, Fort. I practically promised the Prime Minister—not that I find dealing with a Frenchie *easy*, but he's quite reasonable about Canada's position in this war, you know—I practically promised him I'd put you on special assignment. I want to give another troop ship. You've got to find one of our ships that we can spare. And another thing. I want to give equipment. You'll have to consult the defense department about what they need and where we can buy the guns, the ammunition, and so forth. Arrange for delivery. A big job. I've got other ideas, too, all connected with the war effort. Fort, you're needed. I gave my word to the Prime Minister that I'd put you on this."

Geoffrey now interceded quickly, "We've got no ships to spare, Papa."

"Now, let's look at the thing carefully, Geoffrey."

"I mean it! Our spring bookings are filling every ship to capacity. Immigration from England to Canada has gone mad. Partly it's this gold rush in the Yukon. At least half of these immigrants think they're heading up north to make a fortune."

"If England needs help, we must help," Sir Simon said.

"We haven't got a ship to spare," Geoffrey said stubbornly. "I'm as patriotic as anybody—why shouldn't I be? I live there, and I'm closer to the thing than either of you, but we've got our commitments as far as passengers and mail are concerned. We can't afford to lose those mail contracts. And if the service isn't good, we'll do just that."

"Now, wait a minute, Geoffrey. We'd be slowing the service a little, perhaps, but only to help the government. How can they complain about that?"

"We had trouble *getting* the mail contracts last time. Have you forgotten?" Geoffrey persisted.

They were interrupted by Grant, who came in bearing a silver tray. There was a paper on it.

"For you, sir." He presented the tray to Sir Simon.

"What's this, eh? At this time of night?"

"A cable, sir. From the London office, I believe."

Sir Simon opened it. Without reading it, however, he said, "Thank you, Grant. If I need you, I'll ring later."

When Grant was gone, Sir Simon proceeded to read the cable. Then he swore violently.

"What did I tell you? Goddamnit, what did I tell you?"

"What is it, Papa? What's happened?" Fort asked.

"We've been defeated at Ladysmith! That's what's happened. Now do you see? The Boers have got the best of us!"

It was Geoffrey who said the correct thing, breaking the gloomy silence with a vow, no less impressive for the want of timbre in his voice, "By God, we'll find a ship! And to hell with the passengers!"

———

Charles arrived in Montreal on Christmas Eve. It was already getting dark when he engaged a hansom cab outside the railway station. He had the driver stop almost immediately on Peel Street, where, on earlier shopping expeditions, he'd found several gifts for Angela in a toy shop. The proprietor, a wizened but jolly little Frenchman with a wooden leg, imported dolls and toy soldiers from Germany, England, and France.

The night air was crisp and clear. Street lamps made sparkling pools of yellow light on the snow banks piled high along the edges of the road. It had stopped snow-

ing now, but several days accumulation made it difficult
for traffic to move. In the toy-store window there were
branches of green fir decorated with red ribbons, and a
light inside indicated that the owner was still waiting
for late customers. Charles hopped out of the cab.

"Just wait here, driver; I won't be long. I've got a bit of
last-minute shopping to do."

"Certainly, sir. Take your time, sir."

The driver was most agreeable. Of all nights in the
year, this was the one night he could count on a good tip
from a fare dressed like a gentleman. He was happy to
oblige.

Charles found several gifts that appealed to him.
Geoffrey's two small children were visiting, he knew, and
he would need something for them as well as for Angela. He bought a French doll with brown eyes, pink
cheeks, and real hair fashioned into dark brown ringlets.
She was dressed in pink satin with a finely pleated blouse,
a deeper pink satin sash nipping in a lace-edged skirt, and
her boots were real leather. The doll reminded him of
Angela, except that her eyes were cold and shallow while
Angela's were warm and mysterious. He also bought a
drum and a bugle, a wind-up toy in the form of a straw
carriage driven by two tiny dolls and pulled by a goat,
and a peacock run by clockwork. The peacock's tail
opened up and his head moved from side to side while a
music box inside him played a tinkling gavotte.

When Charles was in the cab once more, the driver urged
the horse slowly up the hill toward Dorchester Street and
Pride's Court.

The house was lighted from top to bottom. Lady Court,
Sir Simon, and Geoffrey were decorating a tall fir tree in
the drawing room with glass icicles and balls and candles
in metal holders. After he and Geoffrey shook hands,
Charles asked about Mary. He was surprised to find she
had retired early, until he learned she was pregnant.

"Imagine, Charles, we're going to have a baby here in
Pride's Court once again. I think it's marvelous!" Lady
Court enthused. "Are you exhausted from the journey,
dear? Your father has some eggnog over there. That's
just what you need."

Charles accepted the drink. What he really wanted to
know was whether or not he might go up to the nursery to

see Angela. His mother thought it would be perfectly all right on Christmas Eve, which was, after all, an exception. He decided to give the doll to her tonight. There would be plenty of other toys for all the children in the morning. Lady Court, knowing how much Charles worried about Angela and the scarce attention her mother paid to her, agreed.

"Do give it to her, Charles, but don't wake up Simon or Mildred," she cautioned. "Otherwise, we'll have to give them gifts tonight, too."

He was slightly distressed to find Angela awake, but then she was old beyond her years. It was difficult to realize that the child was only two. She spoke quite clearly in a pompous, but sweet, little voice.

"Oh, Daddy, I'm glad you're back."

He hugged her and presented the doll. She was suitably pleased and took it right into bed, although it was not a cuddly kind of toy. Charles always felt a sense of pain when he saw Angela again after an absence. She was so beautiful, with her huge gray eyes and her black hair already growing long and thick. The remains of her baby fat gave her plump cheeks and dimpled hands and, altogether, she was a most huggable child.

When Charles had first appeared at the nursery door, Mrs. Bigelow had retired to her own room, but she was soon back, hovering suggestively in the doorway.

"We mustn't wake the others," she said in a hoarse, conspiratorial whisper. "After all, Mr. Court, it's very late."

"Well, but it's Christmas," Charles argued.

"I know, but children get so excited . . ."

Angela confided to Charles, "Mildred steals my chocolates and cries a lot. Mrs. Big says she's only a baby."

Angela always referred to Mrs. Bigelow as "Mrs. Big." Although there were many words still too difficult for her she spoke clearly most of the time. She had an unusual memory, too, and could already recite the alphabet, "The House that Jack Built," and "The Twelve Days of Christmas."

When he left the child, Charles went directly to his apartment. He and Venetia occupied separate rooms connected by an adjoining door.

The old familiar weight pressed upon him as he opened

the door to his own sitting room. He wondered if tonight she might listen to his pleas to join the family. In spite of the pockmarks she was still, in his opinion, a handsome woman. People, he told her, would get used to her appearance and eventually forget about her skin. Her eyes were still large and striking, her nose straight, her chin neatly molded. However, instead of being warmly gray, her eyes held a look of tragedy that gave them an added dimension . . . but Venetia, who had once known perfection, wouldn't listen to his arguments. The pitted skin was constantly uppermost in her mind, and nothing seemed to erase her awareness of it.

As Charles opened the connecting door into Venetia's sitting room, the sense of hopelessness almost overwhelmed him. The room, as always, was a cocoon of semidarkness. There was only one candle lit. (Venetia refused, of course, to use the electric lights Sir Simon had installed.)

His eyes adjusted to the abrupt reduction of light, and he saw Venetia sitting by the fire. When he came in, she got up and stood by her chair, distant and waiting. She wore a long, loose robe, a style she had affected since her illness. The neck was high and the sleeves hung down over her fingers. All pockmarks, however, slight, must be covered at all times. The gown was black, another depressing feature of the costumes she wore now. The thick dark hair was pulled forward across her forehead and in front of her ears, covering as much of her face as possible.

"I didn't know you were back, Charles."

"Well, I've only been here a few minutes. I called in to see Angela. Then I came straight along here."

"Perhaps you'd like a drink?" She waved toward a decanter of wine and some glasses on a table by the fire. He nodded an acceptance.

"Will you join me?"

"Yes, please. Since it's Christmas," she said.

He poured out two glasses of wine. When he approached her, she stretched out her arm to take it, keeping him at a distance. She had graceful hands. Nowadays, he reflected, she used her hands a great deal. Every day she embroidered on a huge tapestry that she was designing. It measured at least fifteen feet in width and she was working it in rich colors, and in a pattern that appeared to spring spontaneously from her unhappy mind. From what he had seen, it was alive with mutated animals in questionable poses, exotic acacia leaves, voluptuous women with poppied heads and flowing robes occasionally parted to show limbs turned crippled, gigantic smothering orchids with cannibalistic tendencies—all wound, with fauns and snakes and lions and even bears, into a fretted and frightening fantasy. The frame stood in a bay window facing on a walled garden, and Venetia sat with her back to the light, working on the embroidery during the middle hours of each day. Only Josie, her partially blind maid, ever watched her at work. It was an arrangement that suited Venetia very well.

"I brought you a gift," Charles said now. He had set the velvet box down while he'd poured the wine. Now he picked it up again and offered it to his wife.

She was seated. She took the box and opened it, not hurriedly, but deliberately, as if nothing mattered. She held up the diamond necklace and turned it around so that she could see it more exactly.

"Lovely, just lovely," she said, sighing. "Where did you find it?"

"I ordered it from a jeweler on Notre Dame."

"He must have had it brought from Europe."

"Paris."

"Charles, you shouldn't have done that."

"I thought perhaps you'd wear it for dinner. For Christmas dinner with the family."

There, he'd said it. He'd brought the matter up again. He hoped it wouldn't make her angry. But he had to try. He felt he had to try again. How many times had he tried now? Countless times. Sometimes she didn't reply. Other times, she flew into a temper.

"I won't be down for dinner. Josie will bring me a tray up here. You know that I won't eat downstairs. And let all of them see me? How can I? Oh, Charles, you know I can't. Why do you keep asking me?"

"Because I want so much for you to be with us. To be part of the family. The way other people are. I want you to be my wife. Not to be locked up here like some fairytale character. What about *my* feelings?"

"I'm sorry. I haven't any defense, really."

"What about Angela? What is it doing to the child? She'll realize soon that her mother's different from other mothers. And then what? Do you want to warp her, too?"

"I couldn't face them."

"Let me fasten the necklace on you."

He moved over to the chair and stood beside her. He took the diamonds out of her hand and fiddled with the clasp, opening it.

"It's useless, Charles. Really it is. Don't you see? If I could go down and face them I would. But I can't do it."

Charles stared at the glittering stones for a moment.

"Let me put it on you. It should look beautiful on the black silk."

He thought that if she would wear the necklace it would be an encouraging sign.

"I'm selfish, I know," she murmured. But he heard no trace of regret in her voice.

"Venetia, believe me, I understand. I know what you've suffered. We all know how hard it is for you, and how unfair it is that you've had this sickness. But for me, will you put the necklace on? Please?"

"All right, Charles."

His hope surged. She stood up so that he could put the necklace on, and turned her face away from him. She lifted the mass of dark hair so that he could fasten the catch. As his fingers touched her neck, his face was so close to her own that even in that dim light he saw the deep pits in her cheek. A sick current of despair ran through his chest and he had to swallow hard to keep from showing his agony in his trembling fingers or shaking hand. Still, he knew she sensed his feeling; because he felt her stiffen. He closed the fastening as she began to move away, pulling her shoulders from his touch.

"Turn around so I can see," Charles said. He had stopped breathing. He felt that he was close now to bringing her around to his point of view. His hands were damp. "I deserve that much, surely!"

She turned then. He saw the diamonds flashing on her breast. The black silk clung to her shape so that the necklace sat boldly on the rounded flesh and accentuated it.

"Look, then!" she cried, as he stared at her. "Look, Charles!"

Even in that small area of candlelight, her face was cratered, cruelly roughened with pocks that tore through the white planes of her cheeks, across the wide forehead and the perfect chin. She pulled her hair back with both hands.

"See, Charles? Take a good look now, and know why I will *never* come down to dinner. Not tomorrow, and not ever. Do you think I could live with pity and curiosity? I know what they think. How sad. How tragic. She was so beautiful. Yes, I was beautiful, Charles. I can't forget that. Some people said I was the most beautiful woman they had ever seen. I remember what it was like to have complete adoration, to see surprise and lust in men's faces and envy in women's faces when I came into a room. No matter where I went, there was no woman as beautiful as I. Look at me, Charles. This is what it cost me to marry you, what it cost me to come to this country on your father's ship, what it cost me to be ruled by your father's obsession with money!"

His own temper broke then. He grabbed her and yanked her toward him. The combination of her devastated beauty and his own frustration and need was too much. His hands dug into her shoulders and she tried to push him off.

"I hate your father!" she cried, pounding at his chest.

But he was the stronger, and he tore at the silk gown and the satin underwear, ripping it into ugly shreds until she stood in nothing but the diamonds. His eyes absorbed the delicious white curves of her body, the well-shaped breasts supporting so gloriously the shimmering jewels, the light roundness of her stomach, the dark place below it, the stem of her long legs. He pushed her down on the carpet and threw himself on top of her. She was a statue beneath him. A corpse. A stone angel off some long-dead ancestor's tomb. He was penetrating a dead thing. When he got up again, weeping and sick, he knew it was the last time he would ever make love to Venetia.

━━━━━━

Bishop Lavergne awaited his nephew in his private study. It was a room that somehow combined richness with austerity, a sense of work with a mood of meditation. The bookshelves were crammed with volumes the bindings of which did not match and were slightly worn so that they seemed to have been individually chosen and read with great care. The desk was practical in design, being rectangular and large, but at the same time fashioned of delicate satinwood inlaid with floral patterns. Behind the desk, two tall, narrow windows exposed bare black poplars laced valiantly against the possibility of a high wind. They grew against a stone wall that had been constructed for eternity by careful workmen. Inside the room, browns, beiges, plum, and maroon were mixed with touches of gold, and fragrant pipe smoke blended neatly with burning cedar logs to seduce the senses. The total effect was one of thoughtful elegance and muted authority.

The bishop wore his purple soutane. It was a hue that flattered his skin, and its suggestion of royalty was not lost on him. He folded his hands comfortably over his stomach as the study door opened and Marc was ushered in.

After formal greetings, Marc sat down and waited for his uncle to speak. He had been summoned not as a family member, but on the business of the Church. That much he knew. But exactly what his Uncle Eustache had to say, he could not be sure.

"And how is Camille?" the bishop inquired in his smooth voice. "I understand there is some hope that she might regain partial sight?"

"We still hope so, yes. The doctors say that if it is to happen, it ought to happen soon. She might regain the use of one eye."

"I trust you are putting your faith in prayer, my son."

"Oh yes, my Lord. You can depend upon that."

"Now, Marc, you may relax the formalities," Bishop Lavergne said. "We've been through all that. I am, after all, your uncle."

Marc was only too glad to do so. He had known the bishop all his life, and when Marc was a child and the bishop only a priest, it had always been natural to call him Uncle Eustache. Now it was sometimes difficult to retain the proper attitude.

"Yes, Uncle Eustache. Thank you. Well, the fact is, I spend two hours every morning praying that Camille will have her sight again. I know that she prays constantly for it. She's quite brave, however. She can walk about the house now without help, and when I take her out on the street she manages fairly well."

"I'm glad to hear that's she's bearing up so well. That she hasn't lost her faith."

"No, she certainly hasn't lost her faith."

"Marc, I've been thinking about your future. When I have time from my duties, I do think of the family. I think of my dead sister and her children, and I pray for them. It occurs to me that what you are doing is . . . while I don't doubt the usefulness of it, the necessity of such work being done, you aren't using your full capacities. What do you think?"

"I'd agree with that."

"I took note of the fact that Armand provided you with a house. Armand is doing well, I believe, in business?"

"He's taken hold of the family businesses and he appears to be doing very well indeed. Everything he's tackled has been a success. At least, that's what I gather."

The bishop was silent for a moment. He swung about in his leather chair and stared out at the pale afternoon sky, at the black etching of trees and the gray of the stone fence. His gray hair was growing thin on top but the small cap he wore over it covered some of the baldness. He was five years younger than his brother-in-law Paul, Marc's father, would have been, and was only now approaching the age of sixty. When he turned around again to face his nephew, he put his hands together to form a steeple—a contemplative gesture.

"I am thinking of putting you into a parish again," he said.

Marc had expected something of the kind. He had been punished for his rebellion, that much was understood, and it was only a matter of time before he would be taken back into the fold. However, he did not propose to be sent out into the hinterlands, away from his work and friends and relatives in Montreal. He hoped that his uncle wasn't going to suggest such a thing.

Bishop Lavergne continued, "There is a parish open now, in the city."

"I'd heard that. Father Belliveau is retiring?"

"Yes, that's right. Bonsecours is the parish I had in mind. As it happens, it's right in the area where you've been doing your work, Marc, and you know a great deal about the problems there. You could, to some extent, continue your work with the immigrants, although you might need an assistant. I want to talk to you about some kind of modest organization that might be responsible for that help."

"Believe me, Uncle Eustache, it's needed," Marc said fervently. "The people coming in often need help. They're quite confused, and they have very little money or goods to get started with."

"Guidance," said the bishop softly, "is what they need. And I know you've been doing your best."

Marc wondered what inquiries his uncle had made about his work. In the long run, though, it didn't matter. If he could stay in a parish in Montreal and still do some of the work down at the docks and in Griffintown, he would continue to feel useful.

"There is one aspect of this that we must discuss, however," Bishop Lavergne went on, "and I think we can speak openly about it?"

Marc, knowing something of his uncle's methods, knew that they would not speak *too* openly about it. They would speak around it.

"Naturally we can," Marc said. "What did you have in mind, Uncle Eustache?"

The bishop fenced a little.

"In the last federal election, you and I had a difference of opinion. There is no need to go into details, but you disobeyed the Church. Your advice to your parishioners was not what we had in mind."

Marc waited. There was nothing he could say to that.

"Now, while the Church hasn't taken a notably different stand about politics since that time, we do feel that perhaps we could be a little more—what shall I say?—subtle in our approach. You understand that we haven't changed our minds about what is good for the people. We were right before and we are right now. You have only to look at Laurier's immigration policy to see that! You know what he's about, don't you? All these Protestants and atheists and Jews coming in upsets the balance between the Roman Catholic and the Protestant populations. And Laurier is himself a member of the Church. He errs, my son, he errs." The bishop shook his head.

"I understand that," Marc said noncommittally.

"In any event, if you were to have a parish, Marc, I

would expect you to follow the lead of the bishops in this respect. We will no longer be issuing directives about the political alliances of our flock. Something less obvious is required in these times. There will be a federal election sometime in the New Year. And then we will have to find ways to show people—without preaching at them, without giving them commands—the way they ought to go. That will be our policy. And if that's *our* policy, I would expect my priests to adhere to that."

"I couldn't say that I've actually changed my mind about the Liberal party," Marc said.

"Ah, no. You are too young for that! Too inexperienced! But if *we* don't preach Conservatism, at least *you* would not feel obliged to preach Liberalism?"

"You mean, silence?"

"Hmmm . . . in a way. There is plenty to talk to your people about. Plenty of problems not directly connected with politics. I should think the problems are legion. I should think that the moral questions for people in that parish are abundant."

"They certainly have problems," Marc allowed.

"Then do we understand each other?"

"What you want from me, in exchange for the parish, is my promise not to use the pulpit for the cause of Liberalism?"

"You could put it that way."

The bishop looked a little pained. He much preferred to speak in a roundabout way.

"I'm not unhappy in the work I'm doing now," Marc said.

"But you aren't going anywhere as far as the Church is concerned. You're on a siding, an engine that has been shunted aside while the main express goes through."

Marc had the distinct feeling that Helene must have been talking to Uncle Eustache about his lack of status. He wasn't sure that he really wanted to go anywhere. His ambitions within the Church were minimal. Helping people, trying to understand what it was God had in mind, meditating on the meaning of life, those were things he wanted to do. Being in a position of real authority, like Uncle Eustache, was something else. He wasn't at all sure he wanted that even if it were someday offered to him.

"I suppose I'm not going anywhere in one sense," Marc allowed, "but on the other hand I'm doing useful work."

"I don't doubt it for a moment." The bishop raised his well-kept hands in protest. "Marc, I don't question it!"

"I suppose you want to make this decision soon? Father Belliveau is retiring in a short time?"

"He's anxious to be able to retire, yes. We must find a replacement before he does so."

"I see."

There was silence in the study. Marc's eyes wandered around the room, taking in the details, the comfort in which his uncle lived. It was very pleasant, there was no doubt about that. Would such a setting encourage noble thoughts? Godly thoughts? Would he read more, think more clearly, hear the commands of God? Was this the aim of his life, to someday succeed to his uncle's mantle?

"Naturally, there is a higher salary connected with the parish than the one you're now getting. That was only a . . . stopgap. I didn't want to defrock you, you know. But it was necessary to do something after the way you behaved." Bishop Lavergne allowed himself a sigh.

"Money isn't that important, in the circumstances," Marc said.

"And you'd have an assistant," the bishop went on smoothly. "Therefore you ought to be able to accomplish more worthwhile work."

"You want an answer from me today, is that it?"

"There's no reason why not. It's quite clear, isn't it? I'll have to look around for someone else if you refuse."

There was nothing unreasonable about what his uncle was saying. After all, he didn't have to tell his people to turn into Conservatives, he only had to refrain from selling reached his plateau in the affairs of the Church, had his mind recently about Sir Wilfrid Laurier's policies. It was one thing to believe in Laurier's much-touted "Quebec for French Canadians" policy. It was another to watch in operation an open-handed immigration policy that seemed to contradict the French Canadian interest and also to bring some degree of discomfort and insecurity to the immigrants themselves. Some were equipped to come to a new land and begin again, but many others were only a handicap to progress and needed a great deal of assistance.

That assistance was organized by neither the Church nor the State. What help existed was all haphazard and vague.

Bishop Lavergne waited quietly. He could be watchful and calm when it suited his needs. A man at his age, having reached his plateau in the affairs of the Church, had learned many things about life. One of the most valuable was patience. Bishop Lavergne, exercising this particular talent, thought he might preach a sermon on that subject soon. Patience. Perhaps the greatest of all virtues, if you thought of it in the long view. Yes, over a lifetime, patience might be the most valuable trait a man could cultivate.

After some minutes, Marc said, "Perhaps you're right, Uncle Eustache. It seems to me that this may be God's will."

Bishop Lavergne smiled at his nephew.

"At this time of day—" and he looked out at the darkening sky—"I often think a brandy is a good thing. Would you join me?"

Marc wasn't sure whether he had made progress in the conduct of his affairs or whether he had capitulated. He drank the brandy and listened to his Uncle Eustache discuss some of the affairs of the Church. Wisely or not, he had committed himself, he decided, and he would make the best of what life offered him. He wondered, as he sipped the expensive liqueur, what Camille would say when he told her.

CHAPTER SEVENTEEN

The children had been allowed to stay downstairs after tea so that they could watch their parents' departure for the dinner and grand ball being held by the City of Montreal as part of the celebrations for the new century. Justine and Laurent had come in from St. Cloud, and Helene and Corbin had come down from Ottawa just for the occasion.

In the drawing room, Justine's three children stood in a curious little group beside the fireplace, wide-eyed and watchful. On the other side of the fireplace, Honey's son, Denys, sat on a footstool by himself. (His brother, Michel, was only a year old and had been put to bed because he was considered too young to understand the significance of this night.) It was a rare evening. There wouldn't be another like it for a hundred years.

At the age of nine, Nicolette was tiny and dark with a short nose, playful mouth, and small, coal-colored eyes. This afternoon Justine had ordered her dressed in dark blue velvet—a high collared, deep-yoked creation with stiff frilled shoulders and a broad sash. Beside her, Mathieu looked uncomfortable in a striped cambric sailor blouse and knee-length navy velvet pants. He was stocky and dark like his father, without any of his sister's gamin look, yet on close inspection they would be recognized as brother and sister.

There had been an argument earlier in the day over whether or not Beau should be allowed to stay down with the others. Justine had finally ruled that he might as well be allowed to take part, since he would only fret upstairs if he knew the other children were involved in some excitement. Even at the age of two, Timothée Fitzgerald's son looked different from his half-brother and sister. He was slight of build and had a gypsy's face—narrow, with green, tilted eyes under black, unruly curls. His usual expression was introspective and hinted at some secret knowledge. The seriousness of his look often made the adults around him confused and nervous. He was a difficult child to handle, yet he was clearly his mother's favorite.

All three women were brilliantly dressed for the ball, and each wore carefully selected pieces of jewelry. Justine wore brown silk with gold braid around the collar and cuffs. Helene was in black moire with a deeply flounced skirt that rustled when she walked. Honey had chosen blue satin, which accentuated the blue of her eyes—a gown with a new-fashioned, narrower skirt and a decolletage that was intriguing without being risqué. She wore the antique brooch Armand had given her on their fourth wedding anniversary, a large sapphire surrounded by diamond tears.

Huge fur wraps were brought (muskrat, seal, and fox), for it was bitterly cold and they needed to be warmly clothed even for the short ride to the Windsor Hotel on Peel Street.

When the women bent over to kiss each child in turn, waves of heavy scent, attar of roses or patchouli, swept over the upturned faces. The sensuous brush of silk, the sparkle of diamonds, would one day be fragments of memory. Honey was pleased with the whole mood of expectation. She wanted each child to remember this night as a milestone in history.

The Windsor Hotel, facing the snow-trees of Dominion Square, was ablaze with light. Hansom cabs, carioles, and "drags" (more modest sleighs but quite efficient) dropped befurred ladies, their heads swathed in pastel scarves, and men in tails and tall black hats at the foot of the hotel steps. Scarlet-liveried doormen assisted young beauties and tottering dowagers with equal concern across the slippery sidewalk. The lobby was already a seething crush of Montreal society. Nothing short of complete prostration would have kept anyone from attending, so there were far more guests than could be comfortably accommodated.

Just past the large lobby lay Peacock Alley with its glittering chandeliers and antique velvet settees, a plush avenue between the Versailles ballroom on the right, where couples were already swirling about to a waltz, and elegant Windsor Hall on the left, where later they would dine on oyster-stuffed turkey and French champagne.

Honey's party proceeded at once to a suite on the first floor. Having decided to mix business with pleasure by coming up to Montreal for the New Year's celebrations, Max DeLeon had first tried to book the vice-regal suite and, finding that reserved, had taken the only apartment that was better—the royal suite.

Max opened the door to them himself. Armand performed the introductions (he and Honey were the only ones who had met the DeLeons before), and they all had a glass of champagne. It was difficult for Honey to keep from staring at Velma DeLeon, whom she had not seen since the trip to New York, several years before. The woman was unquestionably vulgar; she looked as if she were made up for a stage show. Towering above her husband, she was molded into an incredible hourglass of tight crimson velvet with a long train and a low-cut neck. A row of round, pink silk roses framed her bare shoulders and led the eye to the great rolling cleavage. Yet she had refrained from wearing the flashing necklace that should have been her obvious choice; instead, a large, egg-shaped diamond sat between two of the roses in the center of her bosom. Her reddish hair was pulled on top of her head in a plump circular pillow stuck through rather dramatically with a diamond spear. Holding aloft her glass of wine, Velma bestowed a smile upon them.

A faint ripple spread over the group like a warm, tropical breeze. Her teeth were not quite perfect, but the lack of symmetry (and it was only slight) gave Velma's smile an added power. Her lips were generous and her eyes, which had up to this point attracted no attention, became suddenly compelling. She swept them all into her gaze and held them there spellbound while Max raised his glass.

"Happy New Year! To all of uz!"

The men talked of railroads and mines, and the women made small talk. Velma's voice was like hot fudge, and all her conversation appeared to revolve around visits she'd made earlier to the Continent or to the Middle East and Asia. Helene's reference to the Governor General sounded dry and mundane compared with Velma's oblique hints about the habits of maharajahs and princes of the blood. After two glasses of champagne, Honey was relieved to go downstairs to the ballroom, where the waltz was the most popular dance of the evening. She had almost forgotten that Velma DeLeon could be so overpowering.

Fort was the first she saw. He was dancing with his wife, and as they passed he said, "We'll talk later, after the dance." She looked at Sydney (this was her first opportunity to see Fort's wife) and found her enigmatic. Charles, she noticed, was alone, watching the dancers. Somewhere she would see her father. That was inevitable And her mother, too.

It wasn't until dinner that she saw her parents. Sir Simon and Lady Court were at the head table (where, Honey could well imagine, Sir Simon was regaling his neighbor with his usual reminiscences about the time Mark Twain had been there as a guest speaker and Sir Simon had made him laugh), and they did not seem to see her. But she knew that her mother was nearsighted.

The courses flowed on endlessly—turkey, great helpings of beef, ham, and mutton; glasses of hock, claret cup, and Moselle; and always, always champagne. It seemed the dinner would never end. Afterwards, the men stayed in Windsor Hall for cigars and brandy, and the women left to freshen up.

Lady Court was sitting on a tall-backed antique chair in Peacock Alley. Honey saw that her mother had aged a great deal in four years and that she was slightly hunched in the heavy blue lace gown. When their eyes met, her mothers' bright blue ones were somehow faded. Honey worked her way through the groups of chattering women.

"Mama!"

Lady Court seemed to draw in a deep breath. Then she held up both hands to take one of Honey's, and pressed it.

"My dear, you look so well."

"So do you, Mama." It was a lie, but a pardonable one.

"I have some problems," Lady Court murmured, her face turned toward her daughter's, her eyes searching the lovely face for signs of something she could not have identified. Perhaps regret. "I have trouble with my hip."

"I'm sorry."

"How are . . . my grandchildren?"

"I wish you could see them. Mama, we can't talk here, it's too noisy, too crowded." Honey could see that already a few of the women around them were looking with curiosity at this meeting of mother and daughter. She felt exposed.

"That's true. Well, your father's taken the vice-regal suite. I should imagine it's empty now, while the men are having brandy in the dining room."

"Could we go up there? That would be much better."

Lady Court rose with some difficulty. Honey thought that her mother ought to be using a cane. She had a slight limp. As they made their way to the stairs, Honey wondered where Velma DeLeon was, and if she ought to make sure that somebody was talking to her. But there was no sign of Max's wife so she quickly abandoned that idea. No doubt Velma was quite capable of looking after herself.

The vice-regal suite, almost as sumptuous as the royal, provided a safe and comfortable place for a chat. Lady Court thought she would like a glass of port. Honey poured them each a glass from the decanter on a well-stocked tray.

"Are your boys beautiful?" Lady Court wanted to know. "Do they look like the Courts? Geoffrey has three children, you know. Mary had the baby on Christmas Day. They're calling him Noel."

"I heard that. Well, I think Denys does look a lot like Papa. He has dark brown hair, not blonde. But his expression . . . yes, I think so."

"Poor Charles," Lady Court said. "Venetia is a recluse. Most peculiar. After that dreadful business of the smallpox . . ." Lady Court closed her eyes as if trying to shut out the memory.

"It must be awful. What about the little girl? Angela, is it?"

"She's so pretty. Such a nice child. But with her mother being so odd . . . I really don't know."

"Mama, I miss Pride's Court. I wish I could come back for a visit. I miss the house terribly, and I miss talking to you, and even Papa's tempers . . ."

"We must talk to your father," Lady Court said.

"I wonder if it's too late," Honey murmured. "Surely not? Do you think that somehow we could patch it all up? If only Papa would *accept* Armand."

They discussed Fort's marriage and Geoffrey's family. And even Honey's ownership of the newspaper.

"It seems most peculiar, your being in business," Lady Court said. "Does Armand approve?"

"I suppose he does, in a way. You know, Mama, I find it quite exciting. I'm writing editorials occasionally. And the paper is growing. We're buying new presses. We're actually making money."

"I'd have no head for business." Lady Court sighed. "But you take after your father, I suppose."

"Not his temper or his prejudices, I hope."

There were years to cover, and as they talked, Honey's longing to return to Pride's Court seemed to grow stronger. She wondered now if her anger at her father's gift of the newspaper and his attempt to use her was justified. Was it so important, after all? Her role in running *Le Monde* was a reality now. No reconciliation with her father would alter that. Yet tonight she felt mellow and nostalgic. How lovely it would be to take Denys and Michel to the house and show them the gardens in summer and the conservatory in winter! To see her own room again and to take tea in the Red Sitting Room. She felt terribly old and weighed down with family problems. How free and happy she'd been as a child at Pride's Court! Thinking back, she wondered why she had been so eager to leave all that for a strange, unfamiliar world that she would never fully grasp even if she lived to be a thousand!

But finally she knew that she must go back downstairs. Armand would be looking for her, and perhaps Velma DeLeon would think her rude.

"Mama, I must go back down. Armand's business partner and his wife are here from New York."

"I know, dear. I think I'll stay here a little while. I'm quite tired. A party is too much for me nowadays."

"Will you be all right?"

"Certainly. Simon will come up after a while. He'll know where I am. You might speak to your father, Honey, and see if you can sound him out. Perhaps we might bring the family together again. Charles would like it, I know. It's so difficult for him now. Except for little Angela, he has nothing but his business interests. And then, while Geoffrey is here it would be nice for you to visit with him."

"I'll try. I promise I'll try, Mama."

She kissed her mother and went through the anteroom to the large white-and-gold door. Thinking, dreaming almost, she opened the door slowly. She was about to go out when she caught sight of a man walking away from the royal suite, down the corridor. It was Armand.

He'd been so deep in thought that he hadn't heard the door open, hadn't looked in her direction. Perhaps Max was in there too, and they'd had another important business meeting. It was so like Armand to use every minute that his partner was here to consolidate more plans. Armand had turned into a thoroughly ambitious entrepreneur. Anyway, she reflected, closing the door and deciding to follow him downstairs, Armand obviously hadn't missed her. She ought to feel relieved.

Just as she was about to walk toward the stairs, the door of the royal suite opened and Velma DeLeon came out. For a moment, Honey was frozen with surprise. Velma's cheeks were flushed, and her coiffure was slightly askew; a number of strands had come loose from the pile of hair.

Velma turned then, and saw her.

"Why, Mrs. St. Amour! Whatever are you doing up here?"

"I was visiting my mother."

"Your mother?"

"My father had reserved the vice-regal suite for some of his guests. We were visiting."

"Oh, I see."

Velma smiled. Honey, joining her for the walk downstairs, wondered if that smile were really quite so ingenuous as she had first imagined. Velma was talking in her silky voice about the food at dinner, about the music. And where were they going to watch the fireworks from at midnight?

"From Dominion Square, I think," Honey said. "The fireworks are being set off from the top of the Mountain. We'll be able to see everything quite well from across the street."

She paid no attention to Velma's reply. In her own mind she was still seeing Armand's quick walk as he'd left the royal suite, and his obvious air of distraction. She felt again the sense of uneasiness, based on instinct rather than knowledge. She saw again Velma's appearance, the hair out of place and the blood beneath the skin, stirred to a flowering crimson. So that by the time they reached the crowds downstairs in Peacock Alley, she scarcely noticed the fact that Velma walked off with Corbin toward the ballroom.

When people began to gather their coats to go outside and see the fireworks, Honey was still standing in a trance. People moved about her, chattering and laughing. When somebody touched her elbow, she forced herself to focus her eyes.

"Mrs. St. Amour. Vy are you stending alone? You vant your coad?"

It was Max DeLeon, looking worried and somehow solicitous. He was a little shorter than she, and Honey found herself looking down into his black eyes and finding there an unexpected communion.

"Yes, I suppose I do, please."

"Ve mide as vell see the firevorks," Max said. "You stay here. I vill get your coad."

He returned carrying her long fox wrap and then helped her into it, muttering at the same time that it was very cold outside. Honey agreed with him politely, thinking how stupid it was that the social graces must be observed, no matter how one hurt inside.

The crowd in the lobby thinned out and now there was space around them, more air to breathe, an opportunity to think more clearly. The doors of the hotel had been propped open and the sound of pealing church bells echoed in the frosty air. Great joyous sounds of proclamation and promise.

"You are nod habby," Max observed, shaking his head.

"I'm perfectly happy."

But he fixed his bright button eyes on her face so that she found herself turning red at her own lie. This man, to whom she had spoken only a few words, had recognized her private grief. She felt naked. She wanted only to escape.

"Ve all haf troubles. I haf stomag trouble. All dis money and I can't ead or drink. Vot good is id?" He shrugged.

"Oh, I'm sorry you feel ill," Honey said. "Perhaps you ought to go to your suite instead of outside. I can go alone to the square. It's only across the road."

"No. I vant to see the firevorks." He paused. Then he said, "Lizzen, I know you haf seen your husband and Velma. I can tell by the vay you look. You know aboud dem."

Honey froze. Looking down into his face, she saw that he too was hurt. But he was also resigned. Now, he wanted to help her, to extend to her some sympathy, some support.

With trembling hands, he began to fasten the buttons on his fur coat. When he had finished, he reached out to her and took her hands in his.

"I am sorry you found oud. I hoped you vouldn't."

"What shall I do?" Honey whispered. "What do people do?" She was close to tears. It was as if the last of her dreams had dissolved. The great love that she had thought invincible, worth every sacrifice, had been exposed as counterfeit. She knew this man understood. For a moment, she hoped he had an instant answer, like a pill one took for a physical ache or pain.

"Dere is nodding to do, my dear, bud go on living."

Then he took her arm gently and led her out into the cold street. Across the road, Dominion Square was alight, the trees coated with snow. Crowds were laughing, singing, shouting. The first dull thunder of exploding fireworks came down from the Mountain. Then the brilliant showers, red rain, blue rain, yellow, green, sprayed patterns on the sky. Honey watched them, holding Max DeLeon's arm tightly. It was a beautiful and exciting spectacle. The mood of the crowd touched her, and as the bells rang out their bright message of promise, she knew Max was right. One went on living. No matter what the pain, she would do just that—go on living.

PART TWO

1910–1914

CHAPTER ONE

By the last week in June, Drake House, on the South Shore of the St. Lawrence, was officially open for the summer. Lady Court was in residence with a large portion of her family. Mary and her three children—Simon, Mildred, and Noel—were already permanently installed with the children's governess, Nora Richmond. Sir Simon and Geoffrey remained in Montreal, of course, journeying out into the country only on weekends. Charles joined them there occasionally.

Fort and Sydney were on the Atlantic that summer. Fort had managed to combine pleasure with business, making a trip over to England to search out half a dozen able superintendents for the rapidly expanding machinery plant that had originally been the highly coveted ironworks. So Landry, their ten-year-old son, and the four-year-old twins, Fenella and Flora, were living at Drake House with their governess, Rose Starkey. Lady Court fussed over them, but it was Mary Court who supervised their care.

As for Venetia, she always stayed on at Pride's Court, drifting about her private apartments and the small, enclosed garden Charles had created for her. Mrs. Card, a woman with extremely strong nerves and even stronger moral convictions, looked after her. Mrs. Card was considered highly satisfactory, and every member of the Court family agreed that it was best to leave Venetia in town. Angela would come to Drake House as soon as she was released from Miss Greenshields' School for Ladies.

Lady Court always felt vaguely guilty about Venetia, but reasoned mildly that her daughter-in-law was no social ornament anyway, and that it was her own choice to separate herself from the family. Out of sight, out of mind, so to speak. (Poor dear Charles, what a dreadful life he'd been forced to lead, and so bad for the child, but Lady Court did her best.)

Sir Simon had been in Ottawa for more than a week discussing a new Royal Mail contract with the minister. Sometimes he passed the Prime Minister, Sir Wilfrid Laurier, outside the House of Commons. This was a situation that, the family realized, could only bring Sir Simon back to Montreal in high bad humor. He couldn't bear Laurier even for a fleeting moment; to merely see the man in the distance drove up his blood pressure to an alarming degree. Laurier was, Sir Simon often said, an upstart who had been knighted for jiggery-pokery in the dim realms of education. Completely inexplicable, the whole thing.

"Things at Buckingham Palace have taken a turn for the worse!" Sir Simon had been heard to exclaim when Laurier's knighthood came up in conversation. "Not like the days of Elizabeth the First! Now there was a queen! Sir Francis Drake *deserved* to be raised up from the ranks. Some *point* in the title, you see? Bringing tons of silver to the exchequer, fighting off the whole bloody Armada single-handed! Some point in a knighthood in those days! But what's it mean now?"

Sir Simon worshiped Sir Francis to such a degree that he had named Drake House in his honor. It had never occurred to him that his hero had, as well as defeating the Armada, plundered a Panamanian mule train, ravaged Valparaiso, sacked Sâo Tiago, and slaughtered countless slaves, townsful of hapless Spaniards, and God only knew how many East Indians.

Drake House was a vast white frame collection of wings, towers, verandahs, porticos, and chimney pots perched high on the banks of the St. Lawrence in the midst of three hundred acres of grass, gardens, and woods. Immense stretches of lawn, cropped by roving geese and an occasional band of sheep, spread down to the water. Directly in front of the main wing were the formal flower beds, shaped into hearts, half moons, diamonds, and stars, and the topiary trees along the great curved driveway. The children didn't play in this area, partly because it was uninspiring and partly because the grass was filthy with goose droppings. They much preferred the riots of flowers on either side of the house, where cosmos, baby's breath, asters, and marigolds fought for space, and where the greenish purple of mignonette smelled sweet after a rain-fall. Beyond these informal gardens there were untrained woods of poplar, pine, and cedar with their neat conical shapes and clean dry ground beneath; the woods were per-fect for hiding or playing Robin Hood in. There was also a natural pool at the back of the house, which the gardeners kept clean. Here, with the governesses to supervise, the children picnicked, played games, and swam.

Farther away still were the real woods—miles of trees and underbrush with no discernible paths, treasure troves of blueberries, the real or imagined haunt of bears, wolves, and foxes. Landry, when he was only six, had reported seeing a bear that had chased him "for miles and miles." No other living soul had seen the bear, but his story was told and retold while the children were warned and re-warned about venturing too far from the gardens.

Those far forests, vast, dark, sometimes swampy, were forbidden territory. Naturally, they became a powerful mag-net: the gloomy measureless preserves of a remote un-reachable planet. Noel had once suggested in a rare flight of fancy, that he seriously suspected the presence of a cave containing a dragon. But the greatest charm of the forest was simply that it was *there*, thus providing un-limited food for speculation, for weird tales and terrifying nightmares.

In the damp heat of a Saturday afternoon, the children were all at the pool. A clump of willows close to the water provided some shade (although it also tended to attract mosquitoes), and the twins were thus out of the sun, dig-ging about in the grass with bent spoons to make race-tracks for unsuspecting ants. Simon and Noel, who at twelve and ten considered themselves much superior to the others, were splashing noisily in the pool, wearing their new navy cashmere bathing suits with the fashionable short sleeves and buttoned shoulders. Mildred, who was eleven sat aloof on one of the picnic benches. She had brought out the gramophone and was now winding the handle strenuously for the first cylinder, a rendition of "The Anvil Chorus" particularly dear to her heart. Actually, there wasn't much choice of music, because so far the adults had only managed to purchase a half dozen cylinders. But Mildred didn't mind. She had a persevering, plodding nature. When she took a fancy to something, she kept at it, and playing the gramophone was now her favorite pastime. In this determination she took after her grandfather. Sir Simon had been known upon occasion to listen to the rousing "The Soldiers of the Queen" nine times in a row, and shared his granddaughter's fondness for "The Anvil Chorus."

"Do we have to listen to that old thumping again?" Simon cried out from the water. "I hate it!"

"So do I," Noel said, joining his brother in a flash of solidarity, meant only to irritate his sister.

"You have no musical taste," Mildred said, repeating a phrase she had heard one of the adults use.

"Yah," young Simon said.

"Let's race to the other side of the pool," Noel offered. "Then we won't hear it so well."

"All right, but you can hear that stupid thing as far as the river. I don't know why they let her bring it down here."

Nora Richmond, sitting on the short wooden dock, was unself-consciously modeling her bathing dress for the silent but secretly admiring Rose Starkey. (Just on the chance that the governess would have to jump into the pool to help one of the children, Mary Court had bought Nora a blue lustre suit with white collar and cuffs, a costume that she considered suitably modest.)

"If you're crossing the pool, just you wait until I get halfway round the shore," Nora shouted at Simon. But both boys had already begun to flail madly toward the middle of the pool. Nora ran lightly around the footpath, a slim, fair-haired girl with small features, a face faintly tanned from the early summer sun, and a curiously husky voice. Her part-time actress mother had taught her to read and write and later arranged for her modest education. She adored serious reading and the acquisition or borrowing of formidable books was her main pastime when she wasn't actually on duty. She was regarded by Rose and the other servants as "well-read." At the moment she was reading *Kenilworth* by Sir Walter Scott, a choice of reading matter that Rose considered incomprehensible.

Rose glanced up from her own book to watch her friend. She didn't swim, but she was envious of Nora's skill and what seemed to her enormous courage. At twenty-three, Rose was plumper than Nora, but she still had the look of a young, untouched girl. Her hair was dark red, very thick, and pulled tightly to the top of her head in a kind of skewered doughnut. Even so, it staged a continuous rebellion against hairpins, giving Rose a perpetual look of slight wantonness. This afternoon she was perspiring a great deal in the white cotton jumper and long-sleeved cotton under-waist that the Court family had selected as a uniform suitable for their two governesses. Lucky Nora, to be wearing a bathing costume in all this heat, Rose thought.

Rose was reading a work by Marie Corelli, a popular romantic novelist and her favorite writer. Although she couldn't know it, she was in excellent company; the Prince of Wales was a Corelli addict. It would have given Rose a feeling of distinction had she been aware of their similar tastes. She was now halfway through *Thelma*.

Mildred took "The Anvil Chorus" off the gramophone and substituted "When Johnnie Comes Marching Home." The boys' swimming race was of no interest to her. As she wound the handle, feeling the spring tightening in her hand, her cousin, Landry, suddenly popped out of the bushes and put something on the table beside her. A toad! She screamed.

Landry brayed at her reaction while the tiny toad hopped toward her, brown and dainty in the sunlight.

Her scream distracted Nora from the swimmers. They, in turn, assumed a disaster on shore, and both boys stopped swimming in mid-stroke. Mildred jumped up and down, partly in horror and partly in anger. The gramophone wheezed out the rousing minor melody of the folksong with its military undertones. A small flock of blackbirds swooped down over the table, possibly drawn by the presence of the toad. Landry hurriedly rescued the toad and put it in a jar; he collected spiders and toads and kept them in boxes under his bed and more than one upstairs maid had threatened to resign over his habit.

There was chaos everywhere. Noel began to flounder, attempting to tread water. He suddenly remembered that he didn't know *how* to tread water, and panicked.

For a few seconds Nora Richmond stood paralyzed on the footpath while Rose Starkey shouted meaningless instructions over the heads of the twins. (They had begun to cry for no reason at all.) Then Nora jumped into the water and swam uncertainly toward Noel. Without thinking clearly she grasped him by the hair, as he spluttered and choked, and tugged him up on the bank.

Noel, after some coughing, threw up in the grass beneath the willows.

Somehow it was all sorted out. Noel was put to bed for an afternoon nap. Mary Court took the twins to one of the cool verandahs to play "Snap" and "Snakes and Ladders," and Mildred and Simon were dispatched to practice their tennis serves.

"Starkey, you take Richmond up to her room and see that she gets dry clothes and some tea," Mary had said, seizing the situation with a bold hand for once. "I'll look after the children for an hour. We mustn't exaggerate the seriousness of this, the children must be more careful in the water. I'll have to talk to Mr. Court about getting a supervisor for them."

"I'm sure Richmond did her best, ma'am," Rose said defensively.

"Of course she did, I'm not suggesting for a minute that Richmond wasn't adequate," Mary said. "But the children must all learn to swim properly. There must be no risks in the future."

"Yes, ma'am."

"Go along with Richmond, then, Starkey."

"Very good, ma'am."

Starkey led her shaken charge up to the third-floor quarters they shared. The tower room was segregated from the other servants' quarters by a narrow corridor. As governesses, the two were in a special position, and it was only correct, they felt, that they should enjoy this touch of privacy. The room had a sink, as well, which made it unnecessary to always use the servants' bathrooms.

Then, too, they provided welcome companionship for each other. Neither had a beau, and they were not likely to meet any young men, at least for the summer, cut off in the country, as they were. Their days off were spent mostly in reading, indoors if it rained and out along the river by themselves if it were sunny. Thrown together thus, and separated by interests and education from the other servants, the two had grown very close.

In their room, with the door closed, Rose began to

help Nora remove her wet bathing costume. Nora was shivering.

"I'm not really cold," she explained through chattering teeth. "I think it's nerves, Rose, just nerves. What if that boy had drowned?"

"But he *didn't* drown. Here, let me help you with the fastenings. You must get out of these wet things and lie down under the covers."

"Yes, I suppose so." Nora stood obediently while Rose's fingers worked at the skirt band to unfasten the buttons. The skirt came off in a sodden heap and Nora stood in the one-piece waist and bloomers.

"I'll get your bathrobe," Rose said. "You must take everything off, Nora. Even in summer you might catch a cold."

She fetched the blue robe made of Turkish material. Nora had rid herself of the wet underwear and stood, pale and damp, in the middle of the room.

"Oh, you're wet. You need a towel," Rose said, all efficiency. She brought Nora's own towel from the rail by the sink. "Let me help you."

And she began to rub Nora's shoulders and arms with the towel, while Nora stood completely rigid, her now white body covered with tiny goose pimples, her usually pale pink nipples hard and deep red with cold.

"What if he'd . . . actually drowned? What would I have done then?" Nora whispered again into the yellow stillness of afternoon sunlight. "I was responsible for a *life*. A *child*, too. And they'd have let me go . . ."

Her fears communicated themselves to Rose, whose hands, filled with white toweling, were sliding over the small, firm breasts and down the flat stomach. She thought very seldom of death, or of what would happen to her if she lost her position. And yet, this afternoon, life in its precariousness had taken on a fresh glow, and made her, and Nora too, seem very fragile.

"We mustn't think about it," Rose said. And yet she could not help thinking of the cemetery through which they sometimes walked, back in Montreal; of its listing, discolored tombstones with dates going back to the early years of the past century, of the names of the people lying below, names now fixed in her own mind.

"Oh, Rose, I'm suddenly frightened," Nora said, as if reading Rose's mind.

Rose held out the bathrobe to her, thrusting it roughly into Nora's hand. She was sharply aware of the strange comfort it had given her to minister to Nora's body.

"Put this on," she said, her voice strained. "I'm going down to get some tea. Mrs. Court said I was to get you tea. Now, you get into bed and wait for me."

"Yes, all right, Rose."

Rose went to the door of the bedroom and opened it, looking back toward Nora, who was climbing into bed.

"I'll shut the door. I don't want the others coming around, poking in here. They're going to be talking, you know. Any little thing causes a big fuss downstairs, so we'll be asked questions."

"Rose," Nora said, still whispering, and sitting up in her bed, eyes unnaturally large with surprise and fear, "will you come and lie down with me? I don't think I can rest if you don't."

"Yes, yes, of course," Rose said.

As she shut the door, and took a deep breath, steeling herself for the prying of the servants in the kitchen, Rose felt an undercurrent of anticipation. Tea with Nora, almost as if they were gentlefolk, in the middle of the afternoon! Then, a comforting rest with her arms about Nora, just to help her sleep a little, to help her over this difficult time. It all seemed more adventurous, more exciting, more dangerous, even, than she could ever have hoped.

The sun was behind the lilacs that surrounded the grass tennis court. Soon it would be teatime, and Mildred, hitting the tennis ball in a desultory manner, was hungry. Her mother had sent her out to hit the ball with Simon, to give them both practice. She was obedient, but it was not a sport that appealed to her. The white lawn dress that hit her leg at mid-calf, the black stockings and black canvas shoes were hot. Simon, she supposed, was even hotter in his knee pants and long socks, but he didn't complain. It was a shame, really, to be sent off after all the excitement of Noel's near-drowning, and then to think that both governesses had been given time off, and their own mother taking on the twins like that! All for nothing, though, if she had to stay out here in the heat and pretend to learn tennis.

"I'm hungry," she said to Simon. "Can't we go in now?"

"I don't know." He stopped then, recognizing in her question an excuse to slack off in his practice. He could blame Mildred if anybody saw them just standing about.

"Aren't you hungry?" she asked.

"I'm thirsty. I wish I had some lemonade. Or some ginger ale, but I suppose they won't give us any until teatime."

"Did you think Noel might die?"

"Yes, for a moment or two." There was a wistful note in his voice, suggesting a valuable opportunity lost.

"They'd only have another baby, I suppose," Mildred said, sighing. "If they lost Noel, I mean. I've noticed that about parents."

"Do you really think so?" It was a new idea to Simon. He was much struck with it.

"Of course! Remember the Mulcasters? That's what *they* did, when Johnny was killed falling off a horse."

"But Noel's ten. Isn't that a long time . . . I mean . . . between?"

"It never makes much difference to *them*," Mildred said wisely, as if she'd thought about it a lot. "Look at Uncle Fort. They waited six years for the twins. And I wouldn't be surprised if they had even more children, yet."

"More? Do you really think so?" Girls, Simon suddenly realized, thought about things differently. He was amazed that Mildred could have formed such definite opinions about a subject that had so far escaped him almost entirely.

"Well, for adults, they're still sort of . . . well, not *young*, but they aren't *old*."

"Don't they ever *stop* having children, then?"

"Oh, sometime," Mildred said airily. She wasn't sure just how it worked. "Look at Grandfather and Grandmother. They stopped."

"That's right."

"We always seem to get sent away when there's any excitement," Mildred observed. "Grown-ups have all the fun."

"There probably won't be anything as exciting as Noel's drowning for ages, either," Simon agreed sadly.

But he was wrong. Just as he spoke, they heard a sound that indicated instantly that something new and perhaps even adventurous was about to happen. It was the sound of an automobile. A visitor had arrived at Drake House.

The fire-engine-red Cutting Model A Tourabout, like a large, elegant bug from some distant star, pulled up with a satisfactory rumble at the front door of Drake House. By the time it had come to a full stop, Mary Court and the twins; the erstwhile tennis players; Mrs. Grouse, the house-keeper; and the houseman, Packley, had all assembled on the front verandah. Lady Court appeared shortly after.

The smiling woman driver wore a long gown of brown silk with a frill about the ankles and long ruffled sleeves, black gloves, goggles, and a brown chiffon scarf tied over her wide-brimmed hat. Beside her sat a young girl with long black hair held in place with a gray silk scarf. Her great gray eyes were revealed as rather opaque, and her mouth was smiling happily. She was an extraordinarily graceful child, filled with the promise of a beauty that painters pursued all their lives. The driver removed her goggles.

"Why, it's Honey!" Lady Court exclaimed from behind Mary Court. "She's brought Angela!"

"Aunt Miel," Simon whispered to Mildred with awe. The children had only met their aunt half a dozen times over the years, but they knew that the nature of her re-lationship with the adult Courts was mysterious and pro-scribed. Aunt Miel (all her nephews and nieces had been asked to call her Miel, as Justine's children did) was a figure of great interest to all the children. Now, to add to her other fascinating qualities—hadn't she eloped with a Frenchman, like in the fairytales? didn't she stand up to Grandfather? didn't she actually own a newspaper?—here she was driving an automobile! And a red one. Not a huge, cumbersome touring car, but a neat little sports car with two bucket seats, a gasoline engine, two oil head-lamps, and a spare tire.

After the first shock wave had passed over the assembly, the questions began. Why had Honey brought Angela? Why had Angela been taken out of school early? Wasn't Charles supposed to make a special trip from the city to deposit her safely with Lady Court in three days' time? It was all very strange, Simon whispered into his sister's attentive ear. Mildred nodded, uncomprehending, suitably mystified.

The seemingly gala arrival did not reveal the nature of the situation. In reality, Honey was doing Charles a favor. He was going through a bad time. Yet Honey looked exhilarated; the red car gave her a sense of adventure. It had been Armand's gift, and like everything he gave her, it was perfect. She was cheered each time she drove it, and today, momentarily, had lost sight of the reason for this journey.

Her brother had telephoned her the day before at such an early hour that she had known something must be wrong at Pride's Court. Charles was not in the habit of telephoning for a chat.

"Honey, it's Charles," he had begun. "I'm sorry to bother you so early, but it's important."

His voice had been trembling a little although she had felt that he was making a great effort to control himself.

"What's wrong, Charles?"

"It's Venetia."

. . . Naturally it would be Venetia. Honey's first fear that something was wrong with Papa or Mama fled. Venetia could be expected to produce a crisis every so often.

"Is she ill? What's happened?"

"She's had a bad fall. The doctor doesn't know yet how badly she's hurt, but we think . . ."

"Oh, Charles, what do you want me to do? What happened?"

"She fell over the balcony outside her bedroom door. You know the one. Mrs. Card was out of the room. Venetia lay on the ground for some time before she was missed. Dr. Brandon thinks she may have broken her neck."

Honey sensed how close Charles was to breaking down. It was terrible, really, how Charles had suffered since his marriage. The strain of his wife floating about the upstairs like some wraith, out of touch with their only child, and certainly no wife to him, was indescribable.

"What can I do to help, Charles?"

"Could you possibly go out to Miss Greenshields' and pick up Angela? I can't leave the city at the moment or I'd do it myself."

"Of course. But what will Papa say if he finds out? Where's Sydney?"

"Sydney and Fort are at sea, returning from England."

"Oh. I haven't talked with anybody for some time."

"Don't worry about Papa. He's still in Ottawa. We don't expect him back for another day or so. Mama is at Drake House, of course, and so is Mary. There's nobody else I can ask to do this, or I wouldn't trouble you, Honey. Geoffrey is no good at this kind of thing. He'd frighten Angela out of her wits. Dr. Brandon thinks she ought to come in and see her mother, just in case. You understand."

"I understand perfectly. And then you'd want me to take her out to Drake House? I presume she was going there for the summer holidays anyway?"

"That's exactly what I'd like."

She heard Charles's voice take on a note of relief.

"I knew you'd understand," he said. "I do hope it isn't too much trouble."

"Armand gave me a car for my birthday. So I can easily manage to pick Angela up this morning."

"Honey, this is kind of you. I don't want to frighten the child, but if you could somehow prepare her for seeing her mother so ill . . . She's in the Royal Victoria Hospital, so if you could just take Angela there and ask for me at the reception desk, they'll tell you where to find me."

Honey was sympathetic. She and Charles had never been particularly close, but she had always felt that he'd deserved something better than the marriage he'd had with Venetia. As for bringing up a child in such an atmosphere . . . she wondered what Angela was really like.

"Let me see the time," Honey said, looking across the room at the clock, "I'll get ready to leave as soon as I can. Do you think they've bothered to install a telephone out at the school? You know how stuffy Miss Greenshields can be."

"I'm not sure. Mama usually makes all the arrangements about Angela's school."

"If they do have the telephone, Charles, you might call ahead and ask them to get Angela packed up. Just tell Miss Greenshields, or whoever is in charge, that there's been a change of plans. That Lady Court would like Angela early. She needn't alarm the child."

Armand, mercifully, had been sympathetic to the plan, and so by ten o'clock in the morning she was driving toward Miss Greenshields' School in the country. During the journey, Honey wondered again what the child would be like. In the past few years her visits to Pride's Court had been few (and all had taken place when Sir Simon was out of town), so she had seen Angela only half a dozen times. On the rare occasions when she had paid visits to Fort's house, Angela hadn't been a guest. Time had passed quickly, it seemed, and Angela was now thirteen, only a year younger than her own son, Denys. It was, therefore, intriguing to speculate on the child's appearance and manner, given the distinctly odd behavior of her mother, the preoccupation of Charles with business, the indulgence of her grandmother, and the bombastic rigidity of her grandfather.

It was a warm, sunny day, a day that threatened to become unbearably hot. In the western distance a leaden thunder cloud cut off half the sky. Honey hoped she wouldn't be caught in a storm, for the car had no top.

The school, she discovered, was at the end of a long line of black poplars. The gravel driveway led to a gray limestone rectangle with tall, narrow, Gothic windows. The woodwork, the portico, the bits of trim around the roofs were painted cream. It was not a welcoming building, Honey reflected. Her view was confirmed when she stepped inside the main foyer, a square of polished floor and furniture that smelled faintly of oil and old wood.

She was ushered into the apartments of Miss Greenshields herself. Here, austerity had given way to comfort and sentiment: green upholstered chairs and sofa, a fern stand bearing an enormous plant, family photographs in gold frames, bric-a-brac and small tables intended to hold delicate teacups and trays of little cakes.

Miss Greenshields was above average in height, tightly corseted and painfully erect. She wore a pleated blue skirt that revealed the ankles of her black boots and a stiffly starched white blouse with a long navy silk tie. Her smallish, sharp face was plain. The steel-rimmed glasses hanging on a black silk cord about her neck indicated that they were needed only for reading.

"Madame St. Amour? Welcome to our school. Angela is ready to leave. Mr. Court telephoned this morning and, fortunately, we were able to comply with his request."

They shook hands briefly.

"Thank you, Miss Greenshields, that's kind of you."

"This isn't an emergency, I hope? We were expecting Mr. Court to pick up Angela in three days."

"No, just a change of family plans, Miss Greenshields. Lady Court is already in residence at Drake House and would like Angela sooner."

Miss Greenshields smiled neatly. She recognized this explanation as a lie, but it was not in her province to question Madame St. Amour. A stray look of curiosity, nevertheless, briefly enlivened her undistinguished hazel eyes.

"I'm so glad there's nothing wrong. Well, here is Angela." She turned and made a slight gesture with her arm toward the child sitting on a high-backed wooden chair.

The child sat quietly, utterly composed, simply waiting. She was a study in black and gray. The color of her dress, a smoky gray, duplicated exactly that of her enormous eyes—eyes so extraordinarily large that at first glance they commanded all the viewer's attention. Almost opaque, they were fringed with long black lashes. Her hair was black and pulled tightly from the temples with a gray ribbon at each side, while the remainder was allowed to hang long in the back. Upon closer inspection, her other features proved to be completely harmonious; a straight nose, a full mouth that promised to be sensuous in adulthood and small, delicate ears. She must resemble her mother, Honey reflected, but she had inherited the best of the Court features as well. There wasn't a disturbing note in Angela's appearance. Her mother had been a classic beauty, and the child was all of that. But she was more. There was a look in the eyes—was it intelligence? sensitivity? suffering?—that gave Angela's beauty an added dimension. And Honey, by this time knowing something of life's thrusts, felt a knife-sharp pain as she thought of what might be in store for this fantastically beautiful and obviously aware little girl.

"Are you Aunt Miel?" Angela said, standing up.

"Yes, Angela, I'm afraid it's quite some time since we met. Let me see—I think you were ten years old. But now, of course, you're almost a young lady."

"I remember *you*," Angela said.

Honey was afraid Angela would elaborate on family problems in front of Miss Greenshields, and so she hurried their departure.

The storm clouds had passed, floating majestically off across the river to the south. Honey was anxious to have a quiet talk with Angela before they reached the hospital. Outwardly, the child seemed composed, but there was a strong possibility that this was just a fragile screen that would quickly crumble when she heard the truth. When they were seated in the car she offered Angela goggles and a scarf, and they drove off. At three o'clock, Honey stopped for tea at Peachum Inn, a respectable hotel on the river road frequented by traveling ladies; there the red Cutting Tourabout caused a mild sensation. They sat outside under a painted green trellis adjacent to the main hotel building, surrounded by a riot of poppies and cornflowers, the humming of industrious bees, and the trills of wild canaries in tall maples.

When the tea tray arrived, Honey poured out two cups. She was careful to avoid any sign of hurry.

"Do you take milk or lemon in your tea, Angela?"

"Milk, please."

Honey handed the cup to Angela. She was pleased to see that Angela wasn't squirming. She seemed a singularly silent child for a thirteen-year-old, and curiously adult in her manner. It came, Honey supposed, from being with older people most of the time.

"Do you mind leaving school early?" Honey asked.

"No, I don't mind," Angela said calmly, refusing a scone and gazing fixedly at her aunt with her great luminous eyes. "There's something wrong at home, isn't there?"

"Yes, there is. Drink up your tea."

"It's Mother," she said.

"I'm afraid so. She's ill."

"It's all right to tell me, Aunt Miel, I understand about Mother. Or, at least, I understand partly. I expect she's . . . *done* something. Is that it?"

"She's had an accident," Honey said quickly, eager to dispel any idea that Venetia had deliberately tried to take her own life. Such a thing was unthinkable.

"What happened, then? How bad is it?"

"She fell off the balcony. She may have a broken neck."

"Is she going to die?"

"The doctor doesn't know. We'll know more when we reach the hospital. But, Angela, your father wanted me to prepare you for seeing her. It may be serious, but on the other hand, it may be something the doctors can fix. When your father called me it was too early to say."

"I suppose she jumped," Angela said. Her voice was low, her lashes brushing her cheeks as she stared into the teacup.

"No, no. You mustn't think that."

"But the railing is high," Angela pointed out. "Aunt Miel, you know that house . . . you lived there all your life. Didn't you? Until you got married? You know what the railings are like."

"Your mother may have been dizzy. She takes medication of some kind, I believe."

"Oh, yes. She does."

"Well, then, she must have fallen over."

Angela sighed slightly and sipped her tea. She was concerned about her mother, of course, and even sad, and perhaps there was a flicker of fear at the idea of Venetia's dying. But she seldom saw her mother, and it was Lady Court upon whom she depended for advice and even for companionship. After a pause, she looked up at her aunt, this fascinating woman who had until now been merely a background figure of romance and adventure in her life. She had a desire to know more about Honey St. Amour, the woman who had given up her secure position in society to marry a man who could only be termed "a foreigner."

"Do you miss Pride's Court very much?" Angela asked.

"Yes, I do miss it. I miss my room, and the conservatory, and the gardens, and the Red Sitting Room where we always had tea . . ."

"I thought you must. It's such a beautiful house. The one you live in now isn't at all like Pride's Court, is it? I've driven past it a couple of times, and Father pointed it out to me. It looks gloomy."

Honey smiled, charmed by Angela's directness.

"I guess the house looks dark, but I've done my best to brighten it. We added a wing to it and enlarged the garden. That helped. But there isn't a house in the city as beautiful as Pride's Court."

"I guess I'll inherit it."

"Probably. Your father certainly will, and since you're an only child . . ." Honey's voice trailed off; she was not sure just how much of the situation Angela understood.

"Yes. Oh, I know my parents don't, well . . . actually live together. Father seldom sees Mother. She mostly embroiders on a tapestry or walks in the garden. Or she prays. She's quite religious, you know."

"How do you get along with your cousins? Your Uncle Geoffrey's children, I mean."

"Oh, all right, I guess. Simon and Mildred are pretty dull. Noel, well, he's a little more interesting, but not much." She shrugged expressively. "Then there's Landry, Uncle Fort's son. They live just along Dorchester from us. Have you met him? He's fun, sometimes. He collects bugs and drops spiders down my neck. Do you realize, Aunt Miel, that he knows the Latin name of every plant you can think of? He says he wants to breed a new plant and he wants to develop some new kind of hardy wheat and be famous. Can you imagine?"

"He sounds different," Honey said. Trust Fort to have the unusual child in the group. "Do you want a scone now, Angela? We may be late with dinner."

"Perhaps I will," Angela agreed, selecting one from the plate.

"What do *you* like to do? Do you study music, or read books?"

"I draw, mostly. I read a lot too, but I like to draw pictures about the things I read."

"That sounds marvelous. What kinds of things do you like to draw?"

"Oh, princesses, and fairies, and forests, and goblins. Dragons, too. That's the only thing Landry likes about my drawing, the dragons. He says the dragon is really a prehistoric monster that got left over and survived."

"Will you show me some of your drawings?"

"If you'd like."

"Do you like music?"

"Some music. I'm afraid I don't hear very much music. At school we study it, and of course the choir sings, too, but the songs are so silly."

Honey could imagine the kind of songs the choir sang at the School for Ladies: "The Lost Chord," "Land of Hope and Glory," some of Purcell's nymphs and shepherds cavorting about on mythical greens.

"It just happens that I have a musician living in my house," Honey said. "Not one of my own children—they're

all at boarding school—but a nephew. I'd like you to meet
him. His name is Beau Dosquet and he's just your age. He
plays the piano beautifully, and the organ too. Even the
guitar."

"Is he my cousin?"

"By marriage, I suppose. He's not a blood relative. He's
my husband's sister's child. So the connection is rather obscure as far as you're concerned."

"He has a nice name."

"I think you'd get along with him. He's a little shy, but
very clever. Finish your tea, then, and we'll go."

"Yes, I'm finished, really. I wasn't exactly hungry."

"Put your goggles on, dear," Honey said as they climbed
into the car. It was entirely surrounded by admiring
youngsters, one with a foot on the commodious running
board, another fingering the red fender, another peering
into one of the brass-trimmed headlamps. Honey shooed
them off and then tied a big chiffon scarf over her hat and
adjusted her goggles. "Try not to worry, Angela," she said
as they prepared to start.

"I'm not exactly worrying," Angela said, tying on her
scarf and fitting on the pair of much-too-large goggles,
"but a I feel a little frightened."

"I'm sure there'll be some *good* news," Honey said.

The car rumbled to life, responding like magic to her
handling, and they glided off. The cluster of children waved
gaily as if the car were part of a parade. Despite this
send-off, an air of grim expectation hung over them as they
rode along.

Upon their arrival at the hospital, however, they found
Charles looking fairly cheerful. "Venetia is much better,"
he said, after kissing them both. "It was only a concussion
and a broken shoulder. Not a broken neck as Dr. Brandon
first thought."

The prognosis was good. It seemed likely that in a few
months Venetia would be able to walk about quite normally. The effects of the concussion, the doctors said,
would probably disappear after a time. Angela was allowed
to see her mother for a few moments, but Venetia was
asleep when she was in the room. After this ordeal was
over the three met to discuss plans for the night.

"I simply can't drive out to Drake House tonight,"

Honey said to Charles. "It's too late. Without a man along to help me, I mustn't risk having a flat tire."

"No, of course you can't," Charles said.

"But Angela shouldn't be alone at Pride's Court. I know Mrs. Card is there, but really, Charles, that isn't very satisfactory. Mary is out at Drake House, so Angela obviously can't go to her house. What do you think about my taking her home with me just for tonight? In the morning I could drive straight out to Drake House. It would save so much time."

"That's a wonderful idea, Honey."

Honey turned to her niece.

"What do you think, Angela? Your father will be staying at the hospital during the evening, and you'd be quite alone at Pride's Court. It would be much nicer if you came to me."

"I'd love to do that!" Angela said with enthusiasm. "I'd love to stay with you, Aunt Miel."

"Then that's settled. Papa won't find out for some time, anyway. Mama won't mind in the least, so it should work out perfectly."

Sir Simon would be angry at such an arrangement. To have his grandaughter taken to a Frenchman's house—*that* Frenchman's—would no doubt be considered treasonous. However, by the time he found out what had happened, enough time would have passed to take much of the sting out of the news.

"Honey, I *do* appreciate your help in all this," Charles said.

He accompanied them to the hospital steps, where the car was parked on the gravel driveway. When they were settled and ready to drive off, Charles bent over and kissed his sister on the cheek.

"Good-bye. Drive carefully."

"Don't stay here too late, Charles," Honey said, pulling on her gloves. "I'll call you when we arrive at Drake House tomorrow. Angela will be perfectly safe with me."

Again there were interested waves from passersby and from Charles, too, as they drove off. Cars were still a novelty, a woman driver even more of one, and Honey always attracted attention. At the wheel of the bright red car, scarf ends streaming behind her in the wind, goggles adding an exotic air to her already exquisite face, she was a startling sight to most passersby. Angela enjoyed the excitement they caused, feeling herself to be very much the center of attention.

In the dying afternoon light, the nursery was a faded daguerreotype; brown with yellow in the center and deep gray shadows around the edge. The slim figure sitting at the grand piano made a silhouette against an open dormer window. A light, hot breeze ruffled the boy's hair, giving him an animated manner. The music was a Chopin nocturne, sweet and painful.

Angela, following her aunt, stood transfixed near the door, caught by the unreal mood of the place. When the nocturne was finished, Honey spoke gently, as if she were afraid to startle the musician.

"Beau?"

He did jump slightly, apparently unaware that anybody had come in while he was playing.

"Oh, Aunt Miel! Come in. I didn't know you were there."

"The music was lovely, Beau. Look, I've brought a visitor to meet you."

The boy rose from the piano bench and stepped forward almost reluctantly. Angela, coming from behind Honey, stared at him, fascinated. He was astonishingly handsome, but not in the accepted fashion. It was more the handsomeness of a leprechaun, she thought. He had a thin face, with pale skin. His eyebrows were black, like the longish hair that curled over the edges of his collar. The nose was hooked at the bridge but in an attractive manner, so that it gave strength to the face. The mouth was full and dark red, as if he had just been eating strawberries. The eyes were rather too narrow, but of an intense, burning green.

"This is my niece, Angela Court. Angela, this is Beau Dosquet."

He smiled shyly. His hand was still touching the piano, as if it were an island of security away from which he would be lost.

"Hello. I'm sorry I didn't hear you come in. I was concentrating."

It was at this point that Angela realized that he was French Canadian. But of course, she thought crossly to herself, if he were Uncle Armand's relative, he *would* be. She had an odd feeling of *déjà vu*. Then it came to her that it was only the situation that struck her as familiar. She saw herself, a Court, meeting this fascinating boy, who was French. It was just like Aunt Miel. How odd.

"Your music was lovely," Angela said, also with some hesitation. It was never easy for her to meet strangers.

"We've turned the nursery into a studio for Beau," Honey was explaining. "There are several rooms on this floor. The nannies and governesses used to sleep here, so Beau has privacy for his practicing and studying. The nursery was always kept in good repair, you see. There wasn't much to do, really, except move the piano up here and do a little painting."

"It's a wonderful room," Angela said, torn between admiration for the old furniture and toys, and the features of Beau himself.

"Do you really like this room?" Beau asked eagerly. His cousins and even his brother, Mathieu, scorned the nursery. He supposed it reminded them too much of childhood and their struggles to escape discipline. "I love it," he went on. "It's the most beautiful room I've ever seen."

Honey interjected, laughing, "I suspect you simply like living in the city. The nursery isn't that fascinating. Beau," she explained to Angela, "comes from a farm. He had to share space with a brother and sister so he loves having all this privacy. My own children don't care to occupy this apartment, so there's no problem."

"Please play something else," Angela said.

"If you're sure you'd like to hear something," Beau said diffidently. "I'm just practicing."

Honey left the children together, reminding them that dinner would be in an hour. Angela found some paper and a pencil on one of the shelves, and sat down to sketch Beau at the piano. As he played a liquid, lilting thing (he later told her it was by Satie, a new and revolutionary composer in Paris) she began to draw. They spent the hour in perfect communion, not speaking, just being together. Eventually, Honey was forced to send a maid up to fetch them to the dinner table.

CHAPTER TWO

The day before had been Dominion Day—July 1. In past years on this holiday weekend Honey had been shoulder-deep in preparations for the family's annual move across the St. Lawrence River to Ile Ste.-Helene. The St. Amours had a summer place on Lac des Dauphins. This year, she had spent the entire afternoon in town, meeting with Beaulne and the new managing editor, Gabriel d'Esterre. That had left her only Sunday to pack her own clothes, organize supplies, round up the servants, and marshal the children for the journey.

The prospect wasn't particularly pleasing. She was exhausted to begin with. She unpinned her hat and threw her gloves on one of the green velvet sofas in the large sitting room. It seemed exceedingly damp and stuffy. God knows, the old French-style architecture had never been designed for letting in fresh air, she thought crossly. Despite all her efforts during the past fifteen years to lighten the heavy effect of the boxed-in rooms, the St. Amour house was still sometimes hot and airless. She sighed heavily, deciding that what she really needed was a glass of lemon squash.

When she had rung for Louise, she reached for the catch on one of the small windows and opened it, although she could detect no hint of breeze outside. Running *Le Monde*, she thought, was a full-time job these days instead of a pleasant hobby. Doubtless if Armand had realized how time-consuming it would become he would have made a more concerted effort to discourage her from taking the reins. But it was too late to turn back now.

It was she who had hired Gabriel, and now she might have cause to regret it. At thirty, he was clearly out to change the world. A Liberal, yes, but quite capable of criticizing the party doctrine when he disagreed. Already he was arguing bitterly with Beaulne about the writing style of

Le Monde and the unqualified support the paper had given the Reform Group a few months earlier in the municipal election. Mayor Laporte, now that he had been elected, would not long remain a knight on a white charger but must be watched, Gabriel pointed out. Once in power, men had a habit of forgetting their promises. Gabriel felt the need to reform the reformers. His intensity and drive made her nervous. He could turn any situation to his own advantage, at least verbally—a reflection, apparently, of his training as a lawyer.

These constant battles with Beaulne were distressing to Honey. Beaulne was getting old, true, and his ideas were no longer *au courant*, perhaps. But he had the wisdom that comes with age. If a change had to be made, how should she make it? Could she afford to trust the future of *Le Monde* to Gabriel, a fiery intellectual with sweeping ideas and little practical experience? Or should she continue with Beaulne's caution, leaving certain stones in both the federal and municipal governments firmly unturned? Gabriel wanted to stir up trouble, to expose issues. And he probably had much right on his side. The Reform Group (originally headed by Alderman Ames and now led by Mayor Laporte) were not without tarnish. They must be watched, Gabriel said. God knew they had achieved some things—ridding the city of five thousand outdoor latrines, recognizing the unions, increasing civic wages from ten to twelve and a half cents an hour, and pushing through on a popular vote the creation of a Board of Control for the City of Montreal that would take over the city's finances, wresting them from a corrupt city council. But would they now rest on their laurels and then, perhaps, slip into the same old ways?

Frankly, she was tired of thinking about these things. She got up from the chair and examined her face in the mirror over the mantel. She looked drawn; her skin was damp from perspiration, her mouth sagging. She was thirty-four years old. She wondered what drove men on in the business world, and if she had the necessary energy to continue. Why was she struggling with these problems instead of attending lawn teas, elegant dinners, and sitting on volunteer committees for good works like the wives of most of Armand's friends?

Louise came in with a tray.

"We'll have high tea in the garden," Honey said. "I expect M'sieur St. Amour in about an hour. And the children will be here, and, of course, Mathieu."

"Yes, Madame."

"Tell the cook we shall need some cold meats, please. We won't have dinner tonight; it's much too hot and I'm too tired. Plenty of rolls, and some fruit pies. And perhaps some of that cold meat pie that slices so well."

"Yes, Madame."

When Louise was gone, her thoughts strayed back to Beaulne. If she *did* fire him she would have to find some other job for him, after all his years of service. Fifteen years. As long as she had been married, almost. She'd either have to give him another position or a small pension. (Sir Simon had always been dead against pensions, she recalled, saying, "Make the devils work for their money. Don't pay a cent for *nothing*. Find 'em an easier job, if you like, but no damned pension!")

Then there was her nephew, Mathieu. Another problem she had unwittingly taken upon herself. At seventeen he was majoring in philosophy and English at McGill. He took no interest in Laurent's farm, and if it hadn't been for Timothée Fitzgerald, who still stayed on, and Laurent's new son-in-law, the situation would have been grave.

Because Mathieu was so uninterested in agriculture, she'd offered him a summer job on the newspaper. Like Gabriel (whom he worshiped), he now wanted to attack local government with a vengeance and remodel the entire writing style of *Le Monde*.

"I'm going to be mayor of Montreal someday, Aunt Miel. You watch!" Mathieu had cried only two days before. "Let me cover the city council for you. I'll show you what can be done to liven up those damned meetings!"

She was on her second glass of squash when Armand came into the sitting room. He kissed her warmly.

"*Ma cherie*, you look tired!" Trust Armand to see that instantly, she thought. He'd never lost his eye for beauty, although she realized reluctantly that it sometimes strayed from home.

"You're working too hard at that newspaper," he went on, helping himself to some of the squash on the tray. "Get yourself a new editor and let the man run it. As long as he follows the general Liberal party line, what do we care? We don't need any more money from that source."

"But some days, Armand, I like running the paper," Honey protested.

"Well, I can't help, then." Armand shrugged. "Anyway, I have a present for you. *Un cadeau. Un cadeau extraordinaire.*"

She immediately came alive.

"What is it, Armand?"

"It is a surprise."

It was at moments like this that she most appreciated Armand, and she wondered why she persisted in the tiring business of running the paper. Why did she need anything more than Armand, this house, and the children?

"Your eyes always light up when I say 'gift'," he said, smiling at her.

"What is it, then? Tell me!"

He had definitely not brought in a box. A small box in his pocket? A jewel, perhaps?

"I should make you wait until teatime."

"Please, don't! Let me have it before the children come in from the air show."

"Oh, are they at the air show? I didn't know. Did you hear the planes flying over the city?"

"We heard them, but we didn't see any of them," Honey said, not wanting to watch because of the editorial meeting.

"All right, I won't make you wait. Here it is."

He took a piece of paper from his pocket: a heavy, official-looking document with a seal upon it. She accepted it, staring. It was not at all what she had expected. But when she unfolded it and read a few words of the printing, she was delighted.

"Oh, Armand, darling, that's wonderful! The deed to the house! To Grande's house where we spent our honeymoon!"

"Are you pleased?"

She kissed him, throwing herself into his arms despite the heat and covering his face and cheeks, eyes and mouth with caresses.

"I always swore to myself I'd buy the house for you if Philippe ever wanted to sell it. Now, my sweet, you can do whatever you like with the house, but I know you were talking about founding a home for fallen women. A phrase that I must say I abhor. Perhaps you can find another description? Anyway, you could put a matron in charge of it and run it quite economically. What do you think of that?"

"It's the most perfect gift I can imagine!"

"Then you are pleased, my love?"

"So pleased that I'm going to spend my spare time at the lake this week making up a list of patrons. I can open a fund through the newspaper. Perhaps I ought to consult Marc and do it through his connections—and of course, I must talk to the bishop. He'll have some ideas."

"Bishop Grise always has a thousand ideas," Armand said with affectionate sarcasm. "He's exactly like every other bishop. Uncle Eustache was the same before he retired. Why are all bishops cut alike?"

"You're very disrespectful," she said playfully. "Actually, Bishop Grise is an old love. I don't mind him a bit. He's a little overweight but aside from that, quite pleasant. Since your Uncle Eustache's day, the bishops appear to interfere much less. Don't you think?"

"I suppose so. When are we having tea?"

"When the children arrive. It shouldn't be long. Mathieu was at the air show, too, covering the story for the paper."

"I meant to ask you about Mathieu. Do you think it was wise to hire him for the summer and have him live here as well?"

"But what could I do?" Honey asked, making a helpless motion with her shoulders. "He didn't want to stay on the farm with his father. They don't get along, you know. It makes Laurent angry that Mathieu isn't the least bit interested in the land. And then, I've had Beau living here, taking his music and going to school, and I can't make a difference between them or Justine would be slighted. I can't let him board with strangers."

They were interrupted by the arrival of Mathieu, who burst into the room like a black tornado, filled with enthusiasm for the newest sensation, the airplane.

"Did you go, Uncle Armand? There were twenty thousand spectators! Can you imagine?"

"I thought it was noisy," Armand said, laughing. "From what I heard in the sky."

"Almost all the machines got off the ground. And at one point there were actually three machines in the air at once. And the Count de Lesseps . . ."

Words appeared to fail him when it came to describing the French count. The swagger and style of the man, combined with his obvious knowledge of his machines (he had brought two over from France for the fee of ten thousand dollars put up by the Air Show Committee), was incredible.

Honey smiled at her nephew. It was pleasant to see such genuine enthusiasm even over such a frivolous thing as a flying machine.

At seventeen, Mathieu seemed already physically full-grown. He had a large frame topped by a head of thick unruly, straight black hair. He had the coarse features of his mother, Justine, combined with the somewhat fuller mouth of his Uncle Armand which gave him an oddly sensuous look. A hint of mustache on his upper lip made him look faintly unkempt no matter how much time he spent in dressing. He had enormous hands that would have been an asset to a farmer, but which he presently employed by waving them dramatically while he made bombastic speeches with all the confidence of youth. On the whole, not a charming young man, but one who made a lasting impression.

"So, was the count as marvelous as his advance notices?" Armand asked, amused.

"Better. Much better," Mathieu said, obviously having found another hero. "I'm not running this story under any dull headline that Beaulne might think up—"

"*You're* not running . . .?" Honey interrupted quizzically.

"Are you the new editor, then?" Armand demanded.

"I mean, Gabriel gave me the assignment and we discussed it. Gabriel feels it must be handled with some excitement. Beaulne will want something like 'Air Show a Success.' "

Mathieu allowed himself a digression in the form of a snort. Obviously the story was writing itself in his head, the words clicking into place with his excitement. He'd seen the count take off along the river, with a bladder fixed to the plane's back to give him buoyancy should he happen to ditch in the water, while his brother, Bernard, had driven along the dusty river road in an automobile, trying to keep pace, and, eventually, failing. The count had executed a series of graceful dives over Montreal's public buildings and some of the imposing private houses to make people suddenly aware of this revolutionary mode of transport.

"The headline I want, Aunt Miel, is 'Count de Lesseps Swoops over Montreal Rooftops.' How do you like that? That'll make them read! None of this old-fashioned stuff Beaulne likes to print. You know, Aunt Miel, Gabriel is right. You must move ahead with a newspaper, you have to move with the times—"

Armand interceded firmly at this point.

"Your aunt is tired. She's been at the newspaper all afternoon, and tomorrow she has to move the family out to the island. I suggest that that's enough shop talk for one day."

Mathieu was instantly contrite.

"I'm sorry. It's just that I get so excited about the paper and about the air show. About everything, I guess. Flying has great possibilities. It must be exhilarating to fly like a bird."

"Don't tell me you want to be a flier, now," Armand protested, laughing. "I thought it was politics. The mayor of Montreal, wasn't it?"

"Oh, I haven't given that up. I *shall* be the mayor. But there are so *many* things to do."

"I wish I had your confidence," Armand said, pouring himself a Scotch and water.

"You've accomplished the things you set out to do, haven't you?" Mathieu challenged.

"Some of them, yes," Armand admitted.

"And you still have plans for the future, don't you, Uncle Armand?"

"Yes, of course I do."

"Well, it's the same thing. I just don't happen to want to build railroads, or open up mines, or buy property. Isn't it true that you and DeLeon are trying to get a charter for a railroad in northern Ontario because you think there's nickel and silver up there?"

"Where did you hear that?"

"These things get around," Mathieu said airily. "We have a geology professor at McGill who's been doing reports based on prospectors' findings . . . it gets around."

"What time is tea?" Armand demanded again impatiently.

"The children will be here any moment," Honey said

soothingly. "Don't fuss, darling. We're having tea in the garden. I hope it will be cooler."

Denys, Michel, and Susan arrived in a flurry of enthusiasm over the air show. Like Mathieu, they were wild about the idea of flying machines. When she could get a word in, Honey said, "After tea is over, you must all pack."

"Father, did you order some repairs on the dinghy?" Denys asked. "It isn't safe, you know. I spoke to Henri myself about it, but he didn't pay much attention."

"I told Henri what to do," Armand said, "and no quarreling between you and Michel over the use of it."

"I'd rather fly, anyway," Michel said. "I'm going to be a flier when I grow up."

Denys, who was planning to study law in university and who fully intended to join his father in business, said coldly, "Just how do you think you can make a living out of flying? Do you realize it costs thousands of dollars? Perhaps millions. Count de Lesseps is rich. That airplane is only a toy to him."

"What do *you* know?" Michel demanded.

"It happens that I talked to some people who know," Denys said with a worldly air, "when I was in the stands. You're too young to talk to strangers."

They weren't much alike, the two boys, Honey thought, looking at them fondly. Denys was fair and tall, with a tendency to chunkiness like his Uncle Charles. He had the dark eyes of the St. Amours, however. Michel, on the other hand, was much like his father. Dark, quick in his movements, with a mischievous grin that stirred people up. Susan, at ten, was still unformed and awkward. It was difficult to tell whether she would be truly pretty. Her hair was brown and held at the moment in two uncompromising braids; her eyes were dark brown, her nose adequate. It remained to be seen how the shape of her face would affect her looks; the baby fat was still on it. There was an air of petulance, of impatience about Susan that Honey did not find appealing. She had a peculiar and persevering interest in everything about the Court family, and often suggested wistfully that she would love to be a visitor at Pride's Court, and why didn't her grandfather want her to come? Honey felt guilty, at times, because the children were deprived of their grandparents. But she and Armand attempted to fill the void with St. Amour family members and various friends. Susan, Honey suspected, identified strongly with her English ancestry.

When they were seated in the garden for tea, Susan began a series of questions about the Courts. She had been away in boarding school the night Angela had come to visit and was deeply conscious of having missed an opportunity to inspect her cousin at first hand.

"How is Aunt Venetia? Is she getting better?" Susan asked through a mouthful of tea.

"Don't speak with your mouth full," Honey said automatically. "Yes, she's improving. She has a broken shoulder and it's mending." She wanted to treat the whole incident casually, as if it were a minor accident. There would be gossip enough, heaven knew.

"Everybody says she's very strange," Susan confided, widening her eyes. "Like the Lady of Shalott. They say she's so ugly she can't go out in the daylight."

"That isn't true. I told you before, Susan, I've seen Venetia myself. She's marked by smallpox, but otherwise she looks just like everybody else," Honey said crossly.

"Humph!" Susan said, dipping into the sandwiches and rejecting one with an egg filling. "What does Angela look like?"

"Angela is very pretty."

"I'll say so!" Mathieu seconded, having caught a glimpse of her at breakfast.

"Beau says you can't imagine how beautiful she is. He says she's like a princess. That's what he calls her. The princess! But you know what Beau's like, Mother. He's a little crazy," Susan went on.

Beau was spending a week with his parents on the farm and was not present to defend himself. His devotion to music, his quiet introspection, his almost adult approach to things made him seem odd to the St. Amour children. They did not really dislike him (although they found it irritating that their mother had given him the whole fourth floor), but they had not grown close to him, either.

"Beau is very talented, not crazy," Honey corrected, but without much hope of making an impression. She had said it so often that it was now a habitual response.

"You have to concentrate, you have to put your whole

self into things, if you want to succeed," Mathieu said, making a half-hearted attempt to defend his absent brother. "Isn't that right, Uncle Armand?"

"Quite correct," Armand said.

"How did Angela like Beau?" Denys asked, injecting another side to the matter.

"I believe they got along very well," Honey said.

"Then she must be strange, too. Probably like her mother," Michel offered. He had no objection to baiting Mathieu a little.

"That's enough!" Honey said with spirit. "All of you can leave the tea table now and get your clothes and equipment packed for the trip to the island. I bought you new canvas shoes, Denys, so there is no excuse for not learning to play tennis. Michel, yours are still wearable. Take some books, too. Now, run along."

When they had gone, she sank back in her chair.

"I suppose it is difficult for them, having their cousins living here," Honey remarked.

"It does no harm," Armand said. He liked the idea of children, and was fond of his own, even warm toward them, but he did not take their likes and dislikes very seriously. There were other, more important matters on his mind.

They sank into their separate silences. Honey began to think about the house, her newly acquired gift. The first flush of pride and joy was wearing off as a new thought occurred to her. She was loath to spoil the effect of the present that Armand had so thoughtfully made to her, but the question of Philippe Grande's plans would not leave her mind. Finally she said, "And what is Philippe going to do for a house now that he's sold that one?"

"Oh, didn't I tell you? He's building a new one, quite large, I think, up on Sherbrooke."

"And what does a bachelor want with a large house? Is he getting married?"

"Not Philippe!" Armand said, grinning. "Not that I know of, anyway. I guess he'll just hire some servants. But you know how much he likes to entertain, and he wants something more sumptuous."

She could imagine why he wanted a large house, Honey thought angrily. To accommodate his huge parties and his gambling and his drinking. No doubt he would hold a perpetual open house for all his friends. And Armand would be one of Philippe's most frequent guests. The old anger rose up in her as she pictured those entertainments. With an enormous effort, she refrained from expressing her thoughts, and, instead, rose shakily from the table and said thinly, "I must go up and sort out my clothes, Armand."

"Of course, darling. I have some bills to look into. I'll see you later, upstairs."

She smiled at him, but it was not a happy smile.

"All right, darling."

As she climbed the narrow stairway to the second floor she choked down the hurt and anger that could still well up inside her and threaten to topple her whole life. Images of Philippe and his friends, with Armand very much in evidence, were strong in her mind. She forced them back down, swallowing hard, and stiffened herself for the packing and the organizing ahead. But her heart was not in it, and all the joy had ebbed from the gift of Philippe Grande's little house, where she had first experienced the pleasures of love.

CHAPTER THREE

Camille knew every detail of her bedroom perfectly. She had a sense of place for each piece of furniture, each window, door, and ornament so that she could move about without help of any kind. When a new servant was hired Camille was careful to explain that everything must be left exactly as it was and that, after cleaning, it must be replaced. This morning, the new girl, Clara, had nervously broken a drinking glass Camille kept on her bedside table. Still, the girl seemed to understand, and it had easily been put right.

Camille's eyesight had improved slightly after the initial total blindness. Within two years of her illness, she had been able to see faint shadows with her right eye, and both she and Marc had hoped desperately at that time that her sight would return completely. It had not. She lived in a twilight world, but she had learned to move, to work, and sometimes even to take pleasure in it.

As she prepared for bed, standing by the open window to breathe in the motionless air of the hot July night, she thought about Honey's visit. It was a new challenge for Marc, this founding of a home for strayed women. And if Marc wanted to assist Honey in the enterprise, then she, Camille, would be a part of it. If Marc were her eyes, she was his heart.

She left the window and walked slowly and with erect carriage toward the bed. The years had left little mark upon her face; it had the expressionless quality of a sleep-walking child's. As if, by screening her from seeing things, life had washed away disfiguring emotions. Her skin was smooth, the face unaltered in shape, the hair caught back simply at the nape and still long and black. Her hands, always graceful, were even more so now that they were her mainstay. As her thigh touched the bed and she made ready to pull down the summer coverlet, she felt something at her feet. A handkerchief she had somehow dropped earlier, she decided, and bent to retrieve it. The cloth was halfway underneath the night table and she thrust her hand forward to pull at it.

Then she screamed as the sharp piece of glass pierced the tip of her finger with an unexpected fierceness.

The sound penetrated the silent house like a dagger. She grasped her cut finger with her left hand and felt the blood pouring out. This frightened her because she couldn't see how badly it was bleeding.

"Marc! Marc!"

She heard him coming quickly along the corridor, shouting her name.

"Camille? What is it?"

He rushed to her, carrying a lamp. When he had set it down, he took her bleeding hand.

"It's a bad cut on the end of your finger," he said soothingly. "It just needs binding to stop the blood. Where did the glass come from?"

"The girl . . . she broke a glass this morning. I suppose she didn't clean it all up."

He tore up a pillowcase for a bandage and quickly stopped the excessive flow of blood.

"Sit down on the bed, Camille, while I get you something for the pain. A little brandy, I think. There you are . . ."

He eased her down upon the bed and saw in the flickering of the kerosene lamp the paleness of her face and how childlike she was, nursing the awkwardly bandaged finger. Her face was uptilted to him, trustingly. So helpless. She wore a summer nightgown of thin white cambric, and he could see the firm shape of her breasts and the slightly darker shadow of her nipples. His hand on her bare arm trembled and he straightened up with a vicious jerk, to separate himself from her physically.

"I'll get the brandy," he said, hearing the huskiness in his own voice and wondering if she knew his struggle. He came back bearing the brandy and a headache powder. She accepted both without moving from the bed.

"Is it bleeding much now?" she asked finally.

He could hear the tremor in her voice. It must be frightening, he thought, to live all alone in that semidarkness.

He felt the pain of Camille's isolation and, as he had so

many times before, asked an unhearing God why this had happened to *her*. Why must they both be caught in the same endless web, caring so desperately and yet being so utterly unable to reveal it even to each other?

He took her injured hand gently in his own.

"I think the bleeding has almost stopped."

"It doesn't hurt quite so much."

"Hold your hand up," he directed.

She obeyed him like a child.

A growl in some far corner of the sky signaled thunder. Marc put her hand gently in her lap, feeling the warmth of her body through the gown. He walked over to the window and looked out. Gray clouds had thickened over the trees, like clotted cream. In the distance beyond the city, a wide flash of shapeless light revealed the general direction of the storm. A small gust of wind whipped the curtains inward.

"A storm's coming," Marc said. It was an unnecessary remark. She always sensed a storm before anyone else, as if this pathetic but special talent had been given her when her eyes had dimmed.

"A breeze," she murmured, and she turned her face toward the window as if toward a sweet-smelling flower.

Marc blew out the lamp, reasoning that if he could not see the tempting thrust beneath her nightgown and the hint of darker pleasures where her hand lay in the folds between her thighs, then his own ache might ebb. But the thread of tension between them refused to vanish.

He did not know what to do except that he could not leave her like this. Yet if he touched her, his hands—sweating as heavily as if he had been digging a field—might behave of their own accord. Hadn't he prayed every single day for all the years of his adult life that he would conquer this wickedness? Hadn't he worked like a galley slave, read books until his eyes bulged, tramped the docks and the slums giving help to others, abased himself before God, to avoid just such a night as this?

In the darkness she whispered, "Marc?"

"Yes, Camille. I'm here."

His mouth was dry. The throbbing pain in his own thighs joined the pain in her more obvious wound.

"Don't leave me. I'm afraid, Marc. I'm terribly afraid."

Her voice was ragged, cracked with tears. He threw himself on the carpet at her feet, and, remembering to be gentle, removed her hands from her lap so that his own head could lie there. His forehead was wet. The heat from her body rose up to meet him and he groaned. She bent slightly over him so that just the tips of her breasts, covered by the thin cloth, touched his cheek. He shuddered.

"Hold me, Marc, I'm so alone in this darkness. I'm so alone—don't go. You don't know what it's like . . . I try to push away the darkness, as if it were a curtain that I could simply remove, but it's always *night*. There's never anything but *night*, Marc . . ."

He helped her to lie down under a single cotton quilt, and he lay beside her, his arms shielding her from the fears of unutterable blackness. As his hands stroked her shoulders and back, the fine mold of her hips, he swore over and over that this was all he would do. This was *all*. He would hold her in comfort. Could that be wrong? If he did not control himself, he would have to leave her again, leave her alone in the abyss and she might . . . she might do anything. She was like a broken doll in his arms, murmuring over and over, "Don't leave me, Marc." They were children again. The years—was it thirty?—had slipped away. Their child-bodies were welded together in a protective stance against the world. If he was aware of the yielding cushion of her breasts between them (not the slim and sexless statue he had held so long ago) and if she was aware of the foreign hardness bursting with a millenium of denial (no longer the tentative organ she had felt when they were children), they did not speak of it.

The night was filled with waking warmth, with delicate pain and fleeting delights, but in the morning he was haggard and she was still a virgin.

"Just what is this terrible sin that weighs so heavily upon you, my son?" Bishop Lavergne asked.

The old man was buried comfortably in the depths of an enormous brown leather chair, his feet on a hassock. Since his retirement, he had found it expedient to receive people less formally. Beside him on a tooled leather-topped table sat a glass of his favorite port. He sipped the wine and studied the ruby color with appreciation. He had offered Marc a drink, but the priest had refused.

"I find it almost impossible to tell you, my Lord."

"Have you dipped into the Poor Box?" the bishop

asked facetiously. "Have you given the Sacrament to an unconfessed supplicant? What have you done that's so wicked?"

The bishop gave his nephew a faint, slightly derisive smile. He considered himself something of an expert in the matter of sin, but over the years he had been discouraged by the lack of practitioners with any talent for the original.

"Will you hear my confession, Uncle Eustache?"

Marc forced the words out and then stared down at his trembling hands, unable to meet the bishop's eye. He couldn't imagine what his uncle would say when he heard the truth; he couldn't begin to guess whether the bishop could withstand the shock.

The bishop didn't reply immediately. Marc waited, conscious of the steady pulse of the grandfather clock in the corner and the urgent plea of a night bird in the garden. He felt the relentless gaze of the painted, sad-eyed Virgin over the mantel accusing him of numberless crimes.

When his uncle didn't appear to be forming a reply, Marc was forced to elaborate on his problem.

"It isn't one specific sin. It's a lifetime of sin!" he cried out at last. "But what good will it do me to confess to you when I'm going to wallow in the same evil?"

Bishop Lavergne perked up. A careful look at his nephew's haggard eyes, pale cheeks, and shaking limbs, combined with the extraordinary statement, secured the cleric's full attention. Here, then, was an unusual offering.

"My dear Marc, of course I'll hear your confession. And we must never assume that the situation is hopeless." He had taken on a kindly, avuncular tone. His right hand was slightly raised as if he were already conferring a blessing, and he sighed as if from the weight of the world's problems.

Marc searched for the right words to make the issue clear and at the same time spare his uncle's delicate feelings. It was a family matter as well as a religious one. He had no desire to be a martyr, but on the other hand if he didn't tell his uncle the truth he would leave this place as sick and desperate as when he'd arrived.

"I have an unnatural love," Marc said quickly. And then, before his courage could desert him, he spilled out the whole story of his attachment to his sister, their attempts to resist the temptations, their separations, their need for each other, and then, after all these years of deprivation and prayer and stern resolve, how he had fallen only last night. Finally he fell silent. He could scarcely breathe.

It was an unusual story, Eustache Lavergne thought, sifting it in his mind. Most unusual. Who would ever have suspected the spartan, hard-working, devout Marc of such a secret? And Camille. So pretty, so sweet, so devoted to her brother. The convenience of the arrangement did not escape the bishop, either—the constant temptation and the interdependence of the relationship. With Camille blind (an added touch) it was impossible to ask for anything more complex; a gourmet recipe for an exquisite sauce, one might almost say. He dwelt upon it.

"There's no way to solve it!" Marc cried out, impatient for some response, even if it were condemnation and eternal hellfire.

"Ah, wait. I think you have mistaken the case."

"Mistaken it?"

"Yes. *You* see it as a result of your own wickedness. *You* see yourself manufacturing your own cesspool, and then wallowing in the filth. Isn't that right?"

"Yes, yes. I've known all along what I was doing. I must convince you of that, Uncle Eustache. I've *known*. But I couldn't give it up. I couldn't leave Camille before, and I certainly can't leave her now. It's quite hopeless."

"Nothing is hopeless," the bishop intoned.

"I can't leave her. Don't you see? And while I'm with her this . . . this *lust* goes on in my head. I shake now, and feel ill when I think of what we did. But at the time . . . she was so afraid . . . oh, my God, my God, everything is lost . . . everything. I'll give up. I can't go on . . . my work . . ."

Bishop Lavergne allowed him to continue in this vein for a little time—it was good for the man to get the poison out of his system—and then he said quietly, but in a firm, resonant voice, "I see it differently, my son."

Marc looked up, astonished.

"Differently? But *how*, Uncle Eustache? Surely there's only one way to see it?"

"As I said, *you* regard this as something of your own making. But I see it from another point of view. This, my son, has been sent to you as a *trial*. God is testing you.

The trial is long and arduous but it is, nevertheless, a trial. You must keep praying, you must keep exposing yourself to this test, you must *keep resisting*."

Marc was so astonished by this version of his problem that he was temporarily stopped in his flow of words. "It is God's will," the bishop said.

"God's will?" Marc repeated stupidly. "I must go on lusting all my life?"

"Camille will be blind all her life, won't she? Other people are crippled all their lives, you know that perfectly well. There is no end in sight for some people's ugliness or disfigurement. Why should there be a time limit on *your* temptation?"

"No, I suppose there's no reason to expect that. I hadn't thought of it like that. But what must I do . . . what if I fall?"

"You must not fall."

"No."

"You must keep praying. Do you understand? Camille is your responsibility. You can't leave her now. And you can't have her, either, not in the complete sense of the word. But you must stay and resist. And, Marc, every time you do resist that temptation, you are accomplishing a marvelous strengthening of the will."

"Can you absolve me?"

"Yes, my son. You have strayed close to the fire. You must promise not to sleep with your sister again—it's much too close to the mortal sin itself. But you must care for her."

"But if it happens again, Uncle?" Marc shook his head, momentarily sliding back into hopelessness. "I can't guarantee that I can fight the temptation successfully."

"God hasn't asked for a guarantee."

"No, he never does," Marc said humbly.

"Say the words, my son. Say the words."

"For these sins, and all the other sins of my past which I cannot now remember, I ask forgiveness."

"You must pray, and you must love, and you must resist," the bishop said softly. "Now, kneel before me."

With his hand on Marc's head, he lapsed into the Latin. Marc, feeling more peaceful than he had felt for many hours, listened with gratitude. Somehow, it was going to be all right. God would make it be all right. God would remain with him, and he would remain with God.

CHAPTER FOUR

The sweet, incandescent sound of a guitar floated on the morning air. It came from the willows up in the hill pasture, and Timothée Fitzgerald heard it where he worked with the stock near the barns. Young Beau was up there by the creek working out a song. Timothée understood the charm music held for Beau. His own folk back in County Cork had included a number of natural singers who had rhapsodized at wakes and swelled the ranks of a dozen local church choirs. He could remember the thin keening of his mother, a sound born of relentless cruelties and numberless ignominies, but always musical. He had marveled at her talented strength of purpose. No, Timothée had felt no surprise when it became apparent that Beau had the gift.

Although Beau had been home for two days, Timothée had scarcely seen him. He left his work now, drawn away by the music. The morning was bright, sparkling with the leftover diamonds of a night rain. With long strides, he walked swiftly uphill toward the clump of trees.

When he first saw Beau he felt the old familiar pain of recognition—the dark, tousled head, the narrow eyes that would be green as grass when he was close enough to discern their color, the sensitive mouth, the clever, quick hands.

"Good morning, Beau," Timothée said casually when the boy had finished his song. "That's a pretty tune. Is it one of your own, then?"

"Yes. Do you like it?"

"Sounds good, all right. But it's a little *triste*, isn't it? Why are you sad on a morning like this?"

He waved his long arms about, taking in the blue sky, the green dripping willows, the clean creek water flowing over pale stones and carrying small twigs to encourage dragon flies.

"I'm quite often sad," Beau said.

Timothée frowned. He'd noticed that the lad looked thin and distressed, but he had put it down to end of term. The boy had been working too hard, he told himself. Now the ancient fear stirred in him, and his antennae signaled that some crisis was at hand.

"We're all sad, I suppose. But when you're young, and have a talent like yours, there's a lot to be thankful for."

He knew it sounded trite, but he wasn't good at talking to young people. Beau was particularly difficult, but he also found it hard to talk to Mathieu, and even Nicolette.

Unsure of his next step, Timothée sat down on a log a few feet from Beau. At close range the sun picked out the similarity between them. Timothée's shock of hair had turned prematurely white, but still there was the shape of the head. The father's skin was brown and lined from weather and his frame bulky while the son was white-faced and thin, but the look in the eyes, the set of the mouth, the *presence,* was much the same.

"Why did you stay on here?"

It came like a gunshot. Timothée was startled. Yes, he'd known it might happen sometime, that Beau would realize the truth. But he had always pushed the thought away. Some other time. Not now. Another day, another week, another year, perhaps.

"What do you mean? I do a good job for your father. He pays me well. I don't plan to leave. Your father doesn't want me to."

"Oh, I know all that," Beau said with the impatience of thirteen years. "I don't mean your work. Everybody knows you're good with the herd. But it's different now. Can't you see that? When I was little, I suppose it didn't matter so much. But now, anybody can *see.*"

Timothée tried to clear his mind. How could he explain to the boy why he had never left? It was simple. Both Justine and Laurent had needed him. He had had nowhere to go. But was it only convenience that kept him? He supposed not. He had wanted to see his son. He knew he'd never marry anyone but Justine, and since it was impossible ever to marry *her*, then he would have to remain single. Surely he had a right to see his son?

"I guess I hoped nobody *would* see," Timothée said finally.

Beau seemed to recognize that as truth. He stared down at his guitar, unable to look into his father's eyes.

"How can they miss seeing it?" he asked. "I know I'm not large like you; I never will be. But I have the same features. People would have to be blind not to notice. And do you know what that makes me? A *bastard*."

He forced the word out. A foreign, ugly word.

Timothée thought with a terrible pang how badly the word fitted the beautiful boy sitting there in the grass. A boy with an otherworldly face (shaped like his own, with some of the same features, true, but with the off-center vision that talent sometimes offers) and illuminated hands. No, you couldn't even conceive of the word "bastard" in connection with this boy.

"No, you aren't. You have a name. Just like every other child. You're a Dosquet."

"He knows, doesn't he? He's always known?"

"Well, for a long time, anyway."

"And he let you stay on?"

There was just a hint of condescension in the childlike voice. For a moment, the man who would one day occupy this frail body, and who had rigid ideas of manhood, had spoken. But the voice shook, and crumbled, and sank to a lower pitch.

"I guess," Timothée said quietly, "he needed your mother and he needed me."

Beau sighed.

"You ought to have gone."

"Perhaps I should have."

"Nicolette will say something. She and Mathieu always hated me because Mother made more fuss about me. They've always been jealous. And as soon as she realizes . . ."

He was clenching his fists, getting angry now.

"I'm sorry," Timothée said inadequately.

"I hate this farm! I hate coming here! I know Nicolette will say something. Then it will all be out. That I don't belong."

"You do belong. You're Justine's child."

"I don't belong on this farm. I'm going back to Montreal

and I'm never coming back! I'm going before Nicolette says anything!"

"Your mother will want to see you. You must come back. She loves you."

"She can come to Montreal to see me."

"Well, maybe."

"Is that why she prays so much? Because she feels so guilty? Is that it?"

"We don't talk about it. I don't know."

The tears were perilously close, and Beau got up and stamped his foot and tried to hold them back. He was turned away from Timothée so that the struggle to contain himself wouldn't be laid bare.

"I'm leaving. I'm never coming back here! I won't listen to the things everybody will say. I hate you!"

"Stop that!" Timothée said, raising his voice for the first time. "Don't ever say that again."

"I hate you and I hate Mother! Why did you do this to me?"

After this cry, he threw himself on the grass and began to sob. Timothée, feeling completely helpless, finally walked off down the hill. He was numb. How could a feeling that had been so precious and so demanding in the long-ago past be transformed into this painful nightmare?

He met Justine that night in the garden. It was the first time in more than thirteen years that they had arranged a rendezvous. She came to him wearing a cross expression that he could see very well in the moonlight.

"What do you want to talk to me about?" she demanded angrily, at the same time keeping her voice down. "You know I don't want to meet you privately."

"There's no need to talk like that to me. It's important, or I wouldn't have asked you to meet me here," Timothée said. They spoke in French. Timothée spoke French well, and since Justine thought in French and, he assumed, felt in French, he always spoke to her in her own language.

"I have worries enough," she said now, in a somewhat softer tone, "without dragging up some problem from the past."

"We all have worries. It *is* from the past, Justine, but believe me, it must be dealt with. Beau spoke to me today about his birth. He knows the truth."

She stared at him without speaking. The ridge between her eyebrows deepened, and she looked older. She had not lost her handsomeness, although she had put on a little weight. The mouth, despite all her hours of prayer, held its familiar sensual lines. The eyes might, if pressed, be capable still of flashing secret wants.

"How did Beau find out?"

"By looking at himself and then at me."

"I should have known this would happen. It's only a matter of time before Nicolette notices and says something, too. And then Luc. She and her husband are so close."

"And then Mathieu."

"Yes, Mathieu."

"Beau is afraid."

"He understands what Nicolette is like. She thinks she owns this farm because she and Luc have helped to run it. She's always been a prig. I don't know how she could have been born such a prig, but I suppose she takes after Laurent."

He was astonished at this outburst against Nicolette. Since the girl had married Luc Barbier they had lived in a second house on the farm and Luc had become a manager of many aspects of the property. However, that Justine recognized the unpleasant side of her daughter's personality was a revelation to Timothée.

"I wanted to prepare you," Timothée explained. "Beau says he's going back to Montreal and he doesn't want to come here ever again. I told him that he must, that you wanted him here at least occasionally. But right now he's angry and frightened."

"We ought to have expected it," Justine said more calmly. "Laurent has never reproached me. Did you know that? I suppose I thought his silence made me safe. I didn't think about Beau looking so much . . . like you."

"How could anybody know that? It doesn't always happen. Mathieu doesn't look much like his father. Many sons don't. Beau could easily have looked more like you, Justine. He could have had your eyes and your mouth, instead of mine."

"Anyway, one of us should have foreseen it."

"And what would we have done differently if we'd thought about the possibility?"

"I don't know," she said with despair.

He suddenly had a vision of the two of them on an argumentative, questioning treadmill for the rest of their lives; should he have left the farm right in the beginning? How had they thought they could get away with this arrangement? Had Laurent suffered because Timothée had stayed on at the farm as a constant reminder—and then, going back one step further, why had they become emotionally and physically involved in the first place?

Justine abruptly changed the subject.

"Laurent is ill. I'm worried about him. You know he hasn't been well for several weeks, but at first we thought it was just an upset stomach or an influenza."

"I noticed he hasn't been eating much."

"I paid little attention at first. Everybody gets upset from time to time. You don't run to a doctor every time you need a laxative or a stomach powder." Justine paused and then went on, still speaking in a low voice because the windows of the house were open to the warm summer air. "But lately he complains of pain at every meal. Even between meals. I know that isn't natural. Perhaps he has a stomach ulcer. Anyway, so far he's refused to see Dr. Goulet, but only tonight, before I came out here to meet you, he agreed to let me call the doctor in the morning. He's in pain. Tonight he began to vomit. I'm very worried about him."

"It sounds serious. He should have seen the doctor earlier."

"Yes, a month ago."

He turned the conversation back to Beau.

"I think you should let Beau return to Montreal, if he insists," Timothée suggested. "Give him time to think about what happened today. If Nicolette does say something to him at this point, he'll be angry. It could do him a lot of harm. I think he needs time."

"Honey and the children are on Ste. Helene Island," Justine said, hesitantly. "Still, I think Armand stays in town during the week, so he wouldn't be completely alone."

"No doubt they keep a maid on in the city. I'm sure you can arrange something."

"Yes, I'll do something. Especially since Laurent is ill.

I don't want any extra strain on Laurent now. There's only so much one can stand."

"At least we're in agreement."

"Timothée, I want to thank you for telling me. For giving me a chance to straighten things out. I'm going to pray to the Virgin for all of us." She reached out to touch Timothée's arm with her fingers, a small gesture of remembered intimacies.

He watched her go back to the house, realizing that his own faith didn't support him in the way Justine's supported her. The Church, he thought, could be a great comfort if one were able to suspend all questioning. Yet somehow he had never been able to embrace the Church's tenets as Justine did. It was a pity. The hurt that lodged somewhere in his gut would not be pacified with the promise of a chat with the Virgin Mary.

The next morning Beau was driven to the railway station and put on the train for Montreal. Back on St. Denis Street, he spent the days alone, practicing, composing, and reading musical history. Sometimes he dined with his Uncle Armand and sometimes with his brother, Mathieu.

Mathieu, if he had noticed Beau's resemblance to Timothée Fitzgerald, said nothing. He played chess with Beau and occasionally deigned to listen to his younger brother's latest compositions. He expounded on local politics and federal politics and Beau listened with half an ear, out of politeness. They were so different that they could occupy the same room without ever meeting in a common interest.

Mathieu made speeches (as if he were already practicing for later public appearances) about Henri Bourassa and his new paper, *Le Devoir*, which took a strong stand against Laurier and his Naval Bill. The Naval Bill sought to establish a Canadian navy that would at the same time act as a link with the Empire, a kind of genuflection to the British Crown. Mathieu explained to Beau that the bill was another nail in the coffin of the French language and the Catholic Church in Canada. *Le Devoir* was supported by the bishops of the Church, and most young clergy were solidly in favor of its tone. Beau didn't understand much of this, but he did know that Aunt Miel's newspaper was solidly Liberal and behind Prime Minister Laurier.

It was an event much more personal, and much closer

to the heart that seized Beau's imagination: a visit from his cousin, Angela.

Angela had come back into the city to spend some time with her mother at Pride's Court. Venetia, just released from the hospital in the care of a private nurse, had decided she wished to see her daughter for a brief visit each morning. Once she left her mother's apartment, Angela was free to amuse herself as best she could until her father came home for dinner.

Without telling the housekeeper or Venetia's nurse, Angela set out for the St. Amour house on the very first afternoon she was back, armed with a box of water colors, drawing paper, and brushes in a canvas bag.

"I've come to paint," she said to Beau when he appeared, breathing heavily, at the bottom of the stairs (he had practically flown down in his haste after the housekeeper had announced Angela's arrival). "I hope you don't mind?"

"No, no, I'm glad to see you."

That was an understatement. He was ecstatic at the sight of her. When he'd first met Angela he had felt they were close, as if they'd known each other always. It had occurred to him, however, that he might not see her again unless he convinced Aunt Miel to invite Angela to the house as a guest. There was no regular visiting between the St. Amours and the Courts. Now here she was, in the flesh, beautiful and smiling. His muse.

"I remembered how lovely the light was in the nursery," Angela explained as they climbed the stairs together, "and I wanted to work here. It won't bother you while you practice, will it?"

"Bother me? No, I'll play much better."

She spread her supplies out on the floor near one of the dormers and fetched water from the nursery bathroom.

"What are you painting?" Beau asked, standing over her work.

"An illustration for a fairy story. It's about three princesses locked up in a tower and the tower is out in the ocean on a rock."

"They're beautiful."

"They aren't quite right yet. I've discovered some new illustrators—very exciting. I borrow books from the library, you know. Father buys them for me, too."

She began to tell him about a painter called Dulac, and another called Rackham. She wanted to learn how to paint as they did.

"It's a fantasy world. There aren't really places like that, but I like to think there are," Angela explained.

"Music is the same way," Beau said.

She nodded and set to work. He was composing a barcarole. They spent the whole afternoon like that, speaking little, but in communion. Beau forgot the problem of Timothée, and Angela forgot the demands of her peculiar mother. After the success of that first day, they spent each afternoon together until Venetia's convalescence ended, her desire for her daughter's visits waned and Angela was taken back to Drake House.

CHAPTER FIVE

Sydney drifted noiselessly from the dressing room to stand still in a patch of moonlight by the French windows. Her long, light hair swung in a thick braid down her back and her upturned face offered only brilliant bones and deep shadows. Her nightgown was pure fantasy—green mist shot with silver, airy shoulder puffs pinched in neatly on the upper arms only to blow out again in pleated circles at the elbow. A gown that suggested brave knights, merry jousts, and pretty troubadours.

Fort, mesmerized by her entrance, would not have been surprised to see bits of moldering bramble clinging to the folds of her skirt (the aftermath of a long walk through a damp, neglected park) or a unicorn's sad eye lurking in one corner of the bedroom.

At this moment he might never have been her husband, never known the earthly pleasures of her slim ivory body, never felt her delicious breasts pleading for attention. Her mystery was so complete at this moment that she might have been a mythical princess, straying briefly from her kingdom.

At the same time, he realized that not one of these impressions was true. The hard edge of reality about Sydney's background, her parentage, was now an ugly part of his life. During his last visit to London he had pursued once again the chimera of her past and had unearthed, at last, some facts.

True, when they'd first met he had told Sydney that he didn't care where she came from, that he had no interest in her childhood, about which she kept unrelenting silence. It had been enough then to satisfy his hungers on her cool yet responsive body. But as the months and years had gone by, his desire to know had sprung to life and grown into an obsession.

The earliest change had come about when Landry had been born and Fort had felt the pride of fatherhood. This was his son. His heir. The boy would be a reflection of himself. Well, yes, and (he had to admit reluctantly) of Sydney too. That had to be taken into account. Going a step further back, the boy was also a reflection of his grandparents, Sir Simon and Lady Court. It followed that he was also a reflection . . . of whom?

If she was simply concealing poverty, why couldn't Sydney say so? Fort began to juggle lunacy with crime. Doubts grew into fears and fears bred nightmares. His mind dredged up an old saying: "Blood will tell." Bad seeds carried. He even resorted to the Bible and recalled part of a passage about the sins of the fathers being visited upon the sons.

What had he unwittingly passed down to his son? And to his daughters, those twin, blue-eyed sirens? Why hadn't he thought carefully about these matters before he'd become embroiled with Sydney? He could have kept her somewhere as a mistress and married a suitable woman for breeding purposes. He secretly mourned his lack of foresight. (Charles had done better because Venetia was at least from solid stock, traceable, and Angela had every appearance of being a worthy addition to the Court name.)

Now, Fort made a superhuman effort to shake off Sydney's narcotic effect by thinking of the facts he'd brought back from London—facts that added a fresh whiff of ruin to the ravaged aura his wife carried with her.

"Sydney . . ." he began tentatively.

She looked at him wordlessly. Waiting. As if she knew beyond question her power over him.

"Why would you never tell me about your parents?"

He knew a few facts now, he wanted to know more, to know everything.

"You agreed in the beginning not to ask."

"True. But now . . . with the children . . ."

"Ah. So now it's different." She sounded disillusioned. "You've been prying, haven't you, Fort?"

They stared at each other, strangers who had shared splendid intimacies but who now stood *en garde* for the real match. After a few moments, she sat down as if she were very tired. The moonlight bypassed her face and fell only on the curious Arabian slippers she wore.

Part of him wanted to abandon this ugly cause and take her, fulfill himself once again with the delights she could so easily provide. Another part nagged at him to hold back, turning him cold.

"Yes. I've been trying to find out about you. Where you came from. Who your parents were. I . . . I'm sorry, Sydney, but I can't seem to help it."

"And did you find out?"

"Only about your mother."

"I see. It's . . . do you understand why I want to forget?"

"Naturally. An awful death. Incredible."

"An awful life," she amended.

"I suppose she was . . . one of *them*?"

He couldn't bring himself to say the word. No, he would not say the word because this woman, this woman whose only distinction was that of being murdered in a dark doorway of Whitechapel by an unidentified lunatic called Jack the Ripper, this woman was the grandmother of his son and his daughters.

"She was a streetwalker, a common prostitute, if you like. Certainly. That's how she came to be killed, as you probably know very well. He only killed those women, they say, though whether it was because they were easily available and not much missed, or whether he had some vendetta against them, who knows?"

"Did you know your mother?"

"A little. I was left with neighbors a lot. I ran away when I was very young."

"And your father?"

She shrugged.

"I've wondered, of course, but there's no way of proving that. When I was very young I pretended that somehow, just *somehow*, my mother had been with a handsome, brilliant, charming man. A man of taste. Educated. Traveled. Through some peculiar circumstance, he spent a night with my mother and I was the result. You'd be surprised how much comfort there was in that."

Her voice was flat, but seemed to hang in the air, disassociated from either of them. He knew now that he would have to stop asking her and stop making inquiries in London. That the hurt was too deep to be reopened like this. He felt ill, but held himself together with great effort and pushed away thoughts of his son.

"I'm sorry."

She didn't reply. Instead, she went to the huge bed and climbed in, pulling the covers up to her neck protectively. Her arms lay on top of the blanket, lifeless as the arms of a doll. She stared into the darkness. Fort forced himself to get into the other side of the bed. They both lay there without speaking. He had opened Pandora's box, and grotesque, forbidden things had flown out, and he was being smothered by them. He wondered how he could carry on tomorrow at breakfast, how he could face Lady Court, how he could face Landry, how he could play with the little twins and laugh. And his father had informed him of a meeting in the afternoon to discuss the government contracts for new ships. Since the passage of the Naval Bill in April (which might eventually help bring Laurier's Liberal government down), tenders were out for six ships. Court Shipping had established its own shipyard in Halifax in 1902, and Sir Simon was just now back from Ottawa, where he had discussed the navy's requirements. All three Court sons were at Drake House for the weekend to discuss plans with Sir Simon and make a number of far-reaching decisions . . .

Lying in the hostile darkness of his bedroom, Fort wondered how he could rid himself of the choking lump in his throat. How could he concentrate on the affairs of the family business unless he controlled his emotions? He could not remember a time at sea, no matter what the dangers of the problems, when he'd felt so overwhelmed by his personal life. Sleep evaded him. And he knew that beside him, lying as stiffly as a swathed mummy, Sydney was suffering the same agony.

After lunch, Fort walked to the grass tennis court to watch the children. Although it was hot, Simon, Noel, Mildred, and Landry were on the court trying to hit the ball, running madly back and forth. The two governesses, Starkey and Richmond, sat on a wooden bench in the shade of a huge elm, watching. The sun on their white dresses and bright hair framed them. How young they looked! And rather sweet. He noticed how friendly the two women were; how they sat together, chattering and giggling, but watching the children at the same time. It occurred to him that Lady Court was lucky in her choice of servants this summer. There seemed to be no dissension below stairs.

When he came closer he noticed that the two women looked hot. There was a film of perspiration on each of their faces. It must be dull work, he thought sympathetically, always talking to children, correcting them, teaching them. Suddenly he felt sorry for the governesses. They worked hard and seldom had any extra time off.

"Good afternoon," he said to them.

They looked up at him at exactly the same time, like puppets who were invisibly attached to a single string, he thought. They both smiled. Their youth pleased him.

"Look, it's hot. I'm going to give the children a few pointers on the game. Why don't you two take an hour off?"

Their smiles widened.

"Oh, Mr. Court, could we really?"

"It *is* hot."

"I'll take responsibility for the children," Fort said kindly. "Where are the twins?"

"With their mother, sir."

"Then you should take the opportunity for a break," Fort said. "Why not ask Cook for some lemonade?"

They rose. He noticed that they touched fingers lightly. How pretty they are and how warm and friendly, Fort thought with enthusiasm. He watched them walk off toward the back of the house, with a feeling of pleasure that temporarily erased his own worry.

He watched Landry carefully while he coached the children at their game. The boy looked like a Court, he assured himself. A bit longer in the face, perhaps, than most of the family, but still he had the Court stamp. He was well coordinated. He was intelligent. Only this morning at breakfast, Papa had said how clever Landry was with plants; how he seemed to know all the names of the garden flowers. He could be another Darwin, Sir Simon had cried with gusto, adding that there was "no need to throw God out with the bathwater as Darwin did. But the chap was clever. Discovering strange animals in the Galapagos, and so on."

Though he had noted, as always, his father's abysmal condescension, Fort had been proud of Landry at that moment. The boy was only ten and he *was* clever about plants and animals and insects. His mind was a regular encyclopedia. There was nothing strange about a young boy collecting insects and toads. All boys did that. He remembered how, back in England, he'd once kept a white rat in a box at his grandmother's place in Devon. Lady Manthorpe had been horrified when she'd found out, and had ordered the pet killed. She had no use, she'd said, for any animal except the horse. Fort could still recall his own pain at the idea and how years later, at his grandmother's funeral, he'd thought only about her cold-hearted destruction of his pet and not about the nice things she'd done for him.

As he called out suggestions to the children, and settled a fight between Noel and Mildred, half his mind was on the coming meeting with his father and his brothers. In a few minutes they'd be waiting for him in the Round Room, a kind of intermediary salon located between the drawing room and the dining room. The Round Room remained particularly bright but cool during the summer months.

When an hour was up, he chased all four children off for a rest period, and followed them across the hot lawn and into the cool depths of Drake House. His father was already expounding on the Naval Bill when Fort entered the Round Room.

"Laurier only created a Canadian navy because he knew bloody well we Conservatives would do it in the next round," Sir Simon was saying. "Ah, there you are, Fort. A bit late, eh?"

"I was giving tennis lessons to the children."

"Good, good. Well as I was saying, the Naval Bill has my approval, but there's no use trying to make a saint out of Laurier. That's the trouble with Catholics—they're all trying to become saints."

Sir Simon couldn't bring himself to give the Prime Minister credit even when Laurier was unquestionably right. A country with two seacoasts needed a navy, and the navy *should* be put at the service of King and Empire if war occurred. At the same time, Canadian naval recruits should be volunteers rather than conscriptees. Sir Simon, as it happened, agreed with every point of the bill. What he couldn't forgive was the fact that a Liberal Prime Minister had proposed such a bill.

"The bill's passed, anyway," Charles said, clipping the end off a cigar, "and Court Shipyards ought to get a contract to build at least one ship for the Canadian navy. Isn't that right, Papa?"

"No doubt about it. I have the Minister of Transport's word. Privately, of course. But he hasn't much choice. Some of the ships must be built in Canada. And he hasn't got a gaggle of Liberal-loving shipbuilders to choose from. Actually, he's left with a Conservative bidder. My guess is that *half* the new ships will have to be built in Scotland."

"Court Shipyards can use the business," Charles remarked solemnly. "We aren't operating to capacity in Halifax, you know. Some fishing schooners. A yacht or two. Hell, we aren't really in a position to order another ship for our own line just to keep the yard busy. I just went over the figures, and I don't think—"

Geoffrey interrupted him. "I want to talk about Court Harvesters."

They all turned to stare at Geoffrey. It was so unlike him to interrupt, or to introduce an item to the agenda. For years, ever since he had entered the family business as a full-fledged partner, Geoffrey had taken orders, run errands, and kept his opinions mostly to himself. Several of those years had been spent in Liverpool, of course, running the British end of the Court Line, ordering ships built in Scotland. Yet even since his return to Canada he had changed very little. In the pause that followed his extraordinary remark, the senior Court and the two younger Courts gazed at the fourth as if he were a stranger.

They saw a man who had gradually taken on stature, who had gained confidence over the years, and who at forty had become almost handsome. He had put on a little weight, and his hair was styled longer, with carefully designed sideburns. The face that had once been placid, evenfeatured, forgettable, had been transformed into one of assurance, ruddiness, and strength. His voice, so seldom heard as to be a mystery, was calm and deep. He looked back at them all without flinching, and, waving a sheaf of papers in his hand said, "You put me in charge of the ironworks two years ago. I've been producing farm machinery for some time, as you well know and now we're on the verge of bringing out a combine—that is, a machine that will reap and thresh. We employ fifteen hundred workers in Montreal alone. We have agents and salesmen in various parts of the country. And God willing, we can take some of the Australian market and possibly some of the Argentinian market away from our competition as soon as the Panama Canal is opened. But we have a serious problem."

"Hard to imagine your problem is more important than getting contracts for ships," Charles said. "But what's on your mind, Geoffrey?"

"Reciprocity," Sir Simon interrupted, growing angry almost instantaneously. "It's that damned Laurier again, and his secret deal with President Taft."

"That's right. Laurier wants free trade. Remove the tariffs. You know what that means to the farm-machinery business? It means we Canadians can't compete. How can we compete with International Harvester? The Americans will dump their machinery on us at low prices once the tariff comes off, and Court Harvesters will close up shop. So will Massey-Harris in Toronto, for that matter. None of us can compete with the Americans if the protective tariff is removed."

"Maybe we ought to get out of the farm-machinery business, then," Fort said moodily. "We've plenty to occupy our time with the shipping line, the railroads, Papa's bank, the various properties. Maybe we ought to get out of machinery and get into mining. There's asbestos in Labrador. Maybe we could expand up there . . ."

"*Give up?*" bellowed Sir Simon, struck almost speechless by such a craven idea. "Give up and let that Frenchie have his way? What about other manufacturers? Do you think that madman knows all the answers, eh? What about England? He'll ruin Canada, sacrifice the country to the Americans, and England be damned, that's what he'll do! He's always had a leaning toward a continental policy, damnit! Give up? Not if I have a breath left in my body!"

Fort, who had merely thrown out a suggestion, retreated hastily. He had no wish to stir up a fight with his father. That was the last thing on his mind.

"The Naval Bill almost brought him down," Sir Simon went on, blithely ignoring the fact that he approved of the bill, "and this Reciprocity Treaty will be the death of him. But just to make sure he dies quickly, we'll help him along!"

"Hear! Hear!" Charles said.

"Laurier is out stumping the west at the moment, but rumor has it he'll make so much noise on Reciprocity when he gets back to Ottawa that he may force a motion of nonconfidence in the government. If that happens he'll call an election for next spring. That suits me," Geoffrey said. "The Liberals have *Le Monde*, and the hybrids, the Nationalists if you like, have their *Le Devoir*, but we have several good solid Conservative newspapers on our side. We ought to play up the threat of the Reciprocity Treaty with the United States. Encourage an election next year so the people can vote on the issue themselves. If they give Laurier a mandate in the election, then he'll go ahead and remove the tariffs. But if he loses, a Conservative government under Robert Borden will keep things as they are. All we have to do is assure defeat for Laurier."

"Excellent. It's about time the pendulum swung the other way," Sir Simon agreed. "People are fed up with Laurier and his mad ideas. There's plenty we can do to help."

"I know where there are fifteen hundred votes to be had," Geoffrey said calmly. "And I can suggest where there are thousands more."

"What block of votes is that?" Sir Simon asked.

"The workers in the plant. *Our* workers."

"But they don't understand the meaning of the tariffs," Sir Simon began doubtfully. "My God, half of them can't read or write."

"They understand jobs. We'll make sure they understand that if reciprocity becomes a fact, Court Harvesters will close down. That will throw fifteen hundred men out of work instantly. We're not the only company to be affected. I'm drawing up a list of other manufacturers who'll suffer when the tariff is removed. The message we have to get across, singly and together, is this: vote for Laurier and lose your job. Let Sir Wilfrid think about that situation for a while."

A murmur of approval passed over the Court men. Charles slapped his brother on the back. Sir Simon beamed. Fort, yanked violently out of his personal dilemma by a concrete plan of action, felt excited about business for the first time in weeks. The circle of Court friends, of business acquaintances, included many large factory owners who would be badly affected by the new Laurier vision. If they stood together, worked together . . . a mood of optimism spread through the meeting so that by dinnertime all the Court men had been restored to good humor. So much so that all the children were invited to take the evening meal with the adults.

While this caused extra work for the kitchen and dining-room staff, it was a blessing for Starkey and Richmond. As governesses, they took dinner alone in the cook's sitting room. Altogether, they could not remember when they'd had such a pleasant working day.

CHAPTER SIX

It was September before Honey found time to visit the old house on St. Urbain Street. Montreal was awash in the tawny yellows of autumn. A lingering touch of green from a few stubborn leaves and a dash of red where a maple had been nipped by early frost only heightened the effect of filtered amber.

The air was cool and clean on the Mountain, but down close to the river, in the Old City, there was a hint of factory smoke, and the sharp, pungent smell of horses. Honey stopped the car on the narrow street and surveyed the house, remembering her first sight of it. It had seemed smaller and snugger then, coated with thick white snow and dripping icicles from every eave. She had been so excited, so afraid, so young.

Today, it looked forlorn in the autumn light. Substantial, but somehow naked in the sunshine. The steep roof, with its double row of dormers, was badly in need of paint. She knew that under the flaking green was a *fer blanc* roof, made up of the linings of tea cases or bully-beef tins that had been flattened to make shingles. The windows needed washing, too, and the front door was sagging.

The car attracted attention, as always. Not only because it was bright red, but because today the stunning woman driver was accompanied by a priest. Honey wore a pale blue woolen suit by Worth, with a navy, wide-brimmed hat secured by two silk scarves. Marc, in his black soutane and round hat, was a discordant contrast.

"There's a small stable behind," Honey said. "I'll take the car around there and put it out of sight."

It wasn't that she really minded people staring, but that Marc might be upset by all the attention.

"The stable will be a convenience if we do turn the house into an institution," Marc said, speaking in French.

The car's thin rubber tires bumped over the rough cobblestones, and Honey thought wistfully of the squeak of cold metal runners on snow, of Armand shouting at the reluctant stable boy, and of her first breathless entry into the house. She brought the car to a stop beside the stable door.

Honey untied her scarves and began to search in her handbag for the key ring. Handing it to Marc, she stuffed the scarves into the bag and climbed out of the car.

"Here, Marc, see if you can find out which is the back-door key."

Marc struck the right key almost immediately. Inside the narrow hall, memories clustered in Honey's mind so thickly that she felt quite light-headed. Ridiculous, of course. The past was the past. She forced herself to open the door to the back bedroom and saw once again the huge pine armoire, the four-poster, the smoky, dark beams of the ceiling.

"This room might make living quarters for the matron," she said to Marc as she crossed the handwoven carpet. "You see, there's a dressing room attached. It could be made quite comfortable. A nice apartment would be an added inducement to the right woman, don't you think?"

Marc followed her, curiously.

"A good idea, yes. Is Grande leaving all the furniture, too?"

"Most of it, I think. He told Armand I could have whatever was here. He's very kind."

The words came hard, but she didn't want Marc to know that she disliked Philippe Grande.

"Now, upstairs, as I recall, there are big attics we could turn into bedroom space for the women we take in. Perhaps there's also room for a nursery," Honey went on, opening the armoire unthinkingly and finding it empty.

"This house is splendid. It seems to be in fairly good shape," Marc said warmly. "Grande is certainly generous. But so are you, Honey, to devote your time to the project and give the house as well."

"Did I ever tell you about the nightmare I had in this room on our wedding night?" Honey asked. When Marc shook his head she went on, "I saw a funeral cortege but I couldn't see who the dead person was. I was terrified. It was only two weeks later that your father died."

"That's strange, I'll admit. You've never mentioned the dream before."

"Do you think there are . . . well, things we don't know about, or understand? You must have thought about that, Marc, being a priest."

"I *have* thought about it. God's will, and the way the universe is constructed, is far beyond our understanding. There are great forces we can't comprehend, and God doesn't expect us to comprehend them. Would you ask an ant to understand the workings of a steam engine?"

Honey laughed a little, feeling more relaxed than she had when they'd begun this expedition.

"I suppose not. An ant couldn't understand that beyond the grass where he crawls, there is a forest."

"The connection between your dream and my father's death may well have been there," Marc said. "I've asked myself a thousand times why Camille had to lose her sight. I've never found the answer. But perhaps there *is* an answer, just the same."

Marc walked out into the hall and toward the front parlor. Honey, wondering about kitchen arrangements, went in the opposite direction, along a corridor that ran beside the wall of the dressing room. There was a wall-papered recess, like a linen cupboard without a door. Shelves lined either end, and in the middle there had been a painting that Philippe Grande had obviously removed. The darker place where it had once hung made a distinct rectangle on the pattern of the paper.

It would have to be repapered, Honey thought. And perhaps it could be closed in to make a more efficient storage space. They would need every bit of storage they could find for supplies and equipment. Would the paper be hard to remove? She examined it closely, stepping into the recess to do so. There was a small hole in the darker area that had once been covered by the picture.

"How odd," she muttered, running her fingers over the opening so that her fingertip eventually slid into the hole. A strange, nauseating pain struck her chest. She bit her lip in an attempt to keep calm. And then, trying not to show any outward signs of unease, she walked back into the bedroom and through to the little dressing room. The small fireplace in the corner, the empty hip bath, the table with bowl and jug were still there. The wall paneling was decorated with carved flowers on narrow pillars that reached up to the ceiling. She touched each pillar, and yes, in the center of one of the flowers a small circle of wood lifted off. Like the cap on a bottle. She took the seemingly inoffensive object in her hand and, clutching it tightly in her palm, walked back into the corridor.

Marc, wandering speculatively along the front hall, looked at her questioningly.

"I'm just thinking about some alterations," she said, hoping he wouldn't notice the tremor in her voice.

Around the corner, out of Marc's sight, she pressed her eye to the opening in the wall. Directly in her line of vision was the hip bath. A flood of anxieties took possession of her, so that she almost fainted. Did Armand know about this device? Who had looked through it on her wedding night when she had undressed and sat so happily in the hot bath? Surely not some friend of Armand's? Could it have been Philippe?

She could not rid herself of the notion that *somebody* had made use of the room's secret on her wedding night. Other visions seized her mind and would not let go—the parties Armand had once attended with Philippe, the stories of strange women, of gambling, of orgies hinted at but never quite described. She recoiled from the knowledge at the same time that she was attracted to it. Were there other odd things about this house? And the new house Philippe was planning—what of it? Armand, doubtless, would be one of the favored guests when that house was finished. She wondered dimly if Velma DeLeon was one of the habitués of Philippe's world.

The remainder of the house tour was accomplished in something of a fog. Part of her mind was consumed with imaginary scenes involving Armand and Philippe's friends. She noted the kitchen facilities and remarked on certain ways in which they could be enlarged. The upstairs attics would accommodate twelve women if they were properly planned. The stable at the back would be useful for visiting priests and doctors, and the rooms used formerly by stable hands and grooms might be utilized in some productive way. Space must be found for nurseries. And for the servants.

While they walked about, Marc made a list of items to be changed, added, purchased. Honey made correct responses to his remark, but her spirit had drained away. She would have to supervise the removal of that device in the wall and at the same time keep the workmen from talking. The secret must not get out and add a tarnish to the house's reputation. Above all, the house must be known in the city, and in the area, as a respectable, charitable, worthy institution. There must be no shadow cast upon it. Otherwise, she couldn't hope to accomplish her aims, to attract the right patrons, to raise money through a newspaper fund. She wanted to shelter unfortunate women, perhaps give them some training so they could find jobs; to care for the babies; and to take away some of the stigma attached to their situation. If the house was thought to be in any way doubtful, her task would be impossible.

When the tour was completed, Honey invited Marc home for lunch. He accepted, and over a cold ham and salad lunch served in the small dining room that Honey had recently redecorated in the new wing of the house, Marc said seriously, "Honey, you're doing a good thing. It's an original notion and a good one. And with your newspaper behind you, I know you can raise money. However, there is an aspect that I'd like to point out. You may not have thought about it."

Honey was trying hard to pay attention to Marc and to push some food down her throat. She must remain calm. When the shock of her discovery had worn off, she would be able to put things in perspective. She would be able to give her full attention to important matters. The sick feeling in her stomach would go away. After all, it was one of her strong qualities, this resilience. This ability to survive disillusionment and hurt.

"What do you mean, Marc?" she forced herself to ask.

She poured strong tea for both of them. Marc, unlike the rest of the family, preferred tea to coffee.

"Well, Honey, you see this as a secular venture. In your view it has nothing to do with any church. Isn't that right?"

"I guess so. Honestly, I didn't think of it."

"That's it. That's what I mean. You see it as nondenominational, and that's fine as far as it goes. But let me point out that there is an advantage to placing your project under the banner of the Church."

"You mean make it a Catholic home? But what about the

Protestant women who need help? Or Jews, or even agnostics?"

"I wasn't thinking so much of the restrictions to be placed upon the applicants," Marc said slowly. "I was thinking of it from a totally different viewpoint. The house must have a proper name, and following that, a proper tone. It mustn't be thought that we're *encouraging* sin, or that these women are wicked. We don't want neighbors looking at the house and whispering about it, spreading stories, so that the poor souls, if they should go out on the street, will be pointed at and gossiped about. We don't want lewd remarks, jokes, and we *do* want to attract the right people as patrons."

"Oh, Marc, I hadn't thought . . ." She was astonished. It was only when she had found out the secret of the dressing room that the reputation of the house had seriously crossed her mind. And then it was for such a different reason that Marc would have (in his turn) been amazed if she had felt free to reveal it.

"You hadn't thought about it. I realize that."

"But do you think . . . ?"

"Working with people the way I've been doing for years teaches a man many things," Marc said sadly. "People are often unkind."

"And your answer is the Church?"

"Yes, that's my answer. Put the house under the auspices of the Church and you solve those problems instantly."

"Is the Church your answer to everything?"

She had allowed a tinge of bitterness to color her words, she thought with instant regret. Poor Marc, she oughtn't to take out her unhappiness on him. He didn't even know about her problems. She sighed and sipped her tea.

"The Church may not be the answer to *everything*, but it does have the answers to many problems," Marc said gently. "You know that Uncle Eustache is retired. But he's still active in many ways. He's a friend of Bishop Grise. He has the archbishop's ear. He could help a great deal to get your project off to the right start."

"I suppose so."

She saw the wisdom of his suggestion but she had certain reservations.

"But, as a non-Catholic, how can I be part of the management of the house if it's to be run by the Church? It's my idea, after all, and my house. I don't want to be pushed out."

"Oh, I wouldn't worry too much. Something can always be arranged. Our family is Catholic, after all, and your children are Catholic. I don't see that it's an impossible situation. Let me arrange a meeting for you with Bishop Lavergne . . . with Uncle Eustache."

"All right, Marc. That can't do any harm. But if he can't find a way to include me in the house's management, I'll have to solve the problem of the house's reputation in a different way."

"Good. I feel satisfied in my own mind that we can work something out."

"Now that you have a parish again, I suppose you see your uncle from time to time?"

"Frequently. He's been a great help to me, a great support in my work. And a comfort when I feel despairing about Camille."

"I'm glad."

"Did I tell you that I've been given the job of organizing the health services for the Congress?"

The Twentieth Eucharistic Congress was being held in Montreal, and this was the first time it had ever taken place in North America. Pilgrims from Europe, Canada, the United States, and South America were expected. A cardinal legate from Rome would be the central figure. The Congress was meeting in two sections: the French-speaking group in Notre Dame Church and the English-speaking group in St. Patrick's Cathedral. It was a high point in the spiritual life of the Catholic Church of Montreal.

Honey came out of her reverie long enough to sense how much Marc had changed in the past few years. He was no longer the rebel. A new acceptance, a new calmness had replaced that fire that had made him go against his bishops and lose his parish so long ago.

"I'm pleased they've given you that job, Marc," Honey said. "I think your idea about the home is a good one, really. You've had so much experience with poor people—I want to listen to you, and make use of that experience."

"Then I can go ahead with the arrangement for a meeting with you and Bishop Lavergne?"

"Please do. I'm at the newspaper most days, but I can easily arrange a time to suit his Lordship. Now that Prime

Minister Laurier is back from his western tour and there's so much talk of an election, there are so *many* decisions to make at the paper . . ."

A new problem had crossed her mind when she'd thought of the coming election. The bishops of the Church, quiet since the election of 1896, were coming out strongly once again in favor of the Conservatives under Borden. The young priests agreed with them, and were now attentively reading *Le Devoir*, which was not only nationalistic in its outlook but strongly anti-Laurier. It might be only a matter of time before the bishops again took a strong militant stand in the politics of the country. If they told their flocks how to vote (and it would be Conservative), where would Marc find himself this time? Would he go with the Church, or would he go with his family?

"Marc, something has just occurred to me. You know how much talk there is of an election in 1911. Where will you stand on that? Are you going to jeopardize your position with the bishops? And if you speak out for Conservativism, where does that leave us?"

"I haven't come to any conclusions," Marc said quickly. "I don't want to be politically involved. I'd much rather work in my own way."

"But they may force you."

"Damned if I'll be forced!" Marc cried, stirred into the first outburst of passion she'd seen in him for a long time. "I did that before! I can't do it again! I can't go against them again, don't you see? It almost destroyed me the last time."

"I'm not asking you to take a stand now," Honey protested, wishing she hadn't brought the matter up. "But I wondered if my being a Liberal supporter might affect the bishop's position on the house."

"I can deal with it," Marc said, cooling off a little and assuming a stubborn expression. "Just let me deal with it."

He didn't want to talk about it now, or think about it. He hated the whole political process and he refused to allow it to ruin his life again. The Church had taken him back, had shown him that despite his errors, he was her son. He would not give that up. He needed that support to enable him to live as he must, trying to do good works. His love for the Church was strong now, and he had no wish to weaken it by ignoring orders from his superiors.

The split with his family over politics, if it came to a split, would be painful, but it would be much more painful to break away from the Church. Let Armand and Honey and Corbin and Helene fight for the Liberal cause if they wished. As for Honey's project, he could only hope that Uncle Eustache, in his diplomatic wisdom, would find a way to reconcile her political persuasion with the benefits the Church could offer to the scheme.

Honey was saying, "I'll look for a contractor to take on the job of renovating the house. I'll find time to supervise the work, Marc, but I do want your advice as I go along, please. We must find a suitable matron, and I have in mind trying to interest two or three doctors who might donate their services. I'll wait until I talk to Bishop Lavergne before I try to find patrons."

Marc went off into the dying light of the afternoon. She watched him walk down St. Denis Street, a little stooped, leaning into the strong wind that had blown up from the river to mix fallen leaves and scraps of paper and clouds of dust with abandon. Left alone in the small dining room, she stared at the lunch things, but saw only the narrow view of the dressing room through the peephole on St. Urbain Street.

CHAPTER SEVEN

Marc came out of the sickroom carrying a covered tray holding what was left of the oil and wine that had been used in the last rites. He met Justine outside Laurent's door, read the question in her eyes, and nodded briefly as he passed along the hall to his own room. He had done what was necessary—heard Laurent's confession; given absolution, the Eucharist, and, finally, Extreme Unction. That was all he could do for the soul of his brother-in-law. Marc had seen death many times over the years and felt certain Laurent wouldn't last the night. For his sister Justine, he felt only gentle commiseration. If there was some way to comfort her, it escaped him.

Justine closed the bedroom door and sat stiffly in a chair beside Laurent's bed. He was semiconscious, drugged with morphia and probably unaware of her presence. The brief flicker of interest in Marc's dispensations had faded quickly.

Whether Laurent was aware of her or not, she made no gesture toward him. His wasted hand lay on the white sheet, but she didn't touch it. She was too meticulous for that. They'd had no physical contact for years, and it would have seemed offensive to make an outward show of affection. She wanted desperately to pray, but now, when she needed it most, the ability to pray had escaped her.

Outdoors, the February night came down suddenly, like a curtain. The Dosquet farmhouse was buried in snow up to its sills, the driveways were covered in drifts, the fences had become stiff, fanciful waves of solid white.

Justine was aware that in other parts of the big house people were busy preparing supper, talking, going about their various tasks. Helene and Corbin (who had come down that afternoon from Ottawa) would be in the parlor with glasses of sherry and a good fire, Nicolette would be overseeing supper, Luc and Timothée would just be coming in from the barns, Marc would be meditating or reading in the room she always kept for his visits. Mathieu was no doubt studying in his room, and Beau . . . he might be anywhere, doing anything. Hearing those inner melodies of his, perhaps. Composing a requiem for the dying man.

If only she could pray—or failing that, if only she had someone close to comfort her. She had been lonely in the past years. There was Beau, but he spent most of his time in Montreal. She saw a good deal of Nicolette, who always seemed to be around the main house instead of in her own smaller place down the road, but Nicolette was prudish. How could a young girl be so rigid, Justine wondered. Now Mathieu, at least, was amusing, although he was blatantly ambitious. But Nicolette was irritating. She sighed inwardly at the seemingly unbridgeable gap between them, and concluded that she had nobody in whom to confide, nobody she could comfortably trust.

It was difficult to grasp that, surrounded as she was by family, she could feel so isolated. Why couldn't she pray at this time when she needed comfort so much? She stared at Laurent's ravaged face—bones showing through the loose, dry folds of skin on his cheeks, eyes sunken like the eyes of a long-dead mummy, mouth almost lipless. Dear God, it was only six months since Laurent had first complained of feeling ill. It was weeks before the doctors had found any definite symptoms of a serious illness. But as he'd eaten less and less, as the pain had increased, as he'd lost weight, the diagnosis had become more obvious, cancer of the stomach.

Laurent had tried to keep busy, forcing himself down to see the herds each day, walking slowly, resting often on a stump, a barrel, a bale of hay, but forcing himself on just the same. Timothée had been supportive, strong, and reliable and always had been where he was needed. What would they have done without Timothée? Luc worked hard, too, but he was so young, so inexperienced. Luc couldn't possibly have handled the farm alone.

Sitting in the shadows, everything was unreal to her. Laurent dying there on the bed, the family waiting downstairs, the funeral to be planned, decisions to be made.

Death seemed real enough when it happened to others, but it wasn't something she could understand in connection with herself. She felt nothing.

Over and over she tried to focus her mind on prayer, but a thousand practical details surged up instead. How could she carry on without Laurent? Mathieu wasn't interested in the farm, and Beau was not only too young but was completely unsuitable. Nicolette and Luc had been helping, but they were far too inexperienced to manage such a large piece of land along with the herds. She assumed that Laurent's will would leave her in charge of everything, but she could not be sure. His lawyer, coming down from Quebec City where he'd been attending a legal conference, had not yet arrived with Laurent's papers. The truth was, she needed Timothée Fitzgerald more than she had ever needed him before. That was a situation she had not yet had the courage to face.

In the midst of these pragmatic reflections her mind slipped to a more emotional one: Laurent's confession. Marc had surely long suspected the truth about Beau's parentage, but what had Laurent said upon his deathbed? Had he told Marc the truth? Once this thought surfaced in her mind, she expected to feel fear. But a wave of resignation swept into her heart and she became accepting and placid. So she continued to sit throughout the night, staring without emotion at the body that had once been Laurent Dosquet and only rising occasionally to put more wood on the fire.

The St. Amours gathered after the funeral. Berthe, Justine's cook, had set out a hot meal for them, and there was a generous supply of wine and brandy. Coming home in the small cutter, with Beau at her side, Justine felt she would never be warm again as long as she lived. The tearing wind penetrated the muskrat coat and hat; her face, half buried in fur, was numb; and her eyelashes were frozen together. The family had huddled in the cold stone church at St. Cloud and after the service they'd driven to the cemetery for the final rites. She had shivered through the entire ordeal.

The day set a record—thirty below zero with a relentless, burrowing wind. Deep snow and frozen earth had made it extremely difficult to dig the grave, and when the task had finally been accomplished, blowing snow had threatened to fill the cavity before the coffin could be lowered.

As the mourners stamped into the farmhouse, they shook the snow off their furs, threw aside their boots, and jostled for places in front of the blazing dining-room fire. The men were into the brandy immediately, the women had sherry, and the children (as much from boredom as from hunger) began to eat the hot chicken Berthe had prepared.

Yes, the entire family had come to bury Laurent, but looking about her, Justine felt completely adrift. She felt no warmth, no comfort, and certainly no love. What good were families anyway, if they brought no solace?

Gritting her teeth, she watched Nicolette fussing over the arrangement of food on the dining table. She heard Nicolette issuing orders to Berthe that were totally unnecessary. She saw that her daughter, although she was only twenty, wore a chronic frown and that her face was pinched and almost mean. Luc did nothing except hover around his wife. Like a pair of vultures, Justine thought angrily. It wasn't love for her dead father that brought the tense look to Nicolette's face. Something else. Worry, perhaps, over the terms of the will. Worry about her share when (Nicolette would argue to herself) Luc had done so much to help Laurent while he was alive. Justine was amazed at her own reaction to her daughter. She hadn't realized how much she disliked the girl.

The other children sounded fretful and nervous. Honey's three—Denys, Michel, and Susan—were sitting with Beau in a corner, and they were all eating chicken legs with their fingers. The adults were too preoccupied to correct them. Denys had taken a glass of wine although nobody had given him permission. Mathieu stood apart from them, being older, and he too was drinking wine and assuming nobody would reprimand him. Justine, eyeing them all with a cold detachment that had come upon her since Laurent's death, saw how much like Nicolette her cousin, Susan, appeared to be. Susan sounded shrill and bossy. How odd that a likeness would come out in those two!

Above the children's chatter, she could hear Armand and Corbin talking politics. Marc stood with them, silent and austere.

"The issue of reciprocity is splitting the Liberal ranks," Corbin was saying.

"A good thing *you* don't have to stand for election," Armand said, with an attempt at humor. "Now that you're a senator, you're above all that, Corbin."

Corbin refused to be sidetracked.

"Seriously, Armand, it's too controversial an issue to be ignored. Laurier believes in it and so do I for that matter, but a large percentage of the Liberal party is against free trade. An election this year will be a dangerous thing for the Prime Minister.

"I wonder when he'll call it," Marc said, joining the conversation. "After the coronation, I suppose."

"Oh, he'll go to the coronation in May, you can be sure of that," Corbin said knowingly. "Laurier wouldn't miss the coronation for worlds, even if his wife is too sick to go with him. He loves the taste of pomp and circumstance he gets in London."

"Well, he'll be forced to call an election by fall," Armand said, refilling his brandy glass. "Can I get you a drink, Marc? A little wine?"

Marc said yes, he'd have wine. He felt exhausted and chilled. The terrible cold at the graveside had penetrated his bones and he would have liked to wrap himself up in a woolen blanket and get into bed. But that was impossible. He was expected to stay here with his family, and perhaps offer comfort of some kind. There was a feeling of tension in the air and he half expected an emotional outburst. He didn't like Justine's calmness, and he liked Nicolette's bossiness even less.

"Even the *Montreal Star* is against reciprocity. Borden is against it. Most of his party is against it. *Le Devoir* with Bourassa shouting at the top of his lungs is against it. The Church supports *Le Devoir*. I understand that's the paper all the young priests are reading, and some of the bishops as well," Armand said.

"I'm *for* free trade," Corbin insisted. "I wish the bishops would stay out of politics. We've got to cut loose from England. We can't have England as a wet nurse forever. If we're to come of age as a country, we've got to treat England like every other country in the world—fairly, but not differently. After all, we're closer geographically to the United States. We can't ignore that fact."

"Now, just a minute, Corbin," Armand said. "I'm not usually willing to agree with Borden and his Conservatives, but there's something in what he says. If we open up the whole Canadian–American border to free trade, it's more likely to bind British Columbia to Oregon, the prairie provinces to the American Midwest, and Ontario and Quebec to the eastern seaboard states than it is to keep Canada together as a country."

"Bah, that's only a theory," Corbin argued. "Look at it this way, Armand. If Engish big business is against free trade you can be sure it's because of self-interest. It has nothing to do with their concern for French Canadians, you can be sure."

"By God, you're right in one way, Corbin. Honey's father made a statement in *Le Devoir* only last week, and the message was that if we opened up the border the Canadian meat packers would be destroyed, Canadian flour millers would be out of business, and—here's the key point—farm-machinery manufacturers in Canada would be finished. I guess you know he's invested heavily in farm machinery."

"That's exactly my point," Corbin said.

Honey, appearing from the hall, joined them at the table.

"Of course my father is trying to protect his investments," she said, "and I understand he's put a great deal of money into *Le Devoir*. But you know, it's always amused me that Papa is forced to come out, politically, on the side of the bishops."

"I trust you're doing your best to counterattack all this in *Le Monde*?" Corbin asked. "Would you like some sherry?"

"Yes, please. Well, we're doing what we can," Honey said doubtfully. "I support Laurier, and as long as I can keep my managing editor under control, *Le Monde* follows the party line. But it isn't easy."

"Do you think Sir Simon will go to the coronation?" Corbin asked. "Your family is monarchist to the marrow, isn't it, Honey?"

"Oh, some of the family will go. I see Angela quite often, you know. She's become very friendly with Beau. And she says the whole family is talking about it. Mary and Geoffrey want to go. I believe Charles is talking about it. And Papa, of course. But Mama isn't well enough to travel."

The kitchen door opened. A great gust of cold air swept

in a shower of powdered snow. Timothée appeared in the doorway, his bulk almost filling it. He slammed it closed and set down his lantern. He threw off his jacket and began stamping the ice off his boots.

Justine, feeling the draft, glanced toward the kitchen to see who had arrived. Timothée, she realized had been down supervising the hired men at the barns while Luc had completely forgotten the evening chores. Justine felt the old familiar gratitude toward him.

Timothée stood in the dining room archway rubbing his cold hands to restore circulation. He looked diffident. His luxuriant white hair was a contrast to the dark-haired people around him, and his green eyes were still bright with energy although the years had caused his shoulders to droop a little. He was uneasy at the intrusion but had felt that tonight he ought to make an appearance at the farmhouse. Besides, he was too tired to cook himself a meal, and he wanted some decent brandy.

Corbin invited him in.

"Have a drink, Timothée. You look frozen."

Corbin's instinctual *noblesse oblige* had only increased with his stay in the capital. He'd always been oblivious to undercurrents and brewing family conflicts. Outbursts of temper and arguments among his relatives constantly took him by surprise. So it was in keeping that he had no notion of Timothée's peculiar position in the family.

"Yes, do come in, Timothée. There's plenty of hot food, brandy, and wine," Justine said, moving slightly toward him in a welcoming gesture. "You look cold! Is everything all right down at the barns?"

Timothée nodded and accepted a brandy from Corbin. He was about to drink some when Nicolette suddenly thrust herself into the center of the crowded room. She looked extraordinarily belligerent and her voice trembled, but it was loud enough to attract almost everyone's attention.

"Mother, how *could* you?"

Justine was taken off balance by the unexpected attack. Seeing the two flaming patches on her daughter's cheeks, the sharp-eyed look of anger, she knew she must put a stop to the scene before it became worse. But how?

"I don't understand your meaning. You're upset, Nicolette. Perhaps you'd better go to bed."

"Why wouldn't I be upset?" Nicolette demanded, her shrill voice on a rising grade so that even the children's attention was secured. "How can you invite *him* here, with Father just buried? It's shameful!"

"Nicolette, you're getting hysterical. Luc, I think you ought to take—" Justine began.

But Nicolette cut her off. She wasn't to be stopped now by any polite protests. Although only some members of the family realized what this horrible scene was about, everyone recognized that mother and daughter were now in an undefined arena.

"Anyone can see what I mean!" the girl cried, looking first at Timothée, with his upraised glass, and then at Beau, who stood by the fire like a frail, dark statue. The white hair, the large frame did not disguise the facial features the two shared. Beau's face was a more delicately carved version of his father's.

"Look at Timothée! Look at Beau! A person would be blind not to know who Beau's father really is! You've let him stay here all these years with poor Father knowing . . . and even dying with Timothée still here! Oh, I've known for a long time . . ."

Justine dropped her wineglass. It shattered on the stone floor. The red liquid splashed her black, woolen skirt where the hem scarcely covered her black boots.

"Nicolette!" Timothée cried out angrily, "keep quiet! Can't you see what you're doing?"

But she wouldn't keep quiet.

"Oh, you've *always* preferred Beau, Mother. Mathieu and I knew even when we were little that he was different. And Timothée . . . staying on here . . . I suppose you've had a fine time meeting secretly all these years . . ."

Justine leaped forward and slapped her daughter's face so hard that Nicolette reeled a little, gasping with surprise.

"Get out! Get out! Go to your own house, and don't come back here!" Justine cried. "Luc, get her out! Take her away. Don't let me see her! Don't let me see her or I may kill her!"

It was Timothée who left the room first, wheeling about quickly and setting the brandy glass down with a crash that bounced off the overhead beams. He was at the back door, hat and coat on, lantern in hand, before Luc had moved to find Nicolette's fur coat and outdoor boots.

Nicolette was crying hysterically. Luc put his arm around her and took her out to the kitchen where they had left their coats. They hadn't intended to walk through the night to their own house, but to stay here in one of the spare bedrooms. With an effort, however, Luc dressed Nicolette and himself, and, finding an extra lantern, they disappeared into the darkness.

Beau began to weep. At first, great tears welled up in his eyes and he struggled to suppress them. Thirteen-year-old boys were not supposed to cry. But the tears escaped and poured down his cheeks, and he crumpled by the fire, sobbing. Honey ran to him and put her arms around him.

"I'll take Beau up to bed," she said to Justine, who was now a violently shaking statue with her hand grasping a chair back for support.

Beau resisted, at first, but she coaxed him. He was accustomed to obeying his Aunt Miel, so, eventually, he got up, rubbing the back of his hand across his eyes, and went with her. She spoke to Mathieu as they left the room.

"Beau should sleep in your room tonight, Mathieu," she said, and when he nodded assent, she added, "He needs company. There's plenty of room with you."

Mathieu was appalled by his sister's behavior and only too glad to atone for her. He was relieved there was something he could do. He'd shared some of her resentment over the years about his mother's special treatment of Beau, but it had taken a different form. He'd become more determined to get attention, had become louder and certainly more ambitious. Tonight he was horrified at Nicolette's exposure of family secrets and her thoughtless treatment of Beau. Beau was a bastard, that much was clear. His mother had committed a terrible sin. But now everybody knew it. Nobody would forget this night. It was unforgivable of Nicolette. Mathieu felt quite ill. He slumped in a corner chair, not speaking. The younger children looked dismayed. They were completely silent.

But it was not over. The final blow had yet to be delivered.

Justine was still trembling with unexpended anger and fear, and in the flood of passion she made a decision. Standing in the center of the room in her high-necked black mourning dress, she looked every inch a tragic figure. Her voice cut sharply into the charged air of the room.

"You may as well know right now, every one of you, that I intend to marry Timothée Fitzgerald just as soon as my period of mourning is over."

Everyone began to speak at once, but she went on over their protests and gasps, "Furthermore, I will not allow Nicolette to enter this house again as long as I am alive."

With that, she left the room.

Berthe cleaned up the broken glass. Helene went upstairs to bed, shooing Honey's three children before her. The men began to drink brandy in earnest.

Honey lay in bed listening to the sounds of the house settling for the night and the wind whistling around the windows. She kept her arms under the quilt and her feet on the hot water bottle, for in spite of her warm flannel nightgown she was cold. Laurent had never installed central heating, so each room depended on a fireplace for warmth. As soon as the fire died down, the room became chilly.

Part of her mind was tuned to any sound that might come from down the hall, where Beau had gone to bed in Mathieu's bedroom. Surely he wasn't desperate enough to do something stupid like run off into the night? He was such a high-strung, volatile child, it was difficult to gauge how strongly he would react to the ugly scene in the dining room. She was furious with Nicolette for her thoughtless raging.

When Armand finally came to bed, she could tell by his dragging footsteps that he had consumed too much brandy. And as he approached the bedside she could smell alcohol and cigar smoke.

"Are you awake?" he asked, beginning to undress.

"Yes. I'm worried about Beau."

"Justine gave us quite a speech after you left to take Beau upstairs," Armand said, hanging his jacket over a chair back. "My beloved sister made two startling announcements."

"What on earth about?"

"She's going to marry Timothée."

"She actually *told* everybody that?"

"Yes. Also, she doesn't want Nicolette back in the house

ever again. How she's going to manage that, is beyond me. I should think Luc and Nicolette will be forced to move if she keeps her word."

"Well, I don't blame her for being angry," Honey said. "It was a ghastly thing for that girl to do. She may have done irreparable harm to poor Beau, and she made Justine look so cheap and horrible."

Armand got into bed.

"There's no way of knowing how it will all come out."

"The pity is that it could all have been avoided if only Timothée had gone away. I don't know why Justine and Timothée couldn't have understood that in the beginning."

"That's true, *ma cherie*, but I suppose they didn't want to part. Certainly, Laurent wanted Timothée here. And now he's more needed than ever."

"Still," Honey insisted, "he ought to have gone away long before Beau was born."

Armand reached toward her and pulled her into his arms. Usually she didn't care much for the smell of second-hand brandy, but tonight she felt frightened and lonely, and it was strangely comforting to know that Armand was the same as he had always been. She had a quick flash of sympathy for Justine in her solitude, and when Armand began to make love to her, she welcomed him with a kind of furious intensity. She hoped, as she slid beneath him and raised the bulky nightgown, that he would be with her for a long, long time.

CHAPTER EIGHT

"I expect I'll have to go to Boston eventually," Angela said dreamily, "if I'm to make any real progress with my painting. *They* won't let me go until I'm eighteen, though. What will you do about your music, Beau?"

They were standing at the observation point on the summit of Mount Royal. Below them, neat, tree-embroidered streets and soundless, bright toy ships seemed a planet away. The sticky August heat was diluted at this height by a pleasant breeze, and birds wheeled and dived between tall birch, maple, and oak trees. They might have been deep in the country except for the carpet of church spires, water, and boat traffic that lay at their feet.

"Perhaps I'll go to Paris," Beau said, tossing the idea out to see what Angela would say. "There's so much I have to learn. Some of the most exciting new composers are working in Paris right now."

"Paris? To the Conservatory, you mean?"

For just an instant, the idea seemed farfetched. But then her imagination made the leap from Boston to the Continent and she was full of admiration for Beau. Boys were always so much more daring, she'd noticed enviously.

"Well, I'd go to the Conservatory if I could qualify," Beau agreed, causing Angela to protest that of *course* he would qualify, he was practically a genius.

"Fauré is director, you know," he went on. "He was a friend of Saint-Saens. Can you imagine it? Debussy and Ravel are in Paris too."

"It sounds much more exciting than London."

"Anyway, I speak French, so it makes sense to go to Paris, don't you think? Not that Parisians think much of our colonial French, I'm told."

At fourteen, Beau sounded quite grown up and sure of himself. It was only a mask, of course, and Angela understood that. She and Beau had survived the uncertainty of their family circumstances because of their intensely imaginative inner lives. Their introspection made them seem outwardly mature, but actually they were both fragile and easily driven into fearful moods. This unspoken understanding bound them together as much as their creative talents. That they were both physically attractive, almost unreal in their unfashionable, otherworldly beauty, did not occur to either. Yet they both loved beautiful things and were unconsciously drawn to each other's extraordinary looks.

"Paris sounds wonderful. Paris." She dwelt upon the word, savoring it, conjuring up visions of carriages, broad, tree-lined avenues, busy outdoor cafés, the sound of idyllic music floating intoxicating air, and fanciful paintings in shining salons. "You *have* to go over there, Beau, I know that. There's only so much we can learn here. I keep discovering new painters, but I can't see their original work. I must look at the great collections, not only the Europeans, but the Chinese and Japanese colorists . . ."

"*They'll* offer you the Grand Tour," Beau said derisively. "Wait and see. You know what adults are like. They'll never let you go to Paris to *study*."

"Maybe I could find a chaperone," she said doubtfully, but she knew as she said the words that Lady Court, Sir Simon, and her father would line up against her. She wondered dimly if she could enlist the support of her Aunt Miel, but then remembered with a sinking heart that Sir Simon did not think well of his own daughter, and that if the scheme were approved by Honey, it was not likely to impress him.

"I'll be lonely," Beau said.

"We could write every day."

"I'm not very good at writing letters."

This was true. His few half-hearted attempts at writing letters or school essays had been dismal failures. He knew that Angela was articulate on paper, and the idea of writing long, descriptive letters would appeal to her. She had shown him some of her verse from time to time, and he found the poems essentially romantic but promising. Like her paintings, they were chimeras, suggestive of a fantasy world.

"You'd learn," Angela said. "I can't imagine not ever

hearing from you, Beau. That would be awful. Anyway, you aren't going away just yet. They won't even allow a *boy* to go until he's seventeen or eighteen. That won't be until 1914 or 1915."

While they were talking, Honey joined them. She had been reading from a file while sitting on a bench in the sunlight. Now she announced that it was time for their picnic lunch. Honey and Angela spread a cloth on the grass and put out the food—chicken sandwiches, sweet pickles, gingerbread, and lemonade. Two young boys, flying a kite nearby, unconsciously provided entertainment with the meal.

"Too bad Denys and Michel couldn't be here," Angela said generously, although she wasn't especially fond of her St. Amour cousins. It was Aunt Miel and Beau who attracted her to St. Denis Street.

"They like it on the island," Honey said, "but I'm sure they come up here sometimes when they're in the city. I'm going back to the island tomorrow, by the way. I only came into town because the Prime Minister called an election last week and Beaulne thought he needed me."

"I'm going back to the country, too," Angela said. "Mother isn't in a visiting mood these mornings, so Father says I may as well go back to Drake House where it's cooler."

After they had repacked the basket, Honey announced that she had some more reading to do and that the two children ought to take a walk through the Protestant cemetery.

"The oldest part of the park was laid out by Olmsted, you know, the man who designed Central Park in New York," Honey told them. "You'll find it especially lovely in the cemetery. A painter's heaven, Angela."

Honey brought out her paper again and settled down to read. Try as she would, it was impossible to keep up with all the events. It was a week since Laurier had called an election on the issue of reciprocity. Speeches in Washington by President Taft, and by Clarke, the Speaker of the House of Representatives had referred to Canada as a possible "annex" to the United States, and there were suggestions that the American flag was about to fly over all of British North America. The stir this kind of talk caused was enormous. The election campaign in Canada, with

Laurier defending the free-trade agreement he'd made with Taft, and the Conservative, Robert Borden, attacking the the treaty had begun the first week in August. In Montreal, there were rumors that *Le Devoir* under the direction of Bourassa had been "bought" by powerful Conservatives. The charge was, perhaps, ridiculous because Bourassa was strongly against Laurier and his policies; he needed no Conservative persuasion. Still, the hints were circulating. Conservative money, people said, had swelled the coffers of *Le Devoir* to the tune of two hundred thousand dollars. Whatever the case, Conservatives and clergy bought the paper, read it, and praised it.

Le Monde, meanwhile, was still very much a Liberal paper under Honey's ownership. Beaulne was uneasy about reciprocity, however, despite his loyalty to Laurier. Gabriel d'Esterre was sitting on the fence. A Liberal by nature, he could not make up his mind about free trade and Laurier's vision of the future. Honey was deeply concerned about the newspaper's direction. At home, things were simpler. Armand and Corbin, when they spoke about the newspaper or the election, entertained few doubts, and none serious. They were Liberals, they supported Laurier, and that was that. During this time, Honey felt she was ill-equipped to make the decisions necessary to guide the newspaper's policy.

"You two run along," she said now, opening the sheaf of papers and searching for something she wanted. "I want to read and concentrate on some problems."

Beau and Angela found the cemetery even more exotic and isolated than Aunt Miel had promised. They saw nobody. Between the ornate granite and marble tombstones, the heavy shade of trees and shrubs created a world apart. There were a few birds. A small animal scuttled somewhere in the underbrush. Eventually they sat on a crypt shaped like a coffin, where the light was a fretwork of green and gold.

"I could write a musical fantasy about this place," Beau said eagerly. "It would be peaceful and harmonious. Not really sad, but restful, I think. Does it make you want to paint, Angela?"

"Oh, yes. I'm coming back some day with my watercolors," Angela said. "It's like the woods in a fairy tale. Not depressing at all, but mysterious and cool. How many shades of green do you think there are . . . without even turning your head? Just look around! I can imagine all sorts of strange things happening in here, can't you?"

Beau grinned. Somehow he always felt happier when Angela was near.

"I wish you didn't have to go away so soon," Beau said, running his hand over the lettering on the crypt. "I like seeing you best when you come to paint in the old nursery, while I practice."

"So do I. But Father says I have to go back to Drake House. I wish you could visit us there, Beau. We'd have such fun. My other cousins bore me."

"I thought you liked Landry."

"Oh, he's better than the others. At least he *notices* what goes on. I draw insects for him, and he likes my paintings of wildflowers. But it isn't the same as being with you."

"Nothing is the same as being together," Beau agreed. "I know how you feel. I love Aunt Miel, but my cousins are just not interested in music. Susan's a bossy girl. Mathieu is kind sometimes, but other times he goes off on some political speech, and I can't listen."

"How do you think it will work out now that your mother is married to Timothée?"

Angela knew all about Beau's family problems, just as he knew all about her troubles with her peculiar mother and her tyrannical grandfather.

"It's good for the farm, I suppose. Mother inherited everything, you know, which left Nicolette raging. She felt that she and Luc had helped run the place and ought to have a share. Now Mother wants to buy another farm for Nicolette and Luc so they'll move away. She won't see Nicolette, and it's all very ugly. Even Uncle Eustache visited the farm to have a talk with Mother."

"Then it must be serious. Won't your mother *ever* forgive Nicolette?"

"Maybe. Uncle Marc swears she will, after a while. Mother has always been a very devout Catholic, you know. Praying a lot and making her confessions. Perhaps she'll find a way to forgive Nicolette, but right now she can't stand the sight of her."

"I can't say that I blame her. After what she did to *you*, Beau," Angela said, shivering.

"I try not to think of it," Beau said, his voice only a

whisper, his chin falling to his chest. He stared down at the damp grass. A butterfly winged past him: orange and black.

"You're right. I try not to think about my mother, either. Drifting about in her apartment in those awful black gowns, never seeing anybody. Poor Father. I'm sure she tried to kill herself last summer, though Aunt Miel denies it. It isn't as if suicide were a mortal sin or anything, not in our church. But people in polite society don't mention suicide. My grandfather can't ever say the word—he just hints that it's despicable."

"Anyway, your mother didn't die so it doesn't matter," Beau said logically. "And nobody knows how she came to fall."

They were quiet for a few moments, absorbing the shifting patterns of light and shadow. Then Angela said, "Beau, are you ever afraid?"

"Sometimes. But you're the only person in the world I'd tell that to."

"Sometimes I'm afraid. Of being alone. Of being dead. Oh, I don't know, all sorts of things. Look what happened to my mother! She had everything, they say, beauty and happiness and love. She lost it all. That's frightening."

"No more frightening than being a bastard," Beau said sharply. "You can't know what *that's* like."

"You aren't one now. Surely now that your mother is married to Timothée, that makes everything all right?"

"Not to the rest of the family. They all *know*. That's what's so hateful." He kicked at a stone with his boot. "I wish I never had to see any of my family again!"

"I wish we could run away together and live in a castle in a wood, and never have to come out. You could compose and I could paint . . . it would be lovely."

"Angela, let's make a pact. Let's promise to be friends always, and tell each other everything, and always come if the other one needs us. Then we wouldn't be frightened."

"What a marvelous idea!" It sounded like part of one of the stories she was so fond of illustrating. Naturally, Beau would be the one to think of it! She felt a sudden flood of love for Beau for his specialness, for his gentleness and understanding.

"How do you make a pact?" Beau asked dubiously. "You should know. You read so many books."

"Let me think a minute. Oh, yes, we swear on something, that's how it's done. People swear on their mother's bones and on their father's Bible, and things like that. We'll swear on this grave, because that's where you thought of the vow. Don't you think that's a good idea?"

"Yes. Let's see who's buried here."

They stood up and peered at the carved lettering on the stone coffinlike tomb where they had been sitting.

Here lies Mary Ethel Wilkinson
Beloved daughter of
John and Adelaide Wilkinson
Born 1870
Died 1888

"She wasn't very old, poor thing," Angela said.

"Not even married, because she wasn't the 'beloved wife' of anybody."

"You see, she was sad and lonely," Angela said romantically, "and perhaps this will make her happy. Our being here and swearing our friendship on her grave."

They held hands and looked at each other for a moment. Angela's huge gray eyes were like oceans into which Beau seemed to fall, making him part of herself. They were both trembling. Beau kissed her awkwardly, a chaste, nervous kiss that had nothing of the voluptuous in it, but was merely a promise of untouched reserves, buried deep. Without saying a word, they returned slowly to the place where Honey sat reading. There was no need to say anything more. They both knew that for them, for always, there would never be anybody else.

CHAPTER NINE

Any windows that could be coaxed open were propped up with books or rulers, but still there was very little relief from the August heat. The old building on Notre Dame had not been designed for comfort in the first place. It had been meant to impress—pink stone imported as ballast from Scotland fashioned into an attempt at a Florentine façade. Over the years, the presses of *Le Monde* had shaken the building into a state of uncertainty, so that many bricks were loose on the outside walls, and on the inside, plaster ceilings were cracked and the paint was peeling.

The editorial offices on the fourth floor had been inadequate even when the building was new, but now they were vastly overcrowded with extra desks, reference books, filed newspapers, reporters, and editors. Honey, occupying the small cubbyhole which she had chosen for herself when it had become obvious how much time she would be spending at the office, sat perspiring in a white summer blouse and navy silk skirt. At seven o'clock in the evening, the air was still not cooling off. She had gone so far as to open the neck of her shirt a little, and she fanned herself vigorously.

Gabriel d'Esterre came in waving a piece of folded newspaper. "Have you seen *Le Devoir*?" he demanded, slapping the paper down on Honey's desk. It was folded ostentatiously at the object of his rage. "He must have told them he was going to make this speech! *We* knew nothing about it, certainly."

"Yes, I've read it." She was, in fact, fanning herself with a copy of the story.

Gabriel did not accept the situation with the same composure as his employer. He was a few years younger than Honey, with the driven manner of a born crusader and the unremitting energy of a contemporary Hannibal. He was extremely short, which might have accounted for some of his zeal, although people tended to forget his stature once he began speaking. His voice was resonant, his vocabulary extensive.

Physically, he was an attractive man, with a mass of black curly hair flowing into an impressive beard. His dark eyes were always alight, easily communicating his beliefs. Their intensity swept other people into the basket of his dreams. It was easy to imagine him, in some earlier time, uniform brilliant with blues and golds, sword up-raised, leading a mesmerized troop of soldiers into doomed and bloody battle.

"What effect do you think this announcement will have?" he went on.

The story concerned Sir Simon and Court Harvesters. Seizing on Geoffrey's idea that Court factory workers ought to be captive votes for the Conservatives, Sir Simon had made a personal announcement to them. They should look to their jobs in the coming election. If Laurier won, he pointed out, the plant would certainly close. It could not compete with American manufacturers on an open market.

"Some of them will vote Conservative anyway," Honey said thoughtfully, "but I'm sure there's a hard core of Liberals at the factory. They're bound to make trouble."

"It's extraordinary!" Gabriel exploded. "Your father making a public statement like that."

"He's an extraordinary man," Honey said, smiling in spite of herself. She still had such mixed feelings about her father that she could think of him fondly even when he was at his worst.

Gabriel shot her a look of complete puzzlement. He found it difficult to understand Honey's relationships with her English family and her French in-laws. But at the same time, he recognized in her something of Sir Simon's tenacity and strength.

"There's another issue here, Madame. And one I think we have to tackle! What happened to democracy? Where are the free elections? What has become of the secret ballot? This is damned close to coercion, to threats! Anybody less important than Sir Simon would be in serious trouble."

"Write an editorial about it," Honey said calmly.

"I will! I will! But at the same time, Madame, I feel there is a news story in it as well. Let me send Jacques down to the plant to find one of these Liberal supporters and see if he'll give us his side of the story. Don't you agree that that's a way to handle the problem?"

"If you like, Gabriel."

She wasn't afraid of stirring up trouble with her father, but a story would undoubtedly prolong the feeling of coldness between the Courts and the St. Amours. The idea that her children were entitled to visit Pride's Court and share in family gatherings never completely deserted her. She knew that from her father's point of view, there was little likelihood of that happening. He couldn't warm toward his daughter who had defected, or his grandchildren who were Catholics. But Honey still had a lingering hope that they could have some kind of relationship short of complete love and understanding. Why not? Denys and Michel and Susan deserved to share their grandparents. They visited their grandmother occasionally, but Lady Court was not well—she suffered from chronic arthritis— and this added to the strain of the visits. How marvelous if her own children could be guests at Drake House from time to time! If they could get to know Geoffrey's children, and Fort's as well. Angela came secretly to the St. Amour house, and there was no doubt in anybody's mind that Sir Simon would be furious if he knew.

Honey gave her consent to the story, therefore, with some misgiving but no fear. She *was* on the other side politically, and religiously too through her affiliation with the Catholic Church. She must accept the consequences.

"I'll put Jacques on it first thing in the morning," Gabriel was saying, moving to the window and looking down at the street. "Have you thought any more about Beaulne?"

She had been expecting this question.

"Yes. I know I must make a decision. It's difficult for me, that's all. You must give me more time. I can't take such an important step in the middle of the election campaign—there isn't time to do all the things that must be done. I haven't another job for Beaulne at the moment. You know that."

"It's equally hard to run this paper without the authority I ought to have," Gabriel said, turning from the window to look at her. "Some days it's impossible!"

"I know. I know."

"If we only had more space, Beaulne could run the printing side of things . . . you know, the orders we get for posters, and pamphlets, and stationery, things like that. It isn't my decision, Madame, I realize that. I'm only the managing editor. But there's money to be made in that side of things if we could handle enough orders. As it is . . ." he shrugged.

Honey leaned over her desk suddenly, her head in her hands. She felt incompetent to deal with all the problems. They were overwhelming. She wanted life to be simple: no fights with her father, no worries about Armand and his roving eye, no confusion about electoral issues. Why was it all so complicated? It was terribly hot. Her head ached. She wished she were going out to some elegant dinner, beautifully dressed and fussed over by an attentive Armand. Instead, she would go home for a late supper by herself. Armand was having daily meetings with Max DeLeon, who was in Montreal now, and she had seen very little of him for almost a week. The children were holidaying on the island. Mathieu was out on assignment, covering one of the preelection rallies. The house would be empty and she would feel depressed.

"What is wrong, Madame?" Gabriel was saying, all concern.

"The heat. I feel a little faint."

"You haven't eaten much today. That must be it."

"Perhaps that *is* it, Gabriel."

"You look so pale. Let me get you a glass of water."

He hurried out of her office and was soon back with water, which wasn't cold, but which she drank anyway. She handed him the empty glass. Their fingers touched momentarily and she looked up into Gabriel's black, hypnotic eyes. There was an odd sense of recognition, of *déjà vu*. Attraction. She repressed it quickly.

"Let me drive you home, Madame. It would make me feel better."

She allowed him to escort her down to the street and to her parked car. They were just getting into the car when the fire engines came shrieking out of Central Fire

Station. She knew by Gabriel's excited expression that he would follow the fire reels and that it would be even later before she had her lonely supper.

———————

Max DeLeon looked up from his cards just in time to see his wife exchange a meaningful glance with Armand St. Amour. He sighed inwardly. So it was still on. He could understand what Armand liked about Velma; in his own day he had been mightily attracted to that voluptuous pink body himself. But now all that was behind him. He made a point of pushing a huge pile of chips into the center of the table, although his cards were not really good enough for the splurge. Max, however, loved to gamble for high stakes. It was one of the few pleasures that didn't give him heartburn.

Some of the guests, as well as the players, stood about in the card room awaiting the dinner bell. It was getting dark and it seemed to most of the revelers that dinner was extremely late. The card room was comfortable, however; it was one of the smaller rooms in that enormous house (Grande's Grandstand, the wags called it), but was by far the most elegant, being lined with tapestries from Belgium and paintings by Turner, Landseer and Brennir. And the wine was excellent.

Tonight Philippe was giving a costume party. Despite the heat, his guests were got up in hussars' uniforms, dandies' tailcoats worn with broad cravats, vast feathered headgear, and marabou capes. Armand had come as Napoleon, and Philippe was an Austrian baron in a tight uniform of peacock blue heavily embroidered with gold and completed by gold spurs and a gold sword. Especially for tonight, he had glued splendid whiskers to his cheeks (his whiskers were reputed to be one of the real baron's most alluring features) and so was almost unrecognizable.

Armand followed Velma out into the central hall, pretending casual conversation about the fabulous decor of Philippe's new house. Velma wore pink velvet cut to expose her round, delightful breasts (slightly rounder with the years, but still eye-catching). Two porcupine ostrich feathers, dyed maroon, extended three feet above her head.

"Have you finished talking business with Max?" she

asked as they walked slowly about, admiring the carvings and the plasterwork. "You were with him all afternoon."

"Not quite finished," Armand said smoothly. "We're working on a complicated real-estate deal. There is a huge tract of land we want to buy for the railroad terminal, but we've got to cover up the purchases with a number of front men. Otherwise, the prices will become ridiculous."

"And who's acting for you?"

"A new man. He's never been connected with us in any way. His name is Guy Jacques."

"I see. It all sounds very exciting. Men seem to enjoy that kind of thing so much."

"We enjoy many things," Armand said.

There were times when he wished to be rid of his addiction to Velma. She was so obvious. Like a confection somebody had created for St. Valentine's Day, or a particularly vulgar bouquet of flowers. Unfortunately, no matter how often he thought his desire for her was dead, it sprang to life when she appeared. He did not *love* Velma. In fact, he almost despised her. But the physical attraction she held for him was a hunger. It gnawed and pained until he fed it.

"When can I see you?" Armand asked.

She shrugged carelessly. "Tonight, I suppose."

"At the hotel?"

"It seems the best plan."

"What time shall I come, then?"

"Why not come around eleven o'clock," Velma said, lowering her voice as a couple dressed like Sleeping Beauty and the Prince passed by. "Max is asleep by that time. I'll tell him I want to leave the party early. He'll be only too delighted because he always feels so ghastly after dinner, poor man."

"He looks much sicker than the last time I saw him."

"Well, his health doesn't improve. But I don't think he gets much worse, either. I suppose one day he'll get so ill he won't be able to eat at all, and that will be the end."

She sounded callous, Armand thought. Yet he knew that Velma was actually fond of Max. She wasn't unaffectionate toward him, and if she needed more attention than he could give her, then surely that didn't negate her good qualities. On the other hand, he was honest enough with himself to admit he would be horrified if Honey ever involved herself with another man.

They took time to admire the great stone staircase that Philippe had had copied from a Moorish castle and which had been constructed by two European workmen.

Velma said, "It's made for a grand entrance, isn't it? Like the stairs in a musical. I can see Lillian Russell sweeping down those stairs in purple velvet."

Armand laughed, wondering if Velma knew how much she reminded everybody who saw her of the singer she had just mentioned.

Though all the windows in the house appeared to be open, the rooms were almost unbearably hot. Velma cooled herself with a pink feathered fan. She looked moistly desirable. Armand found himself glancing at her and becoming restless. Eleven o'clock seemed far away.

The dinner bell rang. The reverberations had barely died away when, from the street, through the open casements, came the sounds of screaming fire engines. A thrill went through the bored guests and they poured out onto the lawn to watch the engines tear past.

It was not clear who started it, but suddenly the entire party decided to follow the reels and watch the blaze. It was somewhere close, down on Dorchester, judging by the direction of the engines. Dinner was abandoned in favor of sport as the costumed guests piled into carriages and automobiles.

In a few blocks, they tumbled to a halt behind the parked fire engines. Armand, sitting beside Velma in a rented car, realized with horror that the burning house was Pride's Court. He could see smoke pouring from the west wing, and to complicate matters, a crowd of protesting workers carrying placards was impeding the work of the firemen.

Momentarily he was stupefied. He caught a glimpse of his wife running up to the gates, followed by her young editor, d'Esterre. Instinctively he went to her aid, leaving Velma in the automobile, and completely forgetting his Napoleonic costume.

Honey was pushing her way through the demonstrators without understanding the exact meaning of the placards. In rough hand printing, the signs proclaimed, "Free Votes.

No Force." "Where's Democracy?" and "Jobs for Votes Is Ilegal." The misspelling caught her eye even as she pushed through the men to get to the door. They were shouting that they wanted to see Sir Simon. There were mixed cries of "Let's talk to the boss!" "We want Sir Simon!" and "Come out and face your men!"

She reached the massive front door and pulled it open. Knowing her father, she expected him to be directing the firemen. She was right. He was outside the west wing, at the back of the house, smoking a cigar and giving orders.

"Drag the bloody thing over there! Can't you see, man?" If you try to come through this way, the hose won't reach!"

Breathlessly, Honey stopped beside her father.

"Papa, do you know what's happening?"

"Of course I know what's happening! The house is on fire. I'm trying to tell these fellows where to place the hoses to best advantage."

"Did you know about the men out front? They want to see you."

"I refuse to see them." He puffed furiously on his cigar. His eyes were hard with anger.

He turned away from her, much too obsessed with the fire to question why she was in Pride's Court. He barked out another stream of orders. It was quite possible, with the house's peculiar construction, he said, to keep the damage to a minimum if only they would listen to him. The firemen were somewhat bewildered.

Gabriel was beside Honey when Armand arrived, looking out of breath and somewhat ludicrous in his costume.

"Is there anything I can do, darling? I just happened to see the engines, and you running through the gates, so I came," Armand said, putting his hand on Honey's shoulder.

She turned quickly at the familiar voice and a tiny smile flitted across her face, knowing he was there. Then she saw how he was dressed. Her expression froze into disbelief.

"Why are you dressed like that?" Honey asked.

"I'll explain later," Armand said hastily, and said to his father-in-law, "Shouldn't we remove some of the paintings and antiques, sir?"

"No need to panic," Sir Simon said, glaring at this reincarnation of Napoleon. But he did not seem surprised.

If his son-in-law, the Frenchman, wanted to prance about the city in such ridiculous attire, it was only to be expected.

"But there might be water damage," Armand said.

"There *will* be thievery, if we put things out on the lawn," Sir Simon pointed out. "There are ruffians out there. I know their kind. Thieves and liars, all of them."

It was Honey who suddenly realized where the fire was centered. She pulled at her father's arm, shouting at him through the increasing noise, "Isn't that Venetia's apartment?"

"Mrs. Card brought Venetia out. The woman's built like an ox and has nerves of iron. Venetia's perfectly safe in the east wing. You don't think I'd be standing here directing the fire hose if the girl was in danger, do you?"

Armand was forced to smile. You couldn't touch Sir Simon when it came to self-confidence and style. There was no use trying. He left Honey to see if he could give the firemen a hand, and Gabriel went with him. Honey stayed with her father. Graves, the Courts' latest butler, came up half running. He looked wild.

"Sir, I think you ought to speak to those men out front. They're threatening to come round to the back and throw rocks. One of them's already armed with a rock. They might even have started the fire, sir, out of spite!"

Sir Simon had not yet considered the fire's origin. In his mind, the demonstration at the front of the house and the fire in the west wing were two separate events. The suggestion put forward by Graves, however, took hold. It was only too likely.

"Yes, I'll speak to them, all right! But not before I call the police! Blackguards! Criminals! I'll have their jobs for this!"

He went into the center wing (much to the relief of the sweating firemen) to put in the call to the police. Honey stayed to watch the fire. They were pouring water into the apartment now and great billows of smoke were coming out of the second-floor windows. An occasional outburst of flame proved that the fire was not out but that it was not spreading, either.

Now at least a dozen firemen, aided by citizens who had been passing by, trained all the available hoses on the open windows. Ladders were put up in two separate places. An air of accomplishment hung over the entire group, and there were encouraging cries of command. Eager faces turned up toward the windows and the still-intact roof of the west wing.

In a moment, the mood flashed to one of horror as a figure appeared in one of the second-floor windows, surrounded by smoke. Merely an outline with a hand upraised, clutching at nothing. Then the smoke swallowed the vision.

A murmur of fear spread through the crowd. Who was it? Then Mrs. Card came running out of the east wing, crying sharply. "She's got away! She's got away and run back into the fire!"

A ladder was shoved to the window where the figure had been glimpsed. A fireman began to climb up, another behind him while a third steadied the ladder at the bottom. Sir Simon rushed forward, trying to climb the ladder as well. He was prevented by Armand and Gabriel, who happened to be close by.

"No, no, sir! Let them do it!" Armand cried in Sir Simon's ear, while he grasped the older man's arm to pull him back. "The firemen have waterproof coats. They're trained to do this. You mustn't try to go up there."

Sir Simon tried to shake him off. He looked very fierce and, for the first time, slightly out of control.

"The firemen will find her," Gabriel added. He was tugging at Sir Simon's other arm. But the old man was incredibly strong. It took both young men to pull him back from the ladder. Finally, he stood glaring up at the firemen climbing toward the window, his face and stance like that of some avenging god.

There was confusion everywhere now. More spectators had found their way to the back of the house. More firemen had appeared, and two policemen as well. In the midst of this, Honey drew Mrs. Card aside. The woman was sobbing, but Honey managed to elicit the information that she had left Venetia for only a moment while she'd gone to find smelling salts. Venetia had seemed stunned and Mrs. Card had thought it only right to revive her. It had never occurred to her that Venetia might run back into the burning wing.

Mrs. Card wept and repeated over and over that she would never have left Mrs. Court if she had known. Time became meaningless. It seemed hours before anything more happened and yet in truth, it could only have been minutes. Then a fireman appeared in the smoky window and handed something out to the fireman on the ladder. The smell of smoke was poisoned with an indescribably disgusting odor. The fireman, carrying his burden, seemed to stagger, and it seemed that he would fall with it.

What he deposited on the grass was surely not a human being. The crowd moved back, recoiling from the sight, from the smell. No, surely not the body of a woman—this curled up, hairless, charred thing with a formless mass where there had once been a face. This melted, cracked face, eyeless and lipless, tucked into the obscene curve of a shriveled body. All traces of the body with its disfiguring smallpox scars were gone. In its place was a black, unrecognizable, and vile-smelling object. But surely, never a beautiful woman?

The fireman stepped back, then rushed off to vomit in the bushes. The space between the thing lying there and the curious onlookers widened. Armand and Gabriel turned Honey toward the east wing, leading her away. Somebody helped Mrs. Card, who was screaming.

It was Sir Simon who shortly came forward with a blanket and covered what was left of Venetia. When he straightened up, finally, he seemed to gather himself together to speak to one of the firemen. A stretcher was brought and the blanketed figure taken away. Sir Simon, moving like a robot, began directing the playing of the hose once more. He stayed until the fire was out and the west wing a gaping, ugly reminder of the awful night.

It was the costume that was responsible. If it had not been for the Napoleonic garb, Honey might have been more anxious to take the sedative Armand offered her. They had returned home after the fire and, since both were exhausted, had gone straight to their own apartment. Armand was drinking brandy. He was convinced that a sleeping potion was exactly what Honey needed.

While she was in a state of shock after Venetia's horrible death and the damage to Pride's Court itself, her eyes were riveted to Armand's ridiculous costume. Part of her longed to escape from the realities of the night, but the suit Armand wore would not let her forget. It stabbed at that remote place in her heart that she had so far managed to isolate from the truth.

"Take this," Armand said, offering her the glass. "You know, it's the one the doctor prescribed when you were having trouble sleeping some months ago."

Honey's eyes glittered. "Please take off that ghastly costume."

He looked down at it, stupidly, having forgotten in the stress of events that he was not normally dressed, having even temporarily forgotten the reason for the costume.

Although he did not like Honey's tone, he said mildly, "I can explain this."

"Do you usually hold your business meetings with Max in stage dress?"

"No, of course not. There was a party," Armand said quickly. "Max was at the party and we had our business meeting before dinner. Actually, we never did get our dinner, because somebody heard the fire engines, and—"

"You must be hungry," Honey said coldly.

"I'm not. The evening has destroyed my appetite."

She understood that well enough. She had not eaten either, but the thought of food was repugnant.

"Perhaps you'd like to return to the party. While I sleep," Honey went on. "Don't let me interfere."

"Really, darling, this is no time to discuss the matter. You are upset. I am upset. I think it best that we talk another time. I was at a rather unusual gathering, but—"

"At Philippe Grande's house, I suppose."

He shrugged helplessly.

"Yes, it was at Philippe's house."

"Where you carry on much of your business with Max, no doubt. And which accounts for your appearance at the fire so soon after the engines arrived. Philippe's house isn't far from Pride's Court. I thought as much."

"I wish you would take this sleeping potion," Armand said. "There is no earthly use in having this out tonight. Neither of us is fit to discuss anything sensibly. How could we be in any condition to reason, after what happened?"

"I don't want to be reasonable," Honey said, her voice forbidding. "I wish to be as unreasonable as possible. I've been reasonable for too long, it seems. Please take that ridiculous thing off. I suppose you keep it at Philippe's house for these . . . *gatherings*?"

"I don't deny that I am in the wrong. I merely state that this is not the time to talk about it."

Armand walked across the room and disappeared into the dressing room they shared. He began to yank at the buttons on the coat, to get it off as fast as possible. He threw it angrily to the floor, piece by piece. The ludicrous aspect of this apparel, in view of the tragedy they had just witnessed, was offensive. As usual, Honey's instinct was perfectly correct. He could well understand her anger.

As she listened to her husband taking off his clothes, Honey debated whether or not to tell him she knew about his relationship with Velma. Should she postpone the moment of truth? It was the wrong time to make an attempt to straighten out so sensitive a situation. Yet she could not seem to hold back her knowledge any longer. His flagrant lies about a business meeting having been revealed, was she to accept the untruth like some docile, idiotic wife with no brain, no place of her own in life? Her pride prevented it. Under other circumstances she might have welcomed sleep just to stop thinking about poor Venetia and the ruin of Pride's Court. Armand's appearance had changed that.

He came into the room dressed for bed. She was sitting in an armchair, already in her nightgown. He stood before her, waiting, seemingly calm, yet obviously defensive.

"Let it wait," he said.

"Was Velma at the party?" she inquired.

He hesitated. It was tempting to lie. He had not told her that Max had brought Velma up from New York on this trip. But she could check the hotel in the morning. He saw that lying would only weaken his case, would cause Honey to lose even more of her respect for him.

"Yes, she was there."

"I assumed so."

"She was with Max. That's quite natural."

"Is it? You didn't invite me."

"I've never taken you to any of Philippe's parties. I have too much regard for you to take you there. You wouldn't go, anyway, you know that perfectly well."

She was aware that she still had a choice. She could turn back even now. It would, possibly, be better for the marriage if she did. Once spoken, things could not be erased. But the gross injustice of the whole affair intruded into her mind. She refused to retreat.

"I know about Velma."

The words jarred the still night air. Armand stiffened as if she had struck him. He said nothing.

"I've known since the New Year's party at the Windsor, that supposedly splendid night when Max and Velma had the royal suite. Do you remember?"

He was astonished that she had known all these years and hadn't spoken. That she hadn't accused him. He was sensitive to the pain in her voice.

"Why didn't you tell me before this?" he demanded.

"Because our marriage . . . our love came first," Honey said. It was difficult to say the words now. She wanted desperately to cry, but she would not let that happen. It was wrong that another human being should have so much power to hurt. It was very, very wrong.

"Our love . . . our marriage *does* come first."

"Apparently not."

"I've never changed. I still love you," Armand said with difficulty. "With Velma, it was something else. I can't explain it, *cherie*. It's impossible for me to explain that feeling. Men are like that. It's my only excuse."

"If you didn't love Velma, what was it?"

"I wish to God I could tell you. But I can't. I can only tell you what it *isn't*. It isn't love."

"Armand, I must ask something of you," Honey said, forcing her voice to remain reasonably calm. "If we are to go on, if I am to respect you at all, if I am to try to recapture some of my feeling for you, you must promise not to see Velma again. Not in *that* way."

How odd it was that in these terrible moments she could hear her father's voice—telling her it would be a good thing to have her own property, to have some sense of independence. How little she had valued his advice at the time. Her love for Armand had been so perfect then. Flawless. Nothing else had mattered. But now, it was a damaged thing. Her ownership of the newspaper bolstered her pride.

Armand said quietly, *"Ma cherie,* I promise."

"Very well, Armand, I accept that. Let's not talk about this again, not ever. That could only do more damage. I want to put the whole thing out of my mind forever. I want to believe in you. I want to love you again, the way I used to love you."

He knew that he ought not to touch her. She moved to the bed and carefully climbed into her own side. He walked to her, offering the sedative, and she drank it. She was glad Armand did not try to hold her. He always recognized the right time for a gesture, a word, a touch. Tonight he did not fail her. She needed strength from somewhere, from God perhaps, to go on. But first, she wanted nothing but sleep.

CHAPTER TEN

Venetia's funeral was a nightmare. The mourners were caught in a summer downpour that had no cooling effect but managed to soak everybody to the skin. The streets teemed with water so that the women's long black skirts were splashed with mud and crimped up about their ankles in undignified fashion. Black veils, meant to protect, were plastered to their cheeks (Angela's eyes were like great, gray pansies peering through sheer, damp cloth), and the plumes on the horses pulling the hearse streamed with water, so that even the horses seemed to be crying.

Christ Church was full to overflowing, not only with friends and business acquaintances of the Courts and dozens of employees given the afternoon off to attend, but with the curious and the morbid. Tales of Venetia had drifted about the city for years; the eccentric rich were always food for gossip, and a grotesque recluse who had once been divinely beautiful was irresistible.

Honey and Armand shared a pew with Fort, Sydney, and Landry. It was only a pretense of family solidarity, but since Honey had accidentally been present when Venetia had died, Sir Simon could not help but invite the St. Amours to attend. Their presence was but one more arrow to pierce his suffering body, he thought disconsolately, comparing himself to the martyred saints he'd seen once in a Spanish art museum. At his side was Lady Court, who hobbled down the aisle on her cane and sank to her seat. She remained seated through the entire service since it was impossible for her to get up and down or kneel during the elaborate Anglican ritual.

Charles seemed to have lost twenty pounds in three days. He looked haggard and rather vague, holding Angela's hand as they went into the church. Angela felt sad, not because she would miss a mother's love (Venetia had offered none) but because she was fearful of the future. She thought constantly of Beau and longed to see him. He alone seemed to understand her. If only she could see him, she knew he would give her comfort during these days.

Even after the funeral, the Courts were constantly reminded of Venetia's death by the ruined west wing. The fire had been controlled but had gutted two floors of the wing, and the ugliness of burned walls and gaping windows was just one of many scars they bore.

Sir Simon ordered work begun immediately to repair the damage. Lady Court was unable to put her mind to the project of restoration, however, and most of the planning was left to Mary, who was, as Sir Simon often said, "slower than molasses in a January blizzard." Sir Simon plunged ahead as he had always done, on all fronts, but he failed to understand why these events had been sent to try a man who was so obviously working day and night for the common good.

Most newspapers in Montreal, especially those with a Conservative leaning, made much of the "mob scene," at the fire. There was more than a hint of blame attached to the group of demonstrators, one of whom had been seen with a rock in his hand. Sir Simon reiterated for *Le Devoir* his statement that he had only been trying to point out to the workers in his factory the facts of life; reciprocity would cost them their jobs because a Canadian manufacturer would no longer be able to compete with American manufacturers on the Canadian market, and there was, as yet, no foreign market developed for some of the products. As for the fire, it was a strange coincidence that it had begun at the same time that the belligerent mob were gathered outside his door. Nothing could be proved, but there had been threats. The ugliness of the implications tainted the whole issue of free trade. Workers who would resort to violence of this kind were not only ignorant but unworthy, it was suggested. Honey had told Beaulne and Gabriel to play down the story in *Le Monde* during the days immediately after the fire. She wasn't anxious to stir up trouble of this kind, and it could only hurt Laurier's campaign.

Four days after the funeral, Angela came to visit the St. Amours. She was sitting on the nursery floor, and Beau was playing the soothing Handel's Water Music, when Honey appeared in the doorway.

"Ready for tea, anybody?" she asked brightly.

"If there's gingerbread," Beau said, stopping.

"Oh, don't stop playing, Beau! I love that music," Honey said. "Finish, and then come down to the garden for some lemon squash."

"I'm ready to eat now," Angela said, getting up from the floor. "I can't make this dragon look at all fierce—he just looks silly."

Honey inspected the painting, and agreed that it was not a very frightening dragon.

"His eyes are too big," Honey said helpfully. "I think if he had small, mean eyes, it would give a fiercer look."

"Yes, perhaps you're right."

"How are things at Pride's Court, Angela?" Honey asked then, since Beau had closed his music and left the piano. "How is your grandmother?"

"Oh, she's very sad. I think she always felt badly about Mother, you know. Everybody did."

"I'm afraid this terrible accident has made things much worse," Honey said. "I don't think those demonstrators started the fire, but I *do* wonder how it started."

"Oh, they didn't start the fire," Angela said matter-of-factly, "and it wasn't an accident, either."

Honey had been about to go downstairs, to let the children follow when they were ready, but she was struck by the calm certainty of Angela's voice.

"How do you know it wasn't an accident?"

"Mrs. Card told me. She made me promise not to tell, though. She thinks that in a way it was her fault. I'm sure she wouldn't have said anything at all, but I happened to find her weeping the next day."

"What did she tell you?" Honey demanded. "Really, Angela, you must speak to your grandfather if you know something. The stories about the fire are so dangerous. All those men lost their jobs, did you know that?"

"I didn't know they'd lost their jobs," Angela said quietly. "How would I?"

"It was in all the newspapers."

"I don't read newspapers," Angela pointed out. "I'm not allowed to."

"No, of course you don't." Honey sometimes forgot that Angela was only fourteen. Both Angela and Beau seemed so adult at times that there was a tendency to put too much responsibility on them. "How did the fire start, Angela?"

"What about my promise to Mrs. Card?"

"Mrs. Card was wrong to make you promise to keep that kind of secret. There are too many people involved."

"I guess it *was* wrong. But I didn't want to think about it. Grandfather will be furious. And Father will be very upset. And Grandmother . . ."

"I can't see how things can get worse," Honey said. "Lies and rumors have never helped anybody. I'm sure that the correct thing to do is tell the truth. No matter how much trouble it brings, it will be less than the trouble brought on by lies."

"All right, Aunt Miel. I'm sure you're right. But it's quite awful. Mother started the fire herself. She set fire to some curtains with a lighted candle. You know how she refused to have electricity, or even kerosene lamps. She always had candles in her apartment."

"You mean she started the fire on purpose?" Honey said, her voice sinking a little with the weight of these implications.

"I asked Mrs. Card if it was an accident," Angela said, "but she said no, she had just come into the room to check on Mother and saw her put the candle to the draperies in the big bay window where the tapestry stood. She dragged my mother out of the room, but Mother didn't want to leave. The curtains went up in a burst of flame. There were some muslin ones behind the velvet. Mrs. Card would never have left Mother alone after that, but she thought Mother was unconscious."

"That's why she went back into the fire!" Honey said in a dead voice. "Because she had planned to die and wasn't going to be frustrated."

"Grandfather will be so angry," Angela said. "He forbade anybody to mention that Mother knew what she was doing when she ran back into the fire. He said the medicine she took had made her dizzy and she didn't know what she was doing."

"But Mrs. Card, apparently, knew differently. She still feels terribly guilty, I suppose, because she wasn't watching over Venetia when she set fire to the curtains. But that's foolish. Venetia could have done it any time, if she made up her mind to. Mrs. Card couldn't possibly be with her every minute."

"I told Mrs. Card that, too," Angela said. "Still, she can't get it out of her head that she should have stopped Mother from lighting the fire."

"How awful."

"It *is* awful," Angela agreed solemnly. "And it just proves that Mother intended to kill herself when she jumped off the balcony. Nobody wants to admit that, Aunt Miel, but you must see that's the truth! Poor Mother. She just couldn't bear the unhappiness of being ugly."

"You must go at once, Angela, and tell your grandfather what you know. He's got to put a stop to the stories about the workmen setting the fire."

Angela looked unhappy. "Do I *have* to?"

"Yes, of course." Honey saw Angela's face crumple. "I'll go with you, if you like. Beau, you can go downstairs and have something to eat by yourself. I'm afraid this is too important to wait, dear."

"Must we go before tea?" Angela asked, making a last-ditch attempt to stall.

"Definitely. Might as well beard the lion in his den and get it over with," Honey said firmly.

Sir Simon and Lady Court were in the conservatory. They were obviously astonished when Graves showed Honey in, although they had been expecting Angela at any moment. She had forgotten to leave word that she would be out for tea. Sir Simon's face instantly took on an angry cast.

"To what do I owe this honor, Madame?" (Sir Simon made a point of calling Honey "Madame," using the French pronunciation, on the few occasions when they met. He always managed to impart a slightly disreputable note to an otherwise polite title.) "The funeral was one thing. Quite proper for you to appear there. Pride's Court is another matter."

"Hello, Mama," Honey said, kissing Lady Court. "Hello, Papa." She was still somewhat in awe of her father but now she could at least maintain a superficial calm. "I've come to see you about something important."

"Thin edge of the wedge," Sir Simon said darkly, "but

you can forget *that*, Madame St. Amour. We are *not* having a truce."

"Oh, Papa," Honey said in exasperation, "I didn't come here for a personal visit. I came to tell you something you ought to know."

Sir Simon, who was under the impression that he knew everything of any importance, was amazed at this suggestion. However, he was a curious man and so he waited for Honey to explain herself while he grumpily poured more tea.

"You know that Angela comes to visit me occasionally," Honey began.

"I have never approved," Sir Simon interjected.

"In any event, she does," Honey went on, "and she happened to mention to me that she knows how the fire really started. Since the story can be corroborated, right here in the house, I think you ought to look into it."

"How can she know that?" Sir Simon said, turning abruptly to Angela and fixing his glare upon her. "What do you know, Angela? Who told you?"

"My dear," Lady Court protested mildly. "You ought to have spoken to *us* if you know something."

Before they could attack Angela and make her even more nervous, Honey went on to repeat the girl's story, and to tell Sir Simon that he ought to question Mrs. Card. It had been most unfair of Mrs. Card to make Angela promise silence on such an important issue, Honey emphasized.

"You're quite right, but all the same, I don't see what can be done about it now," Sir Simon said.

"What do you mean, you can't see what's to be done? For one thing, you can see that the correct story is given to one of *your* newspapers. I think it's your duty to bring out the truth."

"If it *is* the truth. How do we know Mrs. Card isn't hysterical?"

"You can judge that," Honey said tersely. "You can judge people, Papa."

"What good's it going to do now? Bringing it all up again?"

"It's giving the whole campaign a bad odor," Honey pointed out.

"What do I care if Laurier's campaign has a bad odor? Most of it is quite justified, to my mind."

"Papa!" Honey cried, horrified at his stand. "Where's British justice? And the men you fired—shouldn't they be given their jobs back? And an apology?"

"Jobs back? Apology?" Sir Simon turned crimson at the thought, his voice rising to a dangerous pitch. "*Apology?* To those hooligans?"

"I can see you don't intend to correct this mistake," Honey said. "And if you don't, I'll see that it's corrected in *Le Monde.*"

"You'll *what?*"

Sir Simon spluttered with rage and indignation, ending, finally with, "This is a family matter. You'd go so far as to publish *family business* in that rag of yours? Put another taint on Venetia, on Charles, on Angela?"

"You gave me the *rag*, as you call it," Honey shouted back. "Truth is truth, regardless of family, and it's shocking that you can't see it!"

"Don't tell me what's shocking!"

"Somebody has to tell you! Everybody else is afraid of you, but I'm not!" Honey had abandoned all caution in her anger. "I'll print the story, you can depend on it!"

"I'll fire Mrs. Card if she talks to you!"

"And I'll *hire* Mrs. Card!"

"You'd better realize, *Madame*, that I can sink that filthy little paper of yours by lifting a hand! You don't know what in hell you're doing! A woman running a newspaper! Ridiculous! And this is the result!"

"Are you threatening me?" Honey shouted, her cheeks red with temper and temperature combined.

"You print that story, and it'll be the end of *Le Monde*," Sir Simon said, grinding his teeth in fury. "*The end!*"

The story appeared two days later. Angela was forbidden any more visits to the St. Amour household (but of course, she would disobey since she could not survive without seeing Beau, it was simply a matter of waiting until the storm blew over and she could think of a way to leave the house). Two days after the story appeared in print Honey was presented with a notice from the City of Montreal. The building in which *Le Monde* was printed, and which she owned along with the presses, was condemned. It must be evacuated and torn down immediately.

No amount of pressure, no appeals, changed this edict from the city council. Sir Simon had powerful connections in municipal politics. *Le Monde* printed stories (within the bounds of libel laws) hinting at the coincidence between the publication of the story about the fire at Pride's Court and the sudden decision of the council to condemn the building in which *Le Monde* was printed. Nothing swayed the council decision. The building must come down. The presses must be moved. *Le Monde* might be forced to suspend publication. And this in the midst of the election campaign.

By September 15, one week before the election, *Le Monde* was forced to shut down the presses.

"It's just as I said!" Gabriel cried to Honey and Beaulne. "The Reform council needs reforming! Somebody has been bought, any fool can see it!"

Le Monde was silenced until land could be purchased and a building erected that would hold the new, larger presses on the market and meet the city's building bylaws. Gabriel was sent on the land-buying mission while Beaulne went to New Jersey to buy the presses. Honey had decided to make Gabriel editor when the paper published again, and Beaulne would be in charge of printing stationery, advertising posters, and pamphlets of all kinds, as Gabriel had suggested. It was an admirable solution and, except for the election, she would have been reasonably happy. Now there was no way she could throw her influence behind the Liberal campaign. Exactly what Sir Simon had wanted, she realized. She could only hope that *Le Monde* had been effective all along, and that Laurier would be reelected. Such was not the case, however. The Conservatives, under Robert Borden, took power in September, and while the St. Amours and their friends despaired, Sir Simon was ecstatic. Right had triumphed.

CHAPTER ELEVEN

The days immediately before Christmas were not particularly merry ones for the St. Amours. Honey's decision to publish the truth about the fire at Pride's Court had cost her both a great deal of money and loss of prestige when *Le Monde* had been forced to shut down before the election. It had also cost Armand a railroad charter and, in a more circumspect way, the loss of certain pieces of real estate purchased on speculation in Montreal itself.

"It isn't," Armand announced as he meticulously placed his tie pin before the mirror in their shared dressing room, "my idea of the happiest Christmas of them all, *cherie*."

They were dressing for the ritual Christmas Eve with the family downstairs. Later Armand and the children would go to Mass. Honey, hooking up the front of the bottle-green velvet gown she had chosen, was trying to decide whether to wear diamonds or pearls.

"I quite agree. Do I really have to let two maids go, Armand? It's so difficult to run the house on short staff. But I suppose we must economize somewhere. What about letting one of the stable hands go? Really, the children seldom ride, and I haven't time. Neither have you."

"Your economies are to be admired," Armand said, kissing her hand lightly, "but I can't see that they'll help very much. Why don't you consider giving up the newspaper? It isn't too late to cancel orders for the new presses, is it? You could invest the money in something else. The projected costs of the new building seem staggering to me. A small fortune."

His tone was casual. But she caught him up quickly, her voice brittle.

"Give up the newspaper?"

"Well, *cherie*, you must admit that your little trinket has cost you money *this* year."

"It's mine to do with as I wish," she said.

"Yes, of course it is. I'm not asking for help financially—I don't want it. I never will. I told you that a long time ago. Still . . ."

"I know what you're thinking. Papa interfered somehow with that charter for the northern railroad in Ontario. You lost it because he was angry with me."

"You know as well as I do, darling, that even a Conservative minister should have snapped up my offer. Nobody else wants to construct a line up there, and it's all good for the development of the country. Sir Simon must have bought off somebody. I expected to get the charter despite the Liberal defeat. So did Max. He was shocked. I know your dear father had a hand in it."

"I can't let Papa have his own way, don't you see? He wants me to give up. Then he'll bray in triumph. It will just prove everything he believes in. Well, I won't."

"There wasn't just the loss of the charter," Armand sighed. "Unfortunately, I lost a great deal of money on the land speculation. We thought the rail yards would go through that piece of land, and consequently I bought up too much at high prices. I'll never be able to sell it at a profit now that the rail yards are being located elsewhere. I also suspect your father had a hand in that. He and his group. They've got a firm hold somewhere in the city council, I don't know where. I just wish I did."

"Is it really bad?" Honey asked seriously.

"I'm afraid so. We may have to sell the island property."

"Oh Armand, what a shame! I didn't realize . . ."

"Yes, it is. Still, I mean to hang on to this house, and to as much of the railroad as I can. I'll have to talk to Max, that's all. He was counting on opening up that northern strip because he's convinced there's gold there. He's had stakes in northern Ontario for years."

"I'm sorry, Armand. But I had to tell the truth in *Le Monde*."

"And what's it going to cost *you*?" Armand went on, becoming a little more excited as he talked. "Suspending publication will lose readers as well as advertising money. What if you don't get those readers back?"

"We'll get them back. I'm absolutely committed to a new and larger newspaper. I have such plans!"

"I think it's more important to look after this house

and the children and my interests than to win a battle with your father," Armand said flatly.

"It isn't just a battle with my father."

"What is it? I wish you could explain the mystery of this newspaper to me."

He came up behind her and kissed her on the neck. She leaned her cheek against his and looked at the image of the two of them in the mirror. Her gold hair was piled up into a thick topknot, her face was still firm and lovely. Armand, gray at the temples, looked even darker and more fascinating with age. They were, she reflected, quite a handsome couple.

"I can't exactly explain it, except to say that I—as a person, not just as Sir Simon Court's daughter—that I couldn't be satisfied with anything less, now. Don't you see?"

"No."

"Well, do we have to talk about it on Christmas Eve?"

"I forgot. Everything must stop for Christmas. You're still a child in many ways. A romantic child! What if I were to become jealous of Gabriel? What then?"

"Don't be foolish, Armand. I wouldn't look at another man. Gabriel is a friend." She laughed at the idea.

"He's always around," Armand argued. "He's quite attractive, I've heard women say."

"Not to me. Now stop such ridiculous talk."

"I wish I could make you see that our finances aren't good—" Armand began again.

"Perhaps if you'd stop gambling with Philippe . . ." Honey said, becoming irritated at Armand's persistence.

"My gambling losses aren't enough to make any difference," Armand protested mildly. "We're talking about losing millions of dollars, not a few thousand."

"If that's the case, I have no intention of firing any of my maids. Or giving up the horses. And I'll get a new car in the spring."

"I surrender. Let's not talk about these financial matters tonight. The children must be waiting for us."

Denys, Michel, and Susan were already in the drawing room. Susan was playing carols and Armand was serving wine when the telegram arrived. Armand took it at the door, knowing that a message that arrived at such a time could not possibly be good news. He opened it nervously. He read:

Max died this morning. Funeral December 28. Please come. Velma.

A pit of fear opened up before him. He had counted on Max's advice, on his experience, to help him with the financial problems that he had managed to accumulate. He would soon be heavily in debt. Max would have told him what to sell, what to keep. Max had become like a surrogate father to him. There was no way of knowing at this moment how Max had written his will, whether Velma would be the sole beneficiary. Or if so, whether she would help him. He walked slowly back into the drawing room.

"What is it, Armand? What's happened?" Honey asked, seeing his strained expression.

"Max is dead."

"Oh, poor old man!" Honey said quickly, thinking of Max's kindnesses to her.

"Yes, poor Max," Armand said tightly. But he was not feeling pity for Max or concern for Velma—he was thinking only of the tangled state of his finances and wondering desperately how much of the St. Amour fortune he could salvage.

After the funeral, the small group of mourners returned to the house on Fifth Avenue. In her role as widow, Velma wore black velvet under black mink and a matching toque that bound her thick auburn hair. The half dozen men who joined Velma and Armand for a drink in Max's old study did not stay long. They were making a courtesy gesture, and Velma was noticeably restless. It was obvious that each guest (except Armand) was glad to escape.

Despite the appropriateness of her black gown, Velma remained a hothouse flower. None of her lushness had faded over the years. If anything, she was more full-blown. Her skin was still flawlessly pink, her hair a warm red-brown, and her eyes lighted instantly when she smiled one of her enchanting, all-encompassing smiles. They were alone now, and Velma sank into one of the huge leather chairs.

"Bring me a brandy from the bar over there, will you, Armand?"

"I've never known you to drink brandy," Armand said. "Is this a new habit?"

"I feel the need of brandy, that's all."

He handed her the drink. She tasted it and grimaced in dislike. Still, she finished it off rather quickly, he thought.

"You're staying on to dinner, of course? I told Charles to expect two at the table. Not that I feel hungry . . ." She broke off, setting the glass down.

"If you'd like me to stay," Armand said.

"I expected that you would," Velma said rather pointedly.

She gave him a half smile. But even a half smile from Velma was enough to stir his blood. Remembering his promise to Honey of some months before, he resolved that it would be dinner and nothing else. After dinner he would return to his hotel. There was to be no more intimacy with Velma. The irony of this, now that Max was dead and Velma was free, struck him forcibly. He reminded himself firmly that he had given his solemn word to his wife.

Velma visibly relaxed. She leaned back in the chair, looking at him. The black velvet, while uncommonly high at the neck compared with her usual gowns, clung to the outlines of her plump bosom. Armand had never considered a day dress with a high neck and long sleeves particularly tempting. Velma transformed it, though.

"Now for some champagne," Velma said languidly, as if she were losing her tension gradually, allowing the whole funeral, the forced social formalities, to slide away from her. "I'll ring for Charles. We may as well have some caviar as well, don't you think?"

Armand agreed, although he was hesitant to enter too freely into Velma's mood. Her voice, her manner, even her clothes now seemed to be creating a velvety ambience. He knew he was being seduced, yet she had done nothing, really. He could not fault her behavior.

When the champagne had been poured, and Charles was gone, Velma said suddenly, "I suppose you're wondering about the will? If I'm the heiress to all Max's money, his property? Or if I know who is?"

He had been wondering exactly that, and he caught his breath when she repeated so bluntly what was in his mind.

"Naturally," he said calmly, not letting her see that she had made him uneasy. "I'd be a liar if I said I wasn't concerned."

"I've never found you to be a liar."

"I wouldn't have brought it up so soon, that's all."

"Why not?" Velma said, holding out her glass for more wine.

"Out of respect for Max, I suppose."

"Max would understand."

"Would he?"

"There was nobody more practical than Max. Surely you understand that, Armand? Except when it came to you and me. And even then, you could say he was *practical*. He liked you very much, you know. I would almost say he loved you, Armand. As a son. That was his weakness. He couldn't break his business relationship with you even when he found out about us."

"About us?" Armand's voice sounded hollow. He had always hoped that Max did not really know the truth, that he might suspect, but that as long as they were discreet, the old man would never be sure.

"You didn't think Max was in doubt about us, did you?" Velma said with an edge in her voice. "You can't be so foolish, can you?"

"I thought he didn't . . . really know. That if he knew definitely, that would be the end of our partnership. So I just assumed . . ." Armand shrugged helplessly.

"You expected him to buy you out? Or cut you off? Or force you to buy him out, is that it? No, Armand, in his way he loved you. Max was a strange man, but he was kind. I loved him."

"You loved him?"

"There are many kinds of love. Not the way I loved you, Armand, how could that be? But in another way. Max looked after me, cared about what happened to me. He would have done anything for me, given me anything. One *has* to love a person who feels like that."

"And for me? What was it you felt for me?"

Velma sipped her champagne, staring at him not coquettishly but appraisingly.

"A form of love, perhaps. In some ways, Armand, you are extremely selfish. Did you know that? But there is this attraction between us, the way we are together. It's like being desperately hungry and then being offered delicious food. That's how you affect me. You satisfy me. Perhaps that's all there is to the feeling. But it's enough, don't you think?"

"It always seemed to be enough," Armand said. His voice held no enthusiasm. His worries were surfacing, and his promise to his wife was an irritant.

"You may toast the widow, if you like, darling. I'll tell you something. Outside of some bequests to the servants, and a large charity, *I* am the sole beneficiary."

"Very well, I'll drink to your fortune! And also to Max, wherever he may be, for his generosity!" Armand said, holding up his glass of champagne.

Velma smiled at him. He felt almost ill now with a sudden sweep of desire, but he walked away from her. He sat down heavily in a chair that was too far away to allow him to touch her long, well-shaped fingers, draped so casually over the arm of the chair. The diamonds Max had given her over the years—large, ostentatious, brilliant—flashed as she moved. Armand looked away from her to stare at the painting over the mantel.

"You're in trouble, Armand. Max told me."

Her voice brought him back to harsh reality.

"I didn't know Max talked about his business with you."

"That's because I never mentioned it to you. I know quite a lot about your financial problems, my dear."

"It's true," Armand agreed. There seemed to be no use in denying it. "We bought up property in Montreal on the understanding that the rail yards and some of the rail line would be located there. Plans changed, and the property is not worth what I paid for it on the market. That's one of my problems, and there are others."

"You planned to ask Max for help, I suppose."

"I was going to consult him. Max always knew what to do. He was a genius with money. With investments. I depended . . ." Armand broke off. It seemed useless to go on.

"However, the asbestos mine and that railroad into it are still profitable," Velma said coolly, "so you must try to hang on to them, Armand."

She was right. Perhaps Max had said that to her, or perhaps she was cleverer than he had ever given her credit for being.

"I intend to try to do that," Armand said.

He felt like drinking a great deal of champagne. He

felt like forgetting these problems, he felt like losing his sorrows in Velma's lushness. As she leaned back in the shimmering black velvet he became intensely aware of her ripe bosom, her soft graceful neck, her voluptuous mouth as it curled over the edge of the champagne glass. He saw a flicker of pink tongue and remembered its past talents. When Velma shifted sideways in the chair, her gown slid up almost to the knee, revealing a curvaceous, dark-stockinged leg. He flushed with memories of less formal occasions when those loose limbs had wrapped themselves warmly about his thighs.

"More champagne, please," Velma said.

He obliged. He felt himself slipping into his familiar role with Velma. One for which he was so well-equipped. One that provided such sensual delights.

"Are you going to ask *me* for help, Armand?" she asked then, her gaze bathing him in pleasures that his memory knew too well.

"I don't know. I honestly don't know."

"Well, darling, there is such a simple solution to the whole thing, I don't know why we waste so much time on it. Like Max, we ought to be practical. I am *offering* to help you, offering whatever you need. There's no need to worry, really—you will be able to get all the financial backing you require. I trust you absolutely, Armand, and I know that you'll find a way to put your finances completely in order again. My faith in you is . . . complete."

For a moment, it was as if he had been lifted up on some cloud, out of the depths of despair and worry. As if some magician had waved a wand and wiped out all his problems. Then he rose to stand before Velma and looked into her face. He was afraid to ask, but he had to know the truth.

"And in return?" The words came out softly.

She paused a little, letting the beginnings of a smile touch her lips.

"I imagine I will be very lonely here now," Velma said, "and New York is not so far from Montreal. Perhaps you would invest some time and money down here. Just as Max invested time and money up there. The situation is quite reversible, Armand."

Briefly, he saw how life would be. Sharing that vast, downy bed with Velma, making free with that generous body that still called to him, that he could see clearly though she was fully clothed. And the money would be there to use, to plan and to make more money with. His difficulties of the moment would become trivial. The vision shimmered before him so that he almost took her there, almost fell upon her hungrily, needing, wanting, every physical need, every material need folded into that one marvelous flesh-rose.

As he swayed there on the edge of what seemed to be paradise, he thought of that other love, the one that gave him such a different kind of life. Accepting Velma's proposition would destroy his marriage. He knew that. It might destroy his belief in himself as well. He had promised Honey. Velma's way was too easy, it was too convenient—it was lethal.

His hand formed a fist of such anger and such strength that the thin glass in it crumpled. Blood and champagne trickled together across his fingers, to the carpet. The pain brought him to his senses. When Velma had wrapped his cut palm, and Charles had swept up the broken glass, he knew that he would have to solve his own problems without help from Velma. Or he would have no marriage, and he would not be a man.

CHAPTER TWELVE

Dominion Square was an oasis of light and shadow in the heart of the city. The sounds of electric trams, rattling trucks, milk wagons, hansom cabs and glistening private cars making their way along the streets were like the mating cries of unknown birds. Angela and Beau often met in the Square after their lessons—late in the afternoon, but well before teatime.

They sat in silence for a while, watching and listening. When it was almost time to go—Beau (to walk) eastward to St. Denis, and Angela north to Dorchester Street—she finally asked a question that was very much on her mind.

"Everybody is talking about a war. Do you think it will really happen, Beau?"

She looked very grown-up in a long white cotton Crepon dress trimmed with apricot and blue, her black hair pinned up into a thick bunch at her neck. Her skin was as white as Venetia's had once been, smooth and pale and without blemish. Her gray eyes, fastened on Beau, paralyzed him with their beauty and their vulnerability. He thought that he had never seen, and would never see again, anyone as beautiful as Angela.

"Even my piano teacher talks about the war," Beau said glumly. He had a fatalistic view of the subject, as if the war were a book he was about to open and read. It seemed inevitable that the story would unfold. Everyone said that it would.

"Grandfather is looking forward to it," Angela said in a puzzled tone. "He wishes he could go and fight what he calls 'the Huns.' What a fierce old man he is!"

"A troublemaker," Beau amended. He did not care much for Angela's descriptions of her bombastic grandfather. The old man had made so much trouble, preventing them from seeing each other openly, that he could never forgive, or be amused by Sir Simon, as Angela apparently was.

"Well, he's one of the foundations of the Empire," Angela said with a little mischievous look at Beau's serious expression. "He says so himself, so it must be true."

"Greedy old barbarian," Beau said sternly. "Look what he's done to *you*, Angela, trying to keep you from seeing Aunt Miel and me."

"He can't bear to be thwarted, that's all. Aunt Miel went against his orders and he can't forgive her that, ever. He never will get over her putting politics before family. Anyway, Aunt Miel's newspaper has survived, and is making lots of money, so that's the main thing, isn't it?"

"Not to me. Your happiness is the main thing."

"If there's a war, you won't be able to go to Paris to study this winter," Angela said, changing the subject. Beau's projected trip to Paris to study at the Conservatory was uppermost in her mind. Without him, Montreal would be a terribly lonely place. Her life would be emptier than she could imagine.

"I'll try to go to Boston, in that case."

"I might be able to visit Boston. Perhaps I could coax Father into taking me down there," Angela said wistfully. "Now that he has a new wife, he tries very hard to make up to me for what he thinks of as 'not spending enough time with Angela.'"

"How are you getting on with Polly?"

"Oh, not badly. She's rather dull. She and Aunt Sydney spend all their time taking first aid lessons with St. John Ambulance. They plan to do Red Cross work if there's a war. All very patriotic."

"Well, I suppose it's better than the atmosphere when your Mother was wandering about, being so mysterious," Beau said. "But a stepmother isn't the best thing in the world. In your case, it's easier, though. *My* stepfather is really my father, only nobody talks about it."

"What's the war about, Beau? Do you know? I can't make anything out of what they say at home. Grandfather just keeps talking about the Kaiser 'asking for it,' 'so we'll show him.' And then Father and Uncle Geoff tell him it's much more complicated than that, and they all argue about the temperament of the Germans, and I can't figure it out."

"I don't know what it was about a few months ago,"

Beau said, "but now it's about some archduke who was shot."

"What's *he* got to do with it?"

"He was assassinated in Bosnia. Which is near Austria, and it has to do with Austria seizing some land that didn't belong to her. I don't know whether the archduke was responsible or not. Anyway, he's dead. And everybody is sure that means war."

"It's time to go," Angela said, and then added rather sadly, "Not that there's anybody at home to talk to. Polly won't show up for ages and Grandmother is in bed sick. Father and Grandfather are coming home late for dinner every night. They spend a lot of time discussing a plan to make guns out of threshing machines, or something like that, at the plant."

"It must be lonely in that big house," Beau said.

"It is. I hate being alone, particularly in that wing!"

He was surprised. This was the first time Angela had ever mentioned disliking the renovated west wing where her Mother had died three years before.

Angela went on, not waiting for Beau's response: "You know, Grandfather had some of the inside walls moved, and now I have a small apartment for myself. Between mine and the rooms Father and Polly use, there's a sitting room. Nobody ever goes in there."

"That's not surprising, when the house is so big," Beau said calmly. "There are so many rooms to choose from, it's just not necessary."

"I suppose not," Angela said. Then she leaned forward intensely. "If I tell you something, promise you won't laugh?"

"You know I won't laugh."

Angela's gray eyes darkened and she reminded him of an owl as she put her face close to Beau's and whispered, "Promise you won't laugh! Say, 'If I do, I hope to die.'"

Beau humored her, but he was smiling slightly at her serious manner. Around them were people, and traffic, and the pink sun sinking between the buildings of Peel Street, but he and Angela might have been back in the nursery at Aunt Miel's house.

"I'm sure Mother is still at Pride's Court."

Beau was horrified.

"Angela, that's terrible. It's stupid!"

"I shouldn't have told you. You don't believe me."

"You should have told me, but I know you're just letting your imagination run wild. Because the house is so empty."

"Come with me, then. I'll take you up there. You'll find out for yourself."

"I can't go to Pride's Court!" He was appalled at the suggestion. "Your Grandfather would throw me out!"

"He won't know. Nobody will know. I can get in and out of that house without anybody ever seeing me. I do it all the time. I know where all the servants are. Grandmother doesn't leave her room these days. Polly won't be home for two hours at least. It's simple."

He reluctantly agreed to go. Even then it was only to soothe her and quiet his own conscience. If Angela needed some kind of comfort and support, he must give it. But he found that he was nervous and excited as they walked through the gates. Pride's Court, as grand now as it had been before the fire, was bathed in the pink glow of sunset. There was a beautiful assurance about it that defied the smallness of human beings. Beau hesitated, overwhelmed, but Angela pulled at his sleeve and almost dragged him into the garden and then to a side entrance of the house. They were upstairs on the second floor within minutes and they hadn't seen a single soul.

A corridor with an oval, stained-glass window at the end ran the full length of the west wing. The sun struck through the window, casting a blood-red stain upon the patterned carpet. Yet there was a warmth, still, in the last rays of sunlight. August heat did not penetrate the thick walls of the house as it did smaller, less majestic establishments, and this gave the air a pleasant, semitropical shimmer. Except for the red stain, there was nothing intimidating about the corridor. Angela walked ahead of Beau, leading him toward her own apartment and the sitting room she had mentioned. Their footsteps made no sound on the thick carpeting.

First she took him into her own small sitting room with its bright cabbage-rose chintzes, walnut desk, and green landscapes. He was curious. He had often envisioned Angela here, but now he could carry with him the image of this room and see her sitting there in the deep chair reading, or there at the desk working on her lessons, or there by the window painting her fantasies. When he had gazed enough, she said, "Are you ready now to see the other room?"

"Yes, let's go in there." He found that he was whispering.

They went out into the corridor again. The red stain had shifted slightly. Soon it would disappear altogether. Somebody would turn on the electric lights set in bronze holders along the walls and shaded with silk. The walls would be a darker green then. The whole atmosphere would change.

The sitting room was gloomy despite the fact that it had been redecorated fairly recently. The dark greens and browns of the wallpaper and upholstery provided no freshness, no encouragement, somehow, to stay and read, or to light a fire. An alcove with an upholstered windowseat should have beckoned; instead, it provided odd shadows and inexplicable light. The air was dead, completely without movement.

Angela closed the door behind them. Beau noticed that she seemed to walk stiffly, as if she were nervously expectant. He couldn't remember ever seeing her so tense.

Sandwiched as it was between two apartments, the room picked up no sounds. It was another country, and perhaps another time. In the silence, Beau could hear his own breathing. Then he thought he heard a humming sound. Odd. No, more like a drumbeat, he decided. Muffled and far away. Strain as he would, he could not identify the sound.

"Do you hear that?"

"Hear what?" She looked puzzled.

The sound was gone. The room was extraordinarily cold. An impossible chill for August. While the house's thick walls kept out the worst of the day's heat, the corridor had been warm. Beau wanted desperately to open a window, but he could not visualize himself crossing the room. He seemed rooted to the spot.

"It's awfully cold," he said in an attempt to explain his reluctance to stay. "No wonder the room isn't used."

They saw nothing. At the same time, Beau felt a heaviness in the air; he sensed that he was not wanted in this room. It was rejecting him. He could not imagine sitting in any of the chairs, or on the sofa. He could not conjure up a picture of himself lighting a fire, and then turning on a lamp and settling down for a long, cozy read. The room was pushing him away, somehow.

Angela felt it too. He could make out the tightness of her pale face even in the ever-increasing darkness. She gave a little cry, and he caught her hand in his and pulled her to the door, threw it open, and fled with her back into her own sitting room. In the safety of that room, with the door closed, they held each other tightly for a few moments, to stop the trembling that had overtaken them.

"Beau, did you feel it?"

"I felt something, but it's just a . . . a cold room."

"No, it's more than that," Angela said, her voice muffled against his shirt. "She's there. I know she's there. She won't go away, that's the trouble. Oh, I hate that room! She's making me hate Pride's Court, just as she hated it!"

"No, no, it's all in your imagination."

He continued to hold her, his heart jumping now for a different reason. She turned her beautiful face to him and he put his lips gently, warmly upon her mouth. They kissed like that, with their lips closed, innocent of any other kind of caress. They stayed in each other's arms—sealing, without words, the vow they'd made years before.

The new building on Craig Street provided larger, cooler offices for the *Le Monde* staff, but somehow, in the two years since its completion, much of the old atmosphere (the untidiness, the papers and books strewn about waiting to be read or refiled, the extra people who seemed always to be displaced, the ringing telephone, and, underneath, the rumble of the presses) had gradually reappeared.

"I've set up the front page," Gabriel said to Honey. "If word comes before eleven tonight, we'll use the head 'War Declared' on tomorrow's edition."

It was like waiting for the guillotine to fall, Honey thought. You were sure that it *would* fall, you entertained a faint hope that some last-minute miracle would prevent its falling, and at the same time you prayed that it would happen quickly so that the suspense and pain of waiting would be over.

She took the mock-up from him and studied it. While

her mind was partially on the importance of the newspaper's handling of this story, her thoughts were also spread thinly over a dozen personal details. She was worried about Denys. Not so much from her own point of view (he was eighteen, and she could understand why he wanted to join the army if war was declared), but because she knew that Armand would be outraged. She would be forced to take Denys's side, and that would set her against Armand. It could only mean painful scenes and horrible arguments.

It was not only Armand she was likely to quarrel with, either. Gabriel was completely against Canada's sending aid to England in the event of war with Germany. It was no longer the time, Gabriel said, to knuckle under to the "Mother Country." It was time for Canada to stand on her own. To send supplies to the war, yes. Even Red Cross volunteers, and perhaps doctors. But no army, no navy. Certainly no *conscription*.

"We're committed in conscience to supporting England," Gabriel was saying, referring to an editorial he was writing at the moment, "but there are *limits*."

"What do the bishops say?" Honey asked sarcastically.

"I haven't heard. But it will probably be along the same lines. You can't expect Liberal supporters in Quebec— even inconsistent ones—to stand up and cheer at the idea of sending troops to help England. Nor France, for that matter."

"If England needs help, the Commonwealth nations will have to give it," Honey said. "I can't imagine right-thinking people taking any other view."

"Even the Conservatives are divided about the issues," Gabriel warned. "It's not as cut and dried as you think. It isn't all Liberals against all Conservatives. Nor all English Canadians against all French Canadians. Laurier, for example, will want to send as much aid as possible, I expect."

"I never supposed it *was* a matter of all the French against all the English," Honey said crossly. "But I believe Canadians must do everything possible to help England if war comes. Can you imagine what the world would be like if Germany won?" She shuddered.

"Not much different in world markets. Canada might learn to stand on her own feet, which would be good, in my opinion."

Honey was shocked.

"Gabriel! England *defeated*? You don't know what you're saying! You obviously don't know much about Germans. You don't know much about the Teutonic intelligence!"

"What's so marvelous about the way England has treated the nations *she* conquered? Milking them for everything they had . . . look at India! What has England done for India? And as for French Canada . . ." He shrugged, looking angry and a bit wild.

"You were allowed to keep your language and your religion. Which is more freedom than most conquerors have ever given their defeated enemies. Really, it makes me sick . . ."

The conversation was shaping into a classic argument. They had had this debate before and it always ended in exactly the same way. Both were stubborn and so emotionally involved that reason (wherever it lay) did not enter into the picture. In the end, Honey always felt exactly as she had at the beginning, and Gabriel did, too.

"You never learn, you English," Gabriel said, exasperated.

"Watch what you're saying, Gabriel! Remember, while you are the editor, I am still the publisher!"

He picked up the mock front page and stormed out of her office, slamming the door behind him. Honey, tired from the day's tension and expecting fresh problems at any minute, closed her eyes and tried to calm herself. She was fighting with Gabriel here at the office, and she would probably have to find herself a new editor if he insisted on pursuing these anti-British attitudes. At home, she would undoubtedly run into a fierce argument with Armand. There seemed to be no respite.

Yet the success of the newspaper in the face of her father's treacherous behavior years before had been a source of great pride to Honey. She had found another location, hired an architect, and started *Le Monde* again. Gabriel and Beaulne, between them, had purchased the new presses and set up the other side of the printing business: the stationery, posters, pamphlets, and now the Montreal telephone directory. *Le Monde* was more than just solvent, it was steadily making money.

Armand, after Max DeLeon's death, had lost a great

deal of money, and it had only been by tenacity and with good legal advice that he had managed to hold on to some of the railroads the company had controlled. There had been a time, three years before, when the St. Amour fortunes had been at a low point. Now Armand was gradually coming back up the financial ladder. He looked forward to the day when Denys would become a partner, and this was one of the dreams he would see endangered if Denys joined the army. Armand himself would want to help Canada's war effort, (his Liberalism would be set aside in the face of a national cause) and through that help, England. But he would be aggressively against his elder son joining the army and possibly getting maimed or killed. The two things would be separate in Armand's mind. They were not separate in Honey's mind. She quite understood where Denys stood on the matter.

Deep in this reverie, it was some moments before she realized there was a visitor in her office.

"Oh, Marc! I'm sorry, I was involved in my problems, I'm afraid. Come in—sit down."

Marc greeted his sister-in-law with a quick peck on the cheek and took a chair near her desk. Honey saw by Marc's intense, peering gaze that he was upset. She could have lived without *this* visit, she thought rather irritably—on top of everything else. But she prepared to listen.

"I know you're busy," Marc began apologetically. His hands were restless; he rubbed one over the other and stared out the window. "But you're the only person I can talk to about this, Honey."

"Everybody is busy," Honey said, trying to sound kind. "So you may as well come to see *me*, Marc, as anyone else. What can I do? There's no problem about the Church Home, I hope?"

"No, no. The home is running smoothly. Your efforts to raise money this spring were nothing short of a miracle. Mrs. O'Donohue is an excellent matron. As far as I know, there's no problem at the home. The bishop is pleased, too. I saw him two weeks ago. He told me to commend you on the whole project."

"Oh that's good. I must have a visit with Bishop Grise soon. He's rather a dear old man."

"As a matter of fact, I'll be going to see him again myself. Perhaps tomorrow," Marc said meaningfully.

"Then you have some problem about your parish?"

"Not exactly."

It was so like Marc to avoid coming to the point, Honey thought. She would have liked to hurry him up, but he would have looked so wounded—and, in the final analysis, it would only have served to slow him up. She ordered tea brought into the office, giving him time to sort out his thoughts. Finally he said, "I'm sure the bishop will see my point of view. Good chaplains are an important part of the war effort. I'll offer to go overseas. After all, I'm only forty-six."

So that was it. If war came, Marc wanted to go overseas with the troops.

"Good priests are equally important at home," Honey pointed out. "You might do just as much good right here in Montreal."

"It isn't the same thing."

"Well, I'm not going to argue about that," Honey said, sighing. "If you've made up your mind, and that's what it sounds like to me, then there's nothing anybody can say."

"It's Camille I'm worried about."

It had been an agony, making this decision, but he felt driven to it. He was responsible for Camille, he knew, and he had always shouldered that burden willingly, accepting, finally, the temptations it presented. Camille needed him. On the other hand, being with the troops in battle would be the most difficult ministry in the world. And he wanted that difficulty. He *needed* that difficulty.

"I could send Camille out to the farm, but she doesn't like it. She'd be unhappy there. She doesn't get along that well with Justine, and since her marriage to Timothée . . ." He didn't finish the sentence.

"Camille can come to us, Marc. You know that."

"I'd hoped you'd say that."

"But you know we would always take her! There's plenty of room. Even if Beau wasn't going to study in Boston this winter, there'd be more than ample room for her. We have several unused bedrooms as it is. Perhaps she might like to take over Beau's apartment in the nursery —it's one of the nicest parts of the house, I've always thought. Camille used to love it, didn't she?"

Marc felt a stab of pain in his chest. The nursery. Yes,

he and Camille had shared many moments in the nursery. It was like a twist of fate that Honey should offer that particular place as a shelter for Camille.

"Camille loved the nursery. We both did. That would take much of the sting out of my going, Honey. You can't begin to imagine how she'd love that!"

Just the thought of Camille living in the nursery was like the lifting of a heavy weight off his head. He actually felt the muscles of his face loosen, and when he picked up the teacup his hand was no longer trembling.

"She used to write poetry there," Marc said.

"It must be a very special place. Beau has always loved to practice his music and compose there. Angela has painted in it ever since she first came to visit."

"You have no idea what that would mean to Camille. She could wait for me there," Marc repeated.

"We'll find things for her to do besides wait," Honey said. "I know there are many things Camille has learned to do well."

"I'll go along now, then. After I've spoken to His Lordship, I'll tell Camille myself. Oh . . . and Honey, I realize that you'll need somebody to fill my place on the committee for the home. I'll speak to the bishop about that, too. Perhaps the priest who will be replacing me can help."

Marc had been gone only ten minutes when the telephone rang. She picked it up with trembling hands, sure it was the message they had all been expecting, but it was Denys. He had called to confirm what she already knew. He intended to join the army the moment war was declared.

"I'll tell Father tonight," Denys said. "I know there'll be a hell of a scene, Mother. But it can't be helped. As soon as it's official and there's somewhere to sign up, I'll be there."

He scarcely heard her reply, but went right on enthusiastically. "I hear old Sam Hughes is already trying to get troops together. Doesn't Grandfather know him? Perhaps I can join a unit that's going overseas more quickly if you write him a note, Mother. I don't want to waste any time!"

Sam Hughes, Minister of the Militia since 1911, had wanted to recruit during the Boer War when he was nothing more than a member of the House of Commons. Then he had pleaded with the government to let him raise an army that could "go anywhere on a day's notice." War was Sam Hughes' idea of heaven. Since January Sam Hughes had been building armories for his militiamen and staging elaborate military reviews across the country. If any man could raise an army quickly it was Hughes, although whether it would be a well-organized army was another story.

"Yes, your grandfather knows Sam Hughes," Honey said. Sir Simon knew everybody of importance in Ottawa. "It won't be difficult for you to get into the army, Denys with or without Mr. Hughes. The problem will lie with your father."

"I realize that, Mother. I hope you'll support me."

He sounded so grown-up, suddenly. She gave her word to Denys but she shrank inside, thinking of the quarrel she would have with Armand. For her, Armand was still the source of love and security. Every time they argued, whenever she set her will against his, she felt physically ill. Her Court instincts were strong. Power and glory were things she wanted desperately, almost as a man would want them. But Armand would stand for just so much and no more.

"It's all going to be terribly difficult," Honey said. "I'm dreading the whole thing."

"The whole war will be dreadful," Denys said cheerfully. "But I can hardly wait to go, just the same! You don't think it'll be over before I can get overseas, do you?"

"Thank God, if war comes, *we're* in power," Sir Simon said, referring to the Conservatives. "If Laurier and his gang were in control it would be nothing short of a disaster."

The Courts were at dinner. Lady Court had come downstairs for the first time in a week, leaning on her cane and looking drawn and pale. Angela was at the table along with her father and his wife, Polly. Sir Simon had approved of Polly right from the beginning. She came from "good English stock;" the Grahams were an important Montreal family, heavily involved in transportation and flour mills as well as vast pieces of valuable real estate. Polly had been widowed five years before, and she and Charles had been married quietly in the chapel at Christ Church exactly a year after Venetia's death.

Fort and Sydney were also guests at dinner, along with Landry. (The twins, Fenella and Flora, were dining in the nursery with Rose Starkey, as was Geoffrey and Mary's three-year-old daughter, Charity.) Geoffrey, Mary, Mildred, and Noel were at the table, too. Simon was at sea, all the male Courts having decided it was high time Geoffrey's older son apprenticed with the Court Shipping Line. This made twelve for dinner.

"I just hope Laurier doesn't do too much harm as leader of the opposition," Geoffrey said.

"I'm more worried about Simon being at sea," Lady Court said. "If war is declared those Germans are quite likely to sink any ship—Canadian, English, French, or anything else. You can't trust them."

"The *Albatross* is only a day out of Halifax," Sir Simon said, dismissing her worry with a wave of his hand. "You don't think the Huns are hanging about outside Halifax harbor, do you?"

"I wouldn't want to put my faith in them," Lady Court said darkly. She shared her husband's distrust of all foreigners, especially Germans. "I recall reading that they are barbarians, really. It was only in the late nineteenth century that they joined together as a nation. Before that, they were merely warring tribes. Like the Indians, you know. They really are *most* unreliable."

"Well, some Germans are related to King George," Landry pointed out shrilly. "And so is the czar of Russia."

"Most unfortunate," Lady Court admitted, "but none of us can do much about our relatives. Even the king of England."

"I don't think we ought to go into all that, Landry," Sir Simon said, glaring at his grandson. As the rack of lamb was served and the good hock passed around he managed to ride over Landry's observation that hock was a German wine. "Let the bloody Huns come ahead, I say! We're ready for them."

"Not all that ready," Charles protested. "I just wish we were. Sam Hughes is running about like a wild man . . ."

"Hughes is a good man," Sir Simon said flatly. "He knows a good war when one comes along. He was one of the few in government who wanted to send an army to put down the Boers. I haven't forgotten that."

"We haven't much of an army," Fort said.

"It won't take Sam long to raise one," Sir Simon argued confidently. "I just wish I could go myself. It's good exercise."

"Really, Simon, how can you be so bloodthirsty?" Lady Court inquired mildly. "No, Graves, no more wine, thank you. I've had quite enough."

"Won't last long anyway," Geoffrey said. "I was talking to a man the other day who'd just come back from London. If we do get into the fray, they give it six months. At the outside."

"That's a little optimistic," Fort said. "Germany has a navy, you know."

"It'll last long enough for us to make a few thousand rifles at the plant," Sir Simon said happily. "I'm going to give the word to convert the moment war's declared. Off with the threshing machines, on with the rifles!"

"It will take some time to retool," Charles said cautiously. "That's what I've been saying at the meetings for the past month. We can't do it overnight."

"Men can work overtime," Sir Simon said. "War's war."

"You all talk as if war had been declared," Mary said.

"Only being prepared," Sir Simon said.

"Oh, it could still be avoided," Geoffrey said. "There are people who think so."

"Anyway," Lady Court said, sighing, "The boys are too young for this war. And the rest of you are too old. You'll have to be content with being armchair generals."

"Not I," Sydney said.

Since she hadn't spoken all through dinner, they all turned to stare at her.

"Whatever do you mean, Sydney?" Lady Court inquired.

"Polly and I have our badges. St. John Ambulance. I fully intend to join the Red Cross as a volunteer."

"Is that true, Polly?" Charles asked, taking a sudden interest in his wife's daytime activities.

"I told you about the classes, Charles," Polly said, smiling. "You just didn't listen. We can act as assistants in a hospital, if necessary. I just wish I were a fully trained nurse. I'd volunteer for overseas duty."

"Or to be an ambulance driver," Sydney said.

"Congratulations!" Sir Simon said, holding up his glass "A toast to the two Court ladies! Beautiful in peace and brave in war!"

Obviously he was pleased. The only criticism likely to come from Sir Simon would be what he thought of as "slacking." Positive action for the good of king and country was always welcome.

A thoughtful silence had fallen upon the table by the time Graves served the steaming cups of coffee. Each member of the family was preoccupied with his or her own concerns if war should come. For Sir Simon, it was the contract to produce army rifles instead of harvesters; for Lady Court, it was the possible disintegration of her family life as every member scurried off into some corner of the country's war effort; for Mary, it was a peculiar memory of her gentle cousin, Hans, half German and perhaps fated to kill or be killed by an enemy who might be a relative; for Sydney and Polly, the stimulation of working at something useful and meaningful; for Fort, the question of how many troopships the line could provide and still keep Court Shipping functioning; for Angela, the knowledge that if war came, Beau would be prevented from going to France. Graves, having retired after serving the coffee, returned almost immediately to break into the quiet of the dinner table. He carried a silver salver with a letter on it, and he handed it to Sir Simon. The silence, which had been superficial, became profound. Sir Simon's hand shook a little as he tore open the envelope.

"It's from Brown-Levrington, in London."

They waited. Brown-Levrington was manager of the Court Shipping Line's office in the capital and he had been instructed to send a cable the moment England declared war on Germany. Sir Simon stared down at the paper, making the moment long, making it sink into the consciousness of every member of his family as they sat breathlessly waiting.

Finally, he looked up. His voice was a mixture of pride, happiness, awe, and envisioned glory..

"England has declared war on Germany. God save the king!"

PART THREE

1917–1919

CHAPTER ONE

The June heat was oppressive. Honey, jammed solidly in the midst of the anxious, feverish, milling crowd upon the Court Shipping Line dock, watched the troopship *Lydia* tie up. The process seemed infinitely slow. A cordon of policemen held back the restless, shifting bodies. There was a smell of perspiration, discarded rubbish lying in too much heat too long, smoke, tar—a thousand smells mingled horribly together. Beyond the crowd, at the end of the dock, were trucks and ambulances and Red Cross workers. There were flags. There was a brass band.

No amount of flag-waving and martial music could erase the fear and expectancy, however. No trumpet blast or heady drumbeat could conceal the fact that this was a ship bringing back the wounded from the trenches of France. Eventually, after what seemed a lifetime, the soldiers who could walk began to come down the gangplank to the dock. Their eyes were searching for the faces they expected to see, or hoped to see, or feared to see. Their smiles were sad.

Beneath the noisy, turbulent surface ran a dark river of despair. The tide flowed back and forth between the eyes of the soldiers and those of the welcomers on the dock. One by one the straggling, walking wounded caught sight of beloved friends and family members and waved, then found a way to reach and touch. The crowd shifted and swayed, letting new people in, letting others out. There was kissing, hugging, tears and smiles.

Trapped in the crush, wearing a white cotton dress and a small hat that had seemed right when she'd chosen it but now was inappropriately hot, Honey realized that she had made a mistake in coming here alone. In her eagerness, she hadn't thought it through carefully. Armand was still in France, of course, where he was supervising army railroads behind the Allied lines. He was due back in Montreal in a week. Michel was in England with the Royal Air Force. (The Royal Flying Corps and the Royal Naval Air Force had merged under the new name in April.) Susan, at seventeen, was too young, too unpredictable to give support, and might have been a problem rather than a prop. Honey knew now that she ought to have asked Gabriel to come.

But it was too late. The crowd was incredibly thick, too large to allow her to change direction. She couldn't move either backward or forward. She was completely alone yet pressed from every side by an unfeeling, pushing mass of humanity. The heat was terrible, and she wiped her forehead. Her hair was damp and coming unpinned. She was desperately afraid.

The telegram had said "severely wounded." The letter from Denys's superior officer, Major Hanrahan, had not added much information, except to say that Denys would be sent home to convalesce. She had no idea what "severely" meant, or where his wound was. Perhaps he had died on board ship. She shuddered. Denys was twenty-one. She remembered how eager he had been to join the army even before war had been declared. And how she had encouraged him (against Armand's wishes) because she understood. She was a Court still. *Damn the Courts!*

Denys could be dead. Perhaps he'd lost a leg. She tried to imagine handsome, slim Denys with a pair of crutches or a false leg. What if he'd lost *two* legs? No, dear God, not that. What if it were a lung wound? Or a stomach wound so that he was destined to be a permanent invalid? Or . . . there were other things. Terrible things that she'd heard about, read about, seen listed in the casualties, a swarm of unthinkable and unspeakable things people hinted at. She had heard of men who were vegetables. Blind. Disfigured. Armless. Armless and legless. Ghastly visions poured through her head. She felt hotter, and distinctly faint. She felt as if she might vomit, But she could not do that, not in this crowd.

She found a handkerchief and wiped her face. The crowd's surging crushed her against a heavyset man in a dark suit, with a red face, who smelled strongly of beer.

He turned his face toward her and she tried to recoil

because of his smell. But he had a kindly look on his coarse face, just the same.

"Lady, you look a bit green around the gills. Are you all right?"

"I feel a bit faint." Her voice was thin. She felt herself swaying slightly and his hand came up to her arm; beefy, with dirty chipped fingernails, rough-skinned.

"I'll keep you up, lady," he said kindly. "You lean on my arm. That's right."

She leaned on his arm. He was like a rock—thick, solid, hot, not too clean. He gave her a smile from which several teeth were missing.

"I'd get you out of here, but I don't see no way."

"No, I don't either."

"Don't worry, lady."

"You're very kind."

"That's all right, lady. You shouldn't be here alone. It's tough, this kind of thing. Waiting to see them, I mean. Not knowing for sure what's happened to them. I know. My son's on that boat. He lost his hand. Blown off, see? But it could be worse."

Yes, it could be worse. Much worse, Honey thought. Why did I come alone? What am I doing here like this?

"I'm sorry to hear that about your son," she said.

How could people talk about war so casually? How could she have read, published, even edited all those stories about casualties, about the horrors over there, without feeling anything? A hand blown off. Just like that. You said it as if it were the loss of a wallet, a watch, or a ring. A hand blown off. The pain, and the suffering, and then the poor man would have to find work. His family was poor. She could see by the father that they were laborers. He might even work somewhere in Armand's railroads or mines, or in her father's shipping line, or cleaning the bank or something. She wanted to cry. But she could not cry here. And she had, through *Le Monde*, encouraged men to go and fight and get maimed and live in mud and cold without enough food, without hope. The bombardments that deafened them and shattered their nerves. The gas the Germans sent over to paralyze and kill. She had encouraged men to go into all that. But they *had* to. England had to win. The allies had to win. Now that the United States was in the war, the Allies *would* win. Everybody said so. Anything else was unthinkable. But here, now, was the reality of it. Denys coming home. Severely wounded.

The red-faced man was speaking into her ear above the din around them. A band had struck up "God Save the King."

"What's happened to your boy, then?"

"I'm not sure. The telegram said severely wounded."

"That could mean anything," the man said. "But don't worry. Some of them wounds heal up good as new. They do some wonderful things nowadays. I hear the army surgeons are good. You'll see."

"Do you think so? If it were a stomach wound, or a chest wound, it might heal. He could be all right . . . he was going into business with his father . . ." She heard herself babbling and couldn't stop. The sympathetic face beside her didn't seem to mind. She felt a great wave of affection for this coarse stranger. She wondered what his name was.

The band was playing "The British Grenadiers." Somewhere there was a fife. She had always responded to a fife and drum. Armand had laughed at her for that, called her a typical Beefeater. She looked at the men coming off, some of them ambling along with arms in slings, others with head banadages or crutches or canes, but able to navigate on their own. Would Denys be able to walk? Why had the telegram said "severely wounded"? Why not just "wounded"?

She heard the occasional shrieks of recognition as relatives in the crowd spotted the soldier they'd come to greet, and the boy would push his way, somehow, through the cordon, and then there would be tears, hugs, loud cries, back patting, and the spew of emotional turmoil that always accompanied painful reunions.

The stretchers came next. In some cases the faces could be glimpsed and recognized. In others, the heads were so completely bandaged and the bodies so thoroughly wrapped in sheets that there was no way of telling who or what was underneath.

The band was playing "It's a Long Way to Tipperary."

She did not see Denys.

The red-faced man who had been holding her up suddenly let go. He had seen his boy coming down the ramp on a stretcher, with his arms bandaged (so it had been more than a hand blown off, Honey thought sadly). The man forged away from her, ramming himself through the crowd to the stretcher. She lost sight of him almost immediately.

She hung on. But as the crowd thinned she saw the uselessness of her mission and went to a truck marked with a red cross. An officer, a major, was standing by the truck talking to a nurse. In his hand was a clipboard, and he was referring to a list it held. Ambulances and trucks were pulling away as they had been for some time. She spoke to the major. Now, in a slightly calmer situation, she had regained a bit of her lost confidence. She introduced herself and the man became alert.

He found her a place to sit in one of the trucks while he checked the list.

"My dear lady, you shouldn't be here alone. You look pale. Let me see—yes, here it is. He's to go to a convalescent home on Sherbrooke Street. A private house that's been turned into a hospital. Here's the number. I think your best plan is to go there, if you can get a hansom cab." His face looked grim.

"I have a car," Honey said faintly. "It's a little distance away, but I'm sure I can manage to drive."

"I'll find some water for you. Really, Madame St. Amour, you don't look as if you should drive. Are you sure you'll be all right?"

He was kind. He found water in one of the Red Cross trucks and gave her a cup.

"It's the heat," Honey said.

"May I suggest something?" the major said.

"Of course. You're very kind to take this trouble when you must be so busy." He did look distraught.

"Is there somebody you could get to go with you to the hospital? I feel strongly that you ought to have support. When one sees a relative . . . a son . . . wounded, especially . . . it's difficult to prepare the mind for it. I know. I've watched so many."

"Yes, I suppose I could find somebody."

"Then, Madame, please do. With your friend, or relative, drive up to that address. By that time, perhaps we can sort things out. It's very difficult at this point . . ."

"I'll do that."

She would go to the office and find Gabriel. Gabriel would go with her. She felt the strongest desire to see Gabriel now, and to have him beside her. She had been a fool to think she could do this alone. A complete fool.

"I'll be up there myself," the major went on. "You can look for me. Together, we'll find your son. They'll have him located in a ward by that time, and it will be much easier on you, on him. We'll arrange something. Now, don't you worry, Madame. I'll assist you in every way."

"I shouldn't have come alone," Honey murmured, handing back the empty cup.

"No, well, things will work out. Your husband is away, I imagine?"

"He's in France."

"I understand. Will you be able to get to your car?"

She could see that he was eager to get on with the duties that must be of supreme importance to him. She said good-bye and walked through the thinning crowds toward the street. The dock was littered with bits of paper, with torn, small, cheaply made flags. The band was packing up its instruments. She walked slowly toward the car.

The hospital was located in Philippe Grande's large, elegant house. As they drove into the grounds, Gabriel at the wheel of the three-year-old Locomobile town coupe, the fact that Denys would be hospitalized in this house struck Honey as bizarre. Yet she had known for some time that Philippe had turned the house over to the army as a convalescent center. At present, Philippe was living at the Windsor Hotel in the vice-regal suite. She shivered. Thinking of that particular suite always brought unpleasant memories.

The house had already made the transformation from the quiet grandeur of a stately private home to the self-important hustle and meaningless bustle of a public institution. There were trucks, cars, ambulances, and horses parked over the lawns and driveways. People were rushing about with bits of paper, others with luggage or stretchers. She let Gabriel take her arm and help her through the front hall into the foyer. The great stone staircase swept upward as she had imagined it, but the chandeliers were gone, the carpets stripped away. An odor of disinfectant and sickness hung heavily in the summer air. Gabriel settled Honey on a straight-backed wooden chair while he went to look for the officer she had described. Eventually he returned with the major, who was still carrying his list.

"Ah, Madame St. Amour. I haven't quite located your son, but I'm sure it's only a matter of a few minutes. Most of the stretcher patients have arrived."

"Thank you. I'll wait here."

"Yes, just stay there. I'm glad you have brought a friend with you."

Honey made the introductions, and then the major hurried off once more. There was another surprise, however, only a moment later. Charles's wife, Polly, appeared, in a nurse's uniform.

"Honey!" Polly said, stopping abruptly in her quick walk through the foyer. She had been heading for the stairs.

"Polly! Are you working here?"

"Yes, I'm full time now. I've long since passed the volunteer stage, you know. I'm going on duty now—the wards are all full, and there is so much . . ." Her voice trailed off.

She was a thin, narrow-faced girl with blonde hair pulled back into a tight knot at the nape of her neck. She looked terribly efficient and sure of herself. Honey felt a flood of envy. Once, before so many things had happened to destroy her confidence, she had felt like that. As if she could do anything. She had not understood the meaning of fear, of doubt and inadequacy. In those early days, she would have tackled anything. It was not like that now.

"I must go. Why are you here?" Polly asked.

"Denys."

"He was on the ship? I'll see that he's well looked after, Honey, don't you worry. I'll check on him myself."

Polly had always been friendly. She had a calm disregard for Sir Simon's wishes, temper tantrums, and general bluster. Having come to the marriage as a widow, a woman of thirty-five, she was not a schoolgirl to be frightened into submission. Charles had done well, Honey thought, to choose a woman like Polly.

"Have you found him yet?" Polly wanted to know.

"Not yet, but a nice major is looking. He's the one who seems to be in charge of placing the patients. I don't know his name."

"Oh, that'll be Major Morris."

"Probably. Polly . . . are there many . . . *terrible* wounds?"

Polly hesitated, set her mouth in a straight line, and replied, "Yes, some. But don't think about that now. Denys will be all right, I'm sure of it. There are dozens of men who are not badly wounded, you know. They'll recover. They'll be fine. Major Morris will find out soon what's happening. Well, dear, I must run. I'm due up there right now. Perhaps I can help later."

She hurried toward the stairs and climbed swiftly, knowing what she had to do, where she was going.

Major Morris returned in a few minutes looking extremely grave. He had a doctor with him. Both men approached her with calm, but there was nothing in their eyes to reassure her. Honey stood up. Gabriel kept her arm firmly in his.

"You've found Denys?"

Her own voice sounded to her like the voice of a stranger. Her mouth was so dry she thought she would retch. She felt Gabriel beside her and leaned on him a little.

"This is Dr. Smythe," Major Morris said.

After the brief introductions, Dr. Smythe said, "We've found your son."

He was short and stout, and the white coat he wore was slightly soiled. He wore glasses, and peered a little as he spoke, as if he needed stronger glasses still. His face was not unkind, but neither was it softened by any promise of consoling news.

"You can see him, Madame St. Amour. Most certainly. He may recognize you. I'm not sure. Frankly, we are not sure of his exact condition at this moment."

Honey's hand tightened on Gabriel's arm.

"What . . . please tell me about what's wrong."

"Yes. Your husband is away, I presume?"

"Yes, in France. Gabriel is the editor of my newspaper. An old family friend. You'll let him accompany me?"

"Naturally, if you wish."

The dreadful sinking feeling had returned. As if she

were on the edge of a chasm. There was nothing below her to support or help her. She would fall. Yet she must not fall. Denys was in terrible danger.

"He's very sick, then. Is he . . . he isn't dead?"

"No, no. He isn't dead. But yes, he's very sick," Dr. Smythe said.

She saw that the doctor was perspiring. He passed his hand over his forehead. He said, "Your son is badly wounded. At the moment . . . well, you must prepare yourself, Madame. If you are sure you want to see him . . ."

"Of course I want to see him!" Honey cried.

"Very well."

"Let me see him quickly! What if he dies while we're out here talking?"

The desperation rose in her voice to reach an edge that was brutal. She was not the Honey of any other day, but a new, abused, frightened, desperate Honey who was trembling on the brink of some unfathomable disaster.

"Take me to him."

"We will go." Dr. Smythe made a move toward the staircase.

"His wound? I don't even know about his wound!" Honey said, touching the doctor's arm. "Please, tell me that much."

"It is a head wound. A face wound."

The ground almost gave way again. Gabriel took her arm, and they walked up the stairs somehow, in the nightmare pace of the mortally shattered. A head wound. A face wound.

"He's blind?" she whispered to Dr. Smythe halfway up the stairs.

"No, not blind."

"Thank God."

"He can see. We don't know . . . about the other senses."

She did not understand. Not really. Not until she saw the shrouded figure on the bed. The head, entirely encased in bandages, could not be identified as Denys. The face had a strangely flat look. There were slits where the eyes peered out, a slit where the nose had been (*had been*, she thought, understanding suddenly), a slit where a mouth had been. She drew close and looked into her son's eyes.

She heard Dr. Smythe saying, "He does not hear, as

far as we know, or have any sense of smell, Madame. He cannot talk. We are feeding him through a throat tube. Perhaps he recognizes you."

He recognized her, yes. His eyes pleaded with her from the silent, empty trap of his body. His eyes pleaded for the peace of death, glittering first, and then welling with tears so that the whiteness of the bandages around those fearful slits became damp, sodden with the only emotion he could express. He was a living soul, suspended in limbo, purposeless, devoid of hope or future.

Honey, mercifully, fainted.

CHAPTER TWO

Honey lay in bed, the curtains of her apartment drawn against the June sun. She refused food, refused all visitors except Gabriel and Susan, and had it not been for the sleeping potion prescribed by Dr. Miles, she would have been unable to rest. She waited, in a state of suspension, for Armand's return from France as if, in that event, there would be some small consolation. Consolation, perhaps, but no hope.

Even the newspaper, which had long been the driving force in her life, had ceased to matter. Gabriel was managing it alone, making decisions in this particularly difficult time; the aftermath of conscription had brought riots in Quebec, the Allies were facing for the first time the distinct possibility of defeat at the hands of the Germans, the shortage of manpower on the farms was crucial, there were scandals in every part of Canada about tainted grain shipments to the front, of poor boots sent to fighting soldiers, of dud shells and rifles that backfired. None of this mattered anymore.

She lay staring at the ceiling, riddled with guilt. She remembered her own fierce patriotism, blazing through the columns of her newspaper: every able man must fight for Canada, for England, for the Allies. All differences of race and religion must be forgotten. It was their duty to fight. How empty it all seemed now!

If she saw anything on the white plastered ceiling of her room, it was a scene in the trenches. Visions of some German soldier, his face contorted with the need to kill, rushing over the lip of some muddy hole, his rifle yawning, firing into Denys's face. And Denys, his face blown off, collapsing in a dirty puddle of mud and blood. Hatred seethed in her mind. She became obsessed with the idea of Germans as satanic beings. Over and over the ghastly scene was played out. Even when she closed her eyes she saw it. Or, failing that, the eyes of her son helplessly pleading for death's mercy.

Susan tried to talk to her mother, but they had never been close and now they were merely further apart. Dr. Miles begged Honey to get up, to go for walks, or at the very least to sit in the garden. She could not face anyone. A terrible lethargy had seized her. It was all she could do to wash herself and occasionally brush her hair. They were reduced to one maid in the large house, since most of the young women were needed in the war factories, and if it hadn't been for Annette bringing her a change of nightgown, Honey would have continued to wear the same one day and night.

Even word of Michel, now on leave in England, failed to bring her any relief. Only her mind was active. And that continued to focus on German soldiers, on Germany as the instigator of the war, on one, single, ugly, grotesque moment when her son's life had been destroyed. If only he had been killed! How could she ever have dreamed that one day she would long for that! It was incredible. Yet she knew that Denys was suffering indescribably in his mute, helpless state. Death would have seemed to him an angel. His eyes had told her that. Begging her to do something. She had read his message clearly enough. What could she do?

At last, after a week of her torpor, Armand arrived home. That first morning, he rushed into her room and scooped her into his arms. He stroked her hair, kissed her cheeks, wiped away the tears that ran down her face to the ruffles of her nightgown. She could not speak. She could merely cling. He held her like that for a long time and then at last he gently laid her down and crossed the carpet to the bay window. He pulled the curtains back and let in the sun.

"We must have some sun, some air, *ma cherie.*"

She blinked and tried to see him clearly, but at first her eyes were unable to adjust to the sudden light.

"I can't bear the light, Armand."

"Yes, we must have the sun," he persisted.

When her eyes became accustomed to the brightness she saw that Armand looked infinitely tired. The handsome face was drawn, the mouth sagged, there were fresh lines on his forehead and around his eyes.

"You've been working very hard," she said.

"It isn't just the work and the hours," Armand said, his voice having, for the first time in her memory, lost its timbre. "It's the terrible conditions I've seen."

"I'm sorry."

He came back to the bed and sat down, taking her hands in his.

"Remember, Miel, we are together in this. That is the strength. Do you understand? The worst part is when you are alone. Completely alone. Then it's frightening. I've seen men like that . . . crying like babies . . . but they were alone. They felt they had no one to care, to help, to support them. For you, there is still much. There is your husband, your daughter, your other son, your work—many, many, things. Come, *ma cherie*, the spirit of the Courts is not dead yet." He smiled a little.

"Damn the Courts. Damn patriotism."

"No, you weren't wrong. It's just more complicated than we thought," Armand said slowly. "In spite of the many terrible things I've seen behind the lines, and in the trenches—oh, yes, I was in the front lines on my inspections, I insisted on it—in spite of it all, we must go on. We must win."

"You've seen Denys?" she asked, after a moment.

"Yes, I went to the hospital first. To see for myself."

"Then you know how bad it is. He can see. Did you see his eyes?"

"I saw."

"He wants to die. And they won't let him."

"They can't do that, Miel."

"It would be a mercy. You know that, Armand. He begs to die, you can read it in his eyes. He wept . . ." She began to cry.

Armand held her closely until she had calmed down again.

"Now, *cherie*, we will visit him together. As soon as you're feeling well enough. You understand? Meanwhile, you must get up and go out into the garden. There are some roses in bloom."

"Roses," she said in a dull voice.

"You and I will have some tea in the garden."

"All right, Armand." she stood up. "Ask Annette to come up and help me dress."

"In a moment, yes. What is happening with the newspaper? You can't let that fail, Miel. It isn't like you."

"Gabriel is looking after it."

"Still, I'm certain he needs you. He's young yet and requires your guidance. You haven't forgotten all the causes so dear to your heart? What's happening about the grain scandal, for example? I know from first-hand experience that thousands of bushels of grain shipped to our own troops were moldy. You must force the government to look into it. That kind of thing must be stopped. People are making money out of the misery of our own soldiers."

"I know about it, Armand, but I don't care anymore. We did publish stories about it, about the new rich making fortunes out of army contracts, out of supplies. Is it true that some of our own shells are duds? That they don't explode?"

"I'm afraid so. You can imagine what it's like for the men in the line when their own equipment lets them down! One of the worst offenders is the Ramsay rifle. You remember how that business was hushed up? The rifles either won't fire when it rains or they explode in the soldiers' faces. And who makes them?"

Honey looked at Armand defiantly, biting her lip. It was an argument they had had before. She had suppressed some of the stories about the Ramsay rifle and its deficiencies because Sir Simon owned the factory that made them.

"You can't expect me to print that! Papa has given seven ships for troop carriers! It isn't as if he's done nothing. He outfitted a company from his own pocket. What if I spread rumors, even lies, about the rifles, and it wasn't true?"

"We'll say no more about that, Miel. Get dressed, come down, and have tea. Michel may be home one of these days. Soon, I hope. We'll talk about that. How is Susan?"

"She's finishing her last few days at college. Her grades are not too good, but then she was never a very hardworking student, was she? Susan—" and she made a wry little face—"is more interested in marriage. She's looking for a prince. Preferably one with plenty of gold."

Armand allowed himself a smile.

"That's natural enough. Come along then, darling, and we'll have a visit in the flowers. That's what you need. It will restore your feeling that there is some good in life."

They went together to visit Denys this time. Armand held her arm firmly as they walked into the room. Nothing had changed. Denys lay there, a mummy except for the eyes, and again she read the pleading in them and had to look away to keep from breaking down. He could, however, move his hands. His fingers drummed on the coverlet. They moved speculatively over the material, feeling it. It was all he could do, apparently, but it was something.

Honey left Armand in the room and went out into the corridor. She could not seem to sit, so instead she began to pace along the hall, looking at some of the patients who were able to walk. One young man wearing a flannel robe and walking with two crutches came toward her slowly, his face wearing an expression of recognition. She was puzzled. She had never seen him before.

He was about the same age as Denys, perhaps a little younger.

"Excuse me, but are you Madame St. Amour?" he asked.

"Yes, how did you know?" She stopped to look at him more closely, but still had no idea who he was.

"My name is John Illingsworth. Private. Your son was my captain. He showed me your picture, and I know he's here in the hospital, so I knew . . ."

"Oh, I'm glad you spoke to me." Then she realized that he was still waiting, and that perhaps there was something more he wanted to say. "Were you . . . with him . . . when he was wounded?"

"Yes, I was. Madame, I'm so sorry he's hurt so badly. He was a good officer. We liked him. We all liked him."

The boy was trying to console her, she knew that, but she found it difficult to talk. All the pictures that had flooded her mind, the pictures of that awful time when Denys had been wounded, now came back, and here before her was the man who could corroborate them. She said, "Could we sit down?" Her voice was faint.

"Certainly, Madame. I realize this is a terrible thing for you."

He looked at her, waiting. Wondering if she really

wanted to know what had happened there in the mudhole in France. Perhaps she really didn't want to know at all. So he waited.

"Tell me, if you can," Honey said. Her voice was so low he almost didn't hear it.

"It was on the Marne—I guess you know that much. But we were stuck in this mudhole out in No Man's Land. We were trying to advance, but we got stuck. Then we knew we couldn't get back. There were shells falling all around us."

She stared at him, her eyes wide with expectancy, with terror, almost. Ready as she was to hate, the poison of it concentrated somewhere in her stomach. Her fists were clenched. But she didn't speak.

"Well, we hadn't much ammunition left. I mean, we were always short of supplies. There was a rat. I remember the rat. Funny, how you remember things like that. But I wanted to shoot the rat and Denys said, save your bullets . . . they were coming. See, we knew they were coming."

She had to know. *Please God, give me the strength to listen to this. I have to know.* The face of the German was almost real to her now; the scene was taking on the reality of life instead of nightmare.

"Go on. Go on, please."

"Yeah, well, Denys raised his rifle. We saw them coming. You could see plainly enough between the shells and the smoke and everything. You could see the shapes. They were coming. And he was ready to fire because he knew the Hun would get him if he didn't fire first. And he fired."

"Yes, yes, he fired."

"That's what happened, Madame. His rifle exploded in his face. They sometimes did that. We hated those Ramsay rifles, we tried to get rid of them. We used to pick up Hun rifles if we could, or we'd trade off for some other kind of rifle. A lot of them were no good. And anyway, that was what happened . . ." His voice trailed off.

He had expected her to be upset, but after all, she had asked him what had happened. But he had not been prepared for the expression on her face, or the way she rushed out of the hospital. She didn't even wait for her husband. He couldn't understand it. When her husband came out of the room where Denys lay, he tried to explain what had happened. Naturally, she was upset. But neither of them had expected her to act quite like that.

The Court Bank, at 383 St. James Street, was a gray stone fortress with four Grecian-style pillars at the entrance. When she had been very small, Honey had been awed by the shining lake of marble in the foyer, the imported crystal chandeliers that looked too heavy to stay fastened to the ceiling, the elaborate plasterwork of flowers and figures that rimmed the walls. The larger-than-life portrait of Queen Victoria in its heavy gilt frame still dominated the far wall, while flags were draped carefully on others. The doorman and the elevator operator wore uniforms of military style, with gold braid and brass buttons.

Honey knew the bank intimately. As a small child, she had often been brought for visits, and later, as a teenager, she had rushed in to see Papa, flushed with needs and praise and the assurance of a princess. Today, she swept through the foyer with the old instincts, not asking permission to see her father, barely acknowledging the elevator operator in his elaborate cage. For his part, the elderly man had seen many people go up to the top in a variety of emotional states, and he knew better than to chat.

Without a moment's hesitation she walked through the outer executive offices on the top floor and past Miss Robson, a dragon of some years who guarded Sir Simon's inner sanctum. Miss Robson stood up to protest.

"Sir Simon is in a meeting, Madame. Could I tell him . . ."

Honey cast an unseeing look at the woman and walked on. She turned the big brass knob with all the carving, and opened the door to the inner office, before Miss Robson could gather her wits. The Secretary was left openmouthed, and she sank back into her chair. She felt powerless to play out her role of protector.

Sir Simon's office, which doubled as a board room, was as familiar as the rooms of Pride's Court: the huge, polished mahogany table with its row of chairs, occupied now by four men who faced Sir Simon who was seated at one end. Behind her father, his portrait, painted in his youth by Augustus John: impressive, handsome, the archetypal conquering Englishman in the colonies. The Union Jack draped conspicuously on the back wall. The row of windows overlooking St. James, two of them open now to let in the warm morning air and let out the thick cigar smoke. The four men turned almost simultaneously when she entered.

Sir Simon was saying, "We've lost the contract. We'll have to turn the factory to some other purpose. Now what I want from you is some proposal—"

He looked older, more portly, but still fierce. The blue eyes still blazed with determination and suppressed anger. A plan of his had been thwarted. Steps must be taken. His upraised hand froze in the middle of a gesture.

"Hannah!"

"Papa!"

They both paused, like puppets whose strings have been pulled tight and held . . . the old man's arm upraised, the woman's body stiff but her head thrust slightly forward.

"Hannah! What are you doing here? How did you get in?"

The men were all staring at her, embarrassed, silent. There was the cough of the smoker, the shuffling of feet, the scraping of chairs being pushed back, the clearing of throats.

"Do you know about Denys?"

"Yes, I know Denys has been brought back."

"Wounded. Denys is your grandson."

"I know that, Hannah. Surely you haven't come here in the middle of an important meeting to tell me."

"Denys is my oldest son. He is twenty-one years old. Did you realize that? He joined the army the day war was declared. Aren't you proud of that, Papa? The Courts always fight for England, for Canada, isn't that right?"

"I would hope so," Sir Simon said, speaking quickly. "He's wounded. Well, it's an honorable wound."

"Honorable wound?" Her voice was heavy with something more than the announcement of Denys's condition. Sir Simon could not quite puzzle out her peculiar intensity, her powerful stance, her unforgivable lack of manners in breaking into the meeting in this dramatic fashion.

"He isn't dead, is he?" Sir Simon said, his voice rising to its familiar loud level.

"No. I wish he *were* dead."

"You're hysterical." Sir Simon turned to the men at the table. "I'm sorry, gentlemen—"

"I believed he should go, Papa. You taught me that. You taught me well. The Courts are so patriotic. Fight for king and country. God save the king. God save the empire. I fought with my husband over Denys's joining the army so young. Armand didn't want him to go. Oh, well, the French Canadians don't want to fight for England, or for France either. We know that from the riots in Quebec, don't we? But I knew what was right. You taught me that, Papa."

"I don't move an inch from my position," Sir Simon said, his voice once again sure. "We must fight for our country. We must fight the Huns."

"I wish we *were* fighting the Huns."

"What in hell do you mean by that?"

"Let me tell you, Papa. Take time from your precious meeting, and listen." Her own blue eyes raged back at him. The clash of their eyes sent a current across the already charged air of the room. Her whole body was straight, taut, filled with a power that is only rarely called forth in any human being.

The men were unable to decide whether to go or stay. Fascinated, yet at the same time repelled by the intimacy of the scene, they could not seem to come to grips with the situation. They sat, like a Greek chorus, waiting for some cue.

"This isn't the time or the place . . ." Sir Simon began to bluster, trying to regain momentum, trying to seize the initiative that should have been his and not his daughter's.

"This *is* the time. Denys is lying in a hospital bed, unable to hear, unable to speak, unable to eat, and yes, Papa, unable to *die*. He wants desperately to die. I read that in his eyes. He wants to die because he's trapped there, useless, staring at the ceiling. He can't even know there's anybody in the room with him unless that person bends over directly into his line of vision. He wants to die, I read that in his eyes, yes! *He has no face*! His face was blown off. Do you understand what I'm saying? My

twenty-one-year-old son has no face. He's begging somebody to kill him!"

"But Hannah . . . it's terrible . . . but what has it to do
with me? Denys went to war, as the young men of this
country have done. I'm old. I've given ships. I've armed
a whole company. I've loaned executives to help with the
distribution of supplies. I've given my time . . . I'm an
old man, but I work day and night—"

"Yes, you've given, Papa. Where it shows. But let me
tell you that for a while I hated the Germans. When I saw
what had happened to Denys, I spent days and nights
hating the Germans, hating the one German who had
done this thing. Hating, and hating, and hating, until I
was filled with poison. Seeing that beast who blew off
Denys's face!"

"Hating does no good," Sir Simon said. But she cut him
off quickly.

"Hating does *some* good, Papa, because it's brought me
here to this place. You don't know the truth. You've made
millions out of this war in one way or another. God knows
how many millions you've made out of Ramsay rifles. That
scandal, so far, has been hushed up. I've been one of the
people who didn't publish the whole story about those
rifles. Ramsay rifles, which *you* make in *your* factory, are
no good in France. When it rains they don't fire. Sometimes they explode in a man's face. But you went right on
making them, because you're a stubborn old man. A
greedy, stubborn old man. You were told by your own
people that the design was bad. But you went on believing.
You supplied them to the Canadian army, you and your
friends, because you could make money out of them—"

"I believed in the rifle."

"You're a stubborn old fool! But you're a dangerous
one as well. I ought to have published the story every
single day in *Le Monde* until somebody listened. But you
are my father. I didn't do it. And now—"

"We don't know that it's a bad design."

"Yes, we do. Everybody knows it but you."

"Anyway, we've lost the contract. The government has
canceled. We're changing the factory over—"

"Are you?"

Her voice now took on a new tone, a new firmness. She

was strong, and as she filled with this new strength, her father seemed to shrink.

"Are you going to stop making the Ramsay rifle? That's wonderful news, Papa. But it's too late. It's too late for Denys."

"It has nothing to do with Denys."

"It has *everything* to do with Denys. With *your* grandson. Denys is a vegetable not because a German soldier fired at him, but because your rifle exploded in his face!"

The silence then was thick, heavy with the unspeakable. Sir Simon stood as straight and stiff as his daughter, glaring back at her.

"I *hate* you, Papa!"

The ambivalence of the past had vanished. Over the years she had swung from love to hate, from amusement to derision, from need to independence. Yet through it all, her father had somehow remained a gallant figure. His motives, she had felt, were basically correct. He made mistakes, true, because he was pigheaded and iron-willed. At the same time, he loved his family, his church, his country. He was the old breed of Englishman. She had always been torn between the desire to return to the comfort and security of that fold, and the strange world of the St. Amours into which she had married. Despite her love for Armand, still undiminished although it had sometimes been threatened, she had been attached to the Courts by an invisible thread of heredity and instinct. Now the thread had snapped.

She saw Sir Simon revealed. He was a hypocrite. A humbug. A dangerous man who valued power and money above all else. Behind the sham, the cheap façade of patriotism, the title, the glory, the pomp, the circumstance, was a greedy man. An ugly man. The hatred she had brewed and nurtured for that nameless German soldier was transferred now to her father, this man who stood protesting about Denys's life as if it were a damaged ship or a slightly dilapidated railway car.

"I hate you, Papa!"

She turned then, as her cry echoed about the paneled walls, bounced off the polished desk, and struck Sir Simon in the face.

Sir Simon sank down into his chair, still sitting stiffly

erect for a moment as she swept to the door. And then he crumpled and began to weep, great dry, shaking sobs. He was suddenly a very old man.

The men at the table pushed back their chairs and walked numbly out. Nobody spoke. Only the sobs followed them until the door closed, mercifully, on Sir Simon Court.

======

She met Bishop Lavergne in the hospital foyer. Visitors were allowed to come in during the evening when the case was as grave as Denys's. Honey had steeled herself for a short visit after leaving the office.

The fresh disasters of Passchendaele, where the Allies had lost hundreds of thousands of men, were just beginning to be known. The cause seemed lost. The only hope lay in the fact that American troops had recently stemmed a German offensive in the Chateau Thierry area.

"My dear Honey, I'm glad to see you," the Bishop said kindly. "I've just been up to see Denys."

"I'm glad you could, Uncle Eustache."

He touched her arm as if to confer an indirect blessing. As he moved away from her, she saw that he had a slight limp. He was suffering bouts of thrombophlebitis, now which took the form of clotting in a leg vein.

"I've given him the last rites."

Being a non-Catholic, Honey had not thought much about that important ritual for Denys, but she realized that she had been remiss and felt grateful to the bishop if he had brought Denys any comfort.

"Thank you. I ought to have remembered to request it."

"This is a terrible strain for you, Honey, and we all understand that you can't think of everything. In any event, I've done it. I think he was pleased."

"Is he worse, do you think?" Honey asked.

"There isn't much change."

The halls were quiet. Many of the lights had been turned down for the night. Bishop Lavergne said his car (he had recently acquired one, along with a chauffeur) was outside. It was a warm night, and Honey walked out again through the main entrance to see the bishop off. It was odd, but she too felt some comfort in the fact that the bishop had administered Extreme Unction to Denys. The idea calmed her.

When she climbed the stone staircase a few minutes later, she found that very few people were about. The night nurse was sitting in an alcove at one end of the long corridor, taking tea. The girl nodded to her but did not get up. Visitors like Honey were well-known by this time and the nurses usually welcomed their appearance.

Inside the ward, Honey saw that two of the beds were empty. A curious tightness gripped her chest; the empty beds suggested death. These patients had been too ill to recover. The next bed, in which a patient lay, was screened off. The night light burned on a table in a corner, and the room was in shadows.

As she stepped inside the room she felt that something was amiss, but it was impossible to pinpoint what it was. She could see the still figure of Denys under the sheets, feel the depression come down upon her like a mist, as she moved forward. But there was something out of place. She glanced toward the other bed, wondering for just a short moment if the patient was in trouble of some kind. Nothing stirred.

She moved toward Denys's bed, knowing that he could not know she was there unless she bent directly over him. Then she saw what was wrong. Blood. There was blood on the sheet where Denys's arm lay. There ought not to be blood. The dark stain was spreading.

Honey ran across the room and bent over her son. In the semidarkness, his eyes looked up at her from the slits left by the bandages. Pleading. She stared down into his eyes, feeling the pain as she had never felt it before. She looked away from his eyes to the blood, to his wrists. A pair of surgical scissors lay on the floor, giving off a slight glint. Somehow, he had managed to cut his wrists, or at least jab the scissors sufficiently deep into the artery to make a serious wound. He had used the only faculty left to him, his hands, to accomplish what no one else would do for him. The bishop had given him the last rites. That thought went through her brain like a monotonous chant. After the bishop had left, while she had stood downstairs talking to him, Denys had managed to cut himself. The blood was dripping now onto the floor. Soon the nurse would come, and then there would be the emergency cry to save Denys's life. To try to prop up this awful hulk that lay pleading with her to let him die. Honey wavered. She must call the nurse. She must find the doctor. The boy's life was seeping out of his wrists.

Still, she stood rigid, bending over him. His eyes, powerful in their entreaty, fastened and held her. She could not move. There were no tears this time, just force. All the force he could gather from the shattered, immobile body was concentrated in his eyes. She read that hypnotic plea. *Let me die!*

She bent over him for a long time. The drip of blood was faint but real beside her. His eyes began to soften slowly, and she thought (or did she just imagine it?) she read a blessing in them. The sheets were covered with blood. Some touched her gown as she bent over. Then the eyes changed, she could actually see the change, that curious glazing then a flight of intelligence. She straightened up and fled out of the room, crying for the nurse.

"Nurse! Nurse! Come quickly! Get the doctor!"

She was with them when they tried to bandage his poor wrists and stop the flow, but it was too late. Denys was dead.

CHAPTER THREE

Susan spread a blanket on the grass while David Mulqueen set the wicker picnic hamper beside it. They had been forced to leave the car (a green Pierce-Arrow with a wheelbase like a battleship and a forty-horse-power motor) some distance away. The slight promontory on which they had decided to have lunch was sheltered by a small grove of maples and a few scrub pine, and through the trees the sun picked out small jewels on the St. Lawrence River. The steady stream of traffic was evident but they were too high, too remote, to pick up much noise. On the west end of the Island of Montreal, well past the Lachine Rapids, there were few people. The roads were too poor to encourage traffic.

Susan opened the basket and brought out a bottle of chilled champagne.

"Open this, David. I'm thirsty."

She was slim, with brown hair cut short in a sleek molded bob, and brown eyes with a hint of merriment that changed rapidly to boredom and frustration if she met with opposition. She read few books, had decided to drop out of McGill, had acquired very few skills: neither tennis, nor music, sewing, and cooking, nor the handling of money. At eighteen she rode horses, danced as often and as much as possible, and laughed a lot. She liked to shop for clothes. She had one eye on Pride's Court (where she would have liked to be taken up by Sir Simon and replace her cousin, Angela) and one on London, where she visualized herself as fitting perfectly into the fashionable set. She was completely bilingual but she did not care much for the French language. It was as if all her genes, all her instincts lay with the Courts and not the St. Amours. She could scarcely wait to leave St. Denis Street and somehow move to the Mountain. *That*, she felt petulantly, whenever she had a spare moment to think of it, was where she belonged.

David Mulqueen lived on the Mountain. She envied his security of place and his casual ease with money, just as she envied her cousin Angela's situation (what a waste, Angela living in Pride's Court and being able to meet everybody who counted in Montreal, and not taking advantage of it! Angela was such a dolt).

"Here we are," David said, as the cork popped pleasantly and shot off into the grass. "Have we some glasses in that great packing case you brought?"

"But of course. I can't bear to drink champagne out of anything but the right glass!"

She handed him two long-stemmed glasses.

"Mmmmmmm. A good year. A nice little wine," David said, pretending to sip the champagne with a serious air.

"Nectar. Just plain nectar," Susan said. She had picked that word up somewhere. She was inclined to be pretentious, and she had no scruples about picking people's brains, stealing a line or a phrase, pretending to know more than she knew if it suited her purposes.

Over the glasses, they looked at each other. In the warm web of sun and grass, of yellow butterflies dipping light as kisses over blue-flowered weeds, of ocean-green trees that drooped and bowed across the patch of Utopia they had personally chosen, they were exceptionally beautiful. David Mulqueen was long, lean, blond, and supercilious. His lip held a perpetually disdainful curl. Susan was gold and brown, smiling a symmetrical smile, throwing back a neat little well-shaped head to reveal a chin that was proportionately perfect. Her neck was graceful, smooth, exactly right. Her figure was slim, with the erotic suggestion of firm breasts correctly covered with satin beneath the violet-sprayed voile of the thin summer dress. Correctly covered, but there was such a slight defense between those mouth-watering little mounds and the outside world.

David said, "To fun!"

"To fun!"

"Aren't you sick of hearing about the war, the way Frenchies won't join up, and the way government is running everything so badly?" David asked. "I mean, we're young, and where's the fun? I mean, everybody talks about battles."

"Everybody reads casualty lists," she said.

"Well, listen, Susan, today we aren't going to think about all that. We're going to just have this picnic, away from the world. We're going to be happy."

David Mulqueen was considerably older than Susan. One would have expected him, at twenty-five, to be at war, but a vaguely defined lung ailment had ruled that out. Instead, he worked for his father, organizing the shipment of wheat to France. The Mulqueen flour mills were the largest in Montreal. Perhaps the largest in Canada. As recently as yesterday, James Mulqueen had reminded his son it was time to get married, to settle down. He had mentioned a certain Jane Gresham as a likely prospect. The Greshams owned a considerable chunk of the Canadian Pacific Railway. They also had mining interests in Ontario and northern Quebec, as well as a ranch in Argentina. However, Jane Gresham was not quite what David Mulqueen had in mind. Surely, he had told himself, it was possible to combine beauty with a suitable background. Did all those dreadful girls he met at the right dinner parties, at the right dances, have to look like forlorn mares left in a wet field?

"What did your cook put in the picnic basket?" he asked now. He had no intention of eating immediately; he just wondered, that was all. The champagne was good. He wanted to drink enough to feel dreamy, to fly a little, to see in life some kind of vision that was not dreary and dull.

"Chicken," Susan said. "And strawberries. The strawberries are just ripening. They came from our garden."

"Good. I like your kind of picnics. You French know how to prepare food."

She bristled.

"I'm half English. I'm Sir Simon's granddaughter."

"Sorry. Say, how is the old boy? He got out of that Ramsay rifle scandal by the skin of his teeth, didn't he?"

"I prefer not to talk about that. It's not as simple as it sounds, you know. My grandfather would never make bad rifles *knowingly*. Why, he gave a whole company to the army. And troopships. And money . . . all sorts of things. He's very patriotic. People just don't understand."

"Sure. Sure. I know. I'm sorry I said anything."

David Mulqueen backed away rapidly. He had lost a

little ground there by his clumsiness. The effect of one glass of champagne, which he had hoped would soften her, had now been dispelled. She looked stern. Her mouth had taken on an angry line. From what he'd heard, Susan's own brother had been killed by one of the rifles. But then, she obviously felt little closeness to either of her brothers.

"Let's forget it. I thought we were having fun," she said.

"Sure we are. Here, let me fill your glass."

"I love your car, David. I really love it. I want a car. I've asked my father for one, but so far I haven't been able to persuade him. Mother drives, of course. She has for years."

"Your mother is a very . . . what do they call it? 'forward' woman. A kind of suffragette. Does she chain herself to fences or anything?"

"She believes in the vote for women, if that's what you mean. Do you realize that women have the vote in every province in Canada except Quebec?"

David groaned. He had steered her off again into some kind of anger, a kind of militancy that she had probably inherited from her fierce old grandfather. Why couldn't he keep his big mouth closed and just ply her with wine?

"I wish I could take you out in that car on a really decent road. It'll do seventy miles an hour. That's what they told me when I bought it. But on these roads, you'd have your head knocked off and your spine out of joint if you tried it."

Susan relaxed again. She looked away, across the grass toward the river below.

"It's a very impressive river, isn't it?" she said.

"Oh, yes, one of the greatest rivers in the world," he agreed eagerly, suddenly embracing the St. Lawrence as a passion, a passion that he hoped he could turn to his own advantage. If Susan liked rivers, fine. He liked rivers too.

"Are you still at McGill, then?" he asked now.

"No, I left. I'm bored with books. I like to dance. I like to ride. Do you have horses, David?"

"Sure. Out on the farm. Do you want to ride? We'll go out there tomorrow and ride."

"I'd love to go out to your farm. We don't own a farm, but we have a place on Ste. Helene Island, you know. A summer place. The boys learned to sail there."

"Are you hot?" David asked.

"No, are you? There's a breeze here."

"Mind if I take my coat off?" He was wearing a navy blazer with a crest on it. When she shook her head, he removed the jacket and loosened his tie. "Girls are luckier in summer."

"Yes, I suppose that's true."

"Good stuff, this." He was beginning to feel the wine now. Susan looked a little less stiff, too, he thought. He lay on the blanket, his head supported by one arm. "Not that I know much about wine. If it's drinkable, I drink it."

Susan laughed. She had a pretty, light, genuine laugh that came easily and musically. It was one of her greatest attractions.

"They say," David pronounced rather ponderously, making it into an obvious joke, "that French girls are very . . . very . . . well, you know."

"Do they? Well, please keep in mind what I said. I'm not pure French, you know. But if you wish to think of me as, well *different*, I suppose that's all right."

"When I was at Oxford, the fellows all talked about French girls."

"Boys are very stupid at times. They don't know much."

"Oh, I agree. Yes, I do," David said hastily.

"I know the kind of things they say. But it isn't true. It simply isn't true." She finished off the champagne and held out her glass. "I think it's all right to have fun. To enjoy oneself."

"So do I. That's why I like you," David said.

He lay watching her, fascinated. He sensed in her a quality that excited him. He suspected that she was a rebel. Only in a small way, perhaps, but still a rebel. Not stuffy and ponderous like so many of the girls he met. She came from a good family, too. You couldn't deny her being the granddaughter of Sir Simon . . . but the St. Amours were Catholics. That stuck in the gullet. He tried to imagine his father being told that he wished to marry a French girl. He pushed that vision away. Even Sir Simon's prestige wouldn't wipe out the fact that she was Catholic. Damn it all, she was, as far as he could see, the most attractive girl he'd met since he left England. Those days at Oxford had been high living. He hadn't done much work. He'd had a lot of girls. Some rather delightful ones, too.

"What's it like, being a Catholic?" he asked, opening the

second bottle of champagne. "I've always thought all that Popery-mopery must be awfully difficult."

She said airily, "It's boring."

"Do you do all that stuff? I mean, pray on your beads or whatever it is? Confess . . . say, you aren't going to confess about this picnic, are you? We shouldn't be here alone. Your mother wouldn't like that. Neither would your priest."

"Don't worry, David, I don't intend to go to confession. I don't go anymore."

He perked up at that.

"You don't? Why not?"

"It's a secret. I shouldn't tell you. You might tell somebody. How do I know I can trust you?"

"You can trust me, Susan. You know that. Come on, Susan. Aren't you here with me? Aren't we having fun?"

"All right, then. I will."

In the pause, while he refilled their glasses, he began to imagine Susan as his wife. He could picture her at parties and dinners. She'd be a good hostess. She was pleasing. She laughed. She had spirit. She hadn't been afraid when he'd driven too fast. He liked that. And she could ride. He'd like to take her to Paris. To Cannes. To Baden-Baden. All those places where people knew how to enjoy themselves. To bask in the sun. How pretty she looked in the sun. In a swim suit—she'd look very well in that. He looked at her ankles. Yes, she had nice legs. Nice legs . . . and then . . . a nice body. His eyes fell upon the small points of her breasts. The voile dress was so thin it parted from the tips of her breasts. If if weren't for that damned satin, he'd be able to see the curve below. He began to feel excited. His body was stirring. He shifted his legs slightly.

"What's your secret?" David said, moving closer, smelling the faintest tinge of cologne upon her skin. Seeing the sun pick out the fine blonde hairs on her forearm.

"I'm leaving the Catholic Church."

"You are?" He was genuinely astonished.

"Yes, I am. I can't bear all the bowing and scraping, and eating fish on Friday, and confessing, and everything. You've no idea what it's like to have an uncle who's a priest. So goody-goody . . . and then a great-uncle who's a bishop. You just can't think what it's like! And they're such hypocrites! Do you know that Aunt Justine, who was so religious—she was praying all the time, and we thought she was practically a saint—well, she had an affair! With a hired man on the farm! And then praying, and pretending to be so devout. It makes me sick. It really does. I'm leaving."

"No, I guess it's pretty bad, things like that in the family," he managed to say. He could see that she was wound up like a top. Or a music box, rather. And that she would run on until she lost her power.

"Oh, yes, it's awful. Mother has all my cousins in the house all the time. Mathieu lives with us, you know, he works for the mayor. He's going to be a politician, he says. He's crazy. He has so much energy, he frightens me. Do you know what he likes to do? He walks for miles, and runs, sometimes, and he actually likes to upset his buggy! He *makes* it upset! He runs over curbs, and over rocks and things, and makes the buggy upset! It's terrifying riding with him, and then he picks himself up and walks away from it. 'If you haven't had a fall from a horse or a buggy turn-over, you haven't lived,' that's what he says. And then Beau, he lived with us—that's my cousin who's the musician. He doesn't talk much, he just plays the piano all day, or the guitar, and stares into space, and writes music. It doesn't even sound like music. I hate him! But Mother likes him. Better than she likes me. Oh, I hate the whole place. I wish I could leave."

He saw that she was talking like this because of the wine. Her words were a little slurred. They didn't make much sense. He knew about her cousin Mathieu, of course. Everybody did. He was known all over the city for riding his horse at dangerous fences, for going through traffic with no regard whatsoever for the other vehicles on the road. He had wrecked more gigs, more buggies, than any man would try to reckon, and he seldom seemed to get hurt. He was known far and wide as "The Wind."

"He says he's going to be mayor," Susan went on, "but I don't think he can possibly live long enough. Do you? You must have seen him. He rode a horse right through Dominion Square at breakneck speed only the other day and narrowly missed a tram."

"Well, I see why you don't like living at home," David said. "I suppose you couldn't move in with your grandparents?"

"I've thought of that," Susan said, waving her glass a little precariously in the air so that some of the wine spilled onto her dress.

David brought out his handkerchief and began to wipe ineffectively at the gown. He could feel the warmth of her thigh underneath the material. He slipped his hand underneath the handkerchief, and, feeling the firm flesh under the dress, the stirrings that he had tried to put down began again. He gasped a little with the force of his own desire.

"Oh, yes, I'd love to live on the Mountain. Pride's Court is a beautiful house. I wouldn't care if it *is* haunted."

"You do have quite a family. I heard that story about its being haunted. But it doesn't make anybody move out, does it?"

"Grandfather would never move out," Susan said with some pride. "It would take more than my aunt's ghost to move *him*!"

She was talking quickly, and she began to choke on the wine and the words. David moved closer and slapped her on the back. She set the glass down awkwardly, still coughing. He let his hand stay on her back, flat, hot now on the palm. He allowed it to slide down her back to her waist. He could feel the articulation of her backbone.

"You all right?"

"Yes, now I am, thanks."

"You're awfully pretty." His face was close. "And you're a lot of fun. But not everybody would approve of this little picnic of ours. Nice girls don't go on picnics alone."

"I'm a nice girl."

"I know, Susan. I was only joking. You're the nicest girl I ever knew. You're the prettiest, too."

He pressed his mouth to her cheek just near her ear-lobe. She didn't move or push him away. He allowed just the tip of his tongue to touch her ear. He felt her shiver.

"You know what? If this damned war wasn't on, we could go to the Continent. We could go to Biarritz. We could go . . . we could go to Spain."

"I'd like that. I'd like that a lot."

He let his mouth slide down her face to her neck, his lips just under her chin, and still she did not move. In the buzzing heat, and on the gentle drift of wine, life seemed less raw. There was a smoothness here, a silken cocoon of beauty without guilt. A butterfly rested for a moment on the picnic basket.

For just a moment, he let the spell break.

"Would you be an Anglican if you left?" David asked.

"Oh, yes, that's what Mother is. She goes to Christ Church. She didn't become a Catholic. They made an agreement, and just the children . . . and Father . . ." Her voice trailed off.

"We must finish the wine. It doesn't keep," David said.

"I know. Champagne doesn't keep."

"This afternoon won't keep either. I feel the same as the sparkles in that bottle," David said.

"Oh, so do I!"

His blond hair, blond eyebrows, pale blue eyes were close now. A good-looking, laughing, secure kind of face. A face you could trust.

"My, but this is the nicest picnic—" David began. He put his lips to her mouth. She held her face up to him and the winey, moist velvet of secret flesh glided over her tongue.

As she yielded to this kiss, thinking that she must stop soon, must keep something back, David murmured, "Let's get married. Let's do it right away. Then we can have such a lovely time, Susan."

She felt the tightness that had been building up ebb away, and as he moved over her, hovering, she lay back and smiled up at him. He ran a finger over her teeth, over the open mouth, and she closed her lips on it. She could feel his chest on her breasts, just brushing the tips. If she had expected his weight to come down and crush her, she was surprised. Instead, his wily hands unfastened tiny buttons and began to spin a web inside the camisole she wore.

In the bright light, patched with the shadows of leaves, her breasts were small, pointing upward, into his hands and then into his mouth. He shuddered and began to kiss them, moving his mouth hungrily but smoothly over the pale flesh, over the stiff nipples.

From the dream of wanting, she broke through, a swimmer surfacing after a long, delicious dive.

"We can't . . . it's dangerous . . . what if . . . what if . . . oh, David . . ."

"Don't worry, we aren't going to do that. Something else . . . something just as nice . . . trust me . . ."

"I trust you, David . . ."

She wore the new-style step-ins, little shards of silk and lace with a strap between the legs so narrow that it was incredibly easy to insert a hand. His hand was there, and she opened like a flower. He lifted the long skirt, the satin petticoat, and pulled down the ineffectual barrier of the underwear. Instead of the pain she had expected, the force that surely must be the next step—for even in her innocence, she knew that David was far gone in his own excitement—instead of that, his head came down on her golden crotch and she began to move and thrust under the most delightful sensation of her life. She knew, in her ecstasy, that he was doing something to himself at the same time. But her eyes were closed and when she felt relief and the glorious comfort of satisfaction she knew that David had achieved the same thing.

And they hadn't really done anything wrong.

When they had recovered a little, David poured the rest of the wine.

"When we're married, my darling, it will be much more exciting."

"It couldn't be any more exciting, David. I don't believe it!"

"Oh yes, it can. We'll save that, however, until you have no worries. So you see, darling, it can all be very lovely, and we can have such fun, and there's no risk to you. I wouldn't allow anything to happen to you, Susan."

"Oh, yes. I had no idea, David . . . And she began to laugh. "I don't suppose—"

"You don't suppose what, darling?"

"I don't suppose we could . . . would I be greedy if we did it again?"

David laughed this time, and assured her that it would be possible. In a little while, the web could be spun again, in just a little while. He thought, he said, he might eat some chicken now. And then, later, when he was strong again . . . they would have such fun.

CHAPTER FOUR

Although he still retained the asbestos mine and the railroad in southern Quebec, and had managed to scrape through the three years between Max's death and the outbreak of war, Armand's financial situation had been rescued primarily by war contracts. Much of his revenue now came from manufacturing military uniforms, knitted goods, boots, and leather belts. He had become, over the years, one of the few experts in the field of planning and designing narrow-gauge railroads, and, because of this, Corbin in his position as senator had suggested Armand as a consultant to the Defense Department early in the war. In the beginning, when it had just been becoming obvious to the Allies that the war would be long and bitter, Armand had gone to France to assist in planning war-zone railroads behind the lines. The supply lines were constantly being disrupted, shifted, and completely rebuilt. As the war had dragged on, he had spent many weeks in France redesigning various sections of vital railroad systems.

He was standing now with his back to the people in the room, staring out the window at the busy traffic below on St. James Street. In the past two years, Armand and his staff had taken over a suite in *Le Monde* building because it was convenient. He said, still not looking at his audience, "I'm going back to France in ten days."

"You're going back so soon?"

Honey's voice was tired. She had hoped that this time Armand would be home for a few months. She had no real idea why Armand had called Mathieu and Luc to the meeting with her, or why he couldn't have told her this news at home, in more intimate surroundings.

"I'm afraid so, *amie*. I saw the Prime Minister yesterday. We had a meeting with some of the General Staff, and they've explained certain facts to me."

Armand came back from the window and sat down at his desk. He gave Honey a quick smile.

"You, my darling, cannot be told very much. You're in the business of printing news, and all this is very secret, you understand. However, it's generally known that the German eastern front has collapsed."

"But surely that's good news?" Mathieu demanded, speaking for the first time. "That means we have a chance to win at last, doesn't it?"

"Nothing is so simple," Armand said heavily.

"I wish you would explain it," Luc said.

Since he had left the farm, Luc Barbier, Nicolette's husband, had worked for Armand in Montreal. He had begun as a purchaser for the newly built factories, and now he supervised many of Armand's extensive operations. He had learned quickly, and Nicolette liked living in the city. But there was a wistfulness about him that indicated he would have liked to be in the country, doing the kind of thing he had originally been trained to do.

"I'll try to put it briefly, but anything I tell you is to be kept confidential. Don't say anything to Nicolette, Luc. There must be no 'scare,' no 'panic,' you understand. I was given the most definite instructions about that in Ottawa. People will work better, try harder if there's hope. Is that clearly understood?"

"Armand, it sounds so frightening!" Honey exclaimed. "I don't understand."

"Believe me, we—that is, the Allies—are in desperate trouble. At this moment we are close to losing the war."

"But the United States has come in. Surely that will—" Luc protested.

"We hope so. There hasn't been time yet for the Americans to make their strength felt. We're holding our own at the Marne with the help of American troops. But the Allied armies are depleted. We're short of ammunition and food. France is, in many parts, a wasteland. We're having trouble getting supplies to the front lines as it is, and when the fall rains begin, it will be worse. Now, listen to me. We have it from the highest authority that an all-out German campaign is about to begin on the western front. They're moving their army from the eastern front for a total offensive. Now do you begin to see our difficulties? They're going to mass everything they have for one last, grand attack! And while the weather is still fine. There isn't much time left. We're trying to prepare our armies for that coming offensive."

There was silence in the room. Each person seemed to be trying to digest the significance of what Armand was saying. Finally Mathieu said, "Where do *we* come in? Luc and I?"

"My job, along with a handful of others like me, is to keep the railroad supply lines running. They're the only hope we have. Roads in France are impossible. There aren't enough heavy trucks, there isn't enough gasoline. Not even enough horses. Rail is the most reliable way to get supplies up to the front. That's *my* problem. Miles of track are almost useless now. Then, there's a shortage of men who can organize. That's where both of you come in. Luc, you know how to find and order supplies. I want you to come with me to Paris and lend a hand in the Versailles Depot. The very fact that you speak French is an asset. I know there's some difference in language, but we can communicate a thousand times better than most English-speaking people can. You'll be attached to the Ordinance Department. I've practically promised that you'd go. What is your answer?"

Luc hesitated only a moment. He had been disqualified as a draftee because of poor eyesight and had not expected ever to see France. It was a new thought to him, going overseas.

"But naturally, Uncle Armand, if you want me to go I'll go. Our ships do still get across, don't they, in spite of the German submarines?"

Listening to them, Honey felt drained of energy. She saw herself completely alone once more. Armand gone, Luc gone, Marc somewhere with the troops at Cambrai, Beau in England with an army entertainment group. She had Camille, of course, still living in the nursery apartment, but Camille had always been remote. Michel was due home on leave from the Royal Air Force before too long, but she began to feel isolated, wasted.

"What about me?" Mathieu cried, leaping suddenly to his feet. "Surely they want me?"

"Yes, yes, they want you," Armand said impatiently.

"I'm coming to that. The mayor's office will have to get along without your services for a while, I'm afraid. I need you."

"I want to help," Mathieu said. "I can do two jobs, if it comes to that. I was going to run for city council next year. Time to clean up some of the corruption there. But that's beside the point, if I can help with the war."

"You can let older men run the city for another few months, Mathieu," Armand said, smiling in spite of himself. "We can use all that surplus energy in the Defense Department. Stop running your horses and your automobiles into traffic and trees and use your vitality in a good cause."

Mathieu laughed. He knew his Uncle had heard that only that morning his bay gelding had taken a bad fall. But he'd come away, as always, without injury. Nothing but a few bruises to show for it.

"All right, Uncle Armand, what can I do?"

"Some supplies must be found here in Canada. You're going to head a special committee to get shipments off as fast as possible. There's very little time. Everything must be speeded up. It occurs to me that you're just the man to do it. You can work twenty-four hours a day, if you like. Nobody will mind."

"I don't go to France, then?" Mathieu sounded disappointed.

"Not at the moment. I want you here. The lists will be given to you. It will be your job to find the materials and the means to get them across the Atlantic and delivered, where they'll do some good."

"Certainly, if that's what you want. But I could go over, too, you know. My French, if you'll pardon my saying so, is a little more understandable than Luc's. After all, he was a farmer, while I'm educated. There is a difference. However . . ." And he shrugged.

"The irony is, "Armand said quickly, not wanting Mathieu and Luc to get into some ridiculous argument about their abilities. "you'll be dealing a lot of the time with the Courts."

Mathieu allowed himself a guffaw.

"I won't mind that. Your old father doesn't scare me, Aunt Miel.'"

"I'm glad to hear that," Armand went on. "You'll be

trying to find space in Court ships, trying to buy Court ammunition and, probably, Court grain and flour. Or if the material doesn't come from one of the Court enterprises, it comes from some source owned by a friend of theirs. But I leave that to you, Mathieu. It'll be a challenge."

"Where do I report? Who'll I be working with?" Mathieu wanted to know.

"The Army Ordnance Corps. You'll find them desperately short-handed down there. You've got to speed up shipments without causing a panic. Remember that."

"Trust me, Uncle Armand. I can do that and keep one eye on city council at the same time."

"Leave city council to your aunt and Gabriel d'Esterre," Armand cautioned.

Luc and Mathieu left after making arrangements to see Armand later in the day about names and appointments. Armand closed the office door on them with a heavy sigh and turned to Honey.

"Really, Miel, I thought I might be able to stay on in Montreal a bit longer. I know this is a disappointment to you, but you must believe me—it's necessary."

"I realize that, Armand."

She went to him then, putting her arms around his neck and nestling her face against his. There was still comfort in being with Armand, a feeling of solidity in a slipping, sliding world.

Armand put his arms around her and stroked her hair.

"Be strong. There's every chance that Michel will be home soon. He's suffering from fatigue and shock and I don't think they'll try to hold him there. His superior officer did say he'd be back, you know. The fliers take the strain in a different way from other soldiers. He may get a medal. He shot down five planes. At least five."

"I hope so. I hope so. I want to see him."

He continued to stroke her hair.

"You do have Susan, you know. And Camille is in the house. Surely Justine can come in for a few days from the farm?"

"Armand, don't worry, darling. Please don't worry."

They stood like that for a few brief moments. Then Armand pushed her back so he could look at her face, still fine-boned, the eyes still large and blue and compelling at forty-two. A beautiful face, matured, ripened, still strong. He kissed her on both cheeks; she closed her eyes and he kissed both eyelids gently.

"Go along and run your newspaper, and I'll see you at dinner," Armand said. "I sometimes think I'd rather have had a homebody for a wife!"

She knew that he did not mean it. She would not have wanted (not truly) to change Armand, and he no longer wanted to change her. She could see him still as he had been at the ball when they had first met. She regretted nothing.

CHAPTER FIVE

It was a splendid night for a ball. There was a haze in the air; the incense from piles of burning leaves up on the Mountain drifted down gently to the sprawl of the city streets below. Earlier in the day, a brisk wind had blown most of the bits of paper and garbage off the streets around Dominion Square—as if by divine intervention—so that they were miraculously clean. In the square itself, a yellow-green trail of leaves around the benches and walks rustled pleasantly in the dying light. The Windsor Hotel, dominating the street and the square as well, was alight, as if expecting momentarily the first contingent of carriages and motor cars.

The guests came in an exotic mixture of horse-drawn vehicles jingling brass harness and bells, and in polished automobiles sporting blatant horns. A red carpet had been stretched from the curb across the sidewalk and up into the hotel lobby.

Although no one, especially not the members of Montreal's powerful business community, would admit even the slightest possibility of an Allied defeat at the hands of the Germans, there was a shadow of worry behind social smiles. The memory of bloody Passchendaele the summer before, a futile battle fought partly by Canadians for a patch of Flanders mud, had struck deep. That particular battle had cost half a million Allied lives. There had been renewed hope when the Americans had come into the war, pouring forth their men and arms and unbounded self-confidence. But had their entry been too late? Who could predict the outcome of the unspeakable struggle in France between the two exhausted but apparently intransigent armies?

So perhaps it was forgivable if a certain shrillness showed beneath the laughter and if the cries of recognition as the guests arrived were slightly strained. Whatever one thought or feared, however, money must be raised for the Red Cross. That was the purpose of the ball. Supplies, and staff must be sent to the front. Morale must be propped up at home as well. People must be *seen* to be cheerful. Soldiers who had returned or who were about to go must be extravagantly adored. Dances must be danced (there was the excitement of the one-step, the madness of the fox trot), and songs, patriotic and romantic, must be sung.

The guests were, in a sense, a disparate lot.

First there were dozens of army officers with stirring uniforms and confident mustaches. Pipers of the Fifth Royal Scots were opening the ball with the formal march down Peacock Alley to the Windsor Room. In addition to officers from local regiments, there were visiting colonels from various army posts, captains who had been sent home wounded but who had recovered sufficiently to attend, Lieutenants on their way to France who were not old enough to have grown a whisker, even a handful of brigadier generals in various states of preservation.

Mixed with the authority of the servicemen were members of the old guard of Montreal society, both French and English. (There was even a smattering of Europeans and some Americans.) They were all resplendent in tails, and many wore the ribbons of British orders, which proclaimed them to be recipients of rewards for past services rendered. Almost all, however, were slightly glazed with approaching age. The men were accompanied by gray-haired ladies heavily brocaded and satined, thickly plumed and furred, lavishly pearled and diamonded.

In addition to this select core was the sprinkling of social climbers wily enough to attend an important public function even if it cost too much for their pocketbooks.

Lastly, there were the youths, the bright-faced young women with new-cut hair and the bland-faced young men with burgeoning mustaches. They came from the right addresses and the right schools. They knew all the right people, had all the right connections.

The young women wore pale gowns with straight skirts (material had to be conserved), exposing a little too much shoulder and neck. Their small bosoms nudged thin, scarcely concealing silks; tender flesh invitingly wrapped, so near and yet so far from yearning fingers.

The young men were slim, not yet gorged with living, but hardened and browned by tennis, sailing, and riding to hounds. They were, for the most part, civilians, not by choice but because of some hidden defect. They mixed in a seemingly diffident way with the hero-warriors, but at the same time, knowing who and what they were, they remained essentially aloof, like peacocks in a garden.

In the flash of chandeliers and the flush of champagne, all these people were bound together for the evening in a fervid pastiche of patriotism so that, in the end, the ball was transformed. It shimmered, smoldered, glowed, flamed into its own unforgettable ambience.

Honey had arrived with Michel and Gabriel. Michel, just home from England, looked tired, worn out with that particular lassitude that only the very young can display. He was old-young, world-weary. Slouching in his flying officer's uniform, knowing where he had been, what he had done, the risks he had taken, the terrible sights he had seen, he was too exhausted to speak of it. Or too reticent. There was no way of knowing which was true, Honey reflected, when she looked at his face with a mother's eye. The sparkle, the zest, had gone from Michel's gaze. She wondered if it would ever return.

As for Gabriel, he was always around to escort her, to give support, when Armand was away. Honey was so accustomed to the situation now that she seldom gave it a thought. Gabriel had never married; was, if anything, wedded to the newspaper. He was constantly attentive, watchful, polite. There was something beneath the surface, Honey knew, a latent attraction to her as a woman. She recognized that fact, but Gabriel never went too far. There was a lingering of touching fingers at times. Or there was extra care when he helped her on with a cloak, or handed her a batch of papers. There was the holding of doors, the boosting of an elbow as she stepped onto the running board of her car. Were these moments really meaningful? Were they extended a little too long to be correct? Or was it all her imagination? She had no time, no inclination for dalliance. If Gabriel was dangerous, he had never made that fact known. She had come to depend on him in matters concerning the newspaper, and she could not imagine losing him.

Tonight, Honey had chosen light blue silk and diamonds. Armand had given her a sable cape the previous Christmas and she wore that against the coolness of the September night. Her blonde hair was piled high, pulled back gently from high cheekbones. There was a trace of gray in it now.

When the three arrived, the dancing had already begun in the spacious Windsor Room. Michel asked his mother for the first dance, which happened to be a waltz.

"It's a good thing this isn't a fox trot," Honey said as they took the floor. "I haven't learned that yet."

"Mother, it's easy, really. I'll teach you, if you like."

"When did you have time to learn? I thought you were flying, not taking dancing lessons."

"Oh, in London we sometimes had a little time off," Michel said vaguely. "We couldn't fly day and night, you know. They *do* give fliers a holiday."

Michel spoke to his mother in French. He knew that in casual conversation, she preferred it. When it came to an important scene, or a conversation that required concentration and deep thought, Honey still spoke in English. But she was always aware that she must speak French constantly in order to remain fluent. Her children all understood this, and obliged.

"And did you meet some nice girl over there?" Honey probed lightly. She wondered if Michel was longing for some wartime love, and if that accounted for some of his preoccupation.

"Not *the* girl, Mother, If that's what you mean. Perhaps there won't be one girl for me. I'm not a romantic like my father."

Michel managed a smile. Honey sensed the tremendous effort it cost him to attempt this evening. In the vague light of the ballroom he looked only his twenty years. But in the harsher light of Peacock Alley he had appeared much older.

"I hope your father will return soon," Honey ventured. "Is it really so terribly bad over there, Michel? Are we . . . might we lose?" Her voice was only a whisper close to his ear as they danced.

"It's very bad, Mother," Michel said. "Though it doesn't do to admit it to most people."

She felt him tremble. She stopped talking then and went on dancing. Now she was aware of the people around her. So many of the faces were familiar. She saw Emily Ross—she could never think of her as Emily Cuthbertson —chatting with a group of women in a corner. Fort and Sydney were dancing. Eventually she spotted Sir Simon, deep in discussion with a group of men his own age. Lady Court would be at home. She had been in a wheelchair for some time and seldom left her room now.

As they danced, Honey had a sudden and terrible longing to see her mother. She wanted to be a child again, to rid herself of all these terrible burdens and memories. The memories of Armand's defection, of Denys's death. The memory of the scenes with her father after she'd become a wife instead of his cherished daughter. There were so many heartbreaking visions. Why did one have to grow up? Why couldn't she have stayed as she had been the night she'd met Armand? Young and attractive, filled with hope? She wanted desperately to tear herself away from this ball and go to Mama. In her private agony, she tightened her grip on Michel's hand. He looked down at her, aware for the first time since they'd begun to dance that she was another human being like himself.

"What's the matter, Mother?" he said quickly. "Oh, I see. You spotted Grandfather. You mustn't let the old curmudgeon bother you. We're here to have a good time. Remember that, Mother. You mustn't let Grandfather intrude. Promise me that."

She nodded. But the tears were so close to the surface that she wanted to run away. The lump that had formed in her throat refused to dissolve. Her stomach would not settle down. She was glad when, at last, the dance was over and she could sit down on the side. Gabriel joined her.

"I'd like just to sit out this one," Honey said. "Dancing doesn't appeal to me just now."

Gabriel looked surprised, but willingly sat with her. Honey watched Susan arrive with David Mulqueen. They began to dance, and Honey, looking at them, was not happy with what she saw. She was annoyed with Susan, in any event, because she had wanted the couple to come along to the ball in the big touring car with her, Michel and Gabriel. Instead, Susan had insisted on driving with David—alone.

There had been tension between Honey and Susan for weeks. A brittleness had appeared in Susan when she spoke, a remoteness that indicated that while she was physically in the room she was not there mentally. She was completely preoccupied with David Mulqueen, and Honey felt an approaching crisis. She had hoped to stave it off at least until Armand came home to share the trial. So far, there was no word of his return.

For one thing, Susan had stopped going to church. Honey was on the verge of speaking to Uncle Eustache about this problem. While, ordinarily, she would not care about any Catholic falling away from the Church (she had never felt compelled to convert from Anglicanism, herself), she realized that Armand would be upset. There would be family scenes. The children had been brought up in the Church, as Honey had promised when she'd signed the dispensation on her wedding night. Any laxity would be a failure in Armand's eyes.

Susan wore a lace dress, much too sheer, of a light violet color. A row of small velvet flowers with tiny yellow centers circled the neckline. Her arms were bare above her long, formal gloves. She was slim to the point of thinness, yet her legs were long and well-shaped; they were shadowed beneath the thin folds of the dress she wore.

Honey was even less pleased as she watched the pair on the floor. It was not that she had anything against David Mulqueen. She knew his family, how important they were in the English life in Montreal. David had been to Oxford. But it disturbed her to think that she and Armand had not solidified her bond to the St. Amour family through the children. That failure seemed a disloyalty to Armand. She also felt that Susan was a foolish girl, not knowing what she wanted. But Honey knew she was not being logical. She had eloped with Armand when she was only a year older than Susan, and that had been a long time ago. Also, she had never discouraged Beau's friendship with Angela. As she sat, she tried to think clearly about these things. Beau was only her nephew, Angela her niece. Did that have something to do with her attitude? She wasn't responsible for their actions or their problems, not really. Who could expect Beau to be normal, sensible, conventional, with *his* background? Justine was so passionate, so coarse, so forceful, and Timothée was uneducated yet strangely lyrical—and, she suspected, lustful. The son of such a pair would not be ordinary. It was too much to expect Beau's slight frame to hold in all this concentrated potential.

Her attention was diverted, momentarily, to Angela, who had arrived with Thomas McKay. They made what everyone present would surely call a "perfect couple." Angela's dark hair and gray eyes were complemented by Thomas's red-gold curls and brown-flecked eyes. The McKay's owned textile factories along the St. Lawrence. The families of both Angela and Thomas would approve, Honey was sure. Sir Simon would be delighted. Probably he was busy promoting the liaison.

Honey had a sudden thought. Did Angela know that Beau had returned from England? He had arrived at the St. Amour house only that morning, without a warning of any kind. He'd rented a place on Mountain Street, he'd told Honey, a studio. He had realized that Camille was using the nursery apartment and that he would have to live elsewhere. Her conversation with him had been brief. He had been rushing off, and she had been late for an appointment. But even in the short time they had talked she'd seen a difference in him.

Whereas Michel had become languid, uncaring, Beau now seemed angry and hard. The lines of his face had tightened, his skin was brown instead of pale, his eyes were fanatical. He looked more than ever like his father. She would have liked to have talked to Beau then, to have luncheon with him, but she had been already committed. And Beau had seemed in a hurry to pick up some bags stored in the attic; she had seen him off in a cab. She hadn't thought to tell him about the ball or to ask if he cared to come along.

In the midst of these thoughts, Susan and David approached. There was a determination in the way they both walked, as if they were facing an unpleasant situation but were determined to proceed. She felt alarm.

"Mother, David and I have something to tell you," Susan said, as she stood in front of Honey. She always looked pretty, Honey thought, but she was not beautiful. There was a shallow look about her.

"It sounds important," Honey managed.

"It is. *Very*."

"Then perhaps we ought to wait until we get home."

"No, I want to tell you now."

Why are they forcing an issue in public? Honey wondered. David ought not to let Susan do this. She looked up at David and saw that he appeared untroubled. His glance was smooth and lighthearted.

"Susan, I would really prefer to talk at home."

"But we want to make the announcement at the ball," Susan explained.

"Yes, Madame St. Amour, we do want to make this announcement tonight, so we must tell you first," David was saying.

Honey suddenly wanted time to stop. But there was no way she could prevent Susan's next words.

"David and I are engaged," Susan said. "We plan to be married next June."

She thrust out her small, neat hand. She wore a huge square-cut diamond in an elaborate gold mounting.

For a moment, Honey stared at the ring.

"I'm a little surprised," she managed to say, finally, "but Susan, if you and David are sure—"

"Yes, we're quite sure," Susan said. "I'm leaving the Catholic Church, of course. I realize Father will be upset, but we'll have to deal with that later."

"Susan, I do wish you and David could have talked to me first. At home. Not in public like this."

"I'm sorry, Madame—" David began apologetically.

Susan said abruptly, "Surely you have no objection to David?"

"Well, it isn't that . . ." Honey said.

"After all, Mother, *you* eloped. What can you expect? You didn't even tell your parents before you left the house. We all know the story. It sounded so romantic. Well, David and I are telling you now. We want to make the announcement at supper. It's a perfect place to announce our engagement, don't you see?"

Susan continued to talk. They would be married in Christ Church. Grandfather was going to be pleased. He would be sure to approve of her returning to the Anglican

Church. To the English side of the family. Honey knew that her daughter was right, but she felt a stab of bitterness just the same, and her outrage against her father for this additional thrust was only increased. But Susan wouldn't understand that.

"We're very much in love," David was saying. "So please don't worry."

"Congratulations, then, David," Honey said. "I hope, Susan, you'll be very happy."

Honey saw with much pain the look they exchanged. She remembered feeling that way when she and Armand had first met. When the world had turned, blossomed, exploded, or faded on the whim of one man's smile. When eyes said more than lips. When a heart could swoop or dive over the most ridiculous thing. A glorious, heady, and oh, so short-lived time in one's life!

There was nothing to be done but to gather up her strength and pretend to be happy. She could not explain all her misgivings about this union, but she knew instinctively that it was going to create disturbances. She could not envision Susan in the role of a delightfully contented wife and mother. Still, Susan had been right. She had taken a risk herself, and so she must accept the situation without too much protest.

Angela had not intended to go to the ball. However, her grandfather had given her such a stern lecture on the duties and obligations of people in their position that she had relented and accepted the invitation of Thomas McKay. Nothing, Sir Simon had pointed out testily, could keep *him* from the ball, although he would have to go alone since Lady Court was confined to her bed. In addition to the arthritis, she had lately been complaining of shortness of breath and tiredness due to insomnia. There had been some trouble with her heart over the years, but now it was more acute. Occasionally she suffered chest and abdominal pains. Mrs. Card had been retained after Venetia's death, and she assisted with Lady Court's care under a nurse's supervision. She slept in the dressing room off Lady Court's bedroom. Sir Simon knew that he could go to the ball without undue worry.

He had also pointed out to his granddaughter that *all*

the Courts who happened to be in Montreal on this occasion would attend. It was mandatory. Charles and Polly were in Ottawa, but Geoffrey and Mary, and Noel, would be there. Fort and Sydney would attend with Landry (who, at eighteen, was majoring in sciences at McGill). As for Mildred, she had turned into a stodgy, lumpy girl with colorless hair and heavy manners. Sir Simon had arranged an escort for her, however. Paul Bell worked in Sir Simon's bank and while he was attractive enough, he was penniless and docile. It was unfortunate that Mildred wasn't attractive enough to find young men herself, but Sir Simon was not beyond putting pressure on an employee when it was needed. He had given up on Geoffrey and Mary, who couldn't seem to see the point of making suitable arrangements for the girl. Sir Simon was saddened by Mildred's pedestrian qualities (so unlike Angela, who might be a bit strange, but was so lovely that if she merely stood still at the corner of Peel and St. Catherine she would gather young bucks about her as a magnet collects iron filings), but he was resolute. One could not expect all one's grandchildren to be brilliant and beautiful.

Having thus arranged an escort for both his grand-daughters (for entirely different reasons, of course, because it was Angela's lack of interest that created *her* problem), Sir Simon could go to the ball and enjoy the conversation of his cronies. Thomas McKay was quite suitable—right family, right church, right education. Angela could do better, of course. He had in mind taking her to London when the war was over and introducing her to a few proper people there. A few weekends in country homes. These things could be arranged. Some dinners and balls in London, perhaps. That kind of thing. Actually, Angela was worthy of a peer. Again, when it came to the child's parents, one couldn't rely on them. Charles knew what was what, but he was busy. Polly simply didn't take an interest in anything but ambulances, bandages, and raising money for good causes. A nice girl but a bit dull. Sir Simon sometimes thought that the burdens of the entire Court clan, as well as the bank, the shipping line, the railroads, the ammunition factories, the government, and, in fact, the whole war rested upon his shoulders. It was too damned bad, but he was willing to accept it as long as his strength held out.

Angela, however, did not care much for Thomas McKay. During his visits to Pride's Court he had looked at her drawings with pretended interest. He seemed lazy. He drank too much wine. She had heard rumors that he gambled. Certainly she found him insensitive.

Beau had been away almost a year, and during the first weeks after his departure she had received long, passionate letters with every post. They had described his intense loneliness, the bad pianos on which he was forced to practice, the coarse men he loathed in the group to which he was assigned. They had been bitter letters, soul-wrenching, yearning for the sheltered life he had lived in the St. Amour house. He had poured out his anger at this exposure to the crudities of life. He had poured out, too, his need for Angela's love and understanding, and had often reminded her of the vow they'd made in the cemetery and the future plans they shared.

Angela had returned the same kind of letters. She had soaked up Beau's anger like a sponge and returned to him all her own frustrations, her loveless life, the lack of understanding from her own family, her ultimate fear that her mother's spirit still haunted Pride's Court.

She feared the sitting room so much that she had asked her grandfather to move her to the east wing. So far, she had not been successful. Sir Simon was busy with more important things.

As the months had gone by the letters from Beau had changed, and at last they had been reduced to undiluted melancholy. There was in them an edge of despair, a lost drive. Then the letters had become less frequent—and finally had stopped. Beau became almost a dream figure. But there was nobody to replace him.

Painting and reading in her half-lit world of fantasy, Angela had finally given in to her grandfather's pressure to go out occasionally in society. He now brought Thomas McKay home quite often and on the slightest pretext; anybody could have seen through the excuses. But finally she had agreed to go to the ball with Thomas. The entire Court family gave in, eventually, to Sir Simon's will, it seemed.

So tonight she wore a gray watered-silk gown with wide straps and elbow-length sleeves. It had a short, hip-length overskirt of gray satin, and the hem just touched the tips of her gray kid pumps. The pumps were a find, having been imported before the war and mistakenly placed by an inefficient clerk in the storage room of a small shoe shop. Angela had found them and been delighted. She had an eye for beautiful things.

Sir Simon had been pleased with her decision to go to the ball and had prevailed upon Lady Court to lend Angela a pearl necklace, his gift to his wife on their thirtieth wedding anniversary. The pearls were perfectly matched, the necklace bound with an exquisite emerald clasp.

As the ball progressed, Thomas McKay showed his limitless taste for wine, and almost fell down on the dance floor. Angela led him off to the lobby of the hotel, along Peacock Alley, past the dowagers, the crowds of onlookers and gossips, with the idea that he should get some fresh air.

Thomas had a red face, his tie was askew, and his footsteps were uncertain. He had a tendency to lean alarmingly to one side. She was disgusted, but determined. The solution might be a walk in the chilly night air of the square across the road. So she steered Thomas toward the cloakroom and directed him to pick up her velvet cape. He was making a sloppy attempt to drape it around her neck when she was suddenly confronted by Beau, who had just come into the lobby.

Angela was overwhelmed at the sight of him. She was speechless. She forgot about Thomas McKay, who stood, listing slightly, wondering what was keeping her from continuing on toward the door. There was a small buzzing and fluttering from the crowd around them. But Angela paid no attention.

She saw at once that Beau had changed. His fragility had disappeared; the fineness of his face, his look, was toughened now and hardened. The green eyes, always passionate, were alive with a fiercer flame. The mouth was more demanding.

"Where are you going?" he said. He spoke as if they had never been separated.

"I was going to the square. For a walk."

"With this *drunk*?"

He glared at Thomas. Thomas, having drunk enough wine to make him belligerent and at the same time to have made him lose any common sense he'd had, pushed himself in front of Angela.

"Did you call me a drunk?"

"You *are* a drunk," Beau said.

He roughly shoved Thomas aside, as if he were not to be reckoned with, and took Angela by the arm. Thomas reeled back, then rocked forward, his face turning a deeper red than before.

"Where do you think you're going with my girl?"

"*Your* girl?" Beau stopped long enough to stare at Thomas. He pushed the man away once again. "Go home to bed. Sleep it off."

Thomas leaned forward and swung crazily at Beau. A few people standing around had noticed the disturbance. There were clucking sounds, a few uncomfortable coughs. Large ladies with lorgnettes peered with disbelieving eyes. A porter hurried forward, but before he could interfere, Beau struck Thomas solidly on the jaw. He staggered back into the porter's arms.

While onlookers shifted and a hotel manager swept forward to calm the scene, Beau ignored everyone and took Angela once again by the arm. They were on the street before anyone thought to stop them. He hailed a waiting cab, and they drove off.

Angela had no idea where they were going.

She only knew she was where she belonged. With Beau.

CHAPTER SIX

The coach house Beau had rented sat behind a rambling
red brick house on busy Mountain Street. Although there
hadn't been a vehicle on the ground floor turntable in
fifteen years, nor harness in the tack room, the place still
smelled of used leather and stale horses. The empty square,
which had once sheltered some weathy family's elegant
carriage, was covered with a layer of dust. Beau's luggage
lay piled just inside the double doors where he'd planted
it that morning. There had been no time to clean up, buy
furniture, or unpack his things to make the place liveable.

When they stepped inside from the cold night air,
Beau closed the heavy doors and quickly lighted a kerosene lamp that he had had the foresight to place on the
floor. (The coach house hadn't been wired for electricity nor
provided with any kind of heating system.) The orange
lamplight cast a golden glow that gently brought the room
alive. Angela, exhilarated by seeing Beau, instantly endowed it with magical qualities; long ago it had been an
exciting room, bustling with life and importance, perhaps
even with romance. She was enchanted.

In the past she'd never given a moment's thought to
servants' quarters. Stables merely meant horses. These
days the coach house at Pride's Court was given over to
the family automobiles. But what the rooms above the
stables were like didn't interest her in the least. However,
with Beau, in this secret place, she felt quite differently.
The whole building was charming, filled with fabulous
possibilities. With great eagerness she followed Beau up
the narrow wooden stairs that led to the small rooms
above.

One room was a makeshift kitchen containing a few
basic pieces of furniture. The other was a bedroom with

dormer windows, a single iron-framed bed, a nondescript table, and a chest of drawers with one missing handle. Lifting her silk skirt off the floor with one hand, she viewed the room, as Beau put down the lamp, with a mixture of fastidious horror and intense emotion. This was Beau's room! This was going to be his home! Oh, they could do such wonderful things with this coach house. While Beau stared at her she took a moment to redecorate it in her mind, wondering how much furniture she could extract from the attics of Pride's Court.

"Why in hell were you with that clown?" Beau suddenly demanded, breaking the silence. They faced each other across the flickering lamp, curiously stiff in the aloneness that surrounded them. Beau's green eyes looked a little mad.

"Because Grandfather arranged the evening! He insisted that everybody go to the ball. Except my father and stepmother, who happen to be in Ottawa this week. Grandfather arranged for Thomas to be my escort. That's all there was to it."

"I might have known that old tyrant would try to pair you off with one of his own kind. Why did you have to knuckle under to him?"

"Did it occur to you that I might just happen to want to go to the ball?" she cried angrily. "Why shouldn't I? You didn't write to me for months. How was I to know what had happened to you? You might have been dead. How did I know you still cared about me?"

"For Christ's sake, Angela, don't talk nonsense!"

"Why is it nonsense? You didn't even let me know you were back. Have you ever heard of the telephone? You arrive back here, you don't even call, or come, or send a message . . ."

"I wanted to surprise you. What the hell does it matter, anyway? There's nobody else, Angela, and you know that damn well." He ground out the words in a rage that was barely under control. "We promised each other. You remember."

"I remember."

"How could you go to the ball with that fool, then? Have you no pride at all? That stupid drunk! I should have killed him when he put his hands on you!"

"No pride? You don't even know what you're talking about. You don't understand people like the Courts—you never will!"

"Oh, I know how much you think of your precious family. That's all that counts, isn't it? *Who* you are. *Who* your grandfather is. Well, I don't give a damn about all that. You belong to me."

He grabbed her shoulders and began to shake her wildly. She gave an odd little cry, and he suddenly realized what he was doing and dropped his hands.

"My God, Angela, I'm sorry. I'm sorry."

Angela rubbed at her arm where his nails had dug into the bare flesh above her gloves. She looked pathetic; childlike, yet desirable.

"I only went to the ball to please Grandfather."

"I nearly went crazy when I saw you with that idiot. I've thought of nothing but getting back to you, of making some place for myself here so I could be close to you and go on with my music."

"You should have written. How was I to know? I didn't know where you were. What was I supposed to do?"

"Wait."

"Wait? What do you think I've been doing? Thomas means nothing to me. I was only trying . . ."

"Angela, why are we fighting?"

He moved quickly toward her and threw his arms about her, tightening them, pulling her head close to his, almost breaking her bones in his eagerness. They kissed hungrily, a kiss that held nothing of their past affection, but was filled instead with a starved sensuality. Before, when they had parted, they had been children. Now they were full-grown.

In the time they had been apart, the knowledge that they belonged together had only blossomed. When she lay on the narrow little bed naked except for the exquisite pearls belonging to her Grandmother, and Beau began to kiss her whole body, discovering it for the first time, Angela forgot everything else—the ball she had fled, the silk gown thrown carelessly into the dust, the lateness of the hour, and the ferocity of her grandfather's temper should he find out what she had done. Just being with Beau swept up her whole sense of being. She shivered with wonder. At last they were bound together, the vow made a reality with their bodies. Whatever happened in the future, nothing would ever be as meaningful as this.

There was a frosty nip in the morning air, and, despite her velvet cape, Angela was cold. Coming through the back garden behind the conservatory, she sensed that something was amiss at Pride's Court. She had expected to reach the courtyard, and the door leading to the back stairs, without meeting any of the servants. But as she peered out from a protective clump of cedars she saw Frobisher aimlessly raking up leaves and gossiping with Pennington. It was most unusual. Frobisher did this kind of work later in the morning. And Pennington never hung about the garden except to sneak a smoke; his territory was the stable and sometimes the garage. Both men seemed worried and were gesticulating. She could tell that they weren't really working but merely putting in time. When Pennington finally disappeared around the corner and Frobisher went inside the house, she decided to take a chance.

She ran across the wet grass to the courtyard wall and into the square formed by the stable, the outbuildings, and the house itself. Here, her worst fears were confirmed. Three automobiles were assembled; Uncle Fort's, Uncle Geoffrey's, and one she didn't recognize. Fear ran through her, canceling out the exhilaration she'd felt thinking about her night with Beau. If Grandfather had found she was missing he might have reported it to the police! Certainly that would account for a gathering of the family at this early hour. Perhaps he had known for hours that she had left the ball with Beau. But no, Thomas McKay would never have ventured back into the ball for a word with Sir Simon, not looking the fool that he did.

She found the door to the back stairs open and she got inside with a feeling of relief. The first step, at least, had been accomplished. If she ran into one of the maids or Mrs. Card, she could always appeal to them to keep her secret. That would be better than meeting any of the family, or, worst of all, Grandfather.

She managed to get halfway up the stairs, trying to be quiet on the slippery linoleum of their surface, when she realized with a turn of the stomach that somebody was coming down to meet her. It was a moment before she recognized the figure of her Aunt Sydney.

"Angela!" Sydney whispered. "I was coming out to look for you. Where on earth have you been? My dear, you haven't been home to change. Your gown—" She broke off, waiting for a reply.

"What's happening? Why is everybody here?"

Angela followed her aunt's lead and whispered, too. She was startled at what appeared to be some sort of conspiratorial aid from Aunt Sydney. She had never been very friendly with Sydney, thinking of her as cold and unapproachable.

"It's your grandmother. She's had a heart attack. You must hurry and change. Your grandfather knows you were out of your room, but I told him I'd seen you in the garden early this morning. So if you can change . . ."

There was no time to inquire why her aunt was offering her an alibi. The main thing was to get to her room without being seen and change her clothes. But first, she asked quickly, "Is Grandmother very ill?"

"I'm afraid so. You hurry along," Sydney added. "I'm going down to the kitchen for a tea tray. Everything is topsy-turvy this morning, and Fort is waiting for his breakfast. A crisis like this seems to bring out the worst in servants."

They passed each other then, and Angela scurried up the stairs and along the passage used by the servants that led into the main wings of the house, and finally reached her own room. She narrowly missed Sir Simon and Geoffrey, who were conferring as they walked toward the main staircase. They had, apparently, just come from Lady Court's room. They looked grave.

Once inside her own bedroom, Angela shut the door, tore off the offending ball gown, and tossed it in a corner. Opening one of the doors to her wardrobe, she pulled out a woolen day dress and a sweater, found some walking shoes. She must look as if she had been out early in the garden, as Aunt Sydney had reported. Once dressed, she went into her own bathroom and washed her face. She was exhausted. It was only when she lay on her bed, ready for a visit from anybody who might come looking, that she began to worry—first about her grandmother, who had always been kind and who had made some attempt, when she was small, to fill the place left vacant by her own mother; and, second, about the behavior of her Aunt Sydney. She was confused by Sydney's loyalty, although grateful for the protective lie.

Thoughts of Beau intruded into the central well of her concern about her grandmother. How marvelous it had been to find out at last what life meant! But why did everything have to happen in clumps like this? As if fate were determined to cram everything together so she couldn't sort out her life properly.

They gathered in the library to wait for Sir Simon and Dr. Hunter to come downstairs with a report. It was only a few minutes until teatime, but nobody seemed to be hungry. Geoffrey stood over the drinks tray.

"Can I make you a whiskey and soda, Charles? I think I could use one," Geoffrey said, his hand already on the decanter.

"Yes, please. Polly, too."

"Oh, I'm sorry, Polly. I meant to offer you a sherry," Geoffrey said.

"I prefer whiskey," Polly said. It was a habit she had acquired since she and Sydney had begun working at the hospital. Somehow, after a difficult day, sherry did not quite meet the need to settle one's nerves.

"How was Ottawa, Charles?" Fort asked, moving up to the table where Geoffrey was dispensing drinks.

"Panicky."

"As bad as that? What about the contract?"

"Oh, we've got the contract," Charles said with a slight shrug, but he frowned. "The question is, can we find the ships to take the materials over to France? I said we had ships available. But we lost one only yesterday. I suppose you know the *Maryanne* went down off Gibraltar?"

"Yes; I haven't had time to think about it," Fort said. "I'm getting a report tomorrow. With Mama being so ill, I rushed over here and left the office in awful confusion."

"What are they saying about the German push? Is it really the all-out offensive this time?" Geoffrey asked.

"Apparently," Charles replied. "I had lunch with Colonel Brooke . . . you remember him, Geoff? The man we worked with on that contract for uniforms last spring? He says the Canadian army casualties alone may reach fifteen thousand by next month. Our boys are attached to four British divisions and they're driving toward Mons. The Huns aren't about to give in, and they're asking a high price for every inch of ground. I wonder where young Simon is. Have you heard?"

"No," Geoffrey said, looking even more worried than before. "Mary and I have no idea where Simon is right now, except that he's in France somewhere."

While the men talked, Sydney and Polly sipped their drinks near the fire. Mary was drinking squash. She seldom touched alcohol, except for a glass of wine at dinner. On the other side of the fire, apathetically moving chess pieces about, Noel and Mildred sat hunched, without speaking. Landry, the other young person in the room, ignored everybody, preferring to stare out the library window at a gray squirrel dashing up a tree in a fantasy race with some unseen predator. He was always fascinated by the behavior of animals and birds and only turned his attention to the adults in the room when Geoffrey offered him a sherry. At eighteen, he was given that privilege. After this exchange, Mary roused herself sufficiently to say that she thought she might ring for tea.

"Yes, do. The children should have something to eat," Geoffrey said, "and a cup of tea might help the rest of us. Dr. Hunter might be pressed to have some food when he comes down."

Mary got up and pulled the bell rope. She turned to Sydney to ask, "By the way, where are the twins? Still upstairs with Starkey?"

"I sent them up to the nursery when we arrived because there are books and games there. Starkey is with them, yes. We can't expect them to sit around at their age without getting fidgety."

"Still, they'd better come down for tea," Mary said. "I really don't like to ask the kitchen help to take a special tray up to the nursery tonight."

"I'll get them," Sydney offered, rising up from her chair, "and bring them down right away."

Sydney was looking exceptionally pale and drawn. She wore a gray cashmere afternoon dress that was cut rather short, so that her knees were exposed when she sat down. Mary thought it shocking but said nothing.

Although the twins, Flora and Fenella, were twelve,

Rose Starkey had been kept on. The girls scarcely needed a governess since they were in private school and came home late in the afternoon. But Starkey had other uses. It was difficult to get trained help these days because so many women worked in munitions factories and in offices. Nora Richmond, who had been governess to Mary's children, for example, was now employed in Geoffrey's office. She shared a room with Rose on the third floor of Fort and Sydney's house. That arrangement had been made at Rose Starkey's request. Rooms were hard to get in Montreal now, Rose had explained. Decent rooms a woman could afford, at least. It would be a great favor to her, she had explained, if Nora and she could stay together. Since there was plenty of vacant space in the house, Sydney had seen no reason to turn down the request.

The tea wagon had already arrived when Sir Simon, Dr. Hunter, and Angela came into the library together. Angela had been crying. She sat down beside Landry and he took her hand comfortingly. Dr. Hunter was glowering. Sir Simon looked grim and shrunken.

"How's Mama?" Charles asked quickly.

"I wish I could be more optimistic," Dr. Hunter said.

"The news isn't good, I'm afraid," Sir Simon said, pulling himself together with a tremendous effort. "Your mother . . . well, we don't know how long she's got, but she wants to see all of you. I think in family groups would be best, if Dr. Hunter agrees."

"Yes. That's probably best," Hunter said.

Nobody objected to the fact that Lady Court had asked to see Angela alone. It was understood that Lady Court had been a second mother to Angela in the days when Venetia had been so difficult, and that she felt especially responsible for the child.

"What exactly is the situation?" Geoffrey asked, speaking directly to Dr. Hunter.

"There are complications," the doctor said slowly, as if reluctant to impart the details. "Lady Court is suffering what we call congestive heart failure. There are several side effects. She has pain and a lot of trouble breathing. I've given her a sedative and we have her propped up on pillows to help her breathing, but she's . . . I'm afraid she's failing quickly."

Sir Simon cleared his throat ceremoniously.

"Geoffrey, could I have a brandy, please?"

Geoffrey quickly provided his father with a drink. Dr. Hunter said he'd accept some tea, strong and black. Mary poured some for the children as well, weakening it with milk.

Sir Simon, standing almost in the center of the room, stared down at the carpet and then announced to nobody in particular, "She wants to see Hannah."

It was obviously hard for him to say the words. A heavy silence followed, and then Charles stepped forward and offered to fetch his sister.

"Yes, Charles, that would be best. But first, go up and see your mother. Take Polly. Then go and find Hannah."

When Charles and Polly were gone, the twins arrived, looking remote and slightly puzzled. They did not understand what the family gathering was about; Sydney had merely told them that their grandmother was ill. Yet they sensed when they entered the room that there was tension, that the illness was not an ordinary one.

Every family member looked up at them when they entered. They had an undefined quality that attracted instant attention. They stood side by side just inside the door of the library—still, not speaking, identical in their white middies and navy skirts. Like fairytale princesses, they had pale, oval faces, wide-spaced intense eyes, and long golden hair. Only their mother, and sometimes Starkey, could tell them apart with certainty. This fact made the rest of their relatives uneasy. They had poise not usually associated with twelve-year-old girls. While they communicated with each other easily, one often finishing the other's sentence, their conversations with other people were stilted. Except on rare occasions when they actually tricked people about their identity (Flora pretending to be Fenella and Fenella saying she was Flora), they had no sense of fun. There was something disturbing in their very presence.

"Tea, girls?" Mary said from her place by the tea table. "Come in and sit down. You must want a scone or a sandwich."

"Yes, please," they spoke together, as if in a duet.

Their manners were perfect. They sat side by side on one of the sofas, rather straight, knees carefully together, each with a cup of tea on her lap. They took exactly the same amount of milk and sugar. When Flora selected a ham sandwich, Fenella did the same. Even the ribbon that tied each girl's long hair back from her face in a bow at the crown was fastened in an identical fashion—not a fraction of an inch wider or longer.

Sydney, drink in hand, came to sit beside them. It was time to tell them the truth about Lady Court, because they would have to go in soon and see their grandmother for what might be the last time. When she began to talk to them, they turned grave, careful eyes upon her and listened. The others in the room continued with their tea, their awkward conversations, their chess. In a few minutes, the twins had been absorbed into the room, and the brief phenomenon of their appearance passed.

CHAPTER SEVEN

In a sense, this visit was a distillation of all the times she had come into her mother's bedroom as a child—to ask for advice, to gossip, to devise some essentially harmless scheme for fooling Sir Simon. On those long-ago occasions her mother had been elegantly languid in a blue silk bed jacket, leaning on pillows covered with silk, reading a romantic novel. Her thick hair had been done in two neat plaits, her glasses had hung on a blue silk cord about her neck. The bedroom had been designed to enhance her fragility—all silks, frills, and pastel colors.

Now everything had changed. The room had been stripped of its charm and, with a shock, Honey saw her mother propped up on a mound of harsh white linen pillows smothered in the smell of disinfectant. Lady Court was breathing shallowly, with great difficulty. Her eyes were sunken and her skin had an unhealthy, bluish cast. Thin veined hands lay on top of the sheet, too helpless to support a book, and her glance was too vague for reading. But when she saw Honey, her eyes took on interest for a moment.

"I wanted to see you, Hannah."

"Yes, Mama. When I was at the ball last night, I was thinking about you and suddenly I wanted to come here. I ought to have come."

"I wish you had, darling."

Honey knew she ought to have followed her instinct and visited Pride's Court while Papa was so obviously busy. But her distaste at the idea of starting still another ugly scene, should her father find out she had been in the house, had prevented her. And then there had been Susan's startling news.

"If only things could have been different," Lady Court said wearily. There was a wistful sound in her voice de-

spite the shallow breathing. Honey knew exactly what her
mother meant. How different indeed, if only she had married one of her own! The lavish wedding in Christ Church,
her mother's happiness and her father's pride, the whole
safe, comforting blanket of security and place that Sir
Simon had offered her from birth. She had rejected it all
for Armand. And so there had been the estrangement, the
ghastly scenes, the loss of grandparents to her own children. Those were the things that now dwelt in Lady Court's
exhausted eyes. All the might-have-beens.

"Yes, if only it had been different," Honey said, echoing her mother's words.

"I always missed you, Honey."

The tears were close. Honey took her mother's thin
hand and pressed it. But Lady Court began to cough again
and retrieved her hand to hold a white square over her
mouth. Honey saw the blood spotting the linen. When the
bout was over, Lady Court's eyes had grown vague again,
already one step removed from reality. When she spoke,
she seemed to be making a tremendous effort to catch
the stray thoughts as they drifted by.

"I want you to have my sapphire necklace, Honey,"
Lady Court said finally. She paused to breathe, the act
itself consuming all her energy. "Your father bought it for
me. He always liked me to wear it. Get it out of the jewel
case."

Lady Court's diamonds, the tiara she had worn to
court in London, the large matched clips, the pendant ear-
rings, and some of the heavy bracelets were kept in the
family vault at the bank. But she had always insisted on
retaining in the house half a dozen pieces that she wore
fairly frequently. The pearls she had loaned Angela for
the ball and the sapphire necklace were two of the pieces
she kept in her bedroom.

Honey brought out the blue velvet box and gave the
necklace to her mother. Lady Court clutched it for a moment, unable to raise it from the bed. Honey took it back
then, so that her mother could see the intense blue stones.
Lady Court smiled slightly.

"Wear it sometimes, Honey. You're still beautiful, my
dear. It will look nice on you."

Honey wanted to cry, but she felt that if she broke
down now, her mother might somehow die of the emo-

tional strain. Her eyes were filled with tears, but she managed to keep her voice fairly steady. Lady Court had something else to say and was struggling to get it out. Honey leaned closer to her mother.

"I've left some money and property to your children," Lady Court said, and closed her eyes. Honey stood rigidly beside the bed, unable to move, afraid to weep. In her hand she clutched the necklace. She was aware that somebody had come into the room. She didn't turn.

"Honey, perhaps you'd best come out now," Fort said kindly, putting his arm around her shoulders.

He saw the necklace in her hand.

"I'm glad she gave you that," he said. Honey leaned against him but didn't speak. She knew that Sydney was at the bedroom door, waiting to come in, too. She looked again at her mother.

"She's . . . almost gone," Honey whispered.

"There's nothing you can do," Fort said, attempting to turn her toward the door. "You need to sit down, Honey. Geoff will give you a brandy. Go down."

"I don't want to see Papa," Honey said, trembling. "I can't face him, not right now."

They stood for a moment and nothing happened. It was too difficult to know what to do. Then Fort approached the bed to look at his mother. Her eyes were closed. Suddenly he straightened up.

"My God, I think she's gone! Sydney!" he called past Honey to his wife at the doorway. "Go down and get the doctor, and Papa. Please. Right now."

It was too late for Hunter, Fort knew that. There was nothing anyone could do for Lydia Court now.

———

By the first of October, Bulgaria had capitulated and Montreal was filled with hope and rumors of imminent peace. Honey was embroiled in the newspaper stories pouring in as the American military machine and the exhausted British and French and Commonwealth troops at last rolled forward. The German armies retreated. Peace: the word was magic in the air. The American president, Woodrow Wilson, was drawing up his Fourteen Points and getting ready to sit at the table with his peers to bring about an acceptable armistice. Honey was conferring with Gabriel about the front page when the telephone call came from Armand. His ship had docked. He and Luc were back in Montreal.

"Gabriel, he's going to be at the house in an hour! I'll have to leave all this to you, my dear—I must get home and change. I'm a wreck—I've been working in this dress all day and I'm filthy. I'll have to alert Annette to get some food ready. And to put some champagne on ice . . ."

"I understand. Of course you must rush. Don't worry—I'll finish up here."

"Thank you, Gabriel. I don't know what I'd do without you."

"Find another editor, I expect," he said, making a little face at her, "as you did when I replaced Beaulne. It is the cycle of life."

"No, it's different."

"Yes, in a way. Now, you go along. I don't think there will be any more important news before we go to press."

"No, it will be some days before we find out what President Wilson is actually going to offer."

Honey left the office and drove herself home. After giving directions to Annette, she bathed and changed into a new dark blue crepe de chine gown with a beaded skirt, a costume Armand had never seen. She was putting the last touches on the table when Michel came in from his latest escapade out at the small airfield near Lachine. Camille came downstairs, an eager expression on her face. Susan was not to be found. So it was a family party of three that greeted Armand when he came in.

They all embraced warmly, kissing and laughing and asking questions and more questions before the first were answered. The champagne Honey had ordered provided a festive air. She was determined not to mention her mother's death or Susan's engagement tonight. It was enough to have Armand home.

"Is it really true, darling? Are we winning at last?" Honey asked Armand. "I hear so much about the wonderful job you've done with the railroads. Only the other day we had a story come in from a reporter over there, telling about it. You were mentioned."

Armand passed quickly over that. He had been at Mons, he said, doing what he could. "There's no doubt about it now. We're pushing them back. But it was a near thing, Miel. It isn't possible to describe how close we came to losing. If the Americans hadn't come in—"

"Wilson is about to announce his peace terms," Honey said, smiling at Armand. "We're all waiting breathlessly to hear them."

"It may only be a matter of days, Mother," Michel said, as if he had just come from a Washington cabinet meeting.

"I should think that's about right," Armand agreed.

"I'm buying my own plane, did Mother tell you that?" Michel said. "Flying's the thing of the future, in my view. So I'm going to get into it early."

"How do you propose to make money out of flying?" Armand said lightly. He did not like Michel's idea; he had hoped to interest his son in one of the family enterprises, but tonight wasn't the night for argument of that sort.

"There'll be ways. People will want to travel in a hurry, for one thing. Emergency supplies is another. Important documents, important mail. People will be willing to pay to get things done in a hurry."

"I should think they'd prefer to pay for safety," Armand said, thinking of his railways. "But I won't argue the point tonight. What are you using for money?"

He gave Honey an accusing look, as if he suspected she had loaned Michel money out of indulgence. But Michel said quickly, "Grandmother Court left me money in her will. I intend to use that when I get my hands on it."

"Oh, so that's it." Armand did not intend to pursue any of these lines at the moment. He turned to Camille, instead, standing like a thin black ghost with her glass of wine, waiting for the only important news in the world as far as she was concerned. "You'll be wondering about Marc, wondering if I've seen him, Camille. Well, I have. He was at Cambrai, and later at Mons, doing wonderful work. There's talk of an advancement. I should think we'll have another bishop in the family one of these days. He sends his love and expects to be back before Christmas."

It was all she needed to make her smile. Back before Christmas! That was the best news she could think of, much more exciting than President Wilson's pronouncements or Michel's ridiculous plans to buy an airplane. Marc a bishop! That would be truly wonderful. In her semidarkness, she felt a surge of warmth, pride, and hope.

CHAPTER EIGHT

Fort Sydney (as Fort whimsically called Mellerstain when he was in a good mood) was a smaller version of the original in Scotland. The basic design was a square with a crenellated façade, but the Victorians had not been able to resist tampering with the simplicity of the design; there was a north wing four stories high tacked on the back. And it was on the fourth floor that servants were quartered, in a dozen attic rooms with low, white plaster ceilings, dormer windows, and bare wooden floors occasionally covered with scatter rugs. The climb was a long one up a narrow back staircase with too few landings and too few lights. The rooms themselves were sparsely furnished with plain chests of drawers, one armchair for each room, and single beds with hard mattresses.

Despite these shortcomings, Rose Starkey considered the three rooms she shared with Nora Richmond (a bedroom each and a sitting room between them) comparatively luxurious when she glanced at the rooming houses in downtown Montreal. In those run-down, shabby dwellings, the halls were cramped, the neighbors of dubious character, and the rents consistently high. The domestic staff of Mellerstain had been drastically reduced to five for the duration of the war, and so the attics were not crowded. It wasn't even difficult to use the shared bathroom. Nora and Rose had a toilet and washbasin of their own, however, and this, in Rose Starkey's view, was a great convenience.

On a Saturday evening in October, 1918, Rose arrived in the sitting room before Nora. She had extracted a tea tray from Mrs. Hagerman and carried it upstairs so that she and Nora could have some privacy. By the time each Saturday came, Nora was tired and cross. It seemed to Rose that Geoffrey Court's office was always in turmoil and that it was impossible to keep up with the orders for army supplies. Rumors of peace had only compounded the problems because nobody seemed to know whether to rush orders out or hold them back. Rose, whose life revolved around the more placid affairs of Sydney's household, made an effort to help Nora relax when she came home after the long week's work.

Setting the tray on the small table between the two armchairs, Rose took off her day dress, stockings, corset, and shoes. Wearing only her cotton drawers, she put on a blue flannelette wrapper and her bedroom slippers. A corset, no matter how well-fitting, was always binding to her generous bust. She had added a few pounds over the years but she was still far from fat; a little plump, perhaps, but still pink and ripe, her auburn hair without a trace of gray, her breasts an invitation. Now, hovering over the teapot and glancing occasionally at the darkening sky in the square of the dormer, her breasts were almost completely exposed; the cleavage was deep and the wrapper strained to cover them.

She could hear Nora's step on the stairs, and then the door opened and she straightened up expectantly. A sense of relief spread through her, as it always did when Nora arrived. These days, Nora had been coming home from work later and later, and Rose had wondered what was going on. If Nora had, perhaps, some secret life. Glad as she was to see Nora, she could not resist saying archly, "You're late. I think the tea may be getting cold."

"I'm sorry. We were . . . busy at the office."

Nora took off the jacket of her navy wool serge suit and hung it carefully in the closet. The white blouse underneath looked wrinkled, as if it had been a particularly hot day and she had perspiired a lot. She pushed her blonde hair back from her face and kicked off the black pumps she wore to work. Then she collapsed in one of the armchairs beside the tea table.

Rose began to pour tea. But when she handed Nora her cup (already flavored with milk and sugar, exactly as Nora liked it) she looked more closely at her friend's face. She had heard the slight hesitation in Nora's answer. She was finely tuned to Nora and she sensed that there was something odd about the reply and, in fact, about Nora's entire manner.

"You look as if you ran all the way home," Rose observed, sipping her tea and deciding it was still hot enough to be enjoyed. "You'd better have a sandwich."

"Yes, I will." Nora took one of the egg sandwiches and nibbled on it without enthusiasm.

Rose decided that Nora's cup needed replenishing, a "warm-up." She got up and bent over Nora solicitously. Rose gave off a strong whiff of lavender scent (which she always affected in the evening on the assumption that it prevented her from getting a headache after the worries of the day). Her wrapper was still half-open as she bent over Nora with the cup. She made a feeble attempt to pull it closed. She saw Nora staring at her breasts. (Nora, who was quite thin, often admired Rose's figure and declared that she wished she had a bust like hers.)

"You look settled in for the evening," Nora observed, taking her eyes off Rose's decolletage.

"Well, I hate corsets," Rose said defensively. "They pinch."

"I hate them, too," Nora agreed quickly. She didn't want Rose to think that she disapproved of the loose wrapper. They were in their own private rooms and they ought to be able to wear anything they liked.

"Finish your tea, then, and take your things off," Rose suggested. "You'll feel much better. Was it horrible at the office today? What news do you hear about the peace?"

"Oh, everybody says we're going to have peace soon. President Wilson is going to announce what the terms will be. I don't understand why *he's* doing it, instead of the Prime Minister of England or the Premier of France, do you?"

"Because the Americans made the difference," Rose said wisely. "Otherwise, there wouldn't be any peace to talk about."

"I suppose that's it," Nora agreed. "It really was an awful day, Rose. Some clerk lost the bills of lading for a shipment of boots." Nora closed her eyes as if to shut out visions of ghastly catastrophes.

"Well, it's over now," Rose said consolingly.

"Thank goodness. Mr. Court is very patient. It's a wonder sometimes he doesn't lose his temper. But he never does."

"Finish up your sandwich, and I'll run a bath for you. Then you can put on your wrapper. Nobody will be using the tub just now."

"Yes, all right." Nora set her cup down. Her hand was shaking.

As Rose made her way to the bathroom down the hall, Nora said, "I'll be getting dressed again, though. I'm going out for a visit."

Rose's progress was arrested at the door. She turned to stare at Nora.

"Going out? I thought you were tired. I thought you were going to finish your book."

"I was, I was," Nora said.

"Then where, may I ask, are you going at seven o'clock on a Saturday night?" Her tone suggested that this was too bizarre a possibility to be contemplated.

"I'm being taken to meet a family."

"And by *whom*?"

"By a man I met in Mr. Court's office. I mean, he came in, this man, to see Mr. Geoffrey Court about business. It's all perfectly correct, I'm sure. We even know his connections. He lives with his uncle and aunt. He isn't living . . . alone. It isn't improper in the least."

"I'm not saying there's anything improper in it. I'm merely trying to find out what's going on. You didn't tell me you'd met a man, yet you must have seen him often. Otherwise, why would he want to take you to meet his family?"

"I've only had tea with him twice. In Mrs. Hutchinson's Tea Room. The one by the office."

"So that's why you've been late coming home!" Rose cried accusingly. "And then you weren't hungry. I'm not surprised, if you'd already eaten. Why didn't you ever mention this . . . this admirer? If that's what he is."

Nora hesitated. She looked miserable.

"Because I thought you'd be angry."

"Why would I be angry, if it's all proper, as you say?"

"Oh, I don't know, Rose. I don't know. Are you going to run my bath, or not?"

"As soon as I find out who this *gentleman* is."

"He's a relative of the Courts, in a roundabout way. Through Madame St. Amour. That's Mr. Geoffrey's sister."

"Oh." Rose had pulled the top of her wrapper closed defensively and was frowning at Nora from the doorway. All the color had left her face. She looked frighteningly white, and the natural fullness of her mouth had shrunk into a narrow, ugly line.

"Yes, Madame St. Amour's husband has a sister. This man is the son. So he's French. His name is Mathieu Dosquet."

"Which family is he living with, then? Surely not with Madame St. Amour?" Rose inquired.

"Yes, but he has a married sister, too. Her name is Nicolette and she's married to Luc Barbier. Luc is just back from France—he was there with Madame St. Amour's husband. Everyone says that Armand St. Amour worked very hard to reorganize the railways in France. I heard Mathieu say it, and even Mr. Court was talking about it. Anyway, Mathieu's sister lives in Outremont. It's all quite proper."

Rose admitted that she'd heard about the various members of the St. Amour clan from time to time, although it was difficult to keep them all straight. "They have so many children," Rose said. Nora agreed that this was so, but she was reluctant to say anything against Mathieu when he had been kind enough to pay her some attention. She was not really attracted to him, but he was, somehow, an impressive person. She would have liked to describe him to Rose but knew instinctively that Rose would not be happy if she did.

"Mathieu is attached to the Army Ordnance Corps now," Nora said briefly. "He's in charge of organizing supplies. That's how I met him. He comes into Mr. Court's office. He says that one day he'll be mayor of Montreal. Isn't that something?"

"Oh, *that one*!" Rose said scornfully. "Everybody in the city knows about *him*. He's crazy. Always running horses into stone walls."

"Rose, he does not! He does have accidents, but he doesn't deliberately run horses into stone walls. That's a terrible thing to say. Anyway, I think he enjoys accidents."

"What did I tell you?" Rose said triumphantly, "He's crazy. Besides, Nora, he's younger than you are."

There was a sly tone to this remark that Nora didn't miss. She felt guilty and flushed. She was particularly sensitive to the fact that she was thirty and Mathieu only twenty-five. But she didn't look her age, and when she had told Mathieu the truth, he had said it made no difference.

"I told him my age right at the beginning," Nora muttered. She turned away from Rose and walked over to the window to stare at the sky. It was getting late and Mathieu would soon be arriving to take her out.

Rose seemed to sense her restlessness.

"I'll go and run the bath," she said, but her voice was frosty.

Nora left the window and went into her own bedroom, where she undressed. She was slim, with extraordinarily dark, large nipples that consumed much of her small breasts. Rose had occasionally remarked how different Nora's breasts were from her own plump ones. There had never been any harm in these conversations, Nora thought. After all, the two had shared rooms for eight years and had seen each other naked many times. When it was cold at night, Rose had a habit of getting into Nora's bed and putting her arms around her. It was a great comfort to feel Rose's warm bosom against her back and to have Rose's arm about her waist. Yet there was a distinctly proprietary air when Rose spoke to her these days, and that was why she had been afraid to tell Rose about Mathieu.

Nora put on her warmest wrapper, picked up her towel and soap and face cloth. Then she went back to the sitting room to find Rose waiting, her face still deadly white and set in a harsh, uncompromising expression.

"Your bath will be ready now; you'd better hurry."

"Thank you, Rose. I hope you aren't angry?"

"Why should I be angry?" Her voice cracked slightly with the effort to control it.

"I don't know. Because you're going to be alone, I guess."

"I have my book. I mean to finish it."

When Nora returned from the bathroom, Rose was reading determinedly. She did not look up. Nora didn't speak, but dressed as fast as possible and went downstairs to the housekeeper's room, where she would be allowed to receive her caller. Mrs. Hagerman looked surprised when Nora told her about the expected visitor, and Nora knew that as soon as possible the news would spread to the other servants that Nora Richmond had a beau at last.

Mathieu arrived to pick up Nora in a 1915 Mercer Raceabout. It sat uneasily beside the garage at Mellerstain, somehow out of place. Mathieu was much taken with the car—not his first, but the flashiest he had been able to acquire so far because it had belonged to Philippe Grande and Uncle Armand had arranged a good deal for him. Its canary yellow made an unexpected blot against the fading green of the hedge and the gray brick of the four-car garage. He had considered driving it up to the front door—after all, *he* was no servant—but had thought better of it. Nora had told him to come to the side door, the housekeeper's preserve. Better not offend anybody at this point, Mathieu thought grudgingly, although it galled him. Secretly he was intimidated by the Courts, but this very fact made him more bumptious when he was forced to deal with them. In a perverse way, he had often thought of marrying one of these snobbish English. There would be some satisfaction in it. Not one of the rich Courts—that would be too hard to handle, and he had no intention of ever being put down by his wife in his own house. No, not one of *them*. But an Englishwoman, one of the community, like Nora, for example, whose very Englishness was an unbought, unalterable gift. These thoughts occupied him at the door while he waited for Nora.

Nora was suitably impressed with the car—the bucket seats, the long hood, the pretty lamps. (So far Mathieu had not damaged it too much, having merely knocked over one light standard on St. Denis street—this had dented the right front fender—and later having collapsed the spare-tire holder while backing out of his uncle's garage.) She had only driven in automobiles a few times in her life and then as a member of the household staff. Tonight she felt quite grand. But Mathieu's driving soon destroyed *that* feeling as he tore wildly off in the direction of Outremont, the fashionable residential section now occupied by so many of the well-to-do French. His sister Nicolette and her husband, Luc, lived there in a new house.

During the ride they almost ran over a cat, took a sharp

corner across a sidewalk, ripped off part of a hedge, and came to a grinding halt so that Nora was severely jolted. She straightened her hat and was tempted to comment on Mathieu's driving. But something restrained her. Not an attraction to Mathieu, but the idea of having a male friend in a socially superior bracket. Even if he *was* French.

Nicolette received them in the parlor. She looked darkly prissy, and made it clear that she was politely condescending to entertain a woman who once had been a governess. Nora felt uncomfortable. There was a meanness about Nicolette that even her youth could not conceal. She looked discontented and nervous.

"Please sit down," Nicolette said in English. "I've ordered coffee, Mathieu."

When they were seated, rather stiffly, the maid brought in a tray and set it beside Nicolette. Although she was smiling, Nicolette looked faintly displeased. She now spoke to her brother in French, ignoring Nora. "How is your *important* job going?" she demanded. "It's a wonder to me they haven't forced you into the army by now."

"I was medically disqualified by my eyesight. You know that perfectly well."

"But they're so desperate now, they'll take anybody."

She poured strong coffee into large cups.

"My work is considered vital, just as Luc's is. Armand has done fantastic things for the war effort in France, although he's not in the army. But I suppose *you* couldn't understand that."

"Oh, I understand your not wanting to fight for *les anglais*. I don't blame you," she said, switching into English and looking obliquely at Nora as she spoke. "How do you like your coffee, Miss Richmond?"

"With cream and sugar, please."

"And are you still trying to run City Hall?" Nicolette asked next. "I know how ambitious you are."

"I'll be running City Hall one of these days. Meanwhile, I don't have your impatience and bad temper," Mathieu said.

Nicolette handed coffee to Nora. Mathieu took his and glared at his sister. His temper was rising fast. She had always had this affect upon him. She now added fuel to the fire.

"*You* should talk about impatience and bad temper!"

she said with an unmusical laugh. "Everybody knows how impatient *you* are! Stories about you and your accidents are all over the city."

"At least they'll know me when I stand for election," Mathieu said. He found he didn't really want the coffee. He felt like slapping his sister across the face.

"Yes, they'll know you. Well, I may be impatient and bad-tempered, as you say, but I'm not afraid to speak my mind. I'm the only one who dared speak out when Father died. The rest of you stood about like dummies, while that disgraceful—"

"Stop it! We don't discuss family problems in front of other people."

"Oh, don't pretend to be so good, so polite, so grand. Who are you trying to impress?"

"I brought Nora here to meet you. To meet part of my family," Mathieu pointed out, setting down his cup with a clatter. "But it seems impossible to be civilized with you."

"Oh, shut up!" Nicolette said crossly, and turned to Nora. "I understand you were a governess, Miss Richmond?"

"Nora works in Geoffrey Court's office," Mathieu said loudly. "She's considered very clever."

"Oh, really? I thought you lived in the servants' quarters at Mellerstain," Nicolette observed.

"I do, but . . ."

The coffee was very strong. Nora found she couldn't drink it. She disliked the whole atmosphere, the roughness and foreignness of it. She could not help thinking that the Courts, no matter what the circumstances, would never have behaved so rudely to a guest.

"It seems to me, Nicolette, that it is you who are out of place. Nora is doing war work. It seems to me that women who are capable of working in this way ought to do so," Mathieu said.

Actually, he didn't believe what he was saying. In another place, in another time, unstimulated by Nicolette's spiteful words, he would have said exactly the opposite. He preferred women in the home where they belonged, properly subjected to a husband's will. But Nicolette always had this perverse effect upon him.

"I like the work," Nora said firmly. "I feel I'm helping with the war. It's satisfying."

"Yes, and quite a step up for you, too, isn't it?" Nicolette said sharply.

"It seems to me that social position has little to do with helping one's country." Nora looked at Nicolette coldly, determined not to be dismissed in such a way.

"Oh, I see," Nicolette said, retreating slightly.

Mathieu was rather pleased with Nora's calm handling of his sister. Evidently Nora wasn't easily flustered. She was behaving like a lady while Nicolette was acting like a boor. The thought crossed his mind that she would make an excellent wife for a politician. Quite acceptable. Her manners were good, she dressed well enough considering her station, she was pretty, and she spoke a little French, which could be quickly improved if she were given encouragement.

Also, her blondeness appealed to him. He had always liked fair women. He grudgingly asked his sister to warm up his coffee. He was angry, but he was now looking at Nora across the small parlor and seeing her slightly tanned but firm skin, the thick bun of yellow hair that was now held tight with pins but which, when taken down, would doubtless be long and silky. She wore a dark woolen suit that did not quite conceal the small, pointed breasts. Watching her closely, he sipped his warmed-up coffee, and an almost overwhelming desire to possess her swept over him. He could visualize the slim, smooth body under those clothes, the neatly molded little breasts . . . he had seen one or two girls of her type in the brothels. Only they weren't quite so pretty as Nora. He was aroused now and shifted uncomfortably in his armchair.

"We must be going," Mathieu said. He was appalled by his own terrible need to have this slim, cool, intelligent woman. To take her. To be able to take her whenever he wished. He heard his own breathing in the small parlor, oddly out of place in its raspiness. His mind was clouded with pictures of women he had bought in the past. He shot to his feet and waved to Nora. "Come along—it's time to go."

"Must you?" Nicolette asked without much conviction.

"Yes, yes, we must go. I must get Nora home."

They stood at the door, the three of them, in an uneasy cluster. Nicolette could not seem to resist one more thrust, however.

"And what will you do when the war ends, Miss Richmond? Go back into service?"

Mathieu's low boiling point was brought to a pitch by the combination of his sister's barb and his own sexual needs. He was now a walking Vesuvius.

"I may as well tell you, Nicolette, that I intend to marry Miss Richmond!" He heard himself shouting in the hallway. He knew he was behaving stupidly, but he couldn't stop himself. "So watch your manners or it will be unpleasant for everybody!"

"Don't shout at me, Mathieu—you're a ridiculous man!" Nicolette cried, astonished and infuriated by his words.

Mathieu slammed the door in her face and, pulling Nora by the hand, crossed the verandah and opened the car door. Nicolette opened her door again and shouted after them, as they drove away, "Fool! She isn't even a Catholic!"

The drive home was even more erratic than the journey out. Nora was at once astonished by Mathieu's odd proposal and terrified of his driving. She felt ill as they rammed their way through narrow streets and around sharp corners, grinding to shuddering halts, then leaping forward again, jolting, swaying, noisily progressing through the streets toward Mellerstain, as if a devil had taken possession of the little yellow car.

When at last the mad ride came to an end, Mathieu stood beside the hedge near the garage and stared down at Nora. A wind had come up, the cool smoke-scented wind of autumn, and little clusters of leaves swirled and danced around their feet. Light from the windows of the big house made the darkness patchy, but they could see each other's faces clearly when the wind threw back Mathieu's thick black hair and Nora (clutching her hat) pushed back her own pale hair with her free hand.

"I'm sorry about the proposal," Mathieu said. A gust of wind seemed to take the words away up the mountain. "It slipped out. She made me so angry. I mean, I want to propose to you *properly*."

"I don't understand," Nora said. "Really, I don't. I hardly know you."

"Nora, I think you'd make a fine wife for me. I'm proposing to you now, seriously."

He seized her hand impulsively. "Do you know what I'm saying?"

"But your sister is right. I'm not a Catholic."

She had no idea whether she wished to marry him. Buffeted by the cold wind, he looked like a wild man, his dark hair every which way, his black eyes glaring down at her, his huge hand clutching hers, nearly crunching the bones. She was afraid. Actually marrying a man like Mathieu was an idea she had never entertained. He had a certain amount of family prestige and money, of course. She would be able to stop working, not have to worry about money or a place to live. But still . . .

"It doesn't matter about the Catholic thing. My Uncle Eustache is a bishop. He'll know what to do. You know that Aunt Miel is a Protestant, don't you? You must know that if you worked for the Courts."

"Yes."

He dropped her hand. The temporary urge to have her was gone, but it had been replaced by a strong determination to carry through with this plan. Seeing the plan in perspective, he had decided that she was what he wanted, the woman he must have. This Englishwoman, so cool, educated, deliciously fair—and able to handle the difficult Nicolette—was eminently suited to his needs. But he must proceed with caution and not frighten her away.

"I'll buy you a ring. We'll have a formal announcement placed in *Le Monde*. Everything done correctly—once we speak to Uncle Eustache, of course. Tomorrow, I'll take you out to the farm to meet Mother."

"I . . . I don't know."

"Yes, yes, you know. Think of it, Nora! We'll have a fine house. You can run your own house instead of working for people like the Courts. I'll be Mayor one day, that's what I plan. Everything will be fine, you'll see!"

He made no move to touch her again. She looked up into his dark eyes, and felt a chill that might have been the wind cutting through her suit—or might have been a warning. They stared at each other. Then he took her arm and led her to the house.

"Come along, you're freezing."

Nora saw the corner of a curtain flutter as they approached the door. Mrs. Hagerman, no doubt, ever alert to the possibilities of men's wickedness, had been watching.

"I'll call for you at ten in the morning. Wear something warm; it may be a cold drive."

Again she was afraid. But whether it was the prospect of yet another insane drive with Mathieu at the wheel or of marriage to him, she had no idea. She fled inside the house, panting. Mrs. Hagerman was waiting at the door to her little sitting room.

"Oh, is that you, Nora? I thought I heard the car. Is everything all right, dear?"

"Oh, yes, fine."

"You seem quite out of breath."

"It's the wind. It's very windy."

"Yes, it is. I hope—" Mrs. Hagerman paused slightly for effect—"that your friend was a gentleman?"

"Absolutely a gentleman, Mrs. Hagerman."

"Good night, Nora."

"Good night."

She had no intention of talking about this to Rose. Not for a while, at least. Such a change in her own fortunes was bound to upset Rose, and there was no denying that Rose was already cross with her for going out this evening. No, she would have to keep her momentous secret for a while and mull it over. Perhaps she could tell Rose tomorrow. When morning came, everything might look different. It often happened that way.

Rose was just finishing her book when Nora entered the room. She put down the volume and watched Nora take off her hat and coat.

"You look frozen," Rose said.

"It's cold, yes. Windy."

"Did you have a good time?" Rose spoke fiercely, angrily.

"I suppose so. Yes."

"Was he a gentleman? I mean, you didn't have a problem, did you?" Rose persisted.

Rose looked pale and tired. Reading all evening seemed to have produced dark shadows under her eyes. She still wore the blue wrapper, and Nora saw with a tinge of alarm that it was open at the top. She could see Rose's breasts—large, soft, warm, inviting—and she found it extremely difficult to take her eyes away from them.

"There was no problem at all. At least not the kind you mean," Nora said, taking off her shoes. "I'm going to bed. I'm exhausted."

"I'll come along with you," Rose said.

They often chatted at bedtime, visiting back and forth while they undressed. It was a habit they'd formed back in the days when they'd both looked after the small Court children, a habit that (if they had cared to pinpoint it exactly) had grown after the near-drowning that summer day at Drake House.

"All right," Nora said without enthusiasm. Tonight she wanted to have her room to herself. She wanted to think and not to have Rose probing at the evening.

The attic rooms were warm, since Fort had installed hot-water radiators on every floor the year before. Nora chose a thin flannel nightgown from her bureau drawer and laid it on the bed. She began to undress, aware that Rose was watching her and holding her own nightgown in her hand.

"What was the sister like?"

"A snob," Nora said. "They live in Outremont."

"You told me. So it's a new house."

"Quite new. I didn't like it very much."

"You didn't like Mathieu's sister?"

"She's not very pleasant. The two of them don't get along very well. They fight."

"It wasn't much fun, then?"

"No, it wasn't much fun."

The word "fun" certainly didn't apply to Mathieu. She tried to think of how she would describe him and found it difficult. Large, energetic, erratic, quick-tempered, ambitious, and unpredictable. She wondered if he was attractive, and couldn't make up her mind. Certainly if somebody had pointed him out to her in a crowd, she wouldn't have been drawn to Mathieu. Why had she gone out with him in the first place, then? Because he had asked her and she had had nobody else. Because he came from a class above her own and she was flattered. Because he had a car. Because he had more or less swept her along right from the beginning, not giving her time to think. Just as he had done tonight with his proposal.

"Humph!" Rose said with a snort. "Did she give you cakes?"

"No, just coffee. Actually, she wasn't friendly to me. She thinks a governess isn't good enough for her brother. She made that quite obvious."

"I could have told you that." Rose sniffed. "It's what comes of stepping out of your class. Getting above yourself."

Rose took off her wrapper and cotton drawers and threw them casually on the wooden chair in the corner. Nora was suddenly conscious of her friend's lushness. She couldn't remember ever having been embarrassed at Rose's nakedness before, but tonight Rose seemed determined to draw attention to herself. She paused before pulling the nightgown down over her head; the yellow lamplight softly shadowed the rounded pinks and whites of her, her breasts. The dark red hair on her crotch was a compelling magnet for the eye. Nora looked away from Rose's body.

"I'm going to sleep," Nora said.

"I was going to get into bed with you and warm you up," Rose said, her face slack with disappointment.

"I'm tired."

"You haven't told me much about your evening, about Mathieu," Rose went on, sitting on the edge of Nora's bed. "Did he try to touch you, or anything?"

"No, not except to take my hand."

"Well, that's a bit familiar, isn't it? He's quite crazy. Everybody says so."

"You already said that." Nora spoke crossly. She was already pushed to the point of desperation between Mathieu and Rose and the whole evening. She wanted to sleep. But if Rose persisted in questioning her about Mathieu she would be forced to tell the truth. It wouldn't be right to listen to criticism of him if she intended to marry him.

"Why don't you want to talk about it?" Rose demanded.

Nora swung on her abruptly, her voice shrill.

"Because he asked me to marry him! There, you've made me tell you. I wasn't going to tell you but you've forced me, by prying."

Rose stood up on the bedside mat, an oddly plump statue with a dead-white face. Her hands went to her neck as if to fend off some unseen attacker, her legs were planted apart. For a moment she was shocked into wide-eyed, rigid silence. Then she finally managed a few words.

"Marry you? Mathieu? But that's ridiculous!"

"Yes, marry me. Why is it ridiculous? He asked me in front of his sister, right in her front hall. I was astonished, but that happens to be the truth. He wants to marry me."

"And what did you say?"

"Nothing," Nora said truthfully. "But he expects me to marry him just the same."

Rose sat down as suddenly as she had stood up. Nora felt a nest of panic forming in her stomach and creeping up into her throat to almost choke her. Her heart was pounding wildly. Rose looked so stricken, so ill, so strange. As if she might fling herself out the window or onto the floor. As if she might do anything at all.

"And *will* you marry him?"

Nora shrugged, trying to reduce the impact of the scene. Trying to bring Rose's attitude back to reality.

"I suppose I shall," Nora said.

"You *suppose* so?" Rose sounded even more hysterical.

"Why not? It's a good enough marriage, except for the fact that he's Catholic. Why shouldn't I accept? Do you think I want to be a servant all my life? Or work all my life? His family has money and connections. So why not?"

"A Catholic! You'd marry a Catholic?" Rose said.

If she had hoped to calm Rose, Nora was aware that her efforts had been futile. Rose was even more rigid, and now she gasped a single sentence.

"What about *me*?"

There was no immediate reply to that. Nora couldn't think what to say. They had been close, living together for the greater part of eight years (if you counted summers at Drake House and other family holidays), but Rose would have to make her own way now. She could hardly expect Nora to give up an opportunity to marry well just to go on living in servants' quarters and working for wages.

"I know you'll miss me, Rose."

"*Miss* you? It's more than that!" Rose said hoarsely. She began to weep; great tears streamed down her cheeks, and her shoulders heaved. Nora ran across the room and knelt beside her, putting her arms around Rose and trying to comfort her. "I'll be *alone*," Rose said.

She began to shake with sobs so loud that Nora was afraid one of the other servants would hear and come to investigate. What if they found that Rose, for some unexplainable reason, was hysterical because Nora was getting married? How would it sound? Definitely odd. Nora put her arms around Rose. Rose began to repeat over and over that she would be alone.

Finally, Nora said, "Get into bed, then."

She felt as if she were bribing Rose, but she wasn't sure how it could be bribery when she was merely trying to be kind. It was all too much, on top of Mathieu's behavior. The whole night had turned into a ghastly dream. "Don't cry, Rose. We'll find some way. Don't cry. We'll see each other often, I promise. Get into bed while I get you a handkerchief."

Rose mopped at her face with the handkerchief Nora brought while Nora padded to the lamp and turned it off. She was tired. She got into bed and patted Rose's shoulder to quiet her. They lay close together in the narrow bed and Nora pulled the bedclothes up to their necks. She felt the familiar softness of Rose's body, and her warmth. Nora put her arms around Rose and began to stroke her shoulders. Rose gradually stopped sobbing.

Rose reached out and put her arm around Nora's hip drawing her closer. Nora felt the sweet comfort of Rose's breast pressed against her own and had a fleeting vision of herself as a child cradled to a motherly bosom. Her hands, stroking Rose's shoulders, strayed down to the plump, full breasts. Rose unfastened the button of her nightgown and gently pushed Nora's hand into the smooth crevice. Without thinking, Nora's fingers coaxed the large nipples into stiff little erections of pleasure. She could hear the thumping of her own heart as the sweet, pleasant excitement spread downward to the place between her legs. The feeling was so lovely, so desirable, that when Rose slid her hand between Nora's thighs, she opened them and groaned a little. They pressed their mouths together, and Nora swam giddily in ecstasy under the touch of those clever fingers.

Susan had never before visited her grandfather's bank on St. James Street. She had passed it many times, of course, and had been suitably impressed by the tall Ionic pillars, the brass knobs and trim around the entrance, and the classic foyer. As she pushed open the massive door, her heart was pounding. She had made no appointment and consequently had no idea how Sir Simon would receive her.

Sir Simon, to her, was merely a remote figure of myth and legend—fierce, proud, and a dedicated antagonist of her mother's. Susan herself had never been introduced to him, although she had seen him on various public occasions.

Truly, it was a case of bearding the lion. She crossed the marble main floor to find the elevator cage near the back that she assumed led to the offices above. Praying that what she was about to do would be accepted by her tyrannical old grandfather, she got into the elevator. (She had yearned for such a long, long time to be part of the Court world that the audacity of her present visit struck her as crucial.)

The elevator operator was an old man snug in his maroon livery and years of service. He gave her a diffident smile as he assessed her expensive beaver coat and matching hat.

"What floor, Miss?"

"Sir Simon's office."

The operator pulled the gate shut and pressed the button, observing that it was a bitter cold day, down to ten and likely to snow judging from the sky. Susan admitted that he was correct.

"Sir Simon's in, all right," the operator volunteered. "I took him up myself only an hour ago. He's looking a bit peaked since Lady Court died. I don't like the look of him at all."

"Grandfather must miss her very much," Susan said pointedly, hoping to impress him with the fact that it was her very own blood relative they were talking about, but convinced that the old man would think she was lying.

The operator looked suitably surprised and said that he had known Sir Simon and Lady Court personally for twenty years. The cage jogged to an uneven halt and Susan stepped out into a large, carpeted hall. At one end sat a gray-haired woman with a stern countenance. Beyond her was a highly polished door with an impressive brass handle; the door was closed. At the sight of Miss Robson, Susan almost fled, and only the fact that she would look like a complete fool prevented her. Miss Robson rewarded her with an icy smile.

"Can I help you, Miss?"

Susan found her voice with difficulty.

"Yes, please. I'd like to see my grandfather—Sir Simon."

"Your *grandfather*?"

Miss Robson was familiar with all the Court offspring, who at one time or another had been brought to visit or had ventured in unescorted to petition Sir Simon for some favor. He was not known for being overly generous, but it was accepted by everybody in the family that if he decided to do something, for whatever whimsical reason, it would be a *fait accompli*. His grandchildren, therefore, had managed to extract from him from time to time extra allowance money, badly needed cricket bats, new riding bowlers, and more recently, items made impossible to obtain because of war restrictions. Miss Robson did not recognize this young girl as a relative she had dealt with in the past.

"Yes, my grandfather. I'm Susan St. Amour."

"Oh, Madame St. Amour's daughter!" The woman saw the light and looked interested. "I'm Miss Robson, Sir Simon's private secretary. You don't have an appointment."

"I'm sorry, no. I hoped I might see Grandfather for a few minutes, perhaps between his other appointments." Susan could not shake her nervousness. Miss Robson's austere manner did nothing to lessen it.

Miss Robson got up slowly revealing a well-corseted figure in a heavy old-fashioned, floor-length woolen dress. She admitted that she would investigate the possibility of Miss Susan's seeing Sir Simon, but there was a firm indication in her tone that she considered the case to be hopeless.

Susan waited, examining the surroundings as she did so; the fine oak paneling, the exquisite Turkey carpets, the huge paintings—all of which seemed to be snatches of long-forgotten battles in which horses and men were caught in horrible poses of impending agony and death.

Miss Robson came back quickly with the unexpected news that Sir Simon would receive Miss St. Amour for a very few minutes. He had another visitor arriving momentarily.

Susan went toward the partially open door, driven by a dream that had grown from vague longings to be accepted at Pride's Court as the favored granddaughter (supplanting Angela) to the present scheme of getting Angela to move out of the great house entirely, preferably to some other city. She walked uncertainly through the doorway to face the stern old man at the end of a long, polished board table.

"So you're Hannah's daughter!"

Though he was old and stooped, his eyes were still fiery, and he examined her in detail. He wore a beard, almost pure white, and as he hunched toward her, he reminded Susan of a hungry hawk about to swoop down upon some helpless prey. If ever she had wanted to retreat from a situation it was now.

"Shut the door, my dear."

Susan did so at once. He suggested gruffly that she remove the fur coat or she wouldn't feel the good of it when she went outdoors again. Then he told her to sit down near him.

"I don't hear as well as I used to."

So saying, he picked up an enormous cigar—it was two feet long and ridiculously thick—and proceeded to light it.

He chuckled.

"I hope you don't mind cigars? There are so few pleasures left to an old man. Making money, a glass of port, a cigar. My fool of a doctor told me I could only smoke three a day. So I had these perfectos specially rolled. They last four hours each."

"I've never seen a cigar like that! It's funny." And she laughed the tinkling, musical laugh most people found so enchanting.

Sir Simon responded to her laugh.

"You're a pretty thing."

"Thank you."

"But not as pretty as your mother. Now there was a beautiful woman! Entirely wasted on that blasted Frenchie!

That's the trouble with young women, they have no brains. Never had. And you're a Catholic, to boot!"

"Not any longer. I left the Church."

He perked up, puffing giddily to produce thick, perfumed smoke until the end of the table was hazy with it.

"Left the Church? I didn't know you heathens were allowed to do that. Ha ha. Very sensible of you. I think my son, Charles, told me you are engaged to one of the Mulqueen boys. That right?"

"Yes, David. We're to be married next June."

"Good family," Sir Simon allowed. "What did you want to see me about?"

"I thought you'd like to know that I received the diamond bracelet that Grandmother left me in her will. The lawyers sent it round yesterday. I plan to wear it at the Christmas ball."

She spoke too quickly, a little breathlessly, still not sure that her grandfather was pleased by her unexpected appearance.

"That's good. I knew Lydia had left something to you and your brother. She was always saddened by the fact that she didn't see Hannah's children. It was a great shame, Hannah running off like that. I don't think Lydia ever got over it."

"No, I imagine she didn't," Susan agreed. "I wish I could have visited her at Pride's Court. It's such a lovely house!"

"Humph. Yes, it is." He seemed slightly mollified by this admission. "Anybody who admires Pride's Court can't be all bad," had always been one of his maxims.

"I've never cared much for the old French houses, like ours," Susan ventured, sighing. "They're so dark and cramped. Not at all the kind of architecture you see on the Mountain."

"They'll never build houses like Pride's Court again," Sir Simon said. "But why did you really come to see me? Curiosity?"

"Oh, no, not at all! I'm not sure I should have come, Grandfather, but I felt somebody had to tell you, that somebody ought to *do* something."

He was instantly alert, she could see, even through the cigar smoke.

"Tell me? What should I know? Out with it!"

She had guessed correctly. He still liked to have his finger on the pulse of his relatives, his household, his empire. Age had heightened rather than lessened that drive.

"I'm worried about her, and that's the only reason I came here to talk to you. She doesn't seem to realize how this is compromising her."

"Who? Who are you talking about?"

"Angela."

She let the name sink in. She could see he was all attention now, every nerve at the ready—he was like a general about to receive some important dispatch.

"*Angela?*"

The truth was, he had wondered about Angela's behavior in the past two months. She seemed to be out all the time, not painting in the studio at Pride's Court that he had provided for her at great expense and trouble.

"I guess you know some of my mother's French relatives?"

"A few, yes. Geoffrey has been dealing with a fellow called Mathieu in the war supplies department."

"He's my cousin."

"I also recall a madman who tried to kill me years ago—the one who is the priest. But you wouldn't know about that. Before your time. If it hadn't been for Fort, I would have been shot to death in my own drawing room!"

Susan was instantly fascinated by this bit of family lore, but was wise enough to refrain from asking for details. Better to keep the conversation going along the lines she had planned. Inquiries about Uncle Marc's indiscretion could be made later. So she said, "Mathieu has a brother called Beau. Beau Dosquet. Mother took him to live with us so he could study music here in the city. He's one of the family, or at least he was until he went overseas as an entertainer. Now he's back, and he lives in a studio on Mountain Street. Angela met Beau at our house, and since she paints and he plays the piano they've grown very close. They spend every single day in his studio. Without a chaperone!"

Sir Simon stared at her. Then, as the significance of her words struck him, he turned dark red with anger. His granddaughter spending her days with a Frenchman, unchaperoned? It was diabolical!

"Are you sure about this? It isn't just gossip?"

"Oh, I'm sure, all right. They still visit our house—they like my mother. They chat about it all the time. And Mother doesn't see anything wrong with it, but I guess she thinks of them as children. Angela paints at the studio while Beau practices or composes. She cooks for him."

Sir Simon's mind reeled at these preposterous images. That Angela could bring herself to do such a thing appalled him. He'd always known painters and musicians were wicked, licentious, immoral. His family had laughed at him and said he was old-fashioned. But he had known from the time Angela had announced that she wanted to paint seriously that it was an evil turn of events. Women, decent women, did not belong in *that* world. It was despicable! His mind spluttered on and he faced his other granddaughter in a towering rage—a girl who, though half-French, seemed to have a great deal more common sense than Angela.

Susan saw that she had hit her target, but she was alarmed at the fury she saw in her grandfather's face. What if she caused the old man to have a heart attack? Perhaps she ought to have gone to Angela's father with the information. The trouble was, she had counted so much on using this lever to further her ends with Sir Simon. But she hadn't thought about his age or the possible state of his health.

"She'll have to stop seeing him!"

"Just telling her not to see Beau won't work. They're quite devoted, believe me. It's too bad," Susan added slyly, "that Angela didn't go away to painting school in Boston as she planned."

"I wouldn't allow it," Sir Simon confessed. "But *this* . . . this is far worse than any painting school!"

"People may begin to talk," Susan suggested.

"Do you think anybody knows . . . outside the family?"

Susan shrugged. "Honestly, I don't know. But you know how people are."

He did. He had an instant vision of throngs of gossipers clacking mercilessly about his beautiful granddaughter and the French scoundrel. He suddenly foresaw Angela as a poor marriage prospect in the right circles. He allowed his mind to dwell upon heredity; Venetia's mother, after all, had married three times. And she had divorced, a thing unheard of in the Court family. And despite the fact that Julia had married Twickenham, who was an earl, *his* reputation had stretched across the seven seas. No good could come of these degrading alliances; he had always said so. Charles had been a fool to let beauty overcome his good judgment. Sir Simon clamped his teeth upon his cigar and glared ferociously out the window.

"I'll give the matter some thought," he said after a short silence.

"I wish I hadn't brought you bad news, Grandfather, but I felt somebody ought to tell you."

"You did the right thing. Better to know the truth and deal with it, no matter how painful."

His mind was already feverishly tackling the problem. It was not a question of sending Angela to Boston (a solution that still made him shudder), but of getting rid of the damned Frenchman. Removing him from Montreal, that was the ticket! There was little likelihood that the boy had committed any crime, and if he was a Canadian citizen, he could hardly be deported, more's the pity. (Sir Simon's thoughts settled wistfully upon the old days when deportation to Australia or some other godforsaken place had been the obvious answer to many a serious family problem.) No, something more subtle, and legal, was called for here. If this Beau were a musician, if that were the great driving force of his life . . .

"Does the fellow study at McGill? Is he connected with the university in any way?" Sir Simon asked suddenly.

"I think so. The university chamber orchestra is going to perform some music he wrote."

"I suppose this . . . er *Beau*, as you call him, isn't exactly rich? I get the distinct impression that some branches of your family are not overly endowed with money."

"Aunt Justine gives him an allowance, I think. She owns a farm. I don't suppose he gets a lot of money."

"I see. Well, my dear, I'll give the matter my attention. Meanwhile, I wouldn't mention our visit to anybody."

Already he had an inchoate idea. Money, as usual, was the answer. Money, the great miracle-worker. There was comfort in knowing that almost any problem could be solved with money. Still, the whole thing must be done in a careful, roundabout way so that the situation was not made worse. He hoped that Susan would not turn out to be talkative, or connections might be made later by watchful people.

Miss Robson knocked and entered without waiting for Sir Simon's permission. His next visitor, she said firmly, was waiting. Would he be long? Sir Simon, thinking of Angela and visualizing himself enmeshed in yet another travesty of justice brought on by female stupidity, chilled Miss Robson with a look.

"I shall be a moment."

Miss Robson waved her hands in the smoky air with an expression of profound disapproval. Then she stalked out. Waiting until she had closed the door, Sir Simon butted his cigar deliberately, after which he walked Susan slowly out to the foyer. They parted on amicable terms, an unspoken pact of secrecy (which hinged partly on a promised invitation to Pride's Court during the Christmas season) between them.

Susan, dropping down in the cage elevator, felt she had accomplished a great deal in a single visit. It only took a bit of courage. Visions of a wedding at Pride's Court had already begun to fill her mind.

CHAPTER NINE

A bright moon hung like a round yellow ball over the half-frozen river. Its pale light, combined with a fresh fall of snow, gave the streets a curious, buoyant look, magically turning shabby alleys into fanciful cul-de-sacs usually found only in Dickensian prints. Even the old coach house seemed neatly folded in a soft, white shell that covered its urgent need for paint and new roof shingles.

Angela, carrying a wicker basket of food she had managed to filch from the pantry when Cook wasn't looking, opened the heavy double doors of the studio without bothering to knock. Her face stung with frost, but inside she glowed with the sense of anticipation she always felt at seeing Beau.

He was upstairs in the kitchen. When he heard the doors open he rushed down the rickety stairs to relieve her of the basket. He kissed her cold lips and twirled her wildly about before even helping her off with her heavy fur. Angela instantly knew something very important had happened.

"What is it, Beau? Something marvelous has happened. About your Fantasy? About another piece of music? They're going to perform more than one next week?"

"You'll never guess! We're going to celebrate! I bought a bottle of wine. What's in the basket? I'm starving."

"Never mind the basket, tell me your news. I can't wait to hear."

She caught his infectious happiness. Her own heart was thumping expectantly; she smiled, waiting.

"You remember Dr. Musgrave, the dean of the Music School? He called me in today. I thought he wanted to discuss the performance of my Fantasy—I even feared they might cancel it or some damned thing. But no. That wasn't it."

"What, then? Stop teasing."

"Somebody has put up a new scholarship—a year's study in London and actual classes with Sir Thomas Beecham! It's me. *I've* been awarded the scholarship. Can you believe it? Dr. Musgrave told me there was no question about who deserved it. Honestly, Angela, I can't believe my luck."

"Beau, that's wonderful! How exciting!"

She *was* excited. It was a fantastic piece of luck for Beau and a great honor. It would further his career, get him attention in London. Still, a cold, heavy lump was forming in her throat. Beau would be leaving.

"I'm so goddamned excited . . ." He broke off and went to the table where he usually worked on his scores but which now was cleared off. There was an open bottle of burgundy and two glasses. He poured wine for them. The room was warm. A Quebec heater glowed red-pink from a long-burning coal fire. "You *should* be excited, darling," Angela said, consciously stirring her voice to enthusiasm. The lump was growing larger and more solid. "When do you go? In the spring?"

She could hear the unfortunate tremor in her voice, the hint of panic and despair.

"No, that's one of the strings attached. Arrangements have already been made for classes to begin with Sir Thomas right after New Year's. And he's not to be trifled with. You know his reputation as an eccentric. But what luck, to actually work with him!"

"That's almost immediately!" she protested.

"Terribly soon. There's Christmas to be got over. I'll have to go out to the farm. Right after New Year's I've got to get a sailing out of Portland or Halifax."

"But you just got back."

"I have no ties. There was no reason to argue," Beau said, draining his glass and filling it again. "I know it seems soon to you, but we have a lifetime. We have music, and painting—everything!"

"Yes, we have everything. Here's to your scholarship, and London!" She raised the wineglass and produced a thin smile from someplace inside.

"Thank you, darling. It'll be your turn soon. Boston, or London, I hope, maybe even Paris."

Angela sipped at the glass of wine. She said tentatively, "You don't seem to care very much that we'll be separated again so soon. Doesn't it matter?"

"It matters." He was still riding the crest of his triumph, and had not yet detected the change in her mood, the lack of complete acceptance. "Everything about us matters to me, you know that perfectly well. But my music has to come first, particularly now. I'm only beginning. What a chance for a man in my position! If *you* get an opportunity to further your studies I expect you to take it. You *must*. I'd insist on it."

"Of course I'd take it," Angela said.

Her voice lacked conviction, but he wasn't listening. Angela herself realized as she said the words that she was lying. She had wanted to paint seriously for many years and she still did, but if it came to a choice between painting and Beau there would be no choice at all. She had given up the idea of going to Boston since Beau had returned, although she had neglected to tell him. The mere idea of leaving him filled her with nameless fears. He was her anchor, her substitute for a mother who had never really existed, a father who was preoccupied, a grandmother who had been well-meaning but too old to act as a mother, a grandfather who was a tyrant. Beau was everything, her *world*.

"Then don't look so sad. This is a merry occasion. I wish we had some music other than my own playing. A jig! A fiddler!"

He set his glass down, sensing at last her retreat. He tried to take her in his arms. Angela looked up at the familiar handsome face, thinner now that he was older, but with the same eyes with the same burning green intensity, the same sensual and self-indulgent mouth. For a moment she had a revelation of a future filled with pain and despair. Beau would always take what he wanted, do exactly as he pleased, driven by a terrible need to express his personal visions in creative form. Nothing would stop that. His need for acceptance by the world, to counteract his own family's rejection—his bastardy, as he called it— sharpened the hunger for recognition. She pushed him away, terrified at the vision.

"It's not time for *me* to dance a jig," Angela said harshly. "You only think of yourself, Beau, as you have done from the minute you were born. When you were overseas and didn't write, I tried to forget about you. When you came back I let you sweep me along because I loved you. But *you* . . ." She broke off, biting her lip to keep from crying.

"What in hell is the matter with you?" Beau cried angrily, "I tell you wonderful news, and you act as if this were a funeral." He had been so happy—it was to be one of those special nights, all celebration and love. Fellow artists, reveling in luck and their own passionate understanding. The scholarship was a golden fleece, couldn't she understand that? He had to get out of Montreal sometime, he couldn't stay here forever. He must expand his horizons, his experience. God knew he and Angela had discussed this a hundred times.

"You're going off and leaving me again without any thought for *me*. It's not the scholarship I'm talking about, you know that perfectly well. It's the fact that you can do this without caring about the fact that we'll be apart. You only think of yourself."

"That's not true." He grabbed her shoulders and began to shake her. "Not true!" he repeated stubbornly, shouting into her face. "Stop acting like a baby. What do you expect? Music is my life. This is my first great chance. Do you think I'd turn it down?"

She yanked herself out of his grip.

"Take me with you, then."

"Take you with me?" He stood back, stunned. "You know I can't do that, Angela. I have to get myself set up over there. Find my way. See how the money goes. How it all goes. I can't be saddled with looking after a girl. For Christ's sake, what would we live on? I said scholarship, not inheritance."

"I'll get some money. From somebody. From Aunt Miel. From Aunt Sydney. From somebody. How do I know? I haven't thought about it, but I'll get it."

"You're crazy. It isn't just the money. You're too young. You've been sheltered all your life. How could you know what it's like to live without much money? You haven't the faintest idea what I'm talking about. I'm talking about one room, with a bathroom down the hall. If I'm lucky."

"I don't care."

"You'd care soon enough, when you had no money for cabs, or new boots, or furs, or hats. When you had no servants. Do you think this is *real*? Your coming over here with a basket of food? Do you honestly think that's the way people live?"

"Beau, you don't understand—"

"You're crazy!" Beau cried angrily. "Absolutely crazy!"

"You're the one who's crazy, Beau Dosquet! You're selfish and cruel and childish. I don't want any part of you. Go to London and do whatever you like, and leave me alone. I'll find some other purpose in life than being a part-time convenience for you."

She snatched up her coat and pulled it on. Beau stood still, in a fury.

"You're going nowhere." He tried to take her arm.

"Get out of my way." She pushed his hand away and he grabbed her by the coat. She scratched at his face and he put his hand up to it, surprised. His hand was red with blood.

"I never want to see you again as long as I live!" she cried, and she fled into the cold street. He slammed the door shut after her. To hell with her. What did she know about love? A selfish, rich brat, a child, half-crazed as her mother had been. If Angela loved him, as she said, she would have been happy for him.

He picked up the bottle of wine and hurled it across the room. All the happiness had drained out of him.

Angela was ill. Dr. Brunston, given a vague story about her being out at night and not sufficiently clothed, diagnosed it as a kind of influenza. She must stay in bed. She must be given hot soups, kept warm and comfortable. But Angela could not eat. She could not sleep without a sedative. Her temperature fluctuated wildly. There were days when she remained silent and other days when she seemed to be hallucinating. After a week of this behavior, she was exhausted. Her gray eyes seemed suspended inside a moat of shadows. When Polly visited her, she was frankly puzzled. This was not like the influenza she saw at the hospital. Something much more serious was the matter with the girl, but what?

Sir Simon dimly suspected what the trouble was but

would say nothing. Angela would get over it. Puppy love. Thwarted temper, that was all. It had cost him a great deal of money to arrange for the scholarship, not only in terms of the fund but in other ways. To get it pushed through, and secretly, he had promised Dr. Musgrave a fabulous organ to be ordered from Germany in the spring. Then there had been pressure on his friend Lord Ponsonby-Knight, a close friend of Beecham's in London. (Ponsonby-Knight had owed Sir Simon a little favor from years past, and he had never called for payment. Now, at last, he had seen how he could use that old debt.) A promise had been extracted from Beecham to supervise classes at which the young Montreal musician would appear. It had all been a great deal of trouble, but it was worth it to know that the Frenchman was leaving right after New Year's. Angela would recover. These little dramatics were not to be taken too seriously. He could not, however, tell anybody, not even Charles, how the thing had come about. It wasn't safe to reveal secrets of that kind. The promise of the organ would keep Musgrave quiet. And that was the end of it.

By chance, Sir Simon had intercepted a letter from Beau to Angela. What a piece of luck. Angela had no idea the letter had ever existed. Telephone calls had been dealt with more easily. Servants who valued their jobs did as they were bid, and no questions asked.

Meanwhile, Christmas preparations were going forward at Pride's Court. Polly was no substitute for Lady Court, whose decorating flair was famous all over Montreal, but she was trying to do her best. Young Simon would be home any day, and Geoffrey's family would join Charles's and Fort's at Pride's Court. Young Simon had not been wounded. This was one of the few aspects of life that cheered Sir Simon's heart. Simon was a bit dull, but his grandfather was fond of the boy. It was cause for celebration that he was returning from France a whole man. Another heir to carry on the Court businesses, to build the Court fortunes. One must never lose sight of the importance of the males, even though a beautiful granddaughter like Angela could be a valuable asset . . . that is, she could be valuable when she gave up her ridiculous notions about painting and associating with undesirable people. Now, young Susan was a different sort altogether; a charming girl, marrying a Mulqueen, realizing the value of all this. A real throw-back, Sir Simon thought with some comfort, to both his own ancestors and Lydia's. Blood would tell in the end. He had always said so. It was a pity that Hannah had been seduced from her proper rank and station, but women were well-known to be weak-minded and silly. And then getting into business, thinking she could run a newspaper as well as a man. Blaming Sir Simon for things he could not control. That was the worst of it. His own daughter! But he must think of the positive side. Susan wanted to be a Court. He would encourage it. And Simon was coming home.

Angela, however, was still keeping to her room. When Polly or Charles came in to encourage her to get up for Christmas, she sulked. When Sir Simon came in and commanded it, she simply stared at him. When the maid, Addie, came in to run a bath or bring her tea, she flung herself about, making life difficult.

Late on a bleak December afternoon when blue winter night was already wiping out the last traces of a pale afternoon light, Angela lay staring at the wallpaper. She was counting the roses. She had counted them many times. She heard the creak of the opening door. It would be yet another visitor to beg her to get up, to offer another potion or another tray of tea and scones. The door closed Still she refused to look, waiting for the inevitable plea. A silence followed. Not Addie, then. The room was darkening quickly, it was time to turn on a lamp. Well, let Addie do it. But why didn't the girl speak up? Servants were so hopelessly stupid. She turned her head slowly, curious because nothing was happening; no voice, no rattle of china, no running water in the adjacent bathroom.

The room was uncommonly warm. She lay, as usual, with her covers down, her black hair spread out on the pillow around her pale face, all huge eyes now that she was ill. There was a figure coming toward her, a man . . . a man who was . . . she recognized with alarm and relief combined . . . a man who was Beau!

She sat up, whispering, "Beau! how did you get in here?"

Beau whispered too. "Easily. You showed me the way that day we came to the sitting room. I had to see you. You didn't answer my letter. Or my telephone calls."

"Letter?" She had been ill, unhappy, fearful for so

long now that she could not think clearly.

"I wrote to you."

"I didn't get it."

"I telephoned. You wouldn't talk to me."

"I didn't know. They didn't tell me."

They stared at each other, he standing, she half sitting up in the disordered bed.

"It isn't safe here, Beau—they'll be furious if they find you."

"I don't care. I had to see you. I'm going out to the farm soon. And then to London. I had to see you."

He was by the bed now, holding out his arms. As he came close, into the warmth and peculiar mixture of odors (medicine, the eau de cologne Addie insisted on wiping on Angela's face, the close, encircling, drugging smell of slept-in sheets), he saw her face in detail for the first time.

"Angela, what's the matter with you?" His voice was edged with pain.

"Don't ask, Beau. Please don't ask."

He flung himself upon the bed and held her, crushing his face against hers in an embrace that combined love and lust with a new hunger. She opened her mouth to him, unquestioningly. He began to undress. She went rigid suddenly.

"We can't, not here. Addie will come in. Anybody may come in . . . anybody."

He ignored her words, tearing at his shirt, his trousers, and hurling them to the floor. She sank back into the bed, frail and feverish, but giving him back the same passion he was thrusting upon her thin body. His urgency seemed to increase her fever. Beau had never taken her so violently, nor so deliciously, had never been so hard yet so tender. The danger was forgotten for a few minutes. They were both crying, and exhausted, when it was over.

"You'll take me with you, then? You've come to tell me you'll let me go with you? Beau, I can't bear to be left here alone. I'll get the money, darling, don't worry."

They clung together. But then he pushed her back upon the pillows and said, "No, I didn't come for that. I can't take you."

She could scarcely believe him.

"You came just for . . . *this?*" As if their passion were some ordinary need, like a good dinner.

"I couldn't stay away," Beau said simply.

"You came in here because you wanted me *that way*! Not because you love me at all. How could you?"

She began to cry. Beau got up from the bed and began to dress. He was, in bearing, like a very old man. Very, very tired.

"No, it isn't like that. I can't explain."

"Nobody can explain who's only an animal," Angela said fiercely, though she kept her voice to a whisper. "A *dog* can't explain."

"I came to say good-bye," Beau said, standing away from the bed.

"Yes, you did. I told you before never to come into my life again! I was a fool to think you'd ever change. I ought to have known. Once a selfish pig, always a selfish pig! That's all you are. Oh, you can pretend you have a great soul, and you produce beautiful music for the world to hear, but inside you're nothing but a selfish little man. A child who hasn't grown up. Greedy. You're an animal. Get out, get out, get out! I hope you get caught. I hope they thrash you. I hope they kill you!" And she collapsed crying into the sheets while Beau opened the door and walked out into the corridor to find his way to the street.

There are times when life takes on the appearance of a dream and dreams take on the appearance of life. Tangled in a black web of despair and shame, Angela remained in her room except for fitful excursions down the hall to the sitting room where Venetia's presence had seemed to be so strong.

She was a floating soul with such a frail hold on life that there were only sporadic flashes of human need. She ate little and grew thinner until the beautiful face was transformed from the essence of health and energy to that of a sleepwalker. At times she sat still, completely silent. At other times she read frantically—authors like Gustave Moreau and Guy Michaud whose subtle spinnings of despair and cynicism suited her present mood. She found, among the books in Sir Simon's library, translations of Swedenborg's philosophies. So for a time she wallowed in mysticism. Like the decadents at the turn of the century (though her reasons had nothing to do with either boredom or voluptuousness), she fostered a passion for dead beauties. They reminded her of her mother. She tried to contact that tortured soul whose spirit seemed still to be about Pride's Court. In the chill of the gray, unheated sitting room, she would commune with the dead air, trying with tense despair to fasten on some fleeting rapport with the shade of her unhappy mother. There she sensed her mother's profound gloom and saw through drawn gossamer blinds (in her mind's eye) the violent desires of sinful men. Sometimes she actually painted. No longer the stuff of fairytales, but grotesqueries (reminiscent of Venetia's vast, lewd tapestry). No bold princes came forth on virile horses in these new paintings, no princesses swayed mistily in pastel wimples while they awaited rescue from damp and musty castles. There were no castles; only jails. She heard no music but the muted drumbeat Beau had heard in that same sitting room long ago.

In the midst of Christmas preparations, Simon arrived home from England. He came by train, of course, since the St. Lawrence was closed to shipping. He looked pale but sound enough. There was to be a special family party for him on Christmas Eve, after the service at Christ Church. Angela got up and dressed in honor of the occasion but she stayed in a corner of the drawing room, saying nothing. Landry came to sit by her. He had always been her friend, and he took her hand now and held it while the fire blazed and the family talked and everybody drank eggnog. The smell of fir branches was heavy in the air. Young Simon stood before the fire, the center of attention. His grandfather asked him questions about the war. Simon replied easily enough, it seemed.

"By God, I envy you," Sir Simon was saying heartily. "Nothing like a good battle to get the spirits up. The Crimea was *my* turn, you know. Bloody mess, I'll admit, but some good bits of soldiering were done, just the same. Not all jokes, like Cardigan, and Lucan at Balaclava. Plenty of good solid stuff as well."

Fond memories washed through Sir Simon's mind so that he looked remarkably happy for a few moments.

"That gun in the corner, isn't that the one you carried?" Noel asked him, jollying the old man along. They all knew the stories. They'd all heard them dozens of times. But their grandfather loved to relive his battles. He had been a colonel. Had expected to be made a brigadier general, but somehow that hadn't come about.

Sir Simon looked at the gun collection fondly. There were only three kept on a rack in the drawing room. Guns, for the most part were kept in his library, in glass cases. But these three were special, each with a story attached to it. Sir Simon, with this bit of encouragement, walked over to the handgun and took it down from the wall. He handled it fondly, as one would a pet animal or a treasured piece of jewelry.

"Saved my life once," Sir Simon said. "It's a beauty. A bit heavy, but look at the workmanship." He described once again how he had had the gun made to order in London.

Noel took the gun from his grandfather and dutifully admired it. Sir Simon said, "Careful with it—it's not loaded, but I put some blanks in it just in case I wanted to try it out at the farm. To see if it still worked. Makes a hell of a noise if it goes off in a drawing room." He laughed.

Noel had consumed several eggnogs (two while his mother was out of the room) and was clumsy. He began to hold the gun at shoulder level. Sir Simon cautioned him again. Fortunately, the gun was aimed at the ceiling when it accidentally fired. The noise was deafening: as if a thunder bolt had struck the center of the room and lodged there.

Everyone jumped involuntarily, and Sir Simon swore, repeating that he had *told* Noel not to fire the damned thing off in the room. Noel was suitably sheepish. It was a few seconds before they began to realize, one by one, that Simon was cowering under a marble-topped table. He came out, presently, white-faced and trembling, and left the room, with his father, Geoffrey, following. In the silence that fell upon them, Polly spoke finally, a little apologetically, but firmly.

"It's a new war disease," Polly said to the family, none of whom seemed to grasp the meaning of Simon's behavior. "You wouldn't know about it, probably, but it's called shell shock. We had patients like that at the hospital. The noise brings it on, you see. It's a nervous condition." She paused before adding, "Nobody knows what to do about it."

For Sir Simon, this was the last straw. He faced Christmas Day grimly. Without Lady Court, with a granddaughter who seemed half mad and a grandson who was a nervous wreck, he found little to give him cheer. He drank a good deal of brandy. He had fleeting moments of faint satisfaction when he thought about sending Beau away. At least he had accomplished that much. Angela would recover. She was young. There were other fellows about, more suitable. She would get over the itch to paint. Young women were noted for entertaining strange fancies at times, and if he could get her married off to somebody of the right type, everything would straighten out. Simon's problem represented still another challenge. He would, as soon as possible, consult with the best doctors. He would see what could be done. One must never give up hope.

CHAPTER TEN

For Camille, the high point of December had been Marc's return. He had arrived in Montreal by rail on the eighteenth of the month, looking exhausted, older, but distinguished. The dark experiences of his widely assorted flock in the trenches were written on his face. Camille was spared from seeing this particular kind of pain and was enveloped in bliss, hanging onto his arm at every opportunity, constantly begging for stories about his part in the war.

After dinner on his first night at St. Denis Street, he offered to take Camille up to the old nursery after coffee and liqueurs. The visit, to this point, had been a general one. The family had talked about his work in France, about the rumors that he would get an advancement in the church, about Michel's passion for airplanes, about Susan's engagement and Armand's plans for the future. Honey had wanted a description of the troopship on which Marc had returned. She had wanted to know about the morale of the soldiers—grist for her newspaper mill. She meant to write an editorial about Marc and his return, using it as a focal point to tell about the fate of returning war veterans.

By ten-thirty, Marc was eager to be alone with Camille, to share with her the room that had always been so dear to them. "I thought I might sleep in one of the extra bedrooms off the nursery," Marc ventured. "Camille would find it comforting to have me on that floor."

"Of course, Marc, I thought of that. I put you in the old nanny's room we did over when Beau was living here. It's quite cozy. I had Annette light the fires and there's some brandy up there if you want something before you go to bed."

Marc took Camille's arm and they walked up the stairs to the fourth floor, holding hands tightly. Inside the main nursery room it was warm. There was only one lamp on, but Camille didn't need light, and Marc didn't want it. They took separate chairs rather shyly. Camille's face was expectant while Marc's was suffused with subdued passion and happiness at being home again.

"Was it really so terrible?" Camille asked softly.

"Worse than anything you've been told," Marc said, hearing the tremor in his own voice. "Nobody who was there will forget . . . but I don't want to think about the horrors now. I want to think about you and the future. Knowing you were safe in the nursery meant a great deal to me, Camille. That was one of the saving thoughts I carried about with me."

"I was lucky that Honey wanted me here. Imagine living again in this place. It made it easier to bear the loneliness. I'll always love this apartment more than any place in the world. Will you, Marc?"

"Yes. But you know, when I find out the bishop's plans for me, I'll probably be moving again. It's possible I'll be pastor of some large church. Whatever happens, I won't have any choice."

"Armand says they may make you a bishop some day. Because of what you did over there."

Marc laughed, but it had a self-deprecating sound.

"A bishop. That's possible. Even *I've* heard those rumors. Won't Uncle Eustache be pleased? Anyway, I only did what had to be done."

"Armand told us you'd done all kinds of extra missions and that you went right up to the front line sometimes to give the last rites, and even into No Man's Land. And that you saved more than one life by dragging some poor wounded soldier back to his own trenches. I've been so proud, Marc!"

"I did no more than many priests," Marc muttered.

"That's not true."

He'd taken risks, yes. Because he had felt so often that the best thing that could happen to him was to die. That was why he had been so fearless. That was why he'd been able to go into danger and give the kind of support that some of the soldiers so desperately needed. Not only had he not cared what happened to him, he had almost prayed, at times, for death to deliver him. It was a false kind of courage, not deserving of praise, he felt.

"Marc, do you realize I can dimly see you! My left eye has improved in the past year. I can see more distinct shadows. In bright sunlight things look gray instead of black and take on shapes. Even in this light, I can see your outline sitting in the chair."

"That's wonderful news, Camille. Why didn't you tell me sooner?"

"I was keeping it as a surprise."

"Have you been helping at the home? Is Honey still running it under Bishop Grise's auspices?"

"Yes, it's been a wonderful release for me, Marc. I go almost every weekday. There are so many things I can do, you know. One of them is to listen. Some of those poor women need a confidante as much as anything else."

"You were always a good listener."

"Was I, Marc?"

"Have you composed any poetry?"

"Some, yes. I'm saving that for later. What a happy Christmas this is going to be!"

"You're brave."

"No, I'm a coward. Without you, I'd have killed myself long ago. I can't describe to anybody, not even in my poems, what it's like inside this prison."

"Don't say that! Don't think such thoughts!"

He was deliberately postponing what he wanted to do most—to take her in his arms as he had dreamed of doing through the long nights and ugly days in France. Remembering her dependency, the way she leaned on him, how she trusted him, had kept him going.

He went to the table where Annette had set out a decanter of brandy and two thin glasses. His hand was unsteady as he poured, and he could feel the tension from Camille's erect body on the chair across the room. She was sitting upright, her folded hands twisting nervously together and her face tilted up as if to catch his movements, his sounds, and any bit of shadow that he might cast across the near-blankness of her vision. She had aged little. The pockmarks were less obvious around her eyes now and there was a single line down either side of her mouth, but the shape of her face remained amazingly uncorrupted by time.

"A nightcap," he said, handing her the brandy carefully, making sure that her long white fingers were safely around the glass before he released his own hold. Their fingers touched. A spark of electricity seemed to jump between them.

"Thank you." Her voice was a whisper.

"I think we deserve this to celebrate my homecoming," Marc said, trying to sound casual.

"Oh, yes!"

They drank in silence, the years, the visions of other nights and other places, consumed with the brandy. Camille was smiling faintly. She wore a floor-length black velvet gown with heavy-cuffed, bell seleeves because Honey had insisted they dress for dinner on Marc's first night home.

Marc sat down facing her, and they did not speak. The ticking of the clock on the bookshelf dominated the room. Outside, a wind had risen and was teasing the dormer windows. They were close, as close as minds can be, but physically they were ten feet—or ten light years—apart.

"Would you like another?" Marc asked. They had consumed rather a lot of champagne at dinner. He wondered if Camille were ever so slightly drunk. He saw that her hands were still twisting each other aimlessly in her lap whenever she set the glass down.

"Yes, I think I would."

"Haven't had too much champagne, have you?"

"Not enough," she said, trying to sound light-hearted.

"All right, then."

He took her glass, bending over her, wanting to touch the dark hair she had pulled back and tied with a ribbon at the nape of her neck. She looked, in this light, impossibly young and innocent. He straightened up with an effort and went to the table to pour out more brandy. He thought of his bishop's words when he had confessed: that this was his test and that he must bear it and at the same time resist. He wondered if getting drunk might not be the answer to tonight's problem, but when he saw Camille's trusting face, he knew that that was not possible.

The dark, buried passions began to stir again as he sat staring across the space at his sister. The brandy did not deaden but rather heightened the urgent cries of the flesh. He shifted uneasily on the chair. He saw Camille set down her empty glass with tender care and knew that she would come toward him now. He was helpless. He could not move, could not leap up and shrug off the long-sleeping urge or brusquely thrust her back into her appropriate role. She came to him surely and knelt on the carpet at his feet. He managed to put down his own half-empty glass before she put her arms around him and lay, warmly quivering, in his lap. He felt her cheek rubbing across him, her hands dreaming down his body. He could not pretend that he was passive. She knew better, innocent though she was. In the gray-shadowed world in which she lived, touch was her most important ally, and so her hands, running down the sides of his neck and across his chest, were highly educated.

He had learned the horrors of death, and she had learned the horrors of life, and they were both starving. The nursery closed about them with its old familiarity as she unfastened the top of her velvet gown and freed for him the pale breasts. Was it possible, he wondered, to feed and still fast? It was a night to test even that bizarre conception.

———

The St. Amour clan gathered at the farm to celebrate Christmas and Marc's return. Helene and Corbin had come down from Ottawa, Mathieu had brought his fiancée, Nora Richmond, and Beau had arrived alone but bearing a suitcaseful of gifts. He was leaving in early January for London; plans were now set for him to study with Ethel Smyth, the composer whose avant-garde works were being performed by the Beecham Symphony Orchestra under Sir Thomas Beecham. Honey and Armand brought Michel. Susan had bluntly refused to join the family. She was spending Christmas on the Mountain with David and the Mulqueens.

Marc had convinced Justine to patch up her long-standing quarrel with Nicolette. The war had made him sensitive to man's loneliness, his vulnerability, and his ultimate bleak end, and so he could not bear needless pain. If there was a possible solution, he was forced to try to find it. That was his personal commitment.

Justine gave in to his request, finally, after a consultation with Timothée.

"Perhaps they won't want to come," Justine had protested sullenly when Marc had first proposed the idea. "Nicolette still harbors as much ill feeling as I do."

"I disagree with you there. I think Luc and Nicolette want to come back to the farm as visitors. They'll be alone at Christmas if you don't invite them, Justine. It's a perfect opportunity to heal some of the wounds."

"Healing wounds that *she* made," Justine persisted.

"We all make mistakes," Marc said.

"Oh, really, Marc, don't be trite. Keep that for your pulpit," Justine said with an impatient gesture. But she was less harsh in her tone, and he sensed she was weakening.

"I'm sorry, Justine, I don't mean to sound as if I'm preaching. The truth is, I'm so convinced that the unhappiness in the world is so often of our own making that I want to reduce it if I can. There's no need for you to go on with this vendetta. Beau has survived. He's going to London soon and will be away for a long time. He needn't think about Nicolette or what she said. I'm sure he doesn't care much anymore. She behaved badly, but it was a long time ago."

"She may have damaged Beau," Justine said darkly. "He's a strange boy. Very driven. Very mysterious. Right now, he seems unhappy."

"Honey told me that's partly over a woman. It has nothing to do with Nicolette."

"My daughter is a cruel, stupid girl. I don't understand her and I don't care to try."

"She isn't that bad," Marc said, smiling a little at his sister's vehemence. Justine did not seem to change. He had noticed that even now, after marriage, she eyed Timothée with a lurking sense of lust. She was basically coarse, almost animalistic, but she covered it nicely with a sense of the devout. He had seen women like her often in his congregations. Her appetites were momunental, her patience minuscule. No doubt this had something to do with her dislike of her own daughter.

"All right, Marc. For you. Only for you. This is a special Christmas because you're back, and because the war is over. Beau is safe and I thank God for that."

"Justine, you never fail to amaze me."

She ignored that. Her ideas were expansive, though they were shallow. She felt she was behaving like a saint.

"You invite them, Marc."

"No, you must do that yourself. I'll carry a letter to them. I must go back into town before Christmas Day to shop and see the bishop. You write the letter, though. Otherwise, there's no hope of Nicolette's accepting. Luc will do whatever she wants, so you needn't worry about him."

"Oh, very well," Justine said crossly.

It was a triumph Marc badly needed. His ardor in performing good works always increased when his own weakness was most apparent to him. He was happier when he prepared to go back to the station for the city train, he planned to shop for some special wines and sweets to bring to the farm as his own Christmas gifts. For Camille he had an antique necklace he'd brought from France—a fine silver chain and tiny cross supposed to have been blessed by the Pope himself.

CHAPTER ELEVEN

With his usual impatience, Mathieu had set the wedding date for December twenty-seventh, and Justine arranged for the ceremony and the party following to be held at the farm. Uncle Eustache was deemed well enough to officiate, and Marc would assist. Only Nora seemed reluctant, but she did not voice this opinion.

It snowed a good deal over Christmas week, making travel difficult. At the same time, the countryside was still and white and incredibly silent.

By ten o'clock on the morning of the twenty-seventh, the white crepe bridal dress was spread carefully on the bed in one of the guest rooms. It had the latest butterfly sleeves, wide sweeps of silk emerging from the sides above the waist like half-formed wings. A veil of double tulle fastened to a circlet of rosebuds lay beside the gown; it was designed to fall exactly to the fingertips.

"Personally, I think the dress overwhelms you, Nora," Rose said gloomily. "There's too much of it."

Although the sun had now come out and was polishing up the snow fields and gardens, Rose considered it a gray day indeed. As maid of honor, she wore pink silk, and the color enhanced her peach-colored skin and complemented her auburn hair. Her eyes were miserable, however, and her mouth was pouting with unsatisfied desires. She did not look pretty despite the costume.

"Justine chose the dress," Nora said petulantly, referring to her future mother-in-law by her first name, a thing she wouldn't dare do to Justine's face.

"I know, and she obviously sees it on herself. That's different. Madame is a large woman and no doubt that style would suit her, but . . ."

"Oh, what's the use of talking? It's too late to change now," Nora said in a melancholy tone that would have been more suitable to an aristocrat stepping into the tumbril than to a bride. She had gone over her reasons for accepting Mathieu's proposal many times—security, a step up the social ladder, no more worries about jobs or living in servants' quarters. It all made sense. It was just that she had no feelings for Mathieu, unless you counted apprehension. Love, most certainly, did not enter into this bargain.

"You're pale," Rose said accusingly. "I'll have to pinch your cheeks to bring up the color."

It was true. Beneath the light tan Nora had managed to retain from the summer's sun, her face was bleached. Her lips were white and twitched with nerves, and her hands couldn't seem to fasten a button or tie a bow. She wore her blonde hair rolled into a topknot from which the veil would be suspended over her face, to be thrown back for the bridal kiss. A narrow shaft of sunlight from the bedroom window picked out the gentle hills and valleys of her slim body under the thin white chemise and flimsy knickers she wore.

Sounds of last-minute preparations came through the closed door. A group of village musicians were scraping through a tune-up.

"Are you ready to put on the dress?" Rose asked belligerently.

A knock at the door saved Nora from replying. Justine opened it without waiting and pointed out that the bride had exactly six minutes, and why was she still in her underwear?

"I'm sorry, Madame, I'll hurry," Nora said, her husky voice shaking. She was all nerves, she told Rose. Her eyes bore out that statement; they were abnormally large, as if she'd seen a ghost.

"Can you finish dressing her, Rose?" Justine asked. "I'll be back in a minute to see that you have the veil on correctly." Justine wore blue of a particularly startling shade that set off her dark skin but at the same time was too brilliant for so large a woman. She wore a broad-brimmed velvet hat bound with matching blue ribbons.

Rose said she could dress Nora and that they would be ready in less than five minutes. She spoke briskly, anxious to be rid of Madame Dosquet and have Nora to herself for these last precious moments.

"Nora," Rose said, after Justine had left them, "I'm

praying for you. How you will survive tonight is beyond me. Mathieu looks like a brute. Have you thought about that? To be with a man in bed?"

"Not much," Nora said, which was true. Any time the idea of lying in bed with Mathieu had come into her head she had resolutely thrust it away.

"He's huge. And rough. But don't say I didn't warn you. I tried, God only knows, but you wouldn't listen."

They had been over this ground before—an endless ritual of forebodings from Rose, terrible stories of wedding nights related to her by friends and old crones—but nothing had caused Nora to change her mind. Rose had hinted that if Mathieu were truly a beast, Nora could escape back to her rooms at Mellerstain. Rose would take Nora back.

"I think the strap on your chemise has come untied," Rose said. "Here, let me see."

Nora stood obediently while Rose's fingers reached for the ribboned strap and skimmed lightly over her bare shoulders.

"There, that's better," Rose said.

She picked up the wedding gown as if it weighed pounds and pounds, as if she couldn't bear to put it over Nora's head in that final act. Once she covered Nora's shoulders and breasts and let the gown fall into the place, Nora's body would be hidden from her. Afterwards, the next time (if there were a next time), it would no longer be the same body. Mathieu, that dark monster filled with nameless lusts, would have defiled it. But what if Nora *liked* Mathieu's passionate embraces? Rose shuddered with a new fear. She had assumed that Nora would reject her husband's advances. Why had she assumed that? Tonight, after the wedding ceremony, after the dancing, the drinking, the eating, it would be Mathieu who took Nora to bed, Mathieu who . . . she couldn't get past that. She felt ill. Tears welled up in her eyes and as Nora stood rigidly, she kissed the curve where the neck and shoulder were so deliciously molded together. Her tears fell on the soft, golden skin. Nora tensed.

"Stop it, Rose!" Even now her security, her dreams of social importance could be ruined. What if they were seen doing that?

Rose straightened up, sniffling, and lowered the gown

over Nora's head. Her eyes as she picked up the veil were misty.

When Justine returned a few minutes later to check on their progress, she said crisply that it was a good thing she was looking after all the details because obviously Rose was blind—the veil was absolutely off center and would not do at all. Justine adjusted it firmly. Nora did not protest and Rose sniffed in the background.

"Come along then, girls. Corbin is ready to take you to your place, Nora. You go on too, Rose, do be quick! Both of you act as if you were fifteen years old instead of thirty."

This shaft did not go unnoticed by Nora, but she was too much in despair to feel any resentment. Rose blew her nose into a linen handkerchief.

"Please don't cry yet," Justine said, exasperated with what she considered sentimental behavior totally inappropriate to such an occasion. "You can do that during the service, but we haven't begun yet. Nora's a lucky girl. Remember that."

Downstairs, the living room, dining room, the two sitting rooms, and the kitchen were all crowded with relatives and guests. When Nora took Corbin's arm at the foot of the stairs, the fiddlers struck up the wedding march and the solemn ritual churned into motion as it had done countless times before and would do countless times in the future. There was some security and comfort in that very familiarity.

Honey and Armand sought refuge in a corner of the kitchen. They were laughing and out of breath because it had been so long since they'd taken part in a square dance. It was stimulating after all these years to dance so vigorously, swinging about, going through the precise steps, feeling merry. In the large sitting room, cleared for the dance, the fiddlers were still sawing out a familiar dance tune. Several of them had been replaced when they'd drunk too much wine to be able to carry on. Nobody minded. They were all neighbors from nearby farms, or from St. Cloud.

Mathieu, thinking ahead to the day when he would run for a federal seat, perhaps in this riding, kept the voters in mind. One of the things he most admired about Nora was the fact that while she was refined enough for his own taste, she was essentially one of the people. Mayor Médéric Martin of Montreal had taught him the political value of having a wife like that.

Armand pushed back the curtain and looked outside. The snow was gleaming under a clear sky.

"Just look at that moon!" It hung low over the river, almost within reach.

"It reminds me of the night we met," Honey said.

"You *are* a romantic," Armand said indulgently, but obviously he didn't mind. She was as pretty as a young girl tonight, in the light-colored woolen gown with the deep frill around the bottom and the blue ribbons in her hair. Her smile was three-dimensional. He could have stepped into it.

"Is it so bad to be a romantic?" A slight edge crept into her voice in spite of a determined effort to stay calm. She remembered quite suddenly the voluptuousness of Velma and wondered for the thousandth time if Armand had been in love with Velma or if he had merely used her as a cure-all for his wayward desires.

"Not bad, no," Armand was saying, "but unrealistic. Romance doesn't remain when you apply reason. Or perhaps it's merely that I'm getting old. But let's not spoil this evening, *ma chérie*, by philosophizing. You're having fun at the wedding, I know. You look happy."

"It is fun. Justine has done a marvelous job with the arrangements. I wonder what Susan's wedding will be like. She's changed so much, I feel she's almost a stranger to me, and yet . . . what can I say? I did that to Mama. She never got over our elopement, you know."

"Now, darling, don't think about the past. We all do things we regret," Armand said, taking her hand. "It cost you a great deal to love me and to trust me as you did. I hope I've compensated for that in some ways, *chérie*."

"There was nothing else I could do," Honey said. "I had to run off with you or I would have pined away."

She gave him a twisted little smile and he kissed her fondly. She put her arms around his neck for a moment.

Then Armand said, "I don't remember much poetry, but there's a line that reminds me of you. '*Tu portes fièrement la honte d'être beau.*' 'You bear with pride the stigma of your beauty.' "

"Armand, what a lovely thing to say." Honey leaned back against him and said somewhat dreamily, "Do you think Mathieu is making a good choice in this marriage? It seems odd to me. He's such a difficult boy. Imagine spraining his ankle the day before his wedding!" She laughed. Mathieu's accidents constantly amused the family because they were usually ridiculous and he had never yet been seriously injured.

"If you collide with a streetcar you're lucky to get no more than a sprained ankle," Armand observed.

"He put an awful gash in the side of the sleigh," Honey agreed. "And the horse was cut on the shoulder. Just as well he didn't do it in summer with a car—it might have been worse. Do you think he'll stay in one piece until election time?"

"Certainly. Corbin has great hopes for the boy, you know. Speaking of Corbin—now, Honey, you must promise not to say a word about this to anybody, you must *promise*—but Corbin has heard a rumor—"

"Darling, I won't say a word. What is it?"

He almost whispered, "The Prime Minister is recommending me for a knighthood on the New Year's honors list."

"Armand, really? That's so exciting! And darling, you deserve it. Everybody says so. Without you, I think the armies would have starved."

"Now, that's silly, but thanks for your loyalty, *chérie*."

"I'm not the least bit biased," she said fondly.

"Remember, not a word to anybody. Let's get some more champagne."

"You've had quite enough." But she went with him happily to the dining room, filled with a great new pride in her husband.

As they pushed their way through the guests toward the table where the wine was being served, Armand spotted Gabriel d'Esterre. He nudged Honey and whispered conspiratorially, "There's your admirer, darling. Gabriel. And look who he has on his arm! The mysterious Rose. I've never seen Gabriel pay attention to any woman except you, Honey. What do you think it means?"

"I think it means he's polite. Rose has no beau."

But she glanced at them curiously. Truly, it wasn't like Gabriel.

* * *

Mathieu had consumed a great deal of wine. His relatives and friends pressed champagne upon him, slapping him on the back, making toasts, encouraging him to merriment on his wedding night. At one point he felt quite drunk and had to sit down in a corner, where he clapped his hands in time to the music (although he was consistently off the beat) and put his arm around Nora's waist. Nora brought him food and he ate it, his eyes a little wild as he watched her bend over him. Soon he would have his bride to himself, get her away from this crowd. He was sure she was a virgin, and although this might present problems at first, he was certain he could solve them. Eventually, having put aside his plate, he whispered to Nora, "Let's go now. I've had enough wine here. Let's slip away to the farmhouse and have a brandy, just the two of us."

Swallowing hard, Nora tried to speak. Nothing came out. Mathieu took her arm and began pulling her through the crowd to the hall where her new fur coat was hung. Mathieu's wedding gift to her had been a muskrat coat and hat. There was no turning back now, Nora realized as they put on their outdoor clothes for the walk down the road to the isolated farmhouse.

Justine had planned that they spend their wedding night alone in the house once occupied by Nicolette and Luc. Tomorrow the newlyweds would take the train to Montreal, and from there travel to Quebec City for a two-week honeymoon. (With her usual practical view of life, Justine had decided that Mathieu would be in no condition to drive anywhere after the long party and generous supply of wine.) Earlier in the evening Justine had dispatched a hired girl up to the smaller house to light fires and turn down the covers on the big pine bed.

"Join me in a brandy?" Mathieu asked once they were in the small sitting room. A good fire was burning, and he stirred it so that the sparks flew.

"No, really, I've had quite enough wine."

"Not much of a drinker, are you? Well, I'll have one myself then." His eyes were shining, he was smiling, and he didn't look particularly offended that she wouldn't join him.

Nora climbed the stairs, thinking that at least she could

undress before he came into the bedroom. She could not imagine actually taking off her clothes in front of Mathieu. Not with his dark, wild eyes on her. She lighted the candle by the bed and began to take off the wedding gown. Her nightdress was lying on the bed and she hurried into it in an impulsive, last-ditch attempt to postpone disaster. She would get under the covers, she thought, and perhaps Mathieu would have had so much wine he'd fall asleep. She had just accomplished this when she heard her husband's footsteps outside the bedroom door, and, when he opened it, saw his bulky shape swaying a little. He limped into the center of the room, favoring his sprained ankle, but he was smiling still. His eyes fastened on her.

"So there you are, Nora. Already in bed."

"The room is cold," she said defensively.

"So it is. I'll poke up the fire. I thought you were eager to find out what married life is all about."

"No, I'm not." Her voice was a mere whisper. "I'm tired."

Mathieu had reached that state sometimes produced by a combination of too much alcohol and prolonged sexual excitement—like a violin string stretched too tight and about to snap, he was one tingling nerve. Yet his mind was singularly clear.

"You can't be tired on your wedding night."

His laugh was coarse. Outside of Mathieu's breathing, the spitting of the fire, and the sound of his clothes being tossed upon the floor, the house was silent.

"I'm not tired. I've looked forward to this for a long time. Do you realize I've only slept with whores before?"

She could think of no suitable reply to that. She closed her eyes, as if to shut out what would happen next.

"Don't go to sleep yet, Nora, or you'll miss the best part. You must have talked to your girlfriends . . . heard jokes about this, haven't you? You must have wondered what it was like to have a man—well, haven't you, Nora?"

He was stripped to his trousers.

"No, certainly not. Women don't talk like that."

"Oh, come now, Nora, don't lie." Mathieu's voice had taken on a sly tone. "I've got something to show you. Something you've never seen before, I know. Now, don't be frightened!"

He was fumbling with his underwear now. She had

never seen a man in his underwear. Suddenly she wished she'd neglected to light the candle. Her face was warm with a deep blush. As he came toward the edge of the bed, he looked shaggy, his hair long and black, his hands, outstretched toward the sheet, excessively large, his shoulders uncommonly broad. She felt a shiver of fear. She recalled some of the warnings she'd heard from Rose: terrible acts only hinted at, but which sounded crude, even painful.

His chest, she saw, was covered with dark hair that appeared to grow down over his stomach. He had discarded his underwear, and he was naked. He was still smiling, his hands reaching out for her where she lay clutching the sheet.

"You see, Nora? *That's* what it's like! Eh? Don't you want to look? Oh, look, my darling bride. You're a virgin. I knew that. I was sure of it. Well, never mind, this is the secret of marriage. Plenty of it, isn't there? How do you like it?"

She gasped, catching her breath, biting her lip. Whatever it was she had expected a man to have, it was not this seemingly huge, dark protrusion. Why, it would be impossible, she thought crazily, for her to accommodate a thing like *that*. It would never go inside her without tearing her to pieces. What did women do? How could they bear this awful act?

He reached across the bed and pulled the sheet away, exposing her slim body in the satin nightgown. Though she hung on with her fists, the sheet gave way and she lost its pathetic bit of protection. The scuffle only seemed to amuse him. She could see his broad smile. She tried to keep her eyes on his face but they slid, unbidden, below his waist to where the hard, insistent piece of flesh had sprung up between Mathieu and her own body. She began to sob.

"Come on, Nora, for Christ's sake, don't be a fool. What do you expect? Marriage . . . this is it. This is why men get married. So they don't have to look for a whore every time they get stiff. Be a good girl and take off your nightgown. You can see I've got to do something with this thing, can't you? You'll get used to it, you'll like it after a while. You'll be asking me for it."

"No, please. Not tonight."

She could not bring herself to take off the nightgown and show her nakedness to him. She closed her eyes, tears trickling out beneath her lids. But Mathieu was growing impatient.

"I've waited, haven't I? I've been a perfect gentleman all the time we've been engaged. Never laid a hand on you. Never tried to get inside your blouse, did I? Never even put a hand on your thigh, now did I? You must admit—"

Her sobs only increased.

"Come along, I can't wait all night! Let me see that pretty little body of yours, Nora. How often I've undressed you in my mind, how I've thought of feeling those little breasts of yours. Did you think I didn't notice them all these weeks? And as for what else you've got there . . . I want some of that too, my darling wife. Now, I haven't got much patience left, and neither has *he*."

He looked down at himself pointedly, with some pride. He knew from the sporadic forays he'd made into the whorehouses, and the one girl he'd seduced from a munitions plant who had not been a professional but merely stupid, that he had an extraordinary piece of equipment. The girls at the houses had marveled at it, at the size and the hardness and the length of time . . . he stopped thinking about that and fixed his mind on his bride.

"Take your nightie off, Nora."

He was crawling across the bed.

"*No*, please!"

"*No?*"

"I mean, not tonight. I'm so tired after the wedding, after all the excitement, I feel as if I did have too much wine after all, Mathieu. Not tonight, please, Mathieu."

"Are you going to take the nightgown off, or am I?" He made a grab for it, catching a bunch of the thin satin in one big hand. "Damn this ankle, it hurts. Nora, for Christ's sake don't be so difficult."

She didn't reply. Hearing no response, and seeing that by grasping the nightgown at the front he had pulled it up over her waist, Mathieu panted with need and frustration and the throb from his ankle. All his sensations mixed together so that, in a temporary rage, he ripped the gown from her. She lay there cowering against the mattress, her slim body revealed; the small but pointed breasts with their huge dark nipples, the flat white stomach, the secret patch between the legs she now pressed tightly together. He gave a cry and hurled himself upon her, his mouth greedily sucking on the provocative breasts, his hands thrusting her legs apart. She felt the awful wetness of his mouth, and then he lifted away slightly, rearing back so that he could find his way inside her with the huge, dark penis. With a well-aimed thrust, he drove himself in. She felt the uneven tearing of the flesh and then the impossible bloated thing was filling her. She tried to squirm out from beneath his weight, but she could not move. She was suffocating as Mathieu, any kindness vanished in the anger and desire that flooded him, put all his weight on her. As he pounded away at her thin body, seeking his own sweet release, she knew only pain and humiliation. After what seemed a millenium, his animal cry heralded his final triumph. She prayed that he would die. He rolled away from her, finally, panting heavily. The smell of stale wine hung over the bed as she lay in her slough of hatred. She was afraid to move in case he was still awake and would begin again, but at last, deciding that the snores were real, she got out of bed painfully and sought a towel. The splotches on the towel, after she had mopped at herself, were blood. She swore then that she would have her revenge; she remembered the soft, fluttering kisses of Rose Starkey, the way Rose stroked her and comforted her and stirred in her thighs such delicious, undulating waves of pleasure. For her, there would be no beckoning delights in the marriage bed. Not with *that* animal. She longed to put her cheek on Rose's plump bosom and feel those soft hands stroking away the fears and whetting the secret appetites that lurked in dark places. It was to Rose that she would turn, she thought weakly, as she found herself a second nightgown and climbed into bed once more. She lay as far away from Mathieu as possible, nursing the ache between her legs, and yearned for Rose's mouth. Her dreams, then, were of other nights in the attics of Mellerstain. She would go there again, if she survived the horrors of this honeymoon with Mathieu. Yes, she would go there again.

CHAPTER TWELVE

Mornings were the best time. Once Mathieu had left the house for City Hall and she could sit in the bright kitchen with her menus and her shopping lists, Nora would savor her new freedom. Her *own* house, her *own* housekeeping allowance, even a "general" to do the heavy work, and nobody to tell her what time to do things or how long she could spend over her morning tea. Although she had lived in the huge Court houses for many years, Nora liked the smallish house on Avenue Durocher well enough. It was modest, but Outremont was the right place to live; it was an area that was gradually creeping up the north slope of the Mountain with the spread of a prosperous middle-class French population. Justine had given Mathieu the house as a wedding present.

In the pale wintry sun of February, Nora could still look around her and feel astonished; it was two months since the wedding, but she still felt surprise when she gazed at the strawberry-covered oilcloth on the kitchen table or through the arch into the dining room with its golden oak suite. The parlor was especially nice—lace curtains and red upholstery. She built a fire in there every night and gave Mathieu his tea beside it. She had, in some ways, come a long way from the servants' quarters at Meller-stain.

Nora was the cook. She enjoyed shopping and learning to cook and bake new things, although Mathieu was an indifferent eater. He ate as he did everything—passionately, at breakneck speed. As long as there was plenty of food, he didn't notice what it was. Still, that part was the least of her problems. The price she paid for this house, this security, this escape from working for other people, began after tea. (Mathieu always ate dinner at noon with various businessmen and politicians, so Nora seldom served a dinner at night except on weekends.)

She poked at the fire, now, in the small parlor. The house was lighted by electricity, and she had chosen lamps with cream silk shades edged with red fringe to match the divan. There was a large leather Morris chair with a footrest in one corner; there Mathieu read his papers at night. As she was deciding that the blaze she had created was quite satisfactory, she heard the car crunching with its narrow tires through the packed snow of the driveway. Then, steeling herself, she walked to the front hall. Mathieu burst in, already throwing his hat on the hatrack, yanking off his coat, unwinding his scarf. She took his coat—the raccoon one he had bought at Christmas—and hung it up. He had his usual batch of papers. He was red in the face from running up the steps and from the cold nippy air as well.

"Aunt Miel's furious!" he cried, waving a copy of the *Montreal Star* at Nora. "Wait until you see this!"

She took the paper curiously. Her background, necessitating a constant silence at the outside perimeter of family affairs, had not prepared her for the volatile effusions of the St. Amours. When she had lived with the Courts as governess, she had been aware of quarrels, of problems, but they had been as distant to her as the problems of some remote African tribe. There would always be money for her wages. There would always be large Court houses to live in. That was enough; she was never emotionally involved. In the office, when she worked for Geoffrey and lived in Fort's house, it was much the same. She had looked at the families' lives much as she would at a play; they were interesting, but, in the end, had little to do with her life.

Now it was entirely different. The St. Amours (and, because of Honey's connection, the Courts as well) had suddenly become people instead of players. Mathieu was forever bringing home stories of family intrigue, or the political plots of Corbin and Armand, of the somewhat exotic problems of Beau and Angela. She did not find it easy to become involved, but Mathieu insisted on going on about everything that happened in his family, in his life. He was as bombastic in the house as he was outside it.

"Whatever's happened now?" Nora inquired. "Your tea is ready. Will you have it by the fire?"

"Yes, by the fire." He thumped the paper she held. "But read this first. What a slap in the face! That old devil never gives up—he's incredible!"

Nora took the paper and saw where Mathieu had folded it, revealing a story on the editorial page. The name on the story was Sir Simon's. She read it quickly, and grasped why Mathieu was excited.

"Do you see? That old fool, that vicious, diehard old Tory—but we'll get them yet! Next election they'll be out, and he can sweat about that. But it's really directed at Aunt Miel, that's why she's so furious. I telephoned her at the paper as soon as. I read it."

When Sir Robert Borden, Prime Minister of Canada, had submitted recommendations for the New Year honors list, Armand St. Amour's name had been included. Armand was to be knighted for his contribution to the key railroad supply lines behind the Allied armies during the war. He was one of the few French Canadians to be so distinguished. Armand and Honey had already begun to make plans for the journey to London in the spring for the investiture. ("Just imagine," Honey had said when they got the news, "You'll be *Sir* Armand! Darling, I think it's wonderful. You deserve it." And Armand had joked a little, hiding his pride: "Well, you'll be Lady St. Amour, *cherie*. Don't forget that part.")

Sir Simon was writing in the *Star* about the devaluation of English titles. They were, he said in the article, worth less and less when they were given out to "nobodies" who had contributed nothing to the country but a few miles of track. Were knights created at the opening of a mine? he inquired. Or were these honors to be reserved for men who had proven their bravery, their extraordinary courage, their undivided loyalty to the king. Titles were not cakes to be bought and sold. (He ignored the historical fact that various kings had raised great sums of money selling baronetcies over the centuries, and that prime ministers had put prices on English titles that depended upon urgent need in the exchequer rather than jousting in the lists.)

Sir Simon urged the federal government to put a stop to the annual honors list in Canada "unless some inviolable good taste is exercised in the choice of the nominees." It was a direct attack on his son-in-law. The family had expected Sir Simon to be angry about Armand's knighthood, but they hadn't anticipated a public announcement of his scorn. Naturally, Mathieu explained to Nora, his Aunt Miel was livid with rage. Her father had deepened the rift between them.

"She suspects he's had a hand in separating Beau and Angela, too, but she doesn't know how," Mathieu went on. "He'll stop at nothing, she knows that. Look what he did about her own newspaper years ago. Had the building condemned so she had to stop publication and rebuild. There's no stopping the arrogant old bastard!"

"Really, Mathieu!"

"Oh, don't pretend you don't know words like that," Mathieu said, hurling himself into a chair by the fire. "I'll have my tea now. Is it hot? I nearly froze my hands driving home." He was rubbing his hands vigorously and holding them to the flames.

Mathieu crammed meat sandwiches in his mouth and swallowed great quantities of hot tea, meanwhile explaining and gesticulating all the time. Nora watched him, dreading the end of the evening, allowing herself to be drowned in his words as a kind of anesthetic to the coming confrontation in the bedroom.

"Robert Borden and his merry bandits will be out next election, don't you worry! The scandals have done him in as Prime Minister. The war has done him in. I'm going to run for Parliament in a riding west of Lachine, I found out today. There isn't a municipal election for two years, although I'll run for alderman when it happens. But I can't sit around waiting for that. Uncle Corbin is arranging something—a sure-fire seat for a good Liberal. With Uncle Armand's title, and Aunt Miel's newspaper, and Uncle Corbin's influence, I'll be a shoo-in."

He had forgotten about Sir Simon's diatribe now and was off on one of his own. On his way to being mayor of Montreal, he would serve as an alderman. Get himself known that way. Médéric Martin, the incumbent mayor, would be hard to beat. But anything was possible. All he needed was more public exposure. The election for the federal Parliament would help that, and he could take both positions. It had been done before..

When he had finished his tea, Nora took away the tea

things and left Claire, the "general," to wash up. She would gladly have remained in the kitchen herself, but that wasn't proper. Claire would soon get out of hand if Nora became too friendly. The alternative was the parlor and Mathieu. Tonight he had temporarily subsided into the Morris chair with some of his papers. Nora sat on the other side of the fire, embroidering a pillow case. She was conscious of the clock on the mantel, its hands reaching inevitably for nine o'clock. The routine was always the same. Unless she was obviously ill or Mathieu had been at some male gathering, he expected to make love every night.

At nine she rose from her chair.

"I think I'll go up now."

"I'll be up soon. Just a few more papers to read."

"I may be asleep," Nora said without hope.

"Don't worry, I can always wake you up."

He was right. Mathieu's retirement for the night was anything but subtle; a platoon of men trapped in a bog would have been less likely to attract attention. He flung himself up the stairs two at a time, switched on lights, switched off lights, and banged doors until at last he plunged into the bedroom, where he always turned on the lamp, which shone directly into her eyes. Next he threw his shoes across the carpet, where they were bound to land against the baseboard or a chest of drawers. As he tore off the remainder of his clothes, a new banging ensued—closet doors, various drawers, until at last he thumped (even in his bare feet Mathieu was noisy) to the bathroom next door. Here began a new series of noises and flashes of light; running water full out, the fierce cleaning of his teeth, spitting, gargling, the dropping of a medicine bottle, a curse, the flush of the water closet, fresh bangings of the door. Then the same heavy tread back to the bedroom, as if a gorilla had escaped from the zoo and gotten into the house by mistake. Finally the huge and blustering presence appeared again, casting a shadow across her line of vision as he stood by her side of the bed. Even then silence was at a premium, for he almost always boomed, "Here I am, Nora. I've been looking forward to this all day."

The possibility of remaining asleep throughout this sort of performance was as remote as the possibility of taking a nap in a boiler factory.

Nora resigned herself to the inevitable: Mathieu's heavy body thrust down upon her own, the fearful, quick, and driving sex with no tenderness, no love, no understanding. It was the price she paid for the slow, easy mornings, the new importance clerks paid to her when she shopped, the gowns Mathieu bought, the new coat he had promised her. She tried to remember all those things as she lay smothered and angry beneath his impossible weight. She also thought of Rose and her next visit to the room they had shared. She and Rose had tea every Friday evening while Mathieu went to his club. It was, at the moment, a small hold on sanity, but she had no idea how long her relationship with Rose could go on. Or even how long she *wanted* it to go on.

CHAPTER THIRTEEN

Early in January, Susan and David accepted their first invitation to dinner at Pride's Court. The evening was a success, partly due to Susan's charm and partly to Sir Simon's interest in a particular business deal. The Mulqueens, as one of their many business ventures, had manufactured fine carriages since 1875. During the war they had converted the small factory in order to produce primitive truck bodies for use by the army overseas. With the war over, the Mulqueens were unsure what to do with the plant. Sir Simon, ever alert to deals and mergers that might work to his advantage, had a proposition to put to young David Mulqueen.

Charles knew his father wanted to bring this matter up after dinner, and he had no objection. He had no serious objection, either, to his father's enthusiasm for Susan. After all, she was Honey's daughter, part of the family. He shared his father's profound disappointment in Angela. She was still moping about the house, wraithlike, seldom coming down to meals, painting weird things up in her apartment, seeing nobody, accepting no invitations. The doctor could do nothing for her. The family was at its collective wits' end. It was refreshing to find a girl like Susan, so cheerful, so inclined to do the right thing, so correct in her selection of a husband. You couldn't fault her choice of a Mulqueen.

Sir Simon, although he liked Geoffrey's children well enough, could not find in them the excitement, the glitter he felt was almost obligatory in a family of such prestige as the Courts. Poor young Simon was under treatment for his nerves, in and out of the hospital, sometimes able to assist his father in business but more often than not an invalid. Noel was still at school. Mildred was causing worry to everybody: neither elegant, witty, charming, nor pretty; how could they arrange a good marriage for her? (She was too like the Browns of Bootle, Sir Simon told himself darkly.) She was a constant thorn in Sir Simon's side. Even pressure on Paul Bell, a promotion at the bank, and the promise of a bright future had failed, so far, to elicit a proposal of marriage. Age, Sir Simon reflected gloomily, would not improve a girl like Mildred (she would not be a late bloomer, not a hope!), and she must be married off somehow while there was still a bit of youth about her. Mary and Geoffrey merely sat on their hands, doing nothing. It was up to him, as usual, to solve the problem. Now Susan, that was something different. Lively and pretty. Doing all the right things under her own steam—including wresting herself from the grasp of the Papists. Clever, that was Susan. She might be half French (a thought he tried to drown whenever he could), but she had style. Moreover, she admired everything about Pride's Court: the architecture, the gardens, the antiques, the paintings, the food, the entire way of life. Who could resist such enthusiasm?

After that first dinner, the men retired to the library for conversation and brandy. (Polly and Susan took coffee in the drawing room, where Polly described life at the hospital and invited Susan to become a volunteer worker. Susan, seeing instantly the advantage of having Polly on her side, agreed quickly to give her time.)

Sir Simon lost no time in coming to the point. "What are you people doing with the carriage works you own at Lachine? Not still making trucks, are you?" he asked.

David Mulqueen was startled at this turn in the conversation. The carriage works was a minor project as far as the family was concerned.

"As a matter of fact, sir, we don't know what to do. There's no market right now for carriages, or for trucks. The factory is at a standstill. Father is thinking of shutting it down."

"Carriages are dead," Sir Simon pronounced, as he began to fade from view behind a thick screen of cigar smoke. "A few farmers using democrats and buggies, that's about all. No money in that, I can tell you."

"Exactly what my father said," David agreed. "Frankly, we don't know which way to turn. It might be simpler to close up the shop and take the loss."

"I never close anything up and take a loss," Sir Simon said untruthfully. When he wished, he could overlook his few failures as unimportant side issues.

"Well," David began apologetically—and then, catching Charles's eye, he reached an instant understanding that the old man must be humored—"that's good management, I suppose."

"Foresight," Sir Simon said. "That's what you need in business today. You must see what's coming. Do you get my meaning? Look ahead. The automobile is the coming thing, mark my words."

"Aren't roads a problem?" David inquired politely. "There are so few places one can drive a car."

"Politicians will see the light soon. They *always* see the light if it's expedient before election. When they begin to realize that people want cars, roads will be built. The point is, who is going to make the cars, be ready for the market?"

"Are you going into the car-making business, then?" David asked.

"Absolutely. We have several plants we can turn to good use. We were making guns and munitions during the war, but now we'll make cars. We're getting out of farm machinery. Too much competition from the Americans. Let Massey-Harris fight International Harvester, not me."

"That sounds sensible. But why are you interested in our carriage works?" David wanted to know.

Sir Simon, relishing his captive audience, was delighted to explain his situation.

"I'll tell you my thinking. Right now Court Enterprises has a source of iron. Up at Herouxville, you know. Not a big producer, but good-quality stuff. We have railroads under our control to bring it out, and right now we're making rails and a few building products. On a small scale. What I want to do next is get hold of a steel mill. Steel. That's where the future lies. Cars and steel."

"I still don't see what that has to do——" David began.

Sir Simon cut him off. "I'll make cars in my factories. And that's where you come in. If you're interested, you go back to your brothers and your father and tell them I'm interested in a merger. I have the plants to put cars together. You people have the know-how for making bodies. I'll get a franchise from one of the American motor companies, and we're in business!"

As usual, Sir Simon oversimplified the case. But historically, he had every right to do so. Once he formed an idea, no matter how grandiose, it had a way of materializing. Charles allowed himself a chuckle.

"My father will want to discuss your proposition, I know," David said, with enthusiasm. "I'll talk to him right away and call you. I'd like to be part of that myself."

"What do you say, Charles?" Sir Simon asked.

"I agree, Papa. But you'll have to give some of the authority to Geoff. I'm swamped with the new ships, trying to coax along the production of two new luxury liners and half a dozen cargo vessels. Every ship we had deteriorated during the war. The troopships will have to be scrapped, as I told you. We can't run a first-class shipping line with what we have now. I'm doing my best."

"What I need is another son," Sir Simon said, thinking wistfully of young Simon, who was of little use; of Noel, who wasn't old enough; and of Landry, who was only interested in cabbages instead of kings. "And another brandy."

"Another brandy? I thought Dr. Brunston told you to stop drinking. And smoking."

"Never mind Brunston. I'll outlive him, and Dr. Hunter too. The old fools."

Charles shrugged. There was never any use arguing with the old man. He'd just get angry and then pour his own brandy with a little extra for good measure.

"Since you're about to become one of the family," Sir Simon went on expansively to David, "I'll give you a little tip, David. Get into oil. I'm investing heavily in the Middle East."

"You sure? Isn't that risky right now?"

"Risky? How? Look at Anglo-American. The sheiks are leasing for very little now, but later, things may change."

"Oil isn't making much for its investors at the moment," David said doubtfully.

"Where do you think the gasoline is coming from when we produce a thousand cars? And that's only the beginning."

"If we ever produce automobiles on a large scale, I guess you're right, but still . . ." David said.

"Don't forget, my boy, joy riding isn't the only use for motor vehicles. We used trucks during the war. If we'd had good roads over there, trucks would have been of *more* use. But they can be used on farms, you know, and for carrying goods where there *are* roads. I'm in railroads, but I have to be realistic."

"I hadn't thought of it like that," David admitted.

"Now, this newfangled airplane is a different thing. That's for nitwits. I see no future in that except for a few dilettantes who can afford to kill themselves as expensively as possible. I know the Royal Air Force played a small part in the war, we all know that, but in civilian life the airplane is a toy. A game for the idle rich, and nothing more. You won't see me in *that!*"

"Perhaps you're right, sir."

"Now, just a minute, Papa. I've talked to some chaps in aerodynamics who say planes can be made larger. Eventually, they'll be able to carry several passengers and fly long distances," Charles protested.

"Don't you believe it! Icarus all over again. Well, we won't singe *our* wings, Charles. Let somebody else do it. But not with Court money."

"Here in Canada, the weather is against flying," Charles admitted.

"There is no way to make the airplane profitable," Sir Simon pronounced. "And I don't propose to waste my time on them. But automobiles, that's different. At least they travel on the ground like the rest of us. There's some sense in cars."

When Angela read Sir Simon's explosion in the *Montreal Star* about the awarding of titles, her pride collapsed in a desperate need to see Beau again. She would have to see Aunt Miel. She knew Honey would be furious with Sir Simon, and she had formed an idea that this could be useful to her own plans. She had not been outside Pride's Court since Christmas, and the effort of dressing warmly, bundling herself into her furs and boots and getting down to the old city, was tremendous. But Aunt Miel was the one person who could help her.

Angela arrived near teatime, and Honey offered her a

sherry. She was horrified at the paleness, the shadowed look of the girl.

"My dear Angela, have you been so ill? Charles told me you were sulking about something, but I had no idea . . ." Honey felt guilty that she had not tried to see Angela, to find out what the trouble was.

"I didn't want to see anybody," Angela said quietly. "I suppose you know that Beau and I had a terrible fight. You must have seen him at Christmas. At the farm."

"Beau didn't say much," Honey admitted, "but he looked unhappy. Really, Angela, I had no idea the quarrel was so serious."

"I'm miserable, Aunt Miel. All this time I've tried to pretend it didn't matter to me. I was so angry with Beau. But now, I see that I'll have to give in to him. Apparently he isn't going to give in to me. I want to see him."

"I have no idea when he'll be home—" Honey began. But Angela cut her off.

"That isn't why I came. You'll be going to England when Uncle Armand is knighted, won't you? You're planning a trip, I'm sure. Probably taking some of the family, isn't that right?"

"Yes, in April."

"I want to go with you."

"Your grandfather would be outraged if you went with me, Angela," Honey said doubtfully. "You know we aren't speaking. He even ignored my presence at Mama's funeral. And now I'm furious with him over that editorial. But why am I continually surprised by what he does? He's done so many things." And she spread her hands in a hopeless gesture.

"That's exactly what I mean. What do you care if he's mad because I go with you?" Angela said.

"There is your father to consider. And Polly," Honey said. "I don't want the responsibility. I still manage to get along with Charles and Fort, although I don't see them often. But I don't want to antagonize—"

"Father and Polly wouldn't care that much. Anyway, we'd keep it a secret until the last moment," Angela said, begging now. "Please, Aunt Miel. That's what's the matter with me, don't you understand? I don't paint—not the way I used to—I don't go out, I don't eat, I don't *care*. Beau is my whole life . . ."

Honey was slightly shocked by Angela's intensity. She had never realized how wrapped up in each other these two had become. A friendship, yes: a crush, perhaps. But a great and burning love affair? She had never meant that to happen when she had introduced them.

"I can't do it," Honey said firmly. She was tempted, of course. It would infuriate Sir Simon if Honey chaperoned his favorite grandaughter to England for the ceremony. A ceremony he had made quite clear to the world *he* felt was a joke. But she had to think of Charles.

"Please, please, Aunt Miel. I'm begging you," Angela said, tears forming in her great gray eyes. "I *beg* of you."

"It's the rest of the family I'm thinking of," Honey said. "Certainly not my father."

"I'll kill myself if I don't get over there!" Angela said, grinding her teeth in a sudden, angry gesture. "Wait and see! I almost killed myself at Christmas."

"Angela, stop that talk right now! Beau will be back. You've only to be patient. He'll come back and it will all work out. Somehow." She tried to put conviction into her voice, but it was difficult. She thought of herself and Armand and the way life had gone for her when she had left the fold of the family and gone to strangers. And here was Angela, contemplating exactly the same thing. "I wouldn't have done it differently," Honey thought, gazing into the fire, "but I don't wish it on anyone else, either."

"I thought you of all people cared about me," Angela said, putting down her glass and standing up. "Nobody gives a damn about anything but family. Family. Family. Family. It's so insane. What about the people? Who cares what happens to *people*?"

"Please, Angela, don't leave the house when you're angry like this. Stay for tea. I've tried to explain why I can't take you along. You're upset now, but think about it. Beau will come back—probably in' the summer, or, at the latest, in the fall."

Angela walked out into the hall and began to put on her coat. Honey tried to persuade her to stay, but she would have none of it. She stamped off into the cold February night.

Left alone, Honey felt distraught. She wondered if she ought to telephone Charles or Polly and warn them. But this seemed such a betrayal of Angela that she could not bring herself to do it. She was sitting by the fire, undecided, when Susan came in. Honey looked up when Susan entered the drawing room and knew by her daughter's expression that they were going to have a scene. She felt incredibly exhausted. But Susan, seeing her mother's drooping shoulders and tired mouth, was not to be put off. She had come with a little speech. Now she intended to deliver it.

"I'd like to speak to you, Mother. Seriously."

"Couldn't it wait, Susan? I'm terribly tired tonight."

"Since you're *always* tired, I see no point in waiting," Susan said.

"Do I really sound like that?" Honey asked with mild surprise. "Always tired?"

"We're all used to it," Susan said candidly.

"Very well, dear, what is it you wish to talk about?"

Susan sat on the arm of a chair, swinging her leg and tossing back her short sleek hair with a gesture that had long since become habit.

"David and I have been seeing Grandfather. We had dinner at Pride's Court." I know you don't approve, Susan's eyes seemed to add defiantly, but that's the way things are.

Honey felt chilled. Although she and Susan were not close, she had expected a certain degree of loyalty from her own family. Her own feelings were not the only consideration—there was Denys. There was the open challenge to Armand's position by Sir Simon's public denunciation. True, Susan would be married in a few months and living away from home, and would of necessity be part of the English community. But family ties surely meant *something*?

"Susan, how could you?" Honey managed.

"I thought it better to tell you. I don't see why David and I should sneak around as if it were some crime," Susan went on defensively. "After all, the quarrels are between you and Grandfather."

"Not exactly," Honey said, her voice flat. "He publicly attacked your father."

"Oh, Mother, people attack each other in newspapers

every day. It's not the end of the world. Anyway, David is very much a part of that society and I want to be, too. I love Pride's Court. And I want to be friendly with Grandfather."

"I see."

"It's my *right*. It's my right to be welcome in that house, to be part of the family. Just because you threw it all away . . ." Susan broke off, letting the words trail off.

"Yes, I did throw it all away, if you want to describe it like that. I think it was worth it, to marry your father. I hope your marriage will be as happy, Susan."

"Oh, I imagine it will be," Susan said airily. "The point is, Mother, that I see no need for me to hide what I'm doing. I don't want to feel guilty just because I happen to visit my own grandfather."

"The wedding—"

"I don't know just how you and Grandfather are going to manage that," Susan said calmly, "but that's months away. I can't worry about that now."

For a few moments Honey could think of nothing to say. She stared at her daughter, wondering how the girl could be so callous. For if David and Susan were guests at Pride's Court, Sir Simon would most certainly expect to be at the wedding.

"What does your grandfather say about the wedding? Does he expect Armand to be his host, to receive him as a guest after this public attack?" she asked finally.

"Grandfather isn't worried. He says it will all work out somehow."

Ah, so that was it! Papa was behind this new treachery, and she might have expected just such a thing. How like him, to try to influence Susan because she, Honey, had influenced Angela. Honey had never intentionally enticed Angela, nor had she meant Beau and Angela to fall in love, but in all truth, she had taken the girl in and made her welcome. And why not? Angela had had little enough affection even when her mother had been alive. The house was a mausoleum. Susan was just selfish enough, just shallow enough to fall in with Sir Simon's plans. Honey was almost speechless with indignation.

"*He* isn't worried?" Honey managed. "Susan, don't you see how this suits Papa? You're . . . you're only a dupe as far as he's concerned. He knows I'll be angry, he knows it's the very thing to upset me. And you're aiding and abetting him."

"That's actually funny," Susan said, laughing. "If you only knew how wrong that is! I *want* to go to Pride's Court. Grandfather doesn't have to influence me in the least."

She realized how angry and bitter her mother would be if she knew who had sought the first interview.

"Anyway," Susan added, "I left the Church without any help from Grandfather. And I met David, and became engaged to him, without Grandfather. So you can't blame him for that."

"There is a great deal about this I don't understand," Honey said.

"I don't see why, Mother. I don't happen to feel comfortable with the French side of the family, that's all. Why do you have to make a mystery of it?"

"I can't forbid you to see your grandfather," Honey said, getting up to ring the bell for tea. "What would be the use? Do you want something to eat, Susan?"

"No thank you, I'm going out again."

Susan left and Honey sat staring at the carpet, a little stunned. She had thought about waiting for Armand, but now she felt the need for tea, for some familiar routine that would keep her occupied. Before the tray arrived she took out a decanter of brandy and poured herself a glass. Temporarily, she felt beaten and distraught. Her father's every move, it seemed, was meant to make her miserable, to make her pay for the one action he could never forgive: her elopement. But presently, her spirit strengthened a little and she felt a fresh surge of determination. She waited just long enough for Angela to return to Pride's Court. Then she rang the house and spoke to her niece.

"Angela? This is your Aunt Miel. I've changed my mind about our talk today. If you'd like to call again in a day or two, we'll begin making plans for the spring."

Only Sydney, of all the Court family members, seemed to object to Susan St. Amour's being frequently entertained at Pride's Court. With the instinct born of London's slums, she smelled in Susan an opportunist and an ingrained snob. Yet none of this would have bothered her if she had not foreseen that Susan would displace Angela in her grandfather's affections. Angela, who was so unworldly but who would not conform, was bound to suffer. Of that, Sydney was convinced. It was so like the stubborn, rigid old man to prefer a toady like Susan to a sensitive child who simply did not accept all the standards he set.

Angela was not like the rest of the Courts, in Sydney's opinion. The child's sense of values was different; she put a high price on creativity instead of on making money, on beautiful things instead of on bank accounts. She must be insecure, despite Sir Simon's position, having had such an odd mother and a background that had not provided much affection. Angela seemed a lonely person. Sydney knew that feeling very well. Angela ought to develop as an artist in order to give herself a feeling of inner worth. Sydney was far from a vocal supporter of women's rights, but she felt strongly that women needed protection, and protection to her meant inner security. Otherwise, a woman was always the pawn of some man, seeking to give herself a feeling of importance through another human being. None of this feeling was articulated, however. Sydney's identification with Angela was more one of emotion than of pure reason.

Over the years, Sydney had purposely stayed out of Court family arguments and emotional upheavals. She could never, by reason of her background, become deeply involved with property concerns and expanding empires. Consequently, when she raised the question one April night after dinner, Fort was astounded.

"Polly tells me that Susan is spending a great deal of time at Pride's Court. Did you know that?"

"So I gather." Fort laid down his newspaper and stared at his wife. She not only kept silent most of the time, she never indulged in family gossip. "I think Papa likes the idea of more young people about the place. Susan talks to him, pays attention to him. Angela is always off by herself, brooding or painting. He doesn't get much satisfaction out of that. Also, he likes David Mulqueen."

"I think he encourages the child in order to spite Honey."

"Well, I don't know," Fort said hesitantly. "It's possible, I guess."

"Honey must be furious. It will lead to more trouble."

"Papa is genuinely fond of Susan, I'm sure," Fort said defensively.

"And is *she* genuinely fond of *him*?" Sydney asked sarcastically.

"I believe so. You must remember, Sydney, that Susan had left the Church before she became so friendly with Papa. She also became involved with David on her own. Papa had nothing to do with any of that. If she's alienated from her French connections, that's not Papa's fault."

"Fortunately," Sydney said.

"What in hell . . . you can't blame the old man for *everything* that goes wrong. He and Honey seem to have irreconcilable differences, and I can understand why Honey is upset, but we ought to be fair."

"I wouldn't like to see Angela displaced," Sydney observed.

"What do you mean? For God's sake, Sydney, Charles will inherit Pride's Court as the oldest son. After him, Angela will have it. There's no doubt about Angela's place in the scheme of things, but whether she manages to get along with Papa is another matter entirely."

"Do you honestly believe that Susan and David's house will be ready for them by the time they're married? I drove past the other day, and I'd say they won't be able to move in for a year. The next obvious step is to take an apartment in Pride's Court."

"You may be right, but I don't see . . . Papa likes David, after all. We have business interests with the Mulqueens. He's keen on the marriage. You know how he is. I imagine he might think it a suitable punishment for Honey, if he kidnaps her daughter. After all, she did encourage Angela to see that Beau Dosquet, and that caused all kinds of problems." He felt on strange ground with Sydney, and was growing distinctly uncomfortable.

"And in the summer, Susan will be living at Drake House. Just wait and see," Sydney pursued.

"You don't go there much, so why do you care?"

It was an odd thing, but she *did* care. She felt strongly that Susan was mischievous, and at the same time Angela appeared so vulnerable. She didn't want Angela to be pushed out into a place where she was less secure than ever. The poor child was having a difficult enough time as it was.

"I may not know much about families like the Courts," Sydney said icily, "but I do know something about women like Susan."

"My dear Sydney," Fort said, allowing himself a smile that was distinctly superficial, "you don't know what you're talking about. In families like ours property isn't scattered about like a handful of seeds. It's all done according to precedent. If you think Papa would ever disinherit Charles to turn Pride's Court over to Susan . . ." His voice dropped off in a kind of hopeless attempt to explain the obvious.

"I didn't mean the property," Sydney said.

"Then what *do* you mean? Anyway, you needn't worry about the family. I'm here to do that."

He was standing now, having put down his paper. He was still well-built, though slightly heavier now with age. His beard was sprinkled with gray (many men had given up wearing beards, but Fort had not done so) but he was still a vital, attractive man with strong drives and opinions.

"*I'm* not worried," Sydney said coldly.

This was opening the wound slightly, almost against her will. But quarrels often began like that. She knew the subject might bring disaster in its wake, that words once said often tore open a carefully covered sore. Still, she went on.

"You're the one who is worried about *family*, Fort."

She had tossed the idea out. It hung in the air. She hadn't quite said all the terrible words but she had said enough. Also, it wasn't true that she failed to worry. She had been tormented all her life by the need to know who her father was. Her mother had never admitted to knowing. Her mother had never at any time referred to the situation in which Sydney had been conceived.

Yet having lived with her mother in Whitechapel, one of London's pestholes, in a tenement lodging house kept by a tough old woman who was at once grasping and pretentiously moral, Sydney knew only too well the unsavory possibilities. It was an area rank with poverty, disease, drunkenness, and crime.

As a small child she had been surrounded by the scum of London: incredible filth, hopelessly brutalized men and women who made a scant, day-to-day living by hawking live larks, hot baked potatoes, flypapers, whips, sponges, secondhand tea caddies, rat poison, fighting dogs, and used clothes of every description. She had known sewer-hunters who fetched up minute treasures of metal, jewelry, and even coins lost down the city drains, costermongers with barrow-loads of fruit and fish, street vendors who sold old knives, scissors, bootlaces, and leather breeches.

Her childhood friends had been emaciated waifs selling woven baskets bought in Spitalfields, and her nodding acquaintances crooked old women hustling bundles of twigs, live lobsters, and bits of coal dug from the mud of the Thames by four-year-old boys. She had known soot-covered dustmen, crippled crossing-sweepers, desperate sailors, and haggard coal-heavers. All trying to exist on a few pence a day. At night many of these people had slept by the dozen in doss houses or tenement flats riddled with lice and rats—three, four, six, a dozen to a bed. Bed? If you could call a handful of straw on a stone floor a bed, or a filthy bunch of rags, or a cot bought cheap from the defunct smallpox isolation hospital a *bed*. Their only pleasure had been quick, unthinking, undiscriminating sex and cheap gin. They had been a brawling, ignorant, savage bunch, some of them half crazy, all of them half starved.

How well she realized that in the one obscene moment, under some unseeing canopy of rain or stars or sagging ceiling, when her mother had conceived, it might have been with one of *them*. It was more than likely. Her only hope lay in the possibility that some stranger, desperate perhaps for a sexual encounter, had wandered into Whitechapel from a distant realm. A gentleman, perhaps. Drunk, more than likely, but still a gentleman. And that this man, slightly educated, wearing clean clothes and speaking with the knowing tongue of the elite, had taken her mother up against a cold wall in one of the stench-ridden alleys off White's Row. That was the very best she could pray for.

Her mother had refused ever to speak of it. She had only admitted that once she had been a seamstress and that the job had ended with the birth of her daughter. Still, Sydney recalled, her mother's voice had been gentler than that of most of the women about her, and her face had had an aura of prettiness even though she'd been gray and thin and had worn a seldom-laundered gown and old shawl. There had been something different about her, almost erased with the grinding struggle to exist. She had had a single purpose and she had accomplished that: to obtain a job for Sydney, when the child was seven years old, mending clothes in the shop off Rosemary Lane . . .

The shop specialized in secondhand clothes of every kind, which were cleaned and mended before resale. Quite a respectable establishment. Sydney knew she was lucky. It was better than sifting mounds of dust at the yard, sorting out the rags, bones, bricks, and bits of metal to be sold later. That was the lot of many small children in the neighborhood—helping their elders with the strange harvest of the street-sweepers of London. For Sydney, life could have been far worse.

When she was twelve, a few months after her mother's terrible death in Millers Court at the hands of Jack the Ripper (that particular autumn, street women were terrified not of being raped or robbed as usual, but of having their throats cut or of being disemboweled), she was miraculously scooped up and taken away. A gentleman had come into the shop looking for a particular style of long velvet coat. The proprietor called for Sydney to bring the exact article from the back room where she had been mending it.

Sydney at twelve was a pale angel in a ragged green dress. She looked like a nymph escaped from some classic painting. Not even the dress, or her bare legs, could hide the fey look of her—the fathomless eyes, the oval face, the long, ash-blonde hair. The gentleman asked her age and she lied. She was fourteen, she said, sensing that twelve might frighten him. He was an artist, he told her, and she would make an admirable model for him and for some of his friends. Sydney walked out of the shop with him without a word. She took his hand. That was the only trusting thing she had ever done. They walked to a cab and he drove her off to the beginning of a new and convivial life. Not always perfect, but she had come from such degradation that it seemed almost heavenly to her. Still, she saw no need to speak. She seldom said anything even to that first, kind gentleman.

Through it all, the secret of her father's identity nagged her. She kept the fear buried deep under a blanket of more practical matters, but it lingered on. On the one hand she longed to know the truth, but, on the other, she was afraid . . .

Fort had risen from his chair now. He stared at her, caught up in her last remark. Aloud he said, "I don't know what you mean by my worrying." They had often fenced like this.

"You're worried about the children!" She spoke sharply now, exhausted from long pretense. "I've seen you watching Landry! Wondering whether that cleverness is brilliance or madness. Wondering if some lunatic genes are going to appear suddenly in your son! Do you think I don't know? Wondering if he's a potential alcoholic, or thief, or murderer. And the girls. What are *they*, with a grandmother who was a streetwalker? Do you think I don't know how you look at the children?"

He had known she watched him. He wanted to deny it, but that would have been stupid since they'd gone this far.

"What if I *am* worried about the children? Is that so unnatural?" he demanded.

"You're obsessed with it!"

"What if I am?"

There, he had admitted it. He had not meant to admit that, ever. Yet something in Sydney's emotional outburst had freed him from his own promises. He saw her flinch, saw her eyes turn to ice, saw her mouth settle in a straight, unforgiving line.

"You're still searching," she announced.

"Yes."

Although he had sworn to her that her past did not matter, he had never given up the search. It was his secret vice; it held him like the need for a drug. He'd spent a small fortune on the search in London, not only on investigators, but in his own time as well, time that was valuable. He had roamed Whitechapel and Spitalfields, looking for somebody who remembered the murders, the victims. Looking for the landlady who had sheltered Sydney's mother just before she had been killed. Finally he had found an investigator, Griggs, who had the connections necessary for a thorough search through that segment of London society. And recently Griggs had reported that he was very near a major discovery. Not only had he located Sydney's mother's landlady, but one of her oldest acquaintances as well.

"You've reneged," Sydney said. Her voice was flat.

"Yes, I have. I'm sorry. I couldn't help it."

His obsession with his children's ancestors might be typical of a Court, Sydney thought with cold anger. It might be human, too. But it was an open declaration of war just the same.

For ten days they barely spoke. Sydney had retreated into a remote area of herself that was completely unapproachable. She had gone numb. Fort waited for the letter from Griggs, every day a respite that brought some sense of relief, yet every day prolonging the hostilities between himself and his wife.

On a particularly warm June evening, Sydney sat in front of her dressing table unable to decide on what jewelry to wear down to dinner. She was tempted to sweep the boxes off the table to the floor in impotent rage at the stupidity of it all: having all this, and not wanting it, not caring, being afraid, hating her husband, not wanting to speak to her children. It was horrible. And it was all Fort's fault. If only he had kept his promise, if he had left well enough alone, she could have lived with her fears, keeping them suppressed as she had done for so many years, only letting them surface now and then. What a fool she had been to believe that Fort would or could stop himself from finding out the truth! Money gave power. She hated money. Hated this house. Hated the marriage. Hated everything.

She was not good with jewelry. She didn't wear it well and had no real interest in it, but Fort, like many men who have a great deal of money, liked to see her in gold and diamonds and pearls.

Fort came in as she picked up a pendant and stared at it as if she'd never seen it before. She set it down with a clatter, looking into the mirror to see his reflected face. The window beside the dressing table was open. A slight breeze came in, ruffling the edges of her blonde hair.

She knew instantly, from the look his eyes flashed to hers, that he had received the information he had been waiting for. Her hands clutched the edge of the dressing table; her back went rigid.

"Yes," he said to her unasked question. "I have something to tell you. Now, Sydney, don't be upset. Come over here and sit down on the sofa."

He took her arm. She wondered why he felt she needed to sit down on the sofa. He poured out a glass of sherry for her. She took it. Fort sat down on the other end of the sofa with a whiskey and soda.

"I think I'll tell you, rather than let you read the letter," Fort said. "I believe it will work out better that way because, you see, it's a strange story, and I think I can tell it . . . I think I understand it."

She took a mouthful of sherry and swallowed it quickly. "Is it . . . bad?"

"Not bad. I would put it another way. It's quite likely to make you cry. But it isn't bad. Not in the sense you mean."

"Tell me first," she said impatiently. "Tell me that my father isn't—wasn't—any of those things that I worry about. That *you* worry about."

"Not the things you've worried about," Fort said, and his eyes were not fearful, not cold, not angry. She thought, for a man's eyes, that they were oddly compassionate.

"Not *any* of them?" she persisted.

"Not any of them."

He began to reconstruct the story as Griggs had related it. But he knew that told in Griggs's poor English, with his brutal frankness, his factual approach, Sydney would not be able to bear it as easily as if he told it to her as he would a story to a child.

Fort was telling the story, but to Sydney it was unfolding in shattering reality. The scents and sounds and sights of London returned to her, fresh and strong, pushing up from her memory like weeds in a garden. She was back in the city again, could see the narrow dirty streets, the street-hawkers, the reeling drunks as night fell, the crowded lodging houses and tenements, the frightening thrust of the river. She saw her mother.

Her name had been Catherine Bateman, and at her death she was listed as the fifth victim of the killer Jack the Ripper. Nobody cared much who she had been—there were an estimated eighty thousand prostitutes on London streets at the time, and probably many thousands more—so one more streetwalker's death was of little concern.

But she had not always been a streetwalker. Twelve years before her death, Catherine had been a pretty, shy, brown-haired seamstress working in a shop owned by Angus Cameron. Cameron's, as it had been called, had made up clothing in cheap fabric for the great masses who had not been able to afford tailors. The girls had been largely confined to a dismal back room, stitching under the poor light of gaslamps. Carefully supervised and grossly underpaid, still they had known it was considered a step up to work at Cameron's . . .

Catherine was a good girl; they were all good girls. Occasionally, when the front of the shop was very busy, one of the girls from the back was pressed into service to help with customers. Catherine could read and write and do simple figures, so she was rather highly regarded.

She lived not far from the shop, off Rosemary Lane, sharing a tiny room with another seamstress like herself. The girls ate often from the street vendors' carts, and one fall day as she was paying for a meat pie she was followed by a male customer.

He was tall, with good shoulders and strong hands. His suit was rough and not too well-cut, but he was extraordinarily clean, an unusual trait around this part of the city. His country childhood (there had been milk, cream, cheese, and meat) had given him a sturdy constitution, and he didn't have the gray look of the city-born. He had the light, thick hair and the clear blue eyes of the Anglo-Saxon, a straight nose, and a mouth that could be kind or forbidding, depending upon the occasion. But it wasn't just his pleasant look that attracted Catherine, but something in his manner—"an air" was the way she later put it. They struck up a friendly conversation, and the man confided that although he was working a few hours a day in a chemist's shop, he was really an inventor.

She was entranced with this information, and when he suggested that they find a bench to sit upon by the river, she went with him. He confided that he had several inventions for the improvement of certain parts of steam engines that he was patenting. And when he had patented them he intended to go down to Manchester to try to sell them where the engines were made.

His name, he said, was Jamie Ackroyd, and he came from Leicester.

After this first meeting, they saw each other almost every day except when Jamie forgot because he was absorbed in some new drawing, some new aspect of an idea. He lived in a basement room that he somehow managed to keep clean, although the building itself was almost as filthy as every other building in the area. That was one of the things about Jamie that made Catherine love him—he seemed able to thread his way through the horrors of the slums without being touched. None of the ugliness appeared to wear off on him, or to dilute his belief in the importance of his own ambitions.

When Jamie disappeared for a few days, Catherine was patient. She knew he was working and living on no more than bread and tea. Several months went by in this way, and then one evening as they were walking through a wet mist, he told her he was ready to leave London. All his patents were paid for and legally safe. He would have to go out now and try to sell them to the men who made engines. That was when Catherine realized how precarious her happy world was. The stab was so painful that it was as real as a dagger thrust, though it was only words that Jamie had spoken. Jamie was hopeful that he would be back in London in a few weeks, or, at the most, months.

For Catherine, the parting was a small death. She received a few brief letters from Jamie—and then silence. By Christmas of that year she knew she was pregnant. She wrote to Jamie, to the last address she had for him, but there was no reply.

Cameron's kept her on until the baby came, a little girl she called Sydney, but afterwards she couldn't work in the daytime and leave the baby. She tried to find other work. Sometimes she found a job and sometimes she didn't. There were times when she stole bread, or an apple, just to keep alive. At first, she hoped Jamie would come back. But eventually, as the months turned into years, she realized that her dream had vanished. She was alone.

With this realization, she began to pick up men on the streets to earn a few pence for her room, for the child's food, and for the gin she needed so badly. She moved constantly, each time into a worse tenement. When Sydney was seven, Catherine found a job for her in Cameron's and with the extra money (the child did odd jobs, cleaning, running errands, all with the promise that some day she could be taught to sew) managed to get a room for the two of them in a lodging house run by a Mrs. Barker. It was better than most. Catherine was no longer recognizable as Catherine, of course. She was thin, her clothes were patched and ill-fitting, and she drank enough gin to make her look ten years more than her age. She was no longer pretty, but, in those streets, prostitutes were seldom pretty. It made little difference to the clientele.

In the autumn of 1888, a weird series of murders broke out in Whitechapel. The victims were always prostitutes and they were found with their throats cut, sometimes disemboweled, in some narrow, filthy alley. The murderer was dubbed Jack the Ripper; nobody knew who he was, but from descriptions given the police he was "something of a dandy."

The fear of death joined the fear of failure when the prostitutes went out picking up customers, but there was nothing to be done but take their chances.

On a cool October night, Catherine Bateman had left her lodging house as usual and ventured out to make a few pence to buy her nightly tot of gin. But she soon returned to Mrs. Barker's.

The woman was surprised at Catherine's excited behavior. She thought Catherine had been into the gin a bit early.

"I've got to speak to you," Catherine said quickly.

"Well, all right, but wot's the excitement?"

Mrs. Barker had looked out the door and seen a man waiting on the street, an exceptionally well-dressed man, he appeared to be. She closed the door.

"I told you not to bring 'em 'ome," Mrs. Barker said severely. "Nobody is to bring 'em 'ome. Wot you do on the street is *your* business, as long as you pay the rent. But don't bring 'em around 'ere."

"We'll be gone in a minute. What I wanted to know—was there a man looking for me tonight?" Catherine asked breathlessly. "Just after I picked him up—" and she nodded in the direction of the street—"I thought I saw a man I knew. Has anybody been here looking for me?"

"That's another thing. Yes, there *was* a man. I told you wot the rules are. But 'e was a gentleman, that one. Asked for you. Left 'is card. 'Ere it is. James R. Ackroyd. Well, a card! So I took it. But just the same . . ."

Catherine gave a little cry.

"He came looking for me?"

"I said so, didn't I?"

"I saw him, on the street," Catherine repeated, half to herself. "And he looked straight at me and didn't know me! Oh, I'm so ugly, so filthy, so low, Jamie didn't know who I was! Do you realize what that means?"

"Why *should* 'e know you? It beats me," Mrs. Barker observed. She was aware that her tea was getting cold, and that there was a man lingering outside her house. She had handed over the card to Catherine and now she saw no reason to go on about it. Better that the girl go off with the customer and away from Mrs. Barker's lodging.

"He's . . . he's Sydney's father," Catherine whispered.

Even Mrs. Barker was touched and curious. Imagine that! A real gentleman, being Sydney's father, and having a card as well.

"Tomorrow you can find 'im. Wot you need to do is stop drinking gin and clean yourself up," Mrs. Barker said sternly, sensing in the case a rare romantic touch. "Maybe you won't look so bad if you fix up. You can find 'im tomorrow. 'E's in London, judging by the address ain't 'e?"

"Do you think I could?" It was a faint hope.

"Look, send that man out there about 'is business. You get yourself fixed up and find your caller—Sydney's father. That's my advice to you. Don't go out again."

"I need the money," Catherine said. "But this is the last time. I swear it. Tomorrow, I'll buy a new shawl.

I'll tidy my hair and find Jamie. If he knows we have a daughter, perhaps . . . what do you think?"

"My tea's cold. You do as you like. I told you wot I think." With this, Mrs. Barker went into her room and closed the door.

It was the last time Mrs. Barker saw Catherine alive. She joined her customer in the street and walked off with him. The next morning, she was found in Millers Court with her throat cut. Her customer had been Jack the Ripper.

Fort had not quite finished, but Sydney began to weep. Thinking of her mother, and of her awful fate, and of how it might have been avoided if only . . . Fort had never seen Sydney break down and he tried to put his arms around her, but she drew away from him. She looked numb, her face having settled into a rather stupid expression as she wiped away the first tears. She felt relief, knowing about her father. The nightmares would surely disappear now that she knew the truth. Yet she looked at her husband with a hardening expression, gathering herself inwardly. The first flood of tears was over. She was becoming a cold, immobile block.

Fort poured a second sherry for her, but she refused it. Her eyes had changed. Looking at her, feeling puzzled and a little frightened, he saw that her eyes were dead. It was as if her spirit had retreated to some other place.

"What's the matter, darling? Aren't you delighted to hear about your father? To know at last that he was a respectable, perhaps even a brilliant man?"

"And what if he had turned out differently?" she asked in a flat voice. "What then?"

"But he didn't, don't you see? He didn't turn out to be bad at all. So it's wonderful."

She did not reply.

"There's more," Fort said, wanting to finish so they could stop talking about the problem once and for all. "Your father is alive."

If he had expected her to explode into happiness, he was gravely disappointed. All she said was, "Oh?"

"He's retired and living quite comfortably in Leicester. He has a little house and a garden."

"How nice."

"I thought, later, if you wanted to, we might visit. You

might try to see him. It would be good for the children, too, because we've never talked about . . . their grandparents on your side of the family."

"Nice for the children," she said, repeating his words without any inflection. "That's all you care about, isn't it?"

"Not exactly, Sydney. I was worried, I'll admit that. But I knew you thought about the thing, too. Worried about who your father was. I knew it would help if we settled it once and for all."

"Tell me, Fort, what would you have done if my father *had* turned out to be a lunatic or a thief? What then? Would you have sent me away? Would you have disowned the children?"

"Sydney, please listen to me, because you're not making any sense. I've found out that your father was a fine man. That your mother was once quite respectable, and that life seemed to destroy her. I thought you'd be delighted. And all I find is this peculiar attitude—as if I'd done something wrong . . ."

She turned away from him then. He had used her, had not kept his promise. He had risked their marriage to satisfy himself. There was no love, no concern, no pity in that. He had found out the truth, but only for himself.

"Sydney, please listen to me," Fort began, his voice cracking with strain. "I want you to be happy. I wanted tonight to be a celebration. I thought . . ."

She did not reply, but walked into the darkness of the bedroom and lay down upon the bed, staring at the window. From the sitting room, she heard Fort's voice. "Sydney, please. Will you please listen to me?" When she did not answer, the voice was followed by the clink of the decanter on the tray. Fort was pouring a glass of wine.

Fort held up the glass of wine and stared at it. *I am,* he thought, *going to get very, very drunk.*

And as he drank, hearing no sound from his wife in the other room, he went over and over the same recurring theme. He had lost Sydney once more, and somehow from triumph he had fallen into a terrible defeat. He would have to begin all over again somehow, to win her back. And he wondered if he had the strength or the ability to do that.

CHAPTER FOURTEEN

They had taken a suite at the Ritz. London, on the last day of April, 1919, was an exciting city. The long struggle and deprivations of the war were over; there was a resurgence of energy and confidence not only in the capital but in the whole country. The economy was on the upswing and the ties of Empire had never seemed stronger. The Ritz, dominating a share of Piccadilly, had been refurbished, almost returned its prewar elegance.

Armand and Honey were accompanied by Michel, Angela, Helene, and Corbin. Honey had been delighted, although a little surprised, that Michel had wished to come with them. His sole interest now was in flying machines, and social occasions in Montreal had bored him. Here, however, she soon discovered that things were different. An invitation, printed on a stiff card bearing a ducal crown was awaiting them on arrival; it was addressed to Michel, but included the entire St. Armour party.

Michel opened it casually in the sitting room the family shared while his mother watched curiously.

"You must have left some impression in London, darling," Honey ventured, "to have an envelope like that waiting for you."

"It's from Clarissa," Michel said, reading it. "I let her know we were coming. I hope you don't mind, Mother. Clarissa is an old friend. I met her in a canteen during the war."

"She must come from an important family," Honey said, recognizing the crown embossed upon the envelope.

"Yes, actually, her father's a duke. Duke of Burleigh. He's not a bad sort of fellow."

"I *am* impressed," Honey said, smiling. "Are you very friendly, then, you and Clarissa?"

"You could say we're quite friendly." Michel came across the carpet and kissed his mother on the cheek.

She looked at him, waiting to hear more. He was, she supposed, an attractive man, although she hadn't thought of him in exactly those terms before. He was tall and dark, with some of Armand's sparkle. The weariness he had displayed when he'd come back from the war, the slouch, the jaded approach to everything except flying, were all modified a little now. He had Armand's dark eyes. He wore a mustache. She tried to see him with an English girl called Clarissa, a duke's daughter, and found it not quite so outlandish as it might seem. After all, he was Sir Simon's grandson!

"And when is the invitation for?" Armand asked, taking an interest. "Have we missed an important ball? Are we late?" He was treating it lightly, his mind more on his own affairs than on those of his son.

Helene and Corbin had not yet disappeared into the bedroom they were to occupy and were listening intently. Michel had said the invitation included the entire party. Helene said quickly, "Tell us, Michel. Stop teasing. Are we in time?"

"Oh, yes, it's tomorrow night. A dinner and ball at Burleigh House. It's on Park Lane. Very impressive. One of the great houses, I believe. Clarissa took me there a few times. It's larger than Pride's Court. Acres of marble floors and stairs, tons of crystal chandeliers, platoons of stuffy servants in livery. You'll adore it, Aunt Helene. And we haven't missed it. Of course, you may not want to go . . ."

"Certainly we want to go!" Helene said quickly, without consulting Corbin. "Don't we, Honey?"

Honey smiled.

"It's entirely up to Michel. If you let your friend, Clarissa, know you were coming to London, I assume you want to see her?"

"Certainly." Michel laughed suddenly. "We'll all go, if you like." He looked across the room for Angela, but she had already gone into her bedroom and closed the door. He shrugged. It didn't matter to him whether Angela accompanied them or not. That was entirely her own affair.

Michel handed the invitation to his mother.

"Here, accept for all of us, will you, Mother? I'll call

Clarissa tonight and tell her we're coming, but I think you ought to accept formally for everybody, don't you?"

Honey took the card from him and placed it on one of the tables beside a vase of dark red roses. She wondered if the management had sent them or if Armand had thoughtfully ordered them ahead of time.

"They smell so beautiful," she said, sniffing the flowers appreciatively. "Don't worry, darling, I'll send a note to accept. It's terribly short notice. Helene, I think we'll have to send out our gowns for pressing right away, don't you? Heaven knows what the service is like. Since the war everything has gone downhill, people say, and it's only beginning to pick up again."

Helene agreed.

"Then I'm going to take a rest," Honey said. "I'm exhausted."

From the doorway of his own bedroom, Michel said, "Don't count on me for dinner tonight, Mother. If I can get hold of Clarissa on the telephone I'll be taking her out somewhere. She's bound to know where the newest spot is."

Burleigh House was much grander than any member of the St. Amour family had imagined. It was one of the great gray porticoed houses on Park Lane Circle, lavishly lighted this evening for some two hundred guests. The St. Amours entered the great hall, received first by a butler in maroon livery, and found it crowded with men in tails and overdressed women glittering with diamonds. An orchestra was playing in the distance. Platoons of footmen wove through the guests carrying trays loaded with champagne. Michel, Honey noticed, appeared to be unimpressed by the splendor, even a trifle bored. He introduced his family to the duke and duchess, whom he seemed to know quite well; the duke was handsomely gray with a deep, fluid voice and an excessively polite manner while the duchess was dowdy despite her diamonds—a tiara clamped firmly to badly cut hair, a heavy choker, and numberless bracelets and rings.

Clarissa, it turned out, was a figure from the pages of *Country Life*. She only lacked a horse. She was brown-haired and bony, her carriage erect, her handshake firm, her face plain. She shook hands with enthusiasm and firmness. From the first moment, it was obvious that she doted on Michel. When she gazed upon him—at eye level, for they were the same height—her face lighted up, her pale blue eyes sparkled, her smile widened. (She's in love with him, Honey thought with a pang; she wants Michel.)

At one point, while many of the guests were dancing in the second-floor ballroom, Michel and Clarissa found Honey by herself.

"How do you like Clarissa's little homestead, Mother?" Michel asked. He looked very attractive, if a little drunk. Clarissa was hanging on to his arm possessively.

"It's an impressive house," Honey said, looking at the marble staircase and the masses of crystal chandeliers.

"Ghastly, actually," Clarissa said cheerfully. "Frightfully cold in winter. Even tonight, with this crowd, it's hardly comfortable, would you say? We always preferred the country place, as children."

"Mother was brought up in a very large house," Michel said, "so she's pretty hard to impress."

"Nothing so vast as this," Honey demurred. She looked around again, past her son and his companion. "Half the peers in London must be here, Clarissa."

"Quite a few—anybody who happens to be in town," Clarissa said casually. "Farr does know a lot of people. He likes parties and dinners. Being a duke has its advantages. You can always find servants, get credit, and count on loads of acceptances to parties." And she laughed.

Honey looked puzzled.

"She calls her father Farr," Michel explained, "and her mother Marr. His name is Farrant. What does it mean, again, Clarissa? I always forget."

"It's a Teutonic name, actually, meaning 'the fair.' And Farr is certainly handsome, isn't he? Pity I didn't take after him more. The English are always coming up with simply diabolical names for their children—have you ever noticed?—So we've always retaliated by calling them Farr and Marr."

Honey asked, "What are your interests, Clarissa? I suppose you ride?"

"Yes, a lot. I have two horses out at Surrey Castle, not here, of course. I have a new interest, however." She looked up at Michel and seemed to tighten her grasp on his arm. "Flying. Michel has me terribly excited about flying. I'm going to try to talk Farr into investing in an airplane."

Honey knew then that her instincts had been correct. This was a serious affair. She saw that Michel, in his somewhat arrogant, casual way, returned the interest. Whether it was because the girl was from a titled family, and presumably rich, or whether he just liked plain, bony English girls, she had no idea. Well, she thought resignedly, it wouldn't be a bad match, except that she doubted very much if the girl would be Catholic.

Michel, reading her thoughts, said in a drawl, "I know what you're thinking, Mother darling, and you're perfectly right. Except for one thing. She *is* a Catholic. There *are* a few Catholic peers, you know, even in dear old England. And Lord Burleigh just happens to be one of them."

Clarissa said briskly, "That's a very poor way to tell your mother about us! Don't you think, Madame? You must excuse Michel—he's rather self-conscious about the whole thing. I expect he'll get over that presently."

Armand came up then and asked Honey if she'd care to go upstairs to dance. She accepted, deciding she would postpone telling Armand about Michel and Clarissa until later. After all, they hadn't officially announced anything. She felt nothing—not pain, or excitement, or disapproval, or approval. Michel would have to solve his own problems, if he wished to live in the fashionable world, the tight and almost impenetrable world of the English aristocracy. With this alliance there was no religious problem to solve, and that was some comfort, at least.

Angela had begged off the ball. "I've telephoned Beau, Aunt Miel. I can't wait to see him. He wants me to go over to his flat at teatime. We'll probably go out for dinner—that is, if we make up our quarrel. If we don't fight."

Angela was tense, but her eyes were shining, Honey noticed. She had changed her clothes several times in the late afternoon, asking Honey's approval each time. Each time she decided that the outfit wasn't right. "I want to look my best, Aunt Miel."

"Are you walking, or taking a cab?" Honey asked.

"Beau says it's only a ten-minute walk from the hotel. He lives on Half Moon Street, just off Piccadilly."

"Then if it isn't dark, you can easily walk. What time are you setting out?"

"About five."

Honey kissed her cheek. "Good luck, darling. I know this is difficult for you, but I hope it's a success."

The afternoon had sunk into gloom, as it so often does in London. Gray skies threatened to produce a serious downpour so Angela set off carrying a big black umbrella. She found Half Moon Street without any trouble. Beau had rented the street floor of the house, and, with a pounding heart, she stood waiting for an answer to her ring.

When Beau opened the door life stood still for a moment: she, standing in a slight drizzle, a sullen evening light coming down around her face; he, illuminated by a light behind him, tall and rather fierce in the doorway. She stared at him, not quite believing that after all this time she was seeing him in the flesh.

"Come in, come in." Beau's voice was trembling. His green eyes were staring into hers. She noticed that he was thinner. There was a hungry look about him. The look of a caged zoo animal.

She stepped inside, her mouth dry, her hands shaking as they folded the umbrella.

Beau took her coat from her and stood the umbrella in a stand by the door.

"Well, come in by the fire," he said. "You must feel chilled."

"I do feel cold." She huddled herself together, her arms crossed over her breast, her hands hidden in the sweater she wore. She wanted to hide her fear from Beau. She wanted to behave as if this were not the most important moment in the world to her. As if she had not sought him out.

The small drawing room was comfortably furnished with upholstered chairs and a sofa and hunting prints on the walls. A grand piano took up the entire bay window; it was out of scale, but obviously the pivot of the room. There was a tray on a table before the fire, holding a decanter of wine and two glasses.

"Here, let me . . ." Beau began to pour the red wine into a glass. He spilled some. "Damn!"

"Beau . . . I . . . don't know what you think of my

coming here . . ." she began. He thrust the wine at her and she took it.

"I need this," Beau said, drinking some wine.

"Perhaps I do, too."

"You're thin," he said.

"This place looks very comfortable."

"I manage. With my allowance from Mother, and my scholarship money. I don't need much. Once in a while I go out to dinner with some students. To the opera sometimes, and we get free tickets to concerts when Sir Thomas is appearing."

"It all seems very . . . *complete*," Angela said with an effort. "You don't need anything else, I can see that. Are you composing something exciting?"

"Yes, I'm working on an opera. Based on the story of Heloise and Abelard."

"What a dramatic idea!" Angela exclaimed. "Wasn't Abelard a religious teacher? I seem to remember that Heloise's uncle hired Abelard to tutor her and they fell in love."

"That's right. There was a child and they secretly married, but the uncle, who was actually a canon at Notre Dame, decided that Abelard intended to abandon Heloise. He had Abelard attacked by a band of ruffians and emasculated. Later Abelard became a monk and Heloise an abbess in a sisterhood."

"I remember thinking it was a tragic story. It ought to make a beautiful opera, Beau."

"What about you?" Beau asked pointedly. "Are you painting?"

"Not really."

"Drink up your wine. Let me refill your glass." His movements were uncertain, jerky.

Angela stared past his head, avoiding his eyes, at a painting of three hunting dogs with a dead pheasant. She shuddered.

"You look awfully thin," he said again. They were standing close together, separated by only a few inches. His eyes burned with nervous energy and his body was taut; he was like a storm cloud about to burst.

"And what about your music?" Angela asked desperately. "Are you writing beautiful music? Is the opera going well?

Romantic music needs such poignant themes, needs inspiration. Are you finding it?"

Her mouth was dry. She sipped some wine, looking away from Beau, turning her body a little as if to reject him and yet not moving from the place where she stood.

"Goddamnit, I'm not writing any music at all!" Beau shouted angrily. "I sit down every day but nothing comes. I don't hear any *poignant themes*, as you put it. I hear nothing. Do you understand? Nothing."

"It's only temporary," she began, almost reaching out to him and then preventing herself at the last moment.

"What about your painting? Are you painting great pictures? Are they romantic, are they poignant?" His voice was tinged with sarcasm.

"No. I haven't painted anything worthwhile since Christmas. They're . . . horrible. My pictures are horrible."

They stared at each other.

"What's happening to us, Angela?" Beau said harshly. It was not really a question. Or, if it was, he didn't expect an answer from the woman standing so close.

"We've broken the rules," Angela said.

"For us there *are* no rules." Beau snatched her glass and hurled it, with his own, at the hearth. The glasses shattered in the silence, slowly staining the tiles red.

Beau seized her then and without thinking she put her arms around his neck, felt the warmth of his flesh, ran her hands down his back and strained his body to her own. Beau pressed his face so hard against hers that their cheekbones crushed painfully. Their mouths were ravenous, their eyes half glazed, their bodies flushed with need. She felt him hardening against her thigh. They broke apart and began to tear off their clothes. They fell on the carpet by the fire.

Afterwards, dressed again, and sitting on the floor laughing at the splintered glass, Beau said, "We'll have to talk, Angela. You can't go back. Not when Aunt Miel goes. You know that, don't you?"

"I won't go back. She's leaving in only three weeks. Do you think I could face that?"

"I suppose your grandfather was furious when you came away with her? What happened?"

"We didn't tell him until the day before the sailing. I had already managed to get my bags out and over to St.

Denis Street. Aunt Miel called him to make the announcement and he almost ate up the telephone. He was livid."

"I wouldn't have thought Aunt Miel would go along with the scheme to bring you here," Beau said thoughtfully. "Oh, I know she and Sir Simon fight all the time, but still . . ."

"You haven't heard the latest in the feud," Angela said, smiling at him fondly. "First, Grandfather wrote a bitter piece for the *Montreal Star,* denouncing Canadian titles. It was obviously aimed at your Uncle Armand. Aunt Miel was furious. I begged her to bring me on this trip but she said no—you know how she still loves her brothers. Anyway, the next thing was, Susan told her mother she was seeing Grandfather socially and spending time at Pride's Court. Going absolutely against Aunt Miel's wishes! So Aunt Miel was so stricken, she decided to retaliate. That's why she brought me with her. Lucky for me!"

"Lucky for me, too," Beau said, kissing her and holding her again. "Oh, Angela, why do we waste so much time fighting? Darling, let's not fight anymore. Let's just get on with life, with music and painting, things that matter."

"Can I stay here with you, then?" Angela asked, when they had managed to sit up again. "It looks as if you need a housekeeper. Do you always keep such a messy hearth?"

"Not unless I throw my wine glasses in the fire. But you can't keep house, Angela—you're quite useless. We'll have to find money for a 'general' to come in and clean. After a month, I won't be living in this house, anyway."

"What? Where are you going?"

"I've got the loan of an old house in Devon. A musician friend owns it and said I could have it until September. He'll be in Paris, so it won't cost me anything. Except for food and some cleaning help, and fuel."

"Sounds lovely. I could paint there. But I don't have any money, darling."

"You'll have to get some someplace. I haven't much either. The scholarship pays my way as far as rent and lessons go, but there's not much left over. Mother sends me a small allowance, but there's hardly enough for two. Especially since you aren't much of a cook or housekeeper."

"How do you know?" She looked sullen.

"Oh, come on, Angela, how *could* you be?"

"I can learn. I'm not stupid."

"All right, you can learn. Meanwhile, I think you should find a way to get some money. Didn't your grandmother leave you anything?"

"Of course, she left me quite a lot. At least a hundred thousand dollars and some property, but I can't get it until I'm twenty-five."

Beau groaned.

"That's almost four years. That's no help at all. We can't ask Aunt Miel, do you think? She's liable to be quite shocked if we announce we're going to live together in a cottage in the country. She may be quite upset."

"Probably. She didn't count on this when she brought me. She just thought we'd make up, and then, when you came home again, everything would be perfect. She's a romantic, you know. Look what she did with her own life!"

Beau was frowning, obviously thinking hard.

"There must be somebody who could help you. God knows, your family has plenty of money. I suppose your father and Polly will be angry? They won't give you any allowance, will they?"

"I can't imagine it. Father will be almost as furious as Grandfather. Grandfather will do something terrible, like threaten to cut me off forever, and prevent me from ever setting foot in Pride's Court again. I can just hear him now. No use there. I need my clothes, too. I only brought enough for a month. Let me think a minute . . . I know! Aunt Sydney!"

"Aunt Sydney? I didn't realize you were friendly with her, Angela. Rather peculiar, I always thought."

Angela was thinking. She finally said, "Well, there's something more to Aunt Sydney than appears on the surface. Do you know that she helped me, that morning I came in after the ball? Everybody was looking for me and Aunt Sydney made up a story to protect me. I think she likes me. I believe I'll try Aunt Sydney. I just suspect she has some kind of hidden life, or at least, she has some loyalties that don't make sense. She really likes me, Beau. I feel it."

"All right, give that a try. *Somebody* has to get your clothes out and send them over here. I can't afford to dress you, Angela. Perhaps you can get a job illustrating for a publisher. I'll ask around and see if any of my friends know anybody in the publishing business. There must be a way."

Beau got up from the floor, and said, "I'll clean up this mess. By the way, what are we going to tell Aunt Miel?"

"Not the truth, not yet. We can't spoil their holiday and Uncle Armand's investiture. He's so thrilled, and so is she."

"What does she think you're doing tonight?" Beau shouted from the kitchen, where he was looking for a broom and dustpan with which to sweep up the broken glass. "Does she know you're with me?"

"Yes, she knows. But she trusts us. She thinks we're having a lovely talk, and perhaps a few kisses. I don't believe she has any idea about . . . about the way it is."

"Then you'll have to stay at the hotel until they leave," Beau said, bending over to sweep up the glass. "We owe her that much. You'll have to make your confession later on, nearer the end."

"What a waste! I want to stay here with you."

Beau had disappeared into the back of the house again. When he came back to wipe up the wine stains, Angela said, "Did you hear me, darling? I hate to go back to the hotel. What a waste of time."

"Yes, but it's the only way. Just for now, we'll have to sneak around, I'm afraid. Aunt Miel's been good to us. We can't upset her and spoil everything."

"I know."

"Where are they tonight?" Beau asked curiously. "At the theater?"

"No, Burleigh House. Guess what! Michel used to take out a duke's daughter, during the war. There was an engraved invitation waiting for everybody when we arrived. A ball and reception. Your Aunt Helene was beside herself —you know what a snob she is. But how about Michel, and his great and secret love—don't you think that's amusing?"

"I hope she's got money, that's all. Michel isn't about to work hard. All he wants to do is fly airplanes."

"I feel so happy myself, I can honestly say I hope Michel marries her, and she's rich, and he gets to design airplanes for the rest of his life. You see? That's what love does for a person."

"Are you hungry?"

"A little, but I'm not starving."

"Angela, come here. Before dinner, I think we should go upstairs. I haven't really looked at you yet. I haven't really had time to grasp that you're here, that we're together again. Can you wait for dinner?"

"It won't be hard to wait, not at all. Beau, darling, let's . . . let's go upstairs right now."

CHAPTER FIFTEEN

It was Susan's idea. It had come to her in the middle of the night, and no sooner had she conceived of it than she plotted to see her grandfather alone and put the plan into action.

They were sitting in Sir Simon's library before dinner. She had deliberately chosen a time when Charles and Polly were out, so there was little chance that they would be disturbed. Her grandfather sat at his desk, puffing contentedly on one of his huge cigars. Susan had a glass of sherry. Sir Simon was gazing at his latest acquisition, an extraordinary mantel clock with a bronze lion poised on top.

"It's German-made, more's the pity," he growled. "*That* goes against the thing, but I simply had to have it because of the lion. Magnificent, isn't he? Fire-gilded bronze and set on an ebony base. The mechanism is brass plate. It not only tells the hours, the quarter hours, and the phases of the moon, but the days of the week. Chimes every quarter hour, with a big chime on the hour. They have some foreign name for that, I can't remember what it is. But the *lion*. Look at him! Imagine a bloody Hun thinking up a lion like that! He's pure British, and his eyes and mouth work, do you see? There's a driving mechanism in his body. Magnificent, even if it *was* made by a German. It belongs to me now, so I count it English!"

When she told him what she wanted, however, he shifted his interest sharply from the clock to his granddaughter.

"In three weeks?" he bellowed, startled for once by the sheer aggressiveness of a member of his family. "A wedding as big as yours in three weeks? Can't be done."

"Short notice, I know, but think of the advantages."

"What advantages? Tell me that, Miss."

Susan was prepared. She smiled at him slowly, a gleam

in her eye. She knew how he liked to be teased a little, led on, provided there was some point at the end. She had learned very quickly how to handle Sir Simon.

"Don't you realize that everybody is away in England? Mother, Father, and Michel? So obviously if I had the wedding in May instead of June, as we planned, *none of them could attend.* A *fait accompli!* Furthermore, if Mother and Father aren't here, there would be no real need to invite my other French relatives. It wipes out all the real difficulties of the wedding's being held at Pride's Court."

Sir Simon looked at her with genuine admiration. She was an unusual girl. Brains, looks, taste. David Mulqueen was lucky indeed. She'd make him a perfect wife. It was as if all the splendid family traits had come together in her. And by God, she had guts!

"I see what you mean. You're quite right, of course. Frankly, my dear, I never could visualize myself attending the wedding if your mother was in charge. She doesn't want to see *me* and I don't want to see *her.* Most awkward. I simply cannot imagine myself addressing your father as *Sir* Armand, or *Sir* anything else. Now that Hannah has managed to spirit Angela away to England, expressly against my wishes, and no doubt to meet with that despicable Frenchman, I cannot bring myself . . ." he spluttered off, then picked up again with a restrained fury that turned his cheeks purple and made his beard tremble: "Sir Armand. Sir Armand, indeed!"

He became enraged anew. A sudden vision of the wedding, with Honey giving him vicious looks and the upstart Frenchman being addressed by his new title, almost overcame him as he spoke. Even his inflammatory article in the newspaper had failed to rid him of his bile on this subject.

Susan saw that he was about to digress into total fury, and this did not suit her purposes. He was frightening when he went into one of his anger fits, and she suspected he might have a heart attack one of these days. This was no time for Sir Simon to become ill. She needed him to engineer the wedding, to give his strength and prestige to her plan.

"If anybody in Montreal can arrange a big wedding on short notice, Grandfather, it's you," Susan pointed out. "I know you can accomplish anything, move the Mountain itself, if you want to."

He laughed at that, as at a private joke. There had been talk of a tunnel under the Mountain. But Susan wouldn't know about that. He had attempted to outwit the French Brigade, as he called his opposition, on the scheme.

"I'm not a magician," Sir Simon said, although he believed that he was as close to being one as a man using money and power could be.

"Of course you are, Grandfather. You're the most fabulous magician I've ever met, or ever will meet. You can make things happen. I've given this a lot of thought. You could order the invitations printed tomorrow and tell the printer we need them in two days. That will give guests three weeks' notice. I know it ought to be a month, but it can't be helped. As for the caterers, I think the owner of the Windsor is a friend of yours, isn't he? You could put some pressure on him, surely. My gown is already being made, and Polly never makes a fuss about clothes, so *she* won't care much. I can goad the bridesmaids—they're David's friends, really. That just leaves the twins. Aunt Sydney won't like it, but, in the end, she'll cooperate."

"You've caught me off guard. I'll have to think about this for a minute. About the invitations. How many guests are you and David planning to have?"

"Only three hundred, Grandfather."

"Hmmm. Miss Robson could handle that, I suppose. She's a tiger when she gets on to something that has to be done in record time. Gives her a purpose in life. We'll have them hand-delivered to save time."

"Miss Robson would adore it!" Susan said, laughing. "A challenge is good for everybody. Makes life more exciting, don't you think?"

"I can get my wine merchant to arrange for the champagne. But the garden, you'll have to talk to Jameson about the garden. What will be in bloom? Too early for most of the roses, isn't it? Peonies, perhaps. Irises. You'd better talk to Jameson about it. Where do you want the ceremony, by the fountain?"

"Yes, right in front of the fountain. You know that strip of straight path that leads up to it from the east formal garden? With the lily pond behind, it will be perfect. I'll talk to Jameson in the morning about the altar. He can have one of the carpenters make it up. Also, I believe I'll consult Bishop Gregory about a cloth for the altar. He loves that sort of thing. He'll be glad to give his opinion."

So, Sir Simon thought with gratification, she already had Bishop Gregory under her thumb. Clever girl. She didn't waste much time. Knew how to make friends with the right people.

"Susan, I must congratulate you. You appear to have thought of everything. Your solution to the er . . . *family* problems is better than anything I could have imagined. Perhaps my old brain isn't functioning as well as it used to. Now, you go right ahead. I'll take care of Miss Robson. And the champagne and the caterer, too. We'll need extra help, but the hotel may come to our rescue. Leave that to me."

He wrote some instructions to himself on the pad he kept on his desk. Then he butted his cigar.

"I'm hungry. Are we dining alone, my dear? Where is Polly?"

"Polly and Charles are at a hospital fund-raising dinner," Susan reminded him, "so I took it upon myself to order a simple dinner for the two of us. I'm far too excited to eat and you aren't supposed to have rich food. I'll tell Graves we're ready for dinner anytime." She rang the bell to summon the butler. It was as if she were mistress of Pride's Court instead of a part-time guest.

Sir Simon noticed, but did not mind. He had always admired strength and a determined nature. He rose from his desk and walked to the mantel where the new clock sat. He ran his finger lovingly over the lion's head. In some ways, he reflected, fate *had* been a little kind.

———

Everybody was there. Every influential English family in Montreal was represented, every aspect of government, every business of economic importance. The spacious gardens of Pride's Court were quilted with white, pink, and magenta peonies, irises so purple they were almost black, and a scattering of early roses. The sun shone accommodatingly and though the air was humid, there was a slight breeze on the Mountain that found its way through the grounds to the fountain. Susan was a storybook bride in white French lace and a delicate picture hat, after the fashion of those worn by Princess Eugenie in an earlier time. Her bridesmaids matched the flowers, in varying shades of bluish-pink and deep wine. The twins, Flora and Fenella, wore palest pink silk with rather old-fashioned long sleeves dripping little points over their long, thin fingers. They carried nosegays of wallflowers and baby's breath, and each silky blonde head was covered with a bonnet tied under the chin. They were refugees from a mid-Victorian stage. They behaved sedately, exquisitely, their small oval faces passive, their little bobbings and bowings almost anachronistic. The guests were fascinated by them. They never left each other's side, never lost their solemn expressions or their perfect dignity. They made all the right replies. Their manners were beyond criticism.

After the ceremony, while the guests washed down Beluga caviar with Dom Perignon, Sir Simon retired to his library and picked up the telephone. This was one message he did not intend to delegate. He wanted the pleasure of doing it himself. Today he was riding a small crest of triumph in what had seemed a sea of disasters. If he were lucky, he could get the cable off to London before Armand's investiture. The message was simple, but he had made himself wait until the marriage, as Susan had put it, was a *fait accompli*.

Susan and David married today. Pride's Court is in bloom.

He signed it Simon Court.

Let Hannah try to take *that* in her stride. She had kidnapped Angela (even now, despite his new affection for Susan, he felt a pang, thinking of the girl's exceptional beauty and potential) and she had shown him no mercy. He had thought that by getting the damned Frenchman out of the country he had won, but somehow Hannah had outwitted him. Or outmaneuvered him. He would never forgive her for that. So let her take this new blow as best she could. She had missed her only daughter's wedding. Let her weep over it. Let her suffer.

When he had put down the telephone, he glanced for just a moment at his new cloak. It was exactly four. He

walked through the house and out to the terrace overlooking the central formal gardens. His friends and as-
sociates had done well by him, despite the brief notice;
almost nobody of importance was missing. Sir Simon instructed a passing waiter to bring him whiskey. Champagne, he felt, was not called for under the circumstances.
While he surveyed the scene he brought out a cigar,
clipped it off, and lit it. The twins approached him, unbearably delicate, it seemed to him, in the midst of the
milling crowd and the music from the orchestra situated
in the far corner of the west garden.

"You two look like princesses," he said heartily—too
heartily, perhaps, since he never quite knew how to talk
to Flora and Fenella.

"Thank you, Grandfather," they said together, giving
him a small bob. "Why isn't cousin Angela here?"

"You know she went to England," Sir Simon said
gruffly. "She couldn't get back on time."

"We thought there was a letter on the mail tray; it had
a black border. Does that mean bad news, Grandfather?"
Flora asked innocently.

He was startled.

"There was no mail there—I just came past the hall
table myself." He felt a shiver of uneasiness.

Fenella and Flora exchanged grave looks.

"Perhaps we were wrong," Fenella said mildly.

"Yes," Flora agreed. "Perhaps we were."

"Now, see here, you two," Sir Simon said, not being
sure which sister he was looking at, "no jokes. This is a
pretty wedding, and I'm very happy. You don't want to
spoil it for an old man, do you?"

He took the whiskey from the offered tray and swallowed some gratefully. He needed it, but why two such
beautiful children should upset him, he couldn't explain
even to himself.

"No, Grandfather. I'm sorry," Flora said contritely.

"Isn't the bride lovely?" Sir Simon demanded of them.

"We don't like Susan much," they said together.

He was about to reprimand them, but they gave him
a tiny curtsey each and turned away, walking close but
not touching, as if an invisible wire held them together.
Sir Simon drank more whiskey. He found them distinctly
unnerving. He turned his attention to the success of the

wedding, to the brilliant sunshine of the afternoon, to the importance of his guests.

After the wedding supper, Susan changed into a suit for the drive to a country house that had been loaned to the young couple. The silver Rolls was waiting, a gift from the Mulqueens. Susan wore, Sir Simon saw with satisfaction, the diamond-and-emerald pin he had given her. It had belonged to Lydia. He had meant Angela to have it, but that was past now, done with.

———

The view from Angela's hotel room gave on Piccadilly. A weak noon sun spread pale rays through the heaviness of the room, over the ornate furniture and the rather dark patterned carpet. Honey had come in wearing a houserobe of crushed blue velvet. Her hair, still uncut, was molded into a chignon, but in spite of the color of her gown, the elegance of her hairstyle, she looked tired.

Angela said, "I'm sorry, Aunt Miel, I wanted to tell you later. I should have waited. I shouldn't have told you on the telephone."

"It doesn't matter now," Honey said. "Since I got the news about Susan's wedding, all our excitement about the investiture seems to have faded into insignificance."

"Beau and I didn't want to spoil Uncle Armand's day, or yours, in any way. So we planned to wait. But after you got that cable yesterday about Susan's wedding, I knew the damage had been done. I was so angry when you told me . . . Grandfather is just encouraging Susan out of spite. Because you brought me here to England."

"It doesn't do any good to be angry," Honey said wearily. "I've found that out. Susan has her own will, too, you know. But I'm sure Papa has been a strong influence in this whole arrangement. He'd feel it was some kind of retribution, certainly."

"I was so angry, Aunt Miel, that I sent him a cable."

"You did what?"

"I sent him a cable telling him that I was going to stay here and live with Beau. I knew it would enrage him, and I wanted to make him suffer. I suppose I ought to have told Father and Polly first, but it's always Grandfather who engineers things, and so . . ."

"Oh, Angela, I wish you hadn't done that," Honey said.

"He'll be furious. I wanted to punish him," Angela said, "because he deliberately made you unhappy."

"You should have waited. Sent a letter."

"I can just see him gloating when he sent that cable," Angela said, her gray eyes darkening with anger. "And Susan, doing that to you! Can you imagine how they must have rushed around, making all those arrangements?"

"Papa could manage it, all right," Honey said. "I've tried to imagine the wedding if Armand and I were there, as I most assuredly hoped we *would* be, and Papa being invited, and whether he would have come or not. He might have insulted Armand, made a scene. Perhaps . . ." Honey didn't finish the sentence. No matter what rationalization she made, she felt wounded at her daughter's betrayal. She would never forgive her father this last blow. Never.

"Susan is completely under Grandfather's spell," Angela mused, forgetting her own situation for the time being. "She's crazy about Pride's Court and everything it stands for."

"You are the black sheep, Angela, not wanting to be part of the English, not following Papa's wishes and marrying a nice, safe businessman, not adoring the house. He's disappointed in you, and I can understand that. First there was my elopement, then Venetia, and now you. I suppose it's natural that he'd take up Susan, who seems to be everything he wanted."

"Don't make excuses for him," Angela said crossly. "He is willful—and vengeful, too."

"Yes, he's all those things." And more, Honey added to herself, much more.

"But how did Susan get that way?" Angela went on. "I can't see how, being brought up by you and Uncle Armand . . ."

"I don't really know, except she doesn't like her *Frenchness*. That's the way she puts it. She doesn't like any of Armand's relatives. It's a throwback."

Angela's breakfast tray was still on one of the tables. Honey felt the coffeepot experimentally, to see if it were still hot enough to drink. Discovering that it was, she poured herself a cup. Angela refused, saying she wasn't thirsty.

"Putting the wedding aside, Angela," Honey began, taking a different tone, "am I to understand that you and Beau are planning to live together without being married?"

Angela went to the window and stared out at the busy street. Without Beau at her side, she felt nervous when confronted with this flat statement of the truth. She must face the inevitable arguments alone.

"That's right, Aunt Miel. Beau is borrowing a cottage down in Devon for a few months so he can work where it's quiet. Some musician friend of his owns it and happens to be going to Paris. It won't cost much to live there, apparently. Beau can write music and I can paint."

"It sounds idyllic," Honey said with a tinge of sarcasm in her voice, "but I don't think you realize how other people are going to see this. It will put you in a damaging position."

"I don't care what people say," Angela said stubbornly, but her voice did not sound quite as convincing as she had hoped. What Aunt Miel didn't realize was that she had no choice. She must stay with Beau, and Beau did not want to get married. Really, it was simple.

"Someday you may care a great deal," Honey said.

"I doubt it," Angela said. But would she? Would she regret this wild, impetuous step? Once it was done, she could not erase whatever mark it made. Aunt Miel was right, of course; people would talk. She would be considered quite scandalous.

"Putting aside all thoughts of your Grandfather, just for the moment, what about your father and Polly? They'll be hurt, and upset."

"I'm sorry about Father," Angela admitted. "I don't want to hurt him. Polly is another matter. I don't dislike her, you know, but she never paid much attention to me."

Honey sighed. She wasn't making much progress with Angela, she could see that.

"Whatever the case may be, Angela, it's no reason to do something foolish, dangerous even. More than likely you'll be cutting yourself out of your Grandfather's will. He's capable of that, if he's angry enough."

"I don't care. Really, I don't." Angela began to pace up and down the carpet in front of the window. "I must be with Beau, that's all I care about."

"You put *me* in a poor light, you know," Honey pointed out next. "Some chaperone, people will say. I bring you with me, under my protection, and the next thing I know you're running off to live with a man somewhere in the country. Angela, I wanted you to like Beau, and I wanted Beau to like you. I quite understand your attraction for each other, but I never intended anything like this!"

"I know," Angela said, looking miserable. "We couldn't seem to help it. I'm sorry."

"You might think of *me*, Angela."

"I do love you, Aunt Miel, but I was dying without Beau Don't you see? Nothing was worthwhile, so I know what it's like. I can't face it again, no matter what happens. Nothing could be worse than last winter at Pride's Court."

"Then Beau ought to marry you," Honey said firmly.

"He doesn't want to get married right now," Angela said dismally. She had pretended to Beau, of course, that she didn't care. But, in reality, she would have preferred marriage.

"I'm going to talk to him," Honey said.

"Oh, please don't, Aunt Miel. He'll be very angry. He hates people meddling in his business, telling him what to do! Please don't talk to him about this."

"I won't promise. I'll have to think about it."

"Anyway, Grandfather and Father, too, would be angry if I *married* Beau. You know that. They'd see it as a repeat of what you did."

"Marriage would be better than this."

"I don't see why."

"At least I had the protection of marriage. You'll have no protection at all. It's very foolish of you."

"Beau says we're too young. We haven't enough money."

"Then you're too young to live together."

"Beau doesn't see it that way. And if he isn't coming back to Montreal, what can I do?"

"You can refuse to live with him. Surely you could find someplace to live in London, if you insist on staying? Perhaps with family friends. Then if you want to paint, to study, you can still see Beau occasionally. There must be other ways of dealing with the situation."

Honey looked at Angela, seeing before her a fragile creature, only slightly older than the child she had picked up at school one June afternoon. The fine, perfectly shaped face, the huge gray eyes (so trusting, so passionate), the cloud of thick black hair. Like her mother before her, Angela was an extraordinary beauty, and although Honey loved Beau almost as a son, she felt that their plan to live together was very wrong. Certainly, Beau was brilliant and attractive. He was also unstable, volatile, bad-tempered, and undependable. They were like two children indulging in a game: playing "house." The results could be disastrous for both.

"Don't you remember how you felt about Uncle Armand?" Angela asked desperately. "Don't you remember? You gave so much for your marriage, and you aren't sorry, are you?"

"No, I'm not sorry."

"Then why can't you believe that I feel the same way about Beau?"

"Armand and I did marry, you seem to forget that. What if you and Beau have a child? What then? And what about money? Beau's scholarship won't go far. You're not accustomed to thinking about expenses. You've never done housework, or cooked."

"I can learn."

"Oh, Angela," Honey said in exasperation, "it's all childish. No matter what you say now, you'll miss the servants, the money, all the things you've been accustomed to all your life."

Angela was shaking inside. Much that Aunt Miel said was true. She did feel incompetent to deal with some of the problems that would face her if she left Pride's Court and her family behind. She wished Beau were here.

"Won't you reconsider?" Aunt Miel was saying. "Come back to Montreal with us and wait until Beau returns. You're young. You know he loves you, Angela, and surely a few months of waiting won't hurt."

"I can't do it. Because I can't work, or eat, or sleep, or live without Beau. There's no use talking about it. If I could do something else, I would. Don't you see? But I almost killed myself last winter, really I did. I wanted to die. I didn't care about the house, or the servants, or the food, or the clothes, or anything. I'm not going to live like that again. I'd rather be dead."

Her voice was so tight with tension that Honey decided to stop arguing. At least for now.

"Very well, I won't say anything more at the moment,"

Honey said. "But I do want to talk to you again before our sailing date. And I beg of you, Angela, to think well before committing yourself to this plan."

"I'm going to look for work as an illustrator," Angela said quickly, glad to get off the subject. "Beau has met some man in publishing. He thinks I might be able to illustrate children's books."

"Probably you could," Honey said. She was terribly tired. All the joy she had felt at Armand's honor seemed to have drained away. The whole London trip had become empty.

Honey looked past the dark head into the middle distance, thinking, *At least I can depend on Armand. I'm luckier than most women.*

CHAPTER SIXTEEN

Sir Simon received Angela's cable while he was at breakfast. Before him, the plates of smoked finnan haddie, sausages, and bacon and eggs; the toast in its silver rack; the immense pot of tea grew cold as he stared at the blunt message from London. His hand shook as he read and reread it. His temper began at boiling point and rapidly shot toward pure wrath. His head throbbed mercilessly as he crumpled the offending piece of paper in his fist and pitched it violently across the room.

"Hannah is responsible for this!" he cried to the empty room. "I won't stand for it! By God, she's done her last bit of meddling in my affairs!"

Half rising, he shouted for the butler instead of ringing the bell.

"Graves! Graves!"

Graves, lurking behind the green baize door connecting the kitchen area with the breakfast room, came forth quickly, although he quailed at facing Sir Simon's anger so early in the morning. As he pushed open the door he told himself that he'd known the cable was bad news as soon as it had arrived. Talk below stairs had swirled for weeks around the battle between father and daughter over Susan's wedding and Angela's journey to London. No doubt this message would trigger another outbreak in hostilities.

"Yes, sir," Graves said, presenting himself.

"Where is Charles?"

Sir Simon, in the heat of the moment, dispensed with formalities.

"Mr. Charles has not come down yet," Graves said.

"Then go up and bring him down. And Mrs. Court, as well. Instantly!"

Graves hurried off, leaving Sir Simon to fume alone.

This, then, was the result of a lifetime of devotion. His granddaughter, that beautiful child, was to throw her life away—under the influence of his wayward daughter, Hannah. His own flesh and blood was destroying him. Angela was being encouraged to live in sin, to live with the vile Frenchman like any common slut! He wouldn't have it, by God, he wouldn't! Not only would he prevent this sacrilege, he would see that Hannah was punished. He, Simon Court, had had nothing but trouble since the day that filthy scum had made off with his daughter. *Sir Armand*, indeed! That such vermin could be honored by the king of England was past belief! If there was any justice in the world, Armand St. Amour ought to be shot by a firing squad.

As his fury burned the edges of his mind, Sir Simon glared ferociously at the door. Charles came in shortly, followed by Polly.

"What is it, Papa? What's happened?"

"I'll tell you what's happened," Sir Simon spluttered as he pointed to the balled piece of paper he had tossed on the carpet. "There. Pick it up and read it. Blasphemous, that's what it is!"

Charles crossed the carpet, stooped, and picked up the crushed paper, while Polly stood just inside the door, unsure what to do.

"Sit down, Polly, for God's sake. Sit down," Sir Simon told her. "It's a terrible day for all of us. A terrible vengeance on an old man who has tried all his life to do his best for his family and his country. What have I done but give, give, give? Never thinking of myself, never considering my own wishes or my health. I've lived for others. And now my own daughter stabs me *again*. Like Caesar, I am attacked, I am murdered by those who should be nearest and dearest!"

It was unlike Sir Simon to compare himself to a foreigner, but he did not think of Caesar as a Roman so much as an elitist. His only knowledge of Caesar had come through watching Shakespeare, and so he had come to regard the emperor as a fellow countryman, almost, trying to lead a stupid and treacherous horde of idiots. The parallel did not displease him.

"Charles, what in God's name has happened?" Polly whispered, sitting heavily in a chair at the far end of the breakfast table and staring at her husband.

Charles smoothed out the cable. He now needed spectacles for reading and it took him what seemed a lifetime to bring them out of his pocket and place them on his nose. The room, meanwhile, writhed in terrible silence.

"Jesus," Charles said. Turning to Polly, he explained in a thick voice, "It's Angela. For God's sake, she's going to stay in England . . . and *live* with that fellow. Honey's nephew, the one she was mooning over at Christmas."

"Oh, no, Charles," Polly said. She turned very white, knowing how this would hurt Charles, how it would drive Sir Simon into towering rages.

"Yes, I'm afraid that's what it says," Charles said, still looking at the message as if the words might, somehow, change.

"But whatever made her send it today? In a cable? Why didn't she write a proper letter?" Polly asked reasonably.

"I hadn't thought of that," Charles said. "Papa, do you know why she would do this? In this blunt way?"

Sir Simon made a half-coughing sound of protest. He had told nobody about his cable to Honey concerning the wedding. Susan was supposed to write to her mother and explain, although Sir Simon had not inquired whether she had done so.

"It's a kind of revolt. She's under Hannah's spell, I would say."

"I don't understand," Charles said, staring at his father as if the old man had, at last, lost his senses entirely.

"I didn't tell you, because I didn't think it necessary, but I sent a cable to Hannah immediately following Susan's wedding. I wanted her to know what had happened," Sir Simon explained.

"You *what?*"

Charles was shocked. It did not take him long to see in this action of his father's a note of triumphant revenge. Good manners alone would have dictated another way of dealing with the situation.

"I thought she ought to know," Sir Simon said.

"But not like that, surely," Charles said. "You ought to have let Susan tell her mother."

"She's to write a letter," Sir Simon said stiffly. "She said she would do that."

Charles pulled himself up, as if to pit himself against his father. His voice now was stern rather than shocked.

"We'll have to do something about this. Do you honestly think Honey approves of this . . . disgraceful conduct?"

"Approves? I imagine she encouraged it!" Sir Simon shouted, getting up from his chair to pace about. "To spite me! Take my word, Charles, it's all Hannah's doing. No doubt she planned it when she took the girl to London. *I* wasn't consulted. You knew what I'd say if you told me. But you and Polly let Angela go there. You ought to have locked her up. You're too soft, Charles. This is the result. It's always the same when you're dealing with heathens. They must be treated like heathens—there is no other recourse but to deal with the realities. I've said it before. Here is the proof! A young girl's life destroyed. She might as well kill herself as live like that."

"Papa, please, for God's sake, let's not get into an argument here. We must consider what to do," Charles said.

"Yes, we must. But you let Angela go to England, and don't forget it. Behind my back, sneaking out her trunks, letting Hannah buy her ticket. Didn't you know this scum would be there waiting? You're partly to blame, Charles. You're both too soft, you and Polly. But Hannah will pay for this, you'll see! I'm not finished yet!"

"Never mind Honey, Papa, what about Angela?" Polly said, interjecting in spite of herself.

"You get on the next boat and bring Angela back. Drag her, if necessary. Charge this bastard with something. Charge him with anything. Consult our lawyers and see what you can do. Kidnapping, seduction, rape! I don't care. Find any kind of charge, and get rid of him. As for Hannah, I'll look after that *Madame*."

He subsided for a moment, frowning. Then, as Charles poured some tea for Polly, he said, in a more reasonable way, although his voice was still shaking and loud, "Where do we have the most influence? With *Le Devoir*? Isn't that fellow, Holland, somebody you know?"

"Yes, he has considerable influence at the paper. But why?" Charles said. "Polly, do have some tea. You'll feel better. I think I may have some myself."

"Why? Because I wish to give an interview. Everybody is making a fuss about the investiture. There are six Canadians over there being knighted. So it's topical. And this will be the last honors list for some time. Now, I wish to give an interview about some of the men so honored. My title, being hereditary, is in a different category, so I can speak with authority."

"But you did that before. Your editorial was instrumental in getting the law changed," Charles said. "You can't say the same thing again—it isn't news."

"This will be news. I have some unpleasant surprises for Mr. Armand St. Amour. I know things about him, about his business methods. Do you think I didn't take the trouble to find out about his finances? If it hadn't been for that American, St. Amour would have gone bankrupt years ago. Then he turned around and had an affair with the man's wife. That's what we're dealing with here, Charles. I knew what the man was the first time I laid eyes on him. You get me a reporter over here, and a lawyer as well."

"I hope you'll reconsider," Charles said soberly. "We shouldn't wash our dirty laundry in public."

"I've been silent long enough," Sir Simon said, giving the impression that he had lived as a martyr and a saint.

"What about slander? Libel?"

"That's why I want the lawyer. Get that fellow Saunders, the one we used during the election. He'll see that I don't go too far—that's what we pay him for. Get him over here right away, Charles, and the reporter after that. Tell Holland at *Le Devoir* that I want the story in immediately. Before the investiture."

"I wish we could concentrate on what to do about Angela—" Charles began. But his father cut him off abruptly.

"You can do that as soon as you get me the lawyer and the reporter. I've told you what to do about Angela, Charles. Don't be stupid. Get yourself passage on the next ship to London, even if it isn't a Court ship. There is no time to lose. But first things first. There'll be no truce, as Madame St. Amour will shortly find out."

———

Armand was at a business meeting with Corbin and a group of English investors and Honey was alone in her hotel room when the long night letter came from Gabriel. It was a summary of the interview Sir Simon had given that day, much of which was an attack on Armand. Gabriel was asking for instructions. Were they to ignore it, or were they to fight back?

If Honey's rage did not quite match her father's it was

only in volume, not intensity. Armand's honor was at
stake. The great day, to which they had both looked forward, was going to be ruined. She could not believe for a
moment that her father would do this terrible thing when
she had suppressed both the election scandal story in 1896
and later the terrible truth about the Ramsay rifle. Her for-
bearance, however, had brought her no mercy. Sir Simon's
wrath, his need to avenge himself, came first, far above
family ties. She could see that.

She scarcely needed five minutes to decide that *Le
Monde* would, most certainly, fight back. She had no intention of allowing Sir Simon his libelous and dangerous
remarks without a challenge. He would find that he was
not God in the city of Montreal, but a mere citizen like
everybody else. So, without waiting for Armand's return,
she dashed off an unsigned piece to be run on the paper's
editorial page.

In it, she brought up the old bribery charges during the
election of 1896, saying that there was evidence to confirm
it. And she reminded her readers of the Ramsey rifle scandal during the war. In a passionate summation she deplored
Le Monde's silence on these matters but stated that it was
not too late to bring them to the public's attention. She
sent the editorial by night letter with instructions to Gabriel
to have their lawyer check it for possibly libelous material.

When Armand came back, an hour before dinner, she
was still feeling triumphant; she had paid her father back
in kind and defended Armand's name. She showed him the
cable from Gabriel and her own reply to it, expecting his
wholehearted approval. Such approval was not forthcom-
ing. She was glared into silence by a furious Armand.

"Honey, I wish this matter hadn't come up now. Just
before the ceremony, the day we've both looked forward to
for so long. But I'm afraid I must tell you that I'm very
angry."

"You're angry because I wrote that piece defending
you?" Honey was astounded. She could not see why Armand took this view. Surely they could not let Sir Simon
rampage about, saying whatever he chose.

"There are many reasons," Armand began, "and you
ought to have consulted me before doing this. Just as you
ought to have consulted me about bringing Angela on this
visit. You only do these things as revenge against your

father. What becomes of the rest of us is apparently not in the least important to you."

"Armand, that's insane! I think about the family, what everybody wants, all the time! Besides, Ángela begged me to bring her. You have no idea how distraught that girl was about Beau. She was quite ill . . ."

"At first you refused, isn't that right? And your good sense told you to refuse. Another fight with your family was bound to come out of this, and you realized it."

"Well, that's true, of course. But when Papa lured Susan away—" she began, but Armand interrupted her, his face unusually taut, his mouth white around the lips.

"You admit it. You know what I mean. When your father *lured* Susan, as you put it, you wanted to take revenge. What about me? Did you consider what this might do to me? Did you think about Angela?"

"It has nothing to do with you. And yes, I thought about Angela. I told you, Armand, she begged me to bring her. You're being so peculiar, I don't understand you."

"You see nothing, understand nothing but your own obsession. It's been going on for years. Everybody can see it but you, Miel. *Everybody.* You have harmed my business interests before, and you are doing it again. You have no idea what you are bringing down on us with this rash behavior!"

"Armand, how could you speak to me like that?"

"Because it's true, and far past the time when I should have spoken to you, stopped you. You and your father have fought in public and in private since the day we were married. At first, it wasn't so bad, but it's getting worse. I kept hoping you'd stop, that he'd stop! But you're just as bad, each one of you. I think you're a little crazy on this subject, Miel."

"A little crazy, when I think of how he tricked me about the newspaper? Letting me think we were going to make up, and all he wanted was to protect himself? And what about Denys? Have you forgotten how your son died?"

"No, but you have turned that into a personal vendetta. As if Sir Simon himself fired the gun. You know the issue is much more complicated than that . . ."

"Not to me, it isn't."

"Come now, you aren't stupid."

"Apparently you think so."

"Look, this has to stop. This whole duel between you and your father must end! Do you hear me? You're both riddled with pride and vengefulness, and you'll bring all of us down if you go on like this. I tell you, Miel, it *must stop!*"

"I was defending you," she said stubbornly.

"I don't want you to defend me. Not in public, at least. You have no conception of the harm this whole issue may do to my ventures both here in London and back in Montreal. I was on the verge of making some important agreements with men who are, at the same time, involved with Sir Simon's companies. Investors who have a foot in each camp, so to speak. Sir Simon's interview is absurd, anyone can see that. An old man's ravings! But this action of yours, so impetuous, so thoughtless, may have jeopardized everything! Oh, I should have prevented you from bringing Angela. We ought to have ignored his attack about my knighthood last January and done nothing about it. Let him be the one who looks petty. And as for Susan, I am upset, of course—"

"Upset? She's my daughter, my only daughter!" Honey cried. "And she's left us. Can't you see that? He killed Denys, and he's stolen Susan!"

"That's wild talk."

"It's true. Why can't you see it?"

"Perhaps if you had not encouraged Angela, not encouraged Beau and Angela to be together—"

"Are you saying that the fault is *mine*? Are you saying that if I had behaved differently, Papa would have kept his hands off my daughter?"

She was incredulous that Armand could even *seem* to be defending her father. It was so obvious that Sir Simon would stop at nothing, that nothing could deflect him from his vengeful course. Why could he not understand?

"I am saying—" Armand spoke deliberately, his anger barely under control now—"that you must make a decision. You must give up this lifelong feud. You must choose between this fight with your father, and me. My welfare. Do you understand me? I won't stand for this public battle any longer! Or the damage it wreaks on our private lives."

"Armand, you are tearing me apart!"

"You must stop it!"

They were shouting at each other now, and Honey was weeping. Never in all their married life had they fought so openly, so bitterly. She collapsed in a chair.

"Do you care nothing about Susan?"

"Of course I care about Susan!" Armand shouted. "I love her. She's my daughter, too. And I regret more than you can understand that she's left the Church. But I cannot blame your father for all of that. There are other influences—I don't pretend to understand them. Perhaps it's impossible for a French man and an English woman to have children who are not divided in some way. How can I know the answer? I'm just as hurt by Susan's treatment as you are, but you must admit that there is part of Susan in this, and it isn't just your father's persuasiveness."

But Honey, through her bitter tears, did not want reason. She wanted complete allegiance in the battle against Sir Simon. It was impossible to understand how Armand could take any view but her own.

"You can't stop me," Honey began. "I will do as I please."

"If you continue in this way, it will be without *me*!" Armand cried furiously. "You will do it alone. Do you hear me?"

Honey stiffened and sat up, looking at Armand through her tears, trying to keep down the sobs that wracked her.

"Are you threatening to leave me?"

"I am warning you, Honey, that if you persist in this conduct, if you drag this matter into public once more, it will be without me. I can't say more than that."

"How dare you threaten me, when I put up with your tedious little affair with Velma, and your years away at war, leaving me to cope with everything? How dare you, Armand?"

"We are not talking about those things," Armand said coldly, some of his anger seeping away. "We're talking about your idiocy."

"So, now I am an idiot."

"In this respect, yes, you behave like an idiot."

"Armand, what's happening to us?" Honey cried, getting to her feet and coming toward him. "What's happened to the way we felt about each other? Is it all gone?"

Armand shook his head, weary, almost dispirited.

"I don't know. Life has done something to us, or perhaps

we have done it to ourselves. I don't know, Miel. I simply don't know."

Seeing him like that—exhausted and no longer angry, it seemed, but only disillusioned—Honey felt a rush of sympathy and love.

"Armand, if you want me to promise," she began, her voice catching on a sob, "I will promise. I don't know anymore. Perhaps you're right, and I've been vindictive about Papa. If you want me to stop, I'll stop. But let's not fight. I couldn't bear it if I had to live without you, Armand."

He took her in his arms then and they wept. But this time it was different because they wept together, over the same things, and not in anger, and not in separate places.

Honey was dressing. Standing in front of the tall glass, she examined the gray silk gown carefully. Was each tiny covered button fastened? Were her white gloves spotless? Was the small hat with the gray egret feather correct? The stormy scene was forgotten, at least for the time being. Michel, Beau, and Angela were traveling to the ceremony in one car, while Helene and Corbin would go in another. Word had come that the chauffeur-driven Bentley that Armand had hired for the day would arrive on time to pick them up at the door of the hotel and deliver them to Westminster Abbey.

At the appropriate time the car would fetch them back to the hotel for a champagne supper. The weather was clear; Honey would not, therefore, have to struggle with a coat or an umbrella. Armand, reflected in the glass at her shoulder, was as handsome as ever. The silver at his temples only made his eyes appear darker. His smile was still mischievous.

"How do I look?" Honey demanded.

"Belle, ma chérie. Très belle. Je suis heureux."

She continued to survey herself in the glass. Except for stray thoughts that would insist upon intruding, she was reasonably content. She desperately wanted Armand to be happy today, to enjoy the honor and to feel secure in himself. God knew he deserved that much.

Soon now they would be in the car, safely on the way to Westminster Abbey, caught up in the age-old ceremony. Armand would be dubbed a knight when King George V touched him on the shoulder with a sword. He would wear a mantle of rose-pink satin lined with pearl-gray silk, fastened with a cordon of pearl-gray silk with two pink-and-silver tassels. The mantle would be adorned with an embroidered star on the left side.

Today, after all, was the culmination of years of hard work, of tears and agony for both of them. The death of their elder son, the estrangement of their daughter, grave financial crises, wearing months in France as Armand tried to organize broken-down railway lines, lack of respect at times and loss of place—all these things were to be redressed in a single significant accolade.

A knock came at the door.

Armand opened it to a porter.

"Your car is downstairs to take you to the Abbey, sir." He was smiling broadly, obviously pleased to bring such news. Armand thanked him.

"We'll be down in a moment."

When he had closed the door, Armand turned to Honey and took her arm, holding it pressed tightly against him. Then, trembling just a little, they walked out into the corridor to the elevator. They must not be late. A king could never be kept waiting.

NANCY BUCKINGHAM

Valley of the Ravens

When her father died, Sarah returned to her beautiful childhood home, Farracombe, on Exmoor. But soon she felt a curious foreboding. No one really welcomed her, not irascible Joshua Lefevre, her guardian, nor young Jerome, Farracombe's heir, nor his beautiful but crippled wife Nadine. And then there was the child, Ginny, who seemed alternately to love Sarah and then turn against her. Why did Nadine's charming ways seem so false? And what was it that Jerome did on his frequent visits to the abandoned hunting lodge in the Valley of the Ravens?

The Other Cathy

Emma's first meeting with Matthew Sutcliffe on a misty moor gave her no inkling of the trouble to come. She was horrified to discover that he had been convicted of murdering her father and recently returned from fourteen years transportation in Australia, determined to clear his name.

Already Emma's life is tinged with tragedy as her cousin Cathy is dying of consumption but she finds a new life as her hostility towards Matthew changes to love. Their persistent attempts to clear his name lead to a horrifying revelation: if Matthew didn't commit the murder, then someone else in the family did!

CONSTANCE GLUYAS

The House on Twyford Street

In the harsh underworld of Restoration London, Sarah Barry was accounted the lowest of the low. Orphaned by the plague and left destitute by her friends, her exotic beauty could not save her from the gutter, nor from the torments of Newgate and Bedlam. But suddenly the powerful figure of Jason, Lord Witherly, entered Sarah's life. And between the orphan of the streets and the great aristocrat there flowered a rare and lasting love, both passionate and sweet. Secure in her new happiness, Sarah could not know that she was still menaced by a dark figure from her past. A dangerous Bedlam lunatic, obsessed by the thought of her death, was gradually tracking her down . . .

My Lord Foxe

Charles motioned the tall, youthful courtier forward. 'Madame, may I present the Earl of Foxefield.' He smiled. 'I call him my lord Foxe, because he is such a wily fellow.' Thought the Queen to herself, her breast stirred by violent and painful emotions, if only my lord Foxe, instead of Charles, had been King! She longed to shout at him, 'Look at me, my lord. You are such a man as I thought only came in dreams!' But Henrietta Maria, self-willed young French princess, was now Queen of England. Although her duty was to the King, her fancy was caught by the King's friend, the handsome Lord Foxe. It was to be many months before she understood the true secrets of her own heart.

SANDRA WILSON

Alice

Lady Alice is the beautiful heiress of Longmore, a castle standing high above the River Severn. Its strategic position makes it a valuable prize in the endless feuds between the barons of medieval England, and Alice herself is an unwilling pawn in their game. After the unexpected death of her unloving husband, Robert Beauchamp, Alice succeeds in escaping the clutches of his uncle the mighty Earl of Warwick. Seeking refuge at Court she falls under the spell of the King's handsome favourite, Piers Gaveston, and begins to share in the danger and intrigue which constantly surrounds him.

Wife to the Kingmaker

A quirk of fate makes Anne Beauchamp the sole heiress to the greatest Lancastrian fortune – Warwick – during the turbulent Wars of the Roses in 15th-century England. Her husband is the ambitious Richard Neville whose loyalties lie with York; now the earldom of Warwick is his. After wasted years of hate and conflict, Anne and Richard discover a passionate love for each other, and she lends her support to the mighty earl whose dazzling success earns him the nickname, 'the Kingmaker'. Eventually Richard's ambitions cause a rift in the marriage and Anne is destined to fall in love with his brother, John Neville. But theirs is a dangerous love which would prove a powerful tool in the hands of Richard's enemies, and must be kept secret at all costs.

CLARISSA ROSS

Moscow Mists

Elsie, a beautiful New York debutante, pledges her life and love to the handsome Count Alexander of Imperial Russia when they meet in America and London. Full of expectations and dreams she goes with him to become part of the pomp and pageantry of the court of the Tsar, only to discover that they are both caught in the evil grip of the most powerful man in Russia – the insane monk, Rasputin! The family palace is haunted by assassinations and suicides and Elsie knows that her love for Alexander has placed her very life in danger, Only by crushing the hypnotic power of Rasputin can she hope to escape the pain of her marriage and the dangers of the Revolution.

China Shadow

After a tragic sequence of events, the beautiful, young Flora Bain, an English clergyman's daughter, is sold into white slavery – destined for a Paris bordello. But she escapes to Armitage House, a brooding mansion shrouded in a mystery of the darkest Orient. A strange new life begins for Flora at Armitage House, but something, or someone, was destined to ruin her happiness. Suddenly plunged into a maelstrom of terror, love, jealousy and hate that spans oceans and continents Flora realises she must prepare to meet the final challenge of the China Shadow.

More Historical Romance available in Magnum Books

Nancy Buckingham

417 0249	Valley of the Ravens	80p
413 3724	The Jade Dragon	75p
413 3723	Shroud of Silence	75p
417 0194	The Other Cathy	90p

Robert DeMaria

| 417 0356 | Empress of Rome | 95p |

Catherine Dillon

| 413 3694 | Constantine Cay | 90p |
| 417 0226 | Rockfire | 85p |

Richard Falkirk

| 413 3459 | Blackstone Underground | 60p |
| 413 3460 | Blackstone and the Scourge of Europe | 60p |

Constance Gluyas

| 417 0268 | The House on Twyford Street | £1.25 |
| 417 0269 | My Lord Foxe | £1.50 |

Rosalind Laker

| 417 0244 | Ride the Blue Riband | 95p |

Elizabeth Norman

| 417 0292 | Castle Cloud | £1.50 |

Clarissa Ross

| 417 0257 | Moscow Mists | £1.25 |
| 417 0258 | China Shadow | £1.35 |

Sandra Wilson

417 0229	Alice	85p
417 0250	Wife to the Kingmaker	95p
417 0230	The Penrich Dragon	85p